Books by Thomas Fleming

FICTION
Liberty Tavern
The Good Shepherd
The Sandbox Tree
Romans Countrymen Lovers
A Cry of Whiteness
King of the Hill
The God of Love
All Good Men

NONFICTION
1776: Year of Illusions
The Forgotten Victory
The Man Who Dared the Lightning
The Man from Monticello
West Point
One Small Candle
Beat the Last Drum
Now We Are Enemies

Liberty
Tavern

Liberty Tavern

A NOVEL BY

THOMAS FLEMING

Doubleday & Company, Inc.

GARDEN CITY, NEW YORK

1976

All of the characters in this book are fictitious,
and any resemblance to actual persons is purely coincidental,
with the exception of obvious historical figures identified by name.

ISBN: 0-385-04420-8
LIBRARY OF CONGRESS CATALOG CARD NUMBER 74-18795
COPYRIGHT © 1976 BY THOMAS FLEMING
ALL RIGHTS RESERVED
PRINTED IN THE UNITED STATES OF AMERICA
FIRST EDITION

Rebuke the company of spearmen . . .
scatter thou the people that
delight in War.

PSALM LXVIII.30

Liberty Tavern

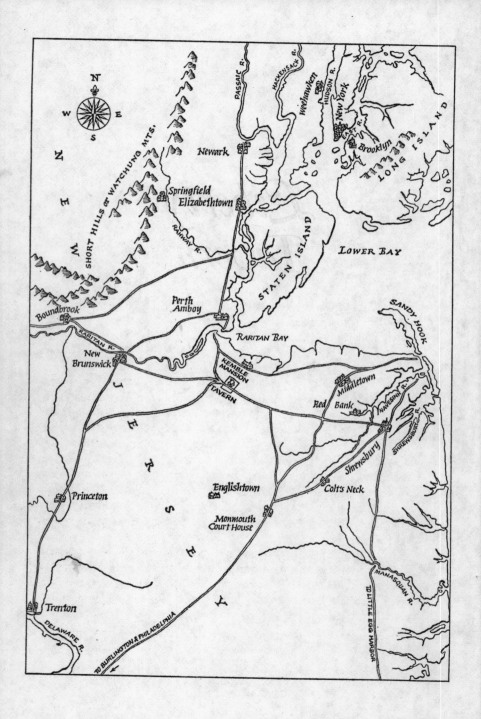

MY DEAR CHILDREN:

Yesterday we celebrated the fiftieth anniversary of our birth as a nation. It was a lavish affair. The mayor and one of our U.S. senators gave speeches, hailing the services of the men and women of New Jersey on behalf of the Cause. A handful of the old soldiers tottered up to accept the cheers of the multitude—and to persuade the senator to increase their pensions. Cannon boomed, church bells rang. I listened, but I did not feel a part of the general emotion. The senator and the mayor made the Revolution sound unremittingly glorious—and incredibly dull.

While the bands were still playing "Yankee Doodle" and our militia strutted down Main Street in their expensive uniforms, I mounted my horse and rode into the country. An hour out of town, I left the handsome new turnpike and was soon negotiating a road full of rocks and ruts that had my wise old horse picking his way. Hard to believe that this was once the King's Highway, the main road to Philadelphia. But practically no one remembers how wretched our roads were fifty years ago. We are in the boastful stage of our national childhood. Everything American must have always been bigger, better, faster, smarter, braver, or wiser than the rest of the world.

I came around a horseshoe bend and paused, my heart pounding. There was the tavern, surrounded by its noble oaks, the swift-running waters of the brook behind it dappled with July sunlight. I felt a quickening anxiety as I dismounted. On my last visit I discovered that neighborhood boys had broken into it. They had done no damage, but it made serious the danger of a fire. You will recall how upset I was when flames destroyed the residence last

11

year. I could see its burnt-out hulk beside the brook as I dismounted.

But all was well in the tavern. The windows were undamaged and the padlock I had added to the front door was still secure. In a moment I was inside, walking with an ever fuller heart into the past. Memories flooded me so precipitously, for a moment I could see nothing as I entered the taproom. I stood there until the great stone fireplace, the massive scarred bar, with its lowered portcullis, the round stone tables became visible again.

Before the bar stood Jonathan Gifford. I saw him as vividly as I see this paper before me, his arms folded over his formidable chest, a rock of a man, so often maddeningly imperturbable, unknowable in his silence, his reserve. With a careful smile on his face he listens to some drunken militiaman, who he knew would run a mile at the first glimpse of a redcoat, roaring out a favorite verse.

> From the east to the west blow the trumpet to arms
> Thro' the land let the sound of it flee
> Let the far and the near all unite with a cheer
> In defense of our liberty tree.

A blink of the eye and he stands in the doorway facing down a mob of liberty boys or a regiment of British infantry, both equally ready to burn the tavern to the ground.

Beside Jonathan Gifford stands his stepdaughter Kate, her red hair flashing defiance in the sunlight. Another blink of my blurry eyes and I see her at the spinet in the parlor of the residence, singing with a delicious hint of mockery one of our more sentimental airs.

> In rapture I gaze when my darling is by
> And drink the sweet poison of love from his eyes
> I feel the soft passion pervade every part
> And pleasures unusual play round my fond heart.

Watching from a distance is her brother Kemble, his dark gray eyes smoldering with headstrong devotion to the Cause. How many times I fought beside him, gun in hand. For a moment it is like a scene from Homer, a glimpse of a hero in the Underworld, the sight of a face stamped forever with grief and failure.

Beside the spinet stands the woman who changed us all,

Caroline Skinner. At first she seems as masked, as impenetrable as Jonathan Gifford. But beneath her composure burned an inner transforming fire. It was no coincidence that I had spent the previous week rereading her diaries, reviewing the extensive notes I had made of my conversations with her in the decade after the Revolution. I have also been talking to Kate, who stands as straight and speaks as saltily at sixty-eight as she did at eighteen. For a month now a wish has been growing in me, and today it has become a resolve.

I shall write it all down. I will fill the tavern and other rooms with the faces, the voices, the passions, and the anguish of those years. Not for publication, but for my own pleasure and your enlightenment. You are all grown men and women now. I cannot see how you would be harmed—and I suspect you might be helped—by knowing the true story of our Revolution.

Perhaps there is a little personal pride in it too—a wish that when I am gone you will think of me as a little more than a dull old country doctor. But let me caution you in the strictest terms against publishing what I write, if by some miracle you consider it worthy of such an expense. The nation is not ready to face the truth about itself that an honest story of the Revolution must mirror. There is another reason for this stricture which you will learn toward the end of the story. Let it pass from hand to hand within the family and rest undisturbed in some vault for a generation or two or three. By then, perhaps, Americans will be able to read the truth without the shock and wrath such a production would engender today.

Above all I hope that the book, if it ever becomes one in some freer future time, will help Americans of that distant era see us not as a set of demigods impossible to emulate, but human like themselves, torn by dissensions without and doubts within, groping toward happiness and repeatedly missing or mistaking it, struggling back from defeat and even from despair, learning painfully to forgive not merely our enemies but our friends and above all, ourselves.

Your loving father,
James Kemble

Book
I

CHAPTER ONE

IN MOST BOOKS about the Revolution you get the feeling that the people had no pasts, they were born in 1775 or 1776. The opposite was the case. The Revolution burst like a hurricane on all our lives, changing most of us forever. But it was only part of our personal histories. Each of us already had a past that complicated or tormented our efforts to cope with the storm. Nowhere was this more visible than the first day of the year 1776, when most of the family met at Kemble Manor in the course of making their annual New Year's Day visits. By the time we arrived the small and middling farmers had paid their respects and departed. Most of the eggnog was gone from the huge Waterford cut-glass bowl which the Squire had set up for them in the center hall.

I was ordered to station myself by the window in the south parlor and sing out when I saw Jonathan Gifford and his stepchildren. They turned up the drive within the hour. Kate sat in the chaise beside her father while Kemble rode beside them on his big black gelding, Thunder. In Kate's lap was an enormous bouquet of red and white roses.

Without a word we bundled ourselves into our cloaks and coats and trooped out to the burying ground on the south lawn. Jonathan Gifford knew why we joined him, as we had last year, in this memorial gesture to his dead wife. It was an act of public defiance, not on his behalf but on behalf of the family. No matter what Sarah Kemble Gifford had done, we were saying that she was still a Kemble and that was more important than anything else, with the possible exception of being a Stapleton or a Skinner. The triumvirate, that was the name humbler folk used to describe our three families.

Two years ago we had laid Sarah in the burying ground on land that was part of the family's original royal grant. With a possessiveness that strongly hinted of resentment, the Kembles had claimed her. Jonathan Gifford had stoically agreed to this alien grave—alien to him, at least—proof, if we needed it, that he was a hard man to know.

Why, you may ask, did Sarah Kemble marry a tavern keeper? Since the turn of the century this trade has been declining in prestige. If the reports I hear from our large cities are accurate, it will continue to fall in public esteem. But in the decade of the Revolution—and for a good many preceding decades—the owner of an American tavern was one of the most influential and respected members of the community. His access to ready money made him a kind of banker with numerous outstanding loans. Circuit judges held court sessions in the tavern's public rooms and gentlemen and ladies filled these same rooms with lively music and witty conversation at spring and autumn balls. On election days the tavern was the local polling place where farmers and tradesmen came in the good old English tradition to call out their support—or sometimes their opposition—to the Squire as their representative in the provincial assembly. Mail was delivered and distributed from the tavern. The militia performed in its front yard each Training Day and got gloriously drunk as further proof that they were true soldiers. A well-located tavern, run by a man who knew his business, could clear a thousand pounds a year—considerably more than many a lawyer made and two or three times the income of the average doctor or clergyman.

But even if Jonathan Gifford had by some strange circumstance been forced into such a business at a time when it lacked social respect, I believe Sarah Kemble Stapleton would have married him anyway. Command, a quiet assurance, emanated from this compact man. It was not in the least diminished by his limp. His shattered knee was an honorable wound acquired in the final battle of the Seven Years' War—the conquest of Havana.

Above all, Captain Gifford was a British officer and he carried with him that special aura of sophistication, power, and romance which to American eyes surrounded these far-traveled guardians of the Empire. He had arrived in our midst, moderately wealthy from his share of the spoils of Havana, bought Strangers' Resort,

18

one of the finest taverns in the state, and within a year had married one of our richest young widows.

This was in my mind—and in other minds—when we gathered at the graveyard to recall for a few moments the sad, bizarre story of Sarah Kemble Gifford. At that time, I, like everyone else, knew only the external face of it—the public fact that her marriage had been unhappy. Even before her death, rumors, often spoken behind hands in the taproom of Strangers' Resort itself, implied that Mrs. Gifford was not beyond sharing her favors with other men. Some said she had done the same sinful thing during her first marriage to Jared Stapleton. This was supposedly why he had gone to sea as captain of a privateer in 1762. He had been killed by a cannon ball from a French West Indiaman, leaving Sarah with two small children—and a whacking fortune.

That this fortune played some part in Captain Gifford's offer of marriage was not likely to shock anyone on our level of society. That this in turn would cause unhappiness—especially public unhappiness—was the surprise. Several times Sarah had all but announced her dissatisfaction with Jonathan Gifford to members of the family, talking recklessly about her fate—to marry unfeeling men whose only interest was money. Once in a particularly wayward moment she told my mother that Jonathan Gifford was more than unfeeling—he was cruel. All this was food for more than a few conversations across teacups. But not even our most inveterate gossips were prepared for Sarah's denouement—her flight to Antigua, her abandonment of her husband and her children—in passionate pursuit of her lover, an army captain who had visited Strangers' Resort on a summer's tour of America and stayed long enough to conquer her. Within two months she was dead, a victim of the fevers that made mortality so commonplace on that pestilential island.

With the malice that seems to be a natural part of consanguinity, the family took sides. Some saw Sarah as the victim of a heartless husband. Others felt that Captain Gifford, who bore the gossip and the humiliation with stoic silence, was a much wronged man. One side noted that Sarah had been careful in her will to sequester all her substantial wealth to her children. Others were quick to point out that Captain Gifford was the will's executor, and the guardian of the children. But those with vicious minds and nasty tongues were unappeased. They even saw the memorial flowers on Sarah's grave as a kind of hypocrisy on Jonathan Gifford's part—a way of fending off the relatives. Litigious as well as avaricious by instinct, they were all too ready to intervene on behalf of their conviction that blood and money were indissolubly mingled.

Jonathan Gifford's thoughts were far from those carpers. He gazed down at the small, sad tombstone and saw nothing, heard nothing, remembered nothing but words that coruscated through his brain and seared his flesh as brutally now as when he first heard them. *I loved you, but not with my whole heart. Just as you loved me.* He tried to erase the pain of those words with other memories—Sarah as he had known her during that first blazing year, the one year in which they had been true lovers, the wildness in her which had seemed to him as American as her glowing skin and violent red hair. He had loved her enough to forget his dream of a gentleman's estate in England, enough to put all the money he had and ever hoped to have—in the prime years of his life— into the difficult venture known as America. But the words still quivered in him like a wound he had received an hour ago.

Dazedly, Jonathan Gifford looked at the circle of faces in the graveyard and then at the small stones with their inscriptions, the first of them a hundred and twenty-five years old. He was gripped by that most unnerving of all anxieties—the sense of being the stranger, the alien in a hostile land. Even more disturbing was the unspoken accusation which he thought that he saw on some of the faces around him. Above all on the face of his stepson, Kemble. He half-knew, half-suspected that Kemble believed he was the real reason why Sarah Kemble Stapleton lay at their feet beneath this frozen January earth. He could only suppose others in this mourning circle felt the same way.

Among the more likely candidates was Sarah's sister, Caroline Kemble Skinner. Five years younger, she was Sarah's opposite in almost every way. She was almost too neat, too composed, too quiet. A dull, mercenary girl, that had been Jonathan Gifford's conclusion when he first met her. He had revised dull to clever in the intervening years, but had not altered the rest of his opinion. Caroline was married to his best friend in America, Charles Skinner. He was at least twenty-five years older than his wife. Such unions of youth and age were as common among wealthy

Americans as they were among the English aristocracy. Sarah had been twenty years younger than her first husband.

Beside his slight dark-haired wife Charles Skinner was a brooding mountain. He and Jonathan Gifford had met during the Seven Years' War (or the French and Indian War, as we called it here in America). Both had joined a corps of rangers organized by the famous American scout Robert Rogers, and later augmented and supported by that beloved, tragedy-fated young soldier Lord George Howe. They had shared a hundred forest fights with Indians and French irregulars. In those years Charles Skinner had been in his prime, an American giant full of incredible strength and daring. A decade and a half of peace had left him ponderous, on the edge of obesity, with a bulging belly, sagging cheeks, and two drooping chins. Among us impudent youngsters in our frequent discussions of our elders, Charles and Caroline were referred to as Henry VIII and Anne Boleyn. Everyone else called him the Squire.

Beside Charles Skinner stood his son, Anthony Franklin Skinner. His middle name was a compliment to the royal governor of New Jersey, not his famous father, Benjamin. Charles Skinner and William Franklin had met in London in the mid-1750s. Both had enjoyed the high life of the great city and produced proof of their pleasures—illegitimate sons. William Franklin had left his son in England with his father, but Charles Skinner had brought Anthony home and declared his mother had been his wedded wife who died in childbirth. Such lies are impossible to maintain, and everyone in the family and out of it soon knew Anthony was a bastard. It became a whisper behind Anthony's back which neither his father's money nor his own savoir-faire could suppress. In the marriage settlement that made Charles Skinner the Squire of Kemble Manor, Anthony was specifically excluded from inheriting the estate. Only children of Caroline Skinner's body, to use the legal phrase, could inherit the manor, commonly considered the finest piece of property in south Jersey.

Anthony was not as tall as his father nor as broad. But he made up in charm what he lacked in strength. As a boy he had had a most engaging manner, and he was obviously intelligent. He had been educated at home, largely by Caroline, whose father had had one of the best libraries in North America. Caroline had doted on him and at family gatherings talked frequently about the books Anthony was reading, the clever, witty things he had recently said.

Now the clever boy was a man, back from two years at Cambridge and a year spent reading law in London. His manner had changed, so it seemed to Jonathan Gifford. There was a condescension in his smile now, a certain arrogance in the angle of his head. He reminded Jonathan Gifford of some British officers he had known in his army days, younger sons of the nobility who thought Irish, Scots, Americans—anyone who was not English—subhuman barbarians. But he admitted to himself that he might be prejudiced against Anthony Skinner. These days he felt utterly incapable of understanding younger Americans.

Captain Gifford may have felt a little more at home after a glance at the next four faces in our semicircle. My father could have sat for a portrait of John Bull. My sister Sally and I were cast in the same mold—hardly surprising since my mother was a Boston Oliver. We were veritable apostrophes to English continuity, with our ruddy beefeater faces and sturdy well-padded physiques. But on second thought, the Captain probably found little comfort from a look at us. Wealth won in America had added pride to habitual reserve. My father would have liked to be friendly, but he was cowed, as usual, by Mother, who was a leader of the anti-Gifford side of the family.

Jonathan Gifford laid on Sarah's grave the bouquet of roses from his greenhouse. There and in his summer garden, to the bafflement of many, he grew roses of every kind and color from cuttings sent to him by friends in the British army around the globe. A soldier who loved flowers! No wonder many people thought Jonathan Gifford was an enigma.

The little ceremony was over. The semicircle of mourners walked out of the graveyard and Charles Skinner put his arm around Jonathan Gifford's shoulder. "I hope you will do more than drink and run, old friend. I've talked the rest of the family into staying for tea. We've still got a case or two of good Dutch bohea before we are driven to brewing maple twigs and strawberry leaves."

"Certainly," said Jonathan Gifford, glancing with just a trace of nervousness at Kemble and Kate. Kemble had heard the invitation and was glaring. Kate was already deep in conversation with Anthony Skinner. The rest of us walked toward the manor house in the Squire's wake. The two-and-a-half-story house of rose-red brick stood in the center of a broad lawn, at the end of a drive lined with huge old elms. Beyond the coast road the gray winter waters of Raritan Bay were visible in frothy turmoil. Behind the house was a formal garden in the latest English style, a deer park which included some thirty acres of cleared woods, and an orchard of six hundred fruit trees. Barns, quarters for two dozen Negro field hands, a carriage house, and a thousand acres of prime topsoil and pasture land completed the immediate estate. About three miles away on Halfpenny Brook stood a mill which ground most of the district's grain and corn. Another large farm, owned by the Squire before his marriage, was thirteen miles away at Colt's Neck. The weight of this property and his reputation as a soldier had long since made Charles Skinner one of the most influential men in New Jersey.

To Jonathan Gifford, Kemble Manor was almost a second home. It was here that he had been welcomed by his old friend Charles Skinner like a prodigal brother, here that he had met Sarah. The parties, the dinners they had enjoyed in those first carefree years. Always they had ended by Sarah calling on him to give the last toast of the evening.

> Here's to all them that we love
> Here's to all them that love us.

With a happy laugh, everyone would join the last two lines.

> And here's to all them that love those
> that love them
> Love those that love them that love us.

What a yearning for peace those words evoked. It was hard to believe they were still singing them only three years ago. Now it all seemed as remote and pathetically quaint as a song from 'Tis Pity She's a Whore or some other primitive play.

Snowflakes began whirling in the air as we reached the front door. In the entrance hall, a grandfather clock bonged four and two black menservants hurried to take our cloaks. The blacks wore the standard Skinner livery, blue velvet suits trimmed with yellow. On their heads were glossy black wigs. Two other servants met us with silver trays on which steamed tankards of mulled wine.

In the drawing room, on a spiral-legged mahogany table, sat a magnificent tea service by the well-known New York silversmith of an earlier age, Charles Le Roux. The furniture in the room was mostly in the Queen Anne style with lovely carved shells on crests and knees, the chairs with those tapering-footed rear legs favored by New Yorkers. The upholstery was all light blue damask embroidered with mythological griffins and swans, a motif repeated in the wainscoting of the room, while the blue was repeated in the paper on the walls.

Charles Skinner stood in the center of this splendid room, beaming on his family and friends. He raised his tankard of mulled wine high. "Here's to the New Year. May it bring us plenty—but above all peace."

We all drank to this thoroughly unobjectionable toast.

"I have another wish," Anthony Skinner said, looking at Kate with a smile on his handsome face. He raised his tankard. "May the most beautiful woman in New Jersey rescue a wretched being from a fate worse than death."

Kate blushed. Kemble glowered. I, who loved Kate with the forlorn hopelessness of fifteen, found it easier than ever to dislike Anthony Skinner.

"Damn me if you look wretched, Anthony," Charles Skinner said. "Though if you had to pay for those clothes you're wearing, you'd be miserable enough."

The Squire was the richest man in south Jersey but he never stopped counting his pennies. It was not easy to be his son, as the look on Anthony's face testified. But there was some truth in Charles Skinner's remark. Anthony's green silk breeches were flowered with silver and gold. His coat was a quilted pale blue satin trimmed with silver galloon, the lapels wide and the pockets huge in the latest London fashion. Lace blossomed from his chest and wrists. The heels of his blue shoes were at least three inches high. His wig was in what London called the macaroni style, sharply raked in the front and rising to an absurdly high toupet.

Charles Skinner more than matched his son's sartorial splendor. His breeches and coat were velvet, covered with small designs in soft shades of red and green, giving a pinkish hue to the eye. His long waistcoat was of corded silk, a shade darker than the coat and embroidered with a flowered pattern reflecting the suit's soft red and green. His shoes were bright green with great silver buckles and red heels.

24

The rest of us were not exactly dressed down. All of us, ladies and gentlemen and boys like myself, wore the brocades and satins and ample lace displayed by the rich in 1776, from the Hancocks of Boston to the Rutledges of South Carolina. Jonathan Gifford wore a suit of dark red satin with a waistcoat of white satin embroidered in several colors. Kate Stapleton wore a brocade gown, blue on the surface and green underneath, with a narrow stripe of green at regular intervals between a running vine pattern of small bright flowers and leaves. It was divided over a quilted petticoat of blue satin fashionably instep length. The skirt was gathered into large festoons à la polonaise, the latest mode. But Kate scorned the absurdly high headdresses of 1776 London, preferring to wear her lustrous hair unpowdered in a loose pile, artfully dressed with twisted scarves to affect a country carelessness.

I should hasten to add that this hair style was also fashionable in England, where only Londoners were slaves to the bizarre whims of Paris. But my mother and sister were slaves to London, and they wore their hair piled a foot and a half high on their round heads, making themselves perfect examples of the satiric poem on the subject:

> Give Chloe a bushel of horsehair and wool
> Of paste and pomatum a pound;
> Ten yards of gay ribbon to deck her sweet skull
> And gauze to encompass it round.

In this gallery of brilliant colors, Kemble Stapleton was a morose island of drab. His hair was unpowdered, and cut so unfashionably short, it had no need of a tie behind. His suit was the plainest imaginable brown broadcloth, without even a cuff or lapel. Not a painted Paris button, such as those that adorned Anthony Skinner's coat, nor a silver buckle on his shoes, nor a single ruffle of lace on his shirt front or cuff. Two years ago, he had departed for college in a blue silk coat, a flowered yellow vest, and fawn breeches as tight as any London macaroni's. But in that same year the First Continental Congress had voted an end to all English imports and called on Americans to abandon the luxuries and ostentation to which we had become alarmingly accustomed.

"Damn me, Kemble," Charles Skinner said, "you look like a Quaker."

"Or a Presbyterian. That's worse in my opinion," Anthony said.

"Benjamin Franklin wears this kind of suit these days," Kemble said. "What is good enough for him is certainly good enough for me."

"That old fraud," boomed Charles Skinner. "I saw him in London at Coronation Day wearing kincob brocade straight from the China coast. Everything Dr. Franklin does is affectation, nothing but affectation. Believe me, my boy. The old rogue is always playing a part."

"I beg to differ, sir," Kemble said. "I consider Dr. Franklin a great man and a great patriot."

"Charles, please. You promised not to talk politics," Caroline Skinner said. She was wearing a surprisingly simple dress for New Year's Day, a rather old-fashioned green taffeta, the bodice laced in front over a white stomacher.

"My dear, I thought I was talking religion," said her husband.

Anthony changed the subject by producing a present for Kate, an English translation of *The Sorrows of Young Werther* the novel by the German writer Goethe that was creating a sensation throughout Europe.

"What is it about?" Charles Skinner asked.

"A young man who falls in love with a beautiful woman who rejects him," Anthony said, looking somberly at Kate. "In despair he kills himself."

"I can't wait to read it," Kate said.

"Are you suggesting a similar fate may be in store for you, Anthony?" Jonathan Gifford asked dryly.

"Who knows, Captain Gifford," Anthony said with a sigh that struck me as patently false. "We are only beginning to understand the mysteries of the heart."

"I have serious doubts about how much understanding you can get from today's novels," Caroline Skinner said. "The characters all seem to have hearts but no heads."

"I could not agree more, Mrs. Skinner," Captain Gifford said.

"I'm safe from the plague no matter what," Charles Skinner said. "The last book Mrs. Skinner tried to get me to read was Hume's history of England. I couldn't get past Alfred the Great."

"I see no point in an American reading such European trash," Kemble said. "If a man must die, let it be for his country, not for some spoiled woman whose only interest is where her next dress is coming from."

"You should really move to Boston, Kemble," Anthony said. "You would be much happier up there with the rest of the fanatics."

"Anthony. *No politics*," Caroline Skinner said.

"It is the simple truth, Mother," Anthony said.

No one disagreed with him. At this point the Revolution seemed like a foreign war to most people in New Jersey. All the fighting had taken place in Massachusetts and we were inclined to blame the cantankerous sons of the Puritans for the trouble as much as the British. Not one man in three agreed with Kemble's contention that the British were using the quarrel with the Yankees to menace the liberties of all Americans.

Caroline began pouring tea into fragile blue Sèvres china cups. Black servant girls wearing velvet dresses that matched the livery of the menservants began passing plates full of cakes and sweetmeats. Anthony Skinner produced the latest copies of *The Gentleman's Magazine* and we listened with fascination to his recounting of two recent London trials in which beautiful women had been defendants in the dock. Mrs. Caroline Rudd had been tried for forgery and Miss Jane Butterfield for poisoning her "benefactor," an old rogue named Scawen who had been keeping her for several years. Both ladies had been acquitted. But the real sensation was the pictures of these not very innocent females. Kate, my sister, and my mother crowded around them to study the latest London styles. Miss Butterfield was in "undress"—without a hoop—and wore an elegant polonaise with studied folds and graceful puffs and a flounced decorated petticoat. The profusion of her ruchings and the length of her elbow laces brought as much comment from the ladies as another topic was stirring among the men.

The King's speech from the throne, closing the latest session of Parliament, had reached Governor Franklin, and he had given a copy of it to Charles Skinner. His Majesty had denounced the "unnatural" rebellion in America and accused the rebels of plotting to set up an independent state. Charles Skinner saw it as the final warning to disband Congress and cease all agitation or face war.

"I expect it will give Dr. Franklin and his friends in Philadelphia an electric shock they will long remember," the Squire said.

Jonathan Gifford was not so sure who would be shocked but he glumly agreed that the future looked grim.

Both these conversations were interrupted by Kemble's sharp, strained voice. Caroline Skinner was holding out a teacup to him. Perhaps suspecting what was to come, she had served him among the last. It only postponed the inevitable. Kemble slowly shook his head.

"I'm sorry, Aunt Caroline. I will have no tea."

"Oh. Would you prefer coffee?"

"No. No thank you."

Anthony Skinner's mouth curled contemptuously. Kate looked as though she might explode. Charles Skinner finished selecting his tidbits and then asked: "Do I detect in this refusal a reproach, Kemble?"

"You know as well as I do, Uncle Charles, Congress has said no man can be a patriot and drink tea."

"But this isn't English tea," Anthony Skinner said. "This is Dutch. Smuggled into good old New York, as we've been smuggling it for most of the century."

"It is still tea."

"Any moment," Kate said mockingly, "we shall have a sermon. Give us a poem instead, Kemble."

Without waiting for him to answer, she recited one for him.

"*No more shall my teapot so generous be*
In filling the cups with this pernicious tea,
For I'll fill it with water and drink out of the same,
Before I'll lose liberty, that dearest name."

"I'm serious, Kate," Kemble said.

"Oh, goddamn you and your seriousness," Kate said.

As usual, my mother was almost giddy with horror at Kate's language. In her native Boston, young ladies—or old ones—never swore. It was unthinkable.

"Dear me, Kate," cried my mother. "If you continue to talk that way, you will have us praying for your immortal soul."

"Why?" asked Kate. "Men talk that way all the time and no one prays for them."

"It's honest American talk, Aunt," Anthony said. "I see nothing wrong with it."

"It is not American talk," Kemble said. "It is English affectation. She thinks that is the way duchesses talk in the country."

"Go to hell," Kate said.

"To soothe your liberty-loving soul, Kemble," Caroline said, "I have made you some tea from Dr. Rush's formula, and some Edenton party cakes."

Benjamin Rush was a young Philadelphia physician who had published a number of pro-American essays in the papers, including a recipe for making tea from twigs of white oak and leaves of sweet myrtle.

"And what may I ask are Edenton cakes?" asked Charles Skinner.

"Cookies baked to a recipe from the ladies of Edenton, North Carolina, a year or so past, at a party in which they drank tea made from dried raspberry leaves," Caroline said.

Caroline passed the Edenton cakes to me, and poured Kemble his patriot's tea from a blue Wedgwood pot. "Jemmy," hissed my mother, but I had popped a cake into my mouth too fast for her to stop me. At fifteen I was old enough to defy my mother and young enough to get away with it half the time by pretending it was just boyish high spirits.

"They look very good," said my sister Sally, who was two years older than I.

"You will have nothing to do with them, my dear," said Mother. "You prefer sweetmeats anyway."

Sally nodded obediently. She had long since succumbed to my mother's New England attitude toward child raising which made parents moralizing tyrants, determined to crush the original sin out of their children. South of New England a much freer, more indulgent philosophy prevailed, and I strove mightily to take advantage of it.

"I'll try one," Kate said, taking a crunchy bite.

"Are you going to report us to the Committee, Kemble?" Anthony Skinner asked.

"No," Kemble growled.

Caroline Skinner passed the Edenton cakes to others while this tense conversation took place. In spite of glares from my mother I declined the bohea and accepted a cup of the patriot's brew. It tasted like dishwater. I concealed my dismay by defiantly narrating what students at Princeton had done to tea drinkers in the vi-

29

cinity of Nassau Hall. Dressed in white to demonstrate their purity, they had forced the weed worshipers to surrender their supplies, which they then burnt in a bonfire in the street.

"Thereby proving the worthlessness of an American college education," Anthony Skinner said.

Jonathan Gifford accepted his teacup from Caroline Skinner. For a painful moment, he had thought of joining Kemble in refusal. But he could never explain such a gesture to Charles Skinner—nor to himself. Something in his nature resented the idea of a Congress, supposedly fighting for the liberty of America, denying him the freedom to drink a cup of tea.

But how could he tell this to a nineteen-year-old who relished arguments and was in love with the sound of his own voice? Jonathan Gifford had never been good at expressing his feelings, but this did not mean he lacked feelings—the conclusion that too many young people seemed to draw when a man resisted enthusiastic impulses. He had grown up in a world that placed enormous stress on self-control, common sense. Kate and Kemble's generation were consciously revolting against this idea. They gloried in throbbing emotions, they read novels and poetry which made them weep—and were proud of it. Jonathan Gifford simply could not understand it. Only a few months ago, Kate had urged him to read a novel by the British writer Laurence Sterne. The fellow made a fool of himself, emoting plaintively over the death of a fly, oozing sighs over everything from old ruins to reckless lovers.

"Haven't you been able to talk any sense into this young man's head, friend Jonathan?" Charles Skinner asked. He picked up two or three lumps of sugar and threw them into his mouth, crunching them into powder with his formidable jaw and washing it all down with a huge swig of tea. Eating the sugar raw was a habit he had picked up from the Dutch when he had spent a winter at Albany during the French and Indian War.

"What?" Jonathan Gifford asked, disconcerted as much by the grinding operation as the question itself. For a moment he was hypnotized by the amount of sugar Caroline and Kate were stirring into their tea. It was twice, perhaps three times the average English portion. Once more he felt himself a disembodied stranger.

"When a young man is nineteen . . ." he said, looking steadily at Kemble.

"—either he has some sense or he doesn't," Anthony Skinner said.

Kemble flushed and glared at Jonathan Gifford as if the cutting words had come from him. For a moment he was almost blinded by a wild mixture of grief and anger. This was the only son he would ever have. Kemble did not bear his name. But he had done his best to be a father to him since the boy was ten. Sadly, Jonathan Gifford remembered the happy hours they had spent together, prowling the marshes in the dawn for ducks, fishing in Raritan Bay, discussing military history before the fire on winter evenings, working together in the greenhouse. All these bonds seemed to be dissolving now.

"Can't we be together for even five minutes without a political argument?" Caroline Skinner said.

She toyed with the death ring on her finger. Jonathan Gifford was wearing an identical ring—gold with a crest of interwoven hands. Sarah had designed it herself as she lay dying of fever in Antigua. It was so like her to insist on this funeral custom. She knew that all the members of the immediate family would wear these rings for at least a year and occasionally thereafter around the anniversary of her death. Caroline could almost hear Sarah saying with confident mockery: *You will never forget me.*

My father was responding to Caroline Skinner with an edge of hysteria in his voice. I suppose he felt especially vulnerable because one of our Kemble cousins was married to the British general Thomas Gage. Her brother, Stephen Kemble, was currently deputy adjutant general of the British army that was cooped up in Boston by some eighteen or twenty thousand Americans under George Washington.

"I would like to have a formal promise from this young man, that anything spoken in this room will never reach the ears of a county committeeman. Or one of their officious lackeys."

"He *is* one of their officious lackeys," Anthony Skinner said.

My mother emphatically agreed with my father. Most of her family had already fled Massachusetts for England. She touched her gauze-wrapped head and huffed: "A proper subordination is what these people must be taught. They should have learned it in the cradle—or soon after—"

She aimed a glare at Jonathan Gifford with these words.

I writhed in my seat, almost ashamed to acknowledge them as

my parents, yet too cautious to be an all-out rebel. On January 1, 1776, no one knew where the Revolution was going. A few thoughtful men may have glimpsed the future. But for most of us it was a murky, New England-spawned cloud into which prognosticators looked and saw what they hoped or wanted to see.

I could see this much—Kemble was about to treat us to some radical fireworks. Jonathan Gifford saw it too. "I will vouch for Kemble's silence—though I personally think it is unnecessary for me to do such a thing."

"I could not agree more," Caroline said, giving Kemble one of those bright smiles that remarkably illuminated her small, ordinarily solemn face. "It's bad enough that members of the same nation have bayonets at each other's throats. I hope we shall never reach the point where members of the same family—"

"God forbid, my dear," Charles Skinner said.

"Which does not mean," Caroline said, "that I think we should abandon the defense of our rights. If we stand firm, I am sure England will give us what we ask."

"I fear that may be a vain wish, Mrs. Skinner," my father said. "If you act the rebel, you cannot expect your sovereign to treat you generously."

"I think history will justify us, Mr. Kemble. You may imply I am a sentimental, foolish woman—but I think we should refrain from calling each other rebels. Or Whigs or Tories or violent democrats or dangerous republicans. Refrain until the last extremity."

"Those names mean something, my dear Mrs. Skinner," Charles Skinner said. "Perhaps they may shock sense into some who need it."

"In my opinion," Kate said, "whether a man is a Whig or a Tory, a radical or a moderate, is not half as important as the quality of his—his heart."

She turned to Anthony Skinner as she said this last word. He smiled and took her hand. Kemble's jaw tightened. He had never liked Anthony and it infuriated him to see his sister in love with a man who was now his political antagonist. Jonathan Gifford wished for the hundredth time that Anthony had stayed in England to practice law, as his father and Governor Franklin had urged him. Caroline Skinner saw some of this on Jonathan Gifford's face and understood his feelings. Few mothers have been closer to the children of their blood than she had been to Anthony when he was growing up. She had taken a personal pride in his precocious interest in law and politics. It had stunned her when he returned from three years in England a convinced Royalist, full of sneers at the men who were leading American resistance to Parliament's greed. He had become one of Governor Franklin's favorite house guests; in fact, the young favorite of all that wealthy circle of judges, customs officers, doctors, and Church of England clergymen who clustered around the governor in Perth Amboy.

A moment after Caroline Skinner looked into Jonathan Gifford's face, an absurd drama performed itself in her mind. It was night. She was in a boat with him, being rowed toward a ship in New York Harbor. She was stepping on board it, his strong arm around her waist. A mate was shouting orders, sails crackled, masts creaked, they were under way for an unknown island, Martinique, Cuba, Jamaica. All in a blinding, impossible flash, invisible to everyone, only freezing her hand on the silver teapot for the briefest moment. Then she heard her own voice asking, "More tea, Captain Gifford?"

"No. No thank you, Mrs. Skinner," Jonathan Gifford said. "I think we had better go. The Committee of Safety is meeting at the tavern tonight. I must see to their dinner."

"You take their paper money?" Charles Skinner asked.

"What else can I do? It's the coin of the realm."

"It's no coin for me, sir. Nothing short of bayonets will persuade me to take it. I am extending credit to every man who grinds at my mill, rather than take it."

"What will you do when you bring your crops to market?" Jonathan Gifford asked.

"I think a British fleet and army will settle that question before harvest time. Don't you yourself think so?"

Before Jonathan Gifford had to answer that difficult question, the beat of a galloping horse's hoofs sounded on the drive. A moment later, a hand pounded on the door. One of the servants opened it and as all of us peered into the center hall, Cortland Skinner, attorney general of New Jersey, burst upon us. He was wearing a dark blue cloak which had done little to protect his breeches and stockings from the mud flung up by his horse's hoofs. Ordinarily a rider in bad weather wore sherryvallies, a long, tight pantaloon that reached to the ankles. Skinner's shirt was soiled, his waistcoat was a greasy leather item he obviously wore when strolling about his farm. The same was true of his square-skirted, sad-colored coat, which he must have inherited from his father. He was wigless and his hair was unpowdered—by and large a strange costume for a man who prided himself on always being in fashion. But the agitation on his face made us forget the attorney general's undress.

"Cousin Charles," he said, "I thought your company would be gone by now. I see I must throw myself on all your mercies."

"What in the world are you talking about, my dear Cortland?"

"I just received a message from Governor Franklin," Skinner said, his sensitive mouth twitching, his sallow aristocratic face contorted with anger and fear. "He tells me his confidential letters to the Secretary of State have been intercepted. In the packet was a letter of mine to my brother William in which I spoke freely about the pretensions of our treasonous friends."

Charles Skinner's face turned an unwholesome magenta. "By God, they have overreached themselves this time. The King's mail—"

"Nothing is sacred or illegal to these people once Congress approves their conduct. Have you not heard about their latest resolution?"

It was obvious that none of us had heard about it. New Jersey did not have a newspaper. We depended on the New York papers, which took several days to reach us.

"They condemned unworthy Americans," Cortland Skinner said, sarcastically reciting the text, " 'who regardless of their duty to their Creator, their country, and their posterity, have taken part with our oppressors.' They said they ought to be disarmed and the more dangerous among them kept in safe custody."

The silence in the room was funereal. Every face, including Jonathan Gifford's, was grim. Only Kemble Stapleton's eyes were aglow with fierce delight.

"Do you think you'll be arrested, Mr. Skinner?" Jonathan Gifford asked.

"There is no question about it. They arrested two judges and a justice of the peace last week in Hunterdon County. Any man who dares to speak his mind against these people is their enemy."

"What did you say in your letter?"

"Much the same thing that the governor said in his letter to the Secretary of State. These people were aiming at independence and nothing would stop them but a British army and fleet."

Confusion now replaced the wrath on Charles Skinner's face. Those words were virtually an echo of what he had just finished telling us. "I don't see how we can keep you concealed here. The servants come and go about the house and gossip with the field hands. They know who you are."

"I realize that," Cortland Skinner said. "I only intend to stay until the night is well advanced. A sloop will pick me up from your beach about eleven o'clock. By morning I should be aboard one of the King's men-of-war in New York Harbor."

"Is Governor Franklin going with you?" Anthony Skinner asked. William Franklin was one of the last, if not the very last royal governor at his post. In North Carolina, South Carolina, Virginia, New York, the governors and other royal officials had retreated to British warships offshore.

Skinner shook his head. "He intends to stand his ground. His lady is almost beside herself with anxiety. I urged him to come. A single man cannot fight a mob."

"I could call out the old militia," Charles Skinner said. "I dare say a good third of the old regiment would turn out. What do you think, friend Jonathan?"

The royal militia and its officers had been dismissed by Congress and a new militia organization created in its place. The old regiment still existed in the minds of many, particularly the officers. But Jonathan Gifford knew from listening and talking to the hundreds of men who drank in his taproom that Skinner was dreaming.

"You would get no more than a tenth, and expose yourself and them to insult," he said.

Charles Skinner obviously did not believe him.

"They have created a government," Jonathan Gifford continued. "Committees of Safety in every county. A legislature. At least half the people support them. It seems to me all we can do is wait and see how this government conducts itself. And what the government of Great Britain does about it."

"I think the Captain is quite right," Cortland Skinner said. "We must bide our time. Let's be consoled by the thought that the longer we wait, the sweeter will be the revenge."

Jonathan Gifford thought Charles Skinner looked dubious at

these words and my father was clearly shocked. A scholarly, rather shy man, Father's deep reverence for the law made the Revolution abhorrent to him. But counterrevolution, the bloody business of attainders and confiscations and beheadings, was even more detestable. Political revenge was equally foreign to Charles Skinner's nature.

"I will most certainly offer you every aid and protection in my power until you leave the house tonight," he said. "A change of clothes, a good dinner, everything and anything is yours to command. As for the rest of us . . ." He turned to our little band of tea drinkers. "Our joking talk about keeping silent about certain matters has now become very serious indeed. I have no doubt that we are all men and women of honor and will say not a word about Mr. Skinner's visit."

He stared particularly hard at Kemble as he said these last words.

"I suggest you get his horse into your carriage house as soon as possible," Jonathan Gifford said.

"Quite right. Tend to that, will you, Anthony?" Charles Skinner said. "Hide Mr. Skinner's saddle in the hay for the time being."

The party was clearly over. Goodbyes were subdued.

Outside the snow was blowing and whirling into a blizzard. Kate was wearing a crimson capuchin lined with ermine. She drew the cloak around her and put the hood over her glowing hair, making a rare combination of colors. My mother and sister Sally looked perfectly ridiculous in huge calashes, hoods of light green silk a foot and a half in diameter. Nothing else fit over their absurd "heads." Kemble mounted his big black gelding, Thunder, and glared while Kate and Anthony Skinner had a final tête-à-tête. Captain Gifford gathered his old dark red officer's cloak around his shoulders and mounted his chaise, where he sat patiently waiting for Kate. With an angry gesture, Kemble swung Thunder's head into the road and cantered off.

Watching, Caroline Skinner felt a rush of sympathy for Jonathan Gifford. "Kate," she said, "your father's waiting in the snow." Kate extracted her hand from Anthony Skinner's grasp and took her seat beside Captain Gifford in the chaise. He handed her a big bearskin muff and arranged her capuchin to give her the best possible protection, then covered her knees with a sable blanket.

Was it all paternal affection, Caroline wondered, or testimony that his love for Sarah was still a living thing? Why, she wondered, did she wish so hard against that last idea? She stood in the doorway, watching them until the chaise turned into the main road and vanished in a whirl of snowflakes that seemed to obliterate everything but the gray, lowering sky.

CHAPTER TWO

FOR MOST OF the half-hour's ride home, Jonathan Gifford and his stepdaughter said little. He was concentrating on safety. The snow covered many of the worst rocks and ruts in the road and he was soon reining in the sturdy little Narraganset pacer between the shafts of the chaise. Ordinarily Captain Gifford traveled at what some people thought a reckless pace, considering the awful roads. But he was an expert horseman, remarkably deft at avoiding obstacles on the road that sent many a chaise and rider into the ditch.

Kate thought her father's silence was caused by what was absorbing her mind. When she finally spoke, it was with caution.

"Anthony pushed me again—for an answer."

"The way you were looking at him, I thought you had said yes."

"I would like your approval."

"Nothing I heard today was likely to change my mind."

"Sometimes I wish I'd never heard the word 'politics.'"

"Wishing doesn't change the way the world turns, Kate," Jonathan Gifford said, giving the pacer his head down a straight stretch of road which he knew was reasonably safe. "Sometimes you sound as Irish as my mother."

"Anthony says these committeemen and their soldiers will run away at the first sight of a British grenadier."

"Maybe they will. But let's hope it doesn't come to grenadiers. I simply don't think you should marry a man with such extreme views in times like these."

"Goddamn it to hell, what am I supposed to do? Grow old and wrinkled waiting for the politicians to settle matters?"

Jonathan Gifford sighed. There was no hope of correcting

Kate's language. Her mother had displayed a similar fondness for oaths that shocked the prim and pious. "Katey, you're eighteen. Give politics a year. Give Anthony Skinner a year. Maybe once the glow of London wears off him, he'll look like a very different fellow."

"What do you mean by that? Are you reminding me he's a bastard, whispering behind his back like all the other damn hypocrites in this state?"

"No."

"I know how he feels. I go through the same thing whenever I go out these days."

"Kate—that is nothing but imagination."

"That's easy for you to say. You don't have to put up with the looks and sniggers. I can practically hear them sneering 'like mother like daughter.'"

"Kate—"

She was looking away from him, knowing she had broached a forbidden subject. "Oh, Father, why don't you like him? I thought you'd appreciate his good manners, his sense of style, his—his manliness."

"Kate. I've told you before, I don't think he's the husband for you. But if your heart chooses him, I will never stand in your way. No man can bind a woman's feelings. Only she can do that. But she may regret it—"

"Yes," Kate said. "I know all about that."

He was tempted to tell her she knew nothing. But that would only bring them back to the forbidden subject. Not that Sarah was literally forbidden. It was the pain she had caused and was still causing that made it impossible to talk about her.

Jonathan Gifford took his eyes off the road to study Kate for a moment. Her face was as beautiful as any idealized image of the court paintings of Louis XV or England's Stuarts at the height of their licentious glory. But it was purified by youth and a peculiarly American innocence of the worldly dross which cast a subtle stain upon European images of beauty. Kate had her mother's dark red hair and green Kemble eyes, full of the kind of light created by sunbeams on deep grass. Her mouth was strong and wide, with a ripe underlip that was said to be proof of a passionate nature. By the more fragile standards of aristocratic beauty, her body may have seemed too solid, almost muscular, especially in the athletic

39

arch of her back and firm, supple neck. But this was an American girl, bursting with a vitality that most European women never experienced in their constricted lives. Did this mean she would be tormented by the same wild, willful spirit that had destroyed her mother? Jonathan Gifford did not know the answer to that question.

Ahead the lights of the tavern and the little village that had grown up around it were visible through the snow. They passed Parmenas Corson's blacksmith shop, Ruben Husted's cooper's shop, the dry goods store of our reigning merchant, Isaac Low, the shops of Auke Wikof, the gunsmith, and Job Allen, our shoe- and bootmaker. Finally there was the tavern looming up in the twilight. It looked even bigger than it really was, with its outline blurred by the gathering darkness. Seeing the blaze from the huge fireplace glowing in the taproom windows, Kate was stirred by a warm rush of memories. How many other evenings had she come home around this time from visiting Sally Kemble or some other cousin or friend and been cheered by the bulk, the solidity of this building.

The tavern sat back from the road a good hundred yards, creating a kind of spacious, comfortable assurance to arriving visitors. Plenty of room, it seemed to say, plenty of room and good cheer inside. In daylight the first-floor walls of thick gray fieldstone gave it a somewhat fortress-like appearance. The wooden upper floor and wooden roof to the stone porch that ran the length of the building added a comfortable companionable touch of home.

Above all else was the sense of order, neatness, command that the place communicated. The wooden upper floor, the trim of the windows, the porch pillars were always pristine white. They were painted twice a year. Kate knew how much time and effort all this took. She knew this man beside her in the chaise was responsible for it. It made her, for a moment at least, grateful for the order, the comfort, the care he had brought into her life, grateful for him and sorry for the pain she was causing him now. She was simultaneously able to forgive herself because the pain he felt, the turmoil she felt was part of this wider upheaval, which Anthony told her would change America forever.

"I'm sorry, Father," she said.

"It's all right, it's all right," he said.

Black Sam, the Negro stableman, was waiting on the porch beneath the tavern's sign. The words Strangers' Resort were painted in blue on a field of white. Above them was the silhouette of a wayfarer hiking along with a staff in his hand. Jonathan Gifford threw the reins to Sam and told him to give the pacer a pint of beer and a good rubdown. The little horse was famous for his fondness for beer and cider.

Sam nodded and put up the fur collar of his matchcoat. Jonathan Gifford had worn it campaigning against the French in Canada. "Mighty busy night, 'spite of this weather. I'd be glad to work at the bar, if you need some help."

"Busy?"

"Soldiers," Sam said, twitching the reins and expertly guiding the horse around the corner of the tavern toward the barn.

"Another recruiting party?"

Lately, recruiters for the four New Jersey regiments of the regular American army had been making speeches in Strangers' Resort two and three times a week. As indignation over the blood spilled at Lexington and Concord faded, Americans were proving as reluctant to sign away their freedom and join the regulars as the British. The recruiters were now using the same tactics Captain Gifford had seen in England and Ireland—equal amounts of liquor and patriotism.

Kemble emerged from the shadows, his eyes bright with excitement. "It's the militia, Father. Our militia regiment."

Jonathan Gifford instantly expected trouble, not from the militia but from Kemble. He brooded for a moment on that sensitive face, only half visible in the glow of the oil lamps on the tavern porch. The large, intense forehead, the fine high-crowned fragile nose, the narrow, stubborn jaw and precise mouth could have belonged to a Puritan squire of the previous century. It was a thoroughbred face, marred by mild arrogance. But this would pass with youth. It was the rest of Kemble's physical self that troubled Jonathan Gifford. Everything about him spelled fragility, from his delicate hands to his narrow shoulders and pinched chest. Raising him had been a perpetual struggle against disease.

There was so much that was fine in the boy, such rich promise. In his first two years at the College of New Jersey at Princeton he had stood at the top of his class. He was doing the same thing in his third year when an attack of pleurisy sent him home. To Kemble's indignation, his father had refused to let him return this year. He feared the effect on his lungs of another year in that icy dormitory. The decision had done nothing to improve relations between him and Kemble. At least, Jonathan Gifford thought, he still calls me father. How much longer would that last? How much longer would anything last?

From inside the tavern came a crash that made Kate cry out with fright. Jonathan Gifford knew the sound. It was a musket shot.

"You'd better go down to the house, Kate," he said.

She looked cross but obeyed him and followed the path down to the high-porched red brick house that Jonathan Gifford had built beside the brook about a quarter of a mile from the tavern.

In the taproom Jonathan Gifford found four or five men at every one of the round stone tables and dozens more at the bar and around the fireplace. There were at least two hundred of them. Their guns were stacked along the wall by the fireplace. A musket close to the blazing hearth had just gone off. Everyone thought it was funny. They grinned while a gaunt man wearing an old bagwig denounced a runty boy of fifteen in a voice that was loud enough to shake the paintings of George III and George II off the walls. "Didn't I tell you not to charge your piece until you heard a positive order, soldier?" shouted Colonel Samuel Breese. "'Pon my word, the liberties of your country may depend upon your obedience to such orders. As a punishment, my man, you will bed down without your supper. Consider yourself fortunate. In the British army you would have a hundred strokes of the lash. Ain't that right, Captain Gifford?"

"Absolutely, Colonel Breese," said Jonathan Gifford. Breese was a veteran of the Seven Years' War, in which he had achieved the rank of sergeant. Like many others, he had fallen in love with soldiering and this explained his present eminence as the commander of a militia regiment. That and his fanatic Presbyterianism, which inclined him to see George III and the Church of England not merely as tyrants, but agents of the devil.

In New Jersey and the other colonies of middle America, a man's religion had a great deal to do with his politics. We were not religiously homogeneous, like New England. Presbyterians were almost all fierce revolutionists. Jonathan Gifford and all our relatives were nominal members of the Church of England, which inclined us toward loyalty or neutrality.

42

Breese had his old army knapsack on his back. Around his waist he was encumbered with a canteen, a cartridge box, a bayonet scabbard, and a sword. He looked ridiculous, but Jonathan Gifford treated him with grave decorum. "What brings you out in such bad weather, Colonel?" he asked.

"Orders," said Breese. About half his teeth were missing, enabling him to snap his upper lip over his lower lip in a style that was more grotesque than impressive. "Secret orders."

He stepped close enough to Jonathan Gifford to say in a stage whisper that was easily overheard by militiamen all around him: "Between us I 'spect it's to arrest some great men for betraying the liberties of their country."

Jonathan Gifford nodded and asked Breese if his men had brought their own provisions. He doubted if he had enough food on hand to feed them dinner.

"They had orders to bring two days' victuals with them," said the Colonel, looking around. "Them that hasn't done it will have to pay their own way. We hoped to be in Amboy this night, but the storm slowed our muster. We must make use of your barns, I fear, and mayhap the floor of the meeting room, when the Committee finishes."

"They are at your service, Colonel."

Jonathan Gifford looked around him at the flushed, excited faces of the militiamen. He saw them with a double vision—as a neighbor and friend, and as a former professional soldier. Many were men he liked, men to whom he had loaned money after more than one bad harvest, men who amused him, like fat, loquacious Private Samson Tucker, who never ceased complaining about the woes of a fallow farm, a sharp-tongued wife, and five daughters. Clinking glasses with him was Captain Nathaniel Fitzmorris, an ebullient young giant who had recently inherited one of the best farms in Middletown. He had spent a year wooing Kate in vain. At a nearby table sat one of Kemble's boyhood friends, John Tharp. He was defying his Quaker parents by shouldering a gun in the Cause.

To the eyes of a former professional soldier, these men raised grave doubts. Instead of uniforms, they wore the loose homespun coats and leather breeches of the average farmer. They were not part of the American regular army. They were temporary soldiers, who were supposed to train several times a month, and be ready to turn out if the British invaded their state. Most of them never showed up for their training sessions, which were boring rehearsals of the manual of arms. Their officers were ignoramuses like Colonel Breese who knew nothing about tactics or strategy. No one had taught them how to use a bayonet, the British army's weapon of choice.

Yet these were the men on whom the Americans were depending if the gunfire that had begun in Massachusetts last April became a war. Americans had been mesmerized by the way the minutemen—the militia of New England—had turned out to batter the British at Lexington and Concord and Bunker Hill. The Continental Congress had decided America did not need a big regular army and missed their chance to recruit one when every man's indignation over the news of Lexington inclined him to be a soldier. They were convinced that patriotism would turn the farmers of America into invincible infantry at the beat of a muster drum.

Jonathan Gifford did not believe it. For Kemble it was an article of faith. To doubt it was tantamount to treason. When Jonathan Gifford showed him a letter from Major William Moncrieff of the King's Own Regiment claiming that the British were outnumbered six to one at Lexington and Concord, Kemble dismissed it as an official lie. He preferred the New England newspaper reports which gave the impression that a few hundred minutemen had routed two thousand redcoats.

Dr. Christopher Davie seized Jonathan Gifford's arm. He was an elf of a man with a head that seemed too large for his body. He wore an old frock coat two decades out of style and an equally old-fashioned bagwig. Dr. Davie had spent twenty years in the British army as surgeon of the Royal Welsh Fusiliers. Like Captain Gifford, he had retired at the end of the Seven Years' War. Meeting him at the house of a mutual friend in New York, the Captain had persuaded the old Scot to settle at the tavern and practice his often unorthodox medicine among us. Dr. Davie had no love for George III. But he had had his fill of rebellions. He had lost half his family in the Scottish risings of 1715 and 1745.

"You are just in time, Gifford," he said. "They were about to start pot-shotting the King's portraits, so help me. Did you ever in your life see anything so damn foolish as pouring liquor into men with loaded guns?"

44

Jonathan Gifford agreed with Dr. Davie. "I wouldn't let these men drink any more if I were you, Colonel," he said to Breese.

"Precisely my opinion," said Breese, who was more than a little drunk himself. "On your feet, lads. We'll muster in the barns for a soldier's supper."

"Another round, Colonel," came a voice from the corner. Instantly it became a chorus. "*Another round. Another round.*"

Breese waggled his head on his long, thin neck. "No, lads, no. We're under orders now. We must be soldiers."

A squat, swarthy man at the table in the bay window stood up. "Damn it, Breese," Captain Daniel Slocum roared, "give them another round. It's the least you can do for fellows ready to stick a bayonet up the King's ass for their country's sake."

A drunken cheer greeted these words. Breese blinked thoughtfully for a moment. "Well. Mayhap it will do no harm. Another round it is. But the last, it must be the last."

Jonathan Gifford ducked behind the bar and nodded to a slab of a man with a red face that seemed to extend, at least in color, to the crown of his bald head. Between Barney McGovern and Jonathan Gifford there was a unique combination of trust and affection. Barney had been the senior sergeant of the Captain's company in the King's Own Regiment.

"What are they drinking?" Jonathan Gifford asked.

"Cider, what else?" growled Barney McGovern. "Except for his nibs, the Colonel. He's on flip. And the great Whig, Captain Slocum. He's drinking stonewall, and plenty of it."

This was a mixture of rum and hard cider, which more than lived up to its name.

"He'll have a headache tomorrow. Who's at the table with him?"

"Who else but more Slocums?"

The Slocums were a family who had attracted little attention until our troubles with England began. Most of them were obscure dirt farmers, scratching out a bare subsistence on cheap, unproductive land in the vicinity of the pine country. Daniel Slocum owned fifty acres of heavily mortgaged but relatively good land in the Colt's Neck neighborhood. This was five times bigger than any other farm in the family and automatically made him the clan leader. In our rising revolutionary ferment, Captain Slocum had pushed his way to the front rank of the liberty boys with his outspoken enthusiasm for total defiance of Great Britain and a ferocious hostility of all those who had a word to say on the King's behalf.

"You pour the cider. I'll do the honors for Breese and Slocum. Has the Committee of Safety arrived?"

"They're in the Crown Room this very moment," said Barney. "Well tended by Black Bertha and me own darlin' wife."

"Good. Have they got their bishop?"

"They have," said Barney. "Piping hot."

Bishop was a favorite New Jersey drink in 1776. It was a mixture of wine, sugar, and oranges served hot in tumblers.

Jonathan Gifford nodded his approval and began preparing the flip. Strangers' Resort had its own recipe, which Captain Gifford had picked up in his travels through New England. The magical ingredients were four pounds of sugar, four eggs, and a pint of cream, beaten well and left to stand two days. Four great spoonfuls of this mixture were stirred into a quart mug filled two thirds with strong beer, then bolstered by a gill of rum.

"Shall it be a bellows top, Colonel?" Jonathan Gifford asked.

"Oh yes, bellows bellows, 'pon my word," said Breese.

A fresh egg was quickly whipped into the tankard, then Jonathan Gifford limped to the fireplace and took from the coals the glowing poker—the "dog" as we called it—and plunged it into the liquid. A creamy white froth rose over the edge of the tankard, a tribute to the late-whipped egg.

Colonel Breese stood by Jonathan Gifford's elbow now, literally smacking his lips. "'Pon my word, Captain Gifford," he said, "I swear there isn't a better flip made between here and Boston."

Jonathan Gifford accepted the compliment with a brief smile. He took a bottle of rum and a jug of hard cider from the bar and walked over to Daniel Slocum's table. The Captain was surrounded by his three oldest sons, his brother Samuel with his two sons, and a half-dozen cousins. All shared the swarthy complexion that gave Slocum his nickname, "Black Daniel." He was describing a patriotic task that he and his fellow liberty boys had performed in Middletown on Christmas Day. They had tarred and feathered a wheelwright named Benson for singing "God Save the King" in front of the local liberty pole.

"We made the tar hot enough to roast the bastard," Slocum said. "You should have heard him yell when we dipped him in it.

46

When we spread the feathers on him, we jabbed a good two dozen of them in quill first. But the rail. Oh, boys, you should have heard him when we hoisted him on that. In a minute or two he was screaming his balls were split for sure."

"He changed his tune, I hear?" asked one of the Slocum cousins.

"Oh, he did, he did. Standing there with the tar dripping off his ass, he told us he was a much deceived man. We were right. George the Third and the British Parliament were enemies of the liberties of this country. He apologized to us and his fellow citizens for his bad behavior and poor understanding."

Everyone at the table laughed heartily. Jonathan Gifford did not join the merriment. He had heard from Dr. Davie, who had visited Benson only yesterday, that the wheelwright had suffered serious burns and might not recover.

"I understand you're drinking stonewall, Captain Slocum," he said.

"I am, Captain Gifford. But I don't expect to pay for it."

"Why not?"

"I'm risking my health on this foul night in the service of the honorable Congress. The least you can do is contribute a drink to the Cause. You ought to do the same for every man in this room."

"I have to charge for what I serve or go out of business, Captain. But you know that I stand a round now and then for everyone who drinks here regularly. We'll consider this"—he filled his glass—"the custom of the house."

In the center of the room, Colonel Breese was holding his flip high and offering a toast. "The liberty of America."

The word came back with an enthusiastic roar. "*Liberty.*"

Jonathan Gifford wondered if any of these men really agreed on the meaning of that magic word. It was such an easy thing to shout. But when it came to the business of everyday life, agreement became very complicated. Inevitably, the word promised different things to different people. Some of these militiamen were indentured servants, Irishmen or Scotsmen who had sold themselves into bondage for five or six years to pay their passage to America. Most of the others were small or middling farmers who toiled ten or twelve hours a day on the thousand and one tasks involved in raising crops and cattle. A few were hired hands

living on thirty or forty pounds a year. Liberty could not mean the
same thing to all these men.

"You'll excuse me, Colonel, the Committee of Safety is meeting upstairs."

"That we know," said Breese. "I believe the General is with
them."

"No. But he will be shortly."

In the doorway of the taproom stood a towering figure in a
thick bearskin coat that made him look even larger than he already was. Fifty-year-old William Alexander was six foot three
and his blue and buff trimmed cocked hat added another two or
three inches to his height. He had a strong, brooding face dominated by a high-crowned nose. One of the richest men in America,
he had been a member of Governor William Franklin's Council
until he accepted command of New Jersey's revolutionary militia
last year. The governor had ordered him to resign from the command or the Council. Alexander had chosen to leave the Council.
Although he did not live in the neighborhood, Alexander often
stopped at Strangers' Resort on his frequent trips to New York,
where he also owned much valuable real estate. He greeted
Jonathan Gifford cordially, and they chatted for a few minutes
about the latest military news from Boston.

"Between the two of us," said Alexander, "Washington is having the devil of a time recruiting men for a year's service. Isn't
that just like a Yankee? Start a fight and then run home, claiming
God told him it was time to warm his backside by his fireplace."
Like many Americans south of Connecticut, Alexander had a low
opinion of New Englanders and seldom hesitated to express it.

"The Committee is in the Crown Room, my lord," Jonathan
Gifford said, giving Alexander the title which everyone in New
Jersey conceded him. He claimed the earldom of Stirling and had
spent years in England arguing his case.

Halfway down the hall, Alexander asked Gifford to send a bottle of claret up to the Crown Room. "My winter visitor is with
me again," he said, holding up his big hand. It was twisted into
the shape of a claw. He had inherited a predisposition to rheuma-
tism from his father and each winter the disease wracked him.

"Immediately," Jonathan Gifford said, studying Alexander for a
moment. He was a committed man, a serious man, close to his
own age. No young hothead. Alexander could have been sitting

48

before the fire in his mansion at Basking Ridge, drinking better claret than he could buy here. His twisted hands must be throbbing with exquisite pain, after hours on the road in the cruel January cold.

The three committeemen were deep into their bowl of bishop when Alexander strode into the room. They were not the most impressive men in New Jersey, Jonathan Gifford thought wryly, as he watched them toast Alexander and declare themselves ready to fight and die for liberty.

Diminutive Lemuel Peters was so excitable, he always looked as though he were about to jump out of his skin. His pop eyes blinked, his button nose twitched constantly. But their activity was somnolent compared to his tongue. Massachusetts-born and Harvard-educated, he had come to New Jersey to tutor the children of several wealthy families. He set up a school and prospered. He closed it and bought a farm, which he proposed to work scientifically. But he spent most of the time riding around the countryside denouncing George III and his ministers while his wife and children did the sowing and plowing without benefit of him or science.

Ambrose Cotter was a large, well-padded man with a mouth that had an odd downward slant which seemed to drag his pendulous nose and languid eyes with it, making him the only human being I have seen who could literally be called two-faced. He was from New Haven, had done a turn as a merchant in New York, went broke, and retreated to New Jersey, where he defended a small farm against numerous lawsuits.

The third committeeman was Jasper Clark, deacon of the local Presbyterian church, a plain, mild-mannered man whose chief distinction was fathering twelve children. He could barely sign his name, and he once admitted to Jonathan Gifford that he had learned this much penmanship only a few years ago. He was a cousin of Abraham Clark, one of the state's delegates to the Continental Congress. The deacon's two oldest sons were in the regular or "Continental" army, serving with New Jersey regiments ordered north to support the American invasion of Canada.

"I thought I should advise you gentlemen of a military order which we are about to execute in this district," Alexander said. "Captain Gifford, you should know about it, too. It may need some explaining to the local folks. Tomorrow morning I expect to place Governor Franklin and Attorney General Skinner under arrest."

"Arrest—the governor?" Jasper Clark said. It was an idea which had obviously never occurred to him before.

"He has proven himself what I long suspected him to be," Alexander said, "an enemy to this country."

"I will second that motion," said Lemuel Peters, downing half a glass of bishop.

"But—what are the charges, my lord?" asked Clark. "I for one feel we must conduct ourselves in the most regular manner."

"Damn manners when the rights of our country are at stake," bawled Peters. "Am I right, Mr. Cotter?"

"Absolutely right," said Cotter, helping himself to some more bishop.

While Jonathan Gifford remained a silent spectator, Alexander told the Committee how one of his men had intercepted the governor's mail. In a report to the Colonial Secretary, Franklin had hinted strongly that many Americans in New Jersey were guilty of treason. The rebels' real goal was not a defense of their rights as Englishmen—it was independence. Another letter in the packet, from Attorney General Cortland Skinner, was even more damning, Alexander said, and recited what the attorney general himself had admitted earlier in the day—his call for a British fleet and army to suppress the rebellion.

"Those are hanging words, yes, they are," shouted Lemuel Peters. "The men of Old England cut off the head of Charles I for less than that."

"I would be satisfied for the present to put our noble governor in a quiet place, where he can do us no harm," Alexander said.

Jonathan Gifford did not know William Franklin well. He had shaken his hand once or twice when he stopped at the tavern en route to a meeting of the Assembly at Burlington. Tall and good-looking, he had a strange mixture of pomposity and familiarity in his nature. He would stand at the bar and drink with the local farmers—but he traveled in a cream-colored coach with the royal crest emblazoned in gold on the doors. He always wore expensive clothes—satins and silks in the latest London style. There was a saying that the governor carried a farm on his back—the price of his clothes would buy a good piece of land. But this caused him no trouble in a country where all the rich dressed lavishly and most men had enough money to satisfy their ordinary wants.

The governor was popular—at least as popular as a man appointed by the King, with no need to stand the test of a vote, could be. He was also a shrewd and skillful politician. Only last month he had presided at a meeting of the legally elected Royal Assembly at Burlington, urged moderation, declared himself a friend of America's rights, and denounced independence. He urged the Assembly to petition the King as the spokesmen of a separate colony, without consulting the Continental Congress. The Assembly had agreeably voted as the governor wished. A rush visit from three Continental Congressmen had persuaded them to change their minds and preserve America's unity. Governor Franklin's performance had obviously convinced the rebel leaders that he was too dangerous to tolerate any longer in his post.

"Shall I go get that bottle of claret, your lordship?"

"By all means, Captain Gifford," said Alexander.

Walking down the shadowed hall, Jonathan Gifford almost collided with Kemble. There was nothing unusual about his being there. He was the secretary of the Committee of Safety, and Jonathan Gifford thought at first he was going to share their dinner. But Kemble had other things on his mind.

"I was listening at the door, Father. You didn't say a word about Skinner. Are you going to help conceal that traitor?"

"I made a promise—as a gentleman—"

"I did not hear you say a word. I didn't say a word."

"As I understand it, we bound ourselves by our silence. If you intended to betray the man, you should have told him."

"What kind of nonsense is that, Father? We're fighting a war."

"We are not fighting a war. Not here in New Jersey. The war is in Massachusetts. Let's hope it stays there."

"I'm going to tell them where Skinner is hiding."

"No you're not."

"Yes I am."

Jonathan Gifford seized his son by the shirt and slammed him against the wall. Kemble gasped with shock and pain. Like many military men, Captain Gifford concealed beneath his habitual calm a tension that could explode into rage. He had spent much of his life struggling to tame this violence that seemed to live within him, like a surly animal. He struggled to control it now.

"A man doesn't betray his friends, Kemble. You grew up with Cortland Skinner's sons—"

He loosened his grip on Kemble's shirt. His son retreated down the hall into the taproom, where the militiamen were thundering a Massachusetts liberty song.

> *"Come swallow your bumpers, ye Tories, and roar*
> *That the sons of fair Freedom are hampered once more;*
> *But know that no cutthroats our spirits can tame,*
> *Nor a host of oppressors shall smother the flame."*

Back in the Crown Room, Jonathan Gifford watched William Alexander, Lord Stirling, demolish the bottle of claret. "Ah," he said, holding up the stiffened fingers of his left hand. "They're coming alive. Yesterday, Gifford, I wasn't able to sign an order."

"Would you like some supper, my lord? We can easily spread another place for you here. These gentlemen will be dining soon."

"No thank you. The Livingstons expect me for the night. I'm damned late already and I'd better push on." He turned to the committeemen. "I'm glad to find you approve of my decision, gentlemen. I am convinced that if Governor Franklin remains at liberty another day, none of us are safe."

"Most assuredly, my lord," said Lemuel Peters. "And that rascal Skinner, too."

"I would appreciate it if you passed a resolution tonight, affirming your support of this decision."

"Consider it passed, my lord," said Peters.

In all his years in Ireland and England, Jonathan Gifford had never heard anyone say "my lord" as deferentially as Peters. Escorting Alexander to the front door, Jonathan Gifford called for his horse. In a minute or two Black Sam led a sorrel stallion from the shadows.

"Have you heard from your old friend Rutherford?" Stirling asked as he mounted.

Rutherford was an ex-major who had married Alexander's sister, Katherine. Jonathan Gifford had had dinner with him at his New York town house several times and they corresponded occasionally.

"I had a letter from him about a month ago," Jonathan Gifford said. "He plans to retreat to his west Jersey house and stay neutral."

"I feared as much," said Stirling heavily. "My son-in-law Watt is playing the same game. It won't work, Gifford. A man must choose one side or the other in this thing."

Jonathan Gifford nodded. "I am afraid you're right."

Upstairs the Committee was settling down to dinner. They ate well, as usual. When they began meeting six months ago, Jonathan Gifford assumed that they would prefer modest fare. Kemble was fond of talking about restoring America's Roman virtue and republican simplicity. But Captain Gifford discovered the Committee preferred to eat like Imperial Romans of the third century.

At a signal from the Captain, Black Bertha, Sam's big, lean wife, and plump Molly McGovern, Barney's spouse, began carrying in dinner. First came oysters and clams and lobsters on beds of ice, then a tureen of clam broth and another of beef broth, then ham, two chickens, a brace of ducks, a side of roast beef, and some lamb pies. Around the fringes of this feast were four or five vegetables, with special emphasis on that favorite New Jersey dish, boiled potatoes. All of this was washed down with quantities of Madeira wine, which Peters and Cotter drank with lip-smacking abandon. Old Jasper Clark was true to the farmer's favorite drink, cider. When the fish and meat were sufficiently ravaged, they were removed and a half-dozen dessert dishes were put down—a jelly full of sliced fruit, floating island, a custard, and a sillabub, a mixture of Madeira wine, sugar, and milk. These, too, were well sampled, and washed down with the last of the bishop. After coffee, fresh bottles of Madeira were brought out, and the gentlemen drank five or six toasts to "the rights of Americans," "General Washington," "the grand American army," "the patriots of New Jersey."

Jonathan Gifford could not help noticing that Kemble, the apostle of revolutionary simplicity, avoided these feasts. He saw in the Revolution only what he wanted to see. Kemble arrived as the last toast was being downed and the table cleared. He opened his minute book and placed a small leather-bound Bible on the table. Lemuel Peters produced a judge's gavel from an inside pocket of his coat and became Mr. Chairman.

The opening witness in the night's first case was an Irish girl with a face pitted from smallpox. Her pursed mouth, by which she tried in vain to conceal her overlapping teeth, gave her a sullen look. She was a bond servant, indentured to the Talbots, one of the more prosperous farmers of the county. Her name was Teresa O'Toole. She had written the Committee a badly spelled letter, claiming that she had heard her master and mistress praising George III and damning Congress. Her master, Richard Talbot, a husky, red-faced, fair-haired man, stood beside her, glaring as she repeated her story in a thick brogue.

"What say you to this charge, Mr. Talbot?" asked Peters.

"I say only this," snapped Talbot. "The girl is a busybody, trying to lie her way out of the four years she has yet to serve on her bond. Not content with cheating me out of full half of the seventy pounds I paid for her, she hopes to avenge herself for numerous just punishments by painting me a traitor."

"Oh, see what he says, sirs," wailed Teresa O'Toole. "He's already vowed to lash me till I bleed for daring to betray him."

"Have you a witness to the words you say Mr. Talbot spoke?" Lemuel Peters asked.

"I went and told their black man, Joshua, the moment I heard it. But now he swears he heard nothing. He fears the lash as much or more as I, your honors."

"Where is Mrs. Talbot?" asked Committeeman Cotter.

"She is—indisposed. The shock of these proceedings has severely indisposed her."

"Sure and that's a shocking lie, your honor," said Teresa O'Toole. "I heard her say this morning that she had no mind to come before you. She called your honors a pack of bankrupt wretches, so she did."

"Is that true, Talbot?" Cotter growled.

"So help me, it isn't. The girl is a most fanciful liar."

"Do you solemnly swear that you support the American Cause?"

"I do. I do most wholeheartedly," Talbot said.

"Wait in the hall," Lemuel Peters said.

The committeemen conferred. Jasper Clark declared himself certain of Richard Talbot's loyalty. He was an old friend. Ambrose Cotter was inclined to believe the Irish girl. So was Lemuel Peters, who found Talbot's behavior "suspicious." But the girl's testimony, without witnesses, was equally suspect. Jasper Clark, who had two bondmen working on his farm, pointed out that it would be a poor example to encourage servants to testify against their masters in such arbitrary fashion.

Jonathan Gifford stood by the door, acting as a sergeant at arms. These hearings against disaffected persons, as they were called, were new. Until a month ago, the County Committees had busied themselves with restructuring the militia and making sure that no one was importing forbidden British goods. Only recently had it become dangerous to criticize the American side of the quarrel with England.

To Jonathan Gifford it was dismaying to see the way the Committees were abrogating that traditional English right—freedom of speech. He was convinced that they were making secret enemies of men like Richard Talbot by forcing him to lie under oath. Jonathan Gifford had no doubt that Talbot was lying. He knew the man well. He had been a major in the old royal militia and had spent more than one night playing cards with him and Charles Skinner here in the tavern. He knew his opinions were not much different from Skinner's—or from Governor William Franklin's, for that matter.

What was the point in humiliating a man like Richard Talbot? No point at all, unless the goal of the patriots or Congress men, as they variously called themselves, was a real revolution, a complete overturn of all government and the creation of an independent state. Richard Talbot had not precisely lied, he had equivocated. Like Charles Skinner, he was a supporter of the rights of America. He did not believe that Parliament had any right to tax Americans, but he also did not believe that the quarrel over this issue was worth a revolution. And he loathed the kind of people who seemed to be in control of this revolution, the Lemuel Peterses, Ambrose Cotters, and Samuel Breeses.

The next two men were accused of casting aspersions on the County Committee. Both had made the statements in the taproom of Strangers' Resort. They were accused by men who had been seated at the same table, pretending to be their friends. Perhaps they were friends, perhaps the patriotism of the accusers was sincere, Jonathan Gifford cautioned himself. But he doubted it. There was too much opportunity for the vicious side of human nature, for meanness, pettiness, jealousy to operate in this system of accusation and intimidation. One man humbly confessed his guilt and begged the Committee's pardon. He was let go with a warning. The second man, a lanky old widower named Clement Billington, admitted everything. He was known locally as "the

Miser" because he loaned money at fierce rates of interest and was not at all hesitant about suing to collect.

"Your honors may put me on the rack, you may do with me what you would, but I will testify with my last breath that you have sitting on your *honorable* Committee a pettifogging welsher who owes me, including interest, forty-eight pounds, ten shillings, twopence British currency. His name is Ambrose Cotter."

"You insult one member of this Committee, you insult them all, sir," Lemuel Peters warned.

"If that is your rule, gentlemen, then I most respectfully insult you all," declared Billington.

"Are you a supporter of your country's rights?" demanded Peters with a judicial frown.

"Most certainly. And I am also a supporter of Great Britain's rights. A large part of our current troubles has, in my opinion, been caused by men who owe vast sums to other Americans or to British merchants and would welcome a revolution to extricate themselves. Mr. Cotter here is a case in point on an infinitesimal scale."

"You impugn my honor once more, sir, and you may have to answer for it at the wrong end of a pistol," Cotter said.

"I decline the challenge. I doubt your carcass would be worth the sum owed," Billington said.

Red blotches of rage were spreading over Cotter's cheeks. He denounced Billington as a liar and a traitor and swore that he had given him power of attorney to collect notes due to him from ex-business associates in New York. Billington insisted it would have taken half his debt in sheriff's fees to collect them. It was a favorite Cotter maneuver, signing over bad debts to cover worse ones.

The Committee found Billington guilty of "disrespect and disdain for his country's cause" and fined him seven pounds. He refused to pay. They threatened him with jail. He told them he would blow out the brains of the first man who came on his property to arrest him. He stalked out of the room. The Committee looked dismayed. Lemuel Peters inflated himself in his odd frog-like way and issued an order to Colonel Breese to arrest Billington and confine him in the county jail. Jasper Clark demurred. It would lead to bloodshed, he declared. Billington had four or five guns in his house and was a dead shot. Peters insisted that Kemble, as secretary of the Committee, write out the order. Kemble told him to write out his own order and declared he would put

56

in the record his disagreement and his belief that Committeeman Cotter should pay his lawful debts.

Jonathan Gifford left them squabbling and retreated to the tap-room, which was, he was glad to see, almost deserted. Barney McGovern had cleared the tables and was polishing the walnut bar. "How goes it with the honorable Committee, Captain?"

"As usual."

"Is it true what I hear from Colonel Breese and his heroes—they're to arrest Governor Franklin tomorrow?"

"It's true."

"Faith, it's a loose game these Americans are playing," Barney said. "You don't dare the English Lion to a fight with clods like Breese to lead you. They'll turn this country into another Ireland, sure as I'm standing here."

Barney was only reciting Captain Gifford's words back to him—a habit that had grown with the years. This was Jonathan Gifford's primary fear. But only a few—those who had come from Ireland and seen the British system in that country—understood it. Not that Gifford had much sympathy for the Catholic Irish—the real victims of the system. They were too crushed, too leaderless, too bewildered to excite more than pity—an emotion far different from sympathy. He himself was Anglo-Irish, the younger son of a Dublin lawyer who had married the daughter of an impoverished Irish Catholic aristocrat. His mother had died when he was a half-grown boy. (One of the reasons he had been glad to play a stepfather's role in America. Strange, the way we often spend our lives repairing the losses of childhood.) From his father, Protestant but an Irish patriot after three generations in the country, Captain Gifford had imbibed the details of England's systematic exploitation of prostrate Ireland.

It was an exploitation based on the most primitive of all laws—the law of conquest. These reckless Americans were giving England a chance to repeat the lucrative performance in America, on a scale that would make Ireland look like a penny-ante game. There were men in England hungry for the chance to do it—powerful men who saw fortunes to be made in confiscated American lands, men whose fathers and grandfathers had made similar fortunes in conquered Scotland and Ireland. Americans were daring them to unleash the British fleet and army, a war machine that had defeated the combined power of France and Spain in the previous decade.

It was madness. Jonathan Gifford poured himself a half tankard of Madeira. Lately it was the only way he got to sleep at night. Barney McGovern poured himself an equal helping of rum.

"Your health, Captain," he said.

"And yours, Sergeant."

"What the devil shall we do, if we find the old Fourth Foot, the King's very own, coming down this bloody road? The way things look, it wouldn't surprise me."

"I don't know," Jonathan Gifford said.

Barney McGovern looked shocked. For almost two decades, he had been used to Captain Gifford deciding with an absolute minimum of hesitation matters ranging from a frontal assault to resigning from the army to serving another brandy to an argumentative drunk. As they finished their drinks, the committeemen came to the door, calling their goodnights and praising the liquor and dinner. Jonathan Gifford presented Lemuel Peters with the bill—$5.50, a week's wages for a farm laborer—and Peters signed it with a flourish no doubt acquired at Harvard. The Provincial Congress would pay—eventually.

A half-hour later, Jonathan Gifford pulled off his sweaty clothes and put on a long flannel nightgown and a flannel nightcap, threw open the window of his room, and slipped beneath the sheets of his big canopy bed. As usual, the sheets were deliciously warm in the otherwise freezing room, thanks to Molly McGovern's hot bricks wrapped in flannel. For a few minutes, Jonathan Gifford lay there, while faces drifted in the darkness— the grim dignity and confident solemnity of William Alexander, Lord Stirling; Ambrose Cotter's slack, shifty face; Lemuel Peters' pompous cartoon visage; the stupidity and earnest honesty of old Jasper Clark; Richard Talbot's rage; Cortland Skinner's fear, a strange sight on that usually arrogant face. Then Kemble and Kate, with their heartbreaking mixture of innocence and anger and pride. Finally, a woman's face—he did not recognize it at first— Caroline, his dead wife's sister, Caroline Skinner looking at him with odd, almost fevered intensity. There was a question in her eyes. What was it, was she asking the same thing everyone else was asking? The Captain seemed to speak only to her: "I don't know what to do," he said. "The truth is, I don't know what to do."

58

CHAPTER THREE

JONATHAN GIFFORD WAS dreaming. It was a familiar dream, and it filled him with dread. He told himself it was a dream and vowed he would awake. But neither vows nor oaths nor promises could free him. He was hurtled along the familiar country road on the back of his dun stallion, Achilles. Beside him on sturdy little Narraganset mares rode a boyish Kemble and a girlish Kate. They were three, no, four years back in time. Magical, the way children suddenly became men and women. They were riding toward the Shrewsbury River. The dreamer knew it and he knew why. But the man on horseback did not know why.

Normally, when he went out for a day's ramble with the children, they would ride to Amboy and gaze at Governor Franklin's handsome house on Amboy Point—perhaps even see the governor and his lady and their guests strolling in the three-acre park around the house, gorgeously dressed in brocaded silk and satin, like figures from a Watteau painting. But today they rode toward Shrewsbury Vale. Was it that romantic poem, recited in the tavern by a young Philadelphian the previous year—did that explain what was about to happen?

> Let Poets the beauties of Ida rehearse
> Of Pathos, of Tempe, which they never saw,
> Make Venus, or Juno the subject of Verse,
> And Pictures of Gods and Goddesses roar:
>> Tho pompous their Diction
>> 'Tis all but mere Fiction
> The plain Truth at last will most cruelly prevail,
>> And even Apollo
>> I'm sure to beat hollow
> When singing the Beauties of Shrewsbury Vale.

How did the rest of it go? He could only remember the last four lines:

> *Here Discord and Faction can never prevail*
> *For Wealth, Titles, Place,*
> *Foul Hearts with fair Faces*
> *Are not to be met with in Shewsbury Vale.*

Ironic, those blithe words, about foul hearts and fair faces. Had he known? Was the truth already lurking somewhere in his blood? Jonathan Gifford twisted and turned in his bed, but there was no escape from the dream. It was hot, June. Perhaps that was the reason Kate or Kemble had suggested a swim. They had stopped at Huddy's tavern in Colt's Neck, bought a picnic lunch of cold ham and cider, watered their weary horses, and ridden on to their favorite cove. Already Jonathan Gifford felt the icy water of the river on his sweaty skin. Perhaps it was he who had suggested the swim. Perhaps he already suspected what he would find on the cool green grass of their cove, shaded by that ancient, tremendous oak.

No, it was purely, totally accidental. He was innocent of fore-knowledge, innocent. But not guiltless, perhaps. What about her? What about the woman he instantly knew was there, although he glimpsed only a flash of whiteness through the green leaves of the riverbank trees? How could she desecrate this place? Fire roared behind his eyes now, the madness that had previously raged there only in his worst hours as a soldier, when he led his company into the thunder-filled gunsmoke at Ticonderoga, Quebec, or Havana. He had whirled in the saddle and told Kate and Kemble, in a voice that even now, in the dream, had death in it, to ride home. Home!

It was too late. They were looking past him up the river road. They saw their mother's horse and beside it the horse of Viscount Richard Needham, captain in the 23rd Royal Welsh Fusiliers.

By the time Jonathan Gifford reached the point in the road where the path ran down to the cove and its bank of lush grass, Sarah had gotten into her shift and was trying to disentangle her dress from some clinging bushes on which she had spread it. Viscount Needham, his too-handsome face twisted in a grimace of dismay or disdain, was struggling with the last button of his breeches. Jonathan Gifford stood at the head of the path, gazing down at them for a long time. Or was it only a moment? It did not matter. Asleep or awake he still stood there, rage clotting his veins, thundering in his chest, blazing in his brain while the ridiculous question repeated itself: How could she bring him to this place, here of all places?

Sarah's hair was wet. It fell in a red sheen down her back. They had come here during their first summer together, and discovered the oak, the cove, the grass. He had taught her to swim. Taught her in the European style, inherited from Greece and Rome, naked. Taught her to love the cool water on sinuous flesh and himself to love the satiny sheen the river left on her exquisite skin.

He began walking down the steep path, faster and faster, like a man with a hurricane at his back. Halfway down, Sarah cried out, "No, Mr. Gifford, please." But he was not even looking at her. She had vanished, perhaps forever. He was plunging toward Needham, who began to back away, crying, "I am prepared to give you satisfaction, Gifford, any time—"

His fist smashed into that arrogant young face. Needham crashed against the massive trunk of the old oak tree. Bright red blood sprang from his nose. "Gifford," he cried, "I am prepared to give you a gentleman's satisfaction. This is low—"

He grabbed him by the throat and smashed him against the tree, once, twice, lifting him off the ground each time. His strength was superhuman. Needham was a well-built man of medium height, and no coward, but guilt and the ferocity of Jonathan Gifford's rage reduced him to helpless terror.

Then something happened that made Jonathan Gifford groan aloud in his sleep. Staring into Viscount Needham's blood-streaked face, into those normally reckless eyes and that mocking sensual mouth, Jonathan Gifford saw himself. For twenty years, he had worn that face, cultivated that same casual sophistication, pursued the same reckless combination of danger and pleasure, wandered the world wearing the King's uniform, taking these sweet multiples where he found them. How could he kill a man for doing what he himself had done? No more than he could explain why he had found his adventurous years strangely empty. No more than he could deny their right to return now and finally empty the years he had hoped like a wishing fool to fill with genuine love.

"Satisfaction," gurgled Viscount Needham, through the vise of fingers around his throat. "As—a—gentleman—insist."

With a snarl of disgust, Jonathan Gifford flung him to the ground.

"You have exactly one hour to get back to Strangers' Resort, pack your trunk, and get on the road. If you are there when I return, I will kill you. Not with a pistol, like a gentleman, but like an innkeeper—by drowning you in my horse trough. Now start running."

Viscount Needham scrambled to his feet, grabbed his shirt and coat off the bushes, seized his shoes and stockings in his other hand, and floundered to the top of the path. He flung on his clothes and shouted a farewell insult.

"I cannot believe you were ever an officer in the King's Own Regiment, sir. I cannot believe that such a distinguished regiment would tolerate such a low, skulking boor in its ranks. You are a liar, sir, like most Americans, a contemptible American liar."

Jonathan Gifford started up the path after him. Needham leaped into his saddle and galloped away. They were alone. He and Sarah were alone. For a moment he almost wished Viscount Needham back.

"Are you going to beat me, too, Mr. Gifford? I am as much at fault as he is."

He shook his head.

"Women are forgiven, like naughty dogs, wayward horses, is that it?"

He shook his head again, asking her to stop now, afraid of what his rage might do.

"We didn't plan to come here, if it makes you feel any better. We met on the road."

With a strangled cry, he seized her by the throat. "What is it—what—is—it you want?"

She stood there utterly passive, willing to let him kill her without a breath of resistance. His hands dropped to his sides. He turned his back and walked away from her, down to the riverbank.

"Put on your clothes," he said.

"Mr. Gifford, in the name of God, do one thing or the other. Kill me or forgive me."

62

He stared out at the broad sun-bright river. "Put on your clothes," he said.

Then came those fateful words. They struck him between the shoulders as if they were fired from a gun. "I loved you, Mr. Gifford, but not with my whole heart. Just as you loved me."

In the dream he could see the two of them in the thick sweet summer air of Shrewsbury Vale, sunlight dappling the grass around them, the trees rustling with a lovers' breeze. He heard her broken words and saw his stiff unyielding back and was filled with regret and pity for the woman who would not and the man who could not love with a whole heart. Pity because that stiff back, that wayward heart seemed fated, a kind of doom descending on those two forlorn lovers, dying, yes, dying at least as lovers before his eyes.

Jonathan Gifford awoke. Gray dawn was filtering through the window on an icy wind. The sheets beyond the immediate warmth of his body were icy. But his body was bathed in sweat. He stumbled out of bed and lit the kindling in his fireplace. After letting the flames warm his clothes for a few minutes, he pulled them on and lit a pipe of strong Virginia tobacco. Outside there was a sheen of ice on road and trees and barns and outhouses. The snow had turned to sleety rain and a strong freeze had followed it. He felt utterly weary, as if he had not slept an hour.

Deep puffs on his pipe sent warmth and spirit tingling through his body. He went downstairs and moved swiftly, noiselessly through the dark silent rooms to the back door that led to his greenhouse. Closing the door behind him, he drew a deep slow breath of scented air. The first faint traces of sunrise were streaking the eastern sky. He lit an oil lamp and walked slowly past the tubs and pots and trays of roses of every shape and size and condition. Some, protected by the roof of glass which multiplied the heat of the winter sun, were blooming. Others were bare twigs, grafts from different types of roses, bound together with cotton cord in carefully tended soil.

He studied with particular care the blooms in his propagation box. Some of the seeds he had planted only two months ago were growing. Others had been in this four-foot-square frame, built of untreated cypress, for two years. Each day the two inches of enriched soil were moistened by rain water. He turned next to study a hybrid he had created from a moss rose which had double

63

yellow blossoms tinged with peach, rather than the usual pale pink. On one mossy-covered stem he had discovered small reddish spots, the beginning of a canker. It had grown overnight. He took a pruning knife, sharpened it on a piece of soapstone, and carefully cut the spots away. Slowly he went from flower to flower looking for other diseases, above all, the dreaded black spot, the unnatural swelling known as crown gall. Growing roses was a perpetual struggle against a host of enemies, from these indigenous diseases to spiders and field mice. It took meticulous care, daily effort, to create these lovely mysterious flowers so rich in historic and symbolic meaning.

At a table in the rear of the greenhouse Jonathan Gifford sat down and clipped with a shears the still-closed bud of an American wild rose. Gently he removed the pale pink petals until he reached the golden center. Now he was at the heart of the flower, the central group of tiny pistils surrounded by rows of stamens. With a tweezers he meticulously removed all the stamens by pulling them off at their bases. The flower was now emasculated. He covered it with a small cotton bag which he tied at the bottom with a piece of cotton string. In two or three days the pistils inside the bag would mature.

From another pot he cut a dark red Tudor rose. This flower was richer in history. Virgil had praised it in 50 B.C. The Crusaders had carried it back to England, where its descendants had become the white and red roses of York and Lancaster. Tomorrow he would remove the red petals and brush the cluster of stamens back and forth with a cluster of pistils left on the American rose. Sometime in June or early July, if the breeding proved successful, a new rose, part English, part American, would be growing in his garden. It was a chancy business. It was almost impossible to tell whether the new plant would thrive, much less match its predecessors in their individual beauty. If the cross failed, the round base of the flower—the hip—would fail to stay green. Instead it would shrivel, decay, and drop off.

While he worked, Jonathan Gifford tried to think calmly about his private and his public concerns. Perhaps it was time to stop regretting the dead and consider the living. He had never been able to discuss that day in Shrewsbury Vale with Kemble and Kate. Was his silence feeding the bitter accusation that obviously smoldered in Kemble's mind? Was it also the reason for the wild romantic visions in Kate's heart? Did that encounter explain in part at least Kemble's fanatic hatred of things British, his insistence on total animosity between America and England—and Kate's infatuation with anything and anyone connected with the glamour and glory of London?

But what about himself? Was there also in that dream an explanation for his deep uneasiness about the mounting revolution around him? Tomorrow—no, today—they would arrest the royal governor. Samuel Breese with his flapping farmer's trousers and drooping homespun coat and squat Daniel Slocum with his brutal mouth and venal eyes were going to inform the elegant William Franklin in his superfine broadcloth coat, silk waistcoat, and satin breeches that he was a traitor. Then Breese was going to surround the governor's house with armed men and dare him to do something about it. If this was not revolution, it was the nearest thing to it.

Was his uneasiness, no, put the right name on it, his dread of this onrushing upheaval also in the dream? Did he see the revolution as an explosion of that primitive American wildness which he had sensed—and sometimes seen—so often in this new continent? Seen and experienced to the bone, the nerve, in his ten years of marriage to Sarah Kemble Stapleton. Not that the Irish—or the English, for that matter—were lacking in wildness. But in Europe it was never more than an outburst, stifled by the stern voice of the church or government. Here there seemed to be nothing to stop the wildness, once it was released, nothing to prevent it from annihilating the peace that he had hoped to find in this tranquil colony of New Jersey, a peace blended of love and modest wealth and honest friends. Long before there was talk of revolution, he had lost the love and that betrayal had cost him more than a few friendships. So what did you have to fear from revolution, really, Captain Gifford?

Perhaps only the fear that this wildness would engulf the two people in this world whom he still loved—Kemble and Kate. But even without a revolution, he had no hope of taming their wildness. It seemed to spring from their American natures. Was it —he flinched from the thought for a moment but forced himself to face it as he peeled away the last petal and looked at the clustered golden stamens of the Tudor rose—was the real fear the reawakening of his own wildness in an America at war?

CHAPTER FOUR

"TREASON! That is what independency is. Treason. And it will end where all the traitors of this century have ended—on the gallows. Those are my principles, and I will state them plainly to any man—aye, to any committeeman—in this county or state."

Charles Skinner enunciated each of these truculent sentences with a crash of his tankard. He was wearing a suit of green silk, with an embroidered blue waistcoat—everyday clothes to him, but he was an island of color among the rest of the drinkers, who wore brown or gray homespun. Neither his heavy hand nor his truculence seemed to impress his listeners. They seemed more interested in the reaction of the man opposite the Squire at the big round table, Daniel Slocum.

"I say you had best sing a different tune, Squire, or the people will teach it to you the hard way," Slocum said.

"The people," Charles Skinner roared. "Do you presume to speak for the people?"

"Not I, but the honorable Committee of Safety does. I have it on good account that they are unanimous for independence and so is the honorable Provincial Congress by a heavy majority."

"Does that mean I should change my opinion because the people have elected a pack of fools to be their spokesmen?"

"Aye, aye," said Dr. Davie, sitting down on Charles Skinner's right. "I half agree with the Boston fellow who said he would rather have one tyrant three thousand miles away than three thousand tyrannical committeemen one mile away."

"Well said, Davie, well said," roared Charles Skinner.

Daniel Slocum looked at the four other men at the table, all middling farmers like himself. None of them had his appetite for arguing with Charles Skinner. But their very silence supported Slocum.

"If the honorable Committee and the honorable Congress be fools, does that mean the people who voted for them are fools also?"

"You may draw your own conclusions about that, if you have a head on your shoulders," the Squire said.

Watching from behind the bar, Jonathan Gifford decided it was time to take his friend home. He heard and understood the rage and frustration in Charles Skinner's voice. Once men like Daniel Slocum had looked to Charles Skinner for their political opinions. But now Daniel Slocum had a title that enabled him to meet the Squire as an equal. Last week, in a little revolution within the larger Revolution, he had been elected colonel of our local militia regiment. It was an ominous sign of what the men with the guns were thinking. They had dumped easygoing Sam Breese because he confessed to some doubts about the wisdom of a declaration of independence.

Jonathan Gifford strolled over to the table. "Gentlemen," he said, "I think you are both getting a little warm. Why don't we let the honorable congresses, Provincial and Continental, settle such mighty matters?"

"Damn you, Gifford," snarled Slocum, who was well into a pint of stonewall, "don't you sneer at Congress. No damned Englishman will sneer at Congress while I have breath."

"I did not sneer at Congress, Colonel Slocum. Let me tell you something else. I do not let any man damn me in public—or private, for that matter."

"I heard a sneer and I will damn you to your face unless you retract it."

"I can't retract what I didn't say."

Colonel Slocum and Captain Gifford were about the same height. For a moment everyone in the taproom thought he was going to see a first-class brawl. Two years ago Jonathan Gifford had barred Slocum from the tavern for a month after a fist fight with a neighbor over a gambling debt.

"What do you think of the honorable congresses, Gifford?" Slocum asked.

"Just that. That they are honorable. There are honorable men on both sides of this quarrel, Colonel Slocum."

67

"Some one of these days, Gifford, you may have to explain just how you find your Tory friends so honorable."

Slocum strode over to the bar. The four other farmers at the Squire's table followed him.

Jonathan Gifford looked up and saw Kemble standing in the doorway, somberly staring. A gust of irritation shook his nerves. Four uneasy months had passed since Colonel Samuel Breese had marched the militia into Perth Amboy and arrested our royal governor, William Franklin. Almost everything that had happened in these four months had made Kemble more and more hostile. The quarrel between the colonies and the mother country had worsened steadily. In February Parliament had passed a Prohibitory Act, forbidding all trade with Americans and giving British men-of-war the right to seize our ships on the high seas. According to another freshet of news from London, the King was hiring foreign troops—German mercenaries—to subdue us.

But New Jersey remained in a state of semipeace. When Governor William Franklin defied his captors and refused to sign a parole which would have permitted him to retire as a neutral to his farm in west Jersey, the Provincial Congress had backed down, leaving Franklin and his wife in possession of their mansion. The colony continued to pay the governor's salary and address him as Your Excellency. It was typical of the way New Jerseyans felt about the Revolution. Most of us were still like Jonathan Gifford, filled with doubts and hesitations about its necessity.

Captain Gifford gave Kemble a long, steady look, then turned to Barney McGovern. "Let's have drinks all around and a toast that every man can drink to."

He sensed as he spoke that he was play-acting for the benefit of those disapproving young eyes in the doorway.

Barney strolled through the taproom, a jug of grog in his right hand and a jug of hard cider in his left hand, swiftly filling glasses.

"To the rights of America," Jonathan Gifford said, raising his glass.

"I'll drink to that," roared Charles Skinner. "Aye, I'll spill the last drop of my blood for 'em."

He emptied his tankard in one tremendous gulp. Jonathan Gifford winced at the sight. The Squire was drinking rumfustian. This drink has gone out of style in America. If it ever returns, farewell tranquillity. It was made with a bottle of sherry, a quart

68

of strong beer, half a pint of gin, the yolks of twelve eggs, nutmeg, orange peels, sugar, and spices. If strangers asked why it was called rumfustian, they were told that rum was also an adjective meaning "strong," and fustian of course meant "high-swelling, inflated"— which was not a bad description of your head after a bout with this concoction.

Lately Charles Skinner had been acting as if he drank a gallon of rumfustian every day. Almost every visit he paid to Strangers' Resort ended in a violent political or personal quarrel. The Revolution had demolished the deference Charles Skinner had been used to receiving when he took command of the big round table in the taproom's bay window—the Squire's table, it was called. Usually, other leaders of our little neighborhood society, lawyers like my father, substantial farmers like Richard Talbot, were there with him to support his opinions. Now they were staying home, wary of compromising themselves in the deepening political argument.

Charles Skinner shoved back his chair and tried to stand up. His first attempt was a failure. The second time he fell backward, missed the chair, and went crashing into the sawdust. There was a gasp, followed by a ripple of laughter around the taproom. At the bar, Daniel Slocum guffawed openly.

"Damn me if that isn't where every Tory belongs—flat on his back in the dirt," he said.

Jonathan Gifford helped Charles Skinner to his feet. "Sir," roared Skinner, shaking a huge fist at Slocum, "if I meet you on my property I will horsewhip you until you beg for mercy."

"We will meet on your property, Squire," said Slocum. "But the begging words won't be in my mouth."

Skinner replied with a hail of curses. Jonathan Gifford managed to get him out of the tavern and calm him down in the cool afternoon air. "Old friend," he said, "you're too drunk to ride a horse. Let me take you home in the chaise."

"The day I get too drunk to ride a horse is the day I hope they bury me," growled Skinner.

"You don't object to a friend riding with you?"

"Of course not."

Side by side they rode home together through the green, glowing countryside. In 1776 New Jersey was called the Garden Colony. It reminded visitors of the English Midlands. Everywhere hillsides fell away in great grassy cascades, blending with meadows that stretched to lines of waving trees. Behind these glistening streams meandered toward bay or sea or a primary river. The ebbing sunshine, flooding down wide streams of light, intensified every shade of color, from the lush green pastures filled with feeding cattle to those emblems of plenty, the huge red or green Dutch barns behind the farmhouses. Every farm had an orchard of three or four hundred trees. Beyond these, fields of wheat and barley swayed in the soft spring breeze.

My God, what a beautiful country they have here, Jonathan Gifford thought. Or should he say *we* have here? Sadly, he had to admit that *they* was more natural. After ten years, he was still an outsider.

Charles Skinner saw nothing of the beauties of New Jersey's countryside. He was submerged in an alcoholic stupor. Three times he was saved from a head-first fall from his saddle by Jonathan Gifford's muscular right arm. Only toward the end of the ride did he return to some semblance of consciousness.

"Why won't they listen, Gifford?" he said as they entered the drive of Kemble Manor. "Haven't they heard the news from Europe? They are mustering the greatest army and fleet ever sent across the Atlantic. 'Tis fact, Gifford, fact from the mouth of Cortland Skinner himself. Tryon has it among his latest dispatches from Whitehall."

William Tryon was the royal governor of New York. At that moment he was a refugee, living aboard H.M.S. *Duchess of Gordon* in New York Harbor. Cortland Skinner had been with him since his January flight. As far as Jonathan Gifford knew, the attorney general of New Jersey had not dared to return to his native state. How did Charles Skinner know what his cousin was talking about?

"Anthony is right, I fear he's right," said Skinner, talking more to himself now. "Nothing but bayonet and ball and a gallows at every crossroad will cure it. Hah!" He glared at Jonathan Gifford, his heavy face flushed. "Wouldn't you like to clap a noose around the neck of that vermin Slocum?"

"He's not the sort of man I'd choose for a friend," Jonathan Gifford said, "but hanging him—he's got children, for one thing."

"Let his brats learn their lesson now, instead of growing up to mock their betters," growled Skinner.

They dismounted in front of the house and one of Skinner's black stable hands led their horses away. "Friend Gifford," said Skinner thickly, throwing his big arm around Jonathan Gifford's shoulders, "we must talk. More seriously perhaps than we've talked since we prowled the woods round Ticonderoga."

"About what?"

"Too drunk now. But when Anthony is here—"

The door opened and Caroline Skinner was framed in the white rectangle. She was wearing a blue silk gown with a red sash. Her lustrous black hair was draped in a casual chignon around her supple neck. On her face was a frown which was strikingly similar to the one Jonathan Gifford had seen on Kemble's face a half hour ago.

"I have been sitting at the table, looking at a cold dinner for the last hour."

"I want no dinner. I am—too tired," Charles Skinner mumbled.

"Too drunk, you mean."

"Yes—I suppose I do mean that. Too drunk." Skinner turned to Jonathan Gifford. "Remember what I said. Make no promises to any man—until you talk with me. Now, if you'll excuse me—"

He lurched past his wife and stumbled up the stairs to his bedroom.

"Can I offer you anything, Captain Gifford? At least a cup of cold spring water?"

"Water would be most welcome."

"I will walk you around to the well."

Jonathan Gifford felt somewhat embarrassed, limping beside Caroline Skinner in his sweaty work clothes, his breeches and stockings covered with the dust of the road. Coolness flowed from this woman. He felt it as distance. He was sure that she had never forgiven him for her sister's death.

Beside him, Caroline Skinner's mind was a world away from such a dolorous topic. She struggled to find the courage to confide in this taciturn man beside her. She did not say a word while they rounded the corner of the house and reached the garden in the rear.

They walked across shaded grass toward the old stone well. "My husband is drunk every day, Captain Gifford," she said. "Do you know why?"

Jonathan Gifford put his hand on the wooden well bucket and

fingered its copper bands. "The times, I think. He doesn't like them much."

"Do you?"

Jonathan Gifford dropped the bucket into the well. The rope hissed through the iron ring on the white frame. A wet thump drifted up to them, a dull, dead sound.

"I've seen what a battlefield looks like, Mrs. Skinner."

"Then you think we should submit?"

Jonathan Gifford began hauling up the bucket. "That's a very different question."

"Which you no doubt think a woman should not ask."

"I know better than to tell a Kemble what to think, Mrs. Skinner."

"Captain Gifford. I feel I need—I must—confide in someone."

Through the trees Jonathan Gifford could see the small graveyard with its cluster of white tombstones. The bucket appeared. He seized the tin dipper and offered Caroline Skinner a drink. Was she trying to involve him in her domestic unhappiness out of a spirit of revenge? Was Sarah's spirit somehow pursuing him?

"I can't imagine—what advice I could give you," he said.

"There is a plan afoot to recruit a regiment loyal to the King. Anthony is trying to involve his father in it."

This information was so totally different from what he had expected to hear, he could only shake his head in astonishment. "Are you sure?"

"No," she said. "I am ordered out of the room whenever they talk about it. Anthony disappears for two or three days at a time. He comes back with marsh mud and weeds on his boots—and guineas in his pockets. One of them fell out and rolled under his bed." She slipped her hand beneath her red sash and extracted a coin that gleamed dully in the mixture of shadow and sunlight. It was a guinea all right, newly minted, with George III's visage in profile upon it.

"Their talk is mostly argument," Caroline Skinner said. "I can tell that much from the sound of their voices. I think my husband dreads the thought of making war on his friends. But Anthony—Anthony relishes it."

There was pain in her voice and on her face as she said this. It was not an easy judgment for her to make. He took a long swallow of the icy water and wished its coolness had some power to calm the emotions swarming inside him. Not that he showed them. Caroline Skinner still saw the same imperturbable, aloof man.

"I don't know your opinion of our quarrel with England. But you're Kate's father, and for that reason alone I thought you should know about this—thing. No. That's not entirely true. Dear as Kate is to me, my strongest feelings are the folly of it—and next the wickedness. I don't know where you stand, Mr. Gifford, but I am for independence."

As she said this she instinctively braced her shoulders, arched her back, and lifted her chin. Pride and passion infused her small figure and dark cameo face with an Amazonian élan. It struck Jonathan Gifford as both touchingly girlish and remarkably serious. Somehow he knew that he would never forget this moment in this quiet garden. He was seeing and hearing in splendid isolation, like the example of a species in a natural history collection, the voice, the image, of American pride. At the same time he felt with a deep-welling sadness his inability to share this pride. Never had he felt his status as an outsider, a stranger, more keenly. He took another long swallow of well water, now wishing it was a drug that would soothe his pain.

"Shall we walk into the park?" he said.

They opened the gate and entered the thirty wooded acres in which Charles Skinner kept a dozen deer. The trees were part of the original forest. Huge oaks threw their shade over slopes and glades unchanged since the Indians roamed them. At first the deer were only shapes in the mingled sunlight and shadow. Tame and greedy, several soon advanced on Caroline Skinner, hoping for sugar—or better, salt. Jonathan Gifford shooed them away with his wide-brimmed sun hat and they strolled through the trees to the edge of a sluggish brook.

"Let's not talk about independence," he said. "You don't want to argue politics with me. Not that we'd necessarily argue on that point. I begin to think it's the only alternative America now has—besides surrender. It's my judgment of—what did you call it?—the folly of Anthony's plan that you want."

"Yes," she said.

"I'm not so sure it's foolish," he said somberly. "I think—if I may say so, Mrs. Skinner—that you overestimate enthusiasm for the American Cause. Especially if Congress declares for independence. I suspect a good half of the people in this neighborhood might be susceptible to an appeal in the King's name— and to this."

He handed the golden guinea back to her. "It looks so much better than Congress's paper."

With an angry cry, Caroline Skinner flung the guinea into the shadowed grass. "Doesn't courage enter into your calculations, Captain Gifford? The courage of free men fighting for their natural rights?"

"I see you have been reading the papers issued by Congress very carefully."

"I've done better than that. I've read John Locke himself."

Perhaps by the time this book is read, John Locke's name will be forgotten and a German or Russian or a Chinese will be considered the fountainhead of political wisdom. For the men and women of 1776, the great Englishman's reasoning on natural rights was the philosophic foundation of American resistance. But few Americans had read the philosopher himself. His books were as dry and devoid of warmth and imagination as an anatomy lesson.

"Ideas can give a man the courage to go to war. But they won't do him much good on a battlefield, if the other side has better guns and better training."

"I can see you haven't made up your mind which side is going to win, Captain Gifford."

"I also have some thoughts about the rights and wrongs, Mrs. Skinner," Jonathan Gifford said. "I'm not a scholar enough to read Locke. But I think Edmund Burke was much to the point when he said last year in Parliament that a great empire and little minds go ill together. Does your husband know where you stand on independence?"

"No. But he suspects the worst. He caught me reading *Common Sense* two months ago and flung it into the fire. I called for my horse and rode straight to Amboy and bought another copy. Tom Paine is my favorite writer. Did you read the *Occasional Letter to the Female Sex* that he wrote in the *Pennsylvania Magazine* last summer?"

Jonathan Gifford shook his head.

"He called for equal rights for American women. He said it was ridiculous for a new country to let one half the human race be robbed of their freedom of will by the laws. That's common sense too, don't you think, Captain Gifford?"

"I—I suppose it is," Jonathan Gifford said.

A startling thought struck Jonathan Gifford. In spirit if not in law, American women were more inclined toward independence than American men. Like most Europeans, he had been amazed by the freedom Americans south of New England allowed their unmarried daughters. He still found himself instinctively protesting when Kate blithely announced that she was off to spend the night skating or sleighing or dancing with Anthony Skinner or one of her several previous beaux and had no intention of returning until the next day.

In Sarah, this freedom of spirit had become sheer willfulness, a continuous, finally exhausting explosion of defiance and bad temper. But Caroline Skinner had her independent spirit under severe control. Perhaps that was why Captain Gifford found himself encouraging her.

"If the King's ministers met a few more American women," he said with a smile, "I think they might change their minds about conquering—you with five thousand men."

"Why don't you say 'us,' Captain Gifford—conquer us? Don't you feel that you belong here yet?"

"I did feel it, Mrs. Skinner, but the terrible thing—that happened." His voice dwindled to a choked whisper. "You know what I mean—"

Now, with even less warning, it was Caroline Skinner's turn to feel a deep throb of sympathy. She saw the intensity of his suffering. "That was not your fault," she said. "I know it wasn't."

"How—how do you know?" Jonathan Gifford asked.

"How?" said Caroline, almost as agitated now as he was. "The way a woman knows—certain things. I also knew my sister, Captain Gifford."

Without thought, moved by the deepest feeling, Jonathan Gifford took her hand. "That means more to me than I can ever tell you."

For a moment, Caroline Skinner saw herself standing beside the bed on which her husband sprawled drunkenly, his muddy boots smearing the blue damask spread. A violent tremor shook her spirit, redoubling her wish to comfort the man who was holding her hand. "I only wish—I had said it sooner."

75

"I must go," he said, releasing her hand.

A chaos churned inside Caroline's mind. She only heard fragments of what he said to her. "Must think carefully . . . extremely dangerous . . . grateful for her . . . confidence." If he had held her hand for another fraction of a second, she was certain she would have flung her arms around him, pressed her lips to his sad, solemn mouth. It was incredible. She was so proud of her good sense, her self-control, above everything else in her life, even, she grimly thought, above her own happiness.

With a gasp of pain, she fled into the trees until she reached the other side of the grove where the brook's waters glistened in the sunlight. Wasn't there a philosopher who said that life was constant change? Nothing stood still and no one ever looked into the same stream twice. There was an enormous change heaving in the depths of America, like an immense child struggling out of the womb. Perhaps this great shapeless thing would transform her life. Perhaps it would even give her dry, bitter, barren self the courage to act, to speak words of love from a living heart before she died.

Why did she dread this possibility? For the same reason that she dreaded the thought of losing her safe, comfortable life as mistress of Kemble Manor? No doubt, no doubt. In calmer moments she could sympathize with her husband's anguish as the world and men changed into shapes and sounds and sizes he despised. But in another part of her spirit, a voice whispered: *Let it come, let it come.*

76

CHAPTER FIVE

At supper that night, Jonathan Gifford asked Kate if she had been seeing Anthony Skinner lately. "No," she said with a pout. "He has become a great man of business. He goes to Amboy for days on end, running goods from the West Indies. He says if things go well, he will be the richest man in New Jersey."

"Have you been to Amboy with him?"

"No. He says it's dreadfully boring and he's probably right. But ships are coming in from the islands, sure enough. He brought me a batch of the latest novels the day before yesterday. And a London baby."

"A London baby?"

"Yes. Would you like to see it?"

In a moment Kate was back with a small doll, perhaps a foot high, dressed in a precisely detailed gown of brocaded silk, covered with tiny ruffles and ruchings and a looped-up kirtle. The powdered hair was twice the height of the little head, with an infinitesimal hat perched on top of the pile. This was the way the latest London fashions were displayed in America in the 1760s and 1770s.

"She's hardly wearing any hoop," Kate said. "I've been telling everyone the hoop would be exploded soon and I was right. Now if only stays would go the same way—"

"The fellow should be arrested," Kemble said. "Smuggling British fashions into the country. Look at her. She's seduced already."

"Oh, he's seduced more than me. He's given a half dozen of these babies to Sally Kemble, the Van Horne sisters, and I know not who else. But you have no need to worry, Mr. Lord Protector. Poor old Bridget Terhune, our favorite New York dressmaker, has

77

been driven out of the city by your friends and has settled in Amboy. She will make our dresses for us. We won't have to import a thing from London but pins."

"Where will she get the cloth?"

"She had the foresight to lay in a great supply."

"I bet. The old harpy is probably in league with Skinner."

"I rode down to Amboy today," Jonathan Gifford said, trying to change the subject. "Great excitement. General Washington is expected tomorrow."

"So I've heard," Kemble said. "On his way to Philadelphia to confer with Congress. I suppose he plans to inspect Amboy's defenses."

"Such as they are," Jonathan Gifford said.

Kemble nodded glumly. "They should have left at least one New Jersey regiment in the colony. I've heard a lot of people saying that Congress has taken advantage of us. Sending twelve hundred of our best men to Canada."

"You should be able to muster ten times that number," Jonathan Gifford said.

"If every man would come out," Kemble said. "But we're lucky to get a third, most of the time. In some districts, it's much worse."

"The colonel of the Shrewsbury regiment resigned, I hear. He couldn't turn out a half company."

"We'll have to march in and disarm that place. They're worse than the Tories in Queens County."

Earlier in the year, militia from New Jersey had been hurried to New York to crush loyalist opposition on Long Island. They had confiscated over seven hundred muskets and arrested a dozen or so leading citizens. Kemble had begged his father to let him go as a volunteer. The general in command, Nathaniel Heard of Woodbridge, was an old family friend and more than willing to have Kemble as his aide. When Jonathan Gifford had said no, a nasty argument had erupted.

Now Kemble revived the argument, insisting that patriotic Americans had a duty to disarm and harass internal enemies. Jonathan Gifford once more told him bluntly that it offended his idea of English liberty, "if you'll excuse the expression," he added with a taut smile.

78

"But we're fighting a war, Father. We can't let internal enemies destroy us."

"No one's declared war yet. The King is sending a peace commissioner."

"That's all a game—to divide us," Kemble said.

"I can't believe anyone named Howe would play such a game." Jonathan Gifford was swept back eighteen years in time. He wore a buckskin hunting shirt and leather leggings. Deep in the forests of northern New York, he warmed his hands before a fire. Beside him sat a young man who personified everything that noble blood was supposed to bestow. Lord George Augustus Howe had thrown aside his stiff regimental uniform and asked the Americans to teach him how to fight in the woods. He had invited a half-dozen spirited young officers to join him. A kind of desperation gripped Jonathan Gifford as he remembered his last attempt to explain to Kemble what he felt about Lord George Howe. *I was perfectly at ease with him. Never once did he make me feel inferior. Yet he was the leader. Always, without question, the leader. His courage was unbelievable. We would take cover behind trees. He would stand in the open, directing our fire. I was only a few feet away from him when he was hit. He fell without a sound. I couldn't believe it. None of us could believe it.*

His voice had choked with tears. Incredible, after eighteen years, he still wept for this man. Now his brother, Lord Richard Howe, was coming to America as a peace commissioner—and also as commander of the British fleet. Another brother, William Howe, was in command of the British army. Kemble—and other pro-independence Americans—were quick to point out the contradictory nature of the Howes' assignments. But Jonathan Gifford could not stop hoping that this second Lord Howe, younger brother of the dead George Augustus, would somehow re-create faith in England's integrity.

Kate touched his arm to interrupt his reverie. "I remember the poem Kemble used to recite. The ode about Lord Howe's death," Kate said. "'The Unfortunate Hero.' Give us a rendition now, Kemble."

"I've forgotten it," Kemble said.

"Father used to give you a shilling every time. I can still see you, taking a deep breath to finish the last stanza—"

Softly, Kemble began to recite:

79

"*But thee, dear Youth, long shall thy Country mourn*
  With grateful tears bedew thy dust
And future ages to thy mem'ry just
Shall dress with Glory thy distinguish'd urn.
Long as these regions know th' insulting Gaul,
  America shall deplore thy Fall."

"Oh, Father," Kate said. "That's worth a guinea at least, now."

"At least," Jonathan Gifford said, forcing a smile that Kemble did not return. Were they both thinking the same thing—the distance, the harsh cold distance that had opened between them in the last two years?

"I can't understand why you are still sentimental about that man, Father," Kemble said. "Didn't you tell me once that you quit the army because a soldier who wasn't an aristocrat had no hope for promotion?"

"I freely admit I'm no admirer of aristocracy as a system," Jonathan Gifford said testily, "but I am not so closed-minded as to despise all aristocrats."

"But you allow one of them to sentimentalize you into neutrality."

Jonathan Gifford could not decide which irritated him most, Kemble's impudent tone or the fact that his son was largely correct. Hearing again the exaggerated language of the old poem, Captain Gifford realized he was not mourning Lord George Howe nearly as much as he was mourning his own youth, his pride in his prowess with pistol, musket, and bayonet, in a body that could match an Indian's endurance, in the sense of importance, even arrogance, that came from belonging to one of the best regiments in the best army in the world. The word "independence" separated him from that past, separated him from memories, history that had continued to give him importance and pride. Yes, he had complacently enjoyed the worship on Kemble's small face when he recited "The Unfortunate Hero." Now that it was gone, gone with the reason for it, he was forced to ask himself why Kemble or anyone else should admire much less love Jonathan Gifford, ex-captain of the King's Own.

"Do you think General Washington may stop here on the way to Philadelphia, Father?" Kate asked.

"I doubt it."

"You met him once, didn't you?"

"No, but we share a friend, Captain Mackenzie of my old Fourth Regiment. He served with Washington in Virginia during the last war. Remember in September he sent me a letter that Washington had written to him?"

"Oh yes," Kate said, "in which he solemnly vowed that there wasn't a man in America who wanted independence. I could have introduced him to a half dozen, including the one on your right."

"I was not for independence a year and a half ago when Washington wrote that letter," Kemble said sententiously. "The English have forced independence on us—"

"Oh, God, not another political lecture," Kate said and retreated to her room.

"Is she going to marry Anthony Skinner?" Kemble asked.

"I hope not," Jonathan Gifford said.

"Why don't you forbid it?"

"What good would that do?"

"She would obey you. I know she would."

"And on her twenty-first birthday she would marry him, no matter what happened."

Kemble nodded ruefully. "You're probably right," he said. "When can I join the army, Father?"

"When you're twenty-one, or a college graduate—whichever comes first."

This last exchange may sound odd to modern readers. Napoleon has taught our era to muster whole populations for war. But in 1776, war was considered the profession or inclination of the martial few. There was no universal compulsion to become part of the national army. Only when a man's immediate neighborhood was invaded was there any expectation of his services. But patriotism was assumed to be sufficiently widespread to provide the country with enough soldiers to maintain the army.

"What will you do if Congress declares independence, Father?"

"I honestly don't know, Kemble."

Jonathan Gifford watched Kemble's hands fingering his coffee cup. He was obviously about to say something that had been churning inside him for a long time. "I think you should know, Father—that if you don't join my country's side, I would consider myself free of all obligation—to obey you in any way."

Jonathan Gifford nodded wearily. For a moment he was overwhelmed with self-pity. Why couldn't Kemble see that all he wanted was peace? Why was he insisting that love and loyalty were indivisible? It was unfair to demand both from a divided man with a withered heart.

That night, Jonathan Gifford slept poorly. He arose with the first light and retreated to his greenhouse to work with his roses. He was in the middle of transplanting five or six fragile plants from the propagation box to individual pots when the door burst open. Kemble stood there, enormously excited.

"Father," he said, "General Washington is outside. He wants to speak to you."

Jonathan Gifford looked with dismay at his dirt-smeared apron and grimy hands. "It can't be more than six o'clock," he muttered. "Does he want breakfast?"

"No. He's waiting in the road."

Outside Strangers' Resort, Barney McGovern and his wife, Black Sam and his wife, Kate and a number of other people were standing at a respectful distance. Washington sat easily on the back of a big bay stallion. The horse was scuffling and skittering impatiently. Washington stilled him with a swift sure motion of the reins. The men around him were all young—in their twenties.

"Are you Mr. Gifford?" Washington asked. "Formerly captain in the King's Own Regiment?"

"I am, sir."

"I was told if I passed this way not to fail to give you the compliments and best wishes of your friend, General Putnam."

This was said with a smile, in a soft, surprisingly light voice for such a big man.

"Thank you, General," Jonathan Gifford said. "I trust General Putnam is his old hearty self."

"Indestructible," Washington said with a slightly broader smile in which several of his aides joined. "He tells me that you were at the Monongahela."

Jonathan Gifford nodded. "I was a mere ensign in those days. I remember you well, though we never had the pleasure of meeting."

"Someday when this business is over, we must spend an hour or two refighting that day, with the help of some good Madeira."

"I'll reserve one of my best bottles immediately, General," Jonathan Gifford said.

The Monongahela was a kind of code word in 1776, particularly among soldiers and their friends. It referred to the battle fought near that western river between the French and Indians and the British-American army commanded by General Edward Braddock. It had been a horrendous defeat for the British, in which the regulars behaved disgracefully. Washington, serving on Braddock's staff as an aide, had been one of the few who distinguished himself on that gory field.

General Washington explained that he must be in Trenton by nightfall. With a smile and nod, he put his spurs to his stallion and led his escort of aides and troopers down the road. Jonathan Gifford looked around him at the mixture of awe and admiration on nearby faces. He was embarrassed. The story would race through the district, making him a kind of hero by association, the last thing he wanted. He would spend the rest of the week explaining to curious inquirers how and where he knew Israel Putnam.

At this point in 1776 "Old Put" was at least as well known and perhaps more admired than George Washington. Putnam had commanded the Americans at Bunker Hill the preceding June in a battle which inflicted fearful casualties on the attacking British, though in the end the Americans broke and ran. "Old Put" had been one of the leaders of the ranger battalion recruited by Lord George Howe. In the intervening years of peace, Putnam had been a slightly comic figure to the Gifford family. The occasional letters he exchanged with his old friend featured some of the most horrendous misspellings in the history of the language.

While everyone else watched General Washington disappear in a cloud of spring dust, Jonathan Gifford turned to Kate and Kemble. "Would you like to help me move the roses outdoors?"

Over the years this had been a family ritual, a welcome to the sunshine of New Jersey's spring. But Kemble was not inclined to become a boy again, even for a few hours. He no longer trusted the man he called Father.

That is what Kemble told himself. Beneath his political antagonism lurked the deeper and more serious grievance of his mother's disgrace and death. He simply could not accept the possibility that it was Sarah Gifford's fault. This wound—there is no other word to describe it—was combined with that natural rebellion against his father that every son experiences as he approaches manhood. Not even the respect George Washington displayed in greeting Jonathan Gifford could change Kemble's mind.

"I'm sorry," Kemble said. "I have some letters to write for the Committee."

"Oh, the Committee," Kate mocked. "The all-powerful, all-important Committee. I would love to plant some roses, Father."

Kate knew what Kemble thought about their mother and stepfather. Sometimes she half-agreed with him. At other times she was sure he was wrong. She did not have the added antagonisms of politics and biology to intensify her feelings. She was able to thrust her mother out of her mind most of the time and let her natural affection for her father control her conduct. After breakfast, she put on an old dress and joined Jonathan Gifford in the garden behind the tavern.

The land ran downhill to the brook. Trees had been cleared away on the left and right to create a broad expanse of sunlight. The slope faced east, so that it drank the richest, warmest sun all morning. In rectangles, ovals, squares, and circles, Captain Gifford had planted a treasury of the world's roses.

At the top and along the sides of the garden were trellises on which climbed the early-blooming Blaze rose of New Jersey. Nearby was the dark red rose of France and the sweet-scented Damask rose of Macedonia, the double yellow Sulphur rose of Persia. There were tea-scented pink and yellow roses of China which only became well known in England and this country in this century, the hundred-leaved Cabbage rose of Holland with its varied double-cupped fragrant blooms, Rosa Alba, the white rose of York, the Jacobite rose for which so many thousands of brave men died in Ireland and Scotland, American Swamp roses from the South and Chestnut roses from India.

Among these like exotic children of a biracial marriage were hybrids created by Jonathan Gifford in his greenhouse. People came twenty or thirty miles to see the rose garden of Strangers' Resort when it was in full bloom in June and July. Already, in this last week of May, the stems were beginning to bud, the leaves of the Sweetbriers were already wafting their apple scent on the soft air.

With the assistance of Black Sam and Bertha, Kate and her father spent the morning and early afternoon setting several dozen shrubs in the moist earth. While they worked, Kate playfully

84

recalled the lectures he used to give them on roses and their history.

> "The rose is the perfume of the gods, the joy of men.
> It adorns the graces at the blossoming of love.
> It is the favorite flower of Venus."

She sighed. "That's Anacreon, isn't it?" With a touch of mockery she inhaled the fragrance of a pink and cream York rose. "That's all I ever want to be, the favorite flower of Venus."

"Perhaps you should imitate that rose," said Jonathan Gifford. "In Ireland we called it 'Great Maiden's Blush.'"

Kate frowned, suddenly serious. "I really do love him, Father. I wish you liked him a little more."

"I like him well enough," Jonathan Gifford said. "If we were living in peaceful times, I'd wish you an early wedding and myself a grandson to welcome in the New Year. These are not peaceful times, Kate. And Anthony Skinner is not, I fear, a peaceful fellow."

"When were there ever peaceful times?" Kate said. "And as for peaceful fellows, would you call yourself one?"

"I guess not," Jonathan Gifford said, gently removing one of his newest Chinese roses from its pot. The small white flowers had only four petals at the head of tall canes with wing-like translucent thorns and lush green fern-like foliage. "Isn't this a beauty? One of my friends in the East India Company sent it to me from Calcutta. He said it came from western China."

"It's beautiful," Kate said perfunctorily. "But you see, Father, I think love is more important than wars or politics. You can't let those things stand in love's way. If you do, you end up like one of the flowers in this garden. Carefully tended, admired, lovely to look at. But with no real life of your own. I'd rather be one of those Blaze roses growing wild there where the woods begin."

What should he say? Jonathan Gifford wondered. Should he preach her a sermon on life, with the rose for a text? Should he sententiously point out to her that the wild rose often blossoms only once, while the garden rose, cut back to the wood in season, blooms again and again? No, she would laugh in his face. It might ruin the fragile web of feeling between them. Sadly he touched the growing thorns of his China rose. He suspected that beneath Kate's affection lurked Kemble's angry judgment against him and in favor of her mother. They shared so few things these days, he dreaded the thought of their differences invading even the roses.

For a moment he had a harrowing glimpse of his father retreating into the garden to escape his mother's lamentations on Ireland's sorrows. Amazing, at forty-seven, he still felt himself in the shadow of that stern, reticent man who had called him into his study on his sixteenth birthday and informed him that he had just bought him an ensign's commission in the King's Own Regiment. He had been stunned. He had wanted to be a lawyer like his older brother, but the practice was not large enough to divide. His father had had the bad judgment to marry a Catholic, which meant he would never be admitted to the inner circle of the government, where the big fees were collected. Thomas Gifford believed that he was doing the best thing for his younger son. He had talked with his schoolmasters, who assured him that Jonathan had not much interest in books, and he had watched him organize and often bully his playmates. *You have the knack of leading others. I don't pretend to understand it. I never had it myself,* his father had said.

"You seem far away, Father," Kate said. "Are you wishing you never came to America and got mixed up with us all?"

"No. Don't be silly."

Kate knelt beside him and put her arms around him.

"I hope you never do feel such a thing. No matter what happens, I will never stop loving you. Even if I marry Anthony and you tell me you hate him."

"My darling, I'm only trying to tell you—" Jonathan Gifford began helplessly.

"Maybe Lord Howe will turn out to be a real peace commissioner. By the end of the summer all those silly men will have to stop playing with their guns and go back to being farmers, businessmen, and husbands again. I really think men love war."

"I'm afraid they do."

Kate giggled. "They'll be terribly disappointed but there won't be anything they can do about it. We'll have peace for a hundred years and you'll end up an old soldier on two canes, hobbling around my house spoiling your great-grandchildren."

"I will consider that an invitation."

He got up and walked down the slope to examine a canker on the stem of the hybrid he had created from the American and the

86

Tudor rose. The petals were a delicate pink, but the hooked thorns of the European rose had vanished, and instead of the orange-scarlet hips of the American rose, these were almost white.

"But what will you do, Kate," he said, fingering the diseased stem, "if things happen the other way? If fighting begins and Anthony sides with the King?"

"Why—I'll side with him, too. What difference does that make? There are plenty of people hereabouts who feel the same way."

"Kate. I mean with a gun in his hand. It won't just be George Washington and his army fighting the British in Massachusetts. They'll be fighting in New York and New Jersey. It's going to be a civil war, Kate, brother against brother, neighbor against neighbor, friend against friend."

It was hard to tell from the expression on her face whether Kate was frightened or angry. "It won't happen that way," she said, shaking her head.

"I hope I'm wrong, but I'm afraid it will, Kate."

Barney McGovern's bulky form loomed over them. "Excuse me, Captain. This gentleman says he'd like to speak personally to you about quartering some horses here."

Barney stepped aside and Jonathan Gifford and Kate looked up at a stocky freckle-faced young man in a blue coat with dark red facing on the lapels, collar, and cuffs. A yellow feather jutted from his sharply cocked hat, which he carried under his arm. He bowed politely to Kate and said, "Good day, miss. Good day, sir. I trust I may speak freely in front of this young lady?"

"Of course."

"General Washington sent back orders to set up a series of relay stations so that dispatch riders might have fresh horses on the way across New Jersey to Philadelphia and back. He fears a British attack on New York, you see."

This was said in a conversational tone, the voice softened by the accents of Virginia.

"I thought it was better to speak to you personally than bring the news into the tavern. It might alarm people. I gather the Tories are pretty thick in the neighborhood, too."

"I understand," Jonathan Gifford said. "How many horses do you have?"

"Four, sir."

"They'll be safe and well taken care of in our barn. You look like you've been on the road a good many hours this day yourself."

The young man nodded and smiled. "They told me New Jersey wouldn't be as hot as Virginia. But I'm not so sure now."

He said this to Kate more than to Jonathan Gifford, and Kate returned his smile. "Wait until July and August," she said.

"By that time I hope we'll have chased the redcoats off the continent for good and I'll be lying on the bank of the Rappahannock with a bowl of punch beside me and a fishing rod in my hand."

"My name is Gifford. I wish I could shake your hand but mine is too dirty."

"I'm sure there is no more dirt on it than there is dust on mine, sir. John Fleming, captain in the First Virginia Regiment."

They shook hands. "This is my daughter, Kate Stapleton," Jonathan Gifford said.

Captain Fleming responded with a deep bow. "I'm more than charmed, Miss Stapleton. The friend who misinformed me about New Jersey's weather also told me that the young ladies were not as pretty as ours in Virginia. I see he was wrong about that too."

"That must be Virginia flattery, when I'm standing here in my oldest dress, covered with dirt from head to toe."

"In Virginia we only flatter ladies when it's necessary. It isn't in your case."

"Could you join us for dinner, Captain?" Jonathan Gifford asked.

Captain Fleming could indeed join them for dinner. Kate absolutely forbade serving it for at least an hour, to give her time to "look civilized again." Ex-Captain Gifford and Captain Fleming adjourned to the side porch of the residence where Barney McGovern soon served them a bottle of the tavern's best Madeira. Captain Fleming talked freely about his current assignment. He was on the staff of Brigadier General Hugh Mercer, who was about to become military commander of Perth Amboy. General Washington planned to create a flying camp of perhaps ten thousand militiamen outside the town to defend eastern New Jersey if the British appeared in force. As far as anyone knew, the British army, which had withdrawn from Boston in March, was still at Halifax, Nova Scotia, awaiting reinforcements.

"We have word, I think, of Canada as their destination," Captain Fleming said. "General Washington sent between five and six thousand men—some of our best regiments—north in the past month."

"A mistake, I think, unless he can spare them," Jonathan Gifford said. "Howe will come to New York, depend on it, Captain. I served for a while on the headquarters staff there in the sixties. We had various plans for dealing with you rebellious Americans. They all presumed an army based in New York."

Captain Fleming's interest in his host increased geometrically. "This could be information General Washington would very much like to hear."

"I doubt if he needs it. From what I hear, he is getting ready to defend New York with all the force he can muster. I wonder if he can do it. He would be better off, I think, if he withdrew his army onto the continent—either into Westchester or into New Jersey. He will be at a tremendous disadvantage in New York, fighting on an island against an enemy with control of the water around him."

"A good many of us have thought about that, I fear," Captain Fleming said with a mournful nod. "But the Congress has given explicit orders to defend New York to the last extremity."

"Congress seems to me to have a bad habit of trying to do everything. A general with sixty heads is a monstrosity that could lose the war for you."

Captain Fleming glumly agreed. "But even if every man now in the army falls a sacrifice," he said, "we will make General Howe pay the kind of price he paid at Bunker Hill. Great Britain will abandon the contest."

"I assure you that General Howe has no intention of paying such a price again. He will fight a war of maneuver, Captain, of flanking movements and siege tactics. I've had letters from several friends in my old regiment discussing Bunker Hill. Putnam and his men were the luckiest soldiers alive. By all the rules of warfare, they should have been annihilated."

An uneasy look appeared on Captain Fleming's face. Jonathan Gifford suddenly wondered if those last words made it sound as if he wished the Americans had been annihilated at Bunker Hill. He emptied the last of the Madeira into their glasses and casually asked the Captain if he'd heard any rumors of Tory regiments being raised in New Jersey.

89

"No," said Fleming, instantly alarmed. "Have you? We have been told that there is a good deal of Tory sentiment in some sections, such as Shrewsbury—"

"A man in my job hears rumors all day long," Jonathan Gifford said. "But I have heard this from—a rather good source."

"Are you prepared to identify the source?"

"No, I am not. It was told to me in confidence."

"At the very least, I think you should inform the County Committee."

"You can do that as well as I, Captain. You can also take some steps to make it more difficult to communicate with the King's ships in New York Harbor. As I understand it, the shoreline at present is unguarded and unpatrolled. A dozen men on horseback, a few guard boats could do a great deal. If more information comes my way, I assure you that I will pass on to you all of it that a man of honor can disclose."

Kate swept onto the porch in a yellow silk dress, two miniature white Chinese roses at her throat. "What are you talking about? But why should I ask? It's the damn nonsensical war. Is there a man these days who doesn't talk perpetually about death and destruction?"

"If you promise to smile at me that way whenever we meet," Captain Fleming said, "I will vow to reform my mind and exclude all such thoughts, even if it leads to my court-martial."

"I see there's no hope of embarrassing you Virginians. There is nothing too extravagant you won't say."

"Would you rather have us worrying all day about the state of our souls, talking through our noses about divinity like the Yankees?"

"Oh no. The Yankees are terrible people, pinchpenny hypocrites, most of them."

"They're a hard people to like, true enough," Captain Fleming said. "But there is something to be said for standing firm for your rights. They helped the rest of us see the necessity for that."

"We are back to talking about the damned war. Another minute and I will insist on that court-martial, Captain."

"Miss Kate," said Captain Fleming, "I haven't heard a woman swear so beautifully since I left Virginia. Being with you is like a visit home."

Jonathan Gifford could almost feel romantic emotion crowding the humid air. Memories of his own conduct when he was Captain Fleming's age filled him with uneasiness. As they sat down to dinner and Kate and Captain Fleming became more and more animated, this worry became almost superficial, compared to the satisfaction Jonathan Gifford felt. He had invited the Virginian to dinner in the hope that he might replace or at least diminish Anthony Skinner in Kate's affections. If he had to worry about succeeding too well, he was prepared to tolerate that burden.

After a dinner of roast sweetbreads, served with mushroom catsup, cold hare pie, and potted swan, stewed in claret with several pounds of fresh butter, the Captain confessed that New Jersey cooking was almost the equal of Virginia. He refused to yield the "almost." Arguing cheerfully, the young couple went for a stroll along the bank of the brook. Jonathan Gifford invited Barney McGovern to sit down with him and finish a second bottle of Madeira. He told Barney what Captain Fleming had just told him about the flying camp planned for Perth Amboy.

"The war is getting closer and closer, Barney. Which side are you on?"

"Can an Irishman stand anywhere but with the Americans? Their cause is Ireland's cause, Captain. If I was ten years younger and I didn't think you needed me here I'd be up there in the Canadian woods with the rest of the boys."

"I'm glad you're not ten years younger."

"'Twill be hard to be neutral, Captain."

"I know it, Barney."

But what should a man do if he was neutral? If his feelings were canceled by opposing memories, by his perpetual sense of being a stranger in every country? What did he owe Ireland? Pity, nothing more. The land of his birth, of his mother's people, to be sure. But the ties of blood were more than balanced by his father's cold British fluids.

Barney went back to work in the taproom. Jonathan Gifford got out his maps of North America, drawn by his old friend Captain John Montresor of the British Army Engineers. For a long time he sat there studying the geography of New York and New Jersey. It was almost twilight when Kate wandered into the room and lit an oil lamp. She teased him about drinking so much Madeira that he thought he could read in the dark. Then she drew aside the gauzy scarf around her throat and said, "Look."

Around her neck was a small gold locket with some lovely filigree work on the cover.

"A gift from the Captain?"

"He bought it in New York. He was going to send it to a young lady in Virginia. But he would rather have me wear it."

Kate strolled to a mirror to study it triumphantly. She seemed more exultant than ecstatic, prouder of it as a trophy than as a pledge of love. Did she suspect what he suspected—that Captain Fleming had bought a half dozen of these lockets? No, Jonathan Gifford decided. Kate always saw herself as an actress in a throbbing drama, a character in a pulsating novel. She had no doubts or hesitations. It was part of her ability to communicate joy, excitement, to the people around her. Looking at her as she fingered the locket, Jonathan Gifford was shaken by an immense fathering love. He yearned to protect her from the hurricane that was whirling toward them. How could he do it? Was Captain John Fleming any safer than Anthony Skinner? Only by a few degrees, measured on the maps of his concern. It was the best he could do. Accept it, he told himself, it was better than nothing.

Above all, it was better than not caring. It was better than turning his face away, walking out of their lives. He had confronted that possibility the day he had found the farewell note in Sarah's bedroom, the warning plea to let her go unhindered. He had confronted it again when they brought her body home in the sealed, lead-lined coffin. He had seen the baffled pain on the faces of Kate and Kemble and said no. He had vowed he would live out the terms of his love for them—and for Sarah, in memory of that first golden year—no matter what failures engulfed him. It was too late to start a new life, to find a new circle of love. More important, he was held here by love, and by the challenge in those bitter words: *I loved you, but not with my whole heart. Just as you loved me.* There was no way to defeat that monster but by living his answer, day by day.

CHAPTER SIX

For the first night in weeks, Jonathan Gifford slept deeply and dreamlessly. Dawn did not find him in his greenhouse, fussing over his roses. He might have slept past breakfast. But a muscular hand shook his shoulder at six-thirty. Black Sam's deep, dark voice penetrated his sleep like a flock of migratory birds plunging down a sunlit sky.

"Captain, Captain, something's happened. Something mighty bad."

"What?" he said, sitting up and involuntarily flinging aside his nightcap.

"Those army horses that Captain Fleming left. Someone cut their throats."

In three minutes, Jonathan Gifford was in the barn. One of the horses, a chestnut mare, was still alive. But with every breath more blood gushed from the gaping slash. One mute eye stared up at Jonathan Gifford, wide with pleading terror.

"They must have done it just before dawn," Sam said. "Else she wouldn't be still alive."

"Is Barney up?"

"Just rising, I expect."

"Get him out here. Saddle three horses. Get three muskets, ammunition, and powder from the armory."

In ten minutes they were riding hard down the Shrewsbury road. They met four or five hired hands trudging to their farms. None of them had seen a group of men, say three or four, armed or unarmed. There had to be a group, Jonathan Gifford reasoned, because the horses were in adjoining stalls and would have been noisily terrified if a single man had done the job. There had been

93

enough men to take up positions beside each horse and at a signal do the vicious deed simultaneously.

They swung down back roads and rode in a wide semicircle around Strangers' Resort. They met only a few soldiers going home on leave, an occasional farmer driving cows or pigs to the Amboy market, and a peddler or two. By ten o'clock they were well to the northwest of the tavern. Reluctantly they turned their horses' heads homeward. The May sun blazed down on them from the deep blue sky. They were hot, weary, and thoroughly disgruntled when they heard hoofbeats and a cheerful voice calling to them. Kemble, out for the morning ride that was part of Dr. Davie's program for rebuilding his health, was soon cantering beside them. His good cheer vanished when he heard their story. He had seen no one suspicious on the road between them and Elizabethtown.

"We may yet run them down," Jonathan Gifford said. As he spoke, they rounded a bend in the road and saw five men in brown loose-fitting homespun farm clothes trudging toward them. They were barefoot and their faces were shaded by floppy, wide-brimmed work hats. Each carried a gun. Not until the man in the center of the line looked up at them did Jonathan Gifford recognize Joshua Bellows, his oldest son George, his two brothers Ben and Abel, and their cousin Harold. The Bellowses owned two middling farms on the north side of Kemble Manor. They were almost family retainers, grinding all their corn and wheat at the manor mill and selling their surplus with Squire Skinner at the best price he could get in Amboy or New York.

The Bellowses drew off the road as Jonathan Gifford and his party approached them. "Good morning, Josh," said the Captain. "You look like you've been on the road a good while."

"Went out for some game, rambled farther than we thought. Ain't that right?" Joshua Bellows said, glancing quickly at the rest of the family. They nodded and muttered agreement. He looked up at Jonathan Gifford again, a triumphant smile on his bony, hollow-cheeked face. They were ready for trouble, Jonathan Gifford thought. George Bellows, known as Pork for the size of his belly, had a finger on the trigger of his musket.

"What were you hunting?" Jonathan Gifford said.

"Why pheasant, squirrel, maybe a deer—anything we could shoot. 'Twasn't our lucky day, was it, lads?"

94

Again there was this nervous glance that demanded assent from the rest of the family.

"Five guns and you couldn't get a single bird? That's pretty poor shooting. You didn't see anybody on the road who looked suspicious, did you? Someone killed four horses in my barn last night. They belonged to the Continental army."

"Is that a fact?" said Joshua Bellows. He almost smiled, but thought better of it. "Why, Captain," he said, "I'm surprised you even let them put such animals in your barn. That could get you in a peck of trouble when the King's troops come to put down this here unnatural rebellion."

"You think so?"

"Why, yes I do. Maybe the ones who done that thing to them horses are your best friends. That could be, Captain. At a time like this it's hard to tell your friends from your enemies."

"That's an interesting thought," Jonathan Gifford said. He swung his horse's head into the road and said, "Have a good day, neighbors."

"Same to you, Captain."

As they cantered away, Kemble caught up to his stepfather. "He did it. Why didn't you arrest him? He was practically laughing in your face."

"They had five guns. We had three."

"They'd never dare to use their guns on you. Or me."

"Maybe not," Jonathan Gifford said with that hard common sense that repeatedly irritated Kemble. "But if they did, we'd never have the chance to repeat the mistake."

Kemble did not say another word on the ride home. His father sensed a sullen accusation in his silence. There was considerable ground for Kemble's assumption that the Bellowses would never dare to shoot a Stapleton. In our era of ever growing democracy, it is difficult to remember how much the America of 1776 was dominated by an elite group of families in every colony. Kemble was the only surviving Stapleton male in our part of the colony, but the family was equally powerful in north Jersey. His father's first cousin, Hugh Stapleton, was a leading Whig in Bergen County. Eventually he became a delegate to the Continental Congress.

Back at the tavern, Jonathan Gifford sent Sam to Perth Amboy with a letter for Captain Fleming, telling him what had happened and offering to pay for the dead horses. He assured the young Vir-

95

ginian that from now on the barn would be locked and guarded at night. Captain Fleming returned a hastily scribbled note that he had no horses to spare. He hoped that Jonathan Gifford would lend his own horses to the army, if necessary. Captain Fleming added that he was sure the incident would persuade General Mercer to take strong steps against the Tories in the area. Just what these would be, he did not know. They only had a single regiment of three hundred men and a hundred of these were sick with camp fever, dysentery, and other "diseases of the season."

The last line of the note was written in a firmer, less agitated hand. *My warmest respects to Miss Kate.* Jonathan Gifford showed it to her. She decided to be cross about it. "Oh, la, am I supposed to be impressed? Twenty lines about dead horses and guard boats and Tories and a single line admitting that I do, after all, exist."

Kemble, who had heard a good deal about Captain Fleming by now, looked surly. But Jonathan Gifford silenced him with a warning wave of his hand and went up to the tavern to help Barney in the taproom. It was Saturday, and the place was full of farmers and hired hands and even a few slaves, who picked up pocket money working in the neighborhood on their days off. Behind the bar, Barney McGovern was busy mixing a huge pitcher of rumfustian.

"George Bellows over there at the Squire's table paid for his first round with this," Barney said.

He took a gold coin from his waistcoat pocket and slid it down the recessed shelf behind the bar. It gleamed dully in the shadow. "Fresh minted in England this year, I'll bet on it. Where would he get that, Captain?"

"I don't know," Jonathan Gifford said.

He took the jug of rumfustian over to the table. Bellows leered up at him. He had a wide flabby mouth and a button nose that seemed to sink into the mottled flesh of his face.

"What do you think, Captain," he said, "do you think the Yankees will stand against the King's troops? I say they'll run away as fast as their legs can carry them—like they did at Bunker Hill."

"They left a good many British unable to run after them," Jonathan Gifford said.

"You must have lost a friend or two in that fight, Captain."

"I did."

"Yet you side with these people. It seems to me a soldier would be fierce for revenge."

"I'm not a soldier any more."

"But you know the profession. You could train other men. Do you know the definition of a trimmer, Captain?"

"No."

"A man who thinks he can throw his slops to windward in a gale."

The remark brought roars of laughter from the ten or twelve drinkers clustered around the Squire's table. Jonathan Gifford noted that several of the laughing men were shippers and wagon masters—important people if an army planned to operate in New Jersey. The man sitting next to Bellows, a razor-faced Yankee type named Cotton, owned three or four coasting sloops. A very useful fellow to know if you wanted to visit British ships in New York Harbor.

Bellows' crafty eyes suddenly shifted from Jonathan Gifford to a man standing to his left, behind him. "Ah, Col—Mr. Skinner, how are you this day in the merry month?"

Jonathan Gifford turned to find himself gazing into Anthony Skinner's saturnine face. "I'm not too well," he said in a voice that could be heard throughout the taproom. "I have just been witness to a terrible sight. Governor Franklin is on the New Brunswick road with an armed guard around him. He is being taken before a committee of Congress in Princeton to be condemned like a common thief."

An excited discussion of this news filled the taproom for the rest of the day. Sympathy for the governor was widespread. Others felt that he had forfeited any right to indulgence by his refusal to accept the offer from Congress to live as a paroled neutral on his farm.

"There will be no way for a man to remain neutral," Anthony Skinner said. "You know as well as I do that the Congress will vote for independence in a few weeks. The violents rule it as absolutely as the Sultan of Turkey rules Constantinople. After they play that damnable card—the last one in their deck—there can be no neutrals. There will only be enemies of the King and supporters of the King. Let me tell you something, gentlemen. I have traveled a good deal around England, Ireland, and Scotland. I have seen what happens to enemies of the King—believe me, I

97

know what I say—His Majesty's vengeance is harsh—and his generosity is great."

At the bar, Barney McGovern whispered in Jonathan Gifford's ear. "That's a recruiting speech if I ever heard one."

Jonathan Gifford nodded. He was more interested in assessing Anthony Skinner's impact on the crowd. Standing there, backed by the burly Bellows and a dozen other men, he looked unbeatable. No one contradicted him. But Jonathan Gifford could see something that Anthony Skinner missed. At least half the faces in the room were in angry disagreement with him. The rest lacked the fervor with which he damned a declaration of independence. They acknowledged what he was saying with glum nods at best. The men who wanted independence were ready to fight for it. Those who disliked the idea opposed it for negative reasons—it would start a war—it opened up an unknown, possibly dangerous future. But they did not hate it. They too were Americans. They shared the undercurrent of resentment at the inferiority implied in words like "colony" and "mother country." The words no longer made sense. America was too big, too rich, to accept an inferior status. It would take a subtle, skillful politician to arouse these cautious men. Jonathan Gifford did not think Anthony Skinner was that politician. He was too angry, too eager for battle.

The rest of May and the first glowing weeks of June slipped by like pages in a book of fables. Unreality permeated the days and nights. When the Jersey wagons with their enormous wheels and teams of four to six horses rolled to a stop in front of the tavern, the travelers who debarked were surrounded by questioners demanding the latest news from Philadelphia or New York. The wagons were called flying machines by their owner, John Mercereau, who boasted in the newspapers of his ability to get you from Philadelphia to New York in a day and a half. We could depend on our travelers telling us fresh news, if they had any.

But our favorite source of information was our post rider, Abel Aikin. Abel's costume was unique. It was usually a blue coat with yellow buttons, a scarlet waistcoat, blue yarn stockings, leather breeches, all topped by a red wig and a blue cocked hat. When he rode on horseback, his saddlebags were stuffed with enough packages and parcels to spavin his poor old mare, all private commissions by which Abel supplemented his small salary. The mare knew the way better than Abel, permitting him to knit stockings and sweaters as he rode.

Abel liked to torment us with hints and rumors. He had his choice of dozens in the month of June 1776. He filled our ears with bad news from the south. The British had a fleet and army poised to attack Charleston, South Carolina. Virginia had introduced a resolution for independence, but fears for the fate of Carolina prompted their convention to vote it down. Charleston was preparing to buy off the British fleet by paying the admiral an immense ransom. All this while he sat in the saddle, needles clicking away. In the tavern, his tongue loosened by free grog, he would admit it was all hearsay.

As we pieced it together from Abel and from soldier and civilian travelers, the news was confusing and alarming. There seemed to be no agreement on independence in Congress. There was, in fact, strong talk of Pennsylvania abandoning the confederation and New York and South Carolina following the Quaker colony. In New Jersey, the Provincial Congress was busy. It resolved by a vote of 54 to 3 to adopt a constitution for the state and a ten-man committee was appointed to write it. It sent a new delegation to the Continental Congress. All were vigorous independence men.

But the most exciting news in that tormenting month came from New York. At about five o'clock on June 29, an army dispatch rider rode an exhausted horse into the tavern yard and asked for a drink of grog and a fresh mount. "The British fleet's in New York Harbor," he said. "There must be three, four hundred ships. It looks like all London is afloat."

"Where are they landing?" Jonathan Gifford asked as Sam led a fresh horse from the barn.

"On Staten Island. They've taken it without firing a shot. That damn nest of Tories greeted them with open arms."

"Any idea how many men they bring with them?"

"Some say ten thousand, others twenty. It looks like there'll be hot work in New York and maybe here in Jersey before summer's over."

This was not the tiny garrison army that the minutemen of Massachusetts had so easily beaten. It was an immense host, committed to a war of conquest. Reports on their numbers multiplied them until they were thirty thousand strong. More than a few of our loudest independence men suddenly became meek. It was one thing to damn the King and sneer at the British army when they were several thousand miles away. Now only a day's brisk marching would put British regiments at the door of Strangers' Resort. For the first time the independence men realized their violent words could cost them everything they owned, possibly their lives. Anthony Skinner was in the tavern every night warning that the punishment for rebellion was the confiscation of a family's land and wealth. The Committee of Safety summoned him for a hearing. He ignored them.

The chairman of the Committee, Lemuel Peters, was among the first independence men to show signs of panic. He drafted a petition and persuaded over a hundred men to sign it, demanding an immediate reinforcement for the defense of eastern New Jersey. In the taproom that night, Peters damned George Washington and the Continental Congress for sending New Jersey's best soldiers to Canada. And what was the point in defending New York and Long Island? Both places were thick with Tories.

But these were trivial issues compared to the major question. Would—should—the Congress declare independence now, when it was clear that the declaration meant war? The number of independence men still wholeheartedly in favor of an immediate declaration dwindled markedly. A startling number now began to think it would be better to wait until the King's peace commissioner, Lord Richard Howe, arrived with—it was hoped—terms that Americans could accept.

A few disagreed, with Kemble Stapleton acting as their fiery spokesman. Although neither of us was old enough to vote, Kemble and I scoured the countryside rounding up signatures for a petition urging an immediate declaration of independence; we collected 211 names in a district where, if unanimity had prevailed, we could have gathered 4,000. We came back dismayed by how lukewarm most men were, how fearful they had become of publicly avowing their opinions in any direction.

"The Tories have them cowed," Kemble said.

"Don't expect so much of the average man, Kemble," Jonathan Gifford said. "Can you really blame them? Most of the state's soldiers are fighting somewhere else. In Shrewsbury and Middletown, able-bodied men are disappearing every night. No one knows where they're going—they may be joining the British—or lying low in the swamps, waiting for a signal to attack. We are practically defenseless."

Jonathan Gifford was startled to find Kemble smiling at this solemn monologue. "What's so funny?"

"That's the first time I've heard you say 'we.' Are you joining our side, Father?"

Jonathan Gifford was standing behind the bar polishing glasses. The taproom was not yet open. "I don't like men who cut horses' throats—especially in my own barn."

What was he saying? Jonathan Gifford asked himself dazedly, picking up another glass. Now was not the time for bravado. Now, above all, with the British army only a day's march away.

Before he could qualify his words, Kemble was asking, "Do I have your permission to join the army now, as soon as I can find a place?"

Jonathan Gifford looked stonily at Kemble's pale face and reed-thin body. He still could not bear to tell him the truth—that he lacked the physical strength to be a soldier. Groping for a path between freedom and obedience, he said, "I've been thinking—thinking of writing to General Putnam—asking if you might serve on his staff as a volunteer. You'd have no rank—but I'm sure you could be helpful. For one thing, you can spell."

"I'll get you a pen and paper this instant," Kemble said.

Ten minutes later, the letter was sealed and Kemble was preparing to depart for New York. Jonathan Gifford vetoed this precipitous plan. They would send the letter to the General by an army dispatch rider. One was certain to come by in the next day or two. Kemble reluctantly agreed to wait for an answer.

Later that day Jonathan Gifford found himself under assault from Kate. She had heard about her brother's plans. Angrily, she pointed out what Jonathan Gifford already knew—Kemble's delicate health made him a poor candidate for army life.

"Kate—give me credit for knowing one or two things. Kemble has been trying to join the army for a year. It seemed to me the best available alternative. If he goes in defiance of me, he'll enlist as a private. You've seen some of the sick creeping home or being carried along the roads."

"But Anthony says that being a general's aide could lead to hanging. He says it is sure to come to that in the end for Washington and his pack of fools."

"Washington doesn't look like a fool to me."

Boots, the tavern cat, came slinking across the room and leaped up on the bar between them. He was Kate's favorite pet and the sight of him brought out her natural affection. She stroked him for a moment. "Well," she said, "there's no point in arguing. Kemble seems to think because you are letting him join the army, you have joined the Congress men."

"That's saying a bit too much," Jonathan Gifford said, "but I don't like the game the loyalists are playing either. I've never let any man intimidate me. I couldn't face myself in my shaving mirror each morning if I did."

"I don't have to face myself in my shaving mirror," Kate said. "Maybe that's why I don't give a damn which side you are on."

She picked up the cat and tickled him under the chin. "I'm like Boots here. Just feed me regularly and I am content."

She looked up and caught Jonathan Gifford frowning. "Oh, look at him, Boots. Can't you just see what he is thinking? What woman has ever been content in her life? Give her ten new gowns and she wants twenty. Give her a fine upstanding Virginia captain and she ignores him."

Kate gave her father an impulsive kiss. "Stop worrying, Father. It will be all right."

She was at the door when she turned with an exclamation. "I almost forgot. Uncle Charles asked me to give you a message. He warned me to tell no one about it, not even Anthony. He would like you to meet him at nine o'clock tonight at the southeast corner of the manor, where it meets the road to Freehold. He will be in the grove of trees that stands just inside the property."

"Do you know what this is about?"

"What else?" Kate said. "Politics."

That night Jonathan Gifford kept his rendezvous with his old friend. Charles Skinner was only a dark blur against the bulk of his bay stallion. "Friend Jonathan," he said, "I'm glad you've come. No one must know about this, not even my wife or my son."

"No one shall," said Jonathan Gifford.

"I'm here to seek advice, friend Jonathan—and perhaps to give some. I know not which way to turn."

"Not many of us do these days."

"Have you brought your pipe? I've got a full pouch of tobacco here. Let's light up and sit down amongst those trees and pretend we're on patrol again in the north woods."

"I have my pipe and I have my own tobacco," Jonathan Gifford said.

When Charles Skinner's match flared, Jonathan Gifford was shocked by the haggard lines in his old friend's face.

"I brought along a bottle of Madeira, too. Let's pass it back and forth as we did with Lord George Howe's best."

"Good enough," said Jonathan Gifford. He could feel the strings of emotion tugging him into the past, where Charles Skinner was trying to go, back to those simpler days when courage and luck were the only requisites for survival.

"Those were the days, weren't they now?" Skinner said. "At least we had them. No one can take them away from us. We had them round and true compared to today—"

Jonathan Gifford felt the bottle touch his knee. He took a pull of the warm sweet wine.

"You know, I suppose, that before they arrested the governor, he appointed my kinsman Skinner major general of the loyal militia?"

"I've heard it."

"He's on Staten Island now with General Howe. I have an offer from him—to be a brigadier."

"What does Anthony say about it?"

"He urges me to take it. The offer came through him. My good wife Caroline vows that she will leave my bed and board if I accept it. Anthony says I should ignore her. But that's easier said than done. She can be as much of a handful as her sister, Gifford, when she so inclines. Not as wayward but every bit as willful."

For a moment Jonathan Gifford was transfixed by the image of Caroline Skinner defying her stepson and her husband.

"But this leads me to the burthen of our meeting, friend Jonathan," Skinner continued. "Anthony has a commission already from Major General Skinner—a colonel's commission, no less—with orders to raise a loyal regiment in this neighborhood. He has been at it apace this last month, and has three hundred good men and true, armed and paid already with the King's guineas. All this time he has been waiting for you to speak your piece."

"What can I do for him? He doesn't need a one-legged soldier."

"You have a following in this neighborhood. You know who comes and goes along the King's Highway. You could be useful, very useful. This is only a small part of my reason for speaking to you in this way, old friend. I fear for your safety. In a civil war there is no quarter asked or given. The tavern, everything you own could go up in flames. You could be driven onto the roads, reduced to beggary."

"So could you."

"What?"

"I said, so could you. Do you think only the King can be ruthless in a rebellion? I think you've lost touch with your own people. There's a savage lurking somewhere inside almost every American. Didn't we see it fifteen years ago in the north woods? We told them to fight like Indians and they did, right down to collecting scalps and torturing prisoners."

"So you won't join us?"

"I won't join out of fear—when fear could be nothing but a mask for folly."

"Folly, folly. What are you talking about? You don't really think Washington's men can stand against the British army in the open field? Those ragamuffins? Look at your map, man. Before the summer is over, Washington's whole army will be caught like cats in a bag."

"They will if Washington's a damn fool. He doesn't look like one to me."

Charles Skinner pulled on his pipe. The glowing bowl momentarily illuminated his haggard face. "So you think I should refuse the King's commission?"

"I do. Unless you're prepared to leave your house and lands and take refuge inside their lines."

"You think I should desert my son?"

"There are sons deserting fathers and vice versa all over America. Look at the Franklins."

"It's easy enough for you to say. You don't have a son."

"I have a boy I've raised since he was ten. He's a son to me."

"A damned hothead. He's as much the reason why you're proscribed as anything."

"Oh? I'm proscribed?"

"You're on a list of those deemed—well—deemed untrustworthy," Charles Skinner said.

"And what does that mean?"

"That you can be—should be—arrested as soon as they have the power, and shot dead if you resist."

"Does Kate know this?"

"Of course not. Anthony has more sense than to tell his business to a giddy girl."

They passed the bottle back and forth again.

"So what am I to do?" Charles Skinner said. "Take the neuter part? I'm a man, Gifford. Besides, I say again this contest will show no quarter for men who are afraid to choose."

Jonathan Gifford heard the accusation in those words.

"I suppose that's true. But not every man can make the choice at the same time. It's a choice that involves the head and the heart, old friend. For some of us the heart speaks with a still, small voice, not easy to hear. Let me assure you when I make my choice it will have nothing to do with calculations about the winning side."

"I know you too well to expect anything else," Skinner said.

The words were cordial, but there was no conviction in them. The tone was empty, flat. With dismay, Jonathan Gifford realized that they were talking more like lawyers than like friends. Another thought crowded into his mind at the same instant, more image than thought, a small, proud woman by a well, speaking words of independence.

"Damn it, Skinner, I can't part from you this way," he snapped. "I can't part from a true friend without telling him what I really think. Didn't you tell me that when you were in London, you never felt more an American? This is your country. It doesn't belong to the English—though they're ready enough to take it away from you, now that they've been given the excuse. Don't you remember the motto of a British officer—to live well and leave a fortune for his heirs? Well, let me tell you, every one of those gentlemen in command of regiments and companies over there on Staten Island is ready and eager to make his fortune in America. What does it matter now that the trouble began with some damn fool puritans in Boston in search of a holy war? Now the war is at your doorstep and there's no place for a man with pride but on the side of his country."

"Even if it means siding with men like Slocum?"

"If you came out for independence, you could take that militia regiment away from him overnight. Have you stopped to think of what you'll have to put up with from those arrogant bastards in London if they win? There'll be a lord lieutenant for America and a standing army in every colony. Your grandchildren will grow up as meek and obedient as their patronizing power can make them. They'll barely know the meaning of the word liberty."

For a long moment the two men sat there, engulfed in darkness and silence. A summer breeze sighed through the branches of the trees above their heads.

"Gifford, you're an independence man. I can't believe it. You're an independence man," Charles Skinner said.

He was on his feet, striding through the trees toward his horse.

"But I'm not speaking for myself, I'm telling—"

The accusation had stunned Jonathan Gifford. The explosion of emotion had not—could not—apply to him, the stranger, the outsider. It had been a compound of wish and hope that he only sought to bestow like a healing balm on the tormented spirit of his friend. But as he limped in the opposite direction and eased his ruined leg over the stone fence to stand beside his horse, he was compelled to face the possibility that his words were the convoluted wish of his own uncertain heart.

CHAPTER SEVEN

For the next seven days, New Jersey oscillated like a pendulum between two mighty magnets—Staten Island with its British army and fleet and Philadelphia, where the Congress debated a declaration of independence. The countryside was rife with rumors of men making fortunes selling fresh vegetables and meat to the British on Staten Island. In Burlington, New Jersey's Provincial Congress was still wrestling with the text of our new constitution. On July 1, two of the delegates from Bergen County stayed overnight at the tavern. They told Jonathan Gifford that some thirty other legislators had decided to go home rather than participate in such a revolutionary business.

The Bergen gentlemen, both stolid Dutchmen who swore picturesquely in their mother tongue, said they did not feel authorized to declare New Jersey independent. Three out of every four men in Bergen detested the idea, they vowed. The Dutch had been treated fairly and had prospered greatly under the King of England's rule for a hundred years now. It seemed to many of them gross ingratitude if they took the side of the New England men in this present quarrel.

The whole trouble began and ended with those damned puritans from Massachusetts and Connecticut, the Dutchmen swore. There were just enough of their brethren in New Jersey to poison the atmosphere. They wouldn't be happy until they made Sam Adams or John Hancock the lord protector of America. All this was declaimed in stentorian tones while the ex-legislators consumed several chickens, a side of beef, a slab of ham, a fleet of vegetable dishes, and several quarts of hard cider.

Such dissension and timidity in New Jersey's legislature made men concentrate even more intently on the drama in Philadelphia. With the British fleet and army in New York Harbor, would the independence men still carry the day? Now that there was no longer any doubt of England's readiness to use force to settle the quarrel, would the men who wished to wait for the King's peace commissioner, Lord Howe, have a stronger voice?

That seemed to be the general opinion in Strangers' Resort crowded taproom during the first two days of July. But it was hard to tell whether the drinkers were a true poll of the neighborhood. There were strangers in the crowd, men who had ridden over from Shrewsbury or Upper Freehold to get the freshest news from travelers on the Philadelphia to New York road. Most of them opposed independence and came out of anxious hope to hear of its defeat. The predominance of this attitude was especially visible on the evening of July 2, when a traveler arrived from Philadelphia with the first news from Congress.

He was a young lieutenant in a Pennsylvania regiment, who had been given leave to help settle his late father's estate. He lived next door to John Morton, one of Pennsylvania's delegates to Congress, and had spoken with this gentleman just before he set out for the Burlington ferry. Morton said that Congress had divided hopelessly, with nine colonies for independence and four —Pennsylvania, New York, South Carolina, and Delaware—either in the negative or abstaining. A wave of exultation had passed through the listeners in the taproom.

Anthony Skinner stood in the center of the room, a dominant figure. Like a good politician, he was quick to improvise on this new development. Even if there was no declaration of independence, there was still a rebellion to be crushed, traitors to be punished.

"Didn't I tell you? Didn't I tell you?" he said. "I always knew those New England hypocrites would fall short with their schemes to turn us all into Roundheads. Let's drink to the loyal, honest men of New York and Pennsylvania, Delaware and Carolina."

Almost every glass and tankard in the taproom was raised. Captain John Fleming, standing at the bar, was one of the few who did not lift his drink. The Captain had become a fairly regular visitor to Strangers' Resort, hoping to improve the advantage he seemed to have gained on his first day. But Kate had begun to treat him with little more than ordinary politeness. She enjoyed his company, occasionally went riding with him, always conversed animatedly with him when he came to dinner—but gave no sign that there was any unusual warmth kindling her heart. Captain Fleming could not compete with Anthony Skinner's assiduous attentions. He invariably combined his political visits to the tavern with a half-hour tête-à-tête with Kate at the end of the evening.

George Bellows saw Captain Fleming's refusal to raise his glass. He roared out a toast. "To the honest men of New Jersey, who know what to do to hypocrites and traitors."

Again, almost every glass was raised. Captain Fleming remained motionless. While Anthony Skinner watched with smiling approval, Bellows strode across the room to confront him. "What's the matter, Captain? Are you afraid to drink to honest men?"

"If you had toasted the honest men of Virginia, I would have gladly done so, sir," said Captain Fleming. "But I must remind you, they are all for independence."

"Damn independence. We'll see how many dance to that word when a British army sets down on *your* coast. Then I'll be damned if you find an honest man in all Virginia."

"I fear you'll be damned and well damned, sir," said Captain Fleming. "You and your redcoated friends will find one or two hundred thousand."

"Did I hear you damn me to my face, sir?" Bellows roared. "There is no man in New Jersey, no man in America who can do that."

"I think you damned yourself," said Fleming in the same quiet voice. "But if you wish to hear the same expression from me, I will most heartily damn your sentiments and call you a traitor to your country, sir. If you wish to repel that charge, I am sure Captain Gifford will supply us with pistols."

"I don't need a pistol," Bellows roared. He raised one of his big fists to smash Captain Fleming in the face. He outweighed the young Virginian by forty pounds and would have given him a fearful beating, but he never struck the blow. Jonathan Gifford, moving with wonderful rapidity for a man with a shattered knee, caught Bellows by the collar of his coat and with a wrench of his powerful arm and shoulder flung him half the length of the bar.

"Get out of here, Bellows. I think you'd better go, too, Mr. Skinner."

Anthony Skinner replied with a mocking bow. "At your service,

Mr. Gifford. It's your tavern, for the time being. As an ex-officer of the King, you should know more than anyone about the penalties of disloyalty."

Jonathan Gifford said nothing as Anthony Skinner turned to the drinkers in the taproom and invited everyone to continue the party at Kemble Manor. There would be a cold supper, country dancing, and drinks for every honest "loyal" man and woman. There was a general exodus that virtually swept the taproom bare. Left in the room were only one or two drinkers too sozzled to care about politics and a scattering of independence men slumped glumly in the corners.

"Do you think he's right, Mr. Gifford?" Captain Fleming asked. "Does the vote in Philadelphia mean the collapse of the union?"

"Tomorrow or the next day could bring very different news," Jonathan Gifford said. "If you Virginians and your friends from Massachusetts are any sort of politicians, you will find a way to satisfy—or frighten—the four who are lagging behind."

"I hope so," Captain Fleming said. "With Carolina to the south and Pennsylvania to the north, Virginia would be in trouble."

"Not half as much trouble as New Jersey, if New York and Pennsylvania fall out," Jonathan Gifford said.

"True enough. From what I saw and heard tonight, we'll have our hands full without that calamity."

Jonathan Gifford nodded again. He took a clay pipe down from the wall, packed it with tobacco from a jar beneath the bar, and lit it. "Do you remember the talk we had about a Tory regiment, Captain?"

"I do. Have you heard any more?"

"I think I know the man you want."

Jonathan Gifford drew deeply on his pipe. The acrid fumes of tobacco swirled in his lungs and coursed on his blood to his brain. It was not an easy thing to do, betray the son of his best friend. But he had come—or been brought—to this moment not by any one voice or incident, not by a mean desire to protect himself— though that was part of it—or by a crude calculation of where his interest lay. No, it was by a medley of voices, faces, and incidents which those last menacing words from Anthony Skinner climaxed. It stretched from that moment by the Shrewsbury four years ago, from the arrogant condescension on Viscount Needham's face, the anger and shame and innocence on the faces of Kemble and Kate, from the big determined Virginian who stopped in the road with greetings from his old friend Israel Putnam, to that small dark cool woman in the shaded park of Kemble Manor. All these things somehow canceled or unbalanced other memories. His father's dry prudence, Lord George Howe's generosity and courage, twenty years of disciplined pride, the 4th Regiment, the King's Own, all seemed as insubstantial as pages from a book dancing in a furious flame.

"Yes," he heard himself say, "if I were you and had a few men to spare—I would put a guard boat in the bay off Kemble Manor and a patrol on the coast road between the manor and Amboy. If you see Anthony Skinner on that road, I would arrest him and search him thoroughly."

Captain Fleming nodded.

"Would you join us for supper, Captain?"

"I had hoped for such an invitation, sir," he said with a warm smile. "But I think you had best simply give Miss Kate my compliments. I have a feeling there is no time to waste."

Jonathan Gifford waited until he heard the hoofbeats of Captain Fleming's horse on the road. He left Barney in charge of the taproom, slipped out the back door into the cool twilight, and strolled through the garden to the family house by the brook. He found the place empty and dark. Lighting an oil lamp in the hall, he saw a scribbled note from Kemble.

Kate has gone off to the Manor with A.S. I saw his performance in the taproom and called him a damn Tory to his face. I'm off to Amboy—where people care about their country.

Jonathan Gifford sighed wearily. The last line was aimed at him, of course. While waiting for a response from Israel Putnam, Kemble had taken to spending his days at General Mercer's headquarters in Amboy, learning what he could about army routine. Jonathan Gifford crumpled the paper and flung it into the cold fireplace. It was just as well. He would spend the evening doing a chore he had been putting off for weeks.

Kate did not return until noon the following day. The party had lasted until 4 A.M., she said. The best dancing and singing she ever remembered. Jonathan Gifford did not ask if one of the songs was "God Save the King."

The next two days were ferociously hot. They drifted by in a kind of suspenseful daze. No travelers appeared from Philadelphia. The tavern was crowded from morning till night with a fluctuating flow from the neighborhood. Independence men came and went in doleful groups, looking ever more tense and anxious. Most of the customers were moderate men whose opinions were not fixed on either side of the dispute, but simply wanted to hear the news.

What they finally heard was news enough—if not the news they expected or wanted to hear. A little after noon on July 4, a group of horsemen appeared on the road in the usual cloud of dust. As they drew closer, loungers in the yard saw Captain John Fleming at their head, his face saturnine. Behind him, between two soldiers, rode Anthony Skinner, his hands tied behind his neck. They dismounted and Skinner was half shoved, half dragged into the taproom. Tensely, Captain Fleming asked where he could find a justice of the peace. Was Mr. Gifford one?

Jonathan Gifford shook his head. "Old Jasper Clark is one," he said. "He's also a member of the County Committee. He lives not ten minutes away. Shall I send for him?"

"Please."

"If you do that, Gifford, you are marked as my enemy, and an enemy of every honest man in this neighborhood," Anthony Skinner said. "This man has no right to arrest me. He's a damn Virginian. So are his men, usurpers in this colony without a shadow of legality. Are you going to let an honest citizen of New Jersey be arrested on the open road while going peaceably about his private business?"

Captain Fleming eyed the crowd in the taproom uneasily. His hand strayed to the butt of his pistol. "I am ready to show these gentlemen your business was neither private nor peaceful, Mr. Skinner. But I prefer to do it legally."

"How can you use that word, you damn hypocrite, when you've driven the legal government out of the colony?"

"Barney," Jonathan Gifford said, "ride over and fetch Mr. Clark. Tell him it's very important."

In twenty minutes, Jasper Clark, dressed in homespun trousers and a loose calico work shirt—a more unjudicial figure could not be imagined—was seated behind a table in the assembly room, his long, lined face solemn, his eyes wide with indignation as Captain Fleming told why he had arrested Anthony Skinner and what he had found in his saddlebags. The drinkers in the taproom crowded the doorway. A visibly distressed Kate and a palpably exultant Kemble sat on the green-cushioned Chippendale couch. Jonathan Gifford stood against the wall in his sergeant-at-arms posture. Skinner, his arms still bound, glared at the boyish Virginian as he spoke.

In a terse, official style that added impact to his words, Captain Fleming told how he had seized Skinner on the Amboy road and found in his saddlebags his commission as colonel of the so-called loyal militia, and commissions for a number of other persons, including Joshua Bellows and his son George. He also found a muster list with three hundred names on it, and three hundred guineas to pay them. The Virginian deposited this evidence on the table before Jasper Clark. The guineas made a faintly musical sound inside their canvas bag.

While Fleming spoke, Jonathan Gifford was studying the faces of the crowd at the door and he was also watching Kate. On the faces at the door, two emotions prevailed. Some resented not being asked to join the loyal militia and some were enraged by its very existence. What Jonathan Gifford saw on Kate's face was more distressing—a mixture of anguish, love, and rage that made him realize how foolish he had been to think that anyone could easily replace this man in her affections.

"Do you have any answer to make to these accusations?" asked Jasper Clark, his Adam's apple moving nervously up and down his throat.

"Yes," Anthony Skinner said. "What is the charge under which Captain Fleming is trying to hold me prisoner? I have committed no crime against any law, as far as I know. My only purpose in recruiting this regiment is to provide a force of honest men ready to protect the lives and property of every man no matter what his political beliefs."

"Do you take me for some kind of fool, young man?" asked Jasper Clark. "You are conspiring against your country. You are guilty of treason and, by God, if you don't hang for it—"

"Mr. Clark, you are talking nonsense. How can I commit treason against a country that doesn't exist? I freely admit I oppose the Continental Congress, that band of political adventurers who are breaking into frightened factions in Philadelphia at this very moment. If you want to arrest me by force, go ahead, take the risk. But it cannot be done by law."

"We shall see about that," Clark said. "Captain Gifford, do you have a strong room in which this prisoner can be safely held for a day or two?"

"All the rooms on the second floor have locks on them."

"I hereby order you to confine this man in one of those rooms. Take pains to make sure there are no limbs of trees convenient to his window, or any other means by which he could escape. What is the distance from the window to the ground?"

"Fifteen feet. A jump would break a man's legs."

"Nevertheless, nail the window shut," Jasper Clark said, staring stonily at Anthony Skinner.

"You will regret this, Clark," Anthony Skinner said. "There will come a day when you will beg me for mercy on your knees."

"Take him away," Clark said. "I have heard enough treason for one day."

"Let's tar and feather him first," shouted someone in the crowd at the door.

"Right," shouted someone else. "There's a tar barrel in the cooper's shop."

Jasper Clark rose to his feet, trembling. Jonathan Gifford thought he was going to collapse. The strain of attempting to govern others was telling on him. With surprising dignity, Clark declared, "We will do no such thing. We will proceed in a decent, lawful manner. No prisoner of mine will ever be abused by a mob while I sit as justice of the peace. I am sure I can depend upon the support of Captain Fleming."

"You can, sir," said Fleming, rising to confront those in the doorway.

Jonathan Gifford took Anthony Skinner's arm. "I advise you to come quietly," he said in a low voice.

For a moment Skinner seemed about to make another defiant speech. But Kate whispered just loud enough for him to hear her: "Go with him, Anthony, please."

Skinner let Jonathan Gifford escort him swiftly through the door which led down a short hall into the kitchen. Captain Fleming followed them. In the kitchen, Jonathan Gifford told Barney's wife Molly to fetch a hammer and nails and some dinner to the corner room on the second floor. They mounted the back stairs and soon had Skinner incarcerated. Jonathan Gifford nailed the window shut and left the prisoner with a bottle of claret and a good pound of roast beef to console himself.

"I will post a man at the end of the hall. That way he should not disturb any other guests," Captain Fleming said.

Downstairs the crowd had returned to the taproom and the tavern yard. Jasper Clark was finishing his letter to the Provincial Congress, reporting what he had heard from Captain Fleming and asking them for directions on how to deal with this alarming discovery of a loyalist regiment.

"They will have to send us men from other parts of the colony," he said. "I doubt we could raise as many as that damn fellow has recruited. Can I borrow one of your soldiers to carry this letter, Captain?"

"You will have to give him directions. They are all strangers to New Jersey."

The messenger was soon on his way to Burlington with the letter. Jonathan Gifford called for his chaise and rode at a fierce pace —even for him—to Kemble Manor. A servant let him into the entrance hall, and Caroline Skinner met him there with a bright smile. She was wearing a simple red silk housedress. Her black hair was woven into two braids that made her look remarkably like an Indian. Jonathan Gifford told her why he had come. Her smile vanished. "Mr. Skinner is in the library," she said. "By this time I am sure he is drunk. He and Anthony had a great quarrel yesterday, before he left. No doubt it was about this business. Did you play a part in taking him captive?"

"No more than you did," he said, eyeing her warily.

She caught the edge in his voice and turned away abruptly to lead him to the library door. The room was full of shadows. The damask curtains were drawn against the bright afternoon sun. In the half-light, the white marble busts of the Duke of Marlborough, General Wolfe, and George III seemed to float like bodiless ghosts on their pedestals between the windows. The heavy Jacobean furniture, fringed with carved coronets, added its touch of the macabre to the scene. Charles Skinner was slumped in a huge dark leather armchair, a decanter of brandy beside him. He was wearing a red velvet skullcap lined with white linen, a blue damask dressing gown, a richly embroidered red satin waist-coat, black satin breeches, and red morocco slippers. He heaved from his chair and stumbled toward his visitor, his voice thick with liquor—and something else, perhaps grief.

"Gifford, old friend, have a glass with me. I was hoping to see you privately. I had it out with the boy. I would sign no paper, join no association that would set me against my countrymen. God knows, some of the dogs warrant hanging. But I thought deep and hard, Gifford. What you said is right, right in the heart as well as in the head. If you don't stand up to these damned inso-lent Englishmen, we shall be truckling servants to them like the Irish. I won't conspire to such a thing, no, by God."

Jonathan Gifford limped to the high windows that looked out on the north lawn and its weeping willows. He pulled back the draperies and filled the room with strong July sunlight. He told his old friend what had happened to his son. Charles Skinner stumbled back to his big chair in the corner, poured himself a tumbler of brandy, and downed it in one long gulp.

"I told him to demand a regiment—two regiments to support him, otherwise damn all commissions and recruiting bounties. What good are they? You can't win wars with gold coins and pieces of paper."

He stared at the bust of George III as he said these words. He swung around, breathing like a man on the brink of an apoplexy. "What's to be done, Gifford? Should I go see him?"

"No. It would only irritate people and accomplish nothing."

"Can I post a bond for him? Let them name any figure. I will write a note for this whole estate if they want it. He's my son, Gifford, my only son."

"I will ask the Committee about the bond. But I think the Pro-vincial Congress may insist on having him transported to Burling-ton, where they can question him."

"Most likely, most likely," Charles Skinner said. He uttered a great groan. "Dear God, Gifford, can you believe this is America? Can you believe we were all as contented as the swains of Arcady a year or two ago?"

Jonathan Gifford nodded perfunctorily. But he thought to himself: perhaps you were happy, but I wasn't. The violence of the denial shocked him. Was this the secret reason why he was

116

turning into a revolutionist? Was he willing to risk a possibly dangerous future because he had no real love for (or in) the past?

"This damn rebellion is already falling apart, Gifford. If it does, the worst of them, people like Clark, Slocum, will be desperate men. We can't leave my boy in their hands. Is there any fresh news from Philadelphia?"

"None."

Charles Skinner seized his arm, pleading like a child. "They'll cut his throat, Gifford. He'd be safer in the hands of drunken Indians."

"I don't think he's in any such danger. The rebels are as opposed to mob law as you are. Some people wanted to tar and feather Anthony. Old Jasper Clark stared them down with the dignity of a chief justice."

"Gifford—promise me this. If the news from Philadelphia is of dissolution and chaos—as I pray to God it will be—if in spite of this they try to take my boy a prisoner to Burlington—then help him. I know you too well to offer money."

"I will do what I can."

In the center hall, Sukey, Caroline Skinner's personal maid, handed him his hat and said, "My mistress would like to see you in the garden, Captain Gifford."

Caroline Skinner had combed out her braids. Her hair was now swept in two wide gleaming bands about her head. She was wearing a red sun hat that matched her dress. It had a wide brim garlanded with white dwarf China roses. She had asked him for some cuttings a year or two ago.

"I see you're putting *chinensis minima* to good use," he said.

She nodded, fingering one of the flowers on the side of the brim. "I love them," she said. Then she dropped all pretense of small talk. "What have you decided?"

He told her that he had promised to help Anthony Skinner if it became necessary. She looked dismayed, and seemed about to say something violent. But she controlled herself with an obvious effort and smiled sadly.

"We seem fated—to make different choices, Captain. I was about to tell you some harsh things Anthony has said against you. But—he is my son. I don't wish him any bodily harm."

Jonathan Gifford nodded. "I'm afraid I've seen and heard him for myself." He told her what Anthony had said to him in the tap-

117

room two nights ago. "But there is a man in there"—he pointed to the manor house—"who saved my life more than once."

"And you saved his. I've heard him tell the story."

"What difference does that make? My dear lady, you don't—I don't think you understand friendship."

"No. I'm only a woman."

"I meant no such thing—"

"But I happen to think this does not disqualify me from advising a man. My husband would rather consult a brandy bottle. I'm only trying to tell you not to risk—too much."

Once again—this time in the most direct and unqualified way—Jonathan Gifford saw the remarkable dimensions of Caroline Skinner's character. It was so totally different from her sister Sarah's personality, he still could only see it without comprehending it.

"I appreciate—your concern."

"It is for Kate and Kemble's sake—as much as yours," she said in a voice so sharp it seemed almost a rebuke.

"I know," he said. "Let's not argue. Let's trust each other—as much as we can."

"Yes," she said. "I like that. As much as we can."

CHAPTER EIGHT

JONATHAN GIFFORD RODE back to Strangers' Resort feeling heavy, mournful, as if he were returning from a funeral. There was so little he could do. But he would meet the responsibility as he had met so many others in his life. As he neared the tavern, he noticed an unusual number of men on the road. Some were on foot, some on horseback. They waved cheerfully to him. Next, he saw an extraordinary number of people in the tavern yard. Black Sam ran out of the crowd as he approached and took his horse to walk it around the back.

"What's happened, Sam?"

"News from Philadelphia. The Congress declared independence."

Jonathan Gifford leaped from his chaise and limped toward the crowd.

"Captain," Sam called, "does it mean everybody'll be free, black and white?"

"We'll see, Sam. We'll see."

Lemuel Peters and Ambrose Cotter were in the center of the crowd. Peters was waving a piece of paper excitedly. "Captain Gifford," he said, "can we use your chaise as a platform?"

"Certainly."

Sam led horse and chaise into the crowd. Peters mounted the chaise and said, "By a communication just delivered to me from the honorable Provincial Congress of New Jersey I am happy to report the honorable Continental Congress in Philadelphia on July 2 declared our independence from Great Britain by a vote of twelve states to none, New York's delegates abstaining only for want of proper instructions from their constituents. A declaration of independence is in preparation and will be forthcoming in a few days."

He handed the paper to Cotter and continued in a more oratorical tone. "I thought it best to tell you this glorious news immediately, since we have an enemy upon our shore. We must rouse ourselves against him and against his depraved and vicious allies in our midst. We are now free citizens of a free country. We need fear no man nor bend our knees to anyone. Are you with me?"

A roar of assent filled the hot July afternoon.

"We have a traitor within reach of a rope at this very moment," shouted a voice from the crowd. It was Daniel Slocum. Aided by a phalanx of his relatives, Slocum shoved his way to the chaise and jumped up on it beside Peters. "What are we waiting for? Let's hang that son of a bitch Anthony Skinner now."

"We are waiting for orders from our elected representatives in Congress," Lemuel Peters said.

"Damn them. What have they done for us anyway? Have they sent us soldiers? Do they care if Skinner and his friends cut our throats tonight?"

"That's enough of such talk," said Peters, visibly shaken. "Let us not disgrace this day with lawless vengeance. Let's celebrate the glorious news."

"He's right," shouted Cotter from beside the chaise. "Let the Congress hang Skinner and send us orders to hang his friends."

Jonathan Gifford pulled himself onto the chaise. "There are drinks inside," he said, "for every man who wants them—free of charge as long as a man can hold his liquor."

That settled it. With a roar of delight the crowd surged into the taproom and filled the other rooms. As an opening ceremony, Kemble cut the portraits of George II and George III from their frames and burned them in the fireplace. Everyone gave three cheers and started drinking. Volunteers were pressed into service as waiters when the family and staff proved unequal to the task. Liquor poured like the falls of the Passaic or the great torrent of Niagara. The walls of the tavern shook with defiant liberty songs.

> We led fair Freedom hither
> And lo, the desert smiled!
> A paradise of pleasure

Was opened in the wild!
Your harvest, bold Americans,
No power shall snatch away!
Huzza, huzza, huzza, huzza,
For free America.

Barney McGovern kept saying that he had never seen anything like it, as he broke open cask after cask of rum and hard cider. When the war began last year, Jonathan Gifford had bought enormous quantities before the prices rose. For a while, even this surplus did not look as if it would last. But about eight o'clock the crowd began to thin.

Barney swore they had served at least two thousand people. "Let's hope they'll fight as hard as they drink," he said.

Kate flung aside her apron and pronounced herself exhausted. "I've done my duty," she said. "Do I have your permission to bring Anthony some supper?"

"Yes, of course."

"If they had hanged him," she said, glaring out at the still populous taproom, "I would have hanged myself beside him."

She vanished through the doorway to the kitchen. A moment later, into the tavern swaggered a new crowd led by Daniel Slocum. The evening was far from over, Jonathan Gifford told himself grimly.

Slocum was already drunk. With him were about a dozen men. Some were familiar to Jonathan Gifford, others were strangers whom he introduced as "honest sailors from Perthtown." They looked like highwaymen to Jonathan Gifford—dirty, rough, ugly, well past their youth.

"Say, Gifford, are you still giving rum away to honest Americans to celebrate the glorious news?" Slocum asked.

"That's right. Step up and drink your fill."

"Ah, Gifford, you know how to get your way, don't you? You know just how and when to trim your sails," Slocum said as he took tankards of rum and handed them back to his friends at their table near the bar.

"I'm not a sloop, Slocum, I'm a man," Jonathan Gifford said.

"You know what I mean," Slocum said. "We've had drink aplenty along the road. This ain't what we come for. We decided to crown the day's celebrations by tarring and feathering and maybe hanging a damn Tory—a traitor to his country."

"Go find one and good luck to you," Jonathan Gifford said.

"What do you mean find one? You've got one upstairs, Gifford, the best possible candidate. Bring him down."

"I can't do that. I have orders from Mr. Clark to keep him in close confinement."

"Damn you, Gifford, didn't you hear me? I'm a colonel of the militia. I want to interrogate this man, pry out of him his hellish plot to cut our throats and burn our houses over us. That's what he was planning to do. Do you deny that, Gifford?"

"I don't know what he was trying to do. I haven't seen the evidence. Neither have you."

"Listen, you goddamned Englishman," Slocum said. "You'd hate to have a riot in here, wouldn't you? Now these gentlemen, Mr. Chandler and his friends, these fine seafarers from Perthtown, they come from Boston originally. There ain't no one knows how to wreck a house—or a tavern—faster than Boston sailors. Right, lads?"

There was no need for Mr. Chandler and his friends to respond. They kept looking at Jonathan Gifford, their eyes as empty as their heads.

Jonathan Gifford reached under the bar and took a black whip from a lower shelf. He took two formidable clubs off the wall and handed one to Barney and the other one to Black Sam.

"Slocum," he said, "get out. Don't finish your drink."

Slocum contemptuously turned his back and picked up his drink. Jonathan Gifford's whip hissed through the thick air. Slocum howled with pain and shock as it curled around his wrist. The rum in the tankard flew into his face and the tankard sailed halfway across the taproom. Slocum ended up on his back in the sawdust. His sailor friends sprang to their feet. One of them seized a chair. But Jonathan Gifford had given considerable thought to the design of his taproom. His chairs were bolted to the floor.

Barney and Black Sam, both big men, advanced around the bar swinging their clubs. "Now, boys, go along, go along and there'll be no trouble," Barney said. "The Captain has two pistols behind the bar. The first man who raises his hand will get a bullet between the eyes. The Captain never misses. There are men in the ground, from Quebec to Havana, from Dublin to Vienna who didn't believe that until it was too late."

While Barney spoke, Jonathan Gifford calmly placed the two pistols on the bar. Daniel Slocum and his sailor friends headed sullenly for the door. "We'll see you soon, Gifford," Slocum said, rubbing his wrist.

"Barney," Jonathan Gifford said. "Tomorrow morning, I think you'd better send someone to Amboy—or go yourself—and tell Captain Fleming our prisoner isn't safe here any longer."

"Why not?"

Kate was standing behind him. She had slipped noiselessly through the door from the kitchen. Jonathan Gifford gave her a calm account of what had just happened. It still aroused violent emotion.

"They won't just tar and feather him, they'll kill him, you know that."

"They're not going to do either one, Kate, not as long as I have anything to say about it."

"They'll kill you, too. Oh, God—"

She vanished into the kitchen again.

"Maybe you'd better ride to Amboy tonight," Jonathan Gifford said to Barney.

Jonathan Gifford shut his doors at eleven o'clock, as usual, sent his overnight guests upstairs with oil lamps, and retreated to his family house by the brook. Walking through his rose garden, he was engulfed by a dozen, two dozen scents. The garden was in full bloom now. It made him wish that a woman waited for him in his bedroom. He had been living like a monk since Sarah's death—by way of expiation, perhaps. But today's news, the fact and the idea that these Americans had declared their independence of all the things that made life steady and regular and secure—King and church and carefully balanced government—this plunge into the unknown stirred him enormously. It awakened in him an awareness of how much of his life had been ruled by the dead hand of the past, submission to his father's dry authority, fear of his mother's violent Irish heart, obedience to the army's hardcased way of doing things, his anxious wish for the approval of men like Charles Skinner, men who stood for old habits, traditional deference, downright standards of conduct. Was it too late to change now? he wondered. Too late even to try to love another woman? Mournfully, not for the first time, he pondered his failure with Sarah, the apparently inexorable decay of love into hate, desire into revulsion. *I loved you, but not with my whole heart. Just as you loved me.*

Jonathan Gifford stood by his open bedroom window. A southwest breeze wafted the scents of the rose garden down to him. The stars glistened in the murmuring brook. For the first time he thought it might be possible to begin again, to love another woman. At least the wish was there. Perhaps it was born of this daring American decision. Or was it simply just the scent of roses and a natural hunger for some kind of love? He poured himself a long drink of Madeira, downed it in an even longer swallow, and put out his light. He was soon asleep to the languid lullaby of the brook. His dreams were a jumble. Daniel Slocum's swarthy face, his mouth hurling those vicious words. *Goddamned Englishman.* Sarah strolling among his roses in another July, then a voice calling his name: *Captain—Captain—*

He sprang from his bed and rushed to the front door. When he opened it, Barney McGovern crashed into the room like a falling tree. Jonathan Gifford lit a lamp. The hall clock stood at 4 A.M. Someone had hit Barney across the face with a club. His right eye was almost closed, his nose was broken, blood oozed from a massive bruise on his right cheek.

"What happened?"

"Skinner," Barney said. "He clubbed me as I led the horse to the barn."

"Just now?"

The clock bonged four. Barney shook his head. "I got back from Amboy about two."

Jonathan Gifford dragged Barney to his feet and half led, half carried him to a chair in the parlor. He got him a glass of brandy and then labored as fast as his bad knee would let him up the slope to the tavern. Up the stairs he struggled to the second floor. The boyish soldier on guard at the end of the narrow hall was asleep on his feet.

"Have you seen him, man, have you seen your prisoner?" the Captain said with a ferocity that welled out of his army past.

"No, sir," said the frightened youngster. "All's been quiet."

Down the hall they went to Anthony Skinner's door, Jonathan Gifford selecting the key, shoving it into the expensive lock—and

124

flinging open the door to an empty room. The nails had been pried out of the sash. A rope, tied to a foot of the bed, dangled out the open window.

"Where did he get it?" Jonathan Gifford asked. "Who came into this room?"

"No one but—your daughter, sir. Miss Kate. She brought his food. So help me, sir, no one else."

The boy wanted to know if he should awaken his fellow soldiers and pursue the fugitive. Jonathan Gifford told him to go to bed. "He took one of my horses. He's five miles away by now."

Back down the garden to his house Jonathan Gifford went, rage whirling in his mind. He mounted the stairs to Kate's bedroom and pounded on the door. "Kate," he said, "Kate, get up."

She opened the door so quickly, it was evident that she had not been asleep.

"Put on a night robe, I want to show you something."

She put on a rose and blue night robe and followed him downstairs. Kemble peered from his door as they passed it. "What happened?"

"Go back to sleep," Jonathan Gifford said.

In the parlor, he forced Kate to stare at Barney McGovern's battered face. "Look at it. Look at what you've done," he said.

With no children of his own, Barney had been almost a second father, certainly a long-suffering, endlessly generous uncle to Kate and Kemble. He had taught them how to ride, tramped through the autumn woods to gather chestnuts with them, tirelessly played games with them.

"Now, Captain," Barney said groggily, "how could Miss Kate—"

"I don't care! I'm sorry, but I don't care," Kate cried. "I brought Anthony the rope and the hammer for the nails. I'm glad I did it. I love him. More than I love Barney, or you, Father, more than I love anything. Let a swine like Daniel Slocum, let all those drunken heroes who call themselves patriots do what they want to me. They can tar and feather me, I don't care. Anthony is free."

"So that's how," said Barney sadly.

Jonathan Gifford seized Kate by the arms. "Keep quiet," he said. "We are not going to tell anybody what you did. You are not going to tell anybody what you did. Do you understand me?"

Almost a full minute passed before Kate numbly nodded her head.

"Go upstairs, get in your bed, and stay there all day tomorrow. You are ill. You know nothing about it. Understand?"

Kate nodded again. Jonathan Gifford turned to find Kemble on the stairs, outrage on his face. "Don't say a word," he said. "Just take your sister to her room. Then come back here immediately."

When Kemble returned, Jonathan Gifford sent him to the icehouse to make a pack for Barney's cheek. With this medication and six or eight ounces of brandy, Barney pronounced himself practically cured.

"I hope so," Jonathan Gifford said. "We're going to need your help tomorrow. And yours, Kemble. When people find out he's escaped, who are they going to suspect?"

"The Englishman, with all due respect, Captain," said Barney with a wincing grin, "Squire Skinner's best friend."

"They may burn the tavern to the ground. When did Fleming say he'd arrive?"

"As early as possible."

"Is he bringing men?"

"No more than an escort."

"That may be enough. We'll tell him the truth. There's no other way he'll trust us."

The uproar began at breakfast. The soldiers spread the word among the guests that Anthony Skinner had vanished. Jonathan Gifford ignored the hard looks that flew in his direction. Captain Fleming arrived with a dozen men and was predictably thunderstruck to discover he no longer had a prisoner to escort. For the benefit of the audience in the taproom, Jonathan Gifford solemnly assured the Captain that he had no idea how Skinner had escaped. When the listeners went back to their morning coffee, Jonathan Gifford invited Captain Fleming to join him in the rose garden. They strolled past the dazzling array of red, white, pink, and magenta blossoms, the summer air thick with scent. Captain Fleming fingered the huge double yellow Persian rose which Jonathan Gifford, fifty years ahead of other horticulturists, had crossed with other roses to give it the strength to survive in our climate.

"How is Miss Kate?" Captain Fleming said.

Stonily, Jonathan Gifford told him what Kate had done. "If you want to place her under arrest—that must be your decision."

Captain Fleming nodded unhappily. They walked another hundred yards in silence to the bank of the brook. "She must love him very much."

"Yes."

"My father once told me never to condemn a person who acted from a wayward heart. I caught a hint that he had loved someone —perhaps did some extravagant thing—foolish thing—"

"It happens," Jonathan Gifford said.

"I regard what you told me as a confidence. A word of it shall never pass my lips, I guarantee you. But how will it affect you, sir? Are you in danger because of it?"

"Perhaps," Jonathan Gifford said. He told him about the ugly scene with Daniel Slocum.

Captain Fleming nodded. "I will write a report to General Mercer and tell him I am staying the night here."

Later that day, the County Committee of Safety issued a proclamation denouncing Anthony Skinner as a traitor to his country and offering a reward of a hundred dollars to the man who captured him. It was a futile gesture. The fugitive was long since on Staten Island, well protected by the British army. The Committee heard testimony from the sentry, from Barney McGovern, from Jonathan Gifford. They also wanted to question Kate but accepted without comment her stepfather's excuse for her—she was "indisposed." The Committee concluded that "a person or persons unknown" had helped Skinner escape. From the looks on the faces of many listeners, not a few thought that unknown person was Jonathan Gifford. But the Committee declined to condemn him without evidence.

Lemuel Peters and Daniel Slocum did not hesitate to voice their suspicions of "the Englishman," however. This vindictive opinion circulated in mutters around the taproom, which was crowded with celebrating independence men. Though the atmosphere was ominous, the night passed without any serious incidents. The presence of Captain Fleming and his soldiers, carefully positioned around the taproom, their muskets stacked in handy corners, undoubtedly had something to do with this lull.

The next morning, July 6, Captain Fleming departed with his men. Jonathan Gifford invited him to breakfast at the family house. Fleming conducted himself like a diplomat, pretending to know nothing while Kate and Kemble exchanged acrid remarks. When the table was cleared, and Captain Gifford departed for an hour's work in his rose garden, the young Virginian asked Kate to join him for a stroll beside the brook. There he told her that he knew what she had done—and was trying to understand it. He knew it meant there was no possibility of her looking on him with the slightest favor.

"I can only wonder, Miss Kate—I suppose 'hope' is a better word—whether your motive was as much sympathy for his plight as it was affection for his person and opinions. I cannot believe anyone with a name as distinguished as Stapleton would declare herself against her country—which is what Mr. Skinner has done."

Kate was more shaken by this shrewd suggestion than she was willing to admit. She took refuge in her professed indifference to politics. "Even if I regretted Mr. Skinner's politics—which I do not, because I avoid an opinion on such matters—I assure you, Captain Fleming, that there was also the strongest possible affection animating my heart."

"I am sorry to hear that. I think you will genuinely regret his political opinions in the months ahead."

With a deep Virginia bow, he withdrew.

That afternoon, a dispatch rider from the Continental Congress stopped at the tavern to change horses and refresh himself. He had a printed copy of the Declaration of Independence which he was carrying to General Washington. Kemble asked the man if he would wait long enough to let him copy it. The fellow was easily persuaded by the extra pint of rum that Jonathan Gifford poured into his tankard. When the dispatch rider departed, Kemble read the Declaration aloud in the assembly room.

The audience listened with great solemnity. Even the more violent independence men recognized that it was a serious document. As an appeal to the popular mind, Jonathan Gifford thought it was masterful. Those opening phrases—declaring every man had a right to life, liberty, and the pursuit of happiness—were the work of a brilliant politician. But the rest of the document, especially the bill of indictment against the King, struck Captain Gifford as fanciful pleading.

The unknown author or authors rescued their argument with a stirring close: *For the support of this Declaration with a firm reliance on the protection of divine Providence, we mutually pledge to each other our lives, our fortunes, and our sacred honor.* But what mattered most to Jonathan Gifford was the pride, the fervor with which Kemble read the Declaration. His thin face was aglow with elation and in its reflection Jonathan Gifford glimpsed in a more direct way the truth he had urged on Charles Skinner. There was something good, yes, enormously good and vastly important in this idea of independence. It *was* time for Americans to shake off those feelings of inferiority, submission, subordination implicit in the very words "colonies," "mother country."

Perhaps in this new land for the first time men were discovering that they did not need to be children all their lives. They did not need a King, a father of the country, to keep them in proper order and obedience. Jonathan Gifford hoped it was true. But when he looked at the men crowding the assembly room, he had grave doubts. He saw greed, mediocrity, stupidity, violence on so many faces. To make this experiment work would require enormous effort, tremendous commitment on the part of gifted leaders. Above all, commitment from the people themselves. Somehow they would have to become the source of their own wisdom, find in themselves the balance and judgment they needed to live in peace and order. They would have to begin finding these difficult things while fighting a war.

Later in the day, the Committee of Safety met to issue summonses to the Tories on Anthony Skinner's muster list. They were soon discomfited to discover that nine out of ten defied the summons servers, the Committee of Safety, and the Declaration of Independence. Lemuel Peters was also unhappy when he discovered that Kemble had already read the Declaration of Independence aloud. This was, Peters pouted, an extralegal act that should have been reserved for the officials of the new nation, not some mere boy, even if his name was Stapleton. Kemble curtly replied that most of his audience had gone home and there would be no difficulty recruiting another group of enthusiastic listeners.

"I think it should be done properly, to impress these damn Tories," Peters said. "Let us turn out the regiment for a military exercise."

Kemble rode off to deliver the order to Colonel Slocum at Colt's Neck. Worse judgment could not be displayed, Jonathan Gifford thought. The less seen of rabble rousers like Daniel Slocum at a time like this, the better.

Three hours later, two hundred militiamen, half the regiment, mustered in the tavern yard. Once more Jonathan Gifford silently lamented their poor equipment and lack of training. Most had no bayonets for their guns. Twenty or thirty had no guns at all. They carried spears and in some cases sticks. The only exercise they could perform with reasonable dexterity was the manual of arms. An attempt at some basic parade maneuvers was a fiasco. Colonel Slocum ordered a march by the right flank. There were collisions, curses, and hoots of laughter from the audience on the tavern porch. This only confirmed what Colonel Slocum already suspected—Strangers' Resort was the local headquarters for Tories and trimmers. He excoriated everyone for laughing at men who were ready to die for their country.

Lemuel Peters mounted a platform of boxes which he had ordered Jonathan Gifford to erect on the porch. He read the Declaration in his broad Yankee twang and Colonel Slocum ordered his men to salute it with a volley. A hundred and fifty guns went off with a mighty crash. As the smoke cleared, one militiaman was seen on the ground writhing in pain. His shoulder had been dislocated by the kick of his musket. Most of our farmers had little experience handling guns. Powder and ball were expensive and hunting with a weapon as inaccurate as a musket was an exercise in frustration. According to militia law, every man was supposed to own a gun. But in most cases the old pieces had hung unused above our fireplaces for decades.

The injured man was carried home by his friends and everyone adjourned to the tavern, where Peters suggested that Jonathan Gifford should serve drinks without charge to celebrate independence. He must have known this gesture had been made two nights ago. There was little doubt of some malice in Peters' method. But Jonathan Gifford mildly agreed to the proposition and the tavern was soon deep in another night of heavy drinking. Independence in our part of New Jersey—and I suspect in most of America—was the occasion of some very bad heads for several mornings after the great news arrived.

In our case, another kind of excess soon combined with the liquor. Daniel Slocum stood in the doorway of the taproom, watching everyone drink, a contemptuous expression on his face. Jonathan Gifford offered him a tankard of stonewall. Slocum said he would be damned if he would take a drink from a Tory. He damned everyone in the taproom for being so gullible, such bad patriots, as to accept Jonathan Gifford's largesse. Lemuel

Peters, sensing a political rival, announced that while he did not share Slocum's opinion, he would stop drinking on the mere chance that it might be true. Slocum launched a political tirade against Peters. The countryside was aswarm with Tories. What had the Committee of Safety done about it? Sent respectful requests for them to appear before them. Requests which they had rejected with contempt. Had Peters or any of the people's guardians discovered how Anthony Skinner had escaped? Had they troubled to search the most likely hiding place, his father's manor house, or questioned the Squire, who was, in Slocum's opinion, the real leader of the plot, a man who would cut his best friend's throat if the price was right?

"If the honorable Committee were any sort of patriots," Slocum roared, "they'd be leading a march on Kemble Manor this very moment. We ought to ransack it from top to bottom, and if we don't find young Skinner, maybe we ought to tear the damn Tory palace to the ground like the patriots of Massachusetts did to the house of their archtraitor, Governor Hutchinson. It would tell every Tory in New Jersey what they can expect if they continue to defy the honorable Continental Congress."

Lemuel Peters glanced nervously at Ambrose Cotter. They had resisted Slocum's demagoguery once. But twice strained their integrity to the snapping point.

"I say Colonel Slocum is speaking sense, good downright American sense," Cotter cried.

"Let's take a vote," Slocum shouted. "All those in favor of forming a committee of inspection answer aye."

"AYE," came a roar that shook the tavern walls. Slocum had a built-in majority. A good half the men in the room were members of his regiment.

"The people have spoken," Lemuel Peters shrilled, and joined the stampede out the door. In a moment there were only about two dozen men left in the taproom. Among them was Nathaniel Fitzmorris. His late father had been a close friend of Charles Skinner. Another was young John Tharp, whose Quaker instincts naturally abhorred Slocum's violence. Several other men were members of Captain Fitzmorris' militia company.

Jonathan Gifford turned to Jasper Clark, who was clearly appalled by what he had just seen and heard.

"Mr. Clark," he said, "do you have the power to keep the peace in this county?"

"Why, I don't know," said Clark. "I don't believe that power was delegated to Committees of Safety. But the president of the Provincial Congress has issued a proclamation, calling on all the members of the old government to keep their offices until the elections in August. That means I'm still a justice of the peace. I can call out the militia in case of a riot. But how can I read the Riot Act, with all those references to the King's power and authority?"

"Maybe you won't have to read it. Everyone here is a member of the militia. Embody these men and give me command of them. I want to protect the life and property of an innocent man. Charles Skinner has had nothing to do with this business of raising a Tory regiment. His son played his own game—in spite of his father."

Jasper Clark thought this over, pulling hard on the lobe of his left ear. He sighed. "The Squire has loaned me money and ground my wheat on credit more than one year when times were hard. He carried my wife to that New York doctor in his carriage in '68, when she was sick half that winter with the pleurisy. Give me a musket, and I will go with you and do what I can. I hope every man in this room will follow us."

"You have me and my friends," said Fitzmorris. He stood up. Six of his men rose with him.

"I'll come," said John Tharp, his Quaker conscience speaking.

Kemble struggled for a moment with his own conscience. Anthony Skinner's numerous insults still rankled. "I'll come," he finally said.

"I will come, too," said Dr. Davie. "I have drunk at the Squire's table too often to let him be insulted by the likes of Slocum."

Jonathan Gifford turned to Barney McGovern. There was no need to argue with him. "Give them muskets and ammunition," he said, nodding toward the volunteers. "Sam, you and I will start saddling horses."

In five minutes they were on the road, riding two men to a horse. They galloped down the opposite side of Kemble Manor, which was shaped like a huge blunted triangle, and cut across an internal road through the fields and pastures to the back of the manor house. By now it was almost dark. There was no sign of Slocum and his mob. They were still a good mile down the road.

Jonathan Gifford posted his men in two ranks, six to a row, and told them to load their guns. "I don't think it will come to shooting," he said, "but if it does your lives will depend on following my orders. Fire only on command. The first rank will fire and fall back twenty paces and reload. Then the second rank will fire and fall back to the house. The first rank will give them one more volley and follow them."

The door opened and a woman's voice called anxiously, "What is it, Captain Gifford, what's happening?"

A manservant carrying an oil lamp appeared beside Caroline Skinner. She was wearing a blue silk dinner dress. Jonathan Gifford limped to the door and told her what was coming. "Is Mr. Skinner—"

"Drunk? Yes. But not too drunk to hear news like this."

Charles Skinner was in the same massive Jacobean chair in the library. He was wearing his usual elaborate at-home clothes, a purple skullcap lined with red silk, a red silk dressing gown. The decanter of brandy on the round table beside him was almost empty. Jonathan Gifford's news brought him to his feet roaring curses upon poltroons and knaves. He lunged around the room like a man in a fiery furnace.

"Mrs. Skinner, get me my pistols."

"I will not. You are too drunk. I'm afraid you'll shoot me—or yourself."

"Too drunk. Sh' right. Too drunk. Will you stand with me, Gifford?"

"I've brought twelve men with me. They're out there on the drive. Your visitors have at least a hundred. Not good odds, old friend."

"We stood—half the Indians—Canada—with—handful."

"We're not fighting in a forest. There's no place to hide. I'm afraid there is only one way to save your house and your life."

"Whaat?" said Skinner, collapsing into the Jacobean chair again.

"Take to your bed. That is where you belong anyway, if I may be honest with you."

Charles Skinner shook his big head drunkenly. "Crazy, Gifford, crazy. Throw myself—on mercy—those bastards. Crazy."

"No it isn't. Take to your bed and say nothing, except a groan or two. Those men outside—I wouldn't guarantee one of them—except my son and Black Sam and Barney—when it comes to defending you. But they'll defend a sick man and a helpless woman."

"I hate that," Caroline Skinner said. "I would almost rather take a gun and stand beside my husband."

"We may have to do a great many things we hate before this is over."

"What if they force their way into the house, Captain Gifford?"

"You will meet them politely in the hall. Explain your husband is too sick to be interviewed. Let them search the house. They won't touch so much as a teacup—if you keep your head."

Caroline Skinner turned to her husband. "He's right, Charles."

A distant sound penetrated the room. Jonathan Gifford limped to the window and thrust aside the damask curtains. Down on the road the head of Slocum's mob was visible. Some of them were carrying torches. They were roaring out the refrain of our favorite patriot song.

Huzza, huzza, huzza, huzza,
For free America.

Charles Skinner crumbled before Jonathan Gifford's eyes. His huge shoulders slumped, his big head drooped. Caroline called for Jesse, the small spare black butler. He and the Captain hoisted the Squire to his feet and dragged him upstairs to his oversized canopied bed. As they walked to the door, Skinner heaved himself up on one elbow. "Gifford," he said.

"Yes?" The room was too dark to see him.

"I depend on you—not to let them insult my wife. No matter what the cost, Gifford."

"I understand," Jonathan Gifford said.

Caroline Skinner was waiting for him at the bottom of the stairs. "What if your plan doesn't work, Captain Gifford? Are you prepared to fight?"

"I am," he said.

"Can we beat them?"

"I broke a mob this size in Ireland, with twenty men. They ran at the first volley. But these men outside aren't trained. And they have no great stake in the business."

"Tell them there's ten guineas in it for every one of them."

"That may help."

"And some liquor. Don't men need liquor before they fight?"

"It's been known to help."

She filled her husband's brandy decanter and handed it to him. "I'm sure they can't afford this at Strangers' Resort. Give every man a round."

Jonathan Gifford found himself admiring her cool courage. "We may make a soldier of you before this business is over. I must go join the reception committee."

As he opened the front door Caroline's calmness wavered. "Captain Gifford," she said, "please be careful."

He gave her a grim, reassuring nod. She was swept by an emotion she had never felt before. She could not put a name on it. No, she refused to name it, refused with an almost desperate effort of her will.

Outside Jonathan Gifford gave each of his men a swig of the brandy decanter and told them what Mrs. Skinner was prepared to pay them if they had to fight. "Load your guns," he said, as Slocum and his mob began pouring through Kemble Manor's gates.

Captain Gifford waited until they reached the oval at the end of the long drive. "Stand where you are, Slocum," he called. "If you come another foot I'll blow your head off."

"You damned English son of a bitch," Slocum roared. "What do you think you're doing?"

"I'm here to protect the house of an old friend, a man who saved my life in another war," Jonathan Gifford said. "He's upstairs in bed, sick with grief for what his son has done. There's no one else in the house but his wife and a few servants."

"We don't have to listen to your damn lies, Gifford."

"I can't believe there's a man among you who would burn a house down over the heads of a sick man and a defenseless woman. If there is, I think he deserves to be shot down. I have a party of brave men back there who agree with me. Their guns are loaded and they're ready to fire at my order."

"Who are they, let us see them," Slocum shouted.

Jasper Clark walked to Jonathan Gifford's side. He blinked into the flickering light of the torches in the front rank of the crowd. "These men are embodied as militia called out to suppress a riot under my authority as justice of the peace. They are all good true Americans and are determined to uphold the laws of their country as well as defend an innocent man and woman."

Clark walked several steps closer to the crowd and spotted Lemuel Peters and Ambrose Cotter beside Slocum. "I am ashamed to see members of the honorable Committee of Safety condoning much less participating in this lawlessness."

"We're not out to break any laws. All we want to do is search the house," Peters said.

"I'm sure Mrs. Skinner will have no objection to the Committee of Safety searching the house," Jonathan Gifford said.

"That's a fair offer," said Jasper Clark. "There's no other reason for a man to set foot on this property and we all know it."

The mood of the crowd was cooling, Jonathan Gifford could feel it. "The last thing I want is bloodshed," he said. "I want to stand with you and do everything in my power to make this a free country. Be sensible. Don't give the British a chance to prove what they're already saying—that Americans are ruled by mobs."

"Peters, Cotter, come on with me," said Jasper Clark.

Sullenly, the two members of the Committee of Safety edged around Slocum and moved toward the house. But Slocum declined to be eliminated. He joined the procession without an invitation. "If we find that traitor, we'll give him tar and feathers and maybe a rope no matter what any damned committeeman says," he shouted.

Jonathan Gifford escorted the inspectors inside the house. Even Daniel Slocum was subdued from the moment they stepped into the center hall. Rose wallpaper, decorated with golden coronets, surrounded them. A portrait of Peter Kemble, the first lord of the manor, stared imperiously at them. They saw themselves in their soiled everyday coats and leather breeches, framed by the delicate gold filigree of a huge mirror on the opposite wall. Caroline Skinner met them with icy politeness.

"Let me say first, gentlemen, that I am a firm supporter of our country's cause. I never dreamt that such support would expose me to a mob."

A mistake. Daniel Slocum fed on opposition. He became his truculent self again. "That is not a mob, madam. It is a gathering of honest citizens in search of a traitor. Who happens to be your son."

"He is not here. You may search the house, but I give you my word he is not here. Parents cannot control grown sons in these times, if they ever could. Look at Dr. Franklin and his son—"

"We had best search the house, madam," Jasper Clark said, honestly sympathizing with her agitation. "There is no other way to satisfy them."

"Where is your husband?" asked Daniel Slocum.

"Slocum," snapped Jonathan Gifford. "You do not address a lady in that tone."

"Oh, don't I, Captain Gifford? Excuse me. But this here is a lady under suspicion of concealing a traitor."

"My husband is upstairs. He is ill. You may speak to him, if you wish to invade his sickroom."

"I fear it may be necessary, madam," said Lemuel Peters.

Caroline summoned the butler, Jesse, who looked at the intruders with unmistakable disdain. "These gentlemen wish to search the house, Jesse. Will you please escort them and open any doors that are locked?"

The search party clumped up the stairs. Jonathan Gifford tried to encourage Caroline with a smile. "I think everything will be all right now," he said.

"Who is that thick, dark man?"

"Daniel Slocum. Our new colonel of the militia."

"I detested him on sight."

"I'm beginning to feel the same way."

Fifteen minutes later the searchers returned. Jasper Clark apologized for disturbing Caroline and her husband. He was sure everyone would now go home peacefully. Outside, Daniel Slocum abruptly turned right and strode over to Jonathan Gifford's little band of defenders. "I just want to see the faces of men who take Tory money to protect traitors," he said.

Several of the men protested nervously that they had taken no money. Slocum had already turned his back on them and was walking toward the crowd in the drive. "There's no sign of the traitor in the house, men," he said. "He may well have been there, until he was warned of our coming by his *friends*."

"Goddamn that fellow," Barney McGovern growled.

"There was no warning given or taken," Jonathan Gifford

called. But it was too late. Slocum had already made his impression.

"For those who want to quench their thirst after such a long march, the tavern will be open until midnight," Jonathan Gifford said.

"And I say that any man who drinks there is no friend of his country," Slocum shouted. "I'm going to drink at Leary's."

"Leary's for me," said Lemuel Peters.

Slocum's friends in the crowd took up the cry and the majority followed Black Daniel toward Leary's, a groggery a mile down the road to Amboy. The place was little more than a shed with a plank on two barrels for a bar. It served cheap, often dangerous liquor, most of which Leary brewed himself. Jonathan Gifford watched them go, then walked back to the door of the manor to say goodnight to Caroline.

"Will he ruin your business, Captain Gifford?" she asked.

He shook his head. "They'll wake up tomorrow feeling like they've been drinking salt water and eating horse manure," he said. "That's what Leary's liquor does to you."

"I would hate to think of you suffering on my—our account."

"I hope Mr. Skinner won't resent the hard choice we made."

"I hope not. He says he doesn't know where to turn now, with independence declared."

"I see no choice but fighting."

"He will never fight his son."

"Then he must try to stay neutral. That won't be easy."

Jonathan Gifford mournfully remembered the dour face and voice of William Alexander, Lord Stirling, as he stood in the doorway of the tavern the night they arrested Governor William Franklin. A *man must choose one side or the other in this thing.* He gave each member of his impromptu company another swig of brandy and told them to go home. He returned the empty decanter to Caroline and rode back to Strangers' Resort. There he was pleased to discover about half of the mob had chosen to walk an extra mile to enjoy good liquor, rather than be poisoned by Leary. Jasper Clark joined the drinkers. He hoisted his mug of hard cider and assured Jonathan Gifford that no one believed Slocum's accusation. This was an overstatement. If Gifford wanted to look on the dark side of the question, every second man had believed Slocum—or was intimidated by him. But he smiled and accepted

Clark's encouragement for what it was—the good intentions of an honest man.

"Kemble," Captain Gifford said. "Would you go out to the greenhouse and fetch a work of art I finished last night?"

Kemble looked puzzled.

"You'll recognize it the moment you see it," his father said. "It's about this big."

The Captain spread his arms wide.

In five minutes Kemble returned carrying the work of art. It was a sign. The border was deep blue. At the top was a rising sun dispensing bountiful red rays. Beneath it, beautifully lettered on a white background were bold blue words: LIBERTY TAVERN

"I thought it was time we changed the name of this place," Jonathan Gifford said. He smiled as he spoke but I caught an ambiguity, an edge of sadness in his voice.

Kemble was much too enthusiastic to notice such things. "I'll hang it up," he said.

Black Sam fetched a ladder from the barn. There was a ready surplus of hands to hold lamps and candles. Teetering at the top of the ladder, Kemble hoisted off the old sign and put the new one on the hooks. Jonathan Gifford stood to one side, watching, the same uncertain mixture of sadness and gladness on his face. Everyone roared out three cheers. He could only wonder if any of them—especially Kemble—understood how much the change meant to Jonathan Gifford, ex-captain of the 4th Regiment, the King's Own.

Book
II

CHAPTER ONE

So we plunged into the chaotic summer of 1776. It began with frantic preparations for battle. Most people believed that there would be one climactic clash and the fate of America would be decided. The British would either lick their wounds, count their dead, and creep aboard their ships to sail home—or America would be prostrate beneath the tyrant's heel. If I seem to be writing fustian, forgive me. That is the way all the politicians spoke that summer.

In Liberty Tavern's taproom the conversation was more down to earth. Samson Tucker stirred his drink with his finger and said, "What is the matter with those damned lobsterbacks? I thought by now I would have made a lane through a hundred or so of'm. Instead, they cower over there on Staten Island like a flock of sparrows within sight of a crow."

Samson was drinking on credit as usual. Next year, always next year, he was sure a fabulous harvest would get him out of debt. He had an incurable weakness for Stewed Quaker, a south Jersey specialty. It consisted of hard cider and cider oil, with a roasted red apple floating on top. It was really a winter drink but Samson consumed it year round. "That Englishman will own this farm before you are through," his wife often screamed. But Samson was safe, no matter how many Stewed Quakers he drank. Jonathan Gifford never foreclosed on a debt in his life. He had an innkeeper's rather than a banker's heart. He also enjoyed having Samson around because his opinions were almost invariably those of the majority at any given moment. Samson was a living political weather vane in his ability to absorb and reflect the prevailing mood.

Through broiling July and steaming August, the British army sat in their tents on Staten Island, with no apparent interest in fighting the battle that would decide America's fate. We attributed their lethargy to two things—their fear of our military prowess and the hope that they could scare us into negotiating peace with Admiral Lord Richard Howe. This gentleman, the brother of Jonathan Gifford's old commander, had arrived in New York about a week after the Declaration of Independence was issued. He had sent letters ashore at Perth Amboy urging Americans to open peace negotiations with him. The gesture was spurned by Congress but it had a debilitating effect on our militia.

"Damn me, if I see any point in chasing Tories in this weather," said Samson, "when like as not we'll patch up a peace with the cowardly bastards before harvest time."

"If you think that way, it only proves your head is stuffed with horse shit," said Daniel Slocum.

He had returned to drinking at Liberty Tavern within a week of his march on Kemble Manor. He had no choice. The effects of Leary's dreadful liquors were just what Jonathan Gifford had predicted, driving even the most dedicated Slocumites back to his tables.

"I agree with Colonel Slocum," said Kemble. "The Tories and the British are playing a deep game. They are using all this peace palavering to disarm us."

"Well, by God," said Samson, "if peace could rid us of those damn Philadelphians, I swear I'd vote for it."

The conversation summed up our multiple travails in the summer of 1776. To help defend New Jersey, Congress issued a call for thousands of short-term militia from Pennsylvania, Delaware, and Maryland. The Maryland and Delaware fellows never arrived. But the Pennsylvanians came by the battalion—and we were soon heartily sick of them. Most of them were from Philadelphia and the thought of sleeping in an open field—even though the weather was warm enough to be called tropical—appalled them. Night after night they crowded every room in Liberty Tavern and often filled the taproom and the assembly room and the halls with their snores.

Simultaneously, we struggled to cope with the Tories—the loyalists, as they called themselves. Everywhere they used the presence of Lord Howe and his offer to negotiate peace to explain their disinclination to join the militia or to swear allegiance to the Continental Congress. At least 50 per cent of the population in south Jersey were ardent loyalists or neutralists like my father. In some areas such as Shrewsbury, the Tories were a strong majority. At first everyone hoped the stirring rhetoric of the Declaration of Independence would sweep them into our camp. When this magical change failed to take place, no one knew exactly what to do with them—except Daniel Slocum.

His solution was brute force. He told our militiamen they could take anything they wanted from a loyalist farm. Leading loyalists were hunted down and ordered to swear oaths of allegiance or accept a coat of hot tar and feathers. The trouble was, it didn't work very well. Slocum made no attempt to discriminate between neutralists like my father, lukewarm loyalists like Charles Skinner, and aggressive loyalists like Anthony Skinner. Instead of adding to our friends, he multiplied our enemies.

This did not worry Slocum. He knew as well as anyone that the loyalists were no military threat without the support of the British army. Slocum's campaign against the Tories was really an excuse to use his militia to take political control of south Jersey in our first elections as an independent state. He nominated candidates for every office on the ballot from justice of the peace to sheriff to delegates to the legislature. Shrewdly he formed an alliance with Lemuel Peters and Ambrose Cotter of the Committee of Safety, which was slated to go out of business when the new government took over. He backed both for judges of the county court.

At first Slocum's candidates were unopposed. For the first time in decades, not a single Kemble, Stapleton, or Skinner or any of their followers was running for office. The triumvirate had collapsed. Kemble, the heir to the Stapleton name in south Jersey, was too young. The Skinners were totally discredited, most of them loyalists. Walter Kemble, Caroline's father, had died in 1773. My father, his younger brother, spent the summer on his farm, torturing his intellect and conscience, trying to decide whether he could support the Declaration of Independence.

Jonathan Gifford persuaded Jasper Clark to organize a slate of candidates to oppose Slocum. Most of them were moderate independence men, who had held minor offices under the old royal government with the support of the triumvirate. To Captain

Gifford's dismay, Kemble pointedly and publicly refused to support them. He let everyone who visited Liberty Tavern's taproom know that he backed Colonel Slocum's slate. To make his stand even clearer, he regularly rode out with Slocum and his militia on their "Tory hunts," as we called them.

Alas, neither Jasper Clark nor any of his candidates came close to matching Daniel Slocum as a politician. They were used to winning elections with the endorsement of the triumvirate, who passed the word of their approval at church on Sunday, at sociable dinners, and on visits to places like Liberty Tavern. This was all a man needed to win an election before the Revolution. No one made speeches or urged people to give him their votes.

Daniel Slocum displayed a new style, one that has become dominant in American politics. He and his friends roamed the county, haranguing the voters at every crossroads. They touted their candidates as true Whigs, statesmen beyond compare. On their election depended the salvation of New Jersey. To this hyperbole they added savage attacks on Jasper Clark and his fellow candidates. They called them Tory stalking-horses. The Englishman, Jonathan Gifford, was behind them and behind him stood the Squire and his son, funneling British gold into their pockets.

To make sure he did not lose the election, Slocum stationed armed militiamen at every polling place in the county. No one was allowed to vote without taking an oath of allegiance to the Continental Congress and an oath disavowing loyalty to George III. These oaths automatically disenfranchised many Quakers in south Jersey who would have voted against Slocum for his violent ways. It was against their religion to swear oaths. Many other would-be voters were frightened away from the polls by outright threats of force, even when they were willing to take the oaths. My father asked to see Colonel Slocum's authorization for requiring the oaths. Slocum pointed to a dozen musket-wielding militiamen. "We will be glad to send you pieces of it," he roared, "as wadding for these here guns. We'll blow it right through your goddamn carcass and you can read it at your leisure in hell, you Tory son of a bitch. We know who you are going to vote for and we won't forget it."

My father retreated to his horse and went home without voting. When Jonathan Gifford asked Kemble what he thought of these tactics, he got an answer that revolutionaries have used to justify breaches of ethics and humanity since time began: "They're necessary," he said.

Slocum's candidates won an overwhelming victory. That night in the residence, Kemble scoffed at Jonathan Gifford's warning that he would regret his support of Slocum. "He's a fighter. He has energy. That's what we need."

"What really disgusted me is the way he used your name, calling you young Squire Stapleton and puffing you as his strongest backer."

"I told him to do it. What do you care? It's not your name."

Kemble had no idea how deeply those words wounded Jonathan Gifford. The Revolution seemed to be carrying his son further and further away from him. The next day a letter arrived from General Putnam, adding physical distance to his sense of separation. In a scrawl replete with some of his finest misspellings, Old Put declared that he would be delighted to have Jonathan Gifford's stepson on his staff. Before the day ended, Kemble rode off to the Amboy ferry with a single change of clothes in his knapsack. They would ship a trunk to him when he was settled in New York.

Two days later, a message from the King's side of the quarrel threatened a similar separation from Kate. Jonathan Gifford was transplanting another American Tudor rose from his greenhouse to the garden when post rider Abel Aikin interrupted him. "Captain," said Abel, "I was told to give this letter direct to Miss Kate without fail, or risk having my brains blown out."

Jonathan Gifford took the letter from Abel's outstretched hand. "Who gave it to you?"

"A man in a green coat, who hailed me from the wood just beyond Wemrock Brook."

"Tell Barney to stand you a pint of Barbados rum."

Jonathan Gifford limped down the hill to the brook and along its bank to the red brick residence. Kate was sitting on the side porch overlooking the brook, reading *The Sorrows of Young Werther*. Tears were streaming down her face.

"Kate," Jonathan Gifford said. "Is there anything wrong?"

She looked up, wiping her eyes. "Oh no, Father. It's such a good novel. Every time I read it, I cry as much as I did when I read *Tristram Shandy*."

Jonathan Gifford sighed. He constantly forgot it was the fashion among Kate's generation to weep over a novel. The more tears, the higher the book was rated.

Kate was wearing an old blue chintz dress. Her feet were bare. Her red hair was streaming down her back, not even tied by a bow. If it was not for the ripe rise of her breasts, the Captain could have imagined himself back in time five years. Kate was innocent thirteen again, she would spring up to give him a daughter's hug, and Sarah, in one of her better moods, would dash out on the porch to add a wife's kiss.

He gave her the letter and told her how Abel had gotten it. "He should have given it to me," Kate said. "I am not a child." "He's an old friend. He still thinks of you that way."

Kate was not listening. She was reading the letter in one swift glance. She looked up and saw sorrow, concern on her father's face. He knew it was from Anthony Skinner. She had seen the same expression on his face when he stood in the doorway of the tavern watching Kemble ride off to join General Putnam in New York. Now she was deserting him, too, Kate thought. Perhaps in a more irrevocable way. Should she show him the letter, ask his advice? She knew in advance what he would say. The same thing he had been telling her to do for a year: wait. But the time for waiting was over. That time ended when she walked into Anthony Skinner's room to help him escape. For Kate that had not been a political act. It had been a blazing personal commitment.

"I must—I must think about this," she said, and retreated to her bedroom to read the letter a second time.

My dearest one:—

I am returned and cannot wait to see you, even if it is only for an hour. Between ten and eleven tomorrow morning, be at the crossroads outside Shrewsbury Town. A friend will meet you there and guide you to our rendezvous. Wear old clothes. We live in the swamps like hunted animals. But our day will come, and until it does danger will add spice to our kisses.

Devotedly,
Anthony

Immediately after breakfast the next morning, Kate called for her horse. She wore her forest green riding habit, with its mannish double-breasted jacket and small black silk tricorn hat. As she mounted in the tavern yard Jonathan Gifford came out on the porch.

"There is no way I can stop you from going?"

"What do you mean, Father? Am I a prisoner? If I am, I surely have the right to sign a parole and go for a day's ride."

"I know where you're going, Kate."

"I don't know what you're talking about, Father."

She gave her horse a lash with her riding crop and left the yard at a full gallop. Jonathan Gifford watched her go thinking: *wildness.*

What should he do about it? Kate's intransigence left him helpless in the grip of conflicting emotions—the angry impulse to treat her like a child—and the need—almost a compulsion to seek her love. Jonathan Gifford was not wholly aware of these impulses. He was not by nature an introspective man. But he did recognize his male helplessness and decided to seek advice from a woman. He too called for his horse and rode south to Kemble Manor.

There he found neither solace nor advice—but chaos. His face magenta, Charles Skinner stamped up and down in the hot still air of his library, already half drunk on his day's decanter of brandy, and half mad with fury. The object of his wrath was Daniel Slocum.

"Look at this," the Squire roared, thrusting a letter at Jonathan Gifford. "I just got it from that damned rogue."

> Sir:—Several complaints have been made to us respecting your conduct, especially that of giving information to a party of Tories and British commanded by your son, Anthony Skinner, now a refugee, by which means your son and his party escaped the pursuit of a body of militia sent to attack them. I do therefore enjoin it upon you that you do for the future confine yourself to your farm at Middletown and do not reattempt traveling the road, under the risk of being treated as a spy.

"He is trying to drive me out, that is what the bastard is doing," Charles Skinner said. "He sent one of his damn family by here only a day or two ago and boldly asked me what price I would take for my land."

At first Jonathan Gifford could not believe it. "Daniel Slocum

149

—wants to buy the manor? Where would he get the money?"

"Aye, where indeed," said Charles Skinner. "But what am I to do, Gifford? If I obey his order, how can I run my grist mill three miles down the road or superintend the Colt's Neck farm?"

"You will have to let the servants run them for the time being."

"I can't do it," cried Skinner, collapsing into a chair. "There is the devil to pay with them, too. They keep asking me why that damnable Declaration of Independence did not free them. I swear to God I am afraid Mrs. Skinner and I may be murdered in our beds."

"I always detested the idea of running this place with slaves," Caroline Skinner said. "I would have much preferred hired labor."

She stood in the doorway of the library, looking grave.

"But you would also prefer that London dress you have on your back, madam," said Charles Skinner. "You would be wearing old clothes, madam, if you tried to run a farm these days paying wages."

"Let us not have that argument again," Caroline Skinner said. "I've told you a dozen times, I would rather wear old clothes. But more to the point, Mr. Skinner, it seems to me the best solution is for me to run the grist mill and the Colt's Neck farm."

"Now you are being totally ridiculous, madam. A woman knows nothing about such matters."

"She can learn. What do you think, Captain Gifford?"

There was a challenge in her words. He had to respond to it even though he knew his friend, her husband, would not agree with him. "I think—it is a very sensible idea—and a generous one. I only hope your health won't suffer from the heat of the season."

"I've never been sick a day in my life, Captain. While Mr. Skinner—you remember the gout kept him in bed most of last summer."

"Madam, it is out of the question," growled Skinner. "No doubt it is generous of you. But I fear the damage done by your incompetence would hardly be worth the gesture."

Caroline Skinner flushed at this insult. She lowered her head and twisted the gold wedding band on her finger. "As you say," she murmured. "But you will have to do something about the servants or you will have none. Jesse tells me Cato has run off."

"What? Goddamn that fellow, why does he tell you instead of me?"

"Because he thought you were drunk."

"Why did you not tell me immediately?"

"I came here to tell you."

"My best field hand. You tell Jesse I'll get a white man to run things around here, a white man with a whip, and Jesse shall be out there planting with the rest of them."

"Then he will run away."

"God Almighty, Gifford, what shall I do?"

"I say you should free them at one stroke and hire them back on wages," Caroline Skinner said. "It would force every Whig in New Jersey to examine his conscience and do the same thing."

"I'm afraid I disagree with you, Mrs. Skinner. It might have a very opposite effect," Jonathan Gifford said. "The British have tried to start a slave insurrection in Virginia. It's on everyone's mind. People might see the same policy at work here. It could bring another mob to your front door—and this time they would not listen to reason."

"You really think—that might happen, Captain Gifford?"

"Men's minds are terribly inflamed," he said. "They have guns in their hands, Mrs. Skinner." He turned to the Squire. "If I were you, Charles, I would begin to pay them. Not full wages if you can't afford it, but say half. If they save their money, they can buy their freedom at the end of a year or two. That's what I did with Black Sam, years ago. It worked well for me. I don't think there's a more dependable man in the state, black or white."

"But paying them—it will give them notions. In a month or two they will be demanding double and double again a month after that."

"I would give Jesse double to start," Caroline Skinner said.

"I do not need advice from you, madam."

Caroline Skinner's mouth hardened. Anger glowed in her green Kemble eyes, but she did not express it. She closed the library door softly behind her. Jonathan Gifford found himself admiring her self-control. A remarkable trait in a woman. Perhaps he could persuade her to communicate her secret to Kate. He spent another ten minutes with Charles Skinner, discussing how to deal with Daniel Slocum. He advised him to write a letter to Governor William Livingston demanding that Slocum charge him with a specific crime or leave him alone. As for the grist mill and the

Colt's Neck farm, he would stop by every second day or so and check on them.

He felt a sense of release, like a man escaping from a prison cell, when he left Charles Skinner. It troubled him. The man was still his friend, no matter how trapped he was by his emotions and opinions. In the hall he asked one of the servants to find her mistress. He was told she was walking in the garden.

He found Caroline Skinner beyond the garden in the park, feeding the deer. She was talking softly to them. He did not get close enough to hear what she was saying. They scampered away at his approach.

"These days I find the company of those dumb creatures more soothing than my own—flesh and blood," she said.

"I don't blame you," he said impulsively, not realizing its implication until the words were spoken. "I—I really came here to—to see you," he stammered. "I have a problem that's"—he smiled ruefully—"beyond the competence of us all-knowing males."

"What a confession, Captain Gifford. Around here I get the feeling that such a dilemma could not exist."

"It's rather serious. It's—it's about Kate."

He told her what he thought—in fact was sure—was happening between Kate and Anthony Skinner. Caroline listened with the gravest concern. "Her mother's child," she said.

She felt two red spots burning in her cheeks. The words came so naturally to her, only after they were spoken did she recall the violent emotions that assailed her the last time she had discussed her sister, his late wife, with Jonathan Gifford.

He seemed equally disturbed. "I'm—I'm afraid you're right."

With unexpected intensity Jonathan Gifford found himself wanting to know more about the past Caroline shared with Sarah beyond the tantalizing glimpse she had given him in their last conversation. But Caroline concentrated on Kate.

"I'm not sure what good I can do," she said. "I fear her mother turned her mind against me a long time ago. I thought—I thought she had done the same thing with you."

"I never heard Sarah say that much against you," Jonathan Gifford said. "She used to call you Miss Solemn Sides. Once she said you should have been a parson. I thought it was a compliment to your good education."

Three does and a fawn moved timidly among the trees. They

were a perfect image of her feelings. With an effort of the will, Caroline looked him in the face. "You don't really mean that, Captain Gifford. You know perfectly well what she meant. I was a dull weed. Something to be thrown aside, dismissed."

He looked past her at the deer. "I learned—rather early—that I could not share all your sister's opinions."

Caroline smiled mournfully. "Yes. I remember Sarah remarking that you didn't listen to her any more than her first husband."

"She did—run on."

"Yes—that's what charmed you all—"

She realized it was impossible to be lighthearted about Sarah. She had hurt them both too much. "My father—was a rather outrageous man. No doubt you heard Sarah talk about him. He wanted a son. He never forgave his daughters for being women. Sarah revenged herself by being outrageously feminine. I—I suppose I tried to be a man. Or at least to show him I had the mind of a man. I see now we were both trying to persuade him to love us."

He nodded. "I—sensed something of the sort. When Sarah was in a temper she would tell me I was just like her father."

"She was a damn liar!"

They stood there in the sun-dappled park, both embarrassed by the turn of the conversation.

"I—I will send Kate to you."

"I will do what little I can."

153

CHAPTER TWO

IT WAS ALREADY too late to give Kate good advice. An hour before her stepfather discussed her with her aunt, she had left her horse in a loyalist's stable and was soon seated in the rear of a riverboat poled by an old weathered fisherman into the marshes along the banks of the lower Shrewsbury. She fingered a metal talisman she wore on a gold chain around her neck. Her mother had given it to her on her sixteenth birthday. Sarah Gifford had been a devout believer in unseen powers. The talisman, two triangles, joined at their apexes, had supposedly been drawn by King Solomon himself. It was called the Third Pentacle of Venus and according to the ancient book in Dr. Davie's library, "This, if it be only shown unto any person, serveth to attract love. Its angel Monachiel should be invoked in the day and hour of Venus, at one o'clock or at eight."

A blue jay's call and what looked like an impenetrable mass of mud and weeds swung open. Behind it stood a husky green-coated sentry with a gun in one hand, a rope attached to the water gate in his other hand. He smiled broadly at Kate and said, "The Colonel can't wait to see you, miss." Another five minutes along a narrow watercourse and the boat grounded on an island in the center of the swamp. Anthony Skinner emerged from a tent and strode toward her. He was wearing buff breeches and a green coat liberally dashed with gold lace. He swept Kate into his arms and gave her a passionate kiss.

"My dearest," he said. "I have lived for this moment."

He stepped back and held her at arm's length. "I didn't think it was possible, but you are more beautiful than ever. It is a tribute to the power of love."

After a twenty-mile ride on a dusty summer road, Kate knew she was not looking her best. But she told herself love permitted this exaggeration.

"I do nothing but think about you, dream about you," Anthony said. "I have your miniature about my neck."

He drew from beneath his shirt an ivory locket containing a tiny portrait of Kate, done by a traveling artist whom Jonathan Gifford had hired a year ago.

Kate found herself almost overwhelmed by Anthony's extravagance. "Is this your uniform?" she asked, touching the green cloth.

He nodded. "If I'm caught without it I can be shot as a spy."

He took her on a tour of the island, which was only two or three hundred yards wide. Three narrow channels ran out to the river and the sea. "We are as safe here as we would be on Staten Island," he said. "But it is not as healthy. Already we have three men sick, out of the thirty I brought with me."

Kate could see—and smell—what he meant. The ground was so spongy, water sprang up with every step they took. The air was thick with the stench of the swamp's decay and the human waste of his men. Anthony led her back to his tent and plunged into a bitter denunciation of British generals. "They won't listen to Americans, they have their own plans and the Americans can go to hell and be done with it, that's what it amounts to." He was even more vehement in his denunciation of Oliver De Lancey, the wealthy New York merchant. "He is the only loyalist the generals consult. His friends are made colonels and majors and our people are left biting their thumbs."

"Goddamn it!" He slapped a mosquito that had penetrated his breeches to his thigh.

"If things are as bad as you say, are you thinking of coming back to—" Kate caught herself before she said "us." She was momentarily stunned by the implication.

"And become one of Colonel Slocum's lackeys? No thank you. We'll win, Kate, in spite of the stupidity of the generals."

"Damn." He swung at another mosquito, this time on his calf. "But for the time being, New Jersey will have to take care of itself. The generals say they need every man to beat Mr. Washington out of New York. With two regiments I could hold this colony from here to Cape May for the King. But you can't expect people to risk anything for you when you offer them no protection from people like Colonel Slocum. That man is doing us more harm than anyone else in New Jersey."

"Jesus!" He slapped another mosquito from his neck. Kate brushed a buzzing brother from her cheek. It was not what she had imagined, this rendezvous. She had seen them in some snug, dry cottage in the pines, the air rich with tangy green scent, a blaze roaring in the fireplace. They talked about their love, the consolation and strength they drew from it. Instead, she was listening to a political speech, while mosquitoes buzzed and mud oozed around her boots and ripe odors crowded her nostrils.

Anthony introduced her to his officers. There were five of them, two captains and three lieutenants. She knew one of the captains, George Kennedy. He was a short, personable redhead from Shrewsbury, an excellent dancer. They joked about the last time they met, at a ball in Liberty Tavern's assembly room. Almost all the enlisted men were from Shrewsbury and Middletown. Some of their faces looked familiar. She had probably seen them in the tavern. They squatted around a fire, cooking their dinner, while Kate chatted with the officers. She noticed how often the men looked over their shoulders at her and exchanged whispered remarks. For a moment she felt enraged, but this passed quickly to an intense sadness.

Ever since her mother's scandal, Kate knew that nasty remarks about her virtue were common in the neighborhood. Was she confirming all the rotten things the hypocrites said about her? Let them think what they please, she told herself darkly. Perhaps she would share her mother's fate. Perhaps she would gasp out her life here in this swamp, as her mother had died in Antigua. For a few minutes she found a gloomy pleasure in the possibility, while Anthony returned to politics.

"There's scarcely a man in Shrewsbury who isn't for the King," Skinner said. "But everywhere to the north we are being destroyed. Slocum's men hunt us down day after day, take away our guns, make us post bonds that will cost a man his farm if he forfeits it."

"Will we stay here tonight?"

The officers stared at their feet, at the sky. Until Kate spoke, Anthony Skinner had no way of knowing her intentions. They might have parted with a kiss, like thousands of other lovers whose lives were interrupted by the Revolution. But Kate, tormented by the gap between reality and expectation, refused to accept the loss. She would make up the difference, repair the deficiency, out of her own self.

"Excuse me, gentlemen," Anthony Skinner said, and retreated to his tent with Kate. "My dearest," he said, kissing her hands. "I was hoping you would give me a sign. I can offer you nothing, Kate. Only the hope of victory. A future as uncertain as a bullet's flight."

"I'm not in love with victory, with the future, Anthony. I love you."

Did he understand? She let him untie the knot at the top of her bodice and fondle her breasts. They exchanged the deepest of kisses while Kate dreamt a separate dream. The future did not matter. What mattered was this moment. She was giving her love to him in its ultimate purity without hope or wish for any kind of gain, not even marriage, that sham reward that most women demanded to their sorrow.

"We can't stay here, not now. I would not let you spend a single night in this pesthole," Anthony said. "We'll stay at the tavern in Shrewsbury. The men will patrol the roads. We'll have a decent supper. A wedding supper."

Anthony Skinner ordered George Kennedy and the other captain, Enos Ruecastle, a lanky man who had a cast in his eye, to muster ten men and join them. They boarded boats and punted up the river with a strong tide to the Shrewsbury Town landing. There, to Kate's amazement, a British sloop of war was tied up, the royal ensign rustling in the evening breeze while sailors loaded her with fresh fruit, beef, pork, barrels of cider, copper cans full of fresh milk. Anthony Skinner strode up to a young officer who was supervising the work. "Damn it, Lieutenant, I told you not to do this business at the public dock. You are going to bring a regiment of rebels down here to terrorize the town. There's a half-dozen coves between here and the sea you could use just as well."

"Too bloody much work for my men, lugging all this stuff across broken ground and into small boats."

"What's more important, the safety of the town—"

"Look, Skinner—that's your name, isn't it?—you have no authority over me. My orders are to get as much fresh provisions as I can carry, and pay hard money for them. That's what I'm doing and I haven't heard a word of complaint from any man with cash in his hand. Is that what you're looking for?"

"You English son of a bitch—say another word and I'll pitch you into the goddamn river."

Anthony Skinner was close to six feet tall. The Lieutenant was not more than five feet three. But the little Englishman sneered at the threat.

"That's just like you damned Americans, full of fine talk about loyalty to the King one second and ready to murder one of His Majesty's officers the next. I dare you to touch me, sir. I will have that gold braid stripped off your coat before sundown tomorrow."

Anthony Skinner and his friends growled, cursed, and walked away. Kate could not believe it. They were afraid of the Englishman. "Load up and be damned," Anthony shouted as he left the dock.

"You can tell your friends I'll be damned if I'll pay this kind of money again. We shall have fair prices once we get our hands on New York and Long Island. Then you Jerseymen can suck eggs."

The Shrewsbury tavern was a dingy little place about one fourth the size of Liberty Tavern. Anthony Skinner told the disheveled, balding landlord to lock the front door. They wanted privacy. He dropped a half-dozen guineas in his hand to pay for any business lost. But the atmosphere in the taproom was not very festive. The English Lieutenant had cast a pall over Kate's wedding supper. Captains Kennedy and Ruecastle got drunk and alternately damned the British and the rebels. Anthony tried to rally them by talking about the power and strength of the British army.

They discussed the chances of raising a regiment around Shrewsbury. George Kennedy was pessimistic. There were too many Quakers preaching sermons against fighting for either side. Anthony insisted they could do it by paying hard money and giving away good British muskets. In two weeks they would have enough volunteers enlisted to defy the rebel militia. He saw Shrewsbury becoming an island of resistance to which New Jersey loyalists could retreat.

Kate listened patiently for an hour. Captains Kennedy and Ruecastle kept getting drunker, and Anthony kept making speeches to them. Finally she stood up. "I think I will go to my room. Perhaps we can have supper there."

"Yes. Good idea. I'm sorry, Kate," Anthony said. "I know how little use you have for all this politics."

Captain Ruecastle heaved himself to his feet and offered a toast. "To the fairest flower of New Jersey. May all our sweethearts be as loyal and true." His wayward eye gave him a shifty look that seemed to cast doubt on the sincerity of his words.

"I'll join you in twenty minutes, Kate," Anthony said as he escorted her to the door. "I must get things settled for the night."

He kissed her hurriedly on the neck and called for the innkeeper's wife. She was a sloppy, toothless woman who wheezed anxiously about the danger of Skinner staying overnight at the inn. She brought some cold mutton and cider with her as she escorted Kate to the room—the last at the end of the second-floor hall. Kate tried to remember the fierce joy, the icy anger she had felt when she walked down the hall in her father's tavern with the implements of Anthony's escape. The rope had been wound around her waist like the cincture of a nun. The hammer had been beneath the copper cover of the main dish on the tray, another symbol, this of her hard cold resolution. Now everything was darker, more confused. This murky hall lacked the brightly burning brass oil lamps of Jonathan Gifford's well-appointed inn. Both her heart and her mind lacked the passionate clarity, the ecstatic simplicity she had imagined for this moment.

In the room she drank some of the cider, nibbled at the mutton, which was moldy, stripped off her clothes, and slipped naked beneath the sheets. It was not the wedding or the wedding night she had imagined, either. A year ago she had seen herself marrying Anthony in her father's garden on a Sunday in July, the white and red and pink and yellow roses nodding their benedictions. Then music and feasting in the tavern's assembly room, farewell dances with a dozen and a half old beaux, ending with her father's favorite farewell toast: *Here's to all them that we love.*

Downstairs, Anthony Skinner and his captains began roaring out a parody of a liberty song.

> *"Come shake your dull noodles, ye pumpkins,*
> *and bawl,*
> *And own that you're mad at fair liberty's*
> *call;*
> *No scandalous conduct can add to your shame,*
> *Condemned to dishonor, inherit the fame."*

Was it eight o'clock? Kate touched the talisman and prayed to the angel Monachiel, ruling spirit of love. Did she really believe in him? He had proved a poor protector of her mother. The darkness filled the room like water. It seemed to flow into her mind, even her body, filling her with doubt, dread. She thought about the strange and violent things her mother had said to her. *A woman isn't born, she is whelped. That is the only conclusion you can draw from the way men treat us.* And her favorite advice. *Be sure your husband loves you with his whole heart.* Her mother was always talking about love. But not once did Kate ever feel the presence, the reality, of Sarah's love. Even as a child, Kate's hugs and kisses were dismissed, repelled. It was Kemble who always got the attention, always won the praise for his intellect, his recitations, his horsemanship. Meanwhile, Sarah Gifford inflicted on her daughter all the tortures suffered by young girls in the name of fashion. From her sixth to her thirteenth year, Kate wore an iron collar around her neck connected to a backboard strapped to her shoulders. Every night she did her lessons standing in stocks with the same collar around her neck. The goal was a perfect posture, absolutely necessary, her mother used to say, to get a man.

Looking back Kate wondered if her mother had hoped to make her cold and hard so she could deal with men as they dealt with each other. If so, the plan was a failure from the start because Kate already loved a man who seemed to contradict all the things her mother said: her stepfather. At least, she had loved him until that moment by the Shrewsbury, when she saw how hard and cold and savage he could be. He was the creator of the silence that had enveloped their house, the icy silence that had driven her mother to Antigua. But how had it happened in the first place? What was the flaw, the failure that had destroyed their love? Was she acting out another chapter in the story, as her mother had acted out her parents' failure? What blind fate had led her back to Shrewsbury? Was that her own voice that spoke this afternoon? Or her mother's tormented spirit?

Downstairs the singing died away. Footsteps came down the hall. Anthony stood in the doorway, a candle in his hand.

"Kate," he whispered. "Have you gone to sleep without me?"

"Of course not."

"I'm sorry. I wouldn't blame you. But those fine fellows have to be caressed, fed, and watered, like the cattle they are. They're discouraged and ready to quit the business, the moment anything goes wrong. For the first time I see how much a general or a politician must lie. If he is honest about his feelings, he undoes his followers."

"Anthony. How many times do I have to tell you I love *you*—not your damn politics."

"This isn't politics, Kate. It's life and death. War. There's nothing more important—to both of us."

"I don't *care*. I love you in spite of life and death and war. I want you to love me the same way."

Anthony put the candle down beside the bed and raised the covers. For a long moment he gazed at her nakedness. "I'll try, Kate," he said. "I'll try."

They were happy that first night. They lived on the capital of Kate's wish, although Anthony Skinner must have known that it was impossible. Perhaps not. Perhaps Anthony had not become the hypocrite into which he was maturing. He was almost as young as Kate and he shared the opinion of most loyalists in the summer of 1776 that the British army was unbeatable. At the very least he may have tried to create for a few hours an ideal island, free of mosquitoes and stench and halfhearted followers, where he and Kate could live and love.

The power of her wish freed Kate from the fear and shyness that so often make a wedding night something less than glorious. She was as passionate as any French or Spanish mistress in fiction. In the dawn Anthony Skinner knew that he had been given something rare and precious. He tried in return to make Kate part of the dominant emotion in his life—his ambition.

"Before the end of the year, Kate, we'll sit down to dinner in a mansion twice the size of Kemble Manor. Perhaps Lord Stirling's palace at Basking Ridge. The rebels have forfeited their estates, if not their heads. I'll be first in line, Kate. No man will have done more to hold this colony for the King."

He kissed her neck and throat one more time and got up to dress. "You'll wear jewels and gowns to match any lady in London, Kate."

For a moment she tried to believe it. She loved London clothes as much as any American girl—perhaps more because she wore them so well. But this talk of ruling New Jersey collided too directly with the other man whose presence still loomed large in her life.

"My father says you're playing a loser's game. You can't possibly win."

"Damn your father. It's he that's playing the loser's game. And goddamn him for persuading my old man to play it with him. They're finished, Kate, all the old ones are finished. They don't know it because they haven't seen what I've seen on Staten Island. It's the finest army ever sent from England, Kate. They'll smash Washington's vermin to pieces."

He was using almost the same phrases that he had recited to the morose captains last night. Kate was too intelligent not to notice it. He saw the dismay on her face and thought she was disturbed by his return to politics.

"I'm sorry, Kate. I know it's all a bore to you."

Someone came running down the hall. "Colonel," said a stranger's voice, "we just got word. Slocum's on the march with two hundred men."

"Goddamn that fellow," Anthony said. "Where is he?"

"Well past Red Bank. No more than a half hour away."

Anthony turned to Kate, anguish on his face. "We must run for the swamp again. We can't make a stand with our handful. You'd best get on the road yourself."

"Why should I be afraid of him?"

"He's a vicious man, Kate."

He pulled on his boots and shrugged into his green coat. He took a crumpled letter from an inner pocket, and handed it to Kate. "Give this to my father on your way home."

He gave her a farewell kiss and was gone. Kate lay there, trying to recapture the man who had loved her during the night, trying to understand why he had reverted in the dawn to the man she had met yesterday in the swamp, the harassed angry soldier-politician. She saw—or at least half-saw—his attempt to unite his wish and her wish. But the naked confession of his ambition also repelled her. All his talk about duty and loyalty to the best of kings did not harmonize with this desire to make a fortune from the rebels' confiscated estates.

She was gripped by the appalling suspicion that she had given her love to a man who neither understood it nor cared about it. For a moment she was shaken by a helpless, pointless anger; it ebbed into a deep dull sadness. It was her fate, she told herself, a woman's fate. Beneath her outbursts of temper, her impudence, her seeming independence, Kate had a low opinion of her worth as a person. Like many beautiful women she did not think of her beauty as a reason for pride. Her looks were accidental; if anything, they complicated her life, making her attractive to men for reasons she deemed superficial. Praise of her snowy breasts, her glowing hair, had nothing to do with the Kate she knew, a rather indolent girl who had grown up perpetually compared to her brilliant brother. Her mother's disgrace had inflicted another wound.

The landlady pounded on the door. "What in God's name are you doing, miss? You'd best get on the road before the devil Slocum arrives."

"All right. All right," Kate said. She dressed and within ten minutes was mounting her horse in the tavern yard.

"He's coming direct down the main road," the landlady said. "I would go roundabout if I were you, miss."

Kate gave her a contemptuous look. "He won't dare touch me."

Fifteen minutes down the main road she encountered Colonel Slocum and his two hundred men. They tramped along looking more like a mob than a regiment, their guns perched at odd angles on their shoulders, their ranks indiscernible. Slocum rode a small sorrel horse, not much bigger than a pony, at the head of the column. Behind him stumbled George Kennedy, his hands tied to a rope attached to Slocum's saddle. Kennedy had already been badly beaten. He had lost half his front teeth. Blood drooled from a swollen eye, a smashed nose. Dragging him on the rope, Slocum spurred his horse into Kate's path.

"Where the devil do you think you're going, Miss Stapleton?"

"Home."

"You are like hell. You're under arrest. We caught this traitor visiting his mama and papa and he told us all about you."

Slocum reached out to grab her bridle. She lashed his hand with her riding crop. Several men from the column lunged toward her. She whipped the first man in the face with the crop and he dodged away with a howl of pain. The man behind him got a backhand slash as she spurred her horse. He sprang forward with a wild snort, knocked Slocum's much smaller animal out of the way, and leaped a stone fence between the road and some open pasture. Kate gave him his head and he streaked across the lush green grass,

163

soared over another fence, and regained the road about a quarter of a mile beyond Slocum's column. No one tried to pursue her; Slocum had the only horse.

At first Kate rode in a daze of fright and anger. By the time she reached Kemble Manor, she was calmer and remembered the letter that Anthony had given her. She rode up the drive to deliver it. Caroline met her in the center hall. The doors to the north and south parlors and the library were shut, creating a strange gloom for midday.

"Mr. Skinner is indisposed," Caroline said. "I will take the letter for him. Where did you get it? Did Anthony come to—to your house?"

"No. I went to him. We spent the night at the tavern in Shrewsbury."

"Is that wise, Kate? Anthony is—a public enemy. There are men on the other side—our side—who may use you to attack him."

"Let them try."

Kate described her encounter with Slocum and his men on the Shrewsbury road. For her it was a clash between Stapleton pride and Slocum poltroonery, between ideal love and the gross mob.

Caroline saw there was no point in trying to teach Kate political caution. "There's another reason for second thoughts, Kate. Your father came here yesterday to ask me to speak to you. I've never seen him so—so unhappy."

"Really? An amazing performance for a man who did not shed a tear over the body of his wife."

Kate was almost as shocked by these words as Caroline. They revealed how much Anthony Skinner was costing her. Suddenly she was back in the rose garden beside her father, talking about love and freedom. Did following her mother's code mean she had to hate this man, who had done so much to fill her life with happiness? For a moment she almost took back the words.

But Caroline could not avoid a harsh reproach. "You don't know what you're saying, Kate. A man like your father does not weep in public."

The hint of condescension—as Kate heard it—the adult talking to the child—gave her the excuse she needed to lose her temper. "I never thought I'd hear such sentimental gibberish from you, Aunt Caroline."

"Kate—I'm twice your age."

"I don't think that gives you any right to lecture me. I may be a fool. But at least when I die I will have this consolation. I tried to love someone. I took the risk. I gave myself to him—with my whole heart."

"I didn't know you were so cruel, Kate."

"Why not? It's the way of the world."

With an arrogance she did not really feel, Kate strode to the door and looked back at the small figure of her aunt in the shadowed hall. Maybe Anthony was right. Maybe all these old people were fading away, their day done. Kemble said the same thing. But whom could you trust, what could you follow? Nothing but her own uncertain heart, so full of love last night, now charged with nothing but venom.

"I feel sorry for you, Aunt Caroline, I really do."

CHAPTER THREE

THAT BITTER EXCHANGE with Kate triggered a night of anguished insomnia for Caroline Skinner. It exposed, with the savage economy of a saber stroke, all the dimensions of her unhappy marriage. Dawn was tingeing the windows with gray, the first birds were twittering, and still sleep refused to close her aching eyes. In the next room, she heard her husband's big feet shuffling across the floor, then the inevitable coughing, spitting, throat clearing, and other physical sounds of the morning. The manor house suddenly became a huge cage in which she was trapped forever. Hastily throwing on a robe, she fled into the park behind the house. Down a curving path she ran, tears streaming down her cheeks, until she reached a bluff overlooking the bay. The sun had not yet started to rise. The great sweep of water was still a murky gulf.

Across the bay came a strange rumble. What was it? A few stars still glittered in the pale cloudless sky. It was not a storm. Then she knew. The British and the Americans were fighting on Long Island. The rumble was cannon fire. She went back to her room, put on her riding habit, and rode over to our house for breakfast. It was an easy way to avoid her husband and his inevitable predictions of a royal victory.

There was another reason—in fact two other reasons for her visit. My father was still immured with his lawbooks, pondering the legality of independence. Most of the lawyers in Monmouth and Middlesex counties refused to recognize it, and had withdrawn from practice in the courts which had begun to function under our new state constitution. Caroline had spent more than a few hours arguing with him about this boycott and his attitude toward the rebellion. Although he was her uncle, only a dozen or so years separated them in age, and they had long been intellectual companions, exchanging books and ideas. They may also have been drawn together by their mutual unhappiness in marriage. Now Caroline pointed toward the distant cannon and told him that the sound made his continued hesitation unthinkable. War had begun.

My father smiled and told her that the war had begun a year ago. Caroline shook her head. "No. That was a war with New England. This is a war with America. King George and his Parliament are making independence a necessity."

My mother warned Caroline that she was talking treason.

"Not any more," Caroline replied.

At the end of a very argumentative breakfast, she asked to see my father privately about a "family legal problem." They adjourned to his study, leaving my mother almost expiring with curiosity. In the study, Caroline told my father about Kate's rendezvous with Anthony Skinner and her encounter with Slocum. "I fear the worst," she said. "Has she broken a law?"

"As yet, no law against treason has been passed by the legislature. But she could be punished under several statutes against public lewdness."

"If she is accused—will you defend her?"

My father hesitated, as usual. To appear before rebel judges would be a tacit acknowledgment of independence. His glance wandered uneasily toward the dining room, where my mother was undoubtedly still sitting over her coffee. "Yes," he said.

At Liberty Tavern, Caroline's fears were proving to be prescient. A few hours after she saw my father, Daniel Slocum strode into the taproom with a warrant for Kate's arrest. It had been signed by one of his recently elected judges. With it was a deposition from the landlady of the Shrewsbury tavern stating that Kate had spent the night there with Anthony Skinner.

Jonathan Gifford studied the accusing documents and struggled to control a mixture of anger and shame. "This has nothing to do with the war, Slocum."

"It has everything to do with it," Slocum said. "You know as well as I do that your bitch of a stepdaughter set Skinner free. Now she's down there in Shrewsbury flaunting her tail with him, and like as not acting as his courier. She's turned an enemy loose at our backs at the very time that we need every man to fight the ones that are likely to be at our throats if the news from Long Island is bad. We are going to make an example of her, by God, we are going to show everyone south of the Raritan what it means to truck with traitors."

Jonathan Gifford looked past Slocum at the men in the taproom. He saw fear and anger on almost every face. Behind their confident talk, the independence men were haunted by a dread suspicion that the British army was unbeatable. It was inevitable. For decades, Americans had toasted and boasted the prowess of the English soldier. He turned to Barney McGovern. "You had better ask Kate to come up here," he said.

Captain Gifford and Colonel Slocum waited in a silence charged with mutual dislike until Kate appeared. She was wearing an old blue housedress and only one petticoat. I was there and saw the lascivious light in too many eyes at the glimpse of Kate's supple body beneath the carelessly flowing cloth as she strode into the room. She stood before Slocum, her back straight as an Indian's, her proud chin high.

"Katherine Stapleton," Slocum said, "I have been ordered by the magistrates of this county to place you under arrest."

"What for?"

"Did you or did you not spend the night with Anthony Skinner at the tavern in Shrewsbury?"

"That is none of your goddamn business," Kate said, color suffusing her cheeks.

"It is my business if anyone in this county, male or female, trafficks with the enemy."

"If there is an enemy around here, it is you."

"You are calling an officer in the service of the honorable Provincial Congress of the state of New Jersey an enemy?" Slocum roared. "You are condemning yourself out of your own mouth, miss. Why don't you make a full confession here and now? We know you helped Skinner escape."

Kate lost all control of her temper. It was exactly what Slocum was hoping she would do. In sixty seconds, all Jonathan Gifford's efforts to protect her lay in ruins.

"I helped him escape because I love him. I went to him in Shrewsbury because I love him. You can do what you want to me. I'm not afraid of you or any of your stupid vicious friends."

"Maybe we shall teach you some fear before long," Slocum said.

"The Good Book tells us it is the beginning of wisdom. Mr. Gifford, you are hereby ordered to confine this girl in the same room where you previously confined her paramour with so little success. If she escapes, you will be responsible."

"I won't have to escape. A man with more courage than you, with more courage than any of you, will rescue me," Kate said, making enemies of everyone in the taproom with one fiery glance.

"If he does, he will have to be bulletproof," Slocum said. "There will be a company of militiamen guarding this tavern day and night. I hope he tries it. We will have no more worries about Mr. Skinner."

By the time Caroline and my father arrived at the tavern, Kate was a prisoner. Jonathan Gifford was grateful for my father's offer to defend her. He looked into Caroline's haggard face and thought he saw the same concern there that was tormenting him. He asked her to talk to Kate. But Caroline did not have the strength for another encounter with her niece. For a moment she struggled with a wish to tell him what Kate had said to her at Kemble Manor on the way back from Shrewsbury. But why should she expect sympathy from him? Her unhappiness was none of his business.

"I think it would be better if you tried to draw her out yourself. She sees me as a kind of model—of what she despises."

Jonathan Gifford was baffled by this statement. He sensed an unhappiness in Caroline Skinner's voice that went beyond Kate's dilemma. But there was no time to explore it now. He turned to my father.

"It's more important for her to talk with you, Mr. Kemble. I'll take you up to her."

A half-hour later, my father returned to Captain Gifford's office, his hands spread wide with hopelessness and helplessness. "She has no interest in defending herself. She will neither let me plead her guilty nor testify in her own defense. She intends to remain silent."

"Then she must learn the hard way. That seems to be the way women must learn everything," Caroline said.

"Women and men," Jonathan Gifford said.

That evening, Jonathan Gifford brought Kate her supper. She sat by the window staring emptily into the darkness. In profile, Kate looked so much like her mother he thought for a moment he could not bear it. Below in the tavern yard militiamen on guard duty guffawed over some joke. Their coarse laughter gnawed at Jonathan Gifford's nerves. They were probably talking about her.

"I think you'll like this, Kate," he said, removing the covers, "cold lobster salad with your favorite India relish, iced tea."

"Take it away. I'm not hungry."

"Do you really think he'll try to rescue you, Kate?"

"Yes."

"How many men does he have?"

"I don't know." She thought for a moment. "About thirty."

"He can't do it. Slocum is using you for bait, hoping he'll try. Why did you tell them everything, Kate? They never could have convicted you if—"

Like the messenger who aroused the King's wrath with bad news, Jonathan Gifford became the focus of Kate's rage for telling her the truth. She suddenly wanted to hurt him as much as he had inadvertently hurt her.

"I'm not a hypocrite like everyone else around here."

"Kate—I'm trying to help you."

"No you're not. You don't care about me. You don't care about anyone or anything but this damned tavern and your reputation as an ex-officer and gentleman. To protect those two things you'll let me go to the whipping post. Just as you let Mother go to Antigua."

"For God's sake, Kate, don't sit in judgment on me."

"I will sit in judgment on you. Because I know the truth. You're like all the rest of them, playing stupid games with guns, worrying day and night about your reputation, your property, while women die all around you. Die from want of love. Because you don't care about it."

"That's not true, Kate. I failed your mother. I don't know exactly how. But I tried—I tried to make it up with you. I thought between us—there was a love."

In the small still room, Kate saw an incredible sight. Jonathan Gifford, the man of iron self-control, was weeping. The shock almost freed her from her despair. She leaped up, crying: "There was—there is—I do love you. Or I did."

"Then how can you say these things?"

She wanted to fling herself into his arms, to beg his forgiveness, to let him hold her as he often did after one of her tantrums when she was a child. But she was a child no longer. Sadly, she touched his wet cheek.

"I'm sorry. I guess I'm my mother's daughter. Forget about me, Father. I'm not worth crying over."

"Kate!" His big hands seized her arms and gave her a shake that almost made her neck snap. "Don't value yourself so low. Your mother was one person—you're another person—separate—different from her."

She shook her head and turned away from him to stare into the darkness again. Another burst of laughter from the militiamen rose out of the night.

Jonathan Gifford spent an hour beside the brook regaining control of himself. Then he went to his office and wrote a letter to Anthony Skinner, telling him what Kate was facing. "She has acted out of a love for you that is more pure and disinterested than a man can conceive. She clings to the hope that you will somehow rescue her. I don't think you have a chance of doing such a thing. Slocum probably has guards posted on all the roads from Shrewsbury. From what I hear, your numbers are too small to fight him. There is only one way that you can shield Kate—by surrendering yourself a prisoner of war and testifying at her trial. Even her part in your escape could be softened considerably if you told the judges that you played upon her emotions."

Jonathan Gifford dispatched Barney McGovern to Shrewsbury with orders to deliver this letter to Skinner personally. He gave him enough money to bribe half the town into guiding him to Skinner's camp. Captain Gifford spent the night pacing his greenhouse, too agitated even to work on his roses. About an hour before dawn, Barney rapped on the door. The sour look on his face announced failure even before he spoke.

"He read your letter and talked it over with his friends. I could hear them clear enough outside the tent, though they didn't know it. They decided it might be good business for them, if the rebels beat a woman. Then Skinner came back and gave me a lot of malarkey about not trusting Slocum and sent me off. If I had a gun with me, I think I might have shot the bastard and taken a chance on running for the swamp."

Early the next morning a dispatch rider from Amboy stopped at Liberty Tavern with grim news. The Americans had taken a terrible beating on Long Island. It was the beginning of that series of disasters in Washington's defense of New York that shook the nerve of almost every independence man in our district. As far as Kate was concerned, it was not a good omen. The possibility of defeat, disgrace, aroused furious rage in many backers of the rebellion, particularly among the Slocums and their followers.

Later that morning, three newly elected judges, Lemuel Peters, Ambrose Cotter, and Samuel Slocum, the Colonel's brother, arrived with Colonel Slocum and a military escort. They formed a three-judge court in Liberty Tavern's assembly room.

My father tried to defend Kate by asking for a specific indictment under the law. Since the state had not yet passed a law against treason, he was hoping to persuade the judges to dismiss the case. But his legal expertise was useless before Slocum's judges. The Colonel had told them to convict Kate and they were determined to do so, no matter what the law said. Lemuel Peters declared the court was sitting as a kind of interim Committee of Safety. There was no doubt that the legislature was planning to pass a law against treason and trafficking with the enemy. In the meantime, public order must be maintained. Peters rebuked my father for attempting to use "legal tricks" to defend an enemy of the people. My father was left momentarily speechless to hear the bench so flagrantly prejudging the case. He could only shrug his shoulders, sit down, and let the charade begin.

The prosecution had all the witnesses. The landlady from Shrewsbury told in simpering detail what she knew—and imagined—about Kate's night there. Two of Slocum's militiamen told the court how Kate had lashed them when they tried to arrest her at the Colonel's order. Slocum himself testified that he had heard Kate confess in Liberty Tavern's taproom that she had helped Skinner escape. A *coup de grâce*—if one was needed—was delivered by George Kennedy. His face still swollen from the beating he had received, he testified in a low defeated voice that Kate had voluntarily joined Skinner and his loyalists in the Shrewsbury swamp.

My father tried the only possible defense—a woman's weak, easily influenced judgment. In effect he said that women had no judgment at all, that they surrendered it to every man who winked at them. I happened to glance at Caroline Skinner, who sat among the spectators, while my father was making this argument. I was startled by the anger visible on her usually composed face. The defense made no impression on the judges or the spectators. The trial ended with Kate's reputation in shreds and her guilt beyond question. The judges conferred and agreed that they could not afford to ignore such outrageous disloyalty. They sentenced Kate to receive thirty-nine lashes on her bare back at noon on the following day. Kate did not show an iota of emotion. We could only admire the stoicism of a Christian martyr, wasted on a bad cause.

Later that night a note wrapped around a rock was flung through the bay window of Liberty Tavern's taproom. It was a message from Anthony Skinner. He had heard about Kate's sentence. Skinner swore before "the most high God" that the man who laid the whip to Kate's back would forfeit his hand. It was a typical Skinner solution, meeting violence with worse violence. Jonathan Gifford showed the note to the judges when they arrived at the tavern the next morning. Lemuel Peters huffed that the people's representatives could not allow themselves to be intimidated in the execution of their duty.

"In this case," said Dr. Davie, who was at the bar pouring himself a morning brandy, "execution should be tempered by mercy. What do you hope to accomplish by inflicting this brutal punishment on an eighteen-year-old girl? You will only make yourself and your cause an object of ridicule and disgust."

"You would do well to confine yourself to medical opinions, Doctor," said Peters.

"All right, here's one," said Davie. "You may kill her. I have seen a hundred lashes kill a man. Thirty-nine may well kill a woman."

Peters shook his head. "It is too late to change our minds now. We must show every man and woman in this state the kind of resolution displayed by the ancient Romans."

"I never heard of a Roman abusing a woman."

"Bring down the prisoner and let us proceed with the business."

A company of militia under Colonel Slocum's command and about a hundred spectators were assembled in the yard. I was among them, I watched, numb with disbelief, while Kate was led from the tavern door. It was a gray cold day. She wore only the old blue housedress in the raw northeast wind. They tied her hands to one of the columns on the tavern porch and cut her dress up the back with a shears. Ten militiamen were ordered to

173

step from the ranks and draw straws to see who would wield the lash. A husky farm boy named Dunlap drew the shortest straw. He said he would not do it, he had never struck a woman in his life. Colonel Slocum lectured him on his duty. The lad still refused. Slocum turned to his youngest son, Peter, who was about Dunlap's age. He reluctantly picked up the short ugly whip, with its nine ugly tails.

Kate cried out at the first blow. Then she did not make a sound. Many in the crowd watched with sick fascination as the whip fell again and again on that proud quivering back. I saw for the first time the hatred and envy that lurked beneath the surface of ordinary life. They were here to see Kate punished not for what she had done, but for what she was in their narrow eyes, a spoiled rich girl with bad morals.

I could see that Peter Slocum was striking her with less than half his strength. Still the cat was taking a cruel toll of Kate's flesh. The skin broke and bled. By the twentieth stroke, her back was a mass of raw oozing welts. Pain engulfed her. She no longer knew where she was, what was happening. On the thirtieth stroke she fainted.

Lemuel Peters, badly shaken—he had obviously never seen anyone whipped before—declared that justice had been done and commuted the rest of the sentence. Jonathan Gifford rushed to Kate, cut loose her hands, and carried her away. She was as pale and cold as a corpse. Upstairs Dr. Davie helped him force brandy down her throat to restore her, then held her arms while she underwent the final agony. Her father swabbed her back with brine —the standard treatment for lashed backs in the British army and navy. It prevented infection, but the salt water in the fresh wounds was hellishly painful.

For the next two or three days, Kate was feverish to the point of delirium, yet it was almost impossible for her to sleep. Every time she moved, pain clawed at her back. Dr. Davie decided to try one of his unorthodox remedies from the medical practice of the previous century. Davie's mother had been a Highland Scot. Half his head followed the scientific tradition of Edinburgh and the other half inclined toward the potions, charms, blessings, and curses of medieval medicine. He had saved the dress stained with Kate's blood. At the foot of her bed, he stirred into a bowl full of water something called the Powder of Sympathy, which turned the water bright green. He added a half-dozen strips of the dress. Within the hour, Kate's pain eased, and by morning it was gone. It was my first glimpse of the power of suggestion as a medical remedy.

Kate's fever passed the following day. But she was far from cured. She stayed in bed for another week, face down like a corpse on a battlefield, staring silently into her pillow. Jonathan Gifford tried the obvious—and wrong—tactic of trying to discredit Anthony Skinner. He told her of Anthony's cynical reaction to the letter Barney had carried to him. This only deepened Kate's melancholy. She ate practically nothing and became alarmingly thin. Her father looked almost as haggard. In desperation, he begged Caroline to make another attempt to talk with Kate.

At first Caroline was wary. She acted the sympathetic aunt, visiting a sick niece. Kate declined to respond to her small talk. Caroline decided to risk bluntness again.

"What are you trying to do, kill your father?"

"Kill him? What do you mean?" Kate answered in a leaden voice.

"He eats no more than you. I don't think he has slept an hour since you were whipped."

"Of course. I've disgraced him. I've failed him just like Mother failed him."

"How did she fail him?"

"She didn't. He failed her. He failed to love her for what she was."

"What was she?"

"A woman. A woman with a heart full of love, a woman who never found a man—worthy of her."

"Kate, I grew up with your mother. I freely admit I was envious of her. That was almost inevitable. She was five years older. I saw early that we were quite different people. Sarah was infinitely more enthusiastic. She won hearts more readily. She was always so ready to give hers. A lovely trait, but only if it is under some control, Kate. There is always the danger that it will become an extravagance, a thing we do for its own sake, for the glory or the pity or the sadness of it."

Caroline paced up and down the room for several moments trying to conceal her agitation. What she was saying went to the roots of her life. "That was your mother's real flaw. In part it was our father's fault. He goaded her to extremes with his awful abuse of our mother for not giving him a son. It was a bad match from the day of their wedding, as far as I can learn. But in the end, Kate, I believe that no one—not even a woman—can blame her fate on anyone but herself. Bound as we are by all the prejudice against us, we still have enough freedom to decide our destiny. But if you lose your faith in that—as your mother did—if you do not develop your mind as well as cultivate your heart, if you see yourself as nothing but a bundle of desirable flesh created to excite a man for fifteen minutes twice a week—if that's all you are, Kate, then everything depends on blind fatality, on whatever man happens to cross your path, and whether or not he chooses to be attracted to you. That is the way to desperation, Kate. You end up flinging your life away for a man who has no more use for you than—"

"The Viscount loved her. I'm sure he did. She wouldn't have gone to Antigua if—"

"He did not love her. He wrote a letter to your father, after she died, swearing he had done his best to send her back. They say she died of fever. I think she died of embarrassment."

This was stunning news, exploding one of Kate's most cherished romantic dreams. But she was not yet ready to surrender to her aunt's realism.

"She was driven to it. He drove her to it. The way he refused to forgive her. The man has no heart, Aunt Caroline." She hesitated, remembering Jonathan Gifford's tears the night before her whipping and plunged willfully to her conclusion. "He searches for one now and then. But he has no heart."

"You are wrong. I know you are wrong, Kate. When he came to me last month and pleaded with me to speak to you, if I ever heard love in a man's voice, saw it on his face, I saw it then."

Stubborn disbelief still confronted Caroline. "Kate," she burst out, "face the truth, for God's sake. Your mother was a fool. A wild, wayward fool who never knew what she felt from one day to the next, who was sixteen years old until the day she died. You are going the same way, or worse. Are you proud of the fact that George Kemble asked the judges to forgive you because you were a typical woman, a creature with a weak will and no understanding? If you had any pride, Kate, any real pride in being a woman, you should have died of shame at those words. I almost did."

Caroline fled from the room, all the deepest, most disturbing emotions of her life thundering in her soul. Her suppressed hatred of her sister, her smoldering resentment against men's treatment of women, and her forbidden yearning for Jonathan Gifford flashed like a series of tremendous lightning bolts across her moral landscape. Outside, one of our northeast storms shrouded the sky with gray and sent a chill wind moaning through the September trees. The blooming beauty of the rose garden was gone. Like a foretaste of fall, the delicate plants were wrapped in burlap, looking like blind mourning statues. An image of your soul, Mrs. Skinner, Caroline told herself as she walked along the bank of the little stream, struggling for calm.

"How is our patient?"

Jonathan Gifford's voice made her start violently. He was the last person she wanted to see. He limped toward her, a serious smile on his face, apologizing for his dirty hands. "I was working in the greenhouse. I saw you come out."

Caroline nodded. She felt frozen by the fear that she might reveal to this man some of the feelings she had just confessed to Kate. "Our patient—our patient is not very well, either physically or spiritually."

"She still loves him?"

"Who?"

"Anthony."

"I don't think—we didn't even mention him. Kate is troubled by something—more serious."

"What is it?"

"I—I'm not sure I can tell you. It has to do with—your wife—with Sarah."

Caroline's heart was pounding. She felt perspiration sheening her forehead. Was she about to faint?

"Oh," said Jonathan Gifford, a stricken look on his face. "I know Kate and Kemble blame me for what happened. As I told you, there is some truth in it."

"Captain Gifford—"

How could she speak without confessing the wild, absurd, implausible, disgraceful love that was raging inside her? Was she going mad like the rest of the world?

177

"I was never the husband Sarah wanted. That is the only defense I can make. We both discovered it—too late."

"Captain Gifford. She was my sister. I knew her well. Perhaps too well. She has paid a terrible price for her— That is why we both hesitate to speak ill of her. But it grieves me deeply to see you blame yourself."

Jonathan Gifford's voice was husky with emotion. "Mrs. Skinner, your sympathy—means a great deal to me. But I have thought about it through more than one night. There's some truth to the charge that I was—less than wholehearted. It is part of my nature and I am afraid part of my profession. A soldier learns very early to control his feelings. In the end he almost loses touch with them."

It was hopeless, Caroline told herself. Even in death Sarah was triumphant. She stared into the dark autumn waters of the brook. "I told Kate she is wrong. Wrong in what she thinks about Sarah. Wrong to imitate her. But of course she wouldn't listen. Why should she, when it comes from me?"

She wanted him to contradict those last words. She wanted him to ask her, at the very least, why she said them.

But Jonathan Gifford only shook his head. "At least you told her the truth. We can't do more than that."

"Yes."

She watched him limp away, back to his roses.

I told her the truth, but not you. When can I tell you the truth? Never, she told her mournful heart, never.

178

CHAPTER FOUR

"Now, BY GOD, we shall have the fight we have been waiting for. I kept Henrietta and the girls up all night making cartridges," said Samson Tucker, taking a hefty swig of his tankard of Stewed Quaker. "Yes, by God, Washington has proved himself a general, has he not, Captain Gifford? Getting his tail out of that damn nest of Tories in New York and joining us here in New Jersey where men are ready to fight?"

"I wish he had done it six months ago," Jonathan Gifford said.

"Ah, six months or six weeks, what difference does it make," said Samson, drawing a bead on an imaginary redcoat with an imaginary musket. "We are ready for'm one way or t'other."

"I hope you are ready for this," said Nathaniel Fitzmorris in the doorway of the taproom. "The Continentals are retreating."

"Retreating," said Samson dazedly. "Retreating where?"

"New Brunswick, they say. Mayhap Philadelphia, for all they know. I brought some beeves and a wagonload of flour to the commissary at Amboy not two hours ago. They flung money in my face and said they had no time to slaughter the cattle. They would run in the midst of their train to Brunswick."

Fitzmorris turned to Jonathan Gifford. "How is Kate?" Natty was a married man, but Kate still owned a corner of his heart.

"She's better, thanks," Jonathan Gifford said. Not many people even bothered to ask about Kate. Everyone was absorbed by the war. They rode or walked to Liberty Tavern every day for the latest rumors and reports. For weeks it had been bad news piled on worse. The American army was reeling from defeat to retreat to defeat. But Fitzmorris' news was the worst we had heard. About a thousand regulars had been guarding the coast against invasion between Elizabethtown and Sandy Hook. Our militia had been depending on them to bear the brunt of any British assault.

"Retreating," cried Samson, "and leaving us without an army? Leaving us to fight the Foot Guards and the Royal Welsh and the King's Own? They'll be ashore at Amboy before the week is up when they hear the place is undefended."

"Unless we go down to stop them," Jonathan Gifford said.

"We?" said Samson. "If you're joking, Captain Gifford, 'tis not the time for it. God's bones, we don't even have a cannon in the whole district. They will haul them line-of-battle ships against the shore and let loose a broadside that will blow us all to Burlington."

Lemuel Peters burst into the taproom, fear pulsing in his bulging eyes and twitching mouth. "The Continentals. I just saw them on the road."

"They are concentrating in New Brunswick," Jonathan Gifford said. "I suppose Washington has no other choice. Abel Aikin tells me he brought only three thousand men with him."

"Washington should be court-martialed and shot," Peters squawked. "The man is playing a traitor's game. He gave New York to the British. Now he's giving them New Jersey."

"There is not much a general can do when his men won't fight," Jonathan Gifford said. "I read you that letter Kemble wrote after the rout at Kip's Bay."

"He should have shot those damn Connecticut cowards wholesale. That's what a real general would have done," Peters said. "That's what Hancock would have done. When I was at Harvard, I saw him drill the Boston Cadets—the best uniformed militia in America."

"Uniforms don't win battles," Jonathan Gifford said. "You had better ride down and tell Colonel Slocum this news. I imagine they will be calling out the regiment."

A half-hour later we stood in the tavern yard and watched the Continental troops trudge past us to New Brunswick. They looked dispirited and beaten. Among them were John Fleming and his Virginia regiment. Captain Fleming concentrated grimly on keeping his men in ranks and did not even glance in the direction of Liberty Tavern. He had heard about Kate.

Other officers were not so diligent. Dozens of stragglers drifted into the tavern for as much rum as they could gulp. They talked bitterly of being "sold" by Washington and the other generals.

The next day we heard from New Brunswick that when they reached that town they took over every tavern and got so disgracefully drunk they turned to rioting and rape. Only violent efforts on the part of their officers restored some semblance of order.

The same day, General Washington, backed by Governor Livingston and the legislature, issued a call for every man on the militia rolls in New Jersey to join the army at New Brunswick without a moment's delay. Dispatch riders posted a copy of the proclamation on the door of Liberty Tavern. Few paid attention to it. In the evening Nat Fitzmorris stopped at the tavern with ten of his company—all he could persuade to follow him. Jonathan Gifford filled their canteens with rum and wished them luck. Colonel Slocum wore out two horses racing through the countryside in search of his regiment, but not even his most ferocious roars had much effect.

That night Slocum sat in Liberty Tavern's taproom, exhausted, cursing everyone and everything, including Washington. "Not a captain besides Fitzmorris. Not even my old company will turn out," he told Jonathan Gifford. "Goddamn Washington. Why won't he stand at Amboy? The men would fight with their farms at their backs. But you can't expect a man to walk off his property, leave his wife and children and livestock behind him, and put himself under the command of some damn general who knows how to do nothing but retreat. We may find ourselves on the far side of the Delaware in a week."

Slocum poured a gill of stonewall down his throat. Barney refilled his mug. "I wish we had your son here, Gifford. They won't turn out for Slocum. They want to be led by an aristocrat, goddamn them."

"I don't think that has anything to do with it," Jonathan Gifford said. "Maybe they're just using their common sense."

"What do you mean by that?"

"I mean they see there's no point to militiamen fighting regulars."

"That's damn treason talk, Gifford," Slocum shouted. "Is that what you're telling people? No wonder I can't turn out a man in this neighborhood."

"I'm not saying anything I haven't said since this war started."

"You've changed the name of your tavern, Gifford, but you haven't changed the color of your coat."

Jonathan Gifford decided to ignore the insult. Slocum was drunk. Barney McGovern disagreed with his forbearance. "Why don't you throw the bugger out on his head, Captain, or let me?"

"No. It's better to let him talk."

The next morning, Slocum rode off to New Brunswick with fewer than fifty men. He was back the following day. "We weren't in camp two hours when the British appeared on the heights of Brunswick across the Raritan. Washington handed us axes and told us to chop down the bridge. He gave us a single cannon to keep the whole damned British army at bay. We get back to camp and find the order to retreat has already been given. Not a man of us would go with them. Why the hell should we march our feet off in the wrong direction?"

Never had Jonathan Gifford seen or heard a more discouraging example of the weakness of militia thinking—and America's folly in depending on amateur soldiers like Slocum to win the war in 1776. Their viewpoint was hopelessly parochial. They simply did not understand the strategy Washington was evolving in the struggle for control of a continent. They could not think beyond their own little patch of America.

"I saw Putnam and the young squire," Slocum said. "He looked poorly, your boy. The old soldier's in a gloom. He thinks all this retreating is the ruin of us. He sends you a message. Your boy's been sick. He's all right now. But the General fears the worst. If he sickens again, he will send for you. The army's doctors are butchers. They kill ten times what they cure."

Jonathan Gifford nodded. The surge of emotion that struck him at the mention of Kemble helped him overcome his dislike of Slocum. He began trying to explain to the Colonel the strategic situation Washington was creating by his retreat across New Jersey. He was giving the British more and more American territory to fill up. But if that territory was pacified, if everyone cowered on their farms, the British would see no need to leave any troops behind them. This meant the full weight of the royal army would be thrown against Washington's handful of regulars. In this new situation, it was vital for the militia to begin fighting a guerrilla war—partisan tactics, as they were called in 1776.

Colonel Slocum was not interested. "It's easy for you to talk, Gifford," he said. "You have trimmed your sails right through the storm. No matter what happens, your flanks are safe. Squire Skinner and his son will protect you for your daughter's sake on the one hand, and your son will speak for you on our side."

"Slocum," said Jonathan Gifford, "I hope before long you will see that those words are as untrue as they are unfair."

"We will see, Gifford, we will see."

The next day, all of us had a chance to see. Clattering into the tavern yard from the Amboy road came forty British dragoons in red coats, huge cavalry sabers jutting from their saddles. In command was a young captain in his twenties. He introduced himself to Jonathan Gifford as Oliver De Lancey, Jr., of the 16th Regiment. Beside him was a far more ominous figure in a green coat— Anthony Skinner. As they dismounted in the tavern yard, Skinner pointed to the new sign. "You see what I mean," he said, "Liberty Tavern? We ought to burn the damn place to the ground right now."

"I am sure the General will tend to such matters in his own good time, Skinner. We have orders to treat everyone as a loyal subject, unless he demonstrates otherwise by his actions," Captain De Lancey said.

"You don't think that sign proves anything?" Skinner said.

"I rather like it," said De Lancey. "After all, I'm in favor of British liberty, aren't you?"

Jonathan Gifford pointedly ignored Anthony Skinner. He introduced himself to De Lancey and told the Captain how much he admired his father's horses. The elder De Lancey's steeds seldom failed to win most of the races run each year at Hempstead on Long Island. "I've made more than one pound betting on them."

De Lancey smiled politely and asked if he and his men could spend the night at the tavern. They were prepared to pay hard money for everything they and their horses consumed.

"Of course you're welcome. But I can't guarantee the conduct of the neighborhood. There are a good many men around here who might be inclined to fight you."

"I understand that," De Lancey said. "We'll have sentries well posted."

"How is my old friend, Colonel Harcourt?"

"Well, thank you," said young De Lancey, obviously startled to

183

discover Jonathan Gifford was on speaking terms with his regimental commander.

"We served together under Wolfe at Quebec," Jonathan Gifford said, casually adding that he had been a captain in the 4th Regiment. De Lancey's politeness warmed to cordiality.

Anthony Skinner's glower deepened. "Where's Kate?" he asked.

"In her room."

"Is it true what I heard, she was given thirty lashes by your damned militia judges?"

"She was."

"And you stood by without saying a word in her defense?"

"You were the one person who might have helped her, Mr. Skinner," said Jonathan Gifford.

"You mean that ridiculous advice you sent me in your letter? No one would have believed me in the first place—"

Captain De Lancey was looking bewildered. There was no point in trying to explain the conversation to him. "I would be honored if you and your officers would join me for dinner, Captain," Jonathan Gifford said to him, "but Mr. Skinner is not welcome in this tavern or in my house."

"Gifford, I will go where I please and do what I please or you will find yourself in irons in the deepest dungeon the provost marshal can find in New York. I'm the colonel of the King's loyal militia in this county and I am here to take command."

"I call on Captain De Lancey to witness the threats you have made against me. I have the right to throw you or any other man off my property, if British law or British liberty means anything. This has nothing to do with rebellion, Captain De Lancey. Mr. Skinner has abused the affection and ruined the reputation of one of the finest girls in New Jersey. Now get out of here before I horsewhip you down the road like a common thief."

I was a witness to this blazing confrontation. I have never seen anything that equaled its intensity before or since. Jonathan Gifford's large head and thick shoulders were impressive, but his brow scarcely reached Anthony Skinner's shoulder. It was not physical force that demolished Skinner. It was moral intensity, the ferocity with which Captain Gifford spoke the truth.

"Are you going to let him insult me this way?" Skinner asked Captain De Lancey.

"I really don't see what I can or should do about it, my dear fellow. As Mr. Gifford says, he has every right to control his own property and the difference between you seems highly personal, to say the least."

"You're only five miles from your own house, Skinner," Jonathan Gifford said. "You'll get a good dinner there."

"Would you like an escort?" Captain De Lancey asked.

"I need no escort, Captain. There isn't a skulking coward in this state who has the nerve to challenge me now," Skinner said.

He strode to his horse, sprang into the saddle, and galloped away. Jonathan Gifford repeated his invitation to dinner and soon sat down with Captain De Lancey and two of his lieutenants in a private room. Without seeming to ask questions, he had no difficulty leading the young officers into a discussion of British plans to finish the war. They were confident that Washington's army would collapse around January 1. The Americans had made the foolish mistake of enlisting their regulars for only a single year. When the regulars quit, General Howe would probably push on to Philadelphia, occupy the American capital, and arrest as many members of the Continental Congress as he could catch. For the time being, young De Lancey thought Washington could scrape together enough men to make a stand on the west bank of the Delaware. The army would occupy all of New Jersey and restore royal government. Lord Howe in his role as peace commissioner would issue a proclamation offering amnesty to everyone who swore obedience and loyalty to the King within the next sixty days. Each would receive a certificate of protection which would guarantee him against prosecution or retaliation.

It was very shrewd. The Howes were using both the carrot and the stick to persuade the Americans to surrender. Young De Lancey, his tongue loosened by wine, told Captain Gifford about the arguments within the British high command. His father, as America's most powerful loyalist, was heavily involved in them. The Howes had deliberately allowed Washington to extricate his army from Long Island and New York, to the vehement disappointment of the elder De Lancey and other loyalists. The Howes' goal was not the annihilation of the Americans, but their eventual reconciliation. By persuading them to an early surrender, they hoped to win some sympathy for them in Parliament, and head off the confiscators and placemen who were eager to punish them in the same profitable style that they had developed practicing on the Scots and the Irish. As an American and a professional soldier, young De Lancey was thoroughly in favor of the Howes' policy.

He expected Captain Gifford to agree with him and was surprised when he said, "There is only one thing wrong with the picture you draw. The Howes are not politicians. They have very little influence in Parliament. What happens if the Americans surrender and the placemen decide to punish them anyway?"

"That is a chance we must take," De Lancey said with the nonchalance of a rich young man whose property would be safe in any event.

"These loyalists like Skinner," said one of the lieutenants. "They are our biggest problem at the moment. They don't want peace. They want revenge."

"Them and the Germans," said the other lieutenant.

"Oh yes, the Germans," said De Lancey with a grim smile. "If any of them come through here, I urge you to hide everything that might conceivably be portable. They were told they could make their fortunes in America, and they seem determined to do it."

A few days later, De Lancey's commander, Colonel William Harcourt, stopped at Liberty Tavern to shake his friend Gifford's hand. He was a lean, handsome example of the British aristocracy at its best. His father was a member of the Opposition in Parliament, a frequent critic of the war. His son felt the same way. He was in America only because his regiment had been ordered to go, and as colonel, he felt he could not desert his men.

Over a glass of port, he made no attempt to conceal his fears, not of defeat, but of victory. "I am afraid we are going to win, Gifford," he said. "I am afraid of what it will do to England. There are men in Parliament who would like to make it impossible for anyone ever again to criticize the government. They could use the army and the spoils they'll win over here to get laws passed, making opposition a crime."

They discussed the Howes' carrot and stick plan to end the war. "If I was an American," Harcourt said, "I wouldn't trust anyone's good intentions—and I'd trust even less a Parliament that unleashes German mercenaries on a free people." He described in grisly detail the way the Germans had looted Long Island and Westchester County.

Harcourt rode back to his regiment. There were even fewer soldiers with his opinion in the British army than there were politicians in Parliament. But it is good to remember that not all Englishmen wanted to conquer America.

The next day Lord Howe issued his amnesty proclamation. It made even more doleful a letter Abel Aikin brought from Kemble —the last letter Abel delivered for some time. The American postal service in New Jersey had ceased to exist. The letter explained why. Washington's army was too small to make a stand anywhere in the state. They were retreating to the west bank of the Delaware. "Where are the militia?" Kemble wrote bitterly. "If they turned out, we could hold the state against the entire British army. What has happened to all those fellows who cheered so madly for independence? I thought Americans were natural patriots. Now I begin to wonder if they are not natural cowards."

Jonathan Gifford shook his head wearily. Was it typical of Kemble—or typical of youth in general—to plunge from extreme to extreme, from blind optimism to blind despair? He sat down and wrote his son a letter.

Dear Kemble,

I don't know where or when I will get a chance to send this to you. Perhaps I will keep it here until you return. I hate to see you lose hope and pride in your countrymen. Most of them are neither cowards nor heroes but simply human beings with normal amounts of courage and honesty. I have led men into battle, and seen them break and run, rallied those same men and seen them perform feats of amazing bravery in the space of an hour. Every man, even the bravest, is prey to panic. Only a rare man will fight if he thinks he has no chance of winning. This is what has struck New Jersey— panic—a general belief that the Cause is lost. Can you blame the poor militiaman if he thinks this way, when the Continentals—the men presumed to be the best soldiers America can muster—have been trounced again and again? If General Washington wins a battle or two, our people will change their minds and take heart. But for the time being, New Jersey is as good as lost.

What Jonathan Gifford saw and heard in the next few days only underscored these words. The talk in Liberty Tavern was thick with defeatism and despair. Lord Howe's offer was frequently discussed. But for the time being everyone seemed anxious to damn it as a British trick to seduce honest men. Leading the damners were our titans of the now defunct Committee of Safety, Lemuel Peters and Ambrose Cotter. Listening to them, Barney McGovern whispered behind his hand to Jonathan Gifford, "What'll you bet me those two heroes will be among the first to throw in?"

"If you find any takers," Jonathan Gifford said, "let me know. I'll cover all bets."

Early in the following week Anthony Skinner sent one of his family's servants to Liberty Tavern with a note for Kate. She was still a semi-invalid. Her back was healing very slowly. Bertha, Black Sam's wife, rubbed it every day with an ointment she had concocted from her herb garden. But she was dolefully certain that there would always be some scars there, and Dr. Davie confirmed this sad prediction. Kate accepted this fate with a stoicism that Jonathan Gifford found more troubling than a tantrum. She had begun to eat again, converse a little at dinner, but most of the time she was silent. She walked beside the brook and sat alone for hours staring at its frothy white water. Now she fingered her lover's letter idly and set it aside. Not for a full day did she open it.

She knew what it contained. Bertha had told her how Jonathan Gifford had ordered Anthony Skinner off the property. It was precisely the sort of challenge Anthony needed—perhaps wanted—to force him into a proposal.

My dearest,

Your father has forbidden me to see you. He accuses me of being at fault in the beating given you by those rebel scum. As if he had nothing to do with it! He stood there, his hands in his pockets, and let you be scourged. My heart was torn to atoms when I heard the news that they had actually carried out the sentence. I could not believe they would ever be so low. I thought it was a ruse to tempt me to rescue you—which I had no hope of doing. The heroes I have the honor to lead are not much braver than their rebel brethren. I swear to God I'm glad I think of myself as more English than American, in spite of my father. If I was a full American I would be ashamed to show my face to a British soldier. The poltroonery of their conduct will make 1776 go down in English history as the year of the cowards.

Now our time has come to rule these people, Kate, rule them with the rod they deserve. I want you by my side. The way my father drinks, he cannot live longer than another year or two. This means that he will die without issue and Kemble Manor will revert to my mother and you and Kemble as your mother's heirs. Kemble will lose his share, and my mother may well lose hers if she acts any further on her rebel principles. I am sure a bribe or two to the right parties will make you and me the owners of the manor. Won't that be a laugh on those hypocrites who tried to deprive me of my just inheritance? With Kemble Manor and the other confiscated lands —you may depend upon it, all the leading rebels will lose their lands no matter what they swear to Lord Howe's silly proclamation—I will have more than enough income to dress you like the queen you are.

In fact I am told the King intends to create an American peerage to equal the Irish one and guarantee a proper respect for class and rank henceforth. I can all but guarantee that you will be Lady Skinner before the decade is out.

Say but the word, Kate, and I will come to get you with enough men to make your father quiver for his tavern and his neck. Let me make you my wife in name as you already are in fact.

Forever yours,
Anthony

Kate suddenly remembered what Caroline had said to her about being displayed as a woman with a weak will and no understanding. With unexpected anger she told herself she was not too stupid to see why Anthony was so anxious to marry her. Aside from her half share of Kemble Manor, he obviously felt that his failure to rescue her impugned his honor. If she married him, it would be an act of public forgiveness on her part. For the first time, she confronted the avarice in Anthony Skinner's commitment to the King. She threw his letter into the fire.

Watching the flames devour it, Kate suddenly found herself wishing she could thrust her hand, her whole body into some magical flame that would consume the old Kate and permit a new one to step forth, purified of the bad temper, the violent willfulness she had inherited from her mother. That talk with her Aunt Caroline had been a shock of the mental or spiritual sort as violent as the one she had received from the whip. Slowly, painfully, over the past few weeks, Kate had accepted the harsh truth at the center of it. She had recklessly, brainlessly given herself away. She had paid a bitter price for it. She did not want to pay it again.

A few days after Kate discarded Anthony's note, a full brigade of British infantry landed unopposed at Perth Amboy and marched up the road toward New Brunswick. At the head of the column, making Barney McGovern a prophet, was the 4th Regiment, the King's Own. A major on horseback swung out of the column and dismounted. He had a round red face and a belly big enough to burst all the buttons off his waistcoat.

"Is this where a certain innkeeper named Gifford resides?" he thundered.

There were timid nods from a number of us on the porch.

"Get him out here," roared the Major. "I'm here to arrest the damn rascal."

A shiver went through all of us. The British were launching a reign of terror. The Major's threats and exclamations did nothing to dissuade us. "Get him out here," he roared. "By God, I'll have his rebel head on a block before morning. Liberty Tavern. The son of a bitch will dance on hot coals to the British Grenadiers or I'll know the reason why."

Jonathan Gifford appeared at the door. A smile leaped across his face. Were we all going mad? we wondered. The officer was grinning from ear to ear, too.

"Brother Jonathan," he roared.

"Brother Billy," cried Jonathan Gifford.

They flung themselves into each other's arms like a pair of long-lost lovers.

"By God," said the Major, "it's worth three thousand miles of ship's bread and salt beef to see you, I swear it."

"That sounds like a British diet to me," said Jonathan Gifford. "You're in America now where a man can eat to his heart's content."

"Which is exactly what I've been doing," said the Major, patting his paunch.

"And the wine cellar on wheels?"

"Right there," said the Major, pointing to a big wagon in the road. "Here," he roared to the driver. "Pull that in here and post sentries at the head and tail. If I find a bottle missing in the morning, they'll get a hundred lashes each."

Dr. Davie was standing in the tavern door watching all this. Jonathan Gifford waved him over and introduced him to Major William Moncrieff. He pointed to the wagon. "In there you will find the finest collection of wines in America. Possibly in Europe. Wherever Moncrieff goes, his wine cellar goes with him."

"He won't need to touch a drop of it tonight," said Dr. Davie.

Captain Gifford smiled. "We have a few bottles downstairs that can challenge his best."

"The devil you say, Gifford. You've got the palate of a peasant. But I am willing to try the experiment, provided we start off with the drink you fellows call rumfustian."

Two hours later, after liberal quantities of rumfustian had been consumed, Major Moncrieff and his old friend progressed somewhat unsteadily down to the residence, where Kate joined them for dinner. It was a feast of pheasant, jugged hare, oysters from Raritan Bay, and lobsters from the Atlantic, the meat flavored by magnificent wine from Burgundy, the fish by a delicate product of the Moselle.

Moncrieff personified only part of that motto of the British officer, to live well and leave a fortune to his heirs. In his case, he lived so well there was no hope of a fortune or heirs for that matter. His conversation was replete with descriptions of magnificent dinners in England, Ireland, France, and Spain. He also talked freely about the war, which he called "a damn silly business started by fools on both sides." As a professional soldier, he had no interest in politics and nothing but contempt for politicians. He soon concentrated on reminiscing about his days as a young officer with his friend Gifford.

"Ah, Havana, Gifford, there was a city. Remember those Spanish girls? Amazing how often their duennas turned out to be nearsighted or blind."

"What?" said Kate archly. "I can't believe my solemn father ever conducted himself as anything but an officer and a gentleman."

"Whoa," roared Moncrieff, almost choking on a lobster claw. "He was in a class by himself when it came to the ladies. Wild ones, they were his specialty. The wilder the better. After a week or two with Gifford, they were tamed for life."

"Father, is it true?" Kate said.

Jonathan Gifford kicked Moncrieff in the shins. "You know how it is with old soldiers," he said. "They tend to exaggerate everything, from their heroism to their—"

"Damn me if I ever exaggerated a thing," thundered Moncrieff. "But you don't understand how it is with a soldier, my dear. Every day of a campaign he risks being laid low by a bullet. And for what? For King and country. So he says to himself, by God, since I take such risks, I deserve a few exemptions and if the King and the country don't agree, why they can go to the devil."

Kate looked at her father and could not believe what she saw. He was blushing.

"And what about Canada, Gifford? Those Frenchies. Remember that one who called herself Solange? By God, I almost challenged you when she dumped me for your damned Irish blarney. That's why I never married, you know," declared the Major, attacking a column of defenseless oysters. "This fellow was always getting the best-looking woman in sight. I consoled myself with the best cook. Before I knew it, I was too damned fat to interest girls your age—or any age. It's all his fault."

"What would you think of a woman who—lived like a soldier?" Kate asked.

"Why," said the Major, "I'd think she was a shameless hussy. But I'd like to meet her."

"I'm serious."

"Now, my dear," said Moncrieff, "I see you have some modern ideas. Women are not soldiers. That's the only excuse we have to offer. Once a man settles down and marries I expect him to be as constant as the most virtuous wife."

"But once a woman sins—I mean acts like a soldier—she can never be virtuous again."

With no idea that the conversation was very personal for Kate, Moncrieff gave her his honest opinion. "A woman's reputation is her stock in trade, so to speak. Like a soldier's courage."

"I think that is hypocrisy!"

"But a soldier doesn't damn a man if he runs away at first then comes back to the fight. No more would he condemn a single fall from virtue in a woman. However, the way of the world—"

"Is hypocrisy," Kate said.

"Since when is that news?" Moncrieff said. He patted her hand. "Ah, my dear, I think you must be troubled by a friend who has been indiscreet with some young fellow in uniform. Don't fret about it. People forget those things quickly in a war. So many other things happen, they haven't got time to remember matters that would keep them indignant for ten years during a peace."

"Do you agree with all this, Father?"

"Absolutely," said Jonathan Gifford, momentarily bewildered by another aspect of war, the constant occurrence of the unexpected. Two days ago, if someone had told him that his old friend Wild Billy Moncrieff would turn into a moral philosopher and say precisely the things Kate needed to hear, he would have laughed in his face.

"I will leave you two veterans to your pipes and port and reminiscences of old conquests."

Moncrieff studied Kate as she left the room. "A fine girl, Gifford. I could never picture you as a father. But from the way she looks at you, I guess you've made me eat my words again. It almost makes me wish I'd quit this damn business when you did."

"I didn't have much choice, Billy. I couldn't march a mile on this knee."

"Ah, with your blarney you could have talked your way onto a general's staff if you wanted to stay. You were right, what you said that last night in Havana when we got drunker than two cormorants in a brewery. There's no future for the likes of you and me in this army. It gets you like a crab apple in the belly, seeing pipsqueak viscounts and fake Irish lords with commissions their fathers bought them."

For another ten minutes, Moncrieff savagely criticized the British army system of selling commissions and giving most of the promotions to noblemen and sons of noblemen who had the necessary cash and influence in London to shoulder aside professional soldiers like himself. Jonathan Gifford was amazed to recall in the voice of this old friend how sharp had been his antagonism to the British system, with its heavy emphasis on aristocracy. It was a bias that pervaded not only the army but all aspects of English life. It was startling to realize how much healthier, freer, America was without it.

When they talked about the war Jonathan Gifford was struck even more profoundly by how different his feelings were. Moncrieff talked of a quick easy conquest and rubbed his hands at the prospect of being rewarded with some choice American lands. Jonathan Gifford had no fault to find with Moncrieff for this attitude. It was the way a professional soldier saw a war in the eighteenth century. The profits should be as high as the risks. But he could muster no enthusiasm to match Moncrieff's glee. It was his country, or at least the country of his son and daughter, that Moncrieff was talking about with such lip-smacking ardor. When the Major said he would depend on his old friend Gifford to keep his eye peeled for one of the choicer rebel estates, he could not resist pointing out that Washington still had an army and the war was not over.

"By God, I think you're half a rebel, Gifford. I thought you just changed the name of this tavern to keep it in one piece until we got here."

Captain Gifford smiled, poured some more rumfustian into Moncrieff's tankard, and the Major soon forgot politics. An hour later, after Wild Billy had staggered off to his room at the tavern, Kate came downstairs to find her father sitting in one of the two wing chairs before the dying fire, his face unusually solemn.

"I like your old friend," she said.

"He talks too much."

"No. No, Father," Kate said, sitting down in the other wing chair. "For the first time I—I feel I know you as—as Jonathan Gifford. Not the man I call Father. It makes me feel a little easier about myself. A little more—forgiving. It's strange, but at first I didn't want you to forgive me. I wanted you to treat me like you treated Mother. But Aunt Caroline helped me see—how wrong I was, how foolish. I realized you did forgive me—but I couldn't forgive myself."

"That's the hardest thing to do, Kate."

"Why couldn't you forgive her, Father?"

"I don't know, Kate. I tried. I said I forgave her. But in the end —I couldn't do it."

"She hurt you—that much?"

"I tried to put that other life behind me, Kate. It wasn't nearly as good as old Moncrieff makes it sound. It was lonely, damn lonely. You'd wake up in the middle of the night, covered with sweat, wondering why you were scared. In Havana just after the siege ended I realized what was bothering me. An ensign in our company—he was only seventeen—was killed in the last night's fighting. I was undone for weeks. I couldn't sleep. I barely ate. I was mourning him—like a son. That's when I understood those midnight sweats. It wasn't getting killed that worried me. It was leaving nothing behind me, Kate. Nothing—nobody—but a few old drinking friends like Moncrieff."

Jonathan Gifford took a poker and stirred the dying fire. It blazed for several moments and Kate could see the grief etched on his face as he continued.

"I thought I'd changed that—found the kind of life I wanted— with your mother. But little by little, she turned from me, Kate, and tried to take you and Kemble with her. She made me feel like a stranger again. I suppose some of it was my fault. There was some calculation in our marriage—your mother had quite a fortune—but it wasn't the main thing. So help me. She made it the main thing by twisting it that way in her mind and heart. What happened at the Shrewsbury—was the end of it, not the beginning. I suppose that's why I couldn't—I had no feelings left for her, Kate."

"But for me and Kemble you still—"

"More than ever, I suppose, after I lost your mother."

"Is it true that Viscount Needham—in Antigua—tried to send her back? He—he didn't love her?"

"He told me that—in a letter. He swore he never encouraged her to—to go."

"What will happen now, Father—in the war?"

"I don't know. I still think the Americans can win. They are starting to panic. That could beat them. But Washington doesn't look like a panicky man. He could make the difference."

"Anthony says Americans are cowards."

"Doesn't that make you angry, Kate? You're an American. They can talk all they want in London about English colonies. Americans are a separate people. Your people. I never tried to talk politics to you, Kate, but this goes beyond politics. Americans are fighting for their self-respect, their lands, their future—all the things the Irish have lost."

"You know, Father, I think you are more Irish than you realize."

"Maybe you're right."

"And more American."

"I wish—I hope that's true."

For another hour they sat there talking about Ireland, England, America, the war, what these large words meant to them as human beings, what they meant to others—Anthony Skinner, Charles Skinner, Kemble. Jonathan Gifford shared memories and feelings with Kate that he had never shared with anyone before. He told her about the day his mother got up from her sickbed and cooked a big meal while his father was at the law courts. She put it in a basket and sent him down to one of Dublin's back alleys to give it to her brother's family. There were ten of them living in two rooms. It was his first glimpse of the savage, demeaning poverty in which the Catholic Irish lived. He told her how strange the Americans seemed to him at first, their wildness and lack of discipline, how long it took him to realize that this was part of their freedom. Gradually that wall of discretion and diffidence which so often frustrates honest speech between parents and children dwindled into insignificance. It would never entirely disappear, of course. Between Kate and Jonathan Gifford there would always be the distance of their very different generations. But that night in the fall of 1776 Kate and her father became friends. For the first time since her mother's death she felt she could talk to him with perfect trust.

"I feel—like I've been on a long journey—and now I'm home," she said as she kissed him goodnight. "Not the same person. But the same home."

CHAPTER FIVE

THE FOLLOWING morning Jonathan Gifford, his head aching from too much rumfustian, saw Moncrieff and his rolling wine cellar off to his regiment's bivouac, somewhere up the New Brunswick road. He had scarcely returned to the tavern when another old friend was confronting him with a very serious expression on his face. Charles Skinner took his seat at the Squire's table in the bay window of the taproom and asked Captain Gifford why he had changed the name of his tavern.

"It says what I think, Charles."

"You are making a mistake, Gifford. It could cost you this tavern, possibly your head."

"Are you telling me that if the British win this war, it will be a crime to use the word 'liberty' in America?"

"I hope not. But you know as well as I do, it has become a party word, a rebel war cry."

"All the more reason for honest men not to abandon it."

"Perhaps you're right," Charles Skinner said, although it was clear that he had no enthusiasm for the political point Jonathan Gifford was making. The Squire took a formal-looking piece of parchment from the pocket of his coat. "I will thank you to post this on your tavern door."

It was a copy of Lord Howe's peace proclamation.

"You may tell all and sundry that I will be here each day from noon until 3 p.m. I have accepted Lord Howe's request to serve as his deputy for this part of New Jersey. All those who swear the stipulated oath before me will promptly receive the King's forgiveness and protection. I hope they know me well enough to be assured that there will be no reproaches, no reflections on anyone's conduct if he agrees to become a peaceful citizen once more. An early peace—the earlier the better—is what we must have, Gifford. It's our only hope."

"Of what?"

"Of restoring civil government. Getting the army off our backs. I hope you will be among the first to accept this pardon, Gifford."

Jonathan Gifford shook his head. "In the first place, I don't think I've done anything that requires a pardon. In the second place, I don't think all the pardons in the world can get the army off our backs. The army is still in Ireland, a hundred years after they surrendered. It'll be the same story here, I guarantee you. If Washington's army breaks up that won't be the end of the war. This country will be like Ireland multiplied by thirteen for the next fifty years. In the third place, I don't think Washington's army is going to break up. I still don't think the British can win the war, Charles."

"You are trying my friendship, Gifford, by God, you are trying it to its utmost."

"I know I am. What are friends for, if they can't tell each other what they think and feel?"

"True enough. But I think you're half mad, Gifford. I think you've let that son of yours destroy your judgment."

"I could say the same thing to you."

Skinner retreated to the assembly room, where he spread his sheaf of blank pardons on the table and waited for customers. The talk of the taproom that day was a threnody on New Jersey's abandonment. Jonathan Gifford tried to fight the tide of defeatism with common sense. He pointed out how much of America remained to be conquered. Pennsylvania alone was five times the size of New Jersey with twice the population. Washington could retreat almost indefinitely, while behind them the supply lines of the pursuing British became longer and longer. A few men listened to him. But more listened to Charles Skinner.

Leading the procession was our Harvard hero, Lemuel Peters, and his confrere, Ambrose Cotter. Not far behind them was Esek Duycinck, the major of our militia regiment. Colonel Slocum's brother Sam resigned as county court judge and swore obedience to His Majesty a day or two later. (I have always suspected he did it on orders from the Colonel, so that he would have a friend on the other side.) Reports from travelers passing through Liberty

Tavern from other parts of the state made it clear that pardon seeking was becoming epidemic. The numbers of submitted were in the thousands. But peace did not return to New Jersey.

On December 21, about two weeks after Charles Skinner began issuing pardons, and just about the time when the pardon seekers were multiplying ominously, a band of masked men attacked Daniel Slocum's farmhouse at midnight. They dragged sixteen-year-old Peter Slocum, the boy who had whipped Kate, into the night. At dawn he was found stumbling about the yard of Liberty Tavern, half mad with pain and horror, his right hand cut off at the wrist.

He was carried into the tavern, where Dr. Davie quickly stanched the flow of blood and cauterized the wound. Kate rushed to the room where he lay moaning in delirium and assisted Dr. Davie until his father and brothers came to take him home in their farm wagon. Daniel Slocum was incoherent with rage and grief. The sight of Kate produced a stream of obscenities. He called her a Tory bitch, a slut, a whore. Kate stood there, head bowed, enduring the tirade. But Jonathan Gifford was not so patient.

"She had nothing to do with it, Slocum."

"But you did, I wouldn't be surprised, you goddamned double-crossing English trimmer."

"This does your lad no good," Dr. Davie said. "He has had a fearful shock. He needs rest, quiet. Take him home."

Slocum let his two oldest sons carry the boy downstairs. His farewell was aimed at Kate. "Tell your Tory hero he will lose more than his hand for this."

A few minutes after the Slocums drove away, Charles Skinner arrived to issue the day's pardons. With undisguised anger in his voice, Jonathan Gifford told him what had happened. Skinner's lips went ashen. He called for a glass of brandy. "I know nothing about it, Gifford, so help me God I know nothing," he said, gulping the fiery liquid as if it were water.

"I'm sure of that. But he's your son. To most people it's beyond belief that you don't know."

"I have no authority over him," murmured Charles Skinner. "This little task I perform for government here gives me no power over anyone or anything."

"You'd better tell him that Americans are not people to take that sort of treatment. If he thinks he can terrify them into obedience, he is very wrong."

"I agree," said the shaken Skinner.

But Anthony Skinner was through listening to his father. He issued a proclamation, announcing himself as colonel of the district's loyal militia. Every man in the county was required to enroll or be considered "an enemy of his King and country." With an escort of loyalists in which the Bellows family were prominent, he roamed the district appointing captains and lieutenants and openly gloating that soon Daniel Slocum and his friends would be standing before royal courts, criminals with nooses practically around their necks.

In Liberty Tavern's taproom, fear was visible on every face. Men talked in low, discouraged voices. Nat Fitzmorris told Jonathan Gifford that now he could not even persuade the ten men who had followed him to New Brunswick to turn out. Daniel Slocum stayed on his farm, drunk most of the time, according to Fitzmorris, who rode down there to ask him for instructions. Jonathan Gifford found himself wishing that Kemble was home. They desperately needed someone who could say stirring things about the Cause.

"I will grant the lobsterbacks this much," said Samson Tucker. "They have behaved themselves. Them tales of ravishing virgins and looting every house on Staten Island had me fearing the worst. After all, a man with five daughters has got to think about such things."

"I'm told we may sing a different song if the Germans come this way," Jonathan Gifford said.

Two days later, the Regiment Knyphausen from Hesse-Cassel marched into Liberty Tavern's yard. We crowded onto the porch to get a look at them. They wore dark blue coats with black cuffs, yellow waistcoats, and white breeches. Their black hats were lined with yellow. The whole effect was darkness and it perfectly matched their manner of marching—like wooden soldiers in an evil fairy tale. British and American soldiers marched alike, slouching along in ragged, irregular lines. Not so these haughty mercenaries. The officer on the lead horse raised his hand. They came to a stop in the yard with a double stamp of their feet. An order was barked in German and they rested their arms and looked around them with greedy, contemptuous eyes. The officer

—a major—dismounted and marched—he was that stiff—to the door of Liberty Tavern, where Jonathan Gifford stood watching the parade.

"You," said the officer. "Food."

"Can you pay for it?"

"Pay?" The officer's stolid features registered bafflement.

"Money. *Geld.*"

Rage transformed the German's face. "Damned American rebel," he snarled.

"No money, no food," Jonathan Gifford said and repeated it in German, "*Kein Geld, kein Essen.*"

"*Hier ist Geld,*" snarled the German and flung a bag of coins at Jonathan Gifford's feet.

He picked it up and asked the German how many dinners he wanted.

The German held up five fingers. Jonathan Gifford took some coins out of the bag and handed it back to him. The Major wheeled, barked an order, and the regiment broke ranks.

The Major was joined by four younger officers. They ate a hearty dinner of ham, veal, fresh fish, and vegetables, washed down by flagons of beer. While they were eating, Charles Skinner arrived, and tried to introduce himself to them. The commanding officer showed no interest in being friendly. "No English," he said, and Skinner retreated, his feelings not a little hurt.

Outside, we were watching the regiment's baggage wagons arriving in the tavern yard. They were loaded with loot—furniture, clothing, bedding—presided over by their camp women, who glared at us and howled curses if we came too close to their treasures. Most of the Germans spread out into the fields around the tavern and began cooking their dinners. Suddenly we heard a scream from the direction of the Gifford residence. We raced toward the sound, followed closely by Jonathan Gifford and Charles Skinner. On the porch we saw Kate wrestling with two grenadiers with oily black mustaches and high-crowned brass caps. They were trying to steal the mahogany chest containing her mother's silver.

One of the grenadiers was about to strike Kate in the face when Jonathan Gifford bounded up the porch steps, moving with amazing speed for a man with a bad knee, and struck him a blow in the jaw that sent the fellow reeling head first off the porch into the December mud. He staggered to his feet, bellowing murder, and his friends in the regiment came running by the dozens. So did the officer who had ordered dinner.

"*Was ist? Was ist?*" he roared. The soldiers cowered before him, jabbering in German. He stamped up on the porch and opened the chest. His eyes came aglow at the magnificent silver imported from England. He turned to the other thieving grenadier. "*Schwein*," he roared, and struck the fellow in the face with his open hand. Then he put the silver chest under his arm and said to Jonathan Gifford, "I will take, rebel."

"You will do no such thing," thundered Charles Skinner, blocking the Major's path. "This man is no rebel. He is a good peaceful citizen going about his business. Even if he is a rebel, you have no right to rob him."

"*Was? Was?*" roared the Major, his pale face flushing. He shouted an order and a half-dozen soldiers seized their muskets, fixed their bayonets, and rushed to his assistance. Mr. Skinner found himself confronting a ring of deadly steel.

"Let him go, Charles," Jonathan Gifford said.

"But it's Mother's—" Kate cried.

"I know—"

The Major strode back to the tavern and displayed his prize to his fellow officers. They murmured their appreciation. Only one of them did not seem to approve his senior's theft. He spoke sharply to him in German. The Major snarled an answer in which the word "rebel" was used several times. He obviously believed that rebels deserved neither mercy nor justice.

After dinner the Germans broke into Isaac Low's dry goods store and hauled out bolts of cloth, spools of ribbons, boxes of pins, bonnets, and piled them into their wagons. Poor old Mr. Low—he was in his sixties—was too frightened to say a word. We filed back into Liberty Tavern, the most dejected, humiliated human beings I have ever seen. I was only a boy of sixteen. No one expected me to do anything. But even I felt the shame of it. It was a sickening sensation. It was centered in the pit of the stomach and seemed to suck energy from the rest of the body. Your head drooped. Your brain felt like a cold, soggy sponge in your head. It was like losing a night's sleep and trying to get through the next day without it. That is how it feels to be part of a defeated people.

We sat there all afternoon while people wandered into the taproom bewailing their losses. The Germans were like a swarm of locusts going down the road. Every farmhouse within a mile of their march was plundered. It made no difference which side a man was on. Richard Talbot lost two cows and a horse and his family's silver. Ambrose Cotter lost all his dishes, even though they were only cheap pewter, and had two windows smashed because he had nothing else worth stealing. Cotter had flourished the protection given him by Charles Skinner. "I might as well have used the bark of one of my trees," he said.

One of Clement Billington's neighbors rushed in looking for Dr. Davie. The Hessians had started looting Billington's house and he had shot one of them. They had bayoneted the old miser a half-dozen times and left him for dead.

"What are you going to do about it?" asked Jonathan Gifford. He spoke in a quiet, almost offhand voice while filling a tankard with ale.

Heads jerked up, eyes blinked dazedly at the question.

"What can we do?" whined Cotter.

"He's right, Captain," said Samson Tucker. "What can a handful do against the whole British army?"

"He's right. He's right," went around the taproom.

"It seems to me you've got two choices," Jonathan Gifford said. "You can let the Germans and Anthony Skinner's friends beat you up and rob you until they are tired of it. Or you can give them a taste of their own medicine. You've still got guns on your walls and horses in your barns."

"Who's to take care of my wife and kids if I'm caught and hanged?" asked a man who had already accepted a royal pardon.

"What will happen to them if they grow up thinking their father and his friends are cowards—if all Americans—and New Jerseymen in particular—are cowards?"

"It's easy for you to talk, Gifford," Ambrose Cotter said. "You stand here pouring out drinks for Whigs and Tories alike."

"I know it," Jonathan Gifford said. He looked him steadily in the face as he said this, accepting the insult—and forcing them to accept the possibility that he was telling them the truth.

A little after eleven that night, after Jonathan Gifford had called out his familiar "Time, gentlemen, time," and the last drinkers were adjusting their cloaks and setting their hats for the cold December night, Black Sam emerged from the kitchen to whisper in Jonathan Gifford's ear. "There's two men over by the barns. They want to see you."

"Who are they?"

"I don't know. I think they're army men. Our army."

"Take them down to the house and give them a drink."

A half-hour later, the front door bolted and the taproom spotless, Jonathan Gifford asked Barney McGovern to join him and they walked down to the house to find two men in blue coats and mud-spattered buff breeches before the fire in the living room. Between them was an almost empty bottle of brandy. The man on the left side of the fireplace was at least six feet four and had two pistols strapped to his waist. He arose, his hand on one of his guns as they stepped through the door. The smaller man on the right was obviously in charge. He was in his late forties with a grim pockmarked face and dour dark eyes.

"Gifford?" he asked.

Jonathan Gifford nodded and introduced Barney. Brigadier General William Maxwell introduced himself and his huge aide, Major Aaron Ogden. Maxwell spoke with a thick Scotch burr. "Washington said you were a safe man. We've got a message for Colonel Slocum and no time to ride about Colt's Neck in search of him."

"Give it to me. I will take it down to him."

"He is to call out every man he can muster and attack the enemy's supply wagons, boats on the Raritan, shoot up their sentries."

Jonathan Gifford told Maxwell the blunt truth. "I'm not sure how many men he can raise. Most people have practically surrendered. They think that Washington has deserted them."

"Not so, not so," Maxwell said. "He is planning a capital stroke this very moment against the Germans posted along the Delaware. But to gain its full value, we must do something around here to make their royal rears feel less safe."

"If you brought some regulars with you—even fifty of them—it would make a big difference."

"We don't have a man to spare—or a shoe to march them in. If you can only raise a hundred men, spread them thin and make the British think it's a thousand. If our plan works, we can clear west Jersey and most of the south. But it all depends on making them think that there's trouble at their backsides."

By the time General Maxwell killed the rest of the brandy, he was a little drunk. He damned Congress for not giving Washington a decent army to fight the British. "You can't get the militia to fight without kissing their goddamned asses," he said. "But we will do it for the country's sake, right, Ogden?"

Major Ogden nodded. He looked at the General with pure admiration on his young face. He was a hero worshiper. But Jonathan Gifford saw a man who was too inclined to let liquor console him for the way the Americans were fighting the war. A professional soldier with twenty years in the British army, Maxwell was enraged by the incompetence of the Continental Congress. He called them "the sixty generals" and denounced their constant meddling in military strategy. The Scotsman's exasperation helped Jonathan Gifford put his own critical attitude toward the American conduct of the war in better perspective. He saw that it was a waste of breath to rant about what had been done wrong.

General Maxwell departed unsteadily for Springfield, where he hoped the Essex County militia was gathering. Jonathan Gifford and Barney McGovern rode in the opposite direction, to Daniel Slocum's farm at Colt's Neck. The small two-story main house was dark, but there was a light in the ell that jutted from the rear. As they dismounted, a voice spoke from the dark part of the house. "Move and you're a dead man. Who are you?"

"Gifford, from Liberty Tavern. Barney McGovern's with me."

In the kitchen they found Slocum's two oldest sons with loaded muskets. Beside them sat their brother Peter, the sleeve of his shirt flopping over his missing right hand.

"Where's your father?"

"In the ell. He's been drunk for two days."

"Take me to him. I've got a message for him—from Washington."

The ell was a series of storerooms. Slocum sat in one of these, a jug of home-brewed applejack—commonly called Jersey lightning —beside him.

"What's this, Gifford? What are you here for?" he mumbled. "Come to 'rest me? Shoot the bastard, boys."

"He ain't come to arrest you, Pappy. He's got word from General Washington."

"Shit on Washington, goddamn Virginia bastard—leaving us here—"

Slocum tried to stand up. He got halfway to his feet and tumbled back into the cane chair.

"Get me a bucket of water from the well," Jonathan Gifford said.

At a nod from his oldest brother Peter Slocum performed this chore. Jonathan Gifford took icy water and flung it in Slocum's face.

"*Goddamn you, Gifford,*" roared Slocum, temporarily sober.

"Sorry I had to do that," Jonathan Gifford said with a grim smile. "General Maxwell left orders from Washington for you at Liberty Tavern. You're to turn out the regiment immediately and attack the British at Brunswick, Amboy, and along the Raritan."

"Who does that crazy bastard think we are, the Iroquois? I can't turn out a man. We're licked, Gifford. They'll hang me and these boys here. You've got friends in the British army, Gifford. Let them do what they want to me, but not the boys—"

"You're not licked. Washington's still got an army and he's ready to do something with it, if Howe spreads his regiments thin enough. That's where he wants you to help. Keep them busy back here so they don't pay too much attention to what's happening on the Delaware."

Slocum shook his head. "Can't turn out a man—"

"You can now. The Hessians came through here today. They looted every farm within sight of the King's Highway. You've got men who are mad enough to fight."

"Is that the truth?" Slocum asked his oldest son.

"I don't know, Pappy. We been here all day on guard."

"It's the truth. I saw it with these two eyes," Barney McGovern said.

Slocum shook his liquor-soddened head. He picked up the bucket and handed it to his youngest son. "Fill it again," he said.

It was December. Though the weather remained surprisingly mild by day, it was seasonally cold by night. Slocum sat there, jaws clenched, and had three more buckets of that icy water flung in his face. He stumbled into the kitchen and bellowed for his wife. A frightened-looking woman in a calico nightgown appeared from a bedroom just off the kitchen. "Get me some dry clothes," said Slocum, "and make me the strongest goddamn pot of tea you've ever made, old woman."

Jonathan Gifford did not miss the irony of the great Whig, Colonel Slocum, drinking tea, but now was not the time for sarcasm about minor matters.

"How many men do you think I can raise, Gifford?" said Slocum, changing his clothes right there in the kitchen while his wife stuffed green tea leaves into a large earthenware pot.

"At least a hundred. Maybe two hundred."

"And then what? We charge the British camp at New Brunswick? Two hundred against five thousand?"

"I think it would be fatal if you tried to operate as a regiment. The Sixteenth Dragoons would hunt you down and carve you up in a day. Better to operate in groups of twenty or thirty with specific assignments. You must put some men on horses and have them patrol the roads so you will know when wagon trains are coming up from Amboy. Station riflemen at likely spots along the Raritan. If they pick off the pilot or the helmsman of a ship, she may run aground and block the channel. Send five or ten men to potshot the sentries at Brunswick and Amboy. It doesn't matter whether they hit anybody. The point is to keep them excited, wondering if they might be attacked the next day by five hundred or a thousand. You must have a central place to gather, where the men can get some food and drink and fresh orders."

"Where would that be?"

"The tavern is dead center. If we work out a system—a hut in the woods where they can stack their arms—I think we might be safe enough."

Mrs. Slocum put a steaming mug of tea in front of her husband. He drank it down in one long swallow.

"All right," he said, "let's get to work."

That was the closest Colonel Slocum ever came to thanking Jonathan Gifford for giving him a plan that was infinitely beyond his own military capacities. Nor did he thank him for volunteering Liberty Tavern as our partisan headquarters. For the first two weeks of December there was, I must admit, little to be thankful about. Captain Gifford's hopes of turning out a hundred or two hundred men proved much too optimistic. The number was closer to twenty-five and never more than fifty. Colonel Slocum took anyone he could get on any terms. I volunteered on his promise that I could serve secretly. My father had forbidden me to join the militia. Captain Gifford decided I might make a rifleman. He spent a day in the woods teaching me to fire one of those long-barreled monsters from Pennsylvania. He had a half dozen of them in Liberty Tavern's armory. I turned out to have some talent as a marksman. Don't ask me why. It has something to do with the mysteries of the nervous system.

In the next few weeks I picked off a half-dozen helmsmen on British sloops coming up and down the Raritan. One ran aground and blocked the channel for two days. It was not the kind of war I had pictured myself fighting in my boyish dreams. It was hard to hate those distant figures on the decks of the ships, hard to believe I had killed or wounded them as they slumped to the deck without a sound. It made a human life seem cheap.

British dispatch riders and officers out for exercise, or on a visit to a young lady with loyalist leanings, frequently heard bullets whistle past their ears. The sentries around Amboy and New Brunswick spent more than one nervous night challenging every breeze that blew a tree branch, after a volley from a half dozen of our boys.

But most people only thought about rescuing themselves from the wreck of the Revolution in that gloomy December of 1776. Pardon seekers continued to stream into Liberty Tavern to stand before Charles Skinner, one hand on the Bible, the other raised high while they swore they had quit the militia and would henceforth remain "in peaceful obedience to His Majesty." Cornelius Talbot, who had been the closest thing to an independence man that the Talbots produced, took a job as an assistant commissary with the British army. Anthony Skinner and his loyalist militia captured Richard Stockton, one of New Jersey's signers of the Declaration of Independence, not far from Liberty Tavern. He was hiding on the farm of a local friend. A few weeks later, we heard that Stockton had signed one of Lord Howe's pardons and issued a statement urging everyone else in New Jersey to do the same thing. When Anthony Skinner mustered his loyalist regiment at Kemble Manor, three hundred men appeared. Skinner told them the war was over, and the time for punishing the "criminals" would soon be at hand.

Early in the fourth week of December, Jonathan Gifford received an invitation from Charles Skinner to join him for "an old-fashioned English Christmas" at Kemble Manor. Kate refused to go. Jonathan Gifford pleaded the extraordinary number of wartime travelers and the not entire untruth that Kate was more or less housebound. Toward the end of the day he rode down to the manor to have a Yuletide drink with his old friend. Captain Gifford found the Squire sitting before the fire in his library, drunk and alone. My father had also made excuses, and with a burst of independence that surprised me, had forbidden my mother and Sally to go without him. Anthony was celebrating Christmas with British army friends in New Brunswick. Caroline was upstairs in her bedroom. She was so disconsolate about the collapse of the American Cause, Mr. Skinner feared for her health.

"To what a pass these madmen on both sides of the water have brought us, Gifford," Charles Skinner said.

Jonathan Gifford nodded and sipped a glass of brandy while his friend descanted upon the danger of women becoming involved in politics. Their emotions were too violent, their natures too fragile.

"And Anthony talks about Americans like an Englishman," Skinner sighed. "I don't remember hating the Frenchies. They were good fellows, brave enough—" His big head drooped. "'Tis this war—a civil war. The worst kind."

Jonathan Gifford picked up the brandy decanter and put it on a sideboard. "Lay off this stuff, old friend," he said.

In the center hall, the moment he closed the library door, a troubled voice called to him. It was Sukey, Caroline Skinner's maid.

"Captain Gifford, do you have any news?"

Sukey's black skin gave her small, heart-shaped face a special solemnity. She was a very intelligent young woman. Caroline had taught her to read and write.

"News of what?" he said warily.

"Of General Washington. Mrs. Skinner is so upset. If there was the smallest reason to hope—"

Involuntarily, Jonathan Gifford looked over his shoulder at the library door. Even a hint of what Brigadier Maxwell had told him about Washington's plans might reach British ears from this house. But he was surprised by the strength of his sympathy for Caroline Skinner. He would trust her.

"Perhaps if I spoke to her in private—"

Sukey led him upstairs and asked him to wait in the hall while she vanished into Caroline Skinner's bedroom. The black girl left the door open a crack and he heard Caroline exclaim, "Oh no, Sukey, no. My hair—my dress—"

He could not hear Sukey's reply. But a moment later she was beckoning him into the room. It was a combination bedroom-sitting room, furnished in Queen Anne style, the draperies and the curtains around the canopy bed in matching light blue. Caroline Skinner was standing by the window fussing with her hair. "I am ashamed to face you, Captain Gifford," she said.

She looked ill. Her face had dwindled, giving it a pathetic child-like cast. Even in the gray light of a late winter afternoon, he could see she was deathly pale.

"Mrs. Skinner," he said, "the Squire told me how troubled you are."

"I can imagine how he put it."

"He may not share your political opinions. But he is genuinely concerned for your health."

She dismissed these words with a despairing wave of her hand. "It is so hard to bear, Captain Gifford. The thought that Americans will be considered contemptible by all of Europe."

"I suspect that is something you are hearing from Anthony."

She nodded. "Perhaps that aggravates my feelings." She looked at him with eyes that seemed close to tears. "Is there no hope?"

"Of course there's hope," he said in a low nervous voice, hoping that Sukey was not listening just outside the door. "Washington is planning an attack in a day or two. All we need is a single victory and the country will take heart again."

"Did you say—'we,' Captain Gifford? I never heard you use that expression before." A smile transformed her face. "I like it."

"I'm glad—but I wish—"

"What?"

"That you wouldn't—allow the fortunes of war to invade your mind—your feelings."

"I can't help it. I used to think that we could control our feelings. Now I begin to wonder if we are really responsible for them."

"Up to a point—we're not, I'm afraid."

"Yes—up to a point," she said, a mournful note rising in her voice.

He touched her hand for the briefest moment. "Goodbye," he said.

Outside, he found sleet blowing on a northeast wind. He turned his horse's head homeward, his mind far away along the Delaware with Washington's men. The river would be choked with ice. It would be difficult to cross. They would move by night. He suddenly wished he was with them, ruined knee and all, a musket on his shoulder. He hated this role he was playing. It made him feel not only dishonest but helpless. He understood (he thought) what Caroline Skinner was feeling—what every woman must feel in war—the helplessness of the spectator, sharpened in her case by feelings that were as passionately hungry for victory as any Son of Liberty in Washington's ranks. Strange how talking to her ignited similar feelings in him.

What else did she ignite, Captain Gifford? he asked himself wryly. She was so different from Sarah. It was still hard to believe they were sisters. But she was a pretty woman and it had been two years now, two long dry widower's years..

The import of what he was thinking, or half-thinking, struck him like a stone flung up by his horse's hoofs. He almost reined in Narragansett Jack at full trot—which might have been fatal to either him or the animal. It was as if his very muscles and nerves cried out *Stop.* Charles Skinner was one of his oldest and closest friends.

I begin to wonder if we are really responsible for our feelings. The memory of those words spoken by that soft, sad voice gnawed at his will. But we are responsible for our acts, he told himself, and drove the rest of the way home in gloom as gray and total as the lowering winter sky.

CHAPTER SIX

JONATHAN GIFFORD DID not sleep very well that Christmas night. He was up at 3 A.M. prowling his greenhouse. Was it a kind of premonition or simply the instinct of a veteran soldier that made him suspect with something close to certainty that this was the night Washington would attack? It was the time when an over-confident enemy would be most likely to expect a peaceful respite. The weather was foul. The northeast wind continued to drive snow and sleet across the state. He shuddered to think of Kemble exposed to such punishment. Kemble or any other American. The regiments he had seen march past Liberty Tavern during the November retreat were wearing summer clothes.

What fools the Americans were, to think that they could end the war in one or two battles and beat the biggest and best army Great Britain ever sent overseas. But reflection softened his asperity. Almost every war began with expectations of quick triumph on both sides. The Americans were new at the game, new at everything. Think how difficult it was to graft two kinds of roses. The Americans were trying to blend thirteen different species into a single immense flower.

The next day, the twenty-sixth of December, the news began to seep across the icebound, snow-swept state like a soft breeze from never-never land. Hearts, hopes, unfroze, rejected the news as impossible, and leaped like colts in springtime when it was confirmed.

"True, aye, true, so help me God," said mud-splattered shivering Abel Aikin at the bar of Liberty Tavern. He took a great gulp of Scotchem, holding the steaming mug in both numb hands. Jonathan Gifford seldom served this drink, which consisted of applejack, boiling water, and a hefty dash of ground mustard. He considered it closer to a medicine than a refreshment. But Abel's half-frozen state justified the potion. Our mailman had become an army dispatch rider when the post office ceased to function in New Jersey. He shuddered as if he were still out there in the winter wind. "True we took the town of Trenton and twelve hundred of those unconquerable Hessian heroes at eight o'clock yesterday morning. Damn me if it isn't true. I saw it with my own eyes."

"By God," roared someone in the back of the crowd, "let's go get our guns and shoot up the British at Brunswick. We can't let Washington do all the work."

There was a roar of agreement and a surge out the door. All across New Jersey, as the news filtered through the countryside, resistance flared. British dragoons carrying mail and messages were shot down on the roads. Anthony Skinner and his friends no longer roamed our neighborhood with such confidence. Shots were fired at the manor house and he stationed a company of his loyal militia on the grounds, at great expense, to guarantee his own safety. There was news of a fierce battle between a militia army and a brigade of British at Springfield and the ambush of a regiment of Germans near that same town, almost directly north of us.

On December 30 came word from New Brunswick that the British were rushing reinforcements across the state. They were determined to smash Washington's army and revenge their defeat at Trenton. Washington had recrossed the Delaware and announced his intention of doing battle with them for the possession of New Jersey. We huddled over Jonathan Gifford's army maps in the taproom of Liberty Tavern, wondering what Washington would do—or could do. Reports had ten thousand British troops advancing on him. Unless the Americans fought far better than they had in any previous battle except Trenton, the prospect was extremely alarming.

Late that night Cornelius Talbot arrived with news that dispelled these larger military matters from the minds of Liberty Tavern's family and friends. You will recall that he had become an assistant commissary—a buyer of food and firewood—for the British army in New Jersey. He had been captured at Trenton but General Washington had given him a parole of honor on his promise to remain neutral for the rest of the war.

"I really think," said the fellow, shivering before the big fireplace in the taproom, "that I got off because he wanted me to deliver this to you, from General Putnam."

Jonathan Gifford ripped open the dirty envelope and read Israel Putnam's scrawl.

Olde Frend,
   Com atto ounce fore yore lad. He is dedlie sicke but wont quitt tho he cann butt breethe. He is withe the arme.
                                                                    Putnam

"Where is the army?" Jonathan Gifford said.

"They may be in the Delaware, for all I know," said Talbot. "I left the morning of the British advance, and a devil of a time I had of it ducking bullets along the way."

Jonathan thanked the neutralized Mr. Talbot and gave him a pint of brandy to warm him on his way home. He rushed across the snowy lawn to the residence and awoke Kate. He showed her the letter. "Will you come with me?" he asked. "Barney's out with the militia. Kemble may need a nurse—"

"When do you want to leave?"

"Now."

"I'll be ready in ten minutes."

"I'll have the sleigh hitched in the tavern yard."

Ten minutes later, Kate climbed up beside him on the sleigh. Bertha, Sam's wife, stood beside it in the snow, declaring she was ready to come too. "I raised that boy from a baby, Captain. If he's sick he needs a mother and I'm the only one he has now."

"Someone's got to run the tavern, Bertha."

Jonathan Gifford turned to Sam, who was standing on the other side of the sleigh. "You're in charge, Sam. Here's the key to the money chest in my office. Keep a loaded gun handy and don't let anybody push you around."

"I'll do my best, Captain," said the dark voice.

Jonathan Gifford flicked the reins of the two-horse team and they trotted into the night, their bells jangling. A saw-toothed wind blew out of the north. Captain Gifford wore a bearskin matchcoat but the cold seemed to penetrate it as if it were summer silk. Kate was wearing a fur muff and fur-lined boots and a cloak lined with marten fur. The same thing happened to her.

Within minutes she was in agony. The cold penetrated each lash wound on her back with devilish skill.

By dawn they were on the Princeton road. They had scarcely gone a half mile when they collided with an incredible sight—the entire British army—ten thousand men—slogging toward them through the snow, staggering with weariness. A squadron of the 16th Dragoons was at the head of the column. A young lieutenant dashed forward, saber in hand. "What the devil are you about, man? Talk fast or I'll hack you in two."

Jonathan Gifford calmly identified himself and told him where they were going. The Lieutenant looked skeptical. He was about to order them to turn around when his commanding officer, Colonel William Harcourt, rode up. "Gifford," he said, "what in God's name are you doing out in this weather?"

Jonathan Gifford explained his mission. Harcourt was immediately sympathetic. "You'll probably find your boy somewhere about Princeton. There was some nasty fighting there yesterday morning. Washington gave us the slip, got into our rear, and tore three of our best regiments apart. I'm afraid he's taught us a damned hard lesson." He sighed. "Not the last lesson I fear we must learn before we quit this detestable war."

Jonathan Gifford carefully concealed his emotions. "Would the rebel army be at Princeton then?" he asked.

Harcourt shook his head. "Only their sick and wounded and some of ours, poor fellows. It was a damn bloody fight. We lost a half-dozen officers and a good hundred men. Washington moved off for New Brunswick. That's where we're heading to protect our stores. We had no alternative but this forced march, which is likely to put half the army in hospital. The countryside is so damn hostile, we were afraid they'd join Washington and storm the place if we didn't get there first."

Colonel Harcourt did not know that his old friend Gifford was one of the prime reasons why the British thought the countryside was so hostile. Our little war of harassment had made a large impression on the enemy high command.

Harcourt held out his hand. "I must get back to the head of the column. I hope you find your boy."

Jonathan Gifford edged his sleigh to the side of the road and pushed west against the flow of the column. More than once he had to rein in his horses to avoid a man who toppled out of the line of march unconscious from cold and exhaustion. He wondered what he would do if anyone tried to seize his sleigh to transport these casualties. A glance beneath the heavy canvas on the floor would reveal two quarts of brandy, warm blankets, a ham, a thick cut of beef, and other nourishing food. But the officers kept the men under very tight discipline. Dropouts were picked up, slapped in the face, given a gulp of rum, and pushed back into the column.

At the rear came forty or fifty British wagons that forced Jonathan Gifford off the road. The first were full of wounded men who cried out in pain at every rut.

"Dear God," said Kate, "it's like watching a procession from hell."

Finally the road was free and a feeble winter sun broke through scattering clouds. Jonathan Gifford used his whip and soon had the sleigh skimming down the road to Princeton. About noon they rested the horses and heated some tea over an open fire. They gulped it down with bread and butter and were on their way again. Toward four in the afternoon they saw the roof of Nassau Hall looming above the bare branches of the trees and were soon on Nassau Street. Jonathan Gifford hailed a sparely built young man who was hurrying past them in the snow and told him whom he was looking for.

"I have so many sick and wounded I could not begin to remember their names," said the young man. "My name is Rush, Dr. Rush. I came here as a volunteer and find myself running a hospital."

"This man had no rank. He was attached to one of the generals, I would think."

He showed him Putnam's note.

"Oh yes, I remember him now. I saw him in Philadelphia. Pale as Banquo's ghost with a wracking cough. I told him he had a fever and should go to bed directly. But he ignored me. Everybody ignores doctors until it's too late."

"Where *is* he?"

"He is in the same house with General Mercer and Captain Fleming. You cannot miss it. It's a big farmhouse on the Trenton road, just this side of the stone bridge. Most of the fighting took place around the barn and orchard—no one has buried the bodies. I fear this young lady—"

"Did you say Captain Fleming was among the wounded?" Kate asked.

"Among the dead, more likely, by now. Do you know him? He was the commanding officer of the regiment. Imagine it, at twenty-one. All the other officers sick, wounded, dead."

"Thank you, Doctor, we'll find the house."

In five minutes they were riding across the battlefield. Grisly memories welled up in Jonathan Gifford, the awful slaughter of Ticonderoga, where the dead and dying lay in piles before the walls; the carnage on the Plains of Abraham, where men were torn apart by murderous point-blank fire; the putrefying corpses around Havana. Now they saw men in red coats, others in blue, and others in simple homespun sprawled in odd frozen shapes, in an orchard, in the fields before it, and around the barn and a rail fence beyond it. Two or three dead horses lay in the midst of this human carnage. Burial parties were at work, picking up the dead and lugging them to wagons in the road for transportation to unknown graves.

"I thought I'd seen my last battlefield," Jonathan Gifford said.

"I hope this is it," Kate said.

They stopped before the farmhouse and sat there for a moment watching the burial parties loading a wagon just ahead of them. "Won't anyone even say a prayer for them?" Kate asked.

"Their mothers and fathers will," Jonathan Gifford said.

In the farmhouse, a fat distracted woman met them by the stairs. She was the wife of the owner of the farm. He had fled British-occupied Princeton and was somewhere across the Delaware. Kemble Stapleton? There were so many sick and dying soldiers in the house, she did not know one from another. They would have to look for themselves.

In the first room they saw General Mercer sitting up in the bed, his face and head gashed by three or four awful bayonet wounds. He recognized Jonathan Gifford and smiled faintly. Captain Gifford expressed his sympathy. Mercer brushed it aside with a shake of his head. "We won the day. That is all that matters," he whispered. He was a dying man.

In the next room, John Fleming lay on blood-soaked sheets, his breath coming in shallow gasps. Kate cried out with grief when she saw him. He looked dazedly up at her. "Is it really you, Miss Stapleton, or am I already in heaven?"

"No, no, it's Kate," she cried, kneeling beside him.

"Stay with him," Jonathan Gifford said. "I will go look for Kemble."

"When I heard—about you and Mr. Skinner, I gave up all hope that you—"

"It was what I deserved," Kate said, tears streaming down her face. "You were right to forget me."

He shook his head. His breathing was becoming more and more shallow. "I wanted to tell you that day in the garden—how serious I thought it was—principles—I was going to say they were—life and death. I thought you would have laughed at me—now perhaps—"

"I have changed—I am changing," Kate said. "I am coming over to—to my country's side."

"That gives me great satisfaction—"

He closed his eyes, as if the sight of her made death almost unbearable for him. "I think I would give eternity for a month in Virginia with you, Miss Kate."

"We may have it yet."

He shook his head. "Hold my hand. Hold it—please."

She held his cold hand and watched him die.

Upstairs, Jonathan Gifford was standing beside another bed. Kemble stared up at him with wild fever-haunted eyes. "You aren't my father. I have no father. Only a two-faced Englishman who says he's my father."

A strangling cough convulsed the thin body and all but obliterated consciousness on the death's-head face. He was little more than a skeleton in ragged filthy clothes. Jonathan Gifford called for Kate. She did not come. He went downstairs and found her kneeling beside John Fleming's corpse, weeping.

Gently, he drew her to her feet. "Kemble's upstairs," he said. "Let's save him—if we can."

Kate was appalled by the pallid ranting skeleton she found upstairs. While Jonathan Gifford held Kemble's arms, she forced brandy down his throat, then wrapped him in clean blankets and helped her father carry him downstairs. Outside, darkness was falling and with it more snow. They laid Kemble on the floor of the sleigh and started home. Before they were an hour on the road, the snow was whirling and roaring in a wild blizzard. Every fifteen minutes or so, they stopped to force brandy on Kemble. But he became more and more listless. His hands and feet were appallingly cold.

"He's dying," Kate said.

"Freezing," Jonathan Gifford said.

Without a word he stripped his bearskin matchcoat from his shoulders, wrapped it around Kemble, and lay down beside him. "I will warm him with my body," he said. "Pile the blankets on top of us." Kate obeyed, creating a furry cocoon. She took the reins and urged the weary horses into the storm. All night they stumbled forward. Jonathan Gifford lay there with his arms around his son, listening to him babble deliriously. Often Kemble spoke to his mother.

"Not your fault. Like all Americans—the British. It was his fault—both their faults. Both British— They will pay. They will both pay, Mother."

Then he would be on some battlefield giving orders, weeping when Americans broke and ran. "My countrymen, my countrymen," he cried.

Next he was back ten years in a boyhood nightmare. His mother had been incurably superstitious. She frequently lamented that Kemble had been born on Whitsunday. There was an old saying, "Born on Whitsunday, born to kill or be killed." There was only one way to lay the supposed curse—the child had to undergo a mock funeral, complete with a coffin, at the age of ten. The sensitive, highly imaginative boy had been terrified by the idea and Jonathan Gifford had sternly vetoed it. This had led to his first violent clash with Sarah.

"Don't put me in the coffin, Mother, I'll be good," Kemble whimpered. Then he was in the West Indies with Sarah, talking about breadfruit trees, the dangers of the tropical sun. Warning her. "Mother, be careful." Weeping again. "You didn't say goodbye—"

A cry from Kate. The sleigh came to an abrupt stop. Jonathan Gifford crawled from beneath the blankets and the matchcoat to find a sizable tree had fallen across the road. In the windy darkness, with fingers that refused to obey him, he had to unhitch one of the horses, lash a rope around the tree and drag it off the road. It took a half-hour to finish the job and get the horse back into harness. Mounting the sled to hand the reins to Kate, he found her crumpled on the front seat, asleep. He tried to arouse her but she was too exhausted to respond. He placed her beside Kemble, heaped the matchcoat and blankets around them, and took the reins himself, with nothing but an old broadcloth coat to protect him from the savage wind.

About an hour later they were challenged by a sharp "Halt. Who goes there?" A British light infantry squad surrounded them. They were on the outskirts of New Brunswick. In the darkness they had missed the Perth Amboy road. Jonathan Gifford drove into the British camp and found his old friend Moncrieff, who swiftly persuaded one of the British quartermasters to exchange two fresh horses for the exhausted team that had been pulling the sleigh. With this reinforcement, they practically flew the last ten miles to Liberty Tavern.

There, all three travelers were ordered to bed by an appalled Dr. Davie. Jonathan Gifford was on his feet in a day or two. Kate took more than a week to recover from the ordeal. But Kemble was the real patient. Dr. Davie found pleurisy in both lungs. The old Scotsman ordered a strong fire in his room day and night and hot flannel on Kemble's chest to be changed every half-hour. "The lad must sweat, sweat, sweat," growled the dour physician. "It's his only hope, and a damn slim one."

Bertha, Black Sam's wife, and Molly McGovern responded magnificently to this challenge. No patient in history ever had more devoted nurses. They abandoned all their duties in Liberty Tavern's kitchen and elsewhere to the hour-by-hour struggle for Kemble's life. It lasted almost two months. More than once in the first six weeks he seemed to be strangling. Blue veins stood out in his temples as he gasped for every breath.

In his desperation Dr. Davie summoned all the powers of light and darkness to aid his patient. He appealed to Archaeus, a benevolent demon, supposed by Paracelsus to look after the body's functions in sleep or delirium. He wrote certain words in Hebrew on a plate, washed them off with wine, added three grains of citron, and forced the mixture down his patient's throat—an old remedy used by Eastern Jews. He hired boys to thrash the woods and drive away any and all owls because their cries supposedly had deleterious effects on a dying man.

If anything saved Kemble, it was the devoted care of his nurses, and Dr. Davie's refusal to bleed him. It was a month before the fever subsided and Kemble recognized anyone. For the next week he was a barely animated corpse, washed, turned, and dressed by the women. He was still too feeble to hold a posset of milk or broth in his hand. Even when he began to breathe freely, he was still listless, engulfed in gloom. Day after day he lay there, saying nothing.

Jonathan Gifford discovered what was wrong. "I suppose you expect me to be grateful to you," Kemble said.

"For what?"

"For rescuing me. So I can live the rest of my life as a British slave."

"What are you talking about?"

"Isn't the war over? The last thing I remember was the fight around the barn at Princeton. The Philadelphia militia broke and ran. I was trying to rally them. I was sure it was the beginning of the end."

Jonathan Gifford shook his head. "Washington rallied them personally. He won at Princeton and the British were so shaken they abandoned west Jersey. They're still in New Brunswick and they've got fortified camps along the Raritan down to Amboy, which means they're all around us here. But they don't control a fifth of the state. Washington is in winter quarters at Morristown ready to contest any move they make."

Life, animation was suffusing Kemble's still gaunt face. "I thought—when I found myself here—"

Jonathan Gifford explained how they had found him at Princeton after the American victory there. "Legally you're a British prisoner. You and the rest of the sick and wounded were captured by the British when the Americans retreated. The British paroled you in Dr. Rush's custody, when they retreated."

"That means I can't rejoin the army?" Jonathan Gifford nodded. Kemble stared at the ceiling. "You're glad, aren't you?"

"Not everyone can be a soldier. Especially in an army that tries to pretend that winter doesn't exist."

"But I want to be part—"

A fit of coughing almost strangled him. His cheeks glowed with unnatural color, sweat glistened on his forehead. Jonathan Gifford helped him sit up in bed so he could get his breath.

"It's all right," Kemble croaked. "The Cause needs support here as much as on the battlefield. New Jersey will be the cockpit as long as the war lasts. Perhaps God has sent me home to be a scourge to Tories and trimmers. They stopped the militia from turning out with their lies and threats."

Jonathan Gifford shook his head. "The militia didn't turn out because they knew they couldn't win. This isn't Massachusetts, Kemble. This British army has twenty thousand men, trained men with cavalry, artillery."

Kemble glared at his father. "You're one of them. One of the trimmers. That's the kind of thinking that's ruined us."

"You've been almost ruined because your pinchpenny Congress wouldn't let Washington recruit an army big enough to give the British a decent fight. You don't win a war with spirit, enthusiasm, Kemble. You win it with trained soldiers, men who know what to do on a battlefield."

"You may have changed the name of your tavern. But deep down you still want those beloved regulars of yours to win."

"That's a damned lie, Kemble. It's the last thing I want."

"Then why are you entertaining them for dinner?"

Kemble had heard Kate and Molly talking about Major Moncrieff's visit.

"I'm entertaining my personal friends. It doesn't matter to me what color coat a man wears."

"It does to me."

In those harsh words Jonathan Gifford sensed future sorrow. Kemble's set pale lips and glittering eyes contained neither understanding nor forgiveness. But he suspected that the greatest sufferer from his son's revolutionary zeal would be Kemble himself.

Book
III

CHAPTER ONE

"FORAGING PARTY COMING from Brunswick."

Kemble Stapleton stood in the doorway of Liberty Tavern's taproom. His words emptied the place quicker than the cry of fire. Outside, men leaped into chaises and onto saddles and headed for their farms. With luck they would be able to drive most of their cattle into the woods and hide any silver or jewelry they were still so foolish as to leave around their houses. Corn, wheat, rye, oats were more difficult to hide and it would be impossible to say no sale to a grim-faced British commissary, backed by a regiment of loaded guns. The unavoidable clink of hard money would be consoling if the seller was an independence man and pleasing if he happened to be among the numerous lukewarm.

At the tavern door, Daniel Slocum clapped Kemble on the shoulder and shouted, "Do what you can, lad, I've got to see to my cows. They haven't gotten a piece of beef from me yet."

As usual Slocum was letting Kemble take the risks, while the Colonel wrote letters to General Washington telling him how vigorously his militiamen were battling the British. Occasionally Slocum joined in the skirmishing, and Kemble insisted he behaved well. But most of the time the Colonel rode off to collect more men or hide his livestock. By the time he was ready to fight, the British foraging party was safely back in Amboy or New Brunswick.

Neither Slocum's bullying energy nor Kemble's fervent political rhetoric could turn out enough men to stop a foraging party. This was hardly surprising. As Jonathan Gifford repeatedly pointed out, we were up to our hips in British soldiers. It would have been insanity to turn out the whole militia regiment, even if the men were willing—and it would have taken the whole regiment to turn back a foraging party. The wagons were usually guarded by a regiment, sometimes by two regiments of redcoats.

The most Kemble could do was harass them with a fusillade from some likely spot for an ambush or snipe at their horses as they returned to camp in the hope of cutting off a wagon. West of New Brunswick, where the militia was supported by Washington's regulars, foragers were often driven back empty-handed after pitched battles involving as many as a thousand men. That made sense. But there was little point in harassing the British in our district. Jonathan Gifford argued that it only gave the foragers an excuse to loot the countryside, something the British troops had refrained from doing at first. The Germans had, of course, continued to rob everyone with methodical thoroughness.

Kemble vehemently disagreed with his father's opinion. For him it was not realism, it was a relapse into passivity, even surrender. It was easy for him to take this zealot's attitude. Thanks to Jonathan Gifford's excellent connections in the British army, there was no need to worry about what a British foraging party might do to his property. The rest of us were not so fortunate. I will never forget the day that foragers arrived at our farm, after fighting a brief skirmish with ten or twelve of Kemble's boys about a mile away. They had two wounded men moaning on the floor of their lead wagon. The Major in command turned out to be none other than William Moncrieff.

My father met him with his usual grave courtesy. "How do you do, sir. My name is George Kemble."

Major Moncrieff was not the jolly visitor to Liberty Tavern. He was a very angry professional soldier now. "I don't give a damn what your name is," he said. "Take us to your barns. We are here by order of His Majesty to pay you good money for your produce and we get ambushed on your property. You had nothing to do with that, sir?"

"I have done nothing to encourage this rebellion," my father said. "I personally believe the violent on both sides are responsible—"

"Damn you and your political discrimination, sir," roared the Major. "I am talking about blood. Go look at the man in the lead wagon with a ball in his chest and tell me who's responsible. Your countrymen."

My father could only open his hands helplessly. "I have no control over them."

Moncrieff snorted his disbelief. "I begin to think this is a damn disloyal country."

The Major demanded some brandy and bandages for his casualties. I was told to get the liquor and cut up one of my old shirts, while he escorted the Major to the barns. A few minutes later I climbed into the wagon and saw my first wounded men. They were not a pretty sight. The man shot in the chest was dying. A red froth bubbled on his lips; the second man, hit in the knee, had drenched his white gaiters and stockings in blood. They were both in terrible pain, writhing like damned sinners on the coals. One of the wagon drivers, a fellow with the dirtiest face and hands I have ever seen, took a healthy swig of the brandy for himself before handing the bottle to the soldiers.

As I went back to the main house, I almost collided with a fat gesticulating figure charging around the corner from the direction of the barnyard. It was our Dutch foreman, Johannes Hardenburgh, so agitated there were tears in his eyes.

"Mister Kemble, Mister Kemple! Dey is steal all der ducks and chicks. I can do notting."

My father had returned from the barns and was being paid by the British commissary, a worried-looking little man with pinched cheeks and rabbit eyes. Major Moncrieff was watching. He gave poor Johannes no excuses, not even sympathy.

"The men are going to eat dinner here. We've got a bloody tenmile hike home with more fighting likely. I told them to eat well."

"I presume I will be paid—"

"You are being paid for your goddamn oats and hay. But if you don't want to see fire coming out of your barns, you will treat my men to dinner, and cook it in the bargain. It may make them look a bit more kindly on you—"

"This is outrageous," my father said. "You have only to command them—"

"I don't want to get shot in the back in our next skirmish, Mr. Kemble. Do you understand me?" Moncrieff said. "The men don't like this skulking cowardly war. They came to this miserable country expecting to set things right in a single campaign. Now a lot of them begin to think they will never see home again."

For the next two hours, our cook and our house servants, and even my mother and sister Sally, toiled in the kitchen roasting chickens and ducks. Three hundred men can eat a stupendous number of fowl. Our normally crowded barnyard was soon as empty as Egypt after the plague.

My father and I and Johannes Hardenburgh and his field hands carried the food out to our conquerors, who sprawled on the lawn awaiting our service. When they finished eating, they roamed about the property, looking for loot. They broke into the smokehouse, stealing at least a dozen hams and several sides of bacon. Next the cellar was invaded and innumerable jars of preserves disappeared into knapsacks. Those with ambitious imaginations dug up the vegetable garden, where unwise people tended to hide their silver and jewels. Poor old Johannes ran back and forth trying to keep track of what was being taken, crying reproofs and calling for my father's support. But Father had retired to his study, where he sat disconsolately fingering the lawbooks and histories he had been studying since the Declaration of Independence.

"You must get that major's name and report him to General Howe," cried my mother. Her face and neck were streaked with kitchen soot, yet she still wore her lofty London "head." Her eyes rolled violently in their sockets. She looked like a refugee from the madhouse. "Didn't you tell him who we are? Who my family is? That we are as loyal subjects as His Majesty can find in America?"

"My dear, they do not give a damn."

"Will you let me join the militia now, Father?" I asked.

"I don't know, Jemmy. Perhaps you should."

Outside muskets banged. We rushed to the window. There was wild confusion among our dinner guests as they scrambled for their guns. Kemble and his skirmishers had crept into the orchard and opened fire on the soldiers who were digging up our garden. One of them, shot in the stomach, was half-walked, half-carried to the wagons.

"My God, they will burn us for sure," my father cried.

He was right. One of the soldiers took a pine knot from our woodpile and stormed into the kitchen. He lit it from the fireplace there and flung it in   our hay barn. Major Moncrieff did not make the slightest attempt to punish him. He bawled an order. The regiment formed ranks with skirmishers on the front, flanks, and rear of the wagon train and they trudged off for camp.

As we fought the flames, Kemble and his friends raced past us. I was torn between a fierce desire to join them, to share the savage excitement that glittered in their eyes, and an honest sympathy for my father, who was in the process of losing three or four hundred pounds' worth of his property, not to mention a good portion of his health, thanks to their guerrilla daring.

I left the fire fighters—it was a hopeless struggle, the barn became an inferno in a matter of minutes—and watched Kemble and his squad pursue the British down the road and blast away at their rear guard until they all disappeared over the first hill. I don't know how long I stood there. I suddenly realized my father was standing beside me. "What do they hope to gain?" he asked.

"It's necessary," I said, and felt within me the exultant coldness of the revolutionary, ready to sacrifice everything to the Cause.

CHAPTER TWO

AT LEAST ONCE a week, Major Moncrieff rode down to Liberty
Tavern for dinner with his old friend Captain Gifford. When he
came alone, he ate with the family in the residence. When he
brought two or three junior officers with him, Jonathan Gifford
served them at the tavern in a private room. More than once, the
junior officers asked urgent questions about his stepdaughter. Was
she as pretty as Major Moncrieff claimed? When would he—why
didn't he—introduce them?

From one point of view it was better to have the officers asking
questions about Kate than about Kemble. But their interest in
Kate put Jonathan Gifford in another quandary. He had no desire
to keep Kate in social isolation. She was alone too much as it was.
Although she had physically recovered from her lashing, it seemed
to have left her with a tendency to melancholy. She spent most of
her time reading. The only person she saw, except for her father
and brother, was Caroline Skinner, who invariably arrived with an
armload of books. Captain Gifford had been a little staggered to
discover that Kate, who had never looked at anything weightier
than a novel or a magazine, was reading John Locke and the
French political philosopher Montesquieu and the English radical
James Burgh and the political-sexual exposés of Junius, the still
unidentified mystery man whose scathing public letters revealed to
a shocked world the depths of English political and moral corruption. He said nothing against this, either to her or Caroline, but
he found himself wondering if it would not do her more good to
be reassured that she had lost none of her feminine charm.

"Would you like me to invite some of the regiment's junior

officers to dinner? Moncrieff has them almost crazy to meet you," he asked one evening.

Kate shook her head. "It would only cause you trouble. Colonel Slocum will call you a traitor. Kemble will call me one."

"Slocum is already calling me a traitor because I serve Tories and British officers. Kemble is only a step behind him. But there is damn little business from Whigs these days. What else can I do?"

"I hope you are not thinking of changing sides, Father."

"What?" Jonathan Gifford said, not sure he had heard his daughter correctly. The determined look on Kate's face reminded him of someone. Kemble? No, Caroline Skinner.

"Changing sides, Father. If you are, I would not be able to follow you. The more I study the subject, the more convinced I am that we—the Americans—are in the right."

Caroline had changed Kate into a revolutionist. Her melancholy was a by-product of this change. It made her regret even more keenly her reckless leap into love with Anthony Skinner.

"I'm not changing sides, Kate. I'm glad to see you have such strong opinions. That means there is even less reason to worry about having dinner with a British officer or two. A girl your age shouldn't spend all her time reading political philosophy."

Kate threw her arms around him and kissed him with some of her old enthusiasm. "You are a dear to worry about me."

A few nights later, Major Moncrieff rode down to dinner with an invitation. "We are going to end the winter of our discontent with a ball," he told Kate. "And we are desperate for eligible young ladies. Say yes or I'll be reduced to dancing with one of my lieutenants. None of them is pretty. In fact, it's a pretty choice which is uglier."

"What do you think, Father?" Kate asked.

"I see no harm in it," Jonathan Gifford said, wishing Kemble was not glowering at the other end of the table.

Major Moncrieff had won a special place in Kate's affections. An invitation from him had extra weight. But it was Kemble who made up her mind. He began lecturing Jonathan Gifford about the dangers of letting gullible women associate with sophisticated English officers.

"Did you call me gullible?" Kate asked.

"It is not simply you. I am talking about women in general."

"You mean we are such nincompoops, we cannot be trusted to have opinions of our own?"

"If you want to put it bluntly—yes."

"Major," Kate said, "I accept your invitation. But let me warn you that I will defend the rights of my country if the conversation turns to politics."

"My dear," said Moncrieff, "if you look at my lieutenants and captains the way you are looking at me now, it wouldn't surprise me if the chuckleheads deserted to Washington in a body. If I was twenty years younger I'd go myself."

"I don't have a decent dress," Kate said. "I mean one that isn't two years old. I don't even know this year's fashion."

"I will not tolerate your buying a London dress," Kemble said. "That is against the law."

"We will supply you with a half-dozen London babies and all the cloth we can steal from the commissary," said Moncrieff. "If necessary, we'll buy a dress from some damn American who just got it off a privateer."

"A bargain," Kate said.

"By God, Gifford," said Moncrieff, "I knew you'd stand up for the old regiment, even if you've turned half a rebel. We shall lord it over those macaronis in the guards and those pretentious chuckleheads on the general's staff now, with the prettiest girl in New Jersey for our dance cards."

The daughters of a good many independence men were forbidden to attend the British ball, to the acute remorse of some young ladies. The shortage of femininity was well known and widely discussed in Liberty Tavern's taproom. Samson Tucker, with five daughters, was a divided man.

"God's bones," he groused, "I wish we could patch up a peace in a fortnight, and before the redcoats sailed home I might pick out a viscount or a baronet for one of my female tribe."

"Samson," said Jonathan Gifford, "I thought you were an all-out independence man."

"Oh, I am," said Samson. "You heard me say I want'm sailing home, didn't you? But why not take a little souvenir of New Jersey with'm? I don't see nothing wrong with having a viscount in the family. I don't believe the honorable Congress has resolved a single word on that subject."

Down at the Gifford residence, the female half of Liberty Tavern's staff was spending most of their time getting Kate ready for the ball. Major Moncrieff procured the latest London baby from New York, and Kate marshaled Bertha, Molly McGovern, and her old removed-to-Amboy New York dressmaker, Bridget Terhune, to remodel one of her 1774 dresses. This involved a vast amount of sewing and stitching. Hoops were continuing to dwindle. Sleeves were now waist length. The bodice remained low enough to shock any lady of the present generation who has forgotten how much flesh was unblushingly exposed by the leaders of eighteenth-century society. The style suited Kate so perfectly, she saw no need to seek refuge in the lace fichu that was often the resort of those to whom nature had not been generous. But she still refused to pile and powder her hair in the London style. In fact, the more she thought about it, the more she inclined toward not dressing her hair at all, but combing it straight down, and tying it with a plain ribbon as a declaration of republican simplicity.

On the night of the dance, I drove my sister Sally over to Liberty Tavern in our chaise. She—or more exactly, my mother—had also accepted an invitation to the dance, and we had spent hard money we could not spare to buy her a dress in New York. We arrived to discover Kate and Kemble arguing furiously in their parlor. Kemble refused to believe that Kate had created her dress out of one of her old ones. He was examining it like a customs inspector, demanding to know where the lace, the ruchings, the rosettes had come from. Kate was telling him to go to hell, it was none of his business.

"Listen to him," she said to me and Sally. "He doesn't even notice my hair."

My sister, with her "head" piled a foot and a half high, and wrapped in gauze spotted with paste jewels, was goggle-eyed. "Oh, I wish I could do the same thing," she said. "This damn thing itches so. And I think it's ugly."

"It is," I said, not even looking at her. I was gazing in rapture at Kate. Her dress was a dark green that both matched and modulated the green of her eyes. I saw not only its beauty, but exactly what she was trying to do—show the British that an American girl could both equal and defy London fashion. I tried to explain this to Kemble after the girls left. But he declined to listen to me.

"Going to that dance is an act of treason," he said. "It will give those damn British officers a chance to spread their charm. You don't seem to understand the real issue in this Revolution, Jemmy. England was corrupting America, seducing her step by step into their rotten luxury and knee-bending to aristocracy. She's still trying to play the game. It sickens me to see my sister—and your sister—succumbing to it."

I was awed into silence by Kemble's intensity. I even managed to work up some indignation against my sister. But my heart could not muster even a flicker of wrath against Kate. I was still half in love with her in a distant hopeless way. Perhaps it was then that I began to separate myself from Kemble, to begin to see the Revolution with my own eyes.

Major Moncrieff and six dragoons arrived to escort Kate and my sister Sally to the ball. In New Brunswick Kate was relieved to discover a surprising number of American girls in the company. The four Misses Van Horne, whose parents were considered staunch Whigs, were a picturesque enclave all by themselves, wearing dresses that were obviously just off a ship from London. Kate had gone to school with one of them in New York. When the girl caught sight of her she nudged one of her sisters and in a moment they were all staring at her as if she were a traveling curiosity. Kate found herself flushing angrily. Her whipping was obviously still hot gossip for the hypocrites.

Before the ball began, the officers staged a play. It made outrageous fun of all the American generals, from George Washington to William Maxwell. Washington was pictured as a dumb, drawling Virginian with a sword so huge it dragged along the ground. He was unable to make up his mind about anything. In one scene, he deliberated for a good ten minutes about whether to feed his horse first and have dinner afterward or vice versa. The innkeeper became so exasperated, he finally told the General to go eat hay with his horse. General Putnam was portrayed as a roaring madman making incomprehensible speeches about liberty, and writing letters so badly spelled he could not read them himself one minute later. William Maxwell was drunk from the moment he staggered onstage. He produced a bottle at a mock council of war and got all the rest of Washington's generals drunk, too. The audience roared with laughter over all this wit at American expense and Kate found herself laughing too, but not whole-heartedly.

At the ball after the play, the officers of the King's Own Regiment swarmed around her. She did not miss a dance. Major Moncrieff, who had been secretly designated by Jonathan Gifford to act as a chaperon, watched on the sidelines, beaming. Everyone was so gallant, so full of attentions, so deft at amusing small talk that an argument about politics became remote, fanciful. Kate had to remind herself that these men were the enemy, that they had given orders to fire the guns that had killed John Fleming and hundreds of other Americans.

For the first time Kate began to understand how her mother had fallen in love with one of these officers. So many of them represented a world of culture and luxury and privileged wealth, a faery world infinitely beyond the humdrum natural beauty of the New Jersey countryside. She also understood for the first time one part of her attraction to Anthony Skinner. With his endless talk of London and living in style, his fascination with rank and titles, he was a colonial imitation of these glittering gentlemen in red coats.

Thinking these thoughts behind her mask of gay chatter, Kate felt a clutch of self-doubt. Was she doomed to imitate her mother down to the final fatality? She was dancing a gavotte with a muscular captain. It was a dance that traditionally permitted another admirer to break in. A familiar face appeared above the Captain's shoulder. Anthony Skinner touched his arm.

Anthony was wearing his green militia colonel's coat with its abundance of gold braid. He wasted no time in getting to the point. "Why won't you see me or answer my letters? Is it your father?"

"My father has delivered all your letters."

"He's using you, Kate, using you against me. Don't you see how valuable it would be politically if we married now? It would make your brother Kemble look foolish. It would squelch those people who blame me for letting you get whipped."

Once more Anthony's overconfidence in his powers of persuasion and his underestimation of her intelligence were appallingly visible.

"I have changed my mind about the Revolution, Anthony. I

235

wish I could change yours. When the war ends, perhaps we can decide how much our political differences matter. For now—"

"I was afraid your father or your brother would turn your head around, Kate. You don't know what you're talking about. Take my word for it. I need you now, Kate, not after the war. I want you now. How could you forget the happiness of that night in Shrewsbury, Kate? It was our wedding night."

Kate began to weep. She saw, felt, her old longing for this man still alive within her, beside her new repugnance. She had not abandoned her desire for him; instead, she had only managed to sequester it in an unvisited part of herself while she filled her mind with politics and philosophy and women's rights. The old Kate was letting her know that she would not be so casually dismissed by new ideas, however interesting.

Major Moncrieff seemed to materialize beside them. "My dear fellow," he said, "you appear to be making this young lady cry. Please go away, or I will be forced to thrash you."

Anthony Skinner retreated. The next partner on Kate's card, a lieutenant of the King's Own, approached her with a bow as the orchestra began a *menuet de la cour*. He was a tall, rather ugly young man named Rawdon. He looked solemn to the point of utter dullness.

"It's hard to believe that these were once lively dances," Lieutenant Rawdon said. "Minuets, I mean." He began giving her a history of the four types of minuets which he claimed should now be classified as slow, slower, slowest, and dead. Even gavottes and allemandes had been slowed to a middle-aged pace. He said it was because royalty had taken over these dances and replaced their zest with ponderous formality.

These were rather startling opinions from a British officer.

"We only dance these things to prove we can do it," Kate said. "Would you like to see how Americans really dance?"

A smile leaped across Lieutenant Rawdon's wide mouth, giving him a rather puckish look. "I would like to see Americans do something besides shoot at me," he said.

"Let us talk to old Jacquelin."

Jacquelin Dupuy was the best fiddler in the neighborhood. He had been recruited into the orchestra. "Jack," Kate said to the white-haired Frenchman. "This gentleman does not believe I can dance him down in a country reel."

236

Jacquelin looked worried. "The General said—"

"I will tend to the General," said Lieutenant Rawdon. "Get to work, old man."

Old Jack stepped to the front of the podium and struck up one of the fastest reels in his repertoire. Most of the ladies looked dismayed. With their absurdly high heads, their panoplies of hoops and stays, such violent activity was beyond them. Reels were only danced at private homes, where women were in "undress"— without hoops. Those who tried to match Kate's pace soon staggered off to the left and right, gasping. Red-faced colonels and puffing majors joined them with relief, aghast at how exhausting an American country dance could be. They were soon joined by spavined captains and lieutenants. In fifteen minutes Kate and Lieutenant Rawdon had the floor to themselves. They might have danced for another hour, if Major General James Grant had not intervened.

Grant was in command at New Brunswick. He was a short squarish man with a pug nose and bulldog mouth encased in rolls of flesh. He stomped to the podium and waved Jacquelin into silence. "I thought I gave an order that we were to have none of these American dances. This stamping and jigging is not appropriate to His Majesty's officers."

Old Jacquelin and the rest of the orchestra seemed to think they might be shot at sunrise. They stammered out an explanation, pointing to Lieutenant Rawdon. "He what?" roared General Grant.

He thundered down the ballroom to Rawdon. "I will see you at my headquarters tomorrow, sir. You will, I hope, explain yourself."

"I can explain it now, General. This American Amazon challenged me to an endurance contest. I felt the honor of the regiment, not to say the army, was at stake."

"Are you jesting with me, sir?"

"Only halfheartedly, General," murmured Rawdon.

"Sir?" roared Grant. "I think you had better retire to your quarters."

"Would you care to join me, Miss Stapleton?" said Rawdon. "We will take along your fiddler, and continue our dance there."

"It is the least I can do," said Kate. She turned to Grant. "It was entirely my fault, General."

237

"I am not interested. Mr. Whatever-his-name—will explain himself to me in the morning."

Rawdon strode to the podium and invited Jacquelin to join them in his quarters. The old fiddler hesitated and said he would lose his night's wages. "I will pay you double," Rawdon said.

As Rawdon walked to the door with Kate, Moncrieff and most of the officers of the King's Own Regiment blocked his path. "It's bad enough that you talk back to a major general," Moncrieff growled. "But if you think you can walk out of here with that young lady—"

"I was about to invite you and the rest of the officers to join us, Major," said Rawdon. "Why else would I hire the fiddler? In my opinion General Grant has insulted me—which he has a right to do—but he has no right to insult Miss Stapleton. As I see it, we have no alternative but to withdraw from this party in a body."

"I have no use for Major General Chucklehead," Moncrieff admitted. "And there's something in what you say about insulting—" He looked anxiously at Kate. "Do you feel insulted?"

"Yes!" said Kate good-humoredly. She was ready to say anything to avoid another encounter with Anthony Skinner.

"Then go we shall."

Rawdon was living with two other lieutenants in a house vacated by a Whig committeeman who had fled New Brunswick ahead of the royal army. Kate retired to a bedroom and dispensed with her hoops. Rawdon stood Jacquelin on a chair and Kate danced her favorite reels with the officers taking turns for another hour or two. Rawdon and everyone else but Kate drank heroic quantities of port between dances. The house was almost as well stocked with liquor as Liberty Tavern.

No one but Rawdon was able to match Kate's pace, which was odd, because he looked and acted so ungainly. But when he started to dance he was all lightness and grace. "You know," he said at the end of one reel, "I think I deserve some reward for defending your honor in the teeth of Major General Grant. I would like it now because I may be shot by tomorrow night."

"You shall have one," said Kate.

She conferred with Jacquelin and with his help began singing one of the favorite songs of the Revolution, "The Banks of the Dee." The song described the plight of a lonely young lady strolling along the river yearning for her lover who had left her to go "o'er the rude roaring billows" to fight the "proud rebels" of America. Kate sang it to Rawdon with the exaggerated gestures and expressions used by the actors in the play when they parodied the Americans.

Everyone thought it was funny except Rawdon, who somewhat drunkenly said he would give ten years of his life if Kate would make the last stanza come true. In a sweet tenor voice he sang this reprise which told how "time and prayers" would restore the hero to his beloved.

> *"The Dee then will flow, all its beauty displaying,*
> *The lambs on its banks will again be seen playing,*
> *Whilst I with my Katie am carelessly straying*
> *And tasting again all the sweets of the Dee."*

"Oh no," said Kate, ignoring his amorous looks, "I will only be content when you sing the American version."

"What's that?" someone asked.

"You haven't heard it?" She signaled old Jacquelin and he took up the melody once more.

> *"Twas winter and blue Tory noses were freezing*
> *As they marched o'er the land where they ought not to be.*
> *The valiants complained of the fifers' cursed wheezing*
> *And wished they'd remained on the banks of the Dee.*
> *Lead on, thou paid captain! Tramp on, thou proud minions.*
> *Thy ranks, foolish men, shall be strung like ripe onions*
> *For here thou hast found heads with warlike opinions*
> *On shoulders of nobles who ne'er saw the Dee."*

The officers roared with laughter. "A hit, a good hit," they cried. She suspected that they were really laughing at Lieutenant Rawdon. He seemed oblivious. He sat there, gazing up at Kate with a drunken smile. "I agree with every word," he said. "Every word."

"We must get this young lady home, or her father will challenge me, and if that happens I'm a dead man," said Major Moncrieff.

The officers commandeered two carriages and drove Kate home singing "Yankee Doodle" at the top of their voices. When they arrived, Liberty Tavern was long closed. But this did not stop them from banging on the door and roaring for the innkeeper. A bleary-eyed Barney McGovern finally opened the door, and Jonathan Gifford appeared, stuffing his shirt in his breeches, a few moments later. He invited his 3 A.M. visitors into the taproom and served them some of his best port—which none of them needed. Kate described Rawdon's clash with Major General Grant, giving an excellent imitation of that pompous martinet.

"You remember the chucklehead, Gifford," said Moncrieff. "He attacked Fort Pitt with eight hundred men in '58, lost four hundred, and got himself captured."

"I was there, and saw him hiding under a bush," Jonathan Gifford said. "Then he gets up and tells Parliament he can conquer America with five thousand men."

"Right. That is our chucklehead," said Moncrieff. "The man's an ass. But this fellow—" He pointed ominously to Rawdon. "He'd better learn the difference between an ass and an ass who's a major general. Damn me if we aren't out hunting hay and oats every day next week, on account of you. Getting potshotted by bloody militiamen, some of them living right here in this tavern, I think."

"Sing us 'The Banks of the Dee' again, Miss Kate," said Rawdon. "So I can at least die happy."

Kate obliged him. Rawdon rose, swaying. "Miss Kate, I must tell you, the Dee is my native river. I was born on its banks."

"Alas the poor Dee," said one of the other officers and began dragging Rawdon to the door.

"But it's not the Scottish Dee. It's the one in Wales. That's the way my luck runs."

They dragged Rawdon into the night, telling him he would need all the luck in the regiment to survive his interview with General Grant tomorrow. Kate stood at the door laughing and waving to them until their voices faded into the darkness.

"You look like you had a good time," Jonathan Gifford said.

"I did. Thank you for making me go, Father."

"How would you like a rum toddy?" he said. "I'm going to fix one for myself to put me back to sleep."

Kate said she would welcome one. They sat and talked as friends as well as father and daughter. Kate told him her feelings about the British officers as she danced with them, how it had helped her understand some of her feelings for Anthony Skinner.

It had also helped her understand a little more what had happened between him and her mother.

"I think without realizing it you became an American, Father. In ten years you became an American and that made you seem dull and foolish to her. And all the time it was she—who was foolish. She must have been hard to love, Father."

"No, it was easy at first. Later—it wasn't all her fault, Kate. I fear I'm not—an especially loving man."

"You will never convince me of that after what I saw at Princeton."

Jonathan Gifford's voice grew thick with emotion. "I was trying to save his life."

"I saw Anthony tonight."

"Yes?"

"He made me very unhappy. I still felt this terrible longing for him, Father. Not as he is now but as—he—we—might have been. A regret for losing him. I'm glad I saved his life, Father. It would have been terrible if they hanged him."

"Yes."

"I've learned a lot in the last six months, Father. But I look at Aunt Caroline and I ask myself, where has all her knowledge gotten her? It didn't help her make a happy marriage."

"People change, Kate. It's hard to see into the future, especially when we make decisions that bind us for life."

Kate started to weep. "That is what I am afraid I have done. I still love him, Father. What am I going to do?"

Jonathan Gifford took both her hands and held them for a long time. "I know how you feel, Kate. It isn't easy to stop loving someone. Maybe it's even harder to stop regretting that you gave your love to someone. We don't have that much control over our feelings. But at your age, there is every reason to hope—to expect —that a new love will replace the old one."

He meditated somberly on his drink for a moment. "Before this is over, Kate, I think you may find it impossible to love Anthony Skinner."

CHAPTER THREE

THE NEXT MORNING, Kate found Kemble waiting for her at the breakfast table. A glance at his furrowed forehead told her he was spoiling for an argument. Jonathan Gifford sat tensely between them, obviously expecting one too.

"And how was it last night in the enemy camp? I heard those drunken louts bring you home well past midnight."

"I had a lovely time in the enemy camp. And they were not drunken louts, they were drunken gentlemen."

"Did you pick up any intelligence worth passing on to General Washington?"

"Oh yes," Kate said, "I was a very diligent spy. I persuaded one of General Howe's aides to take me on a stroll, and while he was distracted by a rebel attack I made a map of their whole camp on my instep with a piece of charcoal. But I made the mistake of dancing a country reel and the whole thing became a sticky blur."

"Very funny."

"It was a perfectly innocent evening, Kemble, I assure you," Jonathan Gifford said.

"I do not share your moral perception of the matter, Father."

"Morals have nothing to do with it."

"I think they have everything to do with it. How am I supposed to rally the patriots in this part of New Jersey when I have a sister who spends her nights dancing with English officers? Who's going to trust me? Can you imagine what the Slocums will say?"

"For the tenth or eleventh time, Kemble, I see no point in this talk of rallying the people when the British army is all around them. Let Washington take care of that in west Jersey. All you've done with your rallying here is infuriate the troops and encourage them to loot and burn."

"And for the tenth or eleventh time, I am telling you that I find this a disgusting doctrine. You have no blood relationship to this girl. If anyone is her elder in this family, I am. I forbid her to see another British officer. If she disobeys me, she may find out again how that lash feels."

Kemble was the complete fanatic now. Kate was stunned by his ferocity, then deeply hurt. She and Kemble had always been closer than the average brother and sister.

"I can't believe you would even say such a thing, Kemble," Kate said.

"I will not only say it, I will do it."

"Kemble," Jonathan Gifford said, "until you apologize to your sister—and to me—you are not welcome at this table. From now on you will eat your meals in the tavern kitchen."

Kemble stalked to the door. "The less I have to do with either of you, the better it will be for me—and the Cause."

"You see, Father," Kate said, "I told you it would cause trouble."

"Let me worry about that," Jonathan Gifford growled. He was finding it harder and harder to tolerate Kemble's headstrong style. He seemed to go out of his way to pick quarrels with his father, as if he were trying to prove something to himself as much as to the Slocums and their followers.

Relations between father and son deteriorated even more over the next two weeks as Kate slipped back into her melancholy isolation. Thomas Rawdon and several other officers of the King's Own Regiment made repeated attempts to see her. Rawdon was particularly strenuous. He sent her bouquets of flowers, jars of perfume, a set of Chinese silk scarves, a gold locket, a silver bracelet, and a pearl necklace.

"The fellow must be New Brunswick's favorite customer," Jonathan Gifford said.

Kate returned all these gifts with polite notes of regret. Rawdon appeared at the tavern and begged to see her. Jonathan Gifford carried his note down to the residence.

"He says he got shot at three times on the way down. He's literally risking his life—"

Kate shook her head and went back to her book.

243

The gunfire was, ironically, Kemble's responsibility. Day and night he rode through the countryside urging real or potential Whigs to join the irregular war against the enemy. It was April, the trees were budding, the bushes thickening. There were hundreds of places between Amboy and New Brunswick where a man could lie by the side of the road and be invisible to an approaching horseman. One shot well placed and the British army was minus a lieutenant, a captain, a major. A company, a regiment was decapitated. Kemble had it all figured out mathematically. If every Whig in the county killed one British officer between now and June, the royal army would be a leaderless mob, ready and eager to surrender.

The loyalists had a reply to this guerrilla resistance. About a week after Kemble's partisans began sniping from ambush, Jonathan Gifford was awakened by a fist pounding on the door of his residence. He looked out the second-floor window and saw that the house was surrounded by horsemen carrying pine torches.

"Gifford," shouted a voice which he instantly recognized as Anthony Skinner's. "Tell your son to come out with his hands up or we'll come in and get him and show him no quarter."

"What are you talking about?"

"He's under arrest for breaking his parole and persuading others to break the King's peace here in New Jersey."

Jonathan Gifford was sure that Kemble, who was sleeping in exile at the tavern, would be awakened by this uproar and have no difficulty getting out the back door and across the brook into the woods. To make sure, Captain Gifford delayed the loyalists for several minutes on the porch by insisting that Anthony Skinner could not enter his house. He allowed Joshua Bellows and a half-dozen other men to search the residence. They found no trace of Kemble but they had better luck the next night. They surprised Nathaniel Fitzmorris in his bed and dragged him off to New York, where he was held without trial in the Sugar House, the worst of that city's several prisons. Two nights later they tried to seize Daniel Slocum but he was ready for them. Guns blazed from every window of his house. With Kemble's help Slocum had gathered a company of militia to defend the place. At daybreak they sallied from front and back doors and drove Skinner's outnumbered partisans into undignified flight.

But not even Colonel Slocum could keep sixty men on duty

indefinitely to preserve his high-ranking skin. For the next few weeks he and Kemble and other militia officers led a fugitive life, seldom sleeping at home and returning to their farms to work by day with guns never far from their hands. About a half-dozen others besides Fitzmorris were captured in spite of these precautions. The loyalists did the same thing elsewhere in the state. Soon there were between fifty and one hundred New Jersey leaders in the Sugar House. Ex-prisoners of war captured in the 1776 fighting around New York and recently exchanged carried back shocking stories of beatings and starvation.

In our part of the state, Colonel Slocum was among the first of the independence men to give the loyalists a taste of their own medicine. On the last night of April he ordered Kemble to organize twenty-five men with horses. Slocum joined them on the road with about ten of his own numerous clan. They rode swiftly into the heart of loyalist territory around Kemble Manor, until they were within a half mile of the Bellows farmhouse. Leaving their horses, they advanced on foot and surrounded the house. At a signal from Slocum, they smashed in the doors and windows with axes and burst into the house, catching Joshua Bellows, his son George and his two brothers asleep in their beds.

They were dragged downstairs to the kitchen in their nightshirts. "Joshua Bellows," Slocum said, "you are hereby arrested by order of the honorable Provincial Congress of the State of New Jersey for the crimes of treason and kidnapping. You are to be transported to a prison in Morris County where I assure you that you will be treated as your British lords and masters are treating Nat Fitzmorris and other patriot captives in New York."

"Oh no, please—" cried a woman's voice from a bedroom off the kitchen.

"My wife is ill, it may be her death," Joshua Bellows said.

"You should have thought of that before you kidnapped men like Fitzmorris, with no regard for his wife and two babies," Slocum said,

"I'll go in his place," George Bellows said.

It struck Kemble and many of the men as a fair exchange. The son was close to Fitzmorris' age. But Slocum had other plans for him.

"No, you shall not go," he said. "But you shall not go scot-free either, you bastard. Where is my son Peter?"

"Here, Father," said a voice in the back. Peter Slocum stepped forward, his right sleeve flapping over his missing hand. It was the first time Kemble realized the boy was with them.

"Was he one?" Slocum asked, pointing to George Bellows.

"He was. I remember the size of that belly." The boy rubbed the stump of his missing hand. "Aye, he was one of them, all right."

"Hand me an ax," Slocum said.

"No, Jesus God, no," Bellows screamed. He tried to break through the crowd and was flung back to the open space before the hearth.

"Take my hand, take both of them," his father Joshua said. "He's learned the weaver's trade this past year. His wife's a Quaker. He's quit the war. He hasn't ridden out with us once since Christmas, I swear it."

"Shut up," Slocum said.

"Spare him, please, in the name of the God of mercy," cried a woman's voice from the hall which led to the front of the house. It was Bellows' wife. Kemble turned to see a small frantic woman struggling through the crowd. She was about seven months pregnant.

"Put his arm on the table there," said Slocum.

No one moved. Most of the men Kemble had brought with him were losing their stomach for this brand of retaliation. But a half-dozen burly Slocums shouldered their way past Kemble's volunteers, flung Bellows into a chair, and pinned his arm to the table.

Colonel Slocum turned to Kemble. "Stapleton," he said, "your sister was the cause of my boy losing his hand. It seems to me you should strike the blow that evens the score."

Kemble looked down at the squirming pulsing piece of flesh on the table. He heard the Quaker wife whimpering and praying a few feet away from him. *Necessary* echoed in his mind like a great tolling bell. For a moment he recoiled from it. Then he looked into Slocum's face and vowed he would match the dark animal strength he saw there.

He touched the blade of the ax to George Bellows' arm just behind his wrist, raised it high, and brought it down with all his strength. The room rang with Bellows' scream.

Through a haze of nausea, Kemble saw Slocum's contorted

face, heard his mouth shouting: "WHAT WE HAVE DONE IS
NOTHING BUT WHAT THE LORD JEHOVAH TEACHES
US, AN EYE FOR AN EYE A TOOTH FOR A TOOTH A
HAND FOR A HAND."

"Oh Jesus Jesus Jesus," sobbed Joshua Bellows. "Staunch the
blood before he—"

They cauterized the wound with a hot iron from the fireplace.
By this time Bellows was barely conscious and felt no pain. But as
they trudged back to their horses they could hear at a quarter of a
mile his wife's wails. Mounting, Kemble saw that Slocum had tied
Joshua Bellows' hands with a long rope and planned to make him
follow his horse on foot.

"Wouldn't it be better to let him get up behind someone?" he
said. "We've got six or seven miles to go and it's only an hour
until dawn."

"He won't stop us," Slocum said. "He will run right along
behind us or lose half the skin off his ass."

"He's an old man. A run like that could kill him."

"Then we'll have one less Tory bastard to worry about."

"Let him ride behind me."

"He'll run on this rope like the dog he is."

"No he won't. We came out to capture this man to force the
British to give Nat Fitzmorris better treatment. It will do us no
good to kill him."

"You are high and mighty tonight, Mr. Stapleton. Did you talk
to General Putnam this way?"

"I didn't have to talk to General Putnam this way."

"Here," Slocum said, and threw Kemble the rope. "Be a milk
and water man."

They rode back to Slocum's farm at Colt's Neck, where Kemble
made sure that Joshua Bellows was given a horse for the rest of his
journey to Morristown, site of the safest jail in New Jersey thanks
to the presence of Washington's army. They watched him ride
away, escorted by a half dozen of Kemble's men. The rest went
home. Colonel Slocum invited Kemble into the house to have
breakfast.

As he sat down, Kemble realized he was alone with the Slocum
tribe. The Colonel's three oldest sons sat opposite him. Sam
Slocum and his two sons sat beside him. Another half-dozen
cousins filled the benches on both sides of the long table. Mrs.

Slocum spooned some unpleasant-looking mush into earthenware bowls and poured water on it.

"Our cows be all in the woods," she said, "too far to carry their milk out."

The Slocums began talking with savage glee about cutting off George Bellows' hand. Suddenly Kemble saw that quivering arm on the table again, heard the sound of the ax. Nausea overwhelmed him. He shoved his bowl of gruel aside. The Slocums stared at him. Most of them were scraping their bowls clean.

"Well, well, well," said Colonel Slocum, "looks like the young Squire don't like our plain fare. It don't measure up to Liberty Tavern. Just like Daniel Slocum don't measure up to his famous father, Captain Gifford of the King's Own Regiment. But he ain't got the guts to stand up to the Tories—and his son ain't got the guts to give them what they deserve. You saw him tonight, didn't you, boys? Like to threw up when he swung that ax. Face as pale as a virgin's on the first night. Then he turns around and tells Daniel Slocum what to do. Gives him orders, as if he's the Colonel."

"I thought you—"

"You haven't got a right to think, young Squire, when you're out under my command. You haven't got a right to shit unless I say so. Let me tell you this. If you ever do that to me again, I swear to God I'll shoot you down on the spot, and stand trial before my military equals in this state and tell them why. Don't think because your name is Stapleton you can tell a Slocum what to do. By the time this war is over, the Slocums are going to be worth a lot more than the Stapletons. Right, boys? Look at these lads. They never went to no college, but they'll own more land than you ever will, comes the day when we're a free country. Now get the hell out of here and think about what I just told you over ham and kidney pie at your daddy's tavern."

Kemble rode home in a state of double shock. He was sickened by the memory of George Bellows' scream, his wife's pleading prayers. He was stunned by the ferocity of Slocum's attack on him. How could Daniel Slocum be part of the Revolution, the fiercest local supporter of the Cause—and at the same time a man who aroused a deep instinctive revulsion in him? In the American future as Kemble envisioned it, there were no Slocums. America, once it threw off the corruptions of British influence, would become a nation of virtuous farmers, like Cincinnatus and Cato and Scipio Africanus, those heroes of the Roman Republic. But if Colonel Slocum resembled anyone, it was Attila the Hun.

The problem was education, Kemble decided. The Slocums lacked the education to see the America he envisioned. He would have to fight the war and simultaneously educate them. Just how he was going to do this remained obscure. He was able to avoid thinking about it because the war was like a wild horse on which we were all being hurtled into the future.

CHAPTER FOUR

THE REPORT OF George Bellows' mutilation deepened Kate's disgust with the war. She retreated even further into melancholy isolation. It was good for neither her temperament nor her health. Jonathan Gifford urged her to ride out each morning for an hour's exercise, to visit Caroline or my sister Sally. To please him Kate agreed to try it. Color began returning to her cheeks. Now and then she got a friendly greeting from travelers on the road. Most of them were loyalists or friends of loyalists. But it did her good to discover that not everyone in New Jersey considered her a pariah.

As Kate was returning to Liberty Tavern on the third or fourth of these outings, she saw a red-coated British officer standing alone beside the road about a quarter of a mile ahead of her. This was odd in itself. Where was his horse? As she neared him she recognized Thomas Rawdon. He had a peculiar expression on his face.

"Miss Stapleton," he said, in a strained voice, raising his right hand while his left remained pressed to his side. "This almost makes it worthwhile—"

"What do you mean?"

"I was coming down to see you. I'm afraid some brave fellow has shot me. My horse ran away. Could you—find me a doctor?"

"There's one at the tavern."

Kate sprang from her saddle and urged him to mount. She would ride behind him. "I've thought of you every day," he said. "Every day since—"

He put one foot in the stirrup and tried to hoist himself into the saddle. He was too weak. Kate tried to help him. As she put her hands around his waist she felt an ominous wet warmth. She withdrew her hand. It was covered with blood. "Oh, my God," she said.

"I'm afraid it's a rather nasty wound. I need a boost—"

Using all her strength, Kate managed to get him into the saddle. She mounted behind him. Fortunately, she was riding Thunder, Jonathan Gifford's big gelding, and he took them down the road without protest at a strong gallop.

"This is a rather mad reversal of the chivalrous ideal, isn't it?" Rawdon said. "Instead of knight rescuing fair maiden, fair maiden rescues knight."

He crumpled in Kate's arms and would have toppled into the road unconscious if she had not held him erect. They reached Liberty Tavern in this condition. Kate called for help and Sam, Barney, and Jonathan Gifford were in the yard within seconds, carrying Lieutenant Rawdon into the tavern. Kate's sleeves, her gloves, were smeared with his blood. She heard her father calling for Dr. Davie. She seized Rawdon's hand and squeezed it fiercely. "You mustn't die," she said. "You mustn't die."

"I'll do my best—to obey that order," he whispered.

Dr. Davie joined them and swiftly cut away Rawdon's blood-soaked waistcoat and shirt. They shuddered at the gaping wound in his side.

"Buck and ball," Jonathan Gifford muttered.

"Aye," said Dr. Davie. "We'll worry about that some other time. It's the bleeding we must stop. Get me some hot tallow."

Rawdon nodded. "I see you know your business."

"Oh?"

"I spent two years at Edinburgh."

"What are you doing killing men instead of curing them?"

"That's a long story."

Jonathan Gifford returned with a flagon of tallow melted in the kitchen oven. Without even a word of caution, Dr. Davie poured the hot wax into the wound. Thomas Rawdon cried out in agony and clung to Kate's hand.

Swiftly, Dr. Davie wrapped clean cloths around the suffering man's waist and ordered him carried upstairs to a fresh bed.

"What are his chances, Doctor?" Jonathan Gifford asked.

"I will tell you better after we probe for the ball. In the meantime, he must have clean bandages every day and all the liquids he can drink. Someone must turn him in the bed every hour or two to stimulate the circulation and prevent putrefaction."

"I will do it," Kate said.

The fact that Rawdon was coming to see her, his lack of rancor at the man who shot him from ambush, the courage with which he bore his pain aroused all Kate's loathing of war and its mindless violence. Lieutenant Rawdon became her battlefield on which she vowed to triumph against the stupidity of random death.

She enlisted Molly McGovern and Bertha to assist her. But they had responsibilities in the kitchen and elsewhere in the tavern. They had abandoned them to nurse Kemble. But they could not turn nurse for every wounded man off the road. It was on Kate that two thirds of the responsibility fell. She accepted it without a murmur. Jonathan Gifford watched with awe and admiration as she rose night after night to spend from midnight till dawn beside the suffering man's bed. She who was so squeamish she could not bear to watch even a chicken being butchered cleaned his pus-oozing wound every day and accepted without comment the other indelicacies of nursing a helpless man.

An infection sent Lieutenant Rawdon's temperature soaring. For days he was delirious and unaware of his surroundings. Then he surfaced like a drowning man and discussed his own case with amazing objectivity. He predicted each step of his ordeal, from the development of a dangerous abscess to a cruel struggle with a sinuous ulcer. He discussed the best treatment with Dr. Davie and they jointly agreed that the scalpel was preferable to the caustic powders such as the red precipitate which doctors spread so recklessly on ulcers. The surgery was painful. Rawdon ordered Kate to strap him to the bed. While Dr. Davie worked, Rawdon talked calmly to his nurse.

"I sometimes think God, if he exists, is determined to make me look ridiculous. I quit medicine because I thought it was all nonsense. Now I am depending on this good man's skill to save my worthless life."

"Why is it all nonsense?" Kate asked.

"We don't know enough. We are lucky to help three patients out of ten. I think half the treatments—especially those damn drugs—kill more than they cure."

"There's many a man in practice who's drawn the same conclusion, laddie," Dr. Davie said. "Fifty years ago, when I began, we couldn't help one out of ten. We're learning, but it's a slow business."

Cutting away the ulcerated flesh, Dr. Davie found still more extraneous matter, bits of cloth and buckshot, which he had to extract from the wound. "Whiskey," Rawdon muttered to Kate. The pain by now was exquisite. She gave him two gills from a flagon on the night table. He gulped it down and struggled for self-control.

"Do you know the point of this or anything else?" he murmured.

"Be still," she said, wiping his forehead with a damp cloth. By now it was May and the temperature in the sickroom was in the eighties most of the time.

"Are you going to suture it, Doctor?" Rawdon asked.

"I am inclined to leave it open, with a tent." Dr. Davie said. "There may yet be more discharges."

"Suture it and get it over with, one way or the other," Rawdon said.

Dr. Davie decided that he had gotten most of the extraneous matter out and closed the wound. Rawdon drank off the rest of the whiskey in the flagon and sank into an exhausted sleep. Dr. Davie looked down on him and shook his head. "A strange one. He knows not whether to live or die."

For the next week, the fever returned and Rawdon was delirious again. He recited whole paragraphs from Goethe's *Sorrows of Young Werther,* as if he thought he really was that doomed young man. At other times he babbled scraps of poetry to Kate. One day he transfixed her with mad glaring eyes and all but shouted:

> *"I prithee let my heart alone*
> *Since now 'tis raised above thee*
> *Not all the beauty thou dost own*
> *Can make me love thee."*

Most of the time his recitations were quieter, but no less melancholy.

> *"Goodnight, my love, may gentle rest*
> *Charm your senses till the light*
> *Whilst I with care and woe opprest*
> *Go to inhabit endless night."*

The third or fourth time he murmured this, Kate lost her temper. "You will do no such thing," she said, "you noodle-headed son of a bitch. After all my trouble to save your damn life."

Lieutenant Rawdon lay there, as silent as death itself for a long moment. With his eyes still closed, he murmured, "What did you say, dearest?"

"I am not your dearest, and I called you a damn silly noodle."

"But you care enough about me to curse me."

"I am cursing the time I've spent on you, when all the while it seems you are in love with dying."

"I am cured," he said. "Tomorrow I will get up."

The next day, Rawdon ate a big breakfast and reiterated his determination to Dr. Davie. The old man was appalled. Two days ago, he had read in Rawdon's skittering pulse the intimation of early death.

"It's much too soon to test your strength, laddie," he said. "There is no rush."

"I am determined to prove to Miss Stapleton that I do not want to die—even if it kills me."

"What?" said Dr. Davie. "What sort of nonsense have you been talkin' with this lad, my girl?"

By this time, Rawdon had struggled erect in bed and put his feet over the side. He stared down at these appendages and spoke to them very solemnly. "Feet," he said, "you are good soldiers, even if everything above you is a military mistake. You are hereby ordered to place your soles firmly on the floor and march." He put his left foot on the floor, and then his right foot beside it.

"Now legs, do your duty, no matter how much you dislike it."

He tried to take a step and nothing happened. He swayed like a birch tree in a windstorm. With a cry, Kate ran to him and threw her arms around him. He reciprocated and they were locked in an embrace seldom seen in a sickroom.

"I begin to think," said Dr. Davie sarcastically, "that you know more about strategy and tactics than you wish to admit, Lieutenant."

Rawdon ignored him. "Today I will walk two steps with your help," he told Kate. "Tomorrow four, the next day eight, the next day sixteen. Before you know it we shall have reached infinity, which is synonymous with heaven according to some philosophers."

"Tell it to your feet," said Kate. "I don't think they are listening."

He leaned over, balancing himself on Kate's arm, and exhorted his immobilized extremities once more. "Feet, I am ashamed of you. Another moment and I will not be able to believe you are English feet. Your duty to your country is clear. Can you hesitate to obey the patriot's call? Consider those toes, ready and willing to die for their country, regretting only that there are but ten of them. As noble as Cato lamenting that single life he was so eager to lose for Rome. Feet, remember what you stand for, the Constitution, English liberty, Protestantism. Can any honest God-fearing feet ignore such responsibility?"

Jonathan Gifford happened to arrive at the doorway of the room in the middle of this soliloquy. Dr. Davie looked at him and muttered, "I think the fever's settled in his brain."

Jonathan Gifford shook his head. "Celtic blood, that's all." The expression on Kate's face—a mixture of amusement and affection—pleased him immensely. He took Dr. Davie by the arm and led him downstairs to worry over a bottle of Madeira.

Upstairs, Kate found it impossible to be the stern nurse, as Rawdon went on lecturing his feet. "If you don't stop," she said, "I will let you go and you will dash your mad brains out upon the floor."

"Wait, I think they are responding. England's honor may yet be saved."

He took one, two tiny steps, then gave up any pretense of standing erect and collapsed. It took all Kate's strength to stagger back to the bed with him. He toppled on the pillows and murmured, "Thank God for American Amazons."

"Mr. Rawdon," Kate said, "I will not tolerate for one instant any goddamn English condescension from you."

"Condescension?" he murmured. "The Amazons were noted for their beauty as well as their strength. If I remember my mythology correctly, the queen of the Amazons sought to marry Ulysses, or was it Ajax? Or perhaps Achilles. My name is Thomas. It means twin. We are famous neither for wisdom nor statecraft nor courage. Our forte is doubting. We have a most peculiar quirk. We love to be called by our name. Would you deign to do that, Your Majesty? A dying man—and a man struggling not to die—can command certain privileges. Would you call me—Thomas?"

"I will think about it," said Kate and began marching from the room.

"It will do me more good than the combined wisdom of the entire medical faculty of Edinburgh—just to hear it now."

Kate paused in the doorway, half-wanting to laugh and still inclined to be stern, and ending as neither. "Go to sleep, Thomas," she said.

CHAPTER FIVE

IF KEMBLE so vehemently disapproved of his sister's dancing with British officers, his outrage would have been spectacular if he had known what was happening in Lieutenant Rawdon's sickroom. But he had no time to pay attention to that private struggle between love and death. He and the rest of New Jersey were too busy coping with a much older, more public passion—war. The sweet warm days of May and early June promised prime campaigning weather. Travelers from Amboy and New Brunswick reported strong signs that the royal army was preparing to march. Wagons and horses were being hired and forage scoured from the already stripped farms around both towns. Finally, the German and British regiments that had been garrisoned in Perth Amboy streamed up the road to New Brunswick to join the head of the army there.

Their numbers utterly cowed our militia. Kemble could only watch the long line of march from an upper-floor window of Liberty Tavern, his face gray with frustration. His father joined him and named the regiments as they passed. The kilted striding Scots of the 42nd Highlanders, the famed Black Watch, the 23rd, the Royal Welsh Fusiliers, the elite Foot Guards, preceded by their band in immaculate white uniforms. Jonathan Gifford noted that the officers no longer wore any insignia, and they had abandoned their silver gorgets and red sashes. It was a concession to the Americans' penchant for aiming at them in battle.

In the center of the column rode a big bulky man on a bay horse, surrounded by a cluster of officers. "That's General Howe," Jonathan Gifford said, recognizing him at once. There was just enough family resemblance—particularly the swarthy complexion

—to make the identification. The General was anything but a carbon copy of the older brother Jonathan Gifford had served. He was closer to a crude imitation, with a heavy fleshy face and a mouth much more disillusioned and sensual than the one Jonathan Gifford remembered. But the Captain realized he was judging a man in his late forties, a man who had spent the intervening years in London dissipation. Perhaps Lord George Howe would look like that if he had lived. Who knew what the years would do to any man? If someone had told Jonathan Gifford in 1758 that he would grow weary of army life, and become a domesticated husband and father, he would have challenged him for impugning his honor.

Did General Howe stop and exchange a word or two with his brother's old friend? No, Howe probably did not know that Jonathan Gifford existed. The commander in chief of a great army lived an insulated life, surrounded by swarms of majors, colonels, and brigadiers. Watching the General and his suite ride past, Captain Gifford could not help remembering George Washington's impromptu visit a year ago. He liked the easy, open style of the American commander in chief and his half-dozen boyish, smiling aides.

There was something oppressive, ominous about Howe, with his solemn dissipated face, his cloud of aides, and his heavy battalions. He did not look like a man who ever had much interest in reconciling Britain and America. In fact, according to Moncrieff and other officers, the General frankly admitted as much and blamed his older brother, the Admiral, for the carrot and stick campaign of 1776.

The following day, a stocky, balding Scot named John Honeyman appeared in Liberty Tavern and asked for Jonathan Gifford. Standing at the bar, he identified himself loudly as a butcher and asked Jonathan Gifford if he was interested in fresh meat. He shook his head. Liberty Tavern raised its own livestock.

"Washington sent me," Honeyman said in a much more confidential tone. "He's desperate to know what the British have in mind. Will they go to Philadelphia by water or land? Or up the Hudson to meet Burgoyne and his Canadians? It's a tough spot he's in because he must march every foot of the way while they can use water."

Jonathan Gifford passed the word to Kemble, and he soon had some twenty dependable militiamen bringing information to the secret room he had fitted out in the rear of the tavern's cattle barn. But the information was confusing. The British seemed to be simultaneously advancing and retreating. Boats filled with soldiers and women were pouring down the Raritan to board transports waiting at Perth Amboy. Regiments from Staten Island and New York continued to join the concentration at New Brunswick.

Washington was so uneasy, three more spies passed through Liberty Tavern in the next week, quizzing Jonathan Gifford. He had been pumping British army officers who stopped in the tavern. But even friends like Moncrieff confessed they were as baffled by Sir William Howe's intentions as everyone else.

As the last of these spies, a young, very aristocratic lieutenant from Philadelphia, explained his mission to Jonathan Gifford, a rumbling sound from the road interrupted them. They went to the door of the tavern and saw a strange procession. Over forty huge flatboats, each capable of carrying sixty men, were moving up the road on wagon frames.

"If that doesn't mean they are marching for the Delaware, I don't know what it means," said the Philadelphian.

"It could mean that or it could be General Howe's way of tempting General Washington to battle. If I were you, I would see what he does with them after they get to New Brunswick."

The Philadelphian condescendingly disagreed. He felt the flatboats were all the proof he needed. He leaped on his horse and rode back to Washington without even bothering to visit Perth Amboy, where the taverns were full of talkative British sailors from the transports in the harbor.

That night, Jonathan Gifford mentioned the flatboats to Kemble and Barney. "Someone's got to get inside the New Brunswick camp," Kemble said.

"It won't be you. Moncrieff and God knows how many loyalists would recognize you."

"I'll go it," said Barney. "I could pretend—"

"They trust Irishmen even less than they trust twenty-year-old Americans."

"Sam?" said Kemble.

"How about an ex-British officer, who's a little low on rum and wonders if the commissary general has any to spare?"

The next morning, when Black Sam brought Jonathan Gifford's chaise to the door of the tavern, Kemble was sitting in it. "If you find out anything, Washington ought to hear about it as fast as possible," he said.

Jonathan Gifford nodded reluctantly. Kemble was right. But it was dangerous. If Anthony Skinner or his friends saw him they would arrest him instantly. He decided not to argue. He flicked the reins and Narragansett Jack went up the road to Brunswick at his usual brisk pace.

The town was almost deserted. During the night the British army had marched toward the Delaware. Jonathan Gifford found the British commissary general and introduced himself, carefully dropping names of friends such as Moncrieff and Harcourt. He asked the Commissary, a rotund, red-faced man named Haliburton who looked as though he ate triple rations daily, if he would be willing to sell him some rum.

"I'm almost dry and I see that you are about to make a march. I thought you might want to lighten your supply."

Commissary General Haliburton huffed and puffed and said that while it was irregular to do such business, it was not impossible. Jonathan Gifford gave him a hundred pounds in hard money and the Commissary's cordiality increased spectacularly. He assured Jonathan Gifford that the rum would be ready for him in an hour. Meanwhile, would he like to have dinner with him? Father and son sat down in the Commissary's tent to a feast of flesh and fowl and good wine which Haliburton drank in large quantities.

"I suppose you don't have a spare wagon left in the camp?" Jonathan Gifford said. "I found my own has a crack in its front axle and I will have a devil of a time borrowing one."

"No trouble, no trouble at all. You can borrow one from me. Just have it back here by sundown tomorrow."

"I thought the General had set out for the Delaware."

"If he has," said the Commissary with a twinkle in his eyes, "he is traveling damn light. He has not a baggage nor a provision wagon with him nor one of those flatboats which he moved here from New York at such tremendous expense."

Jonathan Gifford pretended to be amazed. "What is his plan?"

"If he has one, it is to get Washington down from those damn hills and fight him to a finish. But I don't believe General Washington will be so stupid, do you?"

Jonathan Gifford shrugged. If Commissary Haliburton wanted to praise General Washington, why should he object?

An hour later they were selecting a wagon and hitching a team to it. Around them were several hundred wagons and just beyond these the squadron of flatboats. The moment they were outside New Brunswick, Kemble told his father to stop the wagon. He was going to cut across country and get their discovery to General Washington without wasting an hour. As an ex-soldier, Jonathan Gifford knew how dangerous it was for a civilian to wander through a countryside contested by two rival armies. It was late in the day. A spring chill rose from the shadowy fields. Kemble might have to spend the night in the woods. He was not even wearing a cloak. A father's concern crowded cautionary words to Jonathan Gifford's lips.

He stifled them. Kemble would go anyway. Let him go as a friend, a comrade. "Good luck," he said and held out his hand.

Jonathan Gifford did not get much sleep that night. He saw Kemble falling before the gun of a quick-triggered sentry, perhaps American, perhaps British. Arrested, hanged as a spy. The next day wore away, full of bright hot sunshine, with no Kemble. In the taproom Captain Gifford tried to look interested as Samson Tucker and his friends discussed the war.

The British and the loyalists were more confident now than they were in 1776. They had dismissed Washington's victories at Trenton and Princeton as flukes. This year, 1777, was the year of the gallows, they said, pointing to the three sevens. They were going to smash the Americans everywhere. The fleet was blockading every port on our coast. One royal army was descending from Canada, to break American resistance on the northern front. The main army was supposed to capture Philadelphia, then march north to join the Canadian army for an assualt on the stronghold of the rebellion, New England.

"What do you think, Captain?" asked John Tharp, the burly ex-Quaker turned militiaman. He had been exiled from his father's house and ostracized by his Quaker neighbors. He was living at the Fitzmorris farm, working as a badly needed hand. Nathaniel Fitzmorris was still in prison. "Will General Howe march to join the Canadian army after he takes Philadelphia?"

"If he does, it will be a damn long hike. That's what makes America so hard to conquer. It's a big country."

Jasper Clark came in with a letter from his oldest son, a captain in the New Jersey brigade of the Continental army. "He says Washington is ready to fight. They are not going to let them ramble to Philadelphia."

Listening, Jonathan Gifford was amazed to discover how much his detestation of a royal victory had deepened. How had it happened? he asked himself again. It had something, perhaps everything to do with that thin determined face beside the wheel of the wagon, glaring up at him, defiantly declaring his determination to become a man. He had to help him reach, discover, create—however it was done—that manhood. The need to share his strength with this boy-man cut through all the ambiguity of King's men and Congress's men, cut through to the heart.

Just after dark that night, a young man about Kemble's age appeared in the taproom of Liberty Tavern. He was wearing an expensive dark blue cloak that looked vaguely familiar to Jonathan Gifford. Where had he seen it? Yes—on the shoulders of George Washington. The stranger had a large head on a short stocky body; his eyes were alive with intelligence and a surprising degree of self-confidence for so young a man.

In the tavern office, the visitor introduced himself as Colonel Alexander Hamilton, one of General Washington's aides. "The General sends you his warmest regards. He wants you to know that your son is safe but a little sick. He got lost and spent most of the night in the woods. We intend to keep him with us for a few days. The news he brought was exactly what we needed and hoped to hear."

"I am sure you will make good use of it," Jonathan Gifford said. "Tell the General how much I appreciate his thoughtfulness."

Hamilton nodded. "I volunteered to reconnoiter the situation in Perth Amboy. So far we have gotten nothing but nonsense from the coxcombs we sent there. I only wish I was getting paid as well as they are."

For five days Sir William Howe and his generals maneuvered around central New Jersey, attempting to lure Washington down from the high ground around Middlebrook. General Washington sat tight. Now that he knew the British did not intend to march for Philadelphia, he saw no point in risking his army to attack them. Let the British attack him. On the steep slopes of the

Watchung Mountains they would pay dearly for it. Meanwhile, every ounce of food shipped from New Brunswick was exposed to violent harassment from American regulars and Morris County militia.

At the close of this week of stalemate, Daniel Slocum burst into the taproom of Liberty Tavern with the electrifying news that the British were retreating. At first no one would believe him. "They are on the march," he said. "I saw the head of their column pass New Brunswick. They should reach here in three hours at most."

Slocum had received a message from Kemble urging him to call out every available militiaman. "We must give them the farewell they deserve," Slocum roared exultantly.

"Why not let them go in peace?" Jonathan Gifford said. "If they are going."

"I saw it with my own eyes. They're retreating."

"Hoping Washington will follow them, so they can turn and demolish him. Slocum, you're asking your men to attack an army that's spoiling for a fight."

"Damn you, Gifford. I am the colonel of the militia in this district. If I say turn out, I don't want you arguing with me. If I find out you've told one militiaman not to turn out, I'll hang you for treason. And that includes him," Slocum said, pointing to Barney McGovern.

"The Captain has never said a word to me about turning out or not turning out," Barney said. "He lets me make up my own mind. If you're askin' me if I'll come now, the answer is yes. You're the commander of the regiment and you're calling us out."

"We'll meet at my farm at ten o'clock."

Slocum sent his sons, his nephews, his brother, and his cousins racing through the district. In spite of a steady drizzle some two hundred men turned out under the impression that the British had been routed and were fleeing down the Amboy road in a panicky mob, hotly pursued by victorious American regulars.

About two o'clock, Samson Tucker appeared at the back door of Liberty Tavern, his face streaked with black powder and caked with mud, his eyes bulging with fright and anger. "Where's Dr. Davie?" he said. "We've got poor Tharp over there in the woods with a bullet in his head."

Dr. Davie hustled across the brook. Jonathan Gifford asked

Samson what was happening. He had heard very little firing so far.

"You'll hear even less," said Samson. "I don't know who said them lobsters were beaten. Whoever it was forgot to tell them. They saw us and chased us a good two mile. We lost a half dozen of our boys. There's fifty men over there in them woods. All they want to do is get home as fast as possible."

Rain continued to drip from the lowering leaden sky. Dr. Davie came back, shaking his head. There was no hope for John Tharp. Samson Tucker began to cry. The young ex-Quaker was one of the favorite soldiers in the regiment. "Damn it, Captain, it don't make sense," he said, "sending us to attack a whole army on the march. Is General Washington crazy?"

"General Washington didn't give you that order."

"Then who did?"

"I don't know," Jonathan Gifford said. It would have been easy to blame Slocum. But Kemble was equally responsible for this madness.

"What did the army do, besides chase you two miles?"

"I didn't stop to find out," said Samson.

"Some of the men there in the woods say they're burning every house on the road," Dr. Davie said.

At first Jonathan Gifford could not believe it. It was one thing for a single regiment on a foraging expedition to burn barns and loot. But for a British army under a general's immediate command—especially a general named Howe—to do such a thing was unthinkable. Dr. Davie or the man who told him the story must be exaggerating.

Barney McGovern, equally sodden with mud and streaked with powder, came puffing around the barn to change Captain Gifford's mind. "I've never seen troops in a worse mood, Captain. They're burning and looting everything from churches to outhouses. If I were you, I'd put up the old sign and the old King's face over the bar. If you don't they'll torch us sure as rain is wet."

Jonathan Gifford stood in the center of the empty taproom pondering that sincerely meant advice. Into the silent room filtered the distant sound of drums and fifes. The British were less than a half mile away.

"I've got a better idea—I hope," Jonathan Gifford said. "Help me get three barrels of rum out of the cellar."

In ten minutes of hard work they had the barrels upright in front of the tavern. Jonathan Gifford stove them open and hung a half-dozen dippers from each of them.

"Do you still have your regimentals?" Jonathan Gifford asked Barney.

"Sure I do," said Barney. "There's a few moth holes in them and I doubt if they fit over this belly of mine."

"Get them. And get mine from the closet in my bedroom."

Within two minutes Barney was back wearing a faded red coat with the blue facings and lapels of the King's Own Regiment. There were even remnants of the traditional blue zigzag lace on his sleeves. Jonathan Gifford shrugged into his equally faded red officer's coat. The silver lace on his sleeves was relatively intact. Both coats were ridiculously old-fashioned, with long drooping tails. In 1767, the British army had redesigned its uniforms to achieve a snugger, more modern style.

As the head of the British column appeared on the road, Kate joined them at the post of danger beside the rum. "They won't make Thomas—I mean Lieutenant Rawdon—go with them, will they? It would kill him, I'm sure of it."

"Tell him to stay in bed and look as sick as possible."

A moment later they were surrounded by some two dozen men from the regiment at the head of the British column, all eager for a quick gulp of rum. As Jonathan Gifford had foreseen, the sergeants, lieutenants, and captains made no protest. In fact several of them partook of the impromptu hospitality. While they drank, Jonathan Gifford casually questioned them.

"What's in the wind, lads, are you retreating to New York?"

"Damned if I know and damned if I care if it was all the way to England," said a grizzled old sergeant, helping himself to an extra dipper of rum. "We've marched our shoes off without firing a shot at Washington and his boys."

A major came riding up roaring curses and drove everyone back into the line of march. Jonathan Gifford did not know him. He had the curt manner of those trained in the German school of the British officer corps.

"What the devil are you doing, man?" he bawled.

"I saw no harm in giving the men a little refreshment," Jonathan Gifford said. "From what I hear they've been marching and countermarching until their tongues are as long as their gaiters."

"If you were ever an officer, as that coat you're wearing suggests, I would think you'd know better than to disrupt the discipline of a march," the Major said.

"I would think if you took this coat seriously you would hesitate to talk to me in that tone of voice," Jonathan Gifford said.

"In England we don't consider tavern keepers gentlemen," snarled the Major. "Get these barrels back in your cellar or I'll dump them out myself."

"My name is Gifford," Jonathan Gifford said. "Does that mean anything to you, Major?"

"Gifford of the Fourth?" The Major's manner changed remarkably. "Well, I suppose if you want to give away your damn rum it's your own business."

"Who is Gifford of the Fourth?" Kate asked as another party of redcoats swirled around the rum barrel.

"Only the deadest-eyed, quickest man with a dueling pistol that the British army's ever seen," said Barney McGovern.

Jonathan Gifford whirled on Barney. "Didn't I tell you to forget all that, ten years ago?"

"True enough, Captain, but you just—"

"Well, forget it again."

For the next three hours Jonathan Gifford and Kate and Barney stood by the side of the road handing out dippers of rum to thirsty soldiers. The men were grateful. They flung hurried thanks and blessings on them. But the liquor did nothing to change their attitude toward the houses along the road to Amboy. Columns of smoke soon rose from that direction as well. The reason was visible with almost every passing regiment. Two or three wounded men were being half-carried, half-walked along the road.

But these casualties did not justify such savage vengeance on defenseless civilians. As smoke and flame billowed from his neighbors' houses, Jonathan Gifford grew more and more angry. Toward the rear of the royal army he saw General Howe and his staff officers. There seemed to be even more of them this time, almost enough to make a cavalry troop. They all wore glum faces. The General himself seemed to be staring fixedly at the back of his horse's head without the slightest interest in the burning houses on both sides of the road.

Jonathan Gifford limped into the road, dodged past the horses of the outer ring of aides, and reached Howe's stirrup. "General," he said, trotting beside him, "I can't believe British troops are doing this to peaceful subjects. I had the honor to serve with your brother, Lord George Augustus—"

"These are not peaceful subjects, Captain," Howe said in a thick, dull voice. "They are getting exactly what they deserve."

Behind him, Jonathan Gifford heard one of the aides indignantly asking, "Who is that cheeky fellow?"

"Gifford. A tavern keeper," another aide replied.

Dust from the hoofs of General Howe's horse and the horses of his aides swirled in Jonathan Gifford's throat. He trudged back to his rum barrels, coughing, his face saturnine. A roar of laughter reached him from the road. Major Moncrieff and the King's Own Regiment were arriving, part of the rear guard. Moncrieff was vastly amused by the sight of Captain Gifford in his old red coat. He let the regiment consume Liberty Tavern's rum while he himself went into the taproom for some vintage port.

Moncrieff interspersed his drink with denunciations of General Howe. He swore Howe had lost his nerve at Bunker Hill. "He said as much to me in the boat going back to Boston that day. There was a moment up there I never felt before. That's what he said. He spent last year trying to caress Washington into surrender. Now he doesn't know how to fight him. We should have gone up those mountains after him, let it cost us five thousand men."

"Instead you burn houses."

Moncrieff nodded glumly. "It's not like the last war. That was a good war."

"What are you going to do now?"

"It's common knowledge. We're giving up the colony. The ships are waiting for us at Amboy. We're sailing to Philadelphia."

Jonathan Gifford at first found it hard to believe. "You're really leaving New Jersey?"

"Absolutely. We're under orders to advise all loyal subjects to head for Perth Amboy without delay. You've got one of our lieutenants here. What's his name, Rawdon? Damn fool that got himself shot coming down here to see your daughter. Ignored the General's explicit orders against riding out alone."

"I'm afraid he's still flat on his back. Dr. Davie says it could be fatal to move him."

Moncrieff shook his head. "The noodle's no loss to the regiment anyway. Are you coming with us, Gifford?"

"I think I'll be all right here."

Moncrieff gave his old friend a rueful smile. "I wouldn't walk out on this place either. I might even feel the same way about this damned war if I was in your shoes." He finished his port. "Not bad," he said. "What year is it?"

"Seventeen sixty-five."

"I must remember that."

He shook hands. "I hope it never gets to sighting each other down a gun barrel."

Jonathan Gifford picked up the money for the port and slipped it into Moncrieff's waistcoat pocket. "Good luck," he said.

Outside, a weary Kate and Barney McGovern were still ladling out rum to the British rear guard. Jonathan Gifford joined them for another ten minutes. He stood there, too tired to do anything else, watching the last ranks vanish around the curve in the road a half mile below Liberty Tavern. All around him the air was acrid with smoke from burning shops and houses. Only Parmenas Corson's smithy and Ruben Husted's cooperage were unscathed—a tribute to their proximity to Liberty Tavern's rum barrels.

"Let's get rid of these barrels and see what we can do to help the others," he said.

"I wouldn't believe it if I hadn't seen it with my own eyes," said a familiar voice from the porch. Kemble stood there glaring at them. "While Americans are out there fighting and dying for their country, my father stands in the road giving free rum to the British army."

"They would have burned the tavern, Kemble," Jonathan Gifford said mildly.

"If you really want to be an American, it would have been better for you—and me—if they burned every damned building here."

Jonathan Gifford exploded. All his anger and disgust with General Howe and the British army, with the militia's lack of training and the stupid tactics of Colonel Slocum were flung at his son. "Do you think I liked doing that?" he snarled. "Do you think I like kissing anyone's ass? Who made me do it? Who guaranteed they would burn everything? You and Slocum and your idiotic mosquito attacks."

"You can sneer all you want," Kemble said. "Every burned house makes a family of Whigs."

"That is as simple-minded as your military tactics," Jonathan Gifford said.

Kemble glared at Liberty Tavern with hatred in his eyes. "I'm tempted to burn it down myself."

Those terrible words cooled Jonathan Gifford's rage. He looked into his son's face and saw a dangerous stranger. Still his son, still the thin face asking his permission to be a man. But a wall had risen between them, a wall of war. "We all can't be heroes like you, Kemble," he said.

Kate was standing in the doorway of the tavern listening to this bitter exchange. As Kemble stalked away from his father, he passed her and she whispered, "You are wrong, Kemble, wrong, wrong, wrong."

On the second floor of Liberty Tavern, Kemble was heading for his solitary room when he almost collided with Lieutenant Thomas Rawdon emerging from his supposed sickroom.

"What the devil, sir?" said Kemble, who predictably disapproved of the large amount of time his sister had been spending with this wounded enemy. "I thought you would have departed with your friends?"

"My friends? Oh, you mean the British army. Dr. Davie told me I was not strong enough to survive a march."

"Then you are my prisoner," Kemble said, drawing a pistol.

"I surrender," said Rawdon with mock solemnity. "Now, I pray you, my good man, stop pointing that thing at my middle."

"While we are at it," Kemble said, "I wish you would cease your attentions to my sister. Like all women she is very impressionable—"

"And like most men," said Kate, who had followed Kemble upstairs, "you are totally impossible. If you will permit me to live my own life, my dear brother, I will do my best to let you live yours and welcome to it."

"How can you Americans hope to win this war, with such dissension in your ranks?" murmured Lieutenant Rawdon.

While his children treated each other like enemies, Jonathan Gifford was in his chaise, racing for Kemble Manor. Caroline

Skinner met him in the center hall. He told her what he had just heard—the British were retreating from New Jersey.

"We know it already. Anthony brought the news early this morning. He is with his father now."

The library door crashed open and Anthony Skinner strode into the hall. "What the devil are you doing here?" he said to Jonathan Gifford.

Behind him in the doorway Charles Skinner wobbled unsteadily. Two Negro servants came down the stairs carrying a trunk. "There is no time to pack anything. We must go helter-skelter," he shouted to them.

"Charles," Jonathan Gifford said, turning to his old friend, "I am here to help. The state government will confiscate this property. There is only one way to protect it now. Sell it to me with the understanding that I will return it to you when the war is over."

These words sent Anthony Skinner into a hysterical passion. In one breath he denounced the English, in the next the rebel Americans. "Neither will drive me out of this colony," he roared. "Nor will I stay here and watch a scheming trimmer cadge our property from this old dru—this sick old man."

"Anthony," Caroline Skinner said. "Control yourself, please."

"I'm sorry, Mother, but this is too important for me to keep silent like a dutiful son."

Buffeted by this exchange, Charles Skinner was trembling like a man with a fatal ague.

"Please, please," he said, the tears starting down his face.

"You must do what Captain Gifford says, Charles," Caroline said.

"You will not," Anthony Skinner bellowed. "If you do, I will leave you to get to New York as best you can and consider you no more my father than General Howe."

Charles Skinner struggled to control himself. He could not look Jonathan Gifford in the face. "I don't know, Gifford. I cannot go against my own flesh and blood."

"What about me?" Caroline Skinner asked.

"I told you, madam. This is not a matter for women to decide," Charles Skinner said. "God knows, I respect your intelligence. You have made that a point of honor between us. But—"

"The legislature has already passed a law authorizing the

confiscation of loyalists' estates," Jonathan Gifford said. "You cannot fail to be the first target in this neighborhood. Is it possible that you don't trust me? I have the money. Or I can borrow it against the value of the tavern and my own land. The way prices are rising, the tavern is worth twice what I paid for it—five thousand pounds, at least."

Charles Skinner was staring past him at the lovely carved oak leaves on the lintel above his doorway. "I cannot go against my own son, Gifford. I believe with him that this remove is temporary. I will be back here before the year is out. But I must warn you that I will not come as a friend. I begin to think Anthony is right—there is no way to cut the rebellion out of this people but with a sword."

"If you come back that way," Jonathan Gifford said, "you will have to sleep with a pistol at your side every night of your life. Did you see the smoke hanging over the Amboy road today? People have lost everything they own. They won't forget who did it."

"I started life as a soldier and I'm prepared to end it as one," Charles Skinner said, "if that is what must be done. I have made up my mind, Gifford." Slowly, ponderously, Skinner turned to his wife. "As for you, madam, I cannot let you remain here alone with the countryside so aroused against us. You must come to New York with me."

"I will not!"

The words rang out in the high-ceilinged center hall as fiercely as an Indian yell. "I will not live in that stinkhole of a city as a British dependent. I am an American. This is my family's land. I intend to live on it until I die."

"I *order* you to come, madam."

"You'll have to bind me and gag me and carry me to the carriage."

"You will live here in an abandoned house, madam. I am taking all the servants with me. All the cattle, the horses, the furniture, everything we can carry. And I will not undertake to support you with a farthing."

"You may do as you please. I would rather beg along the roads than live with you in New York."

"Then I give you up. God knows you've never been much of a wife to me. A dry bitch with a barren womb." Charles Skinner sighed. It was like the sound of a dead tree falling. "We must get on with loading the wagons. When did you say we should be in Amboy?" he asked Anthony.

"Two hours. I must get back there to help Mrs. Franklin. The poor woman is almost distracted."

Anthony strode to the door, hesitated, and turned back to Caroline. "I am ashamed of you, Mother, deserting your husband at a time like this."

"As I see it, he is deserting me—and his country—as you are. I'm sorry—"

Anthony Skinner shook his head and slammed the door. Charles Skinner seemed to consider renewing the argument with Caroline, then abandoned the idea. He lumbered back into the library. Jonathan Gifford wanted desperately to follow Anthony out the door but he could not leave without saying something.

"I'm sorry I've intruded. I only thought I was—"

"You came as a friend. Let your conscience rest quiet on that point, Captain Gifford. Anything I said is my own affair."

"I really think—it would be better if you went to New York."

Her face twisted with pain as if he had struck her. "Captain Gifford, please don't say another word. If you turn against me too—"

"I'm only thinking—"

"I know—of my welfare. But I'm not a child, Captain Gifford. I am a grown woman."

"But you can't live here now."

"I *will* live here. I will borrow money and hire a horse, borrow a plow and work enough land to feed myself and Sukey. My father gave her to me. Mr. Skinner can't take her away with the others."

"But the countryside is full of vagabonds—I couldn't sleep at night thinking of—"

"I will not be driven off my land, Captain Gifford. I brought it to him as my dowry. It was why he married me, you know that as well as I do."

"I didn't know—"

"Yes, our marriage was a business arrangement which has now gone bankrupt. I must survive it—as best I can."

"You will need help." He took her hand and held it for a moment. "You have a friend here. A friend who—"

Words, inexpressible impossible words were suddenly crowding in his throat. He stifled them with an enormous effort of his will.

"—A friend who, like all of us at Liberty Tavern, will come the moment you call."

"Thank you. You will never know—"

She turned and fled up the stairs.

Charles Skinner re-emerged from the library carrying the bust of George III. "Did you talk to her, Gifford? I hoped you might change her mind. She puts great stock in your opinion."

Looking up the stairs, Jonathan Gifford slowly shook his head. "I don't think anyone can change her mind, old friend," he said.

CHAPTER SIX

THE NEXT MORNING Kemble and I and my friend Billy Talbot rode to Amboy in the wake of the departed British army. Billy and I were the same age. We shared neutralist fathers and loyalist mothers, and a confirmed hero worship of Kemble Stapleton. But what we saw that morning was so appalling and disheartening, it shook our commitment to the Revolution. House after house was a charred ruin with wives, husbands, children picking dolefully through the blackened, still smoldering boards in the hope of finding a few surviving bits and pieces of value—a plate or a cup, perhaps, a pot or two, andirons. There was little to look for because the British and Germans stripped the houses before burning them.

"My God," I said, looking at the desolation, "is it worth it, Kemble? Maybe my father is right. Maybe we should have paid those stupid taxes."

"It is worth it," Kemble said, looking steadily at a half-dozen burned houses on the outskirts of Piscataway town. "Forget about the taxes. They were never more than an excuse to run those rotten Englishmen out of our country. It's *our* country, Jemmy. We'll build it again without their help, without their corrupt arrogant influence. We're going to build a country different from anything in history. Where every man has a chance to make something of his life if he's willing to work hard. A country where the government exists for the people—"

We listened, mesmerized. When Kemble talked this way, his face became transformed. The shadow of shyness, of intense intellectuality that normally made it difficult for him to speak freely with other men, vanished. He was like a medieval saint preaching a holy crusade, and we became his converts again.

But that day his spell was broken by a bizarre figure. George Bellows' wife Mary wandered out of the woods, her clothes torn and mud-streaked, her hair streaming in fantastic disarray around her face. She and her husband had moved to her family's home on the outskirts of Piscataway. After the birth of her child, her behavior became more and more disturbed. She was often found wandering along the road, weeping. One day she rose at her Quaker meeting and denounced God for taking away her husband's hand.

"Oh, sir," she said, "are you servants of the King? Why didn't you mind our house?"

"We are not servants of the King," Kemble said.

"The soldiers burned our house. We showed them our protection. They laughed and threw it in the fire. Why did they do that, sirs?"

"Because—"

Kemble saw the futility of explaining anything to her.

"From now on I think I will sing 'Yankee Doodle,' " Mary Bellows said. "So will my husband. He'd play it on his flute, if he could. He played a flute, you know, until they took his hand away. Why did they do that, sirs?"

"Take her home," Kemble said abruptly to me and Billy Talbot. He wheeled his horse and rode back to Liberty Tavern.

There he found Daniel Slocum and his clan, surrounded by numerous followers. Slocum was buying drinks—on credit—for the house and roaring a liberty song. You would have thought the war was over and American independence impregnably established. Tiring of his own music, Slocum began contemplating the future with gloating satisfaction. He went down a list of loyalist estates like a Catholic reciting a litany. Kemble Manor was, not too surprisingly, at the head of the list.

"The old Squire's gone, can you believe it?" he said. "Things change faster than anyone expects in a war. Three years ago Skinner's word was as good as law in this district."

"I hope from now on we will have no more squires," Kemble said. "And no man's word will be law. The people will make the laws from now on, Colonel Slocum."

If Slocum was not too drunk to get the point, he was shrewd enough to ignore it.

"Mrs. Skinner is still living at the manor," Jonathan Gifford said. "She refused to go to New York with her husband. She's on our side, and always has been. I would hope this means the estate is not open to confiscation."

"What the devil?" said Slocum. "What does a woman count? She owns no land in the eyes of the law."

"She owned half that manor before she married Mr. Skinner," Jonathan Gifford said.

"Be that as it may, she lost it the second she signed her marriage contract."

"The manor's the least of our worries," Kemble said. "We've got two or three hundred houses to rebuild."

"And about three thousand miles of fences," said Samson Tucker. "I don't think there's a fence rail left in all south Jersey. First the damn Philadelphians took'm and then the lobsters."

"We'll tend to those things soon enough," Slocum said. "But first we've got some scores to settle."

He took out another list, five times as long as the list of loyalists who had fled to New York with the British army. He began discussing who would be charged with treason, who would be heavily fined, and who would simply be taken out behind their barns and beaten up.

"If I were you, Colonel Slocum, I'd try to bring these people over to our side by being generous," Jonathan Gifford said.

"You don't understand a Tory, Gifford," said Slocum. "He don't know the meaning of generosity."

"I agree with Colonel Slocum," Kemble said.

So Slocum and Kemble returned to Tory hunting, guaranteeing the continued antagonism of the loyalists and neutrals. But they did not get much cooperation from our militia. In that humid summer of 1777, few could shake off a daze of disgust and despair when they looked at the ruins the contending armies had left behind them. While Washington prepared to defend Philadelphia, we struggled halfheartedly to rebuild burned-out homes and barns, to refence pastures and reclaim cattle wandering half starved through the woods, to plant fresh seed in ravaged fields in the dim hope that weather would permit a late harvest.

Jonathan Gifford guided a Jersey wagon down to Kemble

Manor, thinking he was on his way to help an isolated woman cope with an even more difficult problem of survival. He brought with him enough furniture to make two or three rooms in the big house habitable. He also brought two pistols and a musket, which he spent several hours teaching Mrs. Skinner to load and fire. He was pleased by the matter-of-fact way she handled these weapons. It made him feel a little better about her safety. With Little Egg Harbor becoming an ever busier privateering port, south Jersey was attracting the flotsam of war, runaway slaves and indentured servants, deserters, merchant sailors who had jumped ship.

Putting away the guns, Captain Gifford spread $500 on the kitchen table to buy a horse and cow and some chickens, and hire a farm hand. "One man should be able to raise enough food and chop enough wood to keep you comfortable," he said.

"Sukey and I can chop our own wood and milk our own cow, Captain Gifford," Caroline said. "Why not loan me five thousand dollars so I can hire enough men and horses to harvest the crop that is in the ground? I will pay you six per cent interest."

"Mrs. Skinner, that would involve a gang of men. You would need a foreman—"

"I will be the foreman."

Jonathan Gifford took a deep breath. This small dark determined woman upset all his preconceptions about the opposite sex. But the admiration that her courage aroused in him made the upset surprisingly tolerable.

"You can have the money interest-free."

"No. I am not asking you to support me, Captain Gifford. I expect to make a good profit on the crop. I can pay interest and I will pay it."

With so many farmers in desperate need of money to repair their own wrecked farms, Caroline had no trouble hiring hands. True to her announced intention, she was her own foreman, riding out each day with the men in an old calico dress and a wide-brimmed sun hat. She got a full day's work for her wages, from the grumbles Jonathan Gifford heard at Liberty Tavern as more than one of her weary toilers stopped for some refreshment on his way home.

Caroline wisely concentrated her efforts on Kemble Manor. She hired Samson Tucker to run the mill and one of Jasper Clark's sons to run the Colt's Neck farm. Both showed a modest profit but compared to them, Kemble Manor was a bonanza. With the help of almost perfect weather, Caroline harvested forty bushels of wheat and ninety bushels of corn an acre. She sold most of the crop—some thirty thousand bushels—to the Continental army. At the end of October, she triumphantly repaid Jonathan Gifford his $5,000 loan at 6 per cent interest, and had about $2,000 left to invest in next year's planting.

"Did my husband ever make as much, with his slave labor?" Caroline asked Jonathan Gifford.

"I don't know. You have had the advantage of high prices," Jonathan Gifford said. "But I'm sure he is—will be—proud of you."

"I am proud of myself, Mr. Gifford. That is more important. A woman has so little chance to do things that give her real pride."

"To be honest, I have never given it much thought. I have been inclined to take things as they are. But Kate has made me think about women. The way you have awakened her mind—"

"What shall she do with it, now that it is awakened? We must make sure this country gives her a chance to use it. How is the war going?"

Jonathan Gifford looked doleful. He had posted a half-dozen proclamations and exhortations on the door of Liberty Tavern, urging the militia to join Washington for the defense of Philadelphia. Kemble rode through the countryside, making speeches that thrilled us sixteen-year-olds. But no one else listened, and everyone stayed home. Kemble almost despaired. Captain Gifford was inclined to be philosophic. He had little faith in the militia anyway.

"I wouldn't turn out if I was a militiaman," he told Caroline. "Not after what the British did to the regiment on the retreat to Amboy. Maybe the men have more sense than the Congress. They're the ones who have left Washington no alternative but militia. I can't believe he really wants them, if he could get regulars."

Caroline Skinner shook her head. "Overoptimism is the great American weakness," he said.

It was very comforting for Jonathan Gifford to find agreement with his opinions at Kemble Manor. When he expressed his doubts about the militia to Kemble, he was usually treated to a tirade about his lack of faith in the people, supposedly rooted in his weakness for aristocracy. Before the argument ended, both men lost their tempers and Kemble went another week without speaking to him.

As our fog of apathy engulfed both enlistments and the Slocum-Stapleton Tory hunts, the loyalists resumed their clandestine trade with the British in New York, and practically rattled the hard money in our faces to prove it. Colonel Slocum decided to change his tactics from brute force to financial chicanery. He suddenly announced a ferocious enforcement of the law about collecting fines from militiamen who failed to turn out when called. He and his officers rode through the countryside, presenting people with bills for immediate payment.

Slocum swore that there was no other way to raise men. Under militia law, the fines became the property of the regiment and were to be divided among the men who did turn out. "There's plenty of money in the district," Slocum said. "People have been selling crops for hard money to the British all winter. They can pay, damn them, and we'll use the surplus to give a bounty to men who'll come to Philadelphia with me."

Kemble agreed with Slocum for the usual reason. It was necessary. But he was a little shocked to discover that Slocum was presenting people with bills for past as well as present failures to turn out. Loyalists in particular got orders for twenty, thirty, fifty dollars depending on how many men of militia age they had in the family. Other loyalists with sons in the royal army got $100 fines. These were large sums to farmers who were always cash-short. For families who had just had houses burned or looted, it was an impossible tax.

For substantial farmers like Richard Talbot and members of prominent families like my father, who had chosen to remain neutral, Slocum had a special treatment. He arranged to have them elected militia officers. Fines were much heavier for an officer who failed to serve. My father got a bill for $250.

Toward the middle of July, about two weeks after Slocum had started his fine-collection campaign, Kate came to Jonathan Gifford in a very indignant mood. She and Caroline had been busy helping some of the most distressed families in the district, ones who had lost everything. Jonathan Gifford had contributed $1,000 to a fund they had set up, to buy food and replace farm tools. Among the most obvious charity cases were the Tharps.

Their house, barn, outbuildings, granary had been burned. Their son John had been killed harassing the British retreat. Tharp had four other sons who heeded the Quaker injunction against bearing arms. They had been toiling twelve hours a day all summer to rebuild their farmhouse.

"Just as they finish it," Kate told her father, "Colonel Slocum arrives and presents them with fines of a hundred dollars each for failing to do their militia duty. When it's against their conscience! That's unjust, Father."

"I agree. Let us see what our favorite foe of tyrants has to say about it."

Kemble said he knew nothing about Slocum fining Quakers. He agreed it was wrong. He rode over to Slocum's farm to ask him about it. The Colonel exploded. "It's none of your damn business," he said. "I fine who I please."

"It doesn't make sense," Kemble said. "You'll never get Quakers to turn out."

It made a great deal of sense to Colonel Slocum, because he was pocketing the fines. This had not yet dawned on Kemble. He still saw the whole thing as a fund-raising operation for the expeditionary force to assist Washington before Philadelphia.

"Goddamn you," said Slocum. "You keep turning into a milk and water man. And now a Quaker. Damn spiritual weeds that ought to be rooted out, or I'm not a good Presbyterian. Can't you see that the more money we raise, the more men we'll turn out? Let me run this regiment, and we may win this war somehow."

Kemble went back to Liberty Tavern and told his father he reluctantly supported Slocum's Quaker policy. "Well, I don't," Jonathan Gifford said, "and I'm writing a letter to Governor Livingston about it today."

Jonathan Gifford knew William Livingston fairly well. He was a New York aristocrat who had moved to New Jersey in 1772. A gifted lawyer, he had handled the probate of Sarah's will, which had involved considerable property owned jointly with the north Jersey branch of the Stapleton family. Livingston was a man of integrity, who had no use for Slocum and his kind. But he had very little authority to intervene in local matters. A dread of executive power had dominated the writers of our state's constitution. They had made the legislature supreme, and Slocum's ability to elect a half-dozen yes men every year guaranteed his immunity there. But the governor was the commander in chief of the militia. Within two weeks a furious Colonel Slocum appeared in the tavern waving a letter from Livingston.

"Look at this. The governor says I am persecuting these damn Quakers. Says they are exempt from militia duty. The same governor that is hauling you off to fight for those damn Philadelphians. I will show him what it means to push Slocum around."

The calls for help from Washington became more and more frantic. The British army had landed at the head of the Chesapeake and was marching on Philadelphia. New Jersey militiamen were ordered to assemble at Morristown and march in a body from there to join the Continental army. Colonel Slocum was appointed a brigadier general commanding troops from Monmouth, Middlesex, and Somerset counties. An express rider was rushed to Philadelphia at public expense to purchase a suitable uniform for our leader. Kemble hurled himself into a round-the-clock effort to turn out more men. On the eve of his departure, Slocum strode into Liberty Tavern and made a stunning announcement.

"The honorable Provincial Congress has passed a law," Slocum said, "forbidding the Monmouth regiment from serving outside the county."

"That's insane," Kemble said.

"They did so as a rebuke to the governor," Slocum said, "after our honorable delegates communicated to them the perilous state of this county, infested as it is by Tories and Quakers, and the governor's interference in our efforts to handle matters as we see fit. Maybe now the governor will learn that we ain't kicked out one tyrant to be bullied by another one."

It was an awesome display of Slocum's political power. He had, I hardly need add, elected his entire slate of candidates in the mid-August elections unopposed. No one wanted to become an enemy of General Slocum if he could avoid it.

To Kemble's dismay, Slocum's coup was very popular among our militiamen. Samson Tucker echoed the prevailing opinion, as usual. "The General's right," he said. "Why should we march a hundred miles to get our tails blown off for those damn Philadelphians? Let's see how they fight for their own country. They sure as hell didn't do much fighting for ours."

This use of the word "country" may strike later Americans as odd. But it was common during the Revolution and for many years after it for a man to call his home state his country.

To further demonstrate his power, General Slocum mustered three hundred men. He gave Kemble command of them and ordered him to patrol the shores against loyalist raiders. Slocum rode off to Morristown, where he politicked his way into the leadership of the eight hundred New Jerseyans (out of a potential sixteen thousand) who responded to Washington's call for help. Unacquainted with our local politics, Washington never learned that Slocum had deliberately left behind him the men for whom he was personally responsible. If the absence of Monmouth men ever arose, Slocum no doubt blamed the whole thing on the legislature. It was easy enough for a man like Slocum to impose himself on the harassed Washington as one of the first patriots of New Jersey.

This nonsupport from New Jersey and an equally poor turnout of Pennsylvania militia—enthusiasm for the Revolution was never high in the Keystone State—undoubtedly played a part in Washington's defeat at Brandywine Creek, which opened the gates of Philadelphia to Sir William Howe's army.

Abel Aikin brought us the news in his usual indirect fashion. "Well," he said, getting off his horse in front of Liberty Tavern, "I am out of a job again."

"What's this, Abel?" said Barney McGovern. "Have they finally found out you're makin' more than the postmaster general, with all them packages and private letters you carry on the side?"

Abel shook his head, added a few purls to a scarf he was knitting, and said, "The postmaster general has gone to parts unknown. The British are in Philadelphia."

"Now all we need hear is Burgoyne is in Albany, and this may yet be the year of the gallows," said Barney.

For the next several days, Liberty Tavern's taproom echoed with new denunciations of Washington. Again, Jonathan Gifford was his chief defender. "He may have been beaten at Brandywine," he said, "but he saved his army. He will do something with it before the campaign is over, I promise you. He understands the main thing. As long as we have an army, we are in the game."

Within two weeks, Daniel Slocum was back in Liberty Tavern telling us about the battle of Germantown. This is listed in the history books as another Washington defeat. But for us, with our

282

desperate need for hope, it was a marvelous restorative. We listened with exultant delight as Slocum described the secret march of the American army, the hammer blow struck at the British camp in the dawn. We all but tore our hair with vexation at the unexpectedly heavy morning fog that threw the American columns into confusion. Whether the American tactics were good or bad, even whether we won or lost, did not mean as much to us as the simple fact that within three weeks of a supposedly ruinous defeat, Washington had come back to fight the British army with ferocious guile.

"Let the lobsters have Philadelphia," crowed Samson Tucker. "What did that damn city ever do for us here in Jersey but suck out our money for gewgaws and luxuries?"

Slocum naturally portrayed himself and the Jersey militia he commanded as the heroes of Germantown. He had them scattering British regiments like leaves in a thunderstorm. Nothing stopped them, not the Foot Guards, the Black Watch, the King's Own. Jonathan Gifford did not believe a word of it. But he let Slocum talk and pretended to be impressed. For the time being there was no way to stop him from puffing his military reputation. He listened patiently while the General threw Washington's name around the taproom, giving everyone the impression that the commander in chief relied heavily on Daniel Slocum's advice.

"Yes," said Slocum, "I told His Excellency about our situation here, exposed to the ravages of that damned banditti on Staten Island and pernicious enemies in our midst. He agreed to send us a regiment of regulars to patrol the coast this winter."

Slocum's already large popularity became immense with this announcement. Not even the news that General Burgoyne had surrendered at Saratoga and his entire Canadian army were prisoners of war created as much of a sensation among us as the arrival of our Continental regiment. They camped about a mile from Liberty Tavern, and we all went down to take a look at them. Jonathan Gifford was not impressed. They were a Massachusetts outfit, commanded by a major named Yates. He was a tall lean Yankee with a stoop to his shoulders and a prow of a nose that gave a disconsolate cast to his solemn face. They all had twangs so broad they sounded as if they were speaking a foreign language. They were only at half strength, barely two hundred men. Their colonel and several captains had gone home to recruit. They were a scruffy-looking bunch of soldiers, confirming what we'd heard about Yankees—they had a dread of soap and water that equaled their fear of hell-fire. But they looked mean enough to fight.

That night, Yates and two captains came down to Liberty Tavern and got pretty drunk. One of the captains was a potbellied ex-shoemaker who had "liberated" some hides from a Bergen County Tory and said he would be glad to whip together some boots for anyone with ready cash. When he got no takers he grew disgruntled and began taunting us about our inability to defend ourselves. "Why from what we hee-uh," he twanged, "the keows in Massachusetts will fight harder than you Jersey men."

"Too bad you didn't tell General Washington that," Kemble said. "He could have used a few of those cows to do the fighting you Yankees forgot to do on Long Island."

"Maybe their keows can run faster than they can," Samson Tucker said, "and like most Yankees don't know the difference between fighting and running. It's all the same to them."

"What's this, Captain Gifford?" Yates droned. "You serve Tories in here?"

"Samson? You can't find a better Whig in south Jersey."

Yates sighed with astonishment. "Why, if he was up in Massachusetts, we would be praying for his immortal soul, yes we would."

"More likely he'd be wearing a Tory overcoat," said the ex-shoemaker who had started the argument. "Hot tar and feathers."

"How many Tories do you have up there?" scoffed Kemble. "Ten, twenty at the most?"

"Yeah," said Samson, "take a march down Shrewsbury way. You will find enough in that one town to chase you and your damn scarecrows all the way to Boston."

"Gentlemen, gentlemen," Jonathan Gifford said, "you are all Americans. This name-calling is childish."

"Amen, Captain Gifford," said Major Yates. "We are all fighting the Lord's battle. I only wish our chaplain was here. He would get these fellows down on their knees, yes he would, and he'd raise them up with the strength of ten."

The next day General Slocum was growling at Jonathan Gifford and Kemble for insulting the Major and his "brave Yankees." But he did not pursue the subject. The General had other things on his mind. With him was a small hook-nosed Scotsman named Andrew McIntosh. "Andy here's as staunch a Whig as walks the earth," General Slocum said, "a refugee from Philadelphia, where he had his own wharf and a fleet of ships running between the West Indies and the main. A half-dozen good Bermuda sloops that he turned to privateering and made him the terror of our coast from the capes of the Delaware to Florida. Now he's here to do another service for his country. His business was salt before the war came. He brought it in by the ton from the Cayman Islands. With Philadelphia closed and the coast thick with British cruisers, the country's running short of it. Believe me, it's as needed as gunpowder. Washington himself said as much to me before I left him. So Andy and me have decided for our country's sake to build the biggest saltworks ever seen in America down on the Manasquan. Between us, there's a chance for a profit that will make your eyes pop. West of Philadelphia, salt is selling for twenty-five dollars a bushel and going up every day. What do you think of investing five or ten thousand?"

"I don't have it," Jonathan Gifford said. "Every cent I've got is out in the neighborhood. People needed a lot of money to rebuild their houses."

"There ain't nobody runs a tavern without a cash reserve," said the General. "Put in with me now and you will have Slocum for a partner. That's something will do you good in this county for a long time to come."

"I'm telling you the truth," Jonathan Gifford said, lying with a clear conscience. He had ten thousand dollars in his strongbox. But he had no intention of going into business with Daniel Slocum.

"Well, that disappoints me," Slocum said. "Disappoints me greatly. But I half-expected it from you."

While McIntosh slurped his ale, Slocum went to work on Kemble. "But I don't expect the young squire here to disappoint me. We need his help. There ain't no one else in the county that can raise the lads we need to work this thing. Andy here says we will need between forty and sixty hands. There ain't no one but you that can make them understand the importance of salt to this country."

"It's the presairvation of the nation, so to speak," said McIntosh with a shrill cackle at his own joke.

"They'll be paid militia wages and be exempt from call-out."

Kemble agreed to help raise the men. Neither he nor Jonathan Gifford realized it at the moment, but they were present at the launching of the great salt boom of 1777. It is one of the more disgraceful and perhaps better forgotten episodes of the Revolution in New Jersey. But I have promised to tell the whole truth about our supposed Golden Age. Salt was one of the few natural resources with which our continent was not blessed. Before the war most of it was imported from Europe or the West Indies. As the British fleet tightened its patrols off our coast, it became more precious than gold. There was no other cheap way to preserve meat and without meat the average American was devoutly convinced then as now that he would wither like a daffodil in September. We are an incurably carnivorous people.

There was one obvious source of salt lapping the shores of New Jersey—the Atlantic Ocean. Heretofore the process of extracting this precious item from the surrounding liquid had been too expensive to compete with imported salt. This was no longer the case and merchants like McIntosh rushed to our shore to make a fortune. General Slocum was determined to be in the vanguard of this column. With Kemble's help he signed up sixty young men in two furious days. They marched south to the Manasquan, convinced that they were joining their General on a military mission. In the next few weeks, other salt entrepreneurs poured into the neighborhood and offered twice, then three times the wages Slocum was paying. The strength of our militia dwindled to the vanishing point, giving the loyalists new grounds for complacency and arrogance.

"Thank God we have the Continentals," Kemble said at first.

But Major Yates and his Yankees began to look less and less like the answer to anyone's prayers except their own. They showed practically no interest in patrolling the shore. Their chief activity, besides singing hymns and listening to three-hour sermons from their chaplain, was serving as escorts to the latest arrivals in our little village—Deputy Commissary Beebe and Deputy Quartermaster Beatty. Beatty was built like a birch tree, with a small head on his narrow shoulders. Beebe was his opposite—fat as a mulberry bush with a pumpkin-size head. They were part of a small army of similar government servants who sat themselves down in every town in New Jersey. The commissaries bought food for the Continental army and the quartermasters forage for its horses.

Beatty and Beebe were armed with thousands of Continental dollars. But this medium of exchange was beginning to lose its appeal to almost everyone, including the stoutest Whigs. Already its value had begun to decline. It took two dollars to buy what one had bought in 1776. It slowly dawned on us that Yates and his soldiers were there to intimidate Whigs and Tories alike into taking paper money for our oats, wheat, corn, and hay.

But the Tories were the ones who learned to dread the approach of Yates and his troops, slouching sullenly beside Beatty and Beebe's wagons. For them the term "Tory" included neutrals like my father. Slocum had supplied Yates with a list of the "disaffected and suspected." We were on it.

My father greeted Yates, flanked by Beatty and Beebe, at our front door with the same philosophic calm he had displayed to Major Moncrieff. Beneath this deceptive exterior, to which he was trained from boyhood, his feelings could be and often were in turmoil. After Moncrieff and his British foragers had left us with our barns in ashes and our hen house empty, he had gone to bed for two weeks with a high fever and other alarming symptoms of apoplexy. He was weak and melancholy most of the summer and was only beginning to take an interest in the farm when these new foragers arrived.

"We are here to purchase supplies for the troops and horses of the Continental army," said Beatty.

"I am prepared to accept your money, gentlemen," my father said. "But I hope you will take into account the depreciation. At New Brunswick I hear it is already over two to one."

Yates shook his head lugubriously, a saint contemplating a sinner lost beyond redemption. "It is almost hard to believe, yes it is," he said. "A man so deep in the toils of Satan, he don't even know it. I vow it makes me think the devil is setting up a church, and the next thing men like this will be declaring themselves *justified.*"

"A little repentance on a rail might do wonders for him," said the shoemaker Captain.

"We don't have time," Yates said. "But we will exact justice from this fellow, in the Lord's name, for the sake of our suffering country."

He took a small black book from his pocket and paged methodically through it, a parody of St. Peter on doomsday. "Yes, here he is, failed to pay the fine of two hundred and fifty dollars levied for refusal to perform militia duty."

"I told General Slocum I would not pay that fine. The courts will decide which of us is right," my father said.

"The time is past when vipers like you can escape the hand of justice by bribing juries and judges," Yates droned. "I have orders to secure from your house chattel goods to the sum of two hundred and fifty dollars, this day."

"I would like to see that order," my father said.

Yates whipped his sword from the scabbard and put the point of it against my father's throat. "Here it is. The same order the Lord sent to Gideon and Joshua. I am ready to deliver it. Say but the word."

My father stood there with the sword at his throat for a full minute. For the first time it dawned on me that in an oblique way he was a man of courage. I think he considered the possibility of dying on that sword.

He finally stepped aside and let Yates and ten of his men troop through our house. My father was a rich man, thanks to the combination of his law practice and a well-run three-hundred-acre farm. Our furniture, wallpaper, rugs equaled the splendor of Kemble Manor, if our house was not quite so large.

"Look at the way this Tory lives while honest Whigs are shivering in tents," Yates said. He put the point of his sword into the blue satin upholstery of a sample chair made by Philadelphia's Benjamin Randolph and ripped it up the middle.

A shriek from the doorway announced that my mother had arrived. "How dare you, sir. How dare you ruin my property?"

"Why, madam, I don't know," Yates said with a clumsy bow. "Perhaps the Lord was guiding my hand. You know what He says, vengeance is mine."

My mother, with a majesty that came naturally to an upper-class Bostonian, began denouncing the Major as a blackguard, a pirate, a hypocrite, and a vandal. He caught the Yankee echo in her tirade. Twenty years in New Jersey had not erased it from her tongue.

"I see you are from New England," Yates said. "What was your family name?"

"Oliver," blazed my mother.

Yates groaned like a branded sinner. "You are one of that nest of Tory vipers that was feeding on the vitals of poor people, swilling from the public trough like the King's favorite hogs for generation after generation? Why, madam, hearing that inspires my sword to wander again."

He whipped his weapon from his scabbard and gouged the blue damask cushion of one of our Philadelphia sofas down the middle from left to right.

My mother ran wailing from the room.

"You may have a legal right to confiscate my property, Major," my father said. "How do you justify this destruction?"

"Why, this is a Tory house," Yates said. "We have been sent down here to prosecute you vermin. It is our duty to rip up every cursed cushion in this house. That is where you are likely to be concealing secret messages, money to recruit your Satan-loving traitors. Get to work, men."

We stood there and watched them rip apart the cushions of every piece of furniture in the parlor, the dining room, the study, Yates with his sword, the men with their bayonets. My father's lips were trembling. Any moment I thought he would collapse.

"Upstairs, men, and do the same job in their bedrooms," Yates said.

Within sixty seconds my sister Sally started screaming. One of the men, a stocky fellow with an inch of dirt on his face, came back downstairs to tell us that the Tory bitch had locked herself in her room. Should they knock down the door? I went upstairs and talked Sally into unlocking the door. She stood there whimpering while they ripped her feather bed apart with their bayonets and flung open the chest where she stored her gowns.

"By Beelzebub, look at this here finery," said their leader, hauling out satin and silk and damask ball gowns. "If that ain't the most sinful stuff I've ever seen, my name ain't Silas Gobble. I think I'll take this one for my old lady."

They each decided to take one for their old ladies.

Sally went almost berserk with rage. "That's stealing," she screamed. "Stealing."

Silas Gobble gave her a Yankee horselaugh. "You can't steal from a Tory, hussy, don't you know that? We are confiscatin' enemy property here."

"Traitors' property," said the stocky fellow with the dirt on his face.

Downstairs we found my father watching Major Yates hacking out of the frame the portrait of my great-grandfather, the first Kemble to come to America. The Major wanted the frame but not the painting. Next, he ordered the men to roll up the Kirman rug on the floor.

"That rug is worth five times the fine you are supposedly collecting, Major," my father said.

Deputy Commissary Beebe and Deputy Quartermaster Beatty had by this time returned from the barns and were available for consultation. They estimated the value of the rug at $50. I informed the Major that his men had just stolen twelve dresses from my sister. "That is their affair," I was told.

The Major wanted to know where our silver plate was. "That is where we shall make up the balance of this fine," he said.

"The British stole it," my father said.

Actually it was well buried behind the barn along with our candlesticks, our tea service, my mother's jewelry, and our Meissen china.

The Major preached a little sermon on the sinfulness of lying and ordered his men to roll up the Persian rugs in the dining room and study. He took a white and gold looking glass from the hall and the white and gold damask draperies from the parlor and the chandelier of Irish cut glass from the dining room. You may wonder how I can remember these details with such exactitude after fifty years. My father methodically made an inventory of his losses. I have a copy of that inventory before me as I write this.

Outside, the Major and his men looted our smokehouse and hen house and slaughtered one of our prime sows for future consumption. As an afterthought, the Major took my sister Sally's pet goat and tied it to the rear of the last wagon. Deputies Beebe and Beatty handed my father several hundred paper dollars, mounted their wagons, and headed back to their camp near Liberty Tavern. We stood on the steps watching them.

"Now you know how the Romans felt when the barbarians arrived, Jemmy," my father said.

One of the soldiers bringing up the rear fell out of the column and began loading his gun. We watched, not quite believing what we saw. He raised the gun, aimed it at the house, and pulled the trigger. We all flinched with terror, thinking he was firing at us. But the bullet crashed through the dining room window. Everyone laughed uproariously at our fright. We could hear them laughing, and Sally's goat bleating in a kind of counterpoint until they were out of sight on the main road.

That night I rode down to Liberty Tavern and told the story to Kemble and Jonathan Gifford. Kemble listened with a mournful expression on his face. "You must keep it quiet, Jemmy, for the sake of the Cause," he said. "There are too many people in this neighborhood who still respect your father. This sort of thing will arouse sympathy for him. And—"

"You are talking damn nonsense, Kemble," said Jonathan Gifford. "Major Yates is an officer in the Continental army. You tell your father to make an inventory of what they stole and send it to General Washington. I will be very surprised if he does not court-martial Major Yates."

This nasty argument was interrupted by the arrival of Slocum's Scottish partner, Andrew McIntosh. He was in an extremely good mood, and ordered himself a bottle of the best Madeira in the house and a dinner of jugged hare and beef à la mode. They were Liberty Tavern specialties. I especially loved the beef à la mode, which was served in a ragout of sweetbreads, oysters, and mushrooms.

McIntosh ate like a man ten times his size. As he demolished the Madeira, he grew talkative, for a Scotsman.

"I hate to tell ye this, Gifford, no doubt it will give ye indigestion for the rest of the week," he said in his squeaky burr. "But we sold our first salt at New Brunswick yesterday. Forty-five dollars a bushel, Gifford. How d'ye like that? Twenty-eight thousand dollars we cleared. How's that for dooin' business?"

"Why, I don't know," Jonathan Gifford said. "There was a man in here yesterday with a wagon and a team of half-dead horses. He'd come all the way from the Wyoming Valley in Pennsylvania he said, looking for salt. They'll starve to death this winter, if he doesn't come back with the wagon full of it. They'd given him all the money they had in their township. The fellow was practically in tears. He asked me if I knew where he could get salt at a decent price. He said it was going for forty-five dollars a bushel in New Brunswick. He couldn't fill a third of his wagon at that price. I told him he might as well buy, and I loaned him the difference at six per cent."

"From the Wyoming," said McIntosh. "You'll never see your money, Gifford. I'll be damned if I know how ye stay in business if that's what ye do with it. I traded with them in the valley before the war. They're poor as Job on his dunghill. All ye'll get will be excuses, and lucky ye'll be to get them."

"Congress set the price of salt at fifteen dollars a bushel."

"Let Congress set till doomsday. The price will follow the market," McIntosh said.

"But if a man can't pay, does that mean his family will starve this winter? This fellow I'm talking about was as honest a Whig as ever lived. He had a son in the Continental army."

"That's a question better answered by a parson," said McIntosh, finishing his Madeira. He reached into his satchel and spread three or four of his twenty-eight thousand dollars on the table and called for his horse.

One of Major Yates's captains burst into the taproom bawling for Kemble Stapleton. Kemble identified himself. "The Major says you must call out your militia. There's a Tory army in the Navesink. Two thousand men, the report says."

"That's ridiculous," Jonathan Gifford said. "No general would send two thousand men anywhere this late in the year." He walked to the window and eyed the gray November sky. "All you need is a little rain and sleet to put half your men in sickbeds. There are a couple of saltworks on the Navesink, aren't there?"

"At least two, possibly three. I haven't been down that way in a month," Kemble said.

"That's what they're after."

"What the devil," squawked McIntosh. "Attacking saltworks. The buggers show no quarter, do they?"

"I'm afraid it's that kind of war," Jonathan Gifford said. "There's no way you can defend those places, unless you build a fort around them, which would eat into your profits, wouldn't it, Mr. McIntosh?"

"It certainly would," said McIntosh. "Get me my horse. I moost get this news to General Slocum."

Jonathan Gifford was right about the raiders on the Navesink. Anthony Skinner had led a mixed force of regulars and loyalists from New York. There were two hundred of them, not two thousand, a pretty example of how fear and rumor combine to confuse the truth in war. They burned the saltworks on the Navesink and

Skinner left behind him a proclamation, denouncing speculators who were feeding on the vitals of the country.

Skinner and his troops departed from that largely loyalist neighborhood without anyone firing a shot at them. Major Yates and his brave Yankees marched desultorily in their direction, but made sure they were long gone when they arrived. Although no one but the speculators who had invested several thousands in the construction of their saltworks suffered, everyone in the county was struck by the obvious fact that our Continental regiment did not exactly guarantee us protection against loyalist raiders. This feeling did not decrease when Major Yates and his infantry failed to return from their march to the Navesink.

"Maybe they went all the way to Little Egg Harbor and shipped out on privateers," Jonathan Gifford said. "They seem more interested in stealing than fighting."

"'Tis no joke to Deputies Beatty and Beebe. They are afraid to venture more than a mile from here without an escort," said Samson Tucker. "To hear them talk, you would think the Tories had fangs a foot long and dined on human flesh."

Days, then a week passed without a word from or a sign of our Yankee Continentals. The southern part of the county seemed to have swallowed them. A freeze filled the rivers and the Atlantic with ice, making us all but immune to Tory raids. Most people began preparing for Christmas and forgot about our missing protectors. Even my father, once he had sent off letters of protest to General Washington and Governor Livingston, agreed it was time to try to forget the war for a few weeks.

At Liberty Tavern Kate neglected Lieutenant Rawdon to spend most of the time in the kitchen with our cooks, Molly and Bertha, boiling calves' feet and rubbing them through a colander for mince pies, her specialty. There was mace to pound, suet to chop, cloves and nutmeg to be added in delicate balance—all this for the mincemeat. There were plum and Yorkshire puddings, Christmas pies and fruitcakes baking in the huge kitchen oven. For years every member of the family had gotten one of the tavern's fruitcakes, made with four pounds of butter, the same weight of currants, thirty eggs, a pint of brandy. No matter how much you ate, they always seemed to last until Easter.

Even Kemble softened under the influence of the rich odors wafting through the tavern from the kitchen. But he was abruptly returned to the reality of the war by a visit from a Quaker farmer, George Evans. His son Emmanuel had volunteered to join Slocum for service in the saltworks. His father had given permission for him to go. He was glad to have a member of his family do something for the country that did not involve bearing arms.

"The lad has come home more dead than alive. Half starved, his arm turned black and blue from a burn. He tells of beatings and threats, working night and day."

Kemble called for Dr. Davie, and they rode down to the Evans farm in the chaise. There they found the father's description was no exaggeration. Emmanuel was a wan skeleton. Dr. Davie had to cut open his arm and clear out a pint of infected matter. Kemble asked him to describe life at the saltworks.

"The fires must go day and night, the General says, so the place is always full of smoke. They fill the kettles to the top and the water boils over. That is how I got my burn. We would all come home in a minute, but the soldiers won't let us."

"What soldiers?"

"The Yankees. They came down to guard the place."

Without saying a word to his father, Kemble mounted his horse and rode south to see for himself. He had no difficulty finding the Union Salt Works. A column of smoke rose into the gray December sky three miles up the Manasquan River. As he dismounted, he was challenged by a Yankee sentry who stood before the gate of a flimsy-looking stockade that surrounded the works on three sides. Kemble identified himself and asked to see General Slocum. In sixty seconds he was in the General's office receiving a hearty welcome.

Slocum was wearing greasy leather breeches, a sad-colored coat out at the elbows, and the dirtiest shirt Kemble had ever seen. "Well, if it ain't the young squire," he roared. "What brings you down here on such a fine cold day? Has your father decided to put some money into our little business? Well, tell him it's too late. But if he wants, I'll let him go a fourth share in a privateer we've got on the stocks at Little Egg Harbor. To be named *Black Daniel*. How do you like that? Captain Hope Willets commands."

"I bring no money, General. I found myself rambling down this way and thought I would stop and see how you and the men do."

"We are thriving," said Slocum. "Let me show you around."

Their first stop was the boiling house. There Kemble gazed in awe at five copper and four iron pans, each weighing upwards of three thousand pounds. The copper pans were fifteen feet across. Beneath each pan was a brick furnace which sweaty, sooty militiamen stoked with wood or peat bricks. Next door to the boiling house was a storehouse which could hold eight hundred bushels of salt and next to that a pump house which gulped the water from the river into the boiling pans or into a huge covered cistern which held about a hundred and fifty hogsheads of water. There were also stables, a dwelling house, a smokehouse, and two barracks. It was a veritable industrial colony.

"How do the men like the work?" Kemble asked as they walked back to Slocum's office.

"I hear no complaints. I believe our rations are as good or better than the Continental army."

As Slocum spoke, about two dozen men trudged in the gate hauling carts of wood they had just finished chopping. They were escorted by a dozen Yankee Continentals with muskets. The wood choppers looked weary and disgruntled. When they saw Kemble their expressions changed to active dislike. One of them, a husky eighteen-year-old named Bayles Platt, spit on the ground near Kemble's feet as they passed.

Slocum whirled and hauled him out of the column by his collar. "What the hell did you mean by that?"

"Why nothing, General, nothing at all," said Platt.

"If you ever do anything like that again, you will go on bread and water. Remember, this is the army. You are under my command."

"Why did he do that, General?" Kemble asked, as Platt rejoined the column.

"He is a damned troublemaker," Slocum said. "We will have to give him a taste of the lash before long."

"Emmanuel Evans did not seem to like the work down here, General."

"Oh, that fellow. I sent him home. He is like every damn Quaker I ever met. God himself won't be able to keep them Quakers happy in paradise, if they ever get there. Personally I think they will all keep the father of discontent company down you know where."

"Do the men share in your profits, General?"

"What the devil are you talking about?" Slocum snapped. "They are here to serve their country as soldiers. They are producing a commodity which the army and the nation need as badly as gunpowder."

"As I understand it," said Kemble in a voice that could be heard a mile down the Manasquan River, "you made twenty-eight thousand dollars on your first shipment. I heard your partner McIntosh telling this to my father last week. Where did that money go, General Slocum? In your pocket and McIntosh's pocket? Do the honorable Congress and General Washington get a share?"

"Why, goddamn you," roared Slocum, "I'm going to put you under arrest. No man can insult General Washington in my presence."

"I had no intention of insulting General Washington," said Kemble, rattled by this unexpected tactic.

"You have insulted him and I intend to arrest you for it," Slocum shouted. "Major Yates, come here this instant, will you please?"

Major Yates emerged from the barracks. His eyes clouded with dislike when he saw Kemble. He did not forget those who cast slurs on Massachusetts.

"Major, this fellow has ridden all the way from Middletown to disrupt the saltworks," Slocum said. "He has accused General Washington of peculation in its profits. I am asking you to witness his damn Tory talk. Now repeat what you just asked me about General Washington."

"I asked you how much money you were making from this saltworks," Kemble said. "My remark about General Washington was sarcasm."

"But you did ask it, you did ask me what General Washington's profits were?"

"I'm more interested in yours."

"Did you hear him, Major?" cried Slocum. "He's at it again, trying to bait me into smearing General Washington's name. Who sent you down here, old Cortland Skinner himself? Damn me if you haven't turned your coat or started working both sides like your father. What do you think, Major?"

"A suspicious character, General, no doubt," said Major Yates.

"What the devil are you doing down here?" Kemble shouted at

Yates. "You were sent to guard the people of Monmouth County, not this saltworks."

"Why this fellow is a marvel, General, he has more brass than a nine-pounder," Yates droned. "He wants to run your saltworks and my regiment all at once."

"How much money is he paying you?" Kemble asked.

Yates drew a deep breath through his nose. "You don't have to say another word to me, General. He has just damned himself out of his own mouth. He has accused an officer of the army of the United States of taking a bribe."

"What should we do with him, Major?"

"Why, we are on detached duty here. My officers and me will be glad to form a court-martial board, with you as chairman. We will have this spying son of Satan ready to hang tomorrow at sunrise, all done so legal-like the lord chief justice of England would split his wits to find a quibble with it."

"Put him under arrest, Major."

Major Yates yelled an order. A half-dozen Yankees marched Kemble to the guardhouse. There he was forced to strip and surrender his clothing and shoes.

"If you are carrying any secret messages, we will have them soon enough," Yates said.

Kemble was left shivering in the unheated guardhouse all night without even a blanket to cover him, and with no supper, not even a glass of water. At dawn, Slocum appeared and flung his clothes unceremoniously on the floor at his feet.

"The Major's disappointed. I won't let him hang you. It wouldn't be that hard to justify. You're a member of a suspected family. Cousins, uncles, aunts on the other side. They burned them saltworks on the Navesink. How do you think they found them? Some damned spy gave them the exact location, how many guards—"

It was clear that Slocum had seriously considered hanging Kemble. Only fear of the consequences restrained him. With all his power, Slocum was still intimidated by the Stapleton name. If Kemble had been a Talbot, he might have ended his life in those gloomy woods beside the gray sluggish Manasquan that December.

"I told you once before not to cross me, lad. Now I'm telling you again, for the second and last time. Go home and keep your mouth shut about what's happening here. We still need your name to turn out the men in the district. But that is all you are good for. You are out of your depth in this war. If you mind your business, when it is all over, Slocum will take good care of you. He'll send you to the legislature, maybe to Congress. You can have your choice of Tory estates. Any place but Kemble Manor. That goes to Slocum."

Kemble finished dressing. He barely noticed that the Yankees had slashed the linings of his coat and cloak, searching for secret documents. He was full of loathing for this gross barrel of a man confronting him, and equally full of loathing for himself. He had collaborated with Slocum to give him the power he was now using to foul our Revolution with his greed. Worst of all, Jonathan Gifford, the man whom Kemble had sneered at and condemned, had been right about Slocum from the start. Partly for this reason, and partly because he clung to his sinking belief in the politics of enlightenment and virtue, Kemble suppressed his loathing and tried once more to speak to Slocum as a friend, an ally.

"There is only one way you can right the wrong you have done here, General. You must sell the rest of the salt you produce below the market price set by Congress and even give away some of it to the poor. You must also share the profits with the men who are doing the work."

"You are out of your goddamn mind," roared Slocum. "Share the profits with them cattle? Slocum is not risking his head in this war for nothing. You rich bastards are all alike. You expect the poor man to risk his neck for glory and when it's all over go back to sweating a bare living on his lousy acres. Well, you can stuff your glory up your ass, young squire. Now get the hell out of here. Just remember, if you say one word against Slocum you'll regret it all your life."

Outside it began to rain. Acrid smoke billowed from the chimneys of the boiling house and swirled through the saltworks. Kemble walked through the drizzle to his horse, still tied to the tree where he had left him. He mounted and turned to Slocum, who was standing at the gate.

"General Slocum," he said. "Did you ever see a letter Dr. Franklin published after Bunker Hill? He wrote it to a friend in England."

"I don't think I saw it. What did he say?"

" 'You are now my enemy and I am yours.' "

With a curse Slocum snatched a musket from one of the sentries at the gate, aimed it at Kemble, and pulled the trigger. The bullet came within a foot of his head.

"There is my answer to you. The next shot won't miss," Slocum roared.

Kemble shoved spurs into his horse and got out of the clearing into the safety of the trees. For the first time he faced the fact that Daniel Slocum was not just an uneducated Whig. He was something much more dangerous—something that did not exist in the American future as Kemble envisioned it—an evil man.

CHAPTER SEVEN

TROUBLES OF A much different sort were absorbing Kate. Lieutenant Thomas Rawdon suffered an alarming relapse. His wound, which seemed to be healing normally beneath Dr. Davie's sutures, suddenly became infected. Dr. Davie had to remove the sutures. This time he left it open with a device known as a tent in it to encourage a thorough drainage.

"I knew I should have left the dumb thing open in the first place," Dr. Davie said. "I almost think the fellow wanted things to go this way. Remember his crazy talk of closing it up and getting it over with?"

From the hall where they were standing, Kate studied Rawdon's flushed feverish face on his pillow. "Is it—serious?"

"No. I think we will save him this time in spite of himself. But there is something going on in that fellow's noggin that I don't understand."

By this time Kate was alternating between the same opinion and a suspicion that she understood Thomas Rawdon all too well. At first there seemed little to suspect. He had stubbornly insisted on fulfilling the first part of his planned march to infinity. He doubled the number of steps he took each day, clinging to Kate's arm, all the while murmuring outrageous remarks. She was defiantly determined to assert her American identity in his presence. Memories of her mother's fate put her doubly on her guard against the seductive powers of the British officer corps. But these antagonistic feelings mingled with the ambience with which a nurse—particularly an amateur nurse—surrounds her patient. It is a kind of love mingled with a certain vexation. It is akin to the feeling a mother has for a difficult child. In the language of the electrical laboratory, there was simultaneous attraction and repulsion—a phenomenon that would seem to defy science and which occurs in no other place but the human heart.

By the time he had completed his first week of promenading in his sickroom, Rawdon had Kate calling him Thomas as a habit. It was all done with jests, a mad extension of his original contention that Thomases doubted everything, even their own identities, hence needed constant reassurance about who they were, hence the need to hear their names frequently. But beneath the witty fooling there were flashes of serious—and seriously troubled—feelings.

Toward the end of the second week of his recovery, Lieutenant Rawdon suddenly fixed Kate with his deep-socketed dark gray eyes and said, "I'm afraid I'm going to have to shoot you, Miss Stapleton."

"Why?"

"You have criticized my taste in poetry. I recited some of the best work of the finest English poets of our era and you called me a damned silly noodle."

"Which is what you were, and I fear still are. But why should I be killed for saying it?"

"In denying my taste in poetry, you're defying the authority of the mother country, who has sent me over here to educate you on a wide variety of subjects. If you refuse to be educated, I will be forced to shoot you. Doesn't that make perfect sense?"

"There is no one in the world who can talk nonsense to match you."

"Precisely what I told my father. For that very reason I argued that he should buy me a seat in Parliament. Instead I found myself gazetted to the King's Own Regiment. My father is a patriot. He sees America as threatening the very foundation of the English Constitution. Those who threaten the Constitution are traitors, and traitors should be shot. That is the kindest thing we can do to them. When our blood is up, we hang, draw, and quarter them. But my father would find it hard to continue his ranting after one look into your eyes."

"What does this have to do with your taste in poetry?"

"Thomas. Your taste in poetry, Thomas."

"Thomas."

"It has nothing to do with my taste in poetry. But I thought you might be interested to know how I came to America and a little about yours truly, the Rawdon family black sheep."

"Who gave you that nasty name?"

"Practically every relative I have. I suffer by comparison with my cousin, you see. Perhaps you've heard of him. Francis, Lord Rawdon. We are the same age. I've gone through life being compared to him. I'm sure, if he were to pay us a visit, you would fall in love with him instantly. He is the perfect soldier, noble, proud, brave. At Bunker Hill he commanded a company of thirty-five men. At the end of the battle there were only five of them left. Can you find a better proof of a man's heroism? Francis is currently General Clinton's aide-de-camp. His ambition is to be a full general at the age of forty. I have no doubt that he will realize it."

"What is your ambition?"

"Ah, Miss Stapleton. That is why I am the family black sheep. I don't have any. I am a hopelessly idle indolent fellow."

"Don't be so cruel to yourself. There is no need for a person to accept the names others fasten on him. Even if they're half true, a person can change."

"That's why I decided to accept my father's challenge and try soldiering. The very opposite of my nature. I told myself by pretending to be ravenous for fame, honor, glory, I would somehow ignite a mild appetite for these things. And what happens? Before I can lead a charge or deliver a summons to surrender, I am shot through by some bumpkin who neither knows nor cares about the great experiment in character development he is interrupting. I fear I am doomed to be a man of futility. I have only one hope left."

"What?" said Kate, rather solemn now, for in spite of his wry tone she sensed a personal pain in this complicated confession.

"To find a woman foolish enough to let me love her. Since I have no talent or interest in anything else, I am prepared to make this the grand project of my life. But what woman will tolerate a man without spirit, honor, ambition, etc.?"

"Have you tried any to find out?"

"One. She led me on until I revealed my abysmal character in all its unlovely nakedness. She rejected me with contempt."

"Damn her for a bitch," Kate said.

"She was another reason why I accepted my commission in the King's Own."

"Yes. I listened to you reciting *The Sorrows of Young Werther* by the yard while you were delirious."

He took her hint. "I was afraid to hope. I had no hope. Until I saw you that night at the dance. You were so full of life and I was so full of death."

"What in the world—are you talking seriously—"

For the first time in years Kate was flustered by a man. She sprang up, blushing. "You are a damn tease, that is what you are."

"I am serious, Miss Stapleton. I love you."

"You don't know anything about me."

"I don't need to know—or want to know."

"Yes you do," Kate said. "I don't believe two people can love each other in defiance or ignorance of the world. Love can't be separated from the life people must live after it's pledged."

Kate had ceased to be a romantic. But Thomas Rawdon, behind his mask of mockery and humor, was in the grip of the darkest, most destructive romantic emotions and he was determined to draw Kate into them.

"I have the money, Miss Stapleton, or will have soon. The money to devote my life to loving you. Do you know what a nabob is?"

"Of course I do. One of those disgusting Englishmen who has made his fortune by exploiting the poor East Indians."

"Precisely. My father is a nabob. He sired me and forthwith departed for the East, where he no doubt sired several dozen unacknowledged dusky little Rawdons, and returned home immensely rich, built himself a noble pile in Cornwall and a town house in Berkeley Square, and went to work on making me worthy of inheriting his fortune."

"This is all mad imagination, like everything else you say."

"I wish it were. I very much want to inherit this fortune. Otherwise it will go to my pompous hero cousin, Lord Rawdon. But it will take management. I have no intention of recovering my health, until this damnable war ends. I have lost all desire to get killed in order to turn Americans into obedient servants of His Majesty. It should not be difficult to remain a prisoner of war until the maniacs on both sides get tired of killing each other. They've captured several hundred healthy officers in Burgoyne's army who will be much more worth exchanging than me. The moment the war ends, I can resign my commission with tolerable honor. We will board the next packet to London where I will introduce you to Father as the American heiress who has saved my life and whom I wish to make my wife. The day before you see him, I will ask you to spend twelve hours swearing. Hopefully you will be all sworn out for the next day or two."

"I knew you were not serious about this."

"I am serious. I have never been more serious about anything in my life."

The old Kate, the Kate who pledged her love so recklessly to Anthony Skinner in the Shrewsbury swamps, might have been overwhelmed by this vision of lifelong devotion backed by a hundred thousand pounds. But the new Kate was wary. She declined to accept the offer—or Thomas Rawdon—at face value. Over the next few weeks she struggled to penetrate his comedian's mask and find out more about him. Why had he left medical school in Edinburgh, for instance?

"I was too good."

"What does that mean?"

"No, that is only half the truth. The other half is what I've already told you about the ignorance of most doctors masquerading as knowledge. And—something else."

Kate sensed his reluctance and pressed him to tell her the whole truth. They were strolling beside the brook. Rawdon stared away from her into the stripped wintry trees of late November.

"I didn't care, I didn't care whether any of the stupid people I was trying to cure lived or died."

"That is why you did not care whether you yourself lived or died?"

"I suppose so. Until I saw you."

"I wish," Kate said, trying to choose her words with extreme care, "I wish I could say I was flattered, simply flattered by such a reaction, Thomas. But I am afraid it also frightens me."

"Why?"

"I don't know how to say it, exactly. Perhaps I don't feel worthy of such single-minded devotion. Perhaps I'd like to see a man do something besides devoting his life to making me happy. There are so many things to be done in this country, Thomas, after we win this war. I'm not sure I want to marry a man who doesn't care enough to be part of the life around him."

"I will care, through you. Your caring will be my caring."

"It's not enough, Thomas. It's not enough and too much at the same time."

From that moment Thomas Rawdon began slipping down into the swamp of melancholy in which he had spent too much of his young life. It had an inevitable effect on his health. Anyone who practices medicine for a few years notices how much our moods, the loss of hope, a sudden grief, affect our bodies. With melancholy came a critical hypersensitivity. Rawdon saw the time Kate spent preparing for Christmas as a rejection of him. He withdrew from all the celebrations of the season and even abandoned his daily exercise because Kate was no longer there to walk with him. In a few weeks, his wound began to swell and an infectious fever returned to disturb his nights.

He said nothing about it. He probably would have allowed the infection to spread inward from the sutured wound until it was too late to help him. Kate, bringing him his breakfast one morning, noticed his nightshirt was drenched with sweat. She told Dr. Davie, who examined the wound, diagnosed the return of the infection, and took prompt steps to combat it.

A few days later, when Dr. Davie pronounced himself satisfied at the rate with which infected matter was flowing from the wound, Kate tried to deal with the other side of Thomas Rawdon's sickness—the invisible unhealed wound in his spirit.

"You must have been in great pain, Thomas, and you knew you had a fever," she said as they sat in the rose garden. "Why didn't you tell me?"

"Why didn't you ask me?"

"You know how busy I've been in the kitchen. Father spends a great deal of his time at Kemble Manor these days. I've also been needed in the taproom."

Without looking at her, Rawdon felt his own pulse, and said, "The fever is almost gone. I will be up in a week."

"You are half in love with dying, aren't you?"

"Sometimes more than half."

"I have been thinking a good deal about love in the past year, Thomas. I didn't think about it much before that. Then I tried loving someone; I made a dreadful mess of it. So did the man I loved. He hadn't thought very much about it either."

With brutal detail she told him the story of her involvement with Anthony Skinner, leaving nothing out.

"For him love was—is—all pride, possession. You seem to think it's pity. I'm sure it's neither of these things. I'm not rejecting your love out of hand, Thomas. On the contrary I've never been happier in the company of any man. But I think we must wait a little longer to see if we can both discover a better kind of love between us."

The calmness, the honesty, the good sense of these words disturbed Thomas Rawdon more than he could bring himself to admit. But he was too deep in his melancholy to escape that deadly swamp along the route Kate was offering him.

"There are some people who cannot change their natures. You must understand that."

"That is what I refuse to admit. People do change. I am living proof. A country can change. If America can have a revolution, why not a person? History is nothing but the story of changes. I believe we are only at the beginning of them in America."

Lieutenant Rawdon did not realize it but he was seeing a phenomenon of our Revolution—the emergence of American women as thinking as well as feeling beings. The books Caroline Skinner had given Kate, the conversations they had had over the past year were bearing fruit. She was becoming her own woman in a very personal way.

Rawdon was too blinded by melancholy and prevailing masculine pride to see this. He still wanted Kate's love on his terms or not at all. In his secret, darkest self, he really preferred not at all.

"Perhaps some people can change," he said grudgingly. "But for others it is out of the question."

Kate almost lost her temper. But she sensed it would be a mistake, possibly a fatal one. She took Lieutenant Rawdon's hand and gave him her warmest smile. "Let's go on being honest with each other, Thomas, and do the best we can."

"You are talking to me as my nurse," Rawdon said.

"As long as you continue to be a patient, how else can I talk?"

Rawdon left Kate in the garden without another word. He strode to Jonathan Gifford's office and asked him if he could borrow a pistol. Captain Gifford politely refused to give him one.

"You are a prisoner of war, Lieutenant."

"I assure you I have no intention of using it for warlike purposes."

"What then?"

"I want to kill myself."

Captain Gifford considered this calmly for a moment.

"Why?"

"No explanation is necessary—or possible."

"Perhaps you can't explain it to yourself—much less to me."

"Perhaps. But that has no bearing on my decision."

"Why not wait a week, Lieutenant? She may change her mind. Women do, you know."

"This goes beyond a woman, Captain Gifford. It involves the nature of the universe. I find it meaningless. It is true I hoped one person could give it meaning for me. But she has failed me."

"Lieutenant, if you are talking about Kate—I know you are— you are being worse than stupid. You are being downright damnably perverse. If you don't appreciate what she has done for you, maybe you ought to shoot yourself. I am almost tempted to give you the pistol. But I won't because I want to keep you alive for her sake. Go down by the brook and take ten deep breaths. That's what we used to do with green lieutenants who started to panic before a battle."

I am not sure whether Rawdon was serious that day. There is a great deal of posturing in romantic self-pity. Kate remains convinced that his melancholy ran deep enough to make his threat genuine. Unquestionably, it became serious on a day soon to come.

CHAPTER EIGHT

Toward the end of January 1778, General Slocum appeared at Liberty Tavern early on a weekday morning. There was no one in the taproom. Slocum ordered his usual pint of stonewall, sat down before the fire, and asked to see Kemble.

Jonathan Gifford sent Barney up to his son's room. Since his return from the saltworks, Kemble had been avoiding his father, agonizing over what he should do about Slocum. He refused to ask his father's advice, which meant that Jonathan Gifford kept a wary distance while trying to find out what was troubling his son. He got little more than monosyllables from attempts to converse and sadly concluded that Kemble's sullen isolation was aimed at him.

Barney returned to the taproom alone. "The lad says he's busy and has no time to see you."

"What the devil," said Slocum, "he's not going to let that little misunderstanding we had a month ago set him down now, is he? Tell him I'm here to make him a fair offer."

"What would that be, General?" Jonathan Gifford asked.

"Why, to buy out his share of Kemble Manor, in advance of sale. And his sister's too."

"If you want to make an offer, make it to me. I'm still Kate's legal guardian. She won't be twenty-one until June."

Slocum hesitated. He had not expected to deal with Jonathan Gifford. "I ain't no lawyer. But I understand they have some share in the place, since old Skinner never managed to sire nothing off his wife—"

"As far as I know, General, the manor isn't for sale."

"It will be soon enough. The honorable Provincial Congress has appointed commissioners to take charge of confiscated estates, and ordered local courts to begin condemnation proceedings without the waste of a day. As I hear it, the manor will be condemned at the first sitting of our court of general sessions next week."

"I wouldn't be too sure of that. Mrs. Skinner has hired a good lawyer, and intends to plead her dowry rights to prevent the condemnation. I believe Kemble and Kate will join her in the suit, declaring themselves ready to yield their rights to her."

Jonathan Gifford did not bother to tell Slocum that he was the architect of this strategy. His surprise at the news of the manor's condemnation was also pretense. He had been expecting this crisis ever since Charles and Anthony Skinner fled to New York. None of this concern was visible in the cool gambler's face he showed to General Slocum. But Slocum was not easily intimidated. "Gifford, don't be a damn fool. What chance have you got? She can quote the Declaration of Independence until doomsday, she's still the wife of the second worst Tory in the state and mother of the worst one. And your daughter ain't exactly a living endorsement of patriotism. If I want to go to the trouble, I can find some hard things to say about your boy's loyalty too. After all, he lives in this damn tavern, which was thick with your fellow British officers for the best part of eight months. He conducted himself as a damn spy when he visited my saltworks, and only my friendship prevented them Yankees from hanging him."

"I don't know what the hell you are talking about, Slocum."

"I'm telling you to sell now, at a good price, and drop that stupid suit. If you let things go on, I will get the whole farm without paying them a cent for it. Do you think there is a judge in this county who don't take orders from me? Ain't they sitting at my appointment? Don't my Continental troops protect them? Wake up, Gifford."

"Maybe the confiscation commissioners will take a different approach."

Slocum laughed heartily. "Do you know who they are? There is Matt Leary as chief, my cousin Joe as the second, and honest George Winston as the third."

Leary was the owner of the grog shop to which Slocum kept directing customers, largely in vain. His cousin Joseph Slocum was an illiterate drunk, one of the few who could tolerate Leary's liquors. George Winston was the major of our militia regiment, a total Slocum toady.

"I see what you mean," Jonathan Gifford said. "In that case, you won't be the only bidder on the manor, General Slocum."

"Oh, who is going to join? Old George Kemble? From what I hear, he will be pawning his plate to repair what is left of his house, after the Yankees paid him a visit."

"I'm going to buy it. I don't see any other way to protect my children's property."

"What the devil, Gifford . . . ?" Slocum added some choice obscenities to this opening curse and then tried threats. "Stay out of Slocum's way, Gifford. There will be a time when you need him—a time when he won't be there."

"The way your brave Yankees are protecting us, I will take my chances with Barney here and Black Sam for a garrison."

Slocum finished his drink and rose for a farewell salute. "Goddamn you, Gifford, you don't want that place for those brats. You want it to hold for that Tory bastard Skinner. He has slipped you the money. At the very least he will have the laugh by forcing Slocum to pay three times what it's worth. You are a goddamn Tory stalking-horse."

Slocum departed, roaring. Jonathan Gifford went upstairs and told Kemble what had just transpired in the taproom. "You are over twenty-one," he said stiffly. "I probably should have consulted you. But since you said you didn't want to see him—"

"You told him exactly what I would have told him."

"You no longer are—enthusiastic about General Slocum?"

"I will not put up with your sarcasm, Father. That is just what I thought you'd say."

"I had no intention of being sarcastic. I—"

"No, it just comes out that way. You can't help it. You must tell little Kemble he is wrong as usual."

"Let's try starting over. What happened between you and Slocum down at the saltworks?"

Kemble told his father the story. His language was full of halting, disconnected phrases. But his anger drove him to the grisly final scene, when Slocum almost shot him.

"The son of a bitch!" Jonathan Gifford said. "He has overreached himself this time, by God. I think we can bring him down, Kemble."

"It will ruin the Cause in this part of the state."

"I hope the Cause is larger than General Slocum. If it isn't we are all in trouble. We'll beat him at the polls, Kemble. We'll tie that saltworks and that Continental regiment around his neck, like a pair of lead anchors."

Those were brave words, but for the time being, General Slocum remained in charge of our political and military affairs. As he predicted, the court of general sessions, meeting with the courthouse surrounded by Major Yates and his regulars, condemned Kemble Manor and a dozen other estates as the property of "virulent enemies of this country" and ordered them sold at public auction. The court also issued an order, putting the Kemble Manor gristmill in immediate control of "the military power of this county"—i.e., General Slocum—in order to assure its continued operation. All fees were to be paid to the General, who would pass them on to the government, after deducting his "expenses." He promptly appointed one of his cousins as his deputy and threw out Samson Tucker, whom Caroline Skinner had hired to run the mill.

That lady did not accept the news of General Slocum's preliminary victory with philosophic resignation. "I will burn this house to the ground before I let that man get his hands on it," she said.

"I hope it won't come to that," Jonathan Gifford said with a smile. He did not stop to analyze it, but he liked her most when she was angry. She was so small and fragile, and her defiance was so large.

"Why are you smiling, Captain Gifford?"

"I'm imagining the expression on Slocum's face if he laid out twenty or so thousand dollars for the manor and then learned you had burned it down."

"It would be amusing if it were not so serious," Caroline said. "Isn't it outrageous, Captain Gifford, that a woman forfeits her property rights the moment she signs a marriage contract? If this country is serious about those opening lines of the Declaration of Independence, they ought to correct that inequality as the first act of the legislature. They ought to correct it now."

Jonathan Gifford nodded wearily. He had had this conversation before. "I told you I would write to Governor Livingston about it. I got his answer yesterday. Every county is practically slavering over loyalists' lands, and a lot of the saliva is coming from the legislators themselves. They are not going to let anyone introduce novel ideas that might complicate things."

311

"In the eyes of the law I do not exist as a person. Do you think that is fair or honest or even sensible, Captain Gifford, especially when I have proved I can run this place at a profit?"

Captain Gifford felt a need to separate himself from that part of the male sex on which her indignation was being so righteously poured. "I am no lawyer," he said. "Let me assure you, Mrs. Skinner, you exist as a person for me."

"I—I hope so," she said, her anger dwindling into feelings so different, and so visible, he could only avoid naming them with an effort of the will.

"I've brought you the latest newspapers," he said, trying to change the subject. He took a sheaf of them from the inside pocket of his cloak. At her request, he had been bringing her periodic collections of American papers for several months now. He had plenty of them, left by travelers passing from east and west, north and south. Soon they were spending several pleasant hours together each week discussing them. He was amazed by her knowledge of English and Continental European politics. She knew all the factions at the court of France and all the party leaders in the English Parliament. Politics had always fascinated Jonathan Gifford and before he realized what was happening, a whole afternoon often slipped away. But when she asked him to stay for supper, he invariably refused, pleading business at the tavern. Much as he enjoyed her company, he obviously feared enjoying it too much.

"Is there any news in them?" she asked, picking up the first few papers and scanning them.

"Rumors of a French alliance, not much else."

"I dislike that idea. I would rather see us win this war with no help from Europe. Then we could begin a real revolution in this country. We would have the authority to root out all the Old World's hypocrisies and prejudices that afflict us."

She was as fanatic as Kemble about the Revolution, Jonathan Gifford thought. But when Kemble talked this way he inevitably felt hackles of disagreement rising. He had never had much faith in changing the world for the better, having grown up in Ireland, where things had changed steadily for the worse for generations. Here he was for some mysterious reason inclined to do the opposite—agree with almost anything Mrs. Skinner said.

"You may be right. I'm sure you are," he said. "But we can't do

312

much about the big war. We must fight our own little battles as best we can. Let's concentrate on keeping Kemble Manor out of Daniel Slocum's hands. If you hear anything about a public sale or receive any notice of one, let me know immediately. Send Sukey on your horse."

"Do you think he will try some trick? The law very clearly specifies a public sale."

"General Slocum has shown very little interest in obeying the law since I've known him. But at the very least, a notice will have to be posted somewhere. I don't see how they could skip the taverns. I've asked every innkeeper in this part of the state to be on the watch for me."

We still lacked a newspaper in our part of New Jersey. The New York papers that we read before the war were now all royalist—and notices in taverns, churches, and other public places were the only way the government could communicate with the people.

Jonathan Gifford seriously underestimated General Slocum's capacity for chicanery. On a cold wet day toward the end of March 1778, we sat around the fireplace in Liberty Tavern's taproom worrying over the alarming rumors about General Washington's army starving at Valley Forge. We were roundly damning the greedy Pennsylvania farmers, who had had their best harvest in years, for refusing to take paper money for their produce. Kemble declared that if he were General Washington, he would seize food from these crypto-traitors at the point of the bayonet. Jonathan Gifford disagreed. One of the things that impressed him most about the way the Americans were fighting the war was Washington's steady adherence to the civilian control of Congress. "Once you give soldiers the right to take anything with a bayonet, it is hard to draw a line. You're on your way to a military dictatorship."

"When you have legislatures that let men like Slocum make fortunes, maybe the only way you can set things right is with bayonets," Kemble said.

A traveler, soaked and shivering from the weather, came in. We made room for him at the fireplace. He was an inspector from the Commissary Department headquarters in Trenton, touring New Jersey to spur the deputy commissaries and quartermasters into activity. We began damning these characters as a disgrace to the

Revolution. Our local pair, Beebe and Beatty, were typical of the breed. They had gotten into politics with Slocum and bought only from farmers who sided with him. Beebe was drunk much of the time and let Beatty buy for both of them. He had been a plasterer in Philadelphia and barely knew wheat from barley. With Slocum's help they had lately gotten into speculating with the government's money. Jonathan Gifford told the inspector how it worked.

"They have resold a lot of the corn they bought to John Burrows, down on Middletown Point. He's got eight or ten barns practically exploding with corn that he's holding for a jump in price."

"What can I do?" the inspector said. "They have friends, do you know what I mean? I just left them an hour ago at Leary's tavern, witnessing General Slocum's buying of Kemble Manor."

"What?" said Jonathan Gifford, leaping to his feet.

"Aye, Leary is commissioner of Tory estates, haven't you heard? They're having the first sale today."

"Kemble," said Jonathan Gifford, "tell Sam to saddle three horses. You and Barney be ready to ride with me in five minutes. And bring your guns."

He limped to the bar, took two beautifully embossed pistols from their box on the bottom shelf, and stuffed them into the waistband of his breeches. In five minutes he and Kemble and Barney were pounding down the muddy road toward Amboy like the leaders of a cavalry charge. They maintained the pace, although Kemble was sure it would kill either them or the horses, until they sloshed to a stop in front of Leary's tavern. Inside they found General Slocum, the three confiscation commissioners, and several followers sitting around the otherwise empty taproom clinking glasses. Deputy Commissary Beebe and Deputy Quartermaster Beatty were in the midst of congratulatory gulps. Slocum and his scrawny Scottish partner McIntosh were presiding over the merry party, looking as smug as a pair of pirates who had just captured a Manila galleon.

"Well," Slocum boomed, "if it ain't my old friend Gifford and his patriot son. How goes the Revolution at Liberty Tavern?"

"I just heard—by accident—that confiscated estates were being sold here today."

"They were," Slocum said, "but the business is done. You're too late, friend Gifford."

"The hell you say," Jonathan Gifford snarled. "What kind of a public sale do you call it when no one in our part of the county has even heard about it?"

"Why, the commissioner here sent a crier along the roads a week or two ago. You must have been busy when he came by Liberty Tavern."

"Mr. Leary," Captain Gifford said to the snub-nosed, slack-mouthed Irishman, "I'm here to bid on Kemble Manor."

"You heard what the General said," replied Leary, "'tis sold. The sale is over. Here's the new owners."

He pointed to Slocum and McIntosh.

"This is a goddamned fraud," Jonathan Gifford said. "What was the sale price?"

"Two thousand six hundred dollars."

About one fifth of what the manor was worth. Kemble had seen his father almost lose his temper in the past. It had been a frightening sight. But nothing in his previous experience compared to the rage that was suffusing Jonathan Gifford's face now.

"We know why you're here, Gifford," Slocum said. "You're playing a little game with your friend the Squire in New York. You protect his property over here in case the Americans win, he protects your neck in case the British win."

"That is a damn lie. It is Mrs. Skinner I am trying to protect."

There were several guffaws. "Why, that's one piece of old Skinner's property you can have, Gifford. Maybe you've already got it. You spend a lot of time with her, from what I hear."

Another explosion of guffaws. Jonathan Gifford stood, head slightly lowered, enduring the derision. In a low strangled voice he asked Commissioner Leary to let him examine the papers covering the sale of Kemble Manor. Leary's eyes darted uneasily to Slocum, who gave him permission with a nod.

"They are all in order, Gifford," Slocum said. "Perfectly legal. There ain't a damn thing you can do about it."

Leary opened a small battered trunk beneath his chair and fished out a sheaf of documents. Jonathan Gifford paged through them carefully. Then with grim deliberation he ripped them into ten or twenty pieces and threw them into the air.

Slocum was on his feet roaring, his followers likewise. But they

315

stopped in mid-lunge. Jonathan Gifford had a pistol in each hand. "This is the only language a swine like you understands, Slocum."

With his left-hand pistol he gestured to Leary. "Get behind your bar, Commissioner, and reopen this meeting. I want to make a bid on Kemble Manor."

Leary looked as though he might faint. His feet remained glued to the floor. Jonathan Gifford placed the muzzle of the pistol under his nose. "This gun has a hair trigger, Leary. It could go off by accident any second."

With a gasp of terror, Leary scuttled behind the long plank table that served as his bar.

"Where is the secretary?" Jonathan Gifford asked Slocum.

Not a man spoke.

"Kemble, you will act as secretary."

Kemble took a seat at a table. He found fresh paper and ink in Leary's trunk.

"Open the sale, Commissioner."

With a gulp, Leary obeyed. Jonathan Gifford bid ten thousand dollars for Kemble Manor. McIntosh offered fifteen. Jonathan Gifford offered twenty. McIntosh offered twenty-five. Jonathan Gifford offered thirty.

Whining mightily, the Scotsman quit the contest. Jonathan Gifford posted bonds for thirty thousand dollars, giving Liberty Tavern and its surrounding acres as surety. He was risking everything he owned in the world. Kemble and Barney were looking at him with disbelief on their faces. How could he explain it to them? It was impossible. A prudent man did not risk everything he had spent his life painfully saving and building because a woman once said to him: *I am for independence.* True, he was protecting Kate and Kemble's inheritance, too, but that could be regained in the courts. He was not thinking about them. It was the pride and the loneliness and the courage of that small straight-backed woman whom he could never touch, it was for her and no one else that he was risking everything.

He was also making a powerful enemy. But any anxiety on that score vanished in the rage that engulfed him when Slocum began shouting. "You'll hang for this, Gifford. Everyone swears you're a British agent. We'll hang you for it."

"Slocum, you keep trying to insult me. You can't do it. A gentleman cannot be insulted by a swine. But you have also insulted the reputation of a lady whom I happen to admire. For that, you will answer to one of these pistols. The other is ready for your hand, wherever and whenever you are ready to meet me."

Slocum looked around the room. It was a test of his courage that he could not dodge, if he wanted to keep his reputation as a soldier. "I am ready whenever you are, Gifford. One of these gentlemen will inform you where and when," he growled.

With another wave of his pistol, Jonathan Gifford persuaded Commissioner Leary to sign the papers, confirming the sale of Kemble Manor. "We will take these with us," he said, stuffing the documents in the inner pocket of his cloak, "and return copies to the commissioner in a day or two. In the meantime, General Slocum, I will look forward to hearing from you."

"You shall, Gifford. And I hope every man here will resolve if I fall to take proper revenge on this British assassin."

The news that Jonathan Gifford and General Slocum were to fight a duel spread through our district as rapidly as a battle report. Only Caroline Skinner in her isolation at the manor house failed to hear of it. Jonathan Gifford did not mention it when he visited her the following day and told her she no longer needed to fear eviction. "I am your landlord now," he said with a smile.

He gave her a much laundered version of his clash with Slocum and his crew. He did not even bother to mention the astronomical price he had been forced to pay. But Caroline's first question was the cost. She was hoping she could pay off the debt with the profits from the next harvest, if all went well. When she heard $30,000, she cried out in shock.

"Mr. Gifford, that is three times what the place is worth."

"We only have to pay fifty per cent in cash," he said, avoiding her eyes. "I can easily raise the money in Philadelphia. If you do as well with your hired hands next year and the year after, we should be able to pay it off."

"But if I don't—if the weather—"

"Land values will boom after the war. We could sell off part of the farm."

"But if prices fall and the state demands the money you would be forced to sell everything you own."

Her voice dwindled away as she grasped the full meaning of those words.

"Life is a risky business," Jonathan Gifford said. "We can only do what we think is right and abide the consequences."

As usual, she begged him to stay for supper. Also as usual he pleaded business at the tavern and retreated. Upstairs in her bedroom, Caroline Skinner gazed into her mirror. Two dark red spots of color glowed in her cheeks. "He did it for you," she whispered wonderingly to that face which had always seemed plain and uninteresting to her, "he did it for you. He loves you."

For a moment she danced about the room, hugging herself in wild exultation. But in another moment she plummeted from this height to the deepest despair she had yet known. He loved her. But he would never admit it. He would never speak the words as long as Charles Skinner was alive.

That evening she sat down to supper at the table loaned to her by Jonathan Gifford. Charles Skinner had taken with him to New York the ormolu clock, the red and blue china vases, the fretted Chippendale mahogany sideboards and cabinets which had once made theirs the most opulent dining room in New Jersey. Caroline was so dazed by the shock she had just received, she paid no attention to the meal, which was one of Sukey's better efforts, a fish chowder full of succulent lobster and crab meat, clams, oysters, eels, and other denizens of the deep.

"Didn't you like it, mistress?" Sukey asked, as she removed Caroline's almost untouched plate.

"It was very good, Sukey. But I have no appetite today."

"I suppose you are worried about Captain Gifford."

"How—how did you know?" Caroline asked.

"I was over at the Talbots' today, teaching their people to read. One of them—the one I told you I liked—George, was just back from the tavern. Everybody's talking about the duel."

"The duel?"

Numbly, Caroline sat there while Sukey told her that Captain Gifford was meeting General Slocum at dawn tomorrow in a field off the Amboy road. "They say the General insulted you when Captain Gifford bought the manor. George asked me if it was true. I told him if he even thought such a thing again I would scratch his eyes out."

In anguish Caroline fled to her room and sank to her knees. She had never been devout. Again it was a reaction against Sarah, who would sin extravagantly one day and repent even more extravagantly the next. Caroline's mastery of herself had extinguished those wild yearnings for the absolute which have become the fashion—and disgrace—of our age. But now love was loose in her soul, awakening a fervor she never knew she possessed. She prayed wildly for Jonathan Gifford's safety. A moment later she was asking herself how she could pray for such a thing when the reason for her plea was a desire to sin—there was no other word for it in the eyes of religion—with the man for whom she prayed. *Dear God, I cannot help it. Please accept both the sin and the prayer in the name of love.*

Until midnight, Caroline paced the floor repeating this strangest of prayers. Then, with an inner certainty that transcended all other realities she knew what to do.

She went swiftly to the back bedroom and knocked on Sukey's door. She was awake in an instant. "Sukey," Caroline said, "I want you to take the horse and ride to Liberty Tavern. Ask for Captain Gifford, no one else, and tell him someone is trying to break into the house."

Sukey was devoted to Caroline. But this command was too strange to obey without question. "How can I get to the barn, mistress?"

"There is no one there. I have to see Captain Gifford, I want to tell him something that—that could save his life. This is the only way I can be sure he'll come."

The March wind howled through the bare trees on the drive. Caroline rushed back to her room and took a pair of fur-lined gloves and an ermine-trimmed scarlet cloak from her clothes press. She gave them to Sukey.

"Wear these. They will keep out some of the cold. You can have them."

Sukey put them on but declined to accept them as a gift. "If it is as important as you say, mistress, I am glad to go."

A half-hour later hoofbeats came up the drive at a furious pace. In a moment Jonathan Gifford burst into the hall, a pistol in his hand. "Where is he, where did you hear the noise?" he asked.

"There is no one—there was no one, Captain Gifford," Caroline said. She was wearing her best night robe, light blue lamb's wool with appliquéd dark red roses.

The winter wind prowled the grounds outside the house. Jonathan Gifford's face darkened. "Then why—"

"Because—because I had to see you, Captain Gifford. I had to be sure you would come. I told Sukey—that lie."

"Why . . . ?"

"Because I just learned that you will be risking your life at sunrise."

"Mrs. Skinner, please don't—"

"—for another lie."

"A lie?" Jonathan Gifford said.

"You are defending—my honor, such as it is. And your own because of insults you received while acting on my behalf. You wish to prove to all the world that you acted from the purest—most disinterested motives. Captain Gifford, I think—I hope—that is a lie."

"Mrs. Skinner, are you out of your senses? There's no reason—"

"I love you, Captain Gifford. For the first time in my life, I am in love. With you. I think—you love me too. I brought you here to confess my love—and to claim yours before you deny it—wipe it out—with blood. If you kill Daniel Slocum tomorrow in my name, we shall never be able to look each other in the eyes again. It will be Mrs. Skinner and Captain Gifford to our miserable lonely graves."

Explosions of disbelief, of refusal thundered in Jonathan Gifford's soul. Memory smashed like a river in spring flood against his rock-hard will. This woman in the sunlit garden saying *I am for independence*; this same small woman in this hall defying her huge angry husband, saying with tears in her eyes, *if you turn against me, too*. Her husband's savage words, *a dry bitch with a barren womb*; her bitter summary of her marriage as a business arrangement now gone bankrupt. Fighting these images was a lifetime of denial, of discipline. He heard himself, a disembodied voice in the echoing hall.

"I have felt—"

The Captain was no wordsman. He took the lady in his arms. No, that is utterly inadequate. He enveloped her in a swooping, annihilating embrace that was both a capture by storm and a surrender on his part—and on the lady's part.

That first night they were as cautious, as uncertain with each other as newlyweds of nineteen. But though their bodies had not yet learned the lesson, their spirits sensed a union of enormous intensity and depth. Jonathan Gifford found it difficult to accept this intensity. It threatened a deep, stubborn reserve of selfhood which had enabled him to withstand the destructive spirit of Sarah Kemble Stapleton. Complicating his feelings was the way Caroline threw aside all the sobriety, the self-control that had seemed to him the essence of her character. The Captain's youthful fondness for wild women had been cured by ten years of marriage to Sarah. He had to learn that the same woman can be both wild and sober, passionate and self-controlled.

"Oh, Jonathan, Jonathan, Jonathan," Caroline said. "How I have longed to call you that. So many times I stood by my window and whispered it to myself. Would you call me Caroline? Not once, but a dozen times."

To his surprise, Jonathan Gifford found it easy to do, twelve times. "And once more for good luck," he whispered. "*Caroline*." Each time the name slipped from his lips, he felt it become a kind of electrical current, a device born of some arcane science, binding him to this woman for the rest of his life. He knew in the same moment that he was putting the thing he treasured most, his philosophic calm, his peace of mind, yes, even his very soul in mortal peril because if her husband returned and reclaimed her, it would plunge him into a torment that would make his agony with Sarah seem almost a benediction.

"When we are alone we must ban 'Gifford' and 'Skinner' from our vocabularies," Caroline said.

This sounds commonplace now, but it was a new idea in 1778. Only in the informal, not to say irregular atmosphere of the frontier did husbands and wives call each other by their first names.

"It is American," she told him with the same awesome intensity. "That perpetual Mr. and Mrs. is a stupid European custom. Oh, Jonathan, I want to love you, I *shall* love you with all my heart."

"Until tonight, I did not think it was possible for me to do that. I tried once—and failed. I never thought—or hoped—I would try again."

"You mean with Sarah. We must not flinch from using her name, even here, Jonathan. She haunts us both. But perhaps we can lay her ghost—by laying her sister. Oh, I've shocked you—"

"No," Jonathan Gifford said, although he was shocked. It was something Sarah might have said. She was as ribald as a Havana whore in bed.

"My thoughts often run to the obscene. Sometimes when I stood in company with you, I stripped you naked in my mind. It was a game Sarah taught me to play. I pretended to disapprove—you had to do that with Sarah or she devoured you."

"Yes," said Jonathan Gifford ruefully, both a confession and a fact. "I see she treated everyone the same way."

"Everyone who tried to love her. That filled her soul with horror—that anyone could love her. Because she knew she was a monster. So she set out to destroy that love, all the time protesting that she could not get enough of it."

"That's enough about Sarah for the time being."

"Let's not regret her, Jonathan, nor mourn her. For all the pain and torment she caused us, she awakened in us both, I think, the idea, the importance of love. So many people go through their whole lives without ever thinking about it."

"I tried to do that," Jonathan Gifford said, remembering his army years.

"Without this—this time with you—I could never have said—what I just said. It would have killed me."

He saw she was forgiving the cruel, reckless woman who had been her sister. How could he do less? For the first time he realized that until he did forgive Sarah, he would never be able to love this woman—or any woman—with his whole heart. It is a strange truism that men are inclined to make one woman become the paradigm of all women in their minds and hearts—and women are equally inclined to do it with men. If that one woman has been a destroyer, a figure of darkness, she can cast a fatal shadow on all the other women in his life, past and future. The strangeness of this is redoubled when we think how readily men accept the fact that some of their own kind are scoundrels or cowards or sadists while others are loyal, honest, generous. Women are equally adept at perusing and judging their own sex without sweeping negative conclusions.

Jonathan Gifford, a man who did not change his mind easily, struggled painfully to accept this wisdom. From the effort came another insight into himself. "I don't think I have ever really believed in happiness," he said. "A modest contentment was all I thought a man could hope for in this world, and I had failed to win even that—until tonight."

He stroked her thick black hair while his other hand found her soft seat of love. "Caroline," he whispered with no urging needed now. "Caroline."

They made love and dozed and made love again.

"Oh, what gluttonous flesh-ridden creatures we are, and I am so glad of it," Caroline said as the first traces of dawn paled the windows. "We have years of unloving and misloving to make up."

"Is that dawn?" Jonathan Gifford said.

"I am afraid it is."

"I must go."

"Where?"

"To meet General Slocum."

"That's impossible! I thought—"

"That I would stay here in bed with you and let him give me the laugh from Amboy to Cape May? I thought, Mrs.—I mean Caroline—you knew me better. What you said downstairs—the words that brought us up here—were true. But they did not eliminate General Slocum from the scheme of things. I have a reputation to uphold—a reputation as a man. You may say it is childish, to rest a reputation on powder and ball, but we cannot completely ignore the ways of the world."

"If he kills you I will hunt him down and blow his brains out."

"You will do no such thing. You will have to take charge of this property and the tavern, too. If the war lasts, you will have a devil of a time saving either of them. Kate and Kemble don't have half a business head between them—"

"Stop! Stop! You are talking as if you were already dead."

"A duel is an unpredictable thing. The best shot in the world can be killed by a fool with a hand that shakes like a case of palsy. I swore I'd never fight another one—after Havana."

He had his breeches on and his boots. He began buttoning his shirt. "I—I had wronged, as they put it, the daughter of one of the best families. She had been more than willing. But—her brother challenged me. They said he was twenty-one. He looked fifteen. His father, or the girl, or someone had obviously put him up to it. He was terrified. I planned to pink him in the arm. But as we fired he panicked and lunged to one side. I hit him in the heart."

Beneath her warm quilts, Caroline Skinner felt cold clutch at her. This was not the man she loved, this stranger who talked in that flat somber voice about killing and being killed. She had seen

323

him as the wounded victim of her sister's cruelty. This man reeked of death. But she vowed that she would love him in spite of it, she would somehow help him triumph over the years of war which had seemed to end for him not in glory but a kind of grim loathing of it all, a loathing that included himself.

"You see what a noble fellow you've fallen in love with. Maybe now you won't be so sorry if General Slocum scores a lucky hit."

"I will die!"

She sprang from the bed naked into the cold to fling her arms around him.

"I promise you—I will do everything I can to prevent it from coming to bullets."

"Let me fix you some breakfast."

He shook his head. "A bullet in an empty belly does less damage. I will get a little rum at the tavern."

He rode away, leaving her in torment. At Liberty Tavern, Barney, Kemble, and Dr. Davie were waiting for him. Barney had the dueling pistols oiled and ready in their ivory case. He was nervous and talkative, Kemble somber and silent.

"Begorra, if it don't seem like old times, Captain, with half the regiment betting everything but their hats on you. I never had the honor to serve you in this way before, not being a gentleman born."

"Don't worry. We're not dealing with a gentleman."

Jonathan Gifford turned abruptly to Kemble. "I hope your new country—our new country—will pass a law, making this a crime."

"Let me second that motion," Dr. Davie said. "I've been on too damn many of these expeditions. I never saw one that made sense."

Kemble did not agree with them. The College of New Jersey was heavily attended by Southerners and he had imbibed their high ideas about honor. "How else can a gentleman defend himself—or a lady—from men like Slocum?"

"I don't know. A horsewhip or a fist seems better on the whole. You may get your hands dirty, but you get dirty dealing with swine anyway. I just want you to know—as your father—that I have done this often enough to loathe it. I hope you never do it."

As usual when Jonathan Gifford and Kemble talked as father and son, the air was charged with suppressed emotion. Also as

324

usual, there was no agreement. "I don't see how I could refuse if someone called me out," Kemble said.

General Slocum and two friends were waiting for them in a field beside a burned-out farmhouse about midway to Amboy. His seconds turned out to be Deputy Commissary Beebe and Deputy Quartermaster Beatty. They were wearing their buff and blue army uniforms. General Slocum was also wearing his uniform. Jonathan Gifford instantly divined their purpose. They were forcing him to fire at a soldier, a defender of his country, in a time of war.

Dismounting, Captain Gifford took Kemble's arm. "Inform these gentlemen that if General Slocum will retract what he said about the lady he has injured, I am prepared to disregard his aspersions on my character. I will even admit equal rudeness to him. We were both speaking in a great temper."

Kemble delivered this message to Deputy Commissary Beebe. He repeated it to General Slocum. His big black head swung to glare at Kemble. "I always knew that goddamn limey had no guts."

"For your information, General," Kemble said, "it is common practice for a gentleman to do everything in his power to avoid the fatal moment in these encounters. A gentleman does not wish to spill anyone's blood."

Slocum guffawed. "Well, I ain't no gentleman. I intend to spill that limey's blood and splash his brains all over this road."

For the first time, Kemble felt a clutch of fear. Slocum's animal courage was up, fueled by a canteen of stonewall which Beebe was holding ready. "If he should by a stroke of luck cut me down, lads," said Slocum, raising his voice even louder, "let it be known far and wide that I died defending my country's rights against this damned insidious agent of the enemy."

"You can depend on us, General," said Beebe.

Kemble returned to Jonathan Gifford, with an anxious face. "He rejected it with contempt."

"So I heard," said Jonathan Gifford, who had been watching Slocum's performance. "You had better load the pistols. I'll take two ounces of rum, Barney, and no more."

Barney handed the pistols to Kemble and took a flask of rum from his saddlebag. He poured it into a leather cup and Jonathan Gifford drank it off in one swift gulp.

"There's only one place a bullet will stop that bugger," Barney said, studying Slocum. "Between the eyes."

Jonathan Gifford shook his head. "I don't want to kill him."

"Then you'll give him a shot at you, sure as I'm here."

"I will have to take that risk."

"I'm told he's been practicing with a pistol three hours a day this whole week."

"I will shoot for his gun arm," Jonathan Gifford said.

The sun had risen, but the sky remained a wintry gray. Ground fog swirled in the nearby fields. Kemble and Beebe met between the two antagonists to discuss the rules. Beebe would call off ten paces, then each man would be free to turn and fire. Dr. Davie spread a white cloth on the ground and calmly laid out his surgical instruments on it.

The pistols were inspected by the duelists. Jonathan Gifford added a few grains of powder to his firing pan. Deputy Commissary Beebe was summoned to General Slocum's side. They conferred and he strutted over to Jonathan Gifford and his party. "The General wishes to be magnanimous," he said with a smile that revealed his bad teeth. "He is prepared to apologize to the lady—if Mr. Gifford will surrender his illegally gotten title to Kemble Manor."

"Not interested," Jonathan Gifford said.

"Oh, kill him, Captain. Kill the bugger," Barney said.

Jonathan Gifford shook his head. He refused to change his plan. He knew that killing Slocum would arouse an army of enemies. Better than any of us, he knew how fickle men were, how inclined they were to hate a man because of his place of birth or his wealth, however modest, or his associations.

General Slocum said he was ready. Jonathan Gifford agreed with a nod. Both men advanced to the center of the field, turned their backs, and waited for Beebe to begin the count.

"One," he called, and they began pacing away from each other. "Two—three—four—five—six—seven—eight—nine—ten."

Kemble's eyes were on his father. A surge of voiceless regret throbbed through his body, almost strangling him. *If he dies believing that I hate him, I won't be able to bear it.*

Jonathan Gifford turned and fired all in one incredibly swift motion. Slocum cried out in agony and his gun fell from his hand.

His right arm hung useless at his side, streaming blood. But Barney had been right. Only a bullet between the eyes would have stopped this man. Slowly he bent his knee to pick up the pistol with his left hand.

"I can fire as well with either hand, Captain Gifford," he said.

According to the *code duello*, Jonathan Gifford had no choice but to stand unflinching while Slocum slowly raised his gun with his left hand. But when he tried to level it, the muzzle wavered. A musket ball does harsh things to any part of the body it strikes. Blood was gushing from Slocum's wounded right arm. His cheek muscles bulged like knotted whipcord as he struggled to control his pain and nausea. With a guttural gasp, he staggered violently and fired the pistol into the ground at his feet.

Slocum fell to his knees. "Stonewall," he roared. "Stonewall." He swung his head back and forth like a beaten boxer.

Deputy Commissary Beebe rushed to give him the benefit of the canteen filled with his favorite drink. Dr. Davie cut open Slocum's sleeve and began examining the wound. The duel was over.

"Another round," roared Slocum after a gulp of stonewall. "I demand another round."

"I am the challenger," Jonathan Gifford said. "I have the right to decline. I am satisfied with the damage done."

"You can expect a challenge from me the moment this arm is ready," Slocum said.

"The next time, Slocum, I will kill you," Jonathan Gifford said.

The controlled ferocity in these words struck Slocum with the force of a bullet. He was mute. Jonathan Gifford walked to his horse. For a moment Kemble felt a fleeting sympathy for Slocum. He too had flinched before that murderous menace he had always sensed in his father. Kemble approached Slocum. The General was glaring straight ahead, his eyes bright with liquor and hatred, while Dr. Davie worked on his arm.

"Is it possible for us to come to some understanding, General? For the sake of the Cause?"

"You are wasting your time, Kemble," Jonathan Gifford said, from the saddle.

"Your pappy is calling you. Get the hell out of here, little boy," Slocum said.

Flushed with anger, Kemble walked slowly back to his horse.

327

"Wouldn't it be better to negotiate with him? Arrange a truce—at least until the war is over?" he said as they rode away.

"He doesn't understand the meaning of the word negotiate, Kemble."

"You mean I don't. I am too stupid."

"If you had done what I told you in 1776—supported honest men instead of him and his toadies, it would never have come to this—he wouldn't be worth shooting."

"I knew you would throw that up to me," Kemble said. "I knew I would be reminded for the rest of my life about my failure to follow the great Jonathan Gifford's advice."

"I will take the satisfaction of doing it, just this once."

It was not Jonathan Gifford speaking. It was the tension and danger of the duel, the memory of Slocum's pistol slowly leveled. By a sad paradox, it was also the memory of what he had experienced last night at Kemble Manor that made death doubly unbearable. This too became part of his anger at this son who seemed indifferent to what he had just risked.

Behind the anger other words fumbled blindly like cattle in a dark wood. *My son, my son, I don't mean— Father, I am sorry. I am proud—* But the words remained unspoken, mute as beasts, as father and son rode silently home beneath the gray sky in the cold March wind of the third year of the war.

CHAPTER NINE

ABOUT A WEEK after the duel, Kate rode down to Kemble Manor to visit Caroline. She instantly sensed that something extraordinary had happened. In spite of the weather continuing to wear its gray March face, her aunt was brimming with high spirits. They had tea in her bedroom-sitting room and Caroline talked excitedly about her plans to raise Kemble Manor's productivity. She had been reading up on crop rotation fertilization, drainage, and other techniques of scientific farming and had concluded that her husband—and most other American farmers—were fifty years behind the times.

"I'm determined to pay off that monstrous debt your father has incurred on my account."

"I think he rather enjoys it," Kate said. "I have never seen him in such a cheerful mood. Nothing else in his life has changed as far as I can see. Prices are still going up by leaps and bounds. Kemble still barely speaks to him. General Slocum's friends are riding about the countryside slandering him. It must be the debt that is making him happy."

"You are teasing me."

"I am trying to solve a mystery."

"You have grown up a great deal, Kate, in the last year. But there are certain things . . ."

Caroline could not bring herself to tell Kate what had happened. After all, she was still her aunt, and Jonathan Gifford was her father. But Caroline found herself wishing she could tell Kate something—no—more than that—everything.

Who else would understand it as well as Kate? She would share it with her, Caroline promised herself. But not now. It was all too unbelievable, it might dwindle away like morning fog at the beach. That forgotten part of the Revolution, our almost unbearable uncertainty, our perpetually clouded future, combined with Caroline's natural diffidence to silence her.

Kate was a little hurt by Caroline's reticence. But her feelings were not inflamed by that natural (or is it unnatural?) resentment that fuels arguments between parents and children. Caroline had lost her parental aura for Kate. In the past six months they had become friends.

A large part of Kate's growing self-confidence had come from the books she had read and discussed with Caroline. At first she had concentrated on the issues around which the quarrel between England and America revolved. Once her mind was made up on these matters, she turned naturally to another topic that absorbed her as much as Caroline. The nature of the Revolution and the future of American women in their new country.

This is a subject that has almost dropped from sight as I write these words in 1826. The first fifty years of our American history have been a triumph of the male ethos. We have succumbed totally to the European idea of the lady and shoved all our women into the shadow of their men. Yet I cannot believe, as long as they can read and understand the opening lines of the Declaration of Independence, as long as they can remember (or learn through history to remember) that a different dream, a yearning for a truly equal partnership, suffused the women of the Revolution, that American women will tolerate this supine state indefinitely.

This consciousness of their unequal status as women was particularly acute the day Kate visited Caroline after the duel. That murderous encounter would never have taken place, Caroline pointed out, if she had retained her legal right to Kemble Manor. "I begin to think there is only one way we can gain our rights, and protect them when we gain them," Caroline said. "We must be free to vote with the men. Then they will have to listen to us."

"They will say we lack the education."

"There is an easy answer to that. When clods like Samson Tucker can vote and you and I cannot."

Kate asked Caroline if she had read the latest political news in the New York *Gazette*, a loyalist paper. The British were preparing to send another peace commission to America. "They say they will give us everything we asked for in '75."

"But now we have added something—independence," Caroline said. "We would be fools to go back to them now. Remember the history of the Dutch fight for independence from Spain. They agreed to a truce, negotiated a new relationship—and as soon as Spain felt strong enough the war broke out again. This happened over and over, until the Dutch finally realized total independence was the only answer."

"Some New York Congressmen who stopped at the tavern overnight told Father the peace commission was a trick to stop us from signing an alliance with France. They said that would mean the end of the war. England will have to call home her army to fight in Europe. They got drunk just thinking about it."

"I'm not so sure they are right," Caroline said. "If the French become allies—that could change the attitude of a great many people in England. The opposition in Parliament has been gaining strength by criticizing the government for making war on the Americans, using foreign mercenaries like the Hessians. If we have the French on our side, that argument is destroyed. It will give the government a cry to arouse all the patriotism that beat the French in the last war."

Kate sighed. "Sometimes I think I will be a dried-out old spinster in a rocking chair when they finally get tired of killing each other."

Caroline laughed. "A woman with your looks need never worry about dying a spinster, Kate."

"I'm not so sure. The only offers I've gotten lately have been from a British officer and a loyalist."

"You mean Anthony?"

Kate nodded. "He writes me a letter a week, so he says. Only a few arrive. He is unhappier than ever. The best rank he could get in Skinner's Greens was captain."

Officially, Skinner's Greens were the New Jersey Volunteers. They were a loyalist brigade, attached to the British regular army. The British took no Americans except career soldiers like young Oliver De Lancey into their home regiments.

"Anthony says the British give the loyalist regiments all the drudge jobs."

"How is—his father?"

"Even more miserable, as far as I can tell. Anthony rarely writes more than a sentence about him. Does Mr. Skinner ever write to you?"

"No."

"Did you ever really love him?"

Caroline shook her head. "I told myself I could love him—eventually. But the marriage was arranged between him and my father. He—my father—told me it was the only offer I was likely to get."

"He would never have done such a thing to a son."

"Of course not."

"That is what infuriates me—the way men feel we are objects they *own*. Anthony is that way. He insists on claiming me. He calls me his wife. It is true, we did speak of that night in Shrewsbury as our wedding night. In my mind I made a promise like a wife. My conscience would not let me do it any other way."

"But now your conscience—"

"Tells me I am free of him. That is one of the strange things about a revolution, isn't it. Things happen that free us."

"Yes," Caroline said. But there was a mournful echo in her agreement. She inevitably compared herself and Kate and saw how much more formidably she was bound to her husband, not only by conscience but by the force of law and custom.

"I'm not sure how I would feel about Anthony if the war ended tomorrow and he came back here to Kemble Manor. At first I thought I owed him the right to that much consideration. But I'm beginning to wonder how much longer I owe it to him. This war could last ten or twenty years."

"The other offer—from the British officer—is more attractive?" Caroline asked, plainly dubious that this was possible.

"Don't worry," Kate said. "Lieutenant Rawdon is not your ordinary British officer. The trouble is—he is not your ordinary anything. I find him delightful company. He makes me laugh—that is quite a feat in these times. But there is an emptiness in him."

Time and the Revolution (and Thomas Rawdon) were steadily eroding the bond Kate had forged with Anthony Skinner in that first passionate commitment. Those who admire romance may regret this. I will not judge it. I am trying to stand aside here, telling what happened both within and without our minds and hearts. No doubt some will (as I did) respond to Kate's first wish that political loyalties could be divorced from the devotions of the heart. But the politics of the Revolution went far beyond those party disputes over the national spoils that divert the readers of newspapers in every country. The Revolution involved a deeper loyalty, the kind that enters the self's essence—loyalty to a nation, a people. This was the real issue in the Revolution—who would decide the destiny of this new people in this new land—the Americans. The Revolution revealed and then released all the feelings this question evoked and they could not be separated from our personal lives because they went too deep.

For Kate the issue was complicated by her new awareness of herself as an independent woman. She was often angered by the lack of interest her father, her brother, and other males of her acquaintance showed in the future of women in America. At dinner the day after she visited Caroline, the conversation turned to a recent newspaper article in which Dr. Benjamin Rush identified three types of revolutionists. Violent Whigs used the Revolution as an excuse to attack personal enemies and justify their hatreds and greed. Staunch Whigs put their country's interests first. Timid Whigs were ready to give up every time the Americans lost a battle. Lieutenant Rawdon remarked that the loyalists could probably be divided the same way. Even the British at home were split along similar lines.

"I find that hard to believe," Kemble said.

"I assure you it is true," Rawdon said. "I am seriously thinking of resigning my commission and going home to turn scribbler and tell the country the truth."

"That would be droll," Kemble said. "Why don't you do it?" Kemble had grown rather fond of Rawdon, thanks largely to his iconoclastic attitude toward British society.

"Miss Stapleton here refuses to come with me."

"I told you I would come as your partner in political crime. But not as your wife," Kate said. "I am not ready for matrimony just yet. I want to complete my education first."

"You can read a book with one hand and rock a cradle with the other one," Kemble said.

"That attitude," Kate said, "is precisely what is wrong with this revolution. I sometimes think it is not a revolution at all. What have you overthrown? Nothing but a few pathetic royal governors and collectors of customs and some pictures and statues of the King. If we are to have a real revolution, it should start in the

333

home. The word 'obey' should be stricken from the marriage ceremony. Women should have the right to go to college and become lawyers and doctors, just like men."

"You are being utterly ridiculous," Kemble said.

"Give me one reason why a woman cannot master the subjects taught at Yale or Harvard or the College of New Jersey."

"She might master them," Kemble said. "But it would bring her mind into contact with a host of subjects—political, theoretical—unsuitable for feminine natures."

"Why unsuitable?"

"Your nerves cannot bear the tension, the discord created by the conflicting ideas you would encounter, the loud clash of masculine opinions."

"I cannot bear tension? Discord?" cried Kate. "I have lived through three years of war. I've looked into the faces of the dead and dying and been given thirty lashes and been denounced as a traitor. I seem to be thriving on it. I fear I am growing fat on it."

"My dear Kate," said Lieutenant Rawdon. "We depend on you women to brighten, to soften our lives. Not darken them with argument and disagreement."

"Listen to him sitting there in his red coat," Kate said. "If that isn't proof that this whole stupid war is about land, greed, money, I've never heard it. The archrebel and the King's officer are in complete agreement about everything else. No matter who wins, not a single slave or a single woman will be the freer for it. You're a couple of hypocrites."

The violence of this assault threw Kemble and Rawdon into some confusion. They turned to Jonathan Gifford for reinforcement. He had been studiously devouring his roast woodcock, trying to pretend he was invisible.

"Let us ask a man of experience," Kemble said. "You have seen the great world, Father. Do you think these ideas make sense?"

"I would say an education for a woman is like the dressing for this woodcock. Without it, the bird is still a pretty good meal. With it, we have a meal to remember."

"Solomon could not have done better, Captain Gifford," murmured Lieutenant Rawdon.

The dressing, made from a secret recipe which contained claret and chestnuts, was superb. Kate looked cross, and said she was not sure she liked being compared to a dead bird. But Jonathan

334

Gifford had escaped the battlefield unscathed. He left the young people to continue their argument over coffee, and rode down to Kemble Manor. There too he heard complaints about women's lot—but they were softened by an ingredient that made them much less abrasive.

As the new owner, it was natural enough for Captain Gifford to spend a good deal of time at the manor. He practically became co-foreman of the laborers whom Caroline hired to plant that year's wheat and corn and barley. Liberty Tavern saw him only in the evenings. Slocum and his faction spread obscene rumors about "the Englishman" and the lady of the manor. If he and Caroline heard any echoes of these noxious mutters, they probably consoled themselves with the knowledge that such people would say the same thing even if there was no truth in it. Like lovers in every age, they were too absorbed in each other to care much what the world was saying. To himself and finally to Caroline, Jonathan Gifford confessed he was amazed by the strength of his desire for her.

"I thought I was past all that at forty-seven," he said.

"It is this dreadful habit of making love in broad daylight that has undone you, Captain Gifford," Caroline said.

They had begun this delectable practice as a concession to the gossips. It was one thing for Jonathan Gifford to spend several hours a day at Kemble Manor and quite another for him to spend his nights there. At first Caroline had been shocked by the idea. It was the universal practice then and now in England and America to make love in the dark with a bare minimum of kisses and caresses. Only those Englishmen fortunate enough to make the grand tour and daring enough to defy the conventions discovered love in the Italian style. In the winter when they began, it seemed to Caroline harsh and almost demeaning. Her naked body did not seem capable of sustaining or inspiring the enormous emotions his touch awakened in her. The immensity of her love for him seemed better suited to the darkness.

But as spring began to soften and enrich the land and thick white sunshine streamed across the room, she began to like it and then to adore it. She rearranged the furniture so that the sunlight fell across them as they lay together on the bed. Swiftly she came to love with almost frightening intensity the solid curve of his muscular arms, the swell of his thick chest with its growth of fine

335

dark hair, the exquisite sensation this hair aroused when crushed against her breasts. Love, Caroline discovered, was both a large immeasurable idea like the night and a precious congery of specific things, of touches, of shapes that repetition makes more precious rather than mundane.

They loved, in the sunlight of that spring, a special ever-to-be remembered spring to them. But it was not all sunlight. Again and again shadows fell on their happiness, the shadow of the war and those two lesser human shadows cast by Sarah Stapleton Gifford and Charles Skinner.

Sarah was only an occasional intruder since they confronted her on their first night. At times, Caroline found her ghost almost benign. The deeper and more intense her love became, the more she found herself thinking about, almost speaking to Sarah, forgiving her again and again for testifying to life's central truth, the transcendent importance of love, a truth that her extravagant nature could not contain or tame, yet a truth nonetheless, a truth that deserved to be shouted from house and mountain tops if the respectable world where so many marriages are made for money or social place or a parent's pleasure would tolerate it.

Gradually, the love Caroline had once felt for her older sister but had long since stifled was reborn. Without realizing it at first, she even began to display some of that native wildness with which Sarah had first charmed Jonathan Gifford. After they made love they often rode out to enjoy the spring countryside. With no warning Caroline would dare him to race her to a distant landmark, an old tree or a meandering creek. Away they would go across pastures and fields, over fences and ditches. The first race ended in a dead heat. Looking at her flushed triumphant face, her glittering eyes, Jonathan Gifford said without thinking, "I haven't risked my neck that way since—since Sarah—"

"At heart we Kembles are all alike, wild, wanton vixens," Caroline said. "But who else can satisfy a satyr like you?"

"Madam," Jonathan Gifford said, "as a man who prides himself on his philosophic mind, I consider that an insult."

"Oh, you are a philosopher all right. A hedonist."

"I begin to think it would be better if women were not taught to read. These American ideas about equality will be the ruination of the race."

"Not of the race. Simply of the male portion of it."

They both began laughing. Between lovers, these ideas lost their aura of acrimony and threat.

Toward the end of May, Captain Gifford brought down to Kemble Manor a dozen new roses to plant around the front entrance. They were as exotic as any flowers Caroline had ever seen, a cross between Jersey Blaze roses and the long-stemmed Chinese roses with their four exquisite petals. The dark red of the Blaze roses now filled the white petals, but they retained their delicate, almost transparent texture. The long translucent thorns had also disappeared, but smaller almost invisible thorns had appeared in the ferny foliage.

"They're beautiful, Jonathan. What do you call them?"

"*Carolinius passionatus,*" he said, with a straight face.

She blushed. "I hope you have not told that to anyone else."

"I hope to, someday."

Playfully, he pointed out certain symbolic similarities between the new flowers and their patron. "The thorns are invisible. But they can give you the devil of a scratch if you handle them too roughly. There is practically no aroma. But when you press the petals, they release a delicious ointment. You must press them very hard. Exhausting work."

"What about their health?" Caroline said. "They look to me as though they will need daily care and attention. If you are not up to it, Captain Gifford, perhaps you could suggest an assistant."

"I'm afraid three or four visits a week is all I can manage. And if I hear any more talk of assistants, I will start oiling my pistols."

A few weeks later, as the weather warmed into summer, Caroline asked him to teach her to swim. The brook that ran through the manor park formed a small cove as it entered the bay. It was surrounded by the tall trees of the original forest, creating a private swimming pool. They swam there almost every day for a month. Caroline learned faster than any adult Jonathan Gifford had ever taught to swim. Her slim, small-boned body was almost designed to cut through the water swiftly and gracefully. She also had the temperament of a natural swimmer. Within a week she had lost all fear and was challenging the choppy waters of the bay.

Often, after an hour in the water, they would put on loose robes and have a picnic under the trees. Caroline confessed that she had been wanting to learn to swim for years.

337

"When I heard about you and Sarah swimming, I wanted you to teach Mr. Skinner and me. But he absolutely refused. He said he had tried it and almost drowned."

Half playfully, half seriously, Jonathan Gifford outlined his theory that the way people swam revealed much about their characters. Those who could not overcome their instinctive fear of the water were liable to be timid in their central selves, even if they covered these feelings with bravado. The man who slid gracefully through the water was likely to slide gracefully through life. The man who loved lolling on the waves probably enjoyed the good things of this world, fine wine, gourmet food, pretty women.

"That was Dr. Franklin's style," Jonathan Gifford said. "I swam with him once in the Schuylkill. We swimmers are a small exclusive club, you know."

"If I see you lolling, I will sink you," Caroline said.

"Why?" he said. "I have good wine and good food every day—and a pretty woman to love."

"You don't have to flatter me, Jonathan."

Jonathan Gifford could not convince Caroline that she was pretty. Her parents had inflicted on her a vision of herself as a plain, unattractive girl, in comparison to Sarah. With some exasperation, he finally gave up.

"All right," he said. "You are not pretty. It is your character I love. I never realized it until I saw you swim. There, I said to myself, goes a woman of good sense, courage, daring."

"How did Sarah swim?"

"Well. But too hard. She'd tire easily and then she'd panic. She had to have someone near her all the time."

Caroline groaned. "She would. She would know exactly how to keep a man."

Jonathan Gifford nodded solemnly. "I am leaving you before you learn to swim faster than I can."

He took her in his arms and kissed her for a long time. They lay together beneath the ancient trees, listening to the occasional cry of a sea bird, the roll of the water against the shore.

"What will we do—if we must leave each other?" Caroline asked.

"I don't know."

"I will not bear it. I will just die."

"That is not very sensible, or courageous. You are destroying Gifford's aquatic theory of character."

"I'm serious, Jonathan."

"There's an old Irish saying, there's no point in breaking your shins against a stool that isn't there. The time may never come. I hope it never does."

Up at the manor house, they found Sukey feeding a young half-starved-looking American lieutenant in the kitchen. Until yesterday, when he had been exchanged for a British officer, he had been a prisoner of war in New York. Charles Skinner had given him a letter to deliver to his wife, and assured him he would be rewarded with a good dinner. He took the crumpled envelope from his pocket and handed it to Caroline.

My dear wife:

Almost a year has passed since our angry separation. I find myself miserable and lonely here in New York, although I often go out in company. I have money enough for the time being. I had to sell all our blacks to the West Indies to get it. My heart bled for the poor wretches but what else could I do? At any rate, money or company mean little to me. I have no friends who lift a man's spirits. How I long to raise a glass with Gifford at his tavern! We wretched refugees from New Jersey do nothing when we meet but denounce the coxcombs and chuckleheads that are running—I should write ruining— the British army. Anthony and his friends are as miserable as we oldsters. He could have recruited men enough for a regiment, but he was told they were not needed. The truth was, and is, that no more colonels are to be made from New Jersey. All the higher commissions go to New Yorkers, thanks to De Lancey's influence. Anthony was told he was lucky to get a captain's commission.

There is talk of a French treaty from Paris and a peace commission from London. Which will come first no one can say. A French treaty will mean another three, perhaps four years of war. I speak to you now as a politician, madam, knowing your enthusiasm for that doleful art, which I devoutly wish you had never imbibed. Surely, now that our most ancient enemy, the foe that has drenched our frontiers in blood, has espoused the rebel cause, you can no longer consider the Congress men defenders of true British liberty and human rights. In their furious and unnatural hatred of our mother country, they have embraced the worst despot in Europe. If all this is true, and I don't see how you can deny it, would you give some thought, madam, to joining me here in New York as my lawful and loving wife? I have rented a small snug house on Dock Street with an upper room which has been kept vacant for your coming. I am prepared to forgive and if possible forget the severe things we said on parting. I cannot believe the spirit of true religion which I know you possess will permit you to do less. I am told by good report that our old friend Gifford has bought the manor, which means it is safe for the time being from the rebel confiscators. Your presence is no longer needed on the property. I cannot believe you will let false politics any longer divide our marriage—or your conscience permit you to ignore the duties of a wife.

With the greatest respect, madam, I am your affectionate husband,

Charles Skinner

Caroline read this standing in the furniture-less main hall of the manor house. When she looked up, anguish twisting in her, she discovered she was alone. Jonathan Gifford had walked into the library and was looking somberly out one of the tall eight-glass windows. For a moment, Caroline hesitated in the doorway, wondering if she should lie, simply stuff the letter in the pocket of her apron, and airily dismiss it. *He wanted to know if you had bought his land. I will write and tell him.*

No, she faced the terrible truth. She could not lie to him about this—or anything else. She had dared him to love her with his whole heart, dared herself to do the same thing. To lie to him about this letter would be a wound that would eventually bleed. If they had a future—and her inability to answer this question tormented her—if they had a future, they must face this together, now.

"What does he say?" Jonathan Gifford said.

The tension in his voice was terrible to hear.

"Read it," she said, holding the letter out to him.

"No. It is private."

"You must read it. There is nothing—between us—that is private."

Almost angrily he snatched the letter from her and stood reading it in the bright sunlight pouring through the window, the same sunlight that was spilling across the empty bed upstairs. His face remained saturnine. He handed the letter back to her and turned away, to stare out the window again.

"You should go to him."

"How can you say that?"

"You should go to him. But if you try it, I will shoot your horse, burn your chaise, and bribe my friend General Maxwell at the Elizabethtown ferry to arrest you and parole you in my custody."

"Oh. Oh." Caroline flung her arms around his neck and wept.

"That was cruel," she said, wiping her eyes. "Does it please you to make me act like a child?"

"I had to say it," Jonathan Gifford said. "I'm sorry, but I had to say it."

She saw he was profoundly serious.

"I owed it to him. He was—is—my friend. Someday I may have to look him in the face."

"Stop, please," she said, putting her fingers on his lips. "I cannot even bear to think of going to him. I would run away to Canada or the West Indies. I would rather roam the world like a wandering Jew—"

In the dining room they tried to calm themselves with cups of strong coffee. Caroline was solemn. "Strange," she said. "I don't really like the idea of a French alliance, as you know. But I find myself liking it now because it gives us a few more years together. See what you have done to me? I was once a woman of principle, of intellect. Now I'm a mere slave of shameless passion."

"It suits you well," Jonathan Gifford said, taking her hand. "Perhaps we all need a touch of slavery now and then, to make us appreciate freedom."

It took courage to joke about either love or politics. Both were intertwined with threats and anxieties of the worst kind. But if there was one thing Jonathan Gifford and Caroline Skinner had in common, it was courage. What a mysterious and little-understood virtue it is. We tend so often to identify it with reckless daring on the battlefield or in the prize ring. But those moments of physical bravado, I am convinced, are often the very opposite of courage. They are wild animal outbursts. True courage involves the mind and spirit. It confronts the fragility of love, the uncertainties of politics, the fearsome face of war without flinching.

Book
IV

CHAPTER ONE

WE COULD TELL by the look on Abel Aikin's face that he had some special news. We were almost ready to tell him what it was, we had heard so much about it. For weeks we had been wondering whether the British peace commissioners, with their supposed concessions to every imaginable American demand short of independence, would win the race with the French diplomats offering us a treaty of alliance.

Meanwhile we enjoyed the beauties of a Jersey spring. The snowy wreaths of the shadbush appeared on the hillsides and in the dry open woods along with trillium, hepatica, and the eggshell-white blossoms of bloodroot. In the woodlands and south-sloping hills arbutus bloomed along with the pale yellow blossoms of the spicebush, the delicate pinkish white nodding clusters of the staggerbush. As the land flowered we sowed corn and wheat, flax and oats in long furrows of moist gleaming soil—a gesture that was in itself a symbol of hope in the future.

This was our chief emotion as we encircled Abel Aikin, who sat smugly in his saddle as usual, his needles clacking away while his old mare rewarded herself with a drink.

"Have the French arrived, Abel?"

"What are the chances of us getting a regiment or two to replace our Yankee heroes?"

"Come, Abel, tell us the news, or we will drown you and your nag in that trough."

"What day of the month is it?" Abel asked.

"The thirteenth of May."

"Nine days ago, the honorable Congress announced its ratification of the treaty of alliance with France."

With a cheer we trooped into Liberty Tavern to celebrate. Jonathan Gifford stood the house to a round of French brandy. We toasted King Louis XVI and Dr. Franklin, who negotiated the treaty for us. Everyone confidently predicted that the war would be over by September.

Captain Gifford seemed to agree with us. "I would not be commander in chief of the British army for all the money in the Bank of England," he said, running his finger across his maps. "They have done exactly what I always thought they would do to conquer a country as big as America. Spread themselves thin. They have garrisons in Rhode Island, New York, and Philadelphia. Even if the French send no troops, but only a strong fleet, we can gobble them up one by one."

Sir William Howe had resigned as commander in chief of the British army. His successor, Lieutenant General Henry Clinton, was also studying maps. He decided to abandon Philadelphia and concentrate his army at New York. Fearful of an attack by a French fleet, he chose to travel by land. For us in New Jersey, especially those who lived south of the Raritan, this meant the return of war in all its mindless fury. They came straight at us, thirteen thousand retreating redcoats and Germans in the ugliest possible frame of mind.

Washington and the main American army pursued them. Dispatch riders thundered into Liberty Tavern's yard with orders to call out every militiaman on the rolls. We were to swarm on their front and flanks like our native mosquitoes, to slow their march and let Washington bring them to battle. When General Slocum tried to execute the order, he found himself in a very embarrassing situation. Not a militiaman who had slaved in his saltworks, nor any of their friends or relatives, would turn out. Too many others remembered what had happened when he persuaded them to attack the British on their last retreat from New Jersey.

"Where's Washington and his regulars? Show them to me and I might turn out," was the cry.

"Tell Slocum to put some of his salt on the lobsters' tails," was another frequent comment.

Others invoked the law Slocum had wangled from the legislature, barring Monmouth militia from serving outside the county. They declined to turn out until the British army was inside our borders. If the British took an alternate route, let the militiamen in other counties do the fighting and good luck to them.

Slocum rode hastily to New Brunswick, where we were ordered to collect, leaving Kemble and others to argue with our recalcitrant stalwarts. We eventually mustered about a hundred—a heavy percentage of them youngsters like myself, who had just turned sixteen or seventeen and were coming out for the first time. I had expected a fearful argument with my father, but he surprised me. He let me go without a word of reproof, and silenced my mother when she attempted to lecture me into inactivity. My best friend, Billy Talbot, had a much more difficult time with his family. He had to steal one of his father's muskets and with Kemble's help hide out in Liberty Tavern's barn.

There were about twenty of us new militiamen from Liberty Tavern's neighborhood. Ever since the British departed, we had drilled with guns loaned to us by Kemble from the tavern's armory. He was our leader, awesome in his relentless devotion to the Cause, a man who had fought and almost died at Trenton and Princeton, battles that meant more to us than Thermopylae or Pharsalia. In the past few months he had taught us to despise General Slocum. We did not know it as we marched to New Brunswick, but the stage had been set for tragedy.

At New Brunswick we found nothing but heat, dirt, and confusion. The quartermasters complained that people in Middlesex County would not take their paper money. We lived for two days on food better suited for pigs. Meanwhile, rumors swept our little army of one thousand men, most from north Jersey. The British were coming our way and we would have to stop them on the banks of the Raritan. The British were not coming our way, they were marching north, toward Hackensack. They were plodding through the pines of southern Monmouth.

On the morning of the third day, it was clear that the British were not coming near us. They were heading for the coast by the shortest route, miles to the south. But General Slocum gave no order to march. We sat there in the heat, eating our rotten food, growing more and more disgusted. Kemble went to Slocum's headquarters and demanded to know why he was doing nothing.

"Every report says the enemy are slipping past us," he said.

"We have gotten no orders," Slocum said.

"Since when does Washington give orders to militia? He ex-

347

pects us to be there when we are needed. I think you are a damn coward. You remember what the regulars did to you last year, and are afraid to go near them."

"I will go right through them, sword in hand," roared Slocum, "if I get an order. Until I get one we will stay here."

"You will. There are others who think differently."

"Damn you. I will have you court-martialed and shot," Slocum shouted.

Kemble ignored him. He strode back to our camp and made a furious speech, denouncing Slocum and asking our regiment to follow him south. Only our band of sixteen- and seventeen-year-olds stepped forward, eager to march. No one else had much appetite for tangling with the British army, without a guarantee of support from Washington's regulars. Kemble called them cowards and marched us south. Only then did he realize that the heat was ferocious, and we had no food in our knapsacks. He decided to stop overnight at Liberty Tavern, where he could get provisions, and continue our march in the cool of the early morning.

Jonathan Gifford regarded our detachment with unconcealed dismay. It was obvious that Kemble had no idea what he was attacking. He did not understand that an army on the march through enemy country is like a huge serpent out of a nightmare, a beast with a thousand deadly claws, and a murderous sting in its tail.

"Let the regulars do the fighting, Kemble," he said. "Washington is supposed to have thirteen thousand men."

"Militia trapped Burgoyne at Saratoga," Kemble said. "We can do the same thing to Clinton. We can end the war, end it here in New Jersey. I don't think you can stand the thought of your beloved regulars being beaten by militia, Father."

"From what I hear, it was Daniel Morgan and his riflemen—three-year veterans—who stopped Burgoyne," Jonathan Gifford said. "If you must go, Kemble, for God's sake stay away from the British army until you find Washington. He'll have officers detached to work with militia. They'll know what they're doing."

Again, inadvertent words cut deep. Kemble's mouth grew sullen at the (to him) implied insult. "Yes, Captain," he said ironically. "Depend on it, we will obey your orders."

The next morning we marched south, boisterous boys on a glorious adventure. The weather was still hot but we called it tolerable for born New Jerseyans. Some of us filled our canteens with rum, courtesy of Barney McGovern. The rum passed through the ranks, and soon we were all acting more like skylarkers on a picnic than soldiers marching to battle. We blazed away at rabbits and pigeons to supplement our rations and roared out songs that mocked British presumptions.

> "I'll sing you a song, as a body may say,
> 'Tis of the King's regulars, who ne'er ran away
> Oh, the old soldiers of the King
> And the King's Own regulars."

I marched beside Billy Talbot, tall and fair-skinned with hair so blond we called him Whitey. His hair streamed down to his shoulders. Mine was almost as long. Hair was one of several ways we defied our neutralist parents. We scorned the use of a wig, or even of a little powder, knowing this galled our fathers. Kemble encouraged this hirsute defiance—and all other forms of rebellion. In recent months he had spent most of his time with boys our age. It was to us more than to anyone else that he preached his conviction that the Revolution would launch a new era. If Americans succeeded in defeating the aristocrats of England and Germany here, poor and disenfranchised Germans and English at home would rise against their masters. America would be the leader of this age of republican virtue. She alone was qualified because she was relatively untainted by old Europe's corruption. When the war ended, we would achieve a state of social perfection unparalleled in human history. Slavery, that blot on America's national honor, would be abolished. Demagogues like Daniel Slocum would be chastised or banished. There would be a limit to the amount of wealth a man might possess before he was forced to share it with his less fortunate brothers.

This last idea brought growls of disagreement from us as we sat in the woods eating our dinner. Kemble agreed that such an idea sounded ridiculous. But that only proved how important it was for us to free ourselves from European habits of thinking and feeling. The older generation was hopeless. Men like our fathers were trapped in the past—even when they pretended to support the Revolution. This was why it was necessary to keep our feelings toward them under the harsh rein of revolutionary necessity. "You cannot love what you don't admire," Kemble said. We accepted the dictum with the cold ecstasy of the mind, never for a moment considering the violence it must do to the heart. We were very young. In some ways Kemble was the youngest of us all.

Our talk turned to our military mission. Kemble gave us a lecture on courage. That was all we needed to show these mercenaries that free men were determined to protect their home soil. Nothing could be more important than this battle, Kemble repeated. Anyone who died here would be remembered as a hero for as long as America endured. We did not take this talk of dying very seriously. At sixteen we were convinced of our immortality and invulnerability.

We were not invulnerable to the heat. By 4 P.M. we were exhausted and Kemble let us retreat from the open road to the shade of a grove of maple trees, where we camped for the night. Sundown brought no relief. We sweltered through the hours of darkness. Not a breath of cool air stirred.

The morning was more of the same. Most of us drained the last rum from our canteens and the water drinkers—there were a few —finished their supply with our hasty breakfast.

Kemble assured us that we would find fresh water from farms along the road. But we got alarming news on this score from the first farm we tried. The farmer was a Quaker, a small spare man who was doing his best to keep his temper as befitted his creed. He had no water. Some horsemen arrived last night with saddlebags full of horse dung, rotten entrails of pigs and chickens and flung this garbage in his well. They were doing the same thing to wells for miles around.

"It is to prevent the British from getting water," said the Quaker. "But thy friends do not seem to realize that thee and I and other Americans also need water."

We marched on, our tongues thick with thirst. We were soon in pine country, miles upon miles of hot silent woods, the beginning of the great stretch of pine barrens that runs south through the heart of New Jersey almost to Cape May. The road beneath our feet was no longer the firm dusty earth of our native district, but soft shifting sand that wearied the legs with every step. The heat was intense. Local historians claim thermometers soared past a hundred that day. We had begun marching at dawn. About eight o'clock we heard hoofbeats on the road and scattered into the pines. The riders turned out to be Americans. They wore the blue and white uniforms of the Philadelphia Light Horse. As we approached them, we quickly learned they were part of the well poisoning squad. They stank of horse dung and rotten guts. We asked them where the British army was.

"Go down this road about a mile and mount the rise to the west. You will see it clear enough," one of them said.

We did as they told us, cutting through the woods to reach the long pine-crowned hill that rose against the sky to the west. From its crest the pines dwindled into scrub and a kind of sandy plain full of coarse grass and bushes opened to our view. On a road about a half mile away was the British army, creeping along like that great beast to which I have already compared it. Its size was awesome. We could see neither the head nor the tail of the beast, only the groaning creaking center with its thousands of wagons and squads of blue-coated Hessians trudging at intervals beside them and faster-moving squads of red-coated cavalry outpacing them.

Where was the American army? We were baffled by our lack of information. Throughout the spring we had heard that Washington's army was growing by spectacular leaps. We had envisioned a host surrounding the harried enemy with a gauntlet of fire. Nothing was troubling those British or Germans below us on the road but the heat—which was also tormenting us. We did not understand that this was only half the British army guarding their immense supply train. The other half was preparing to attack Washington.

Kemble was studying his map. "That is the road to Middletown," he said. "They are heading for the coast—"

A shot rang out.

"Who fired that? Who fired without orders?" Kemble cried.

Lewis Simmons, one of the more brainless members of our little band, came sidling through the trees, grinning through his crooked teeth. "I just wanted to make them jump," he said.

"A waste of ammunition," Kemble said. "You can't hit anything with a musket at a half mile."

"I just wanted to make them jump," Lewis Simmons said, pouting now.

"They are jumping all right. Look."

A squad of men in short green coats was moving up the hill toward us, their guns leveled.

"Jägers," said Kemble. "Let us give them a taste of American marksmanship."

None of us, Kemble included, knew that the Jägers, which was the German word for "huntsmen," had become the best skirmishers in the British army. They were equipped with short-barreled rifles, much more accurate than our crude muskets.

We fired a volley at the Germans from the edge of the woods and did not hit a man. This did nothing for our self-confidence and a great deal for theirs. They raced along the face of the hill and into the trees about a hundred yards above us. They came toward us like so many ghosts in the hot dim stillness. We hastily retreated and formed an irregular line—poor tactics for fighting in the woods.

For the first time, Kemble realized he should have paid more attention to Jonathan Gifford's military advice. As a revolutionary leader, Kemble was superb. But as a soldier, he scorned to learn even the rudiments of tactics. Enthusiasm, bravery, these were more important, he thought. He was wrong. Both were important. I don't condemn him for it. It was a belief shared by many other Americans at the time. We paid dearly for our ignorance that day in the woods.

The Germans never made a sound as they came toward us, except for their commander, who gave orders with a series of sharp calls on a whistle. We imitated Kemble's example and shouted defiance to them. "Come on, you German buggers. Come on and taste some American lead. Come on, you goddamn sauerkraut eaters."

All this while we blasted away at them—or better, at their shadows. One of their first return shots came within an inch of my head. Then Lewis Simmons, at the end of our ragged line, fell, screaming, "Oh, Jesus, my guts, my guts." Tom Nelson, the man —or boy—nearest Simmons, ran to help him and another Jäger rifle crashed. Nelson gave a brief animal cry and fell on top of Simmons, blood gushing from his head. More rifles crashed and Joe Carter at the opposite end of our line dropped his gun and stumbled away, clutching a shattered shoulder. Calvin Morse howled with fear and pain as a bullet ripped into his thigh. "They're behind us," he cried.

The Jägers were using a standard tactic, working around our

flanks. In a panic, the rest of us loaded and fired with ever more frantic haste, guaranteeing our inaccuracy.

I heard a groan from my right. I turned and saw Billy Talbot, lying on his side clutching his leg. Blood seeped through his homespun trousers. As he knelt to fire, a ball had smashed his knee.

Another series of sharp whistles from the German commander. The Jägers slipped away through the trees. Three or four of us leaped up to pursue them, shouting victory slogans. The leader, George Stout, did not get ten feet before he went down with a bullet in his chest. Kemble called the others back before they met the same fate.

We counted our losses. Nelson was dead. Stout and Simmons were too badly wounded to walk. The other wounded could limp or stagger.

"We must get these men to a hospital," Kemble said.

We rigged litters from our blanket rolls to carry Stout and Simmons. They were both heavy lads and by now it was well over a hundred degrees in those pine-scented woods. My friend Billy Talbot hobbled along with me, clinging to my shoulder. Much chastened, we resumed our march. Within ten minutes we were almost frantic with thirst. The wounded were the worst sufferers. Perhaps nature is attempting to replace some of the precious fluid that has oozed out through the wound, perhaps it is simply a wish for some small physical consolation. But their pleas made us painfully aware of our own thirst.

Around ten o'clock we heard the boom of cannon and the crash of musketry some distance from us. Only later did we discover that these were the opening guns of the battle of Monmouth Court House. We were approaching the place from the rear of the British army—a fact which explained why we had thus far seen only a few rambling Americans. It was rugged country, the woods broken by deep ravines and sandy washes. Not by accident was it often called "the desert" by New Jerseyans. Water was as scarce as human beings in this part of the state.

We were by no means the only group of wandering militia that day. There seems to have been no attempt by anyone—neither a high-ranking officer of the state militia nor a staff officer from the Continental army—to coordinate our amateur efforts. The British were well aware that militiamen were roaming on their flanks and rear. They had two regiments of dragoons—some six hundred horsemen—to guard them from harassment while they assaulted the main American army. Ignorant of all this, we emerged from our tongue of woods to find ourselves on a kind of bluff above a swampy ravine. A rivulet trickled in its center. The sight of water sent us all berserk. Down the bank we tumbled to plunge our faces in the little stream. Alas, it was brackish, like so much water in that sandy country. But we drank it anyway and gave it to our wounded.

We were just finishing this liquid repast when an ominous sound reached our ears: the jingling of numerous bridles. We leaped to our feet. A company of British dragoons was at the head of the ravine.

"Up the bank into the woods," Kemble said, pointing to the other side of the ravine, which was steep enough but not a sandy precipice like the one we had just descended. We ran for it.

That is, some of us ran. I had Billy Talbot clinging to my shoulder. Eight others were carrying the two litters with the badly wounded Stout and Simmons.

"Charge," cried the officer at the head of the dragoons in a high piping voice. He was a boy not much older than we were.

The British were at least a quarter of a mile away when they began. But running in the sand was slow work and our wounded charges suddenly became mortal burdens. On came the dragoons, roaring with battle fury, raising those fearsome sabers.

"For God's sake, run," I gasped to Billy Talbot.

"I—I can't—" He was sobbing with fear and pain.

The less burdened were already scrambling up the bank toward the sheltering trees. Kemble turned back to urge us. "Run," he shouted, "run."

Then came that terrible moment when we saw we could not do it. The dragoons loomed larger and larger above the wild-eyed heads of their huge horses. Their sabers seemed to be touching the blazing blue sky. My mind dissolved. With a whine of terror I abandoned Billy Talbot and scrambled for the woods. The litter bearers did the same thing.

"Shoot, shoot," I heard Kemble shouting to those in the woods. He was on his knee aiming his musket. As I reached the pines I turned my head and saw Billy, his arm upraised, hobbling on his musket, at the very moment when the officer in the lead brought his saber down on his head. Bright red blood drenched Billy's white hair. He fell without a sound.

Others were screaming. I had had a lead on the litter bearers. They were trapped by the rest of the dragoons. Some of them ducked the first saber strokes and begged for mercy. But there was no mercy in those British hearts that morning. Their friends were fighting and dying in the murderous heat only a mile away. They regarded us as skulking cowards out to stab them in their backs. The dragoons even trampled and hacked the writhing bodies of the wounded on their litters.

I was too paralyzed to fire my gun. Part was horror at the carnage, but more, oh, much more, was horror at myself for having abandoned my friend. How many midnight hours over the years have I paid in sweat and tears for that moment of cowardice.

Hitting a target ten or twenty feet below you with a musket is almost impossible. Most of our bullets whistled over the dragoons' heads. But the sound alarmed them to their danger and their bugler quickly sounded retreat. They galloped out of range, leaving behind them a nightmare scene.

Eleven bodies lay in the sand oozing blood. Behind me I could hear some of our survivors vomiting. Tears were streaming down Kemble's face. Ignoring the danger of the dragoons returning, he threw aside his gun and stumbled down the bank toward the victims. One by one he turned them over. They were all dead, their throats slashed, their skulls smashed by those terrible sabers.

Mastering my fear at last, I followed him down the hill and knelt beside my friend. "I'm sorry, Billy, I'm sorry," I sobbed.

His sightless eyes said nothing, neither words of forgiveness nor accusation.

Kemble was speaking to me. "Now you'll have something to fight for." He turned and shouted to the survivors, who were emerging from the pines to stare down at the bodies of their friends. "We all have something to fight for. We will revenge these men, I swear it."

There was no response. We had had enough war for one day. Some had had enough for the rest of their lives. Kemble saw the sullen accusation in their downcast eyes and drooping mouths. He had led them. The blood of these boys was on his head and hands. I saw the truth shiver his soul like a saber stroke.

"But we can—we can do no more today," he said. "We have suffered enough. I will stay here—with them."

No one argued with him. There were no heroes left in our warrior band. Kemble told me to find Black Sam and guide him back with a wagon for the bodies. In the distance, the thunder of Monmouth's guns continued. We turned our backs on the sound and trudged homeward through the heat. Not even darkness seemed to cool the burning air. It was eleven o'clock when we reached Liberty Tavern. Jonathan Gifford had out his military maps and was in the midst of discussing the possibility of trapping the British army. Everyone leaped up at the sight of us, hoping we brought news from the battlefield. The story we blurted out changed their anticipation to anguish and dismay. "Twelve dead?" was the cry. Almost every man in the room was related to one of the boys. Saddest of all was Patrick Simmons, the father of Lewis. He groaned in agony as we mumbled his son's name among our little list of the dead.

"And Kemble?" Jonathan Gifford asked, his voice trembling with suppressed emotion.

"He is with them," I said. "He hoped you would send Sam with a wagon."

"I will go myself," Jonathan Gifford said.

"If I may say so, Captain, 'twould be better to wait till mornin'," said Barney McGovern. "There's a good chance of getting killed wanderin' across a battlefield in the night."

"I will take the chance," Jonathan Gifford said.

He knew, with a father's instinct, what none of the rest of us understood at the time—what was happening to Kemble, what he would have to face when he came home. He could have stayed safely inside his tavern and talked distantly of his murderous blundering stepson. But for Jonathan Gifford love meant standing together, sharing pain, bearing blows when necessary.

"Come on, Jemmy," he said to me. "You can sleep in the wagon."

He filled the wagon with hay while Sam hitched the horses. Barney McGovern strode out of the darkness and said he would feel better if he came along. He had two pistols at his waist and a musket in his hand.

Jonathan Gifford shook his head. "It will be safer if just the two of us go—without a gun."

Barney thought this was madness and said so.

"One or two guns won't do us any good if we run into dragoons in an ugly mood. It's better not to give them an excuse to butcher us."

He mounted the wagon and told me to lie down in the hay. On the road, he gave me a long swig of rum from his canteen. It was all I needed. I was numb with exhaustion and shock. But my sleep was troubled. I lived again and again and again that moment in the ravine when I abandoned Billy Talbot. I saw his wide-eyed pleading face.

"I'm sorry," I sobbed. "I'm sorry. Please, Billy, I'm sorry."

Jonathan Gifford's big hand shook me awake. It was almost dawn. We were in the pines.

"You will have to show me the rest of the way, Jemmy," he said. "But tell me what happened first."

I poured out my disgrace to this strong, serious man. I literally wept with shame on his shoulder—I who had never shown an iota of emotion with my own father.

"Jemmy," he said, "every soldier runs away at least once."

"And leaves his friend behind?" I sobbed.

"It wasn't you that left him behind. Your heart was still with him. It was your legs that wouldn't stay. It's not easy to control your body in a battle. Do you know what I did at the Monongahela?"

I shook my head.

"That was my first battle. When those Indians came at us from all sides, I wet my pants. I was only nineteen. If I'd been a private, I wouldn't have stopped running till I reached Philadelphia. An officer had to be an example to his men. But the fear had to come out some way."

He placed his big hand on my shoulder. "I never told that to a living soul."

We both knew it was a secret I would never reveal while either of us lived. I tell it here only because I know it will not be read until I am long gone to dust.

"You won't run the next time, Jemmy," Jonathan Gifford said. "Now let's find Kemble."

We reached the ravine about nine o'clock. The sun was already scorching the sandy earth, bounding off the walls and the pine trees at their crests, creating an inferno. Kemble hunched there, eyes bloodshot, two days' stubble of beard on his lean haunted face. For almost twenty-four hours he had maintained this vigil like some primitive saint of slaughter.

When he saw Jonathan Gifford at the reins of the wagon, he sprang up, trembling from head to foot. "I told you to bring Sam," he shouted at me.

"I thought it was better if I came," Jonathan Gifford said.

"Why? To examine the battlefield? See what I did wrong? Give me more of your goddamned advice?"

"No," Jonathan Gifford said. "I thought—I thought it was my place—to come. The last thing I thought—was to criticize— Jemmy here told me what happened. It was—one of those accidents."

"No it wasn't," said Kemble. "Don't lie to yourself or to me. You told me not to come. You predicted—this."

What could Jonathan Gifford say? Kemble was about to hear far worse things. He had come to support him in his hour of anguish, to shield him if possible. Now he saw it was not possible.

"I thought it was better if I came. I thought I could deal with British patrols better than Sam. He might wind up on a slave ship to the West Indies. Where are they?"

Kemble pointed up the bank into the pine trees. "I was afraid some Germans might—strip them. I brought Nelson down from the other piece of woods . . ."

His voice trailed away and torment regained its grip on his face. "It was a long night. I kept remembering what Mother used to say about me. Born on Whitsunday. Born to kill or be killed."

"That's damn nonsense, Kemble," Jonathan Gifford said.

"Is it? I used to think so." He gazed at the darkness beneath the pine trees for a moment. "You'll have to get them, I—I can't."

He walked away from us down the ravine. Jonathan Gifford gestured to me. We labored up the bank and found them just inside the woods on a carpet of dead pine needles. They were not a pretty sight. Without Jonathan Gifford, I would have vomited or run away. The heat had swollen the bodies and turned the faces black. Kemble had arranged them in a row. Now I can picture the awful task he performed to protect them from further insult, dragging them up the bank, laying them there in the scented woods, struggling for a mile through the other woods from the place where we skirmished with the Jägers, Nelson's body on his back. I was too overwhelmed by sight and smell to think about Kemble then. Jonathan Gifford saw me start to tremble. He seized my arm in a grip that almost made me cry out.

"They are not your friends, Jemmy, not any more," he said. "Death is a thief. A thorough thief."

Billy Talbot was the first body. With the help of those words, I was able to pick him up by the legs while Jonathan Gifford lifted him beneath his shoulders. One by one we carried them down the bank, laid them in the straw in the back of the wagon, and covered them with canvas.

On the road home we encountered a dozen other Jersey wagons returning from Monmouth with loads as melancholy as our own. In a few the wounded lay with the dead, groaning in agony. We had not been the only militia to collide with British cavalry or light infantry patrols.

No one spoke until we were within a mile or two of Liberty Tavern. Then Jonathan Gifford placed his hand on Kemble's shoulder. "The parents will take it hard, Kemble. You must be ready for some cruel words."

"I know," said Kemble.

But he did not know. None of us could have known the compound of fury and grief we encountered in the yard of Liberty Tavern. Mothers as well as fathers were waiting. They wept and groaned and shrieked as we lifted the bodies out of the wagon and laid them on the stone porch. Mothers kissed and fondled those black putrefying faces. Then one woman—I think it was Lewis Simmons' mother—turned to point at Kemble and scream, "There he stands. There's the murderer of our babes."

"Aye, aye," cried another woman.

"I wish we had a rope to hang the bugger," roared George Stout's father, who looked his name.

Kemble said nothing. He faced them, a suffering rejected savior.

"That's not true," Jonathan Gifford said in his strongest deepest voice. "I went down to see for myself what happened. It was bad luck and nothing else. The cavalry trapped them in a ravine. It could have happened to me or any man here."

"Oh yes, you'll stand by him, won't you, Jonathan Gifford," cried Mrs. Simmons, her narrow face twisted with grief. "Your creature. You sent him on this evil journey like as not, and you're gloating now in your damn British heart, as he may well be for all his talk of independence. It's a deep game you're playing, deep in blood."

Without Jonathan Gifford's impassive, rock-like presence, I hate to think what kind of violence might have been sparked by this pathetic woman's hysterical slander. He simply stood there beside Kemble, letting her rant, making no attempt to answer the vicious things she was saying against him. In the same calm, sympathetic voice, he reiterated his defense of his son.

"You are not the only ones who've suffered," he added. "We saw a dozen other wagons with dead and wounded on the road coming back."

"Aye," said Barney McGovern, who had been standing beside Captain Gifford as a silent supporter. "And the Continentals have at least a hundred men dead and three times that many wounded. Jasper Clark's two lads are among the dead. We just got word from their colonel."

How odd it is, that people can bear a calamity better if they know its victims are numerous. The wrath of the mourners subsided and they began gathering up their dead to depart. Jonathan Gifford urged Kemble to go down to the house. He shook his head. He was determined to drink the cup to its dregs.

Richard Talbot and his oldest son arrived in a wagon to take Billy home. Mr. Talbot burst into tears when he saw Billy. Jonathan Gifford and Kemble had to endure a tongue-lashing from his neutralist point of view. "Now you see where all this brave talk about independence and war leads— Will independence give me back my son? I say damn you and your Congress and your committees. We were a peaceful people until you started your yapping."

Tenderly the Talbots placed Billy's body in their wagon and they too departed. They were the last. Kemble and his father stood alone in the tavern yard. "Come in and have a drink, Kemble," Jonathan Gifford said.

He started to put his arm around his shoulders. Kemble twisted away from him. "Haven't I told you," he said, "haven't I told you I don't want your goddamn consolation?"

CHAPTER TWO

THE FOLLOWING DAY an extremely handsome man of about forty
strolled into Liberty Tavern. He was wearing enough lace on his
shirt to finance a country wedding. His red silk suit and blue satin
waistcoat seemed immune to the dust of the road and the heat of
the day.

"Are you Gifford?" he asked Barney McGovern. Directed to the
Captain, he introduced himself as Dr. William Shippen, Jr., Director of American Hospitals. "The army is marching north to cooperate with the French fleet in an attack on New York," he said.
"We have a good three hundred wounded from the fight yesterday at Monmouth Court House. General Washington thought
you would know of some houses in the neighborhood that might
be converted into hospitals. Confiscated Tory property perhaps."

Jonathan Gifford knew Dr. Shippen was one of Philadelphia's
most distinguished physicians. "The few places that haven't been
sold are pretty badly smashed up," Jonathan Gifford said. "But I
have a house—you may know it. Kemble Manor."

Dr. Shippen had been speaking to Jonathan Gifford in his most
condescending Philadelphia aristocrat's style. He suddenly became
almost cordial.

"Of course. I visited Charles Skinner there before the war. You
are the new owner?"

Jonathan Gifford nodded. "Mrs. Skinner is still living there.
But I have no doubt she will agree to it. She is as strong for the
Cause as any man in New Jersey."

"We will begin moving the men in tomorrow," Dr. Shippen
said. "Do you have some pipes of wine and perhaps a cask or two
of brandy we might buy for them? I would like to husband our

present supply for the push on New York. We fear it will be bloody."

"You can have my whole cellar if you need it," Jonathan Gifford said.

"The doctor in charge will negotiate a price with you," Dr. Shippen said, and departed.

Caroline instantly agreed to convert the manor house into a hospital. But she surprised Jonathan Gifford by refusing to move to a room in Liberty Tavern or to his brookside house.

"In the first place, I am needed here to supervise the farm. I also have some skills as a nurse. I cared for my father through his last illness."

"But a military hospital—it's not a healthy place. These men may be only wounded now. But they bring with them smallpox, putrid fever, God knows what."

"I have been inoculated against smallpox. No one knows how we catch fevers. But I seem immune to them."

Jonathan Gifford started to object all over again, his concern mingling with masculine habit to make him determined to have his own way. Caroline stopped him short with a flash of Kemble temper.

"I have been wondering when we would have a quarrel. I *want* to do this, Jonathan, and I will *not* be told I can't. Loving you does not make you my lord and master."

His feelings not a little bruised, Captain Gifford retreated to Liberty Tavern, to meditate on the female temperament. At dinner Kate noted his gloomy silence and asked him what was the matter.

"I am worried about your aunt—Caroline," he said. He told her of his offer of the manor as a hospital and Caroline's decision to remain there.

"She can't stay there alone, Father. I will join her."

"You will not. I have no authority over Caro—your aunt. But I hope I still have some over you. A military hospital is the most dangerous place in the world. It is worse than a battlefield."

The same determination that had furrowed Caroline's brow now added wrinkles to Kate's forehead. "Father, you are talking to me as if I were a child."

"I am doing no such thing. I am trying to protect you—"

"But I don't want to be protected. That is one of the things

362

that must change. You must stop thinking about women as creatures to be protected."

"Kate—I have no objection to your ideas—or your aunt's ideas —about education, a woman's rights. But when they start to endanger your life—"

"I agree completely with Captain Gifford," said Lieutenant Rawdon. "I would not let any female relation of mine into a military hospital."

"It is a good thing I am not your relation—and am not likely to be," Kate said.

Leaving him thoroughly demolished, she turned to Jonathan Gifford. "I *want* to go, Father, and I *will* go, tomorrow."

The following day, while Lieutenant Rawdon and Jonathan Gifford watched dolefully, Kate went, her trunk beside her on the chaise. At the manor, she found chaos. There were thirteen Jersey wagons in the oval at the head of the drive, loaded with wounded men. Those who could walk or stagger had gotten out of the wagons and sprawled beneath the shade trees on the lawn. A half-dozen orderlies were lugging hay from the barns to spread on the parquet floors. It was murderously hot. Caroline and Sukey were going from wagon to wagon with buckets of water from the well. The wagon drivers sat behind their teams, watching them and the orderlies.

"Where are the doctors?" Kate asked.

"They rode up to the tavern for breakfast."

"What about these men? Have they had breakfast?"

"They have eaten nothing for two days, some of them. The only food they brought with them is in that first wagon. Take a look at it."

Kate climbed into the wagon and opened a barrel marked salt beef. She gasped with disgust. It was swarming with maggots. Other barrels contained corn meal that was covered with green mold. A barrel of potatoes was as wormy as the beef. The condition of the men was not much better than their provisions. Most had not even had their wounds dressed. Only two with legs amputated showed any evidence of medical attention. They had all been lying in the wagons on thinly scattered straw for twenty-four hours. The stench and filth were nauseating.

"Can't we get them out on the lawn?" Kate asked the wagon men.

"Not our job, miss. Go ask the orderlies."

The Sergeant in command of the orderlies, a fat little man from Virginia, by his accent, absolutely rejected the idea. He only had six men and they were half dead from the heat already. They would be lucky to get all the hay for bedding into the house before sundown.

Kate joined Caroline and Sukey in wielding a water bucket while the orderlies plodded from the house to the barn and back again. About noon they stopped. The wagon men got down from their seats and began building a fire to cook their dinners. The orderlies joined them. No one offered a bite to the wounded. They lay in their straw with a resigned silence that Kate found unbearable.

By this time the doctors had returned from Liberty Tavern. Caroline introduced Kate to them. Dr. Benjamin Ladd was in his twenties. His thin frame seemed hunched by disappointment and his pinched face wore an expression halfway between anger and sadness. He was from western Pennsylvania. Dr. Ephraim Lummes was in his forties. He was a comfortably built man with a wide complacent face featuring a large red nose. He was from Rhode Island.

"Are many badly wounded?"

"Hard to say," Dr. Ladd said forlornly. "It doesn't make much difference as far as I can see. We have about two hundred and eighty here. If half that number live, it will be a miracle. I will be content with fifty."

"Now, now," said Dr. Lummes, "you are too impressed by our troubles of last year."

He explained that Dr. Ladd had worked in the main army hospital at Lancaster during the winter of 1777. The mortality had been exceptionally heavy. "God works in mysterious ways. He chastised us severely there. I don't know why," Dr. Lummes said.

"I keep thinking of that Virginia regiment," Dr. Ladd said. "They brought in three hundred of them with light fevers. Only forty came out alive."

"Can we begin bringing some of them into the house, so we can wash them?" Kate asked.

Dr. Lummes stared at her. "Why in the world, miss?"

"To reduce the chances of infection."

"Why, I didn't know we had a medical scholar on our hands,

364

Dr. Ladd," said Lummes. "What is your theory of infection, miss?"

"I have none," Kate said. "But I've been trained as a nurse by a doctor who studied at Edinburgh."

"No doubt he has theories coming out of his nose," said Dr. Lummes. "But I have more faith in practice. A good purge and an open vein is a better cure for infection than all the theories in the world."

Kate saw that Dr. Lummes was an ignoramus. She and Caroline were encountering the American army's medical department. It killed three times as many men as British gunfire in the Revolution. Ignorance was only part of the problem. Pride, greed, and politics often competed with incompetence for the soldiers' lives.

Trying to be diplomatic, Kate asked Dr. Lummes if he objected to washing the men before they were put to bed. "Cold water," Dr. Lummes said, "even warm water, can shock the system of a wounded man. I am afraid I must object, miss. If you wish to assist us in this hospital, you must remember that I am in charge."

By the time they got the wounded men into the house, it was dark. Sukey and Caroline had baked some bread for them. Most of the seriously wounded were too weak to eat it. But this was a minor worry compared to their accommodations. Kemble Manor was a spacious house. But two hundred and eighty soldiers crowded it dismayingly. The men were shoved and in some cases dropped onto their beds of straw, thirty and forty to a room. Dr. Ladd and Dr. Lummes made no attempt to examine them. They rode off to Liberty Tavern for the night, leaving the Sergeant and his orderlies in charge.

Kate asked them if they had any hospital clothes for the men. The temperature continued to hover in the nineties. Light linen clothing, shirts or pantaloons or both, was what they needed. The orderlies said they did not know what she was talking about. After supper they wandered down the road to Leary's groggery, leaving Caroline and Kate in charge of the house.

By this time, Kate was so furious she could barely speak. Her temper did not improve when the orderlies returned about midnight, mostly drunk, and began capering around the lawn roaring out liberty songs. Kate seized a candle and went out on the front steps to give them a lecture. They were not impressed. They had heard all about her down at Leary's, they said. She was a Tory bitch. While they insulted her, the Sergeant circled around in the darkness beyond her candle's feeble glow, leaped up on the steps, and threw her into the hands of his confederates.

"Let's see what's under that dress, boys," he yelled.

Something hard and cold was suddenly jammed into the Sergeant's back. "Let her go," Caroline said, "or I will shoot you dead."

"Let her go, boys, the lady's got a gun," squawked the Sergeant.

Under the muzzle of Caroline's musket, the orderlies were marched into the house and forced to distribute water to the wounded. Two of them spent the rest of the night on duty, under Caroline's command, performing other necessary nursing chores. They did these with the worst possible grace, cursing every man who asked for help with a call of nature, muttering threats to anyone who asked for a second drink of water. The orderlies were the scum of the army. It appalled Caroline that the lives of the wounded were in such hands.

In the morning she had a conference with Kate. Caroline was not sure how far they could go in disobeying or evading Dr. Lummes' authority. "Let's see how much we can get away with," Kate said. "I will go back to Liberty Tavern and get a real doctor down here to argue for us."

She arrived at Liberty Tavern as Dr. Lummes and her father were concluding a very tense conversation. "You can put down whatever you please in your account book, sir," Jonathan Gifford said, "but in mine it will be exactly what you pay me."

"Damn you, sir, haven't I explained the system to you?"

"I am not sure I like the system. I wonder what the Congress thinks about it."

"The Congress knows a man must live."

"Add another hundred dollars and you could have two pipes of wine for that price."

"Goddamn you, I will let Dr. Shippen know the part you are playing. You will never do a speck of business with our department."

"I'm not sure if I want to do any business with your department. I intend to find out from General Washington himself what he thinks of it."

Dr. Lummes stormed out of the tavern, muttering curses.

"What was that about?" Kate asked.

"He wanted me to charge him five hundred dollars for a pipe of wine—when it would only cost him three hundred. He and Dr. Shippen keep the difference, I gather."

"That is all I need to turn me into a Tory again," Kate said.

She summoned Dr. Davie from his morning drink at the bar and gave him and her father a vivid description of conditions at Kemble Manor hospital.

"Six orderlies for three hundred men," Jonathan Gifford said. "In the British army every company of invalids—every thirty-six men—has that many."

"They sleep on straw, you say?" Dr. Davie asked, unbelievingly. "No hammocks? Forty to a room?"

"The food is the first thing we must do something about," Kate said. "Can Kemble take one of our wagons and ask the people in the neighborhood to donate something?"

"I will see. He is in such a gloom—"

"And you, Dr. Davie, you must come down and help us."

"I don't see how I can," said Dr. Davie. "I have no authority."

"Damn authority," Kate said. "If Dr. Lummes complains, we will run him down to Shoal Harbor and throw him in the bay. Where is Lieutenant Rawdon?"

"I believe he's in the rose garden."

Kate found Rawdon rereading—for the hundredth time—*The Sorrows of Young Werther*. "I wish you would throw that damn German lamentation into the brook," she said.

"Every time I read it, I find it more moving than the last time."

"And I find it more boring."

"I don't understand you, Miss Stapleton. Why do you treat me this way? I don't deserve this hostile tone."

"I am not hostile, Thomas. Just impatient. I haven't the time to fuss over you now." She told him what was happening at Kemble Manor. "You know more medicine than those two fools who are running that hospital put together. Come down and help us."

"It would be a violation of my parole."

"Damn your parole. Who's going to know it? You can borrow a suit from Kemble and we will give you a different name. There are men dying down there, Thomas. Doesn't that mean anything to you?"

"There are men dying in New York, in London, and there's

probably a man or two dying down the road. We are all dying, for that matter."

"That is the most miserable sophistry I have ever heard in my life."

"What would my father say if he heard I was working in an American hospital? He would disinherit me on the spot."

"So? You've talked about resigning your commission and going home to tell the British people the truth about this war. Have you done it? You will sit here in this rose garden, spinning out this idea and that idea and doing nothing about any of them. All the time thinking, because you can hold my hand and steal a kiss now and then, that you are living. Well, let me tell you something, Thomas. I saved you from dying. Now I begin to think it was a waste of my time and strength."

"Kate, it was your love—the hope of it—that made the difference between my living and dying. Doesn't that mean anything to you?"

"It did at first. But now I am sickened by it. I don't want a man who lives off my flesh like a vampire. I want a man who has roots of his own in life."

She strode down to the edge of the brook, only a few yards away, and uprooted from the marshy bank one of the pink, five-petaled rose mallows that were just beginning to bloom there. "Look at yourself," she said, and threw it at his feet.

Back in Liberty Tavern Jonathan Gifford reported that Kemble had eliminated himself as the man to raise food for the wounded men. "He thinks he's obnoxious to the whole countryside," Jonathan Gifford said sadly. "He may be right for the time being. But don't worry. I will find someone—or do it myself."

Dr. Davie agreed to return to Kemble Manor with Kate. "We are going to save those men. Save every one of them," she said.

"Be realistic, Kate," her father said.

"All right. Nine out of ten. Instead of killing nine out of ten."

Down at the manor they found Dr. Lummes had departed for the main army. Perhaps he had become uneasy about Jonathan Gifford's reference to General Washington and had decided it would be safer to sever his connection with the hospital and leave Dr. Ladd to deal with any future charges of corruption. Before the year was out, a major scandal shook the army's medical department, involving Shippen, Lummes, and numerous other doctors who were defrauding the government and lining their pockets with money stolen from the medical budget.

Dr. Ladd was easy for Kate to handle. She introduced Dr. Davie to him as one of the great geniuses of Edinburgh. This was far from the truth, but Davie did know how to run a military hospital, thanks to his twenty years in the British army. He was appalled by what he saw on a brief tour of Kemble Manor. The sun was rising high in the summer sky and the crowded rooms increased the heat to oven temperature. The air was foul with the sweat of unwashed bodies and other even less pleasant odors.

"We must empty out these rooms, Dr. Ladd," Davie said. "We must get all but the worst wounded outside. Every man here must be washed as clean as he would be on his wedding day. We must give them clean linen outfits to wear. We must get rid of this straw and set up hammocks. Straw on a hard floor is the worst thing in the world for a wound. A hammock lets a man rest easy and draws the flesh together. They must have wine three times a day and all the fresh food we can gather."

Dr. Ladd hesitated. This advice contradicted everything American doctors had been doing. But their results had been so murderous, he was ready to change his mind.

"Dr. Ladd," Kate said, "last night you told me you were so discouraged you were ready to give up medicine. Why not make this an experiment?"

"We cannot do worse than we have been doing," Dr. Ladd said.

Such impromptu procedures may seem unbelievable in our more organized modern age. But the Revolution—especially the medical side of it—was a very disorganized war. Washington had to use all his slender manpower to maintain his fighting army. No one had much interest in or time for the medical department. Its record was so awful, I suspect the generals were inclined to stay as far away from it as possible. This explains why the Kemble Manor hospital was allowed to go its own unorthodox way.

Before the end of the day Jonathan Gifford's efforts to raise food bore fruit, literally and figuratively. He had gone to the leader of the Quaker community in Shrewsbury and described the situation at the hospital. The Quakers responded with the generosity for which their sect was famous. They saw it as an opportunity to erase the stigma of disloyalty which violent Whigs like the

Slocums had fastened on them. A procession of wagons came up the drive. Black Sam led it with a pipe of wine from Liberty Tavern. Behind them were loads of fresh apples and peaches and pears, dozens of loaves of freshly baked bread, a whole wagonload of hams, sides of freshly slaughtered beef.

Dr. Ladd could not believe it. "My God," he said, "these fellows will eat better than the King of England."

"And what is wrong with that?" Kate asked.

"It seems a waste on dying men."

"They are not dying," Kate said.

Dr. Ladd was only echoing the prevailing opinion in the American army. His attitude explained the strange passivity of the wounded men. For most of them the words "wound" and "hospital" were synonymous with death. It explained the low quality of the orderlies, the indifference of doctors like Lummes. Kate and Caroline and Dr. Davie fought this pessimism day and night. It was exhausting work. Sukey was their only assistant. When she collapsed from fatigue, Caroline recruited me. I went reluctantly and found myself working twelve to fourteen hours a day. No one else volunteered to help us. Everyone was too frightened by the stories of rampant death and disease in other army hospitals.

Kate did persuade the women of our neighborhood to cut up their silk and linen petticoats and sew them into shirts and pantaloons for the wounded men. Jonathan Gifford journeyed to Little Egg Harbor and bought three hundred hammocks from a warehouse in that busy privateering port. By the end of the week the stinking straw was gone, half the men were wearing light silk or linen pantaloons and jackets and the other half at least had had their filthy clothes washed along with their even dirtier skins. This was exhausting work in the savage heat of midsummer. Think about washing two hundred and eighty men, two hundred of them too weak to help themselves. Their wounds had to be examined and dressed. The orderlies refused to do any washing. They said it was damn nonsense. Dr. Ladd was totally ineffectual when it came to giving them commands. Sukey and I took turns working with Dr. Ladd in the kitchen while Kate and Caroline worked with Dr. Davie in the dining room.

Dr. Davie was in his sixties. He was semiretired when the war began and was not used to such extreme exertion. On Saturday night he looked desperately weary as he finished examining the last patient on our muster roll.

"You must go home this instant," Kate said. "And stay in bed all day tomorrow."

"What about yourself?" he said. "I don't like your looks any more than you like mine."

He was right. Kate was staggering with exhaustion. She had been working all day and sitting up half the night with some of the most seriously wounded, trying to ease their pain, giving them water and wine whenever they wanted it, talking to them, trying to strengthen their tenuous grip on life.

"I am not sixty years old," Kate said.

"I think I will rest like the Lord Jehovah on the seventh day," Dr. Davie said, putting on his coat and walking heavily to his chaise. "On Monday we can begin to practice some medicine. The first thing we must do is replace all those damn rag bandages with lint, good clean lint. Nothing better speeds the digestion of a wound—"

Kate walked with him to his carriage. He climbed into it with the gasping effort of a man mounting a steep ladder or an almost perpendicular hill.

A half-hour later, Jonathan Gifford was sitting in the taproom at Liberty Tavern listening to Daniel Slocum telling everybody that the war was as good as over. In a week or two at most, the French fleet would help the Americans capture New York and destroy the British army. A shout of alarm from Black Sam drew the Captain and others into the yard. They found Sam standing beside Dr. Davie's chaise, gently shaking him.

"He's in a powerful sleep, Captain Gifford. I can't wake him up."

"Get Lieutenant Rawdon from the house," Jonathan Gifford said. "He knows something about medicine."

Rawdon came on the run. They carried Dr. Davie into the taproom and Rawdon felt his wildly fluttering pulse, noted the twitching of Davie's right hand and cheek, and diagnosed apoplexy. He forced some wine down his throat and helped carry him up to his bed.

"Is there anything you can do?" Jonathan Gifford asked, as Molly and Barney McGovern tried to make Davie comfortable.

"We might do a number of things," Rawdon said. "Some people recommend blowing sneezing powders up the nose or tobacco smoke down the throat from an inverted pipe, clysters up the rectum, taking twelve ounces of blood from the arm and eight from the jugular. I think they are all forms of torture. That is why I quit medicine, Captain Gifford. I prefer to let nature heal in her own way."

"Rawdon!" Davie called. He managed to open one eye. His voice was thick, his breathing ratchety. "Rawdon," he said, "you must go down there to the hospital and help those lads. They need a real doctor. You must make the ladies—Kate—rest—or—"

"Kate? What is wrong with Kate?"

"Go—go. Don't argue with a dying man."

"You are not dying," said Rawdon. "This is a second-degree apoplexy. You will have some palsy as a result of it. But you'll be back to work in a month."

"If you're right—you can expect a horsewhipping in that time if you don't—go."

"I will go—for only one reason. To prevent the flow of extravagated blood to the base of your brain."

In medical terms Rawdon was telling Davie he was in danger of having apoplexy of the third degree if he did not keep quiet. He strode out of the room. "I knew it," Davie muttered. "I knew it from things the fellow said to me after he was shot. He's a better doctor than I am."

Thomas Rawdon rode down to Kemble Manor through the moonless darkness of that night, his mind a bitter blank. He was still furious with Kate for the accusation she had flung at him in the rose garden. With that objectivity which was one of the most unexpected aspects of his character, he admitted she had told him the truth. He had carried that rose mallow back to his room and left it on his night table. More than once he picked it up and watched it die. The green stem withered, the petals drooped and crumbled. He was doing the same thing, he told himself. Those violent words had ripped up his fragile roots. This time he would not bother to ask Jonathan Gifford for a gun. He would steal one of the dueling pistols from behind the bar. In the center of the rose garden he would blow out his brains. They would find the note in his pocket, accusing her of his murder. Werther and his self-pitying sorrows had wandered to America.

This was still Lieutenant Rawdon's frame of mind when he arrived at Kemble Manor. It was after midnight. A single candle glowed on the hall table. Although the worst odors had been banished, the house was still permeated by the presence of two hundred and eighty sweating men. I encountered him as I came out of the kitchen with some fresh wine. "Where is Kate, Jemmy?" he asked.

I pointed to the south parlor.

He took the wine from me and entered the parlor. The room was full of restless, groaning men. The only illumination was two candles in sconces on the wall. In this flickering light he could see Kate, standing beside a hammock, dipping a cloth in a bowl of water and patting it on a man's forehead. Lieutenant Rawdon also saw a number of less visible things.

This woman had the weight of the world's suffering on her weary face. But she bore it gladly, almost proudly because she was not simply enduring it. She was fighting it, fighting the suffering he had fled the teaching hospitals of Edinburgh to avoid. For the first time he faced the inner pattern of his life. He saw why he had refused to accept this gift of healing which his teachers in Edinburgh had assured him that he possessed in the highest degree. The bitterness that had swelled cancer-like inside him for so many years burst at the thought. The arrogance of God or Fate or whatever it was controlling our little destinies to inflict this gift on him after all those arid loveless years of growing up with disapproving relatives and those dry, moralizing letters from the man who signed himself Father. He would show them all, father, aunts, uncles, God, by doing nothing whatsoever with this gift. That had been the real uprooting, the beginning of his romance with death. The drift into the stupid game of first infuriating then pleasing Father. Accepting a commission to fight in a war he despised.

Yet here was this girl with no special gift except her beauty, something that a man dying of bitterness might justly expect as consolation, like Father's inheritance, here was this girl who had had a monster for a mother, had fallen in love with the wrong man, been abused brutally by her own people, here she was, ravaged by exhaustion, giving herself, her sympathy, her presence to that suffering man in the hammock. The girl had become a woman, a woman with the strength to do this incredible thing. How could he explain it?

Standing there in that fetid room with the sounds of suffering beating against him, Thomas Rawdon did not know the whole answer. More important for him at that moment was what he saw large. This woman's sympathy, caring, tenderness while he had nothing but his posturing bitterness. She had discovered a fundamental secret, the multiplication of love—while he had learned nothing but subtraction, the amputation of the roots of life.

In that same searing moment Thomas Rawdon glimpsed the possibility of not merely understanding but sharing this new love —new for him at least—that he recognized on Kate's face. Something he had not experienced for so long he had forgotten the name stirred in his soul—hope, personal hope, without the usual echo of self-mocking laughter. He walked down the lane of hammocks to Kate's side.

"Allow me," he said.

She was amazed but almost too tired to show it.

"What are you doing here?" she said leadenly as he lifted the man's head and placed the glass of wine to his lips.

"What are his symptoms?"

"He calls for water constantly. He seems to have a violent fever. I thought some wine—"

"Get a candle from the wall and bring it over here."

Kate obeyed. With the added light he noted the man's eyes were yellowish and inflamed, his face bloated. He was breathing with difficulty. "Do you have a sharp pain in the back?" Rawdon asked.

The man nodded.

"I think it is spotted fever. We will know that for certain by tomorrow. By then it may be too late. We must move him out of this room immediately. It is highly contagious."

Fortunately the man only had a shoulder wound. He was able to walk. They took him into the manor's empty carriage house, hung a hammock for him, and left him with enough wine and water to last until morning.

On the way back to the manor house, Rawdon told Kate about Dr. Davie. Kate wept from grief and weariness. "It's my fault. I should have known he was too old—"

"No. It's my fault. If I had come when you asked me—"

"No, that is my fault too," Kate said. "I was too cruel in what I said. I could see how much it hurt you. I still have a terrible temper, Thomas. When I get in a passion I'm an ignorant foolish girl all over again."

Rawdon shook his head. "You're a woman. If you give me a chance, Kate, I will try to become a man to match you."

CHAPTER THREE

FOR THE NEXT two months, Kate worked beside Thomas Rawdon seven days a week as he struggled with fevers, infections, ulcers, gangrene, and the constant indiscipline of the orderlies. The results they achieved soon converted Dr. Ladd and everyone who visited the hospital into disciples of Rawdon's approach to medicine, with its stress on cleanliness, good food, affectionate care, and a minimum use of strong drugs. By the middle of the summer, two hundred wounded were on their way to full recovery. Thirty-six remained in doubt. Only forty-four had died. There was not another American army hospital that could match this record.

Kate deserved a major share of the credit for this achievement. Most of the responsibility for running the hospital on a day-to-day basis fell to her. As the summer advanced, Caroline became heavily involved in the Kemble Manor farm, the mill, and her Colt's Neck property. A carper might say she spent inordinate amounts of time at Liberty Tavern discussing these matters with her business partner, Captain Gifford, but Kate was no carper. Besides, she was too busy buying food, helping Sukey supervise newly hired white and black servants in the kitchen, berating the orderlies, and helping me nurse the more serious cases.

The experience was a turning point in Kate's life. It gave her a new sense of self-worth, a genuine self-confidence. At least as important was the change she saw in Thomas Rawdon. From a man absorbed in his own melancholy he became a doctor with a genuine passion to heal. Within a month she was convinced that it was no mere performance for her sake. No actor could feign the anguish she saw on his face when a patient died, or the compassion when a suffering man begged him for opium to ease his pain.

With Kate's help he kept voluminous records on each patient. During hours when he should have been sleeping, he discussed these with a convalescent Dr. Davie, comparing standard diagnoses and prognoses with what he saw in the record, trying to learn the only way a good doctor learns, from experience, the unflinching analysis of visible evidence.

Listening to these discussions, and daily becoming more adept at recognizing and grouping symptoms, Kate found herself fascinated by the mysteries and challenges of medicine. She began reading textbooks in Dr. Davie's library and soon persuaded Rawdon to conduct little seminars on the front steps of Kemble Manor in the evening for herself, Dr. Ladd, and me.

Rawdon had a truly original mind and the courage to condemn stupidity and malpractice wherever he saw it. Above all, he rejected the standard, so-called heroic approach to treatment, with its reliance on bleeding and dangerous drugs. He was even more iconoclastic about current practice in childbirth and infant care, where mortality was shockingly high. On this subject, Kate had a hundred questions. Dr. Ladd and I had done most of the talking when Rawdon discussed the latest medical thinking about wounds, infections, fevers. But we could not match Kate's hunger for knowledge about a branch of medicine which affected the health and happiness of almost every woman. She was intrigued to learn that British doctors were educating midwives. American doctors were trying to drive them out of business. Rawdon thought making better use of the midwives was sensible, because modesty made most pregnant women prefer to deal with a woman. Besides, intelligent midwives knew more about childbirth than the average doctor, whose knowledge of anatomy (female or male) was too often rudimentary.

By the time our seminars ended, I knew I wanted to be a doctor. So did Kate. Before long, I hope Americans shall see the end of the prejudice that bars women from a profession to which they are so naturally suited. But in 1778, a realistic woman—which was what Kate had become—knew she could never win acceptance from either the public or the medical profession. She realized that she would have to be satisfied with a participation in the art of healing, through her husband.

When the last wounded man left for the army in late October, our hospital closed. Kemble Manor became Caroline Skinner's private home again. While the orderlies loaded the wagons and cleaned up the sickrooms, Kate and Rawdon walked in the park. The air was rich with Indian summer sunshine.

"What will you do now, Thomas?" Kate asked.

"Marry you," he said.

"Oh? It is nice of you to tell me in advance. When is this great event to take place?"

"As soon as possible."

"A British officer marrying one of the enemy? What will the King say?"

"Damn the King. I will resign my commission tomorrow. I will become a citizen of the United States and take over Davie's practice. I will put my roots down here, Kate, with you."

"And your father—your inheritance?"

"Damn them both. You are worth ten times more than a hundred thousand pounds to me, Kate."

She took both his hands and raised them to her lips. "Thomas, I love you. I love these hands for the comfort they bring the sick. I want them to—to comfort me. You have had my heart from the day you first persuaded me to call you Thomas. But we must be realistic. As long as the war lasts, an ex-British officer cannot practice medicine here. People like Slocum will slander you as they are slandering Father. Worse."

"What is the alternative . . . ?"

"Wait. The war cannot last another year, now that we have the French on our side. In the meantime, let me be your pupil. I would like to be more than a wife to you. I would like to be your partner in medicine. Especially in treating women and infants. Don't laugh at me—"

"I like the idea. But what if the war ends tomorrow?"

"I would still like a year of study before I begin rocking cradles. Nature complicates life for us more than for you, Thomas."

"Is there any other reason for waiting, Kate?"

They both knew what he meant. Anthony Skinner was still writing forlorn passionate letters to her from New York. There was not even a trace of hesitation in Kate's answer.

"None."

"All right," Rawdon said. "But let me warn you that you will be studying with the most dangerous professor of anatomy in the history of medicine."

There was only one thing wrong with this arrangement. The war showed no sign of ending. Kate's confidence in victory within twelve months was the product of our first euphoria over the French alliance. She had forgotten Caroline's prediction, that France's entry into the war would arouse British patriotism. She was also out of touch with what the French were doing—or rather not doing—to help us. Kate would have gotten a far different vision of the future if she visited Liberty Tavern's taproom as I did, the night the hospital closed.

Everyone was sitting around in a fog of gloom. The previous night, the British and Tories had landed on Middletown Point and burned the house and barns of John Burrows, our so-called "corn king." He had made a tidy fortune buying corn from all comers (including our crooked commissaries) the previous year and reselling it when the price rose. Dozens of farmers had sold him their corn this year on promissory notes that offered them twice the market price, betting that old John would repeat the performance. Instead, Anthony Skinner and his loyalists had loaded John and his corn into their boats. Burrows was in a British prison and Skinner and company were probably counting the hard money they had made selling the corn to the British army in New York. General Slocum, who was (according to rumor) a silent partner of Burrows, tried to call out the regiment. No more than one hundred men responded. They tiptoed down to Middletown Point, fired a round, and ran for their lives when the loyalists came after them three hundred strong.

"Where is that damned French fleet?" Samson Tucker groaned. "Why ain't they protecting our coast?"

Nat Fitzmorris shook his head. The ravages of eighteen months in a British prison were all too visible on his face. He had been exchanged about a month ago.

"They're doing just what the limeys in New York said they'd do," Nat said. "Caress us until we rejected the peace offer and then sail for the West Indies."

No longer were toasts being drunk to Louis XVI. Our disillusion with our French allies was intense. Historians will undoubtedly find many arguments for their strategy. We only knew that our soaring hopes of an early end to the war had looped to the ground like boyish kites in a sudden calm.

First the confident talk of capturing the British army in New

379

York went glimmering when the French admiral declined to risk his ships to batter his way past the British men-of-war blocking the Narrows. Next the attempt to capture the British garrison in Rhode Island collapsed when the admiral could not agree on tactics with the American general, John Sullivan. Whereupon the French fleet had departed for the West Indies to grab off a few sugar islands, leaving us exactly where we were in 1776, with the royal army breathing down our throats from New York and Staten Island. To complete our sense of abandonment, Washington recalled Major Yates and his regulars to the dwindling main army.

Infuriated by Congress's rejection of the King's peace offer, loyalists and regulars dismissed all hope of reconciliation and launched a war of unrelenting destruction. We in New Jersey were their logical—that is to say nearest—targets. They struck almost at will up and down our long, exposed coast, burning and looting with savage energy. Not a few previously staunch Whigs lost heart and made secret agreements with the British to lapse into neutrality for a guarantee of protection. Even among those who did not "take a protection," to use the phrase of the day, despair amounting to collapse prevailed. Many abandoned their farms and moved west, considering the Indians a lesser risk than our implacable royal enemies. Recruiting officers who appeared in the taproom were insulted to their faces and were lucky to get away without physical bruises.

Jonathan Gifford fought this undertow of defeatism with all his strength. Again and again he repeated a favorite maxim of Washington's—"We cannot lose as long as we stay in the game." But he could not control another major cause of our collapse—which ironically undercut his influence: our money.

In the closing months of 1778, the Continental dollar began to sink in value with frightening rapidity. By mid-1779 it had dwindled away until it took twenty Continentals to buy what one had bought in 1776. The Congress printing presses in Philadelphia continued to spew a river of dollars into the nation, making the money in circulation worth even less. For a man in business like Jonathan Gifford, this meant the price of everything went up in great leaps. A quart of flip which cost a shilling—about twenty cents—in 1776 now cost two dollars. The price of food became even more outrageous. The British on Staten Island and in New York continued to buy tons of food from our loyalist neighbors, paying hard money—which made patriot farmers demand extortionate amounts of paper money for their meat and grain.

It was difficult enough for Jonathan Gifford to endure the unpopularity and accusations of profiteering that the soaring prices brought down on him. He also took an economic beating from his fellow patriots. As I mentioned earlier, he was, like many tavern keepers, a banker to farmers in the neighborhood, loaning them cash when they ran short. Sometimes the sums amounted to a mortgage on a man's farm. When the Revolution broke out and the royal courts were suspended, it became impossible to collect many of these debts. Jonathan Gifford never dunned a single man as far as I know. In a time of social convulsion one could not expect debts to be paid. More than one man had borrowed additional sums from him to replace a burned house or barn or a stolen wagon or a runaway slave.

With Deputy Commissary Beebe and Deputy Quartermaster Beatty flooding the district with Continental dollars to buy supplies for the American army, camped not far away at Middlebrook, more than one man decided there was nothing wrong with paying off his debt in this almost make-believe money. They insisted on their right to pay at 1776 ratios, roundly declaring it was Jonathan Gifford's patriotic duty to accept Continental money at its face value. Hadn't Congress said so? Jonathan Gifford could only swallow hard and accept the bundle of bills the man was handing him. Some refused to take such shameful advantage of him, I'm happy to say. Samson Tucker, for instance, denounced those who were doing it one night in the taproom, in stentorian tones. But there was a formidable phalanx around Daniel Slocum, who whispered behind Jonathan Gifford's back about the profits he was making from Kemble Manor and the tavern. All this justified paying debts to "the Englishman" with cheap money.

Among those who began to strut in Slocum's entourage were such discredited patriots as our turncoat committeemen, Lemuel Peters and Ambrose Cotter. They had taken advantage of an offer made by Washington to give those who had succumbed to British pardons a chance to recant. But for a year they had cowered on their farms, shunning and being shunned by their neighbors. Now the general malaise induced by our French hangover enabled them to emerge without meeting the slightest odium.

There was no local spokesman to uphold the purity of the Cause. We were left with Daniel Slocum and his venal clan for leaders. Jonathan Gifford had hoped that Slocum could be defeated at the polls in the summer of 1778. His profiteering at his saltworks, his illegal land-grabbing—he had purchased the estate of another leading loyalist, John Taylor, in an equally fraudulent sale only a month after Captain Gifford had frustrated his attempt to seize Kemble Manor—the rapacity with which he collected militia fines had antagonized a substantial bloc of voters. But we needed Kemble and the power of his name to rally this formless group. Only his angry rhetoric could have given them the courage to withstand Slocum's bullying.

Kemble was a brooding hermit, seldom emerging from his room except to wander through the woods or along the shore like a solitary leper. Night after night, as he bolted the front door, Jonathan Gifford heard his son's footsteps in the room above the entrance hall, pacing up and down, up and down.

Kemble was experiencing something Americans cannot endure —failure. Someone had to be blamed for it—that is the way Americans think. Since there was no one else available, Kemble blamed himself—another common American mental contortion. Europeans with their sense of history's rises and falls, idiosyncrasies and absurdities, find this difficult to comprehend.

Jonathan Gifford had discussed Kemble with Caroline several times in the previous year. Carefully, without ruffling Captain Gifford's formidable temper, she had pointed out to him his tendency to give too much advice. No matter that it was good advice, Kemble felt smothered by it. After the Monmouth tragedy she felt that the situation was too serious to be diplomatic. She saw how hurt Jonathan Gifford was, how much anger was mixed with his love for his son. She urged a dangerous solution.

"You must go to him, Jonathan. You must take the risk of more insults."

Jonathan Gifford's face darkened. He shook his head. "I have had enough of that—that shit," he said.

"There is no other way. I was able to talk to Kate—as one woman to another woman. I don't know what one man says to another man at a time like this. But you have to try, Jonathan."

Captain Gifford thought about those words for a week. He was still thinking about them as he knocked on Kemble's door. *You are a damn fool—woman's advice—what does she know?* Fragments of negative thoughts skittered through his mind.

"Who is it?"

"Me—your—your father. Can I come in?"

"Why not?"

Kemble stood with his back to him, staring out the window into the darkness. There were no words in Jonathan Gifford's mind. For a moment he almost panicked.

"I've got some news you'll enjoy. The British have burned Slocum's saltworks."

"Oh."

"They sailed right up the Manasquan. No one fired a shot at them."

"Oh."

"There are plenty of other saltworks. I think we are free to gloat, don't you?"

"I suppose so."

There was a long silence.

"You don't sleep well."

"No. How do you know?"

"I see the light in your window."

Another long silence.

"Why can't *you* sleep?" Kemble asked.

"I keep thinking about you."

"Why?"

"I can't believe what you're doing."

"What am I doing?"

"Quitting."

"If the militia is called out, I will march."

"I'm not talking about *that*. Any fool can do that. I'm talking about being a leader."

Kemble laughed. "How can you even use that word—for me?"

"Because that's what you've been. You've been a leader for the people around here—and a pretty good one. I didn't agree with everything you said or did—but that's to be expected. The situation is so new, so strange. A war and a revolution in one bottle—but now when your friends need you—when your country—"

Kemble was no longer listening. He was letting his eyes drown in the darkness outside the window. For a moment Jonathan Gifford saw him dissolving into that darkness.

"Goddamn it," he roared in a voice that woke sleepers throughout Liberty Tavern. "Do you think you're the only one who's ever lost men in battle? The only one who's ever tormented himself about it? See this knee? Every time I limp on it, I'm reminded of a worse failure. There was a Spanish strong point outside Havana that had been blocking our advance all during the siege. I convinced our colonel we could storm it by night. I was wrong. I lost half my company. My lieutenant, a close friend, was killed. And my ensign, a boy only seventeen. The next day the Spanish surrendered. Our attack had nothing to do with it. They were starving. All those deaths—were wasted. I wasted them. Oh, son—"

Kemble was stunned to see tears in his father's eyes. They were deep in it now, that dark world of pain and loss that surrounds the glittering panoply of war. Jonathan Gifford was entering it again, facing the dead men and the blood and the grief, to drag Kemble back into the light before the darkness swallowed him. He was dealing with feelings too deep for an inarticulate man to express. Kemble could not see the connection between him and that long-dead boy Captain Gifford had mourned in Havana, could not understand or even hear the spiritual resonance in that word "son." But the violence of his father's feelings penetrated his despair.

"All right," he said. "All right. I will stay in the game."

The bitter grudging tone made it clear that it was a minimum concession. Kemble could not free himself from his obsessive indictment of this man. He refused to heed Jonathan Gifford's urgings to return to active leadership in our county—which practically guaranteed our decline into apathy. Slocum's conduct—or the lack of it—at Monmouth had destroyed the little popularity he had left. But Kemble turned his back on our smaller world and rode over to Washington's headquarters in the nearby village of Raritan to offer the General his services.

This was primary among the several reasons why Liberty Tavern became a headquarters for American intelligence agents in the winter of 1779. Another reason was the parlous state of the American army. To stay in the game, Washington had to know what the British were doing and thinking. His army had dwindled to the point where a single defeat would have shattered the Cause.

By this time the General had become a spymaster extraordinary. He had a half-dozen networks operating on Long Island and

Staten Island and in New York City. Since New Jersey swarmed with British spies, couriers from these networks could not chance being recognized entering or leaving the American camp.

One morning General Washington rode down our way, seemingly out for nothing more than a little exercise. He stopped at Liberty Tavern for coffee and in five minutes' conversation with Jonathan Gifford arranged for couriers to leave their messages with him. Kemble took them on the last stage of their journey to the Wallace house, where he often delivered them to Washington personally. In the course of a few months, he got to know the General well. The next step was almost inevitable.

In the spring of 1779, Washington stopped at the tavern at his usual early hour—about seven-fifteen—and sat down to coffee with Jonathan Gifford. They talked for a few minutes about the war. Washington was gloomy. There seemed to be no hope of raising enough men to drive the British out of New York. Then the General asked, "Does your son still have good nerves?"

"I would say so."

"I need someone to visit a friend in New York, immediately."

"There are refugees there—friends from New Jersey—who might recognize him."

"We will give him a disguise—some forged papers."

The thought of Kemble dying a spy's death made Jonathan Gifford hesitate.

"He wants to go," General Washington said.

"I'm not surprised at that."

"I thought you should have—a veto."

"I appreciate that very much, General," Jonathan Gifford said. "But he is a man in his own right. He must make his own decision."

"I wish we had more like him."

Washington told Jonathan Gifford how Kemble had ridden into his headquarters on Christmas Day, 1776, and volunteered to cross the Delaware with him. "There were men with rank—high rank—who found it convenient to fall sick that day."

"He has never said a word to me about this, General. I am glad —proud—to know it," Jonathan Gifford said, his voice husky with feeling.

Like Captain Gifford, Washington had a stepson and no natural children. But his stepson sat home on his plantation, contributing nothing to the war. His mother was said to dote on him so much, the General could not bring himself to insist on his service. Perhaps this was why he offered Jonathan Gifford a veto. Perhaps he also wanted to study a little more closely this ex-British officer who was becoming an important part of his intelligence system.

They talked for several more minutes about the war. Washington candidly admitted to Captain Gifford that his "greatest mistake" was not insisting on the right to recruit a thirty-thousand-man army for the duration of the war when patriotism was burning fervently in 1775. "I keep saying that we cannot lose this thing, as long as we stay in the game. But between you and me, Captain, I worry about doing even that much."

Jonathan Gifford was loath to put another burden on Washington's mind. But he could not resist talking frankly to him about the situation in south Jersey. He bluntly placed the blame for the widespread disaffection and apathy on Daniel Slocum. Washington sighed. "Your son has hinted as much to me. But the army cannot interfere in the politics of New Jersey. I have no authority over General Slocum." For a moment Washington's face became saturnine. "I could name you Slocum's counterpart in Connecticut, New York, Pennsylvania, Delaware, Maryland. I hope the time will come when we can root out such men."

"There is one thing you could do, General," Jonathan Gifford said. He described Major Yates's rampage in my father's house and urged Washington to court-martial him. Washington brought his fist down on the table and made a sulphurous comment about thieving Yankees. He swore (literally) that he had never seen my father's complaining letters. (An officious aide, perhaps cajoled by Daniel Slocum, had apparently pigeonholed them.) The General rode back to his headquarters at Raritan, and a court-martial board was hearing testimony against Major Yates within the week. My father and I were the chief witnesses. In spite of the Major's plea that he was only doing the Lord's work, he was found guilty of looting and cashiered.

Meanwhile, Kemble began making regular trips between Liberty Tavern and New York. Each time he wore a different disguise —a brown or a black wig, a Quaker's plain brown homespun and broad hat, a German-Swiss farmer's black boots and a bright waistcoat, a Dutch burgher's red cloak. He concocted most of his disguises himself and soon became an expert. From locks of Kate's hair he constructed mustaches in the German style which he glued to his upper lip. He stuffed the linings of his coats and breeches with wool to make him look fatter, and added inches to his height by reconstructing the inside of his boots. In a month or two he had perfected a half-dozen accents.

Sometimes he would put on his latest disguise and visit Liberty Tavern's taproom, fooling everyone, even Barney McGovern. One day he appeared as an Irish tinker with a mop of red hair that spilled into his eyes and side whiskers in a style Barney had not seen since he left Ireland. Kemble had copied them from an old print that hung on the wall in Barney's cottage. They talked for fifteen minutes and Kemble convinced Barney that he was from his home village, Ballymahon. Of course he was using information he had gleaned from Barney over the years.

The tinker was so good, Kemble made him his favorite disguise. Most of his contacts in New York were with an Irish tailor named Horace Monaghan who made uniforms for General Clinton and his staff and picked up juicy bits of gossip while measuring them.

Yet for all Kemble's skill, these trips to New York were no joke. He was in deadly danger every moment. There were at least a hundred loyalists from our neighborhood in the city who might penetrate his disguise by recognizing his voice, his walk, the shape of his aristocratic nose. For someone with Kemble's fragile health, the physical hardships alone were dangerous. He traveled on foot through rain and sleet, sleeping in cold barns. He came back from every trip exhausted, racked with a cough which made Dr. Davie look grave and his father haggard. But there was no hope of persuading him to stay home. He had found a new way to serve the Cause that satisfied him strangely.

Now I realize that Kemble's disguises were a kind of flight from the man he had to face each morning in the mirror with the memory of that Monmouth ravine in his eyes. Jonathan Gifford had restored Kemble to the Cause, he had tried to share with him the pain of guilt and failure, to tell him these things were inevitably part of war and revolution. But Kemble's mind had been molded by too many American influences. He could accept the forgiveness of others but he could not forgive himself. So he fled into disguises, into the solitary life of the spy, into constant flirtation with death. He soon discovered that others caught in the vortex of the war were possessed by even more dangerous demons.

CHAPTER FOUR

In the summer of 1779 a young Irish girl, her skirts brown with the dust of the road, wandered into Liberty Tavern. She had the face of an innocent child and the body of a mature woman, hair black as the night, and exquisite hands and feet. I know not what part of the feminine anatomy will be fixed upon as the sign of beauty by the generation that reads this book. But ours placed great stress on these extremities. They were supposedly proof of aristocratic blood.

There was no hint of aristocracy in the story Margaret O'Hara told. She was the wife of a veteran sergeant who had been captured in the storming of the British fort at Stony Point on the Hudson—the only victory of consequence won by the Americans in 1779. Rather than starve or sell herself in New York, she had paid a boatman to ferry her from Staten Island to the Blazing Star landing in Woodbridge. With the American army nearby, the tavern was crowded with hungry officers every day. Molly McGovern declared she could use another hand in the kitchen. Jonathan Gifford agreed to hire the girl. Her face and figure made her a favorite waitress and she was soon walking out with several young officers. Barney McGovern lectured her sternly about the dangers of such attachments. They would use her and discard her.

"Isn't that the way of men everywhere?" she replied.

A few days later, Lieutenant Rawdon was strolling beside the brook with Kate. Margaret O'Hara was washing some sheets in the swift-running water. Kate said hello and got a perfunctory smile.

"Extraordinary," said Rawdon, looking over his shoulder. "That girl. I'm sure she is my cousin's mistress. Is her name O'Hara?"

"Yes."

"What in the world can she be doing here?"

Unfortunately Jonathan Gifford had left the previous day on a trip to Little Egg Harbor to buy liquor and wine for the coming winter. Kate told Kemble what Rawdon had said. He quickly answered the Lieutenant's question. "She's probably a spy."

Kemble summoned Margaret O'Hara to his father's office. She came wearing a dress soiled from kitchen work. Her face was flushed with the heat of that hot place compounded by the July day.

"Lieutenant Rawdon says you are not the wife of a sergeant—but the mistress of the Adjutant General of the British army, his cousin, Lord Rawdon."

"I was," she said. "But he discarded me when I did not get on with General Clinton's mistress, Mrs. Baddelly. She's as Irish as I am. But I'm twice as proud."

Kemble found these words astonishing—and strangely moving. The girl seemed to mean what she said. How could she talk about pride, standing there in her soiled kitchen smock?

"What brought you here, then?"

"I was taken up by Major Beckwith. In his English way he decided I could be useful as well as pleasurable, I suppose. He sent me here with the assurance that your father was a secret friend and would protect me. I am to learn what I can from the soldiers, and await instructions. I gave your father a letter from one of his friends in New York the day I arrived."

Two years ago Kemble might have lost his head at this news and suspected Jonathan Gifford of treachery. But he no longer had any doubts about his father's commitment to the Cause. This freed him to concentrate on the woman before him. She disturbed him profoundly. Her honesty stirred a wish to protect and rescue her. By instinct Kemble was a savior, tormented by the world's disinclination to be saved.

He said he would talk to his father when he returned. Then he sprang from his chair and paced the room. "Why are you doing this for them? When they have treated you so badly—and treated your country—"

"I knew perfectly well what my fate might be, Mr. Stapleton," she said. "I chose it in spite of my mother's tears and my father's curses. It was better than a cold cabin in a Mayo bog. All my brothers were outlaws. Why should not I become one such, in my own way?"

"But now you are in a free country," Kemble said. "There is no need—"

"You have no more use for us than the English so far as I can see."

"That's not true."

She knew precisely what his words implied. She accepted them with a cool smile. "Be that as it may. I have made my bargain."

Kemble's agitation brought on a coughing fit. Margaret O'Hara hurried to the taproom and returned with rum and water. As she handed it to him she saw bright red flecks of blood staining his handkerchief.

"Oh, dear God," she said.

"You must tell no one about that. Promise me."

"You have an O'Hara's promise. That was once worth more in Ireland than a monk's vow."

"In what way?" said Kemble, betraying his ignorance of Ireland.

Anger blazed on Margaret O'Hara's face. "Ask Barney McGovern to come here," she said.

Kemble called Barney from the taproom. Margaret O'Hara stepped back as he entered. The scullery maid vanished. Something in the way she stood, the angle of her head, transformed her.

"McGovern," she said, "who was Liam O'Hara of Kildare?"

"Why, the greatest man in the west of Ireland," said Barney McGovern. "He had a house twice as big as this tavern. A dozen poets and a hundred musicians lived upon him. His word was law for a hundred miles. There was not a wedding or a funeral in all that space without a gift from him. Are you—"

"He was my grandfather."

"Begorra, how we have fallen."

"We will rise again."

For a moment, Kemble thought a battle cry would leap from Barney's lips. For another moment he saw him bending his knee before her like a warrior before a princess of the blood royal. But Barney had spent too many years in the British army. He had long since resigned himself to Ireland's fate.

"God willing," he said.

"Whether He wills it or not, in spite of His heaven or His hell."

Kemble saw the depths of her bitterness and despair. It would

390

have been better for him if he had fled the room, the building, the state. But he sent Barney back to work and spent the next three hours talking to Margaret O'Hara. She told him the truth. She made no attempt to disguise or excuse herself. The truth was, of course, the best possible excuse as far as Kemble was concerned. He never saw what was apparent to many others—it was no excuse to Margaret O'Hara. That afternoon she talked as only the Irish can talk—with a mad, bitter gaiety that both mocked and magnified her despair. Her story was the fall of the O'Haras—but it was also the destruction of Ireland—the methodical brutal reduction of a whole nation to beggary—done with consummate British legality.

Her grandfather had sought to remain neutral. Not one of his sons or his retainers raised their hands against British rule. But he might as well have been the greatest rebel in Ireland, for all the good it did him. Every Catholic Irishman was an enemy and their lands, their houses were prizes ripe for picking after the defeat of the old aristocracy at the battle of the Boyne in 1690. Twenty years later, Liam O'Hara was executed in Dublin Castle on a trumped-up charge of treason, sworn by false witnesses. His lands were forfeited. The remnants of the family clung to cabins on the fringe of the old demesne. In one of these cabins with mud for a floor and straw for a bed, Margaret O'Hara was born.

Not until she was a girl of thirteen did she taste meat. Her father lived in a fog of alcoholic despair. Her brothers were goaded into joining the Whiteboys, guerrillas who murdered landlords and constables in the night. Two of them died on the scaffold at Kildare before she was ten. At thirteen she became a scullery maid in the great house her family had once owned.

"When I saw how they lived, with fires to keep them warm and every kind of food upon the table, I vowed I would have it, no matter what I must do. I cursed God, cursed Him for turning His face from us when we had done nothing to offend Him. I told the priest as much when he came out of the bog to confess us. I had looked at myself in a mirror for the first time, you see, and I knew what I had to offer."

At sixteen the landlord's son took her to London. He dressed her in silks and satins and displayed her to his friends "like you might a blood horse." To his dismay, she soon left him for "a real Englishman," a member of Parliament, no less. She left him for Lord Rawdon, and he had brought her with him to America.

No stain of this sordid journey appeared on her exquisite face. Stunned with sympathy, Kemble was convinced that her spirit had somehow survived the transaction. He was wrong. The person named Margaret O'Hara had survived and so had her beauty, thanks to assiduous care. But with every day, week, month, and year of her journey, the personal hope on which the heart must live dwindled and the heart itself withered. She had sold herself to the English service and she was left with faith in nothing except their power. When Kemble began telling her there was a future for her in America, she laughed in his face.

"You will never beat them. The French have saved you for a year or two. But they will beat you as surely as they have beaten everyone else. I knew that the day I saw London. It lies there on the Thames like a great smoky monster feeding on Ireland, Wales, Scotland, America, Africa, India. They are the Romans come back to life."

"No. We are the Romans."

With a violence and an eloquence that momentarily silenced her, Kemble preached her a sermon on the future glory of America. The virtue and the valor of the Roman Republic would be reborn here when Americans became truly free. Every trace of Europe's corruption would be expelled from their minds and hearts. This entire continent—this half of the world—belonged to them.

It was the first time that Kemble had spoken this way since Monmouth. Margaret O'Hara was entranced by his eloquence, and his violence stirred an echo in her own lost soul. But she did not believe a word of it.

"No wonder your father must play a double game. With a son like you, there is no other hope of saving his head."

"I'm telling you the truth."

A tremor passed through Margaret O'Hara's body, a softening smile illumined her face. She touched her fingertips to his cheek. "You are as wild a lad as I've ever seen. I think you are a match for me. Don't lock your door tonight."

"There is no need—"

"Need? Who speaks of need? I only think of pleasing myself—and perhaps you."

"Don't come—if you won't speak of love."

"We will speak of that too. Of its impossibility."

The word "love" had been ripped involuntarily from Kemble's throat. Most people—particularly passionate intellectuals such as Kemble—have only fleeting glimpses of their real motives. Much of what takes place in a man's spiritual self—or a woman's—remains obscure to him, although the real nature of his innermost desires and fears can become visible to a person who knows him well. I am convinced that for Kemble, Margaret O'Hara was a chance to love a woman like his mother—a chance to prove to himself that it was possible to succeed where his father had failed.

I am sure that Kemble had never known a woman before. With all their freedom in riding and walking out and dancing the night away, American girls were extraordinarily skillful at avoiding the final concession until they were certain they were dealing with a future husband. Only scoundrels deceived them and they were comparatively few in our circle. Kemble, with his altitudinous devotion to honor and virtue, was certainly not one of them.

In his room he was assailed by a fundamental masculine doubt. What if he could not please this wild creature? For a while he was tempted to lock the door. Then he thought of the cold cabin of her childhood, remembered her despairing anger, and told himself that America—that he—must and could save her. He would prove the possibility of love to her. He left the door unlocked.

A few minutes past midnight there was a knock. Kemble opened the door. Margaret O'Hara stood there, with two cups of steaming liquid on a tray. In the dim light of the room's single oil lamp, the dark hall behind her, she looked like a priestess. On her head she wore a fresh lace cap. Her dress of blue silk was as pressed and clean as a ball gown. A rich perfume filled the room as she entered it. The scullery maid was no more. This was another woman.

"I have brewed us some of my favorite tea. 'Tis better than whiskey."

Even her voice had changed. It was soft, almost a whisper. " 'Twas vanity that made me bring this dress. I knew it was dangerous. No sergeant's wife could ever afford it. But something told me I might have a use for it. I always listen to such voices."

"Is that what brought you here—another voice?" Kemble said.

"Yes," she said. "Your voice."

The tea tasted strongly of herbs. Kemble asked her what was in it. She smiled and said it was her secret. An old Irish formula inherited from the Druids. "Drink it slowly," she said. "You can be sure it does no harm. It only brings joy. Or makes it possible."

"What if you are a witch?" Kemble said.

"And perhaps you are the devil."

By the time Kemble had finished his tea, a strange lightness, a sense of air charged with electricity, began flowing from his fingers and his lips down through his body and up into his brain.

"What is it? What is in this?"

"I told you. Joy or at least the chance of making it possible for a little while. It's a kind of escaping."

"I like it."

"From now till morning we shall forget such things as time and war and revolution, England and Ireland and America. There shall only be the two of us in our dream."

"That's not the kind of love I want," Kemble said.

"Let us try it and see if you ever want any other kind. But first we must read the leaves."

She took his cup from his hand while dark memories welled up in Kemble. This had been one of his mother's favorite superstitions. She had kept him in a perpetual state of anxiety, seeing in the tea leaves a tragic death for him one day and great wealth or great fame the next day. As Margaret O'Hara bowed her head over the cup, Kemble heard Sarah Gifford's voice, felt again the aching mixture of love and awe and fear.

"I see a great victory in your future. Marching men by the thousands, and you in control of them. And then I see— ochone."

"What?" said Kemble, with a smile. He no longer cared about the future. The herbs were working their subtle magic in his body. He felt free, freer than he had ever remembered feeling. It was a freedom without fearing or even caring about tomorrow.

"I see a great hurt, sorrow and—"

Kemble picked up her cup. "Strange, because I see in your cup the very opposite. A defeat where you've never been defeated before. And the discovery of something you don't believe in—happiness."

Margaret O'Hara became very serious. "It is bad luck to laugh at the leaves. They never lie—especially at a time like this."

"Who's laughing at them?" Kemble said. "I believe in what I

see—just as much as you. I think you are afraid of Americans. Afraid of this happiness we talk about."

"No, oh no," Margaret said, leaning toward him. "It is your wildness I fear. You are as wild as the Irish at the heart of you. I see it now leaping in you, freed by the sweet drink. You hold it back by the force of your mind, but once let go you may never bind it again. Does that concern you?"

Kemble's answer was his lips upon her mouth. She met him with her own harsh passion, then softened incomparably in his arms. The wild American that hid in Kemble's puritan soul burst forth with terrific power, fierce delight. Margaret O'Hara matched it with her own doomed wildness.

"Oh, 'tis a man, 'tis a man among men you are and a match for me," she murmured in the dawn, naked in his arms. "Let us be lovers and the world be well lost."

"We will have both—world and love," Kemble said.

"I will not hear a word of politics here," she said, freeing herself from his arms. "I must go, at any rate. Your self-appointed Irish stepmother, Molly McGovern, would flay me if she knew I spent the night here."

"And tonight and tomorrow night and the night after that," Kemble said.

"If I am not sent back."

"Back where?"

"To New York. I must go when I'm summoned."

"You are going to stay here the rest of your life. You are going to stop crying over Ireland, stop thinking of yourself as Irish. You are going to change your name to Stapleton."

"The drink is still with you. I have never seen it last so long."

"I know exactly what I am saying."

"I know exactly what I must do. Go back to New York."

For a moment Kemble glimpsed his tormented future. But he could not, would not believe the love he felt for this bewitching woman did not affect her in the same way. It would take months of intermixed joy and pain before he realized that she did not believe or trust anyone or anything except blind malignant fatality.

Later that Day, Jonathan Gifford returned from Little Egg Harbor. Kemble found him alone in his office, counting a mountain of paper money. "If this stuff depreciates any more," he said, "I'm going to have to build another barn to store it in, like hay."

"Margaret O'Hara is a spy. I gather you know about it."

Jonathan Gifford nodded, avoiding his son's eyes. "Yes, she told me the day she arrived."

For a moment suspicion leaped in Kemble's veins. "What did you do?"

"I told General Washington immediately. At his request I didn't tell you. He likes to keep his intelligence operations in separate compartments."

"Of course, I—I should have known."

"She brought a letter for me from Moncrieff, and another from Major Beckwith, one of their intelligence men. The information will be left here sealed with a special crest—the head of a sphinx. The girl will carry it to New York in the lining of her dress."

"General Washington is going to permit this?"

"Of course. The letters will be addressed to no one. They will only be recognized by the seal. So Beckwith had to give me a precise description of it complete with a drawing. We've had an engraver in Philadelphia make us an exact duplicate. Everything will be read and if necessary rewritten before going to New York. Washington has a fellow on his staff who can imitate anyone's handwriting after a half-hour's study."

"A forger?"

"A counterfeiter. He was condemned to death in Philadelphia. Washington arranged a reprieve. I like the way he beats the British at their own game. They've been playing it for years in London, you know. There's a secret staff at the post office who work nights opening and copying diplomatic and political mail. Even letters of Members of Parliament."

"So she will be—Margaret O'Hara will be—going back to New York."

"Beckwith made it rather clear that if we arrested her, he would arrange to make a bonfire of this tavern within the week."

Kemble retreated, dismayed by the contradiction raging within him. He exulted at the way the British were being gulled and hated it with his next breath. He loathed the idea of Margaret O'Hara returning to New York to the arms of Major Beckwith. He knew with scarifying clarity that this would be an inevitable part of her journey. It was an unspoken promise in the last thing she had said to him.

The next day, a small talkative man with a squint in his left eye arrived from Philadelphia, full of news about the Congress and rumors from Europe. Congress was about to withdraw the almost ruined Continental dollars. A revolution and a French invasion were threatening England. The war would end before Christmas. The Squinter, as Barney McGovern called him, dispersed this news with numerous toasts to honest Whigs. He was a merchant en route to the coast in search of salt to sell at the price set by Congress. No speculator he. From the sound of him, a better patriot never existed. But at the end of the night, he found Jonathan Gifford in his office and handed him a letter sealed with the head of a sphinx.

"The girl must leave first thing in the morning. There is urgent matter here," he said.

As veteran players of the intelligence game, the British were trying to give the Americans no chance to do any clandestine copying. The Squinter would loiter about the tavern tomorrow morning until he saw Margaret O'Hara on the road. Any delay would arouse deep suspicions.

Jonathan Gifford told Barney to have a horse saddled immediately. He hurried upstairs to Kemble's room. In his haste he gave only a perfunctory knock and threw open the door. Kemble stood at the window, Margaret O'Hara in his arms.

"There are Tory raiders on the Raritan," Jonathan Gifford lied. "They are calling out your company of militia."

As they walked to the barn, Jonathan Gifford told Kemble that he must get the sealed letter to Washington and have it back in the tavern, resealed and ready for forwarding to New York, before dawn.

As Kemble mounted, Jonathan Gifford tried to decide whether to say anything about what he had just seen in the bedroom. He remembered what Caroline had told him about giving too much advice and said nothing. But Kemble answered the unspoken question as he swung his horse's head toward the road.

"I love her, Father."

He galloped into the night, leaving Captain Gifford to meditate sleeplessly on those words.

CHAPTER FIVE

KEMBLE WAS BACK well before dawn, the spy's report copied and doctored for delivery to his British employers. By eight o'clock Margaret O'Hara was telling Molly McGovern and the rest of the kitchen help that she had a message from a militia captain on duty at the Blazing Star ferry landing. Her husband had escaped and was in New York waiting for her. Captain Gifford had been good enough to procure her a pass from General Washington so she could go see for herself if the story was true. By nine o'clock she was on her way.

Kemble stood in the tavern doorway, mind and body drained by his sleepless night, watching her with haunted eyes. A few hours later he went down the same road in his Irish tinker's disguise. He caught up with her at Perth Amboy, where she waited for the boat that came from New York twice a week with exchanged prisoners and mail. He struck up a conversation with her and for an hour he chatted in his cracked brogue about Ireland's troubles and his hopes of getting to Long Island or New York, where a man could earn hard money at his trade. She advised him to slip across narrow Arthur Kill at Elizabethtown—which was precisely what he intended to do.

"But I know not a soul in the city," whined Kemble the tinker, "and I hear the price of food would drive a man mad."

"Come to me and you shall have your dinner for a night or two, till you get work. There's no doubting you can find it, and at sky-high wages, too. Ask for Major Beckwith's house on Bowrie Lane. There's a fine snug barn in the back for your sleeping."

"God bless you, my girl. You've given me new courage. I've had enough of these Americans with their damn paper dollars."

Two days later, Kemble was in New York. He stopped at Horace Monaghan's place of business and told the excitable little tailor to prepare a report. A few minutes later he was in Bowrie Lane asking strollers which of the fine town houses belonged to Major Beckwith. Every visit to New York depressed Kemble. The Americans had set fire to the city in 1776 when the British drove them out. Few of the six hundred houses—a fourth of the city— destroyed by the flames had been rebuilt. In many cases their crumbled ruins were still visible on their lots. The streets swarmed with off-duty British and German soldiers and loyalist volunteers, in a mad medley of uniforms. Soldiers drove huge wagons through the streets, cursing civilians. Sentries paced before houses where generals shuffled papers. It was no longer the New York that Kemble had known and loved. It was a military depot. His gloom was increased by the splendid brick three-story house that was Major Beckwith's home away from home. At the back door he persuaded the fat black cook to find Miss O'Hara for him.

The scullery maid's clothes she had worn on her journey were gone. She wore an elaborate green silk dinner dress trimmed with white lace. Her hair was piled high on her head in a London coiffure. Sausage curls were draped behind her ears and a bright red ribbon held a mixture of curls and feathers in place at the crown. A glistening string of pearls wound through them.

"Ah, so you made it safe," she said before Kemble could remind her of who he was. "There's many a pot in here that could use some work. Nancy will hand them out to you. Happy am I to help a countryman. I've learned from sad experience there is no one else to help us if not each other."

Kemble God-blessed her in his best brogue and praised her expensive new clothes. "I had no idea I was talkin' to a foine lady there at the ferry slip."

"You must forget you saw me here or there if you value my friendship."

"Why, have you no friends on the other side?" asked Kemble. "A young lady as clever as you?" He gave her a sly wink. "We Irish must play both sides, the way I see it. We care not a tinker's dam which of them wins, do we now?"

Margaret O'Hara's face darkened. "We must do—we must do what we must," she said. "Go along with you now. You can sleep in the barn. I'll tell the Major."

A half-hour later, while Kemble was brooding over a half-dozen pots given him by the cook, Margaret came out to the barn. She wore a green pelisse that matched her gown. On her face was a green silk mask. They were commonly worn by city-bred ladies of the era to protect the complexion when they went out.

"Here's money for a bit of drink and food. The cook will give you nothing and it's just as well. She ruins everything she puts over a fire. That's why we are going out to dinner."

Kemble had to strangle a fierce wish to reveal himself, to accuse, demand, denounce. He hated himself for his deception and her for her betrayal of their love. He had to remind himself that she had promised him nothing but a temporary dream, a night separate from the rest of their lives.

Around ten o'clock he heard the sound of horses' hoofs and voices. A few moments later, the downstairs windows of the town house came aglow. Staying well beyond the light they cast, Kemble walked softly down the alley to look through the windows. Three British officers were in the parlor with Margaret O'Hara and two other women. They were all a little drunk. The other women wore coiffures as high and elaborate as Margaret's. Their faces were stained by a moral emptiness. They were not quite women of the street. But they were on their way to that sordid destination.

Margaret O'Hara was pouring port into long-stemmed crystal glasses. She served each guest with a playful curtsy. The last to receive a glass was probably their host, Major Beckwith. He was a husky thick-jawed man of about forty. She handed him his drink with an even more elaborate mock ceremony. He gave her a rather perfunctory smile and raised his glass in a toast. Glasses were raised in response. Margaret proposed a toast and Major Beckwith accepted it with the same cold smile. To Kemble outside in the darkness it was a pantomime that told him everything he had already known but refused to believe.

Back in the barn he glued the guinea she had given him to the bottom of a heavy pot. He was going to pitch it through the window, shout "British whore," and run. He would teach her shame at the very least. Then he remembered the ragged, hungry girl in the bogside cabin, remembered he had left his bedroom door unlatched, remembered the shadow on her face as she said *We must do what we must.* Again he told himself that he would somehow save her.

Margaret O'Hara returned to Liberty Tavern a week later with a sad tale about being misled, her husband was still a prisoner, it was another Sergeant O'Hara who had escaped. Kemble waited until he found her alone, washing clothes in the creek.

"How are all your friends in Bowrie Lane?" he asked.

"What?" she asked, amazed.

"Has Nancy's cooking gotten any better? Does she still burn everything she puts over a fire?"

"Dear God, you're in league with the devil," she cried, springing up.

"No, I think his name is Beckwith."

She backed away, really frightened now. "You could—you could be right. But how do you know?"

"Come to my room tonight."

"You have only to ask," she said softly. "There is no need to terrify me this way."

When she arrived with her midnight tea, Margaret found not Kemble but the tinker with his bushy red hair and side whiskers. She gasped as he greeted her in a perfect brogue. "Good evenin' to ya. We Irish must stick together now, isn't it the truth?"

"You *are* the devil," she said, putting down the tea on a chest of drawers.

"If I was," Kemble said, flinging aside the wig and the rest of his disguise, "I would be rejoicing over your lost soul. What I saw the other night—"

"What were you doing there, damn you?"

"The same thing you are doing here. Learning what I can. But I don't do it for money. I do it for my country."

"You have a country."

"So do you. It's all around you. Margaret, when I think of that cold-eyed bastard touching you—"

For a moment her face was wet with tears. But only for a moment. "You can beat me if you like. I have never let a man strike me. But you—"

She stood there, her dark head bowed.

"I don't want to beat you," Kemble said. "I love you."

"You're a fool!"

401

Her head was up, her eyes ablaze with blue fire. All her despair, the terrible cold uncaring that had emptied her heart, was in those words.

"I will—I will go on being a fool," Kemble said.

He was not mocking her. He was telling her the truth. He picked up the cup of tea and inhaled its rich strange odor. "Little by little you will fall in love with this fool," he said. "Little by little this fool will teach you that you don't need this. You don't need Major Beckwith. All you need to do is trust—your American fool."

"I wish to God I could, I truly wish I could," Margaret O'Hara whispered. She kissed him, caressed him with an abandon that he more than matched. They were lost in each other, two dark stars exploring a universe of wonder and delight. In the dawn she chanted poetry to him, an ancient Gaelic cry written for long-dead lovers.

> *"Between us and the fairy hosts*
> *Between us and the hosts of the wind*
> *Between us and the drowning water*
> *Between us and the shame of the world*
> *Between us and the death of captivity."*

To Kemble she was as exotic as a creature from the South Sea Islands. It was impossible to believe she was not as innocent. Kemble's politics were radically modern, but his attitude toward women was medieval. He saw them as will-less, almost mindless creatures, to be protected, rescued, adored. He was sure that he could save Margaret O'Hara not only from the British but from herself.

A week later, the Squinter was back with another packet of news about Philadelphia. Kemble almost went berserk when Margaret O'Hara told him she was leaving for New York early the next day. After a week of love, he had convinced himself she would refuse. In a fury he told her he would follow her again and haunt Beckwith's house in a new disguise. If she let the Major touch her, he would shoot him. She matched his rage with a tantrum of her own. She swore she would betray him to the provost marshal and have him hanged as a spy if she saw him anywhere near the house.

"I don't believe you," Kemble said.

"Try me."

It was a mad, dangerous game they were playing, each with their empty, reckless hearts. Kemble donned his tinker's disguise and followed her to New York. The day she arrived he knocked on the back door of the house and asked for her. She slammed the door in his face. But she did not betray him to Beckwith. That night Kemble stood in the darkness beyond the house lights once more and watched her play hostess in a bright red gown trimmed with gold. He did not shoot Major Beckwith.

When Margaret returned to Liberty Tavern, she brought with her an ambiguous peace offering. Major Beckwith had told her he was about to become acting chief of British intelligence. The current chief was sailing south with the British commander, Sir Henry Clinton, to attack Charleston, South Carolina. This was important news. Kemble rushed it to Washington's headquarters. The General immediately alerted all his spy networks to find out more about the expedition and warned South Carolina to prepare for the assault.

For a while, as Kemble rode back to Liberty Tavern, he was exultant. Then he saw how totally Margaret O'Hara had outmaneuvered him. He would never be able to object to the time she spent with Beckwith now. In the name of the Revolution he was being forced to accept what his soul detested. But what troubled him even more was the knowledge that Margaret O'Hara did not detest it. She clearly considered it a triumph over him.

Kemble was encountering the darkness in the depths of Ireland's defeated soul. It was redoubled by the darkness which is part of so many women's souls. Is it because they are also in a way a defeated people?

For a week Margaret O'Hara did not enter Kemble's room. It was her time of the month. Kemble found sleep impossible. One night, seeing a light in the greenhouse, he went down to find his father working among his roses.

"What's keeping you awake these days?" he asked.

"Worry."

"About what?"

"About the war, for one thing. No one seems to care whether we win or lose any more. Money is the only thing they talk about. Slocum's privateer captured two transports a few weeks ago. They say he made a half million dollars. Most of the day laborers in the district are heading for Little Egg Harbor to ship out. We can't hire men to work at Kemble Manor for double last year's wages."

Kemble was barely listening. He had lost interest in the war we were fighting in south Jersey.

"Then I worry about things closer to home. You and that girl, for instance."

In a rush of stumbling sentences, Kemble told his father what was happening. Jonathan Gifford saw the resemblance between Margaret O'Hara and Sarah Kemble Stapleton. He understood Kemble's feelings of anger and helplessness all too well.

"You have to let her go, Kemble. There's nothing else you can do," he said.

He was back five, no six years now, standing in the bedroom of the residence, reading Sarah's farewell note. He could have called for his horse, galloped to Amboy, dragged her off the ship like a common criminal. She was his wife. In the eyes of the law that made her his property, as much as one of Charles Skinner's slaves. But he had not wanted that kind of wife. He had wanted a woman he loved, who loved him. That woman had ceased to exist.

Kemble heard the sad echo in his father's voice. For a moment he almost understood what it meant. But he was too deep in his own torment to think about the past. He took the literal words as good advice—which they were, up to a point.

The next time Margaret O'Hara came to Kemble's room, he said nothing about New York or Beckwith. Instead, he told her how pleased he was to find her bringing him such valuable information. It meant she was changing sides, didn't it? She was becoming an American.

"I must go to New York tomorrow," she said.

"Why?" Kemble asked. He had seen no sign of the Squinter from Philadelphia.

"There is a soldier in the American camp on British pay. He put these papers in my hand today. I met him a mile from here, on the road."

She held up three or four sheets of soiled paper.

"Give them to me," Kemble said. "We must have them copied before you go."

"You want me to go, do you now?"

"I've decided not—not to stop you."

"You damn liar," she cried and ran from the room.

Kemble saw she had wanted him to forbid another visit to Major Beckwith. She wanted him to sacrifice his beloved Cause, his fanatic devotion to America, to her. Margaret O'Hara was a forerunner, one of those daring souls like Lord Byron who swore allegiance to nothing, neither to God nor to country, but only to their own shrouded selves and their intricate passions, hates, loves.

A great sadness engulfed Kemble's spirit. For the first time he recognized how little a man can change a woman in the name of love. He was repeating his father's experience on an even deeper level of personal anguish. His commitment to the Revolution added a dimension that Jonathan Gifford never had to face. Kemble took the papers with their careful descriptions of brigade camps and regimental strengths, and walked out to the barn. Saddling his horse, he rode to Washington's headquarters, where the figures were multiplied to awe the British into passivity and the camp descriptions, the locations of fortifications and other useful details were altered to confuse a potential attack. Margaret O'Hara went to New York the next day, and did not return.

Kemble waited two weeks. Then it was time for him to go to New York again as an American spy. He stopped at Horace Monaghan's shop, collected the latest scraps of information from the nervous little tailor, and was soon knocking on Major Beckwith's back door.

"Go away," Margaret O'Hara said when she saw him.

"I will stay here until you talk to me—or they arrest me—"

"We have nothing to say to each other."

"I love you," Kemble said.

The scene could not have been more grotesque. Two lovers whose passion deserved a wild valley, a mountaintop, or some other setting of high romance standing in a New York back yard with chickens hopping about them, goats bleating, cows mooing, pigs grunting nearby, and the hero disfigured by a red wig, red side whiskers, and a drooping mustache.

"You may come here each week," Margaret told Kemble. "Or whenever you please. I will tell you what I have learned from them. That is all you want from me, is it not?"

"You know that isn't true. If you come with me now—"

"There will be great boasts in the taproom, boasts and toasts to young Stapleton who pirated away a British major's punk."

405

"What are you talking about?" Kemble said, staggered by her self-hate.

"The truth. That is the only talk I care about now. We will live on truth. Your use of me and my use of you. That is what it was from the start. I went to your bed because I wanted protection if your side wins this cursed war. You wanted a bit of play with an Irish piece. All the rest was lies."

"All this is lies—"

"I still want protection. You must promise me I will have it, and a lump sum of hard money at the going rate for this kind of work. You will get your information. Here is the first of it. There will be raids this winter the like of which you have never seen. They will smash up your outposts in Westchester and New Jersey to prove to the people your soldiers protect nothing. In New Jersey, the Tories will take the lead."

"I will come here each week," Kemble said. "But I will come to see you. Not for anything else. If you want to give me information, that is your business. I will come anyway."

"I didn't see you stopping your ears just now— You mean I am to get nothing, neither money nor protection for it?"

"You will always have my protection, whether you ever tell me another thing worth carrying to General Washington."

Each week for the next six months Kemble came to New York. Margaret O'Hara never failed to have information for him. For her it was obviously a point of honor to force Kemble to accept it as the reason for their meeting. Her information was frequently valuable. Twice she saved isolated outposts in northern New Jersey and Westchester from annihilation. Another time she helped frustrate a daring attempt to kidnap General Washington. Perhaps most startling was her discovery that an American major general was in secret correspondence with the British about defecting to their side.

The value of her information made Kemble's agony exquisite. His conscience would not permit him to stop seeing her as a spy— which was the only way he would ever see her as a lover. With deepening desolation Kemble sacrificed his feelings to the Cause.

The winter of 1780 was one of the worst on record. Howling blizzards piled snowdrifts ten feet deep on our roads. The Hudson, the Raritan, Long Island Sound froze so that men, horses, wagons, even cannon could cross them without risk, except for the danger of frostbite, pleurisy, pneumonia. Kemble risked all these and the worst of all diseases for someone with his weak chest—consumption. Dr. Davie began asking him point-blank if he was coughing blood. He denied it. The doctor did not believe him and asked Molly McGovern to watch for bloodstains on Kemble's handkerchiefs. But Kemble had long since taken to cutting up some of his shirts into rags which he burned in the fireplace in his room.

The Great Cold, as we came to call it, was almost unbearable. For over forty days the thermometer remained below zero. From Morristown came word that the army was starving. Farmers were being robbed at bayonet point by hunger-crazed soldiers. Even those paradigms of lethargy, Deputy Commissary Beebe and Deputy Quartermaster Beatty, were stirred to action. On direct orders from Washington, they seized cattle and grain from farmers in our neighborhood. They paid with promissory notes. By now Continental money had depreciated so laughably it took almost a wagonload of it to buy a wagonload of food. The phrase "not worth a Continental" became ominously current. Men used them to light their pipes. Contemptuous remarks about Washington, Congress, Governor Livingston were common in Liberty Tavern's taproom.

Never had the Cause seemed so close to final collapse. Kemble's gaunt, cough-racked body was a symbol of the wasting disease that seemed to be consuming the glorious hopes of 1776.

Thomas Paine said that the last months of 1776 were the times that tried our souls. I trust that great prophet of the rights of men —and women—will permit me to make a slight correction in those historic words. In 1776 our nerves were tried; 1780 was the year our souls were tried. Only the truly committed such as Kemble did not waver. The rest of us were preserved in our slough of indifference and passivity by British inertia. So at least it seemed in New Jersey during that awful winter.

Only a few of us knew how sick Kemble was. I was privy to the secret because as the winter waned to a still-freezing spring, he persuaded me to accompany him to New York. He was afraid he would collapse on the road, or worse on a street in New York. One of these trips was all my nerves could stand. Every minute I spent in New York I saw myself swinging from a gallows. Kemble understood my distress and excused me thereafter. But on that one visit I saw him meet Margaret O'Hara in Sam Francis's tavern near the Bowling Green. Kemble was disguised as a Queens County Dutchman, complete with accent, heavy black boots, and a wig of flaxen hair. I was wearing a similar costume.

"Are you Van Ness?" Margaret O'Hara asked, tapping him on the shoulder as he stood at the bar.

Whenever he wore a new disguise he gave her the name that went with it. He nodded, and she asked him if he had chickens to sell. I was openmouthed at her beauty. She was wearing a purple cloak over a dark green sacque dress cut low on her bosom.

"Come, Jemmy," said Kemble, clapping me on the back. "Ve go show dis preddy lady our fat birds."

Outside Margaret O'Hara turned to me. "Who is this boy?"

"A friend."

"He's no friend of mine in that case. I trust neither you nor your friends. You know that."

We walked toward the Bowling Green. The thin sunshine failed to warm the chilly wind. My attention was devoted to the pedestal where George III had ridden in gilded splendor in the robes of a Roman emperor until he was smashed to the ground and beheaded by the New York mob. I preferred to look at almost anything except Kemble and Margaret O'Hara.

"How much longer are we going to keep torturing each other?" Kemble asked.

"Do you call this torture? I call it sport. Your trouble is a sentimental mind."

"And your trouble?"

"I have none. I am as happy as ever I—"

She could not finish the sentence. "Oh, damn you, goddamn you," she said, dabbing at the tears on her cheeks. She took a deep breath and regained her self-control. "Do you want your information?"

"Yes. But I want you, too."

"You cannot have both. You will never have both."

"Then tell me the information."

The defecting major general was using the name Anderson in his correspondence. There was talk of an expedition to destroy the headquarters of New Jersey's privateers, Little Egg Harbor. Loyalists in western Connecticut were ready to rise and seize the highland forts if the British promised them protection.

For ten minutes she continued this mixture of fact and rumor. Kemble wrote nothing down. But he remembered every word of it.

Even with my adolescent eyes I could see the fantastic mixture of love and hate boiling beneath the surface of these mercenary words. They agreed on where and when to meet next and parted.

As they turned their backs on each other and walked away, Kemble began to cough. It was a bad fit. The veins bulged in his thin neck and gaunt forehead. I saw a gout of blood stain his rag handkerchief. His whole body shook with the racking sound.

My eyes were on Margaret O'Hara. She had whirled with the first cough. A slash of pure anguish leaped across her face. Involuntarily her hand reached out toward Kemble. She withdrew it and clasped it to her waist with her other hand as if it were a disobedient child.

Kemble stopped coughing. He straightened his hunched shoulders and gestured to me. Without so much as a glance in her direction he walked away. I looked back as we neared Sam Francis's tavern. Margaret O'Hara was still standing there looking after him. Behind her was the empty pedestal of George III's statue.

On our way home, Kemble swore me to secrecy about his sickness. But he was so weak when he returned, he sent me to army headquarters with the information in writing and took to his bed for ten days. While Kemble lay helpless, intimations of disaster swirled through the state from South Carolina. Sir Henry Clinton had trapped a five-thousand-man American army inside Charleston and was methodically reducing it to surrender by siege. The fall of the queen city of the South, the loss of those precious troops cast a pall over the rest of the country.

The night the news arrived in the taproom, Jonathan Gifford predicted, "Victory in the North will be their next order of business."

"And you know where they will try for it," said a voice from the doorway.

It was Kemble, out of his sickbed for the first time.

"I wish I did know. I would tell George Washington," Jonathan Gifford said with a forced smile.

"You told me yourself a year ago. You said they would come back to New Jersey someday. What better time than now?"

Jonathan Gifford knew what Kemble's words meant—another trip to New York. He could only nod mournfully.

With literally feverish energy Kemble flung himself on his horse the following day and rode to army headquarters at Morristown. He was back the next morning, his pale cheeks flushed with excitement. "General Washington is of the same opinion," he told Jonathan Gifford, "but there is little he can do about it. He only has thirty-five hundred men—and scarcely a horse to pull a wagon or cannon. We must know where they are coming—or they will be through the Watchung passes before he can move."

The Watchung Mountains were the ramparts of New Jersey. There were two main passes through them—one behind Elizabethtown, the other behind Amboy.

It was early in the morning. Father and son were alone in the taproom. The portcullis was still lowered over the bar. Kemble gazed through the wooden interstices at his shadowy image in the mirror behind the bar. A ghostly prisoner. Was that his future—or his present state?

"I must go to New York."

"Let me go with you."

"Don't be ridiculous. There are a thousand people in that city who would recognize you the first—"

"Give me a disguise."

"No."

Never in his life had Jonathan Gifford felt so helpless. Fatherly words crowded to his lips. *You should stay in bed. You need rest, medicine.* But he could not say them to this son who was now a man.

"I want you to know—know how proud I am of you."

Kemble smiled—the same crooked-lipped smile that had illuminated his small face at nine.

"Thanks," he said.

Instinctively, Jonathan Gifford started to put his arm around Kemble's shoulder. But Kemble moved abruptly beyond his reach. They were allies. But they were not yet father and son. Something deeper and more painful than war and politics still separated them. Jonathan Gifford knew what it was. With a sigh he withdrew his arm and murmured, "Good luck."

CHAPTER SIX

By the time Kemble reached New York he was so weak he did not have the strength to walk uptown from the ferry slip to Major Beckwith's house. He stumbled into the nearest tavern—a disreputable dive named the Anchor, patronized by sailors and bargemen. He was wearing his Irish tinker's disguise, which enabled him without too much risk to send a messenger to Horace Monaghan's shop. The diminutive Irish tailor hurried down to see him in his smelly, vermin-ridden room.

Kemble asked him to carry a message to Miss O'Hara at Major Beckwith's house. The little Irishman's thick eyebrows elevated. Like a good secret agent, Kemble had never revealed to Monaghan this other source of intelligence.

Monaghan had news of his own. "There is talk of a mighty effort in New Jersey. The whole army to go from here."

"When?"

"I wish I knew."

That night, Kemble met Margaret O'Hara in the Anchor taproom. She was furious. "You swore to protect me. Now you have revealed me to that little double-talking Protestant."

In a dry, factual voice, as if he were discussing a piece of military information, Kemble told her how sick he was. Before she could say a sympathetic word, he was giving her an assignment.

"You must find out the exact day and hour they are going to invade New Jersey."

"I will obey no orders from you. I tell you what I please when I please."

"Find out—or I will write a letter to Major Beckwith."

"You would do that. We have come that far."

No, Kemble wanted to cry out, *no*. But he had become adept—too adept—at masking his emotions.

"We have come that far."

"Will you stay here?"

"Until I recruit my strength."

Two days later, Margaret O'Hara returned to the Anchor. The innkeeper told her that Mr. Kelly—Kemble's assumed name—had not been out of his room since her previous visit.

"Go away," Kemble said, in response to her knock.

"It's Margaret. Open the door."

The key turned in the lock. The door opened. Margaret cried out in shock. Kemble's shirt was covered with blood. So was the pillow on the bed. He had had a hemorrhage.

"You're dying," she cried. "Oh, my love, you are dying."

"What—what did you say?"

"My love," she said, tears streaming down her face. "What else can I call you? I have tried to hate you. But I will lie no longer, to you nor myself."

"This makes it—" He gestured to the blood. "—almost worthwhile."

He stumbled back to his bed. "I'm not going to die," he said. "Not yet. But I must find some place where I can get decent food and rest for a few days. This place is vile. The food is poison and at night it is more a brothel than an inn."

Margaret thought for a moment. "You must pose as my cousin and come to Beckwith's house. There is ample room. He uses but a third of that big place."

The daring of the idea appealed to Kemble. "Where shall I come from?"

"Galway Town. Beckwith has never been west of Dublin. You were a mate aboard one of the supply ships that just sailed for home. You took sick and the captain left you on shore, damn the heartless bastard."

"All right," Kemble said.

So they began a week of consummate subterfuge. Major Beckwith accepted Margaret's story with a shrug and a nod of acquiescence. Kemble spent the week living on fresh meat and milk from the Major's larder. Each midnight, Margaret crept up the stairs to his third-floor room and held him in her arms. He was too sick to do more than promise an early return to their ardent nights at

Liberty Tavern. By the end of the week, his pulse was normal and he was well enough to spend most of the day out of bed. Margaret seemed more troubled than pleased by this recovery. She caressed his cheek with her delicate hand.

"I feel a doom on us. I don't know what it is. But I feel it."

She could find out nothing from Beckwith. Officers who visited made passing remarks about "action" and "drubbing the rebels." An American loyalist came to the house early one morning and argued with Beckwith for over an hour. Listening at the door, Margaret could only hear snatches of the conversation. "The people are demanding action," the loyalist said. General von Knyphausen, the Hessian officer whom Beckwith served as aide, could become "the man who conquered America."

By now Kemble was strong enough to walk a half mile of counted paces up and down his room each day. But Margaret preferred to let Major Beckwith think he was still sick. It avoided the problem of a face-to-face meeting with the Major, where embarrassing questions might be accidentally asked. This possibility prompted Kemble to give some thought to a hasty departure. He had Margaret bring him fifty feet of rope from the barn.

"I may have to leave some night when your friend is entertaining."

"But will it support two of us?" Margaret said playfully. "If I have anything to say about it, you shall not leave without me."

The following day, the third of June, Margaret was in the front hall arranging some flowers in a vase when the door opened. There stood Major Beckwith and Brigadier General James Pattison, who was in charge of the military police in New York. Behind them was a squad of soldiers with fixed bayonets.

She greeted the General as an old acquaintance—he was an occasional dinner guest. His reply was a frown. "This is not a social call, my dear girl. We are here to arrest a spy."

In that terrible moment all the alternatives must have thundered in Margaret O'Hara's mind. She could pretend ignorance, knowing that Kemble would lie to protect her until the moment of his death. She could tell part of the truth and plead for mercy, sobbing that she only thought she had been helping a sick young man she had met in New Jersey. Irish stupidity, woman's weakness would be her whines. But she chose a third way, a way that must have been filled with special terror for her, having seen two brothers die on the gallows. She whirled and raced to the stairs.

"*Kemble! They are coming for you! Run, my love, my love, my love! Run!*"

With a growl of rage, Beckwith dragged her from the stairs and smashed her in the mouth. "You Irish bitch," he snarled.

"Up the stairs," Pattison was roaring to the soldiers. "Take him alive if you can."

In his room, Kemble had been reading a copy of the extraordinary *Gazette* which the British had just published announcing the fall of Charleston. He was filled with gloom. Margaret O'Hara's cry lifted him from his chair and set his mind on fire. He understood what had happened, what she had done. Should he join her? Meet the soldiers with knife and pistol in hand?

No. What he knew, what he might yet find out about the British invasion of New Jersey was too important. A deep infusion of his father's realism steadied his careening soul. He flung open his window, seized the escape rope and dropped it down the side of the house. But it was still daylight. He had no hope of descending unseen. Pursuit in New York's streets crowded with off-duty soldiers would be brutally brief.

His racing mind saw only one totally daring possibility. He ripped off his red wig and mustache and flung them on the bed. He locked the door and stepped into the room's clothes cupboard. In it were an old uniform or two that belonged to Beckwith and three or four dresses of discarded mistresses. He left the double doors slightly ajar. In a moment the British soldiers were pounding on the door of the room. They smashed at the lock with the butts of their muskets. The wood splintered and they rushed inside, bayonets ready.

"The devil," swore the Lieutenant in command. "He's gone out the window."

"Look 'ere on the bed. A red wig," said one of the soldiers. "His disguise."

The Lieutenant peered out the window. "Now we don't even know what the bastard looks like. Ah! I see a fellow skulking about a half block off. That may be him. Quick, downstairs and make that Irish bitch tell us—"

Their feet thumped on the stairs. The last soldier out of the room paused in the doorway and eyed the clothes cupboard. With a quick look over his shoulder to make sure the Lieutenant was gone, he walked softly over to it, opened one door, and whipped out a dress. His hand came within six inches of Kemble's face. Stuffing the dress under his coat, he hurried after his fellows.

Through the open door Kemble heard them asking Margaret O'Hara what he looked like.

"I will tell you nothing, you goddamn English buggers."

The sound of blows. A scream of pain. Then a wail that made sweat spring out all over Kemble's body. He had never heard an Irish keen before. A wild, wordless lament filled the house. Margaret was weeping for herself, for their love. It took all the strength of Kemble's formidable will to remain silent in the clothes cupboard.

The keening ceased abruptly. Doors slammed. The house was silent. There was not even a sound in the kitchen. The Negro cook must have been out marketing. Kemble emerged from the cupboard, pulled off his boots and breeches, and donned one of the dresses he found there, a plain brown taffeta garment. He ripped the skirt in one or two places. In a second-floor cupboard he found a wide flat sun hat with a hood that draped the back of his neck and tied beneath his chin. He looked unbelievably grotesque—the most unfeminine creature ever created. In the kitchen he added to this impression by rubbing fireplace soot on his face and hands. Then he crept under the back porch and lay there thinking of Margaret with mounting misery until darkness fell.

In twenty minutes of rapid walking, Kemble reached Horace Monaghan's shop. It was dark. But a light glowed on the second floor. Kemble went around to the rear, hiked his skirts to his waist, and climbed some thick trailing vines to a second-floor window. It was open. Knife in his mouth, he came into the room like a pirate. Monaghan heard him and screamed once. He did not scream again because Kemble had the knife at his throat.

"They came for me, Monaghan. They took Margaret O'Hara away. It was you who told them."

The little Irishman's eyes bulged with terror. "Sure, I knew you'd get away. It was only the girl I was giving up. What's she to you? An Irish whore she was, selling her immortal soul for British suppers."

"You miserable bastard," Kemble said and smashed him in the mouth with the back of his hand.

"And a Catholic," mumbled Monaghan, "an Irish Catholic."

"I should kill you, Monaghan. I should cut your throat."

"They picked me up on suspicion. I had to tell them something to set me right. I swear I didn't know you were there. I only found out when they pulled me downtown not an hour ago to ask what you looked like. I said I'd never heard of you. The girl was there. She said nothing. There was death on her face. Bloody. They swung a noose in front of me. I'm not a brave man."

"I won't kill you, Monaghan, if you can find out for me within twenty-four hours the day they are coming into New Jersey. If you don't find it I will come back and kill you, even if there's a regiment of British soldiers guarding you. I'll get past them using a disguise. You'll never suspect a thing until the knife is in your guts."

"How will I get word to you? They may set a watch on me."

"I will come to you. In the meantime I will leave word with other friends in this city. If they arrest me in or near this shop, you're a dead man."

"You have nothing to fear from me. I swear—"

"Shut up and get busy. Get on your hat and start visiting taverns. Strike up a conversation with every officer you recognize. Pay special attention to the ones who are drunk."

Kemble took enough money from Monaghan to buy some food. The next day was the King's birthday. Salutes thundered from the forts and the warships in the harbor. A stream of elegantly dressed gentlemen and officers headed for Sam Francis's tavern at three o'clock for a formal banquet. Beribboned and belaced generals and their aides predominated, of course. It was a gorgeous demonstration of British opulence. Kemble thought about the starving tenants in their Irish huts, the war-weary small farmers in New Jersey, and vowed he would defeat this monstrous imperial arrogance that so casually ground innocent victims beneath its feet. Over and over again he repeated like a man obsessed, "In the name of Margaret O'Hara, in the name of Margaret O'Hara." It was his tragic banner, his private emblem.

That night he returned to Horace Monaghan's shop the same way—through the second-floor window. Monaghan was beside himself with fear. "You should have come to the door," he wailed.

"What have you found out?"

"In a day or two or three at most. I heard it from a major at the Anchor last night and from a colonel when I was fitting him today."

"Not good enough. We have to know the exact day. Militia won't turn out to stand guard. They will go home and refuse to come out at the real alarm." Kemble took out his knife. "I'm going to cut your throat, Monaghan. You deserve it."

"No. No. Give me another day. I swear I'll find out."

"And how they are coming? We must know that too. Is it Amboy or Elizabethtown?"

For another day Kemble wandered New York waiting and watching. He saw ominous signs of military preparations. Dozens of sloops sailed down the East and Hudson rivers to dock near the Battery. Army wagons rumbled through the streets to the wharves and men loaded dozens of barrels of powder, cannon, food onto the boats.

That night Monaghan had the information. "Tomorrow night, weather permitting. I don't know where they are to land. I could only ask such a question under risk of my head."

"How can I get off this island?"

"You don't have a hope. They are guarding every foot of the shore. The usual routes—forget them."

"Who told you it was tomorrow night?"

"Two colonels. They were gabbing away as if I had no ears. And Beckwith, no less. He came to thank me for—the girl."

Monaghan's voice dwindled. The look on Kemble's face made him realize he had said the wrong thing.

"What are they doing to her?"

"They're not hangin' her. Beckwith was for it, but others thought it would trouble the Irish soldiers in the regiments. So they're sending her to the West Indies—for the troops there."

"Monaghan," Kemble said, "if I die and find my soul in hell, my only consolation will be seeing you there."

"Now what do you mean by that? I don't know any man who tries harder to be a good honest Christian. Not a man do I cheat. I stay away from loose women. I drink little if any—"

Kemble was gone, leaving Monaghan to whine his Pharisee's lament into the night.

A tour of New York Island's shores soon convinced Kemble that Monaghan was right. Every cove was guarded by a detachment of loyalists. At one of them he was startled to hear a familiar voice denouncing the British army. "Here we sit in the mud like so many lackeys while they go marching off to glory. Goddamn them all, I say, from generals to privates." It was Anthony Skinner.

The night drained into the dawn with Kemble still in New York. Bands playing, regiments swung down the Broadway from their camps outside the city. There was no longer any question that the army was assembling. Staten Island became Kemble's only hope. If he got there, he could cross it on foot and swim the narrow channel to the Jersey shore at Elizabethtown. He loitered at the lower wharves and finally approached a British sentry. In simpering broken English, he managed to convince the redcoat that he was the wife of a soldier in the Von Lossburg Regiment.

"Von Lossburg whoos-bond?" he said over and over again, pointing to Staten Island and giggling idiotically.

The sentry told him (her) that he (she) was a piece of German trash if he ever saw one. Kemble smiled and nodded as if he (she) thought it was a compliment. The bored sentry pointed to the outermost sloop on the wharf. "Get in that boat there."

The sloop was a guard boat which made regular trips about New York Harbor with orders, prisoners, supplies to the various posts. The captain was obviously used to transporting German soldiers and their wives and paid no attention to Kemble. Within two hours he was on Staten Island. It took him another three hours to trudge six miles to the swampy shore opposite New Jersey. He found the narrow channel called Arthur Kill thick with British patrol boats. He had to wait until dark to swim it. The water was cold and the current was dangerously strong. By the time Kemble crawled into the marsh grass on Elizabethtown Point he was exhausted. It took him a half-hour to find the strength to stumble another mile to the village. At a crossroads on the outskirts he was challenged by a nervous sentry. After a tense dialogue about the password, Kemble walked toward him with his hands up, repeating "American—friend, American—friend."

In five minutes, he was face to face with General William Maxwell, commander of the New Jersey brigade of the Continental army. They were guarding the shore around Elizabethtown against British and Tory raiders. Maxwell's fondness for the bottle had not declined since his visit to Liberty Tavern in 1776. His nose, his cheeks were the color of ripe cherries. But his tongue was blunter than ever. His face grew dour as Kemble told him about the imminent British invasion.

"They won't bring less than six thousand men. Our brigade doesn't have six hundred, scattered from here to Newark. If we don't get some help from the militia, the bastards will be eating dinner at Washington's table in Morristown tomorrow night, and we will be across the Delaware—what's left of us—back where we were in '76."

Maxwell glowered at Kemble. "Where are you from?"

Kemble told him. The Scotsman grunted sarcastically. "One of Slocum's heroes. Where would we be if every county had a law forbidding their militia to leave home?"

"General Slocum got that damn law passed for personal reasons," Kemble said. "Nobody asked him to do it."

"Can you get them to come up here?"

"Give me a horse. If I can't, I'll find someone who can."

"Talk to Gifford at Liberty Tavern. He's a good man."

Kemble reached Liberty Tavern about 2 A.M. He was almost as spent as the half-starved army nag he was riding. He awoke Jonathan Gifford and told him about Margaret O'Hara's capture and the British invasion. He brushed aside his father's sympathy. "We can do nothing for her," he said. "Except revenge her. How can we get the men to turn out?"

Captain Gifford thought about it for a moment. "Tell them what Maxwell said to you. Tell them that the army considers Monmouth men a bunch of cowards because they won't leave their county to fight."

"Will you do it?"

Jonathan Gifford shook his head. "I'll come. But you are the only one who can talk to them."

"They will laugh in my face."

"Not if you tell them what's at stake. No speeches. Just the simple truth."

He poured Kemble a drink of French brandy. "Take a good stiff one. Then let's go to work."

All night Kemble and his father rode from farm to farm challenging our militiamen. Kemble made no speeches about the glorious Cause and the rights of man. He simply told them what Maxwell had said about Monmouth men, and what would happen if the British got across the Rahway River and through the Watchung passes.

"They'll smash Washington and take New Jersey. I'm going to fight them. Will you come with me?" he said.

This was not the febrile orator who led boys to their deaths at Monmouth. At dawn, no less than three hundred men gathered in front of Liberty Tavern. Jonathan Gifford rolled out two barrels of rum from his cellar and we filled our canteens.

As our drums beat and our fifes began to swirl, the boom of a distant cannon reached our ears. On the Watchung Mountains fire signals blazed into the dawn, summoning militia from Essex, Middlesex, Morris, and Somerset counties. A horseman clattered into the tavern yard. An angry General Slocum demanded to know what the hell was happening.

"Who called out the regiment without my orders?" shouted the General.

"I did," Kemble said. While we stood there listening, Kemble repeated General Maxwell's insult. "I hope you'll come with us, General, and help us show the rest of the country we are not afraid to fight."

Slocum could only mumble that he was ready to march.

"We will take no orders from that son of a bitch," shouted Samson Tucker from the middle ranks of the regiment.

"Who said that?" Slocum roared. "I will stand him up against the wall and shoot him."

"Try it," shouted another voice in the rear ranks. "We'll see who gets shot."

"We want Captain Gifford to command us," I shouted.

"Aye, Gifford, Gifford," shouted enough voices to compose a chorus. "Let's elect him colonel."

Jonathan Gifford shook his head. "A one-legged colonel is worse than none at all. Kemble will ask General Maxwell for a regular officer to command you."

"I will be happy to take his advice," said Slocum in a voice that sounded as if someone had a hand around his windpipe.

We marched north, with Kemble and Slocum riding at the head of the regiment. It was past noon when we reached the battlefield. All morning the New Jersey Continentals and the Essex County militia had been fighting the British in the village of Connecticut Farms. As we arrived, the entire British army of six thousand men was beginning an aggressive advance. Kemble and Slocum galloped to the center of the American line and found General Maxwell's command post on a hill near a white steepled church.

The General greeted Kemble with a grim nod. "Don't tell me you've brought Slocum and his heroes with you."

"Three hundred of them, General."

"Well, this excuse for a soldier won't command them as long as I am in charge of this fight," Maxwell said, glaring at Slocum. "He was supposed to support me at Germantown. He got lost until the shooting was long over. At Monmouth he never came at all."

Slocum mumbled something about a fog at Germantown. Maxwell snorted and offered Kemble a drink of rum from a leather flask in his saddlebags. Kemble politely declined and said, "My father—Captain Gifford—thought you would give us a regular officer."

Maxwell looked almost agreeable and inquired about Jonathan Gifford's health. Kemble said he was well, except for his crippled knee, which was why he was not with them on the battlefield. It was an unreal conversation, with cannon booming, muskets crashing only a few hundred yards away.

General Maxwell took a hefty snort of rum and was putting the bottle back in his saddlebags when his huge aide, Major Aaron Ogden, came racing up on a lathered horse to tell him that the Essex militia were giving way on the right.

Maxwell cursed spectacularly for a full minute. "Well, you are in luck, Ogden, this fellow here has brought you another three hundred sprinters. Do what you can with them. You," the General added, pointing to Kemble, "shall act as his second-in-command. As for you, Slocum, go find General Washington and kiss his ass. That is the only thing you are good at."

Choking with rage, Slocum wheeled his horse and rode away. Maxwell pointed to a long narrow defile thick with gunsmoke. Shadowy figures moved through the haze. At times the firing was continuous. "My regulars can hold them down there for another hour or two if they don't flank us," Maxwell said.

He whipped a map from his saddlebag and began discussing it with Ogden. Kemble could make nothing out of it. But to the two regulars it was a battle plan. For the first time Kemble was seeing what his father meant when he talked about the importance of military knowledge.

"Take this farmhouse and barns, first, there's good cover there." Their fingers traced swift lines across the map anticipating the enemy's movements as well as their own.

"Have you ever commanded militia?" Maxwell asked Kemble as he put away the map.

"Not really. I am not a trained soldier."

"You have lots of company. The trick is to get them to retreat without running away. That is the most you can hope for. Don't ask them to attack. They can't do it. They must have woods or some fences to fight behind or they won't stand at all. If the other fellows come at you with the bayonet, give them one volley and get out of there. But King George's boys haven't shown much appetite for that sort of thing today. They want to keep their casualties low. They are as worn out by this damn war as we are."

Kemble led Major Ogden to the woods where we were resting from our forced march. Within ten minutes we were fighting two British regiments in and around a deserted farmhouse and its barns. As General Maxwell predicted, the redcoats showed no appetite for charging us. They had long since abandoned those Bunker Hill tactics. Instead, they wheeled companies to our left and right and pressed hard on our flanks, firing rapid volleys and shouting insults and threats of imminent death.

Nothing rattles amateur soldiers more than fire from the flanks. As the man beside me toppled to the ground, blood streaming from his throat, I felt a gust of confusion and terror run through us. My legs almost betrayed me again. But Major Ogden was there with an order to carry the wounded man to the rear, and another order shifting men from the center of our line to support us and match the enemy's fire power. My treacherous legs regained their courage, along with those of my comrades, and we held our ground for a good hour. Only when the British threw in two more regiments did their superior numbers force a retreat.

Here, Major Ogden's presence was crucial. He withdrew us by companies, giving the order in a calm, easy voice, although bullets were flying around us thick as bees in a swarm. "We're not losing, we're just falling back to a better place to fight," he said.

This was the way we fought throughout that long hot afternoon, slowing the enemy's advance to a crawl, making them pay for the ground they gained. Once, Kemble asked Ogden's permission to counterattack. The British fire had slackened. They were apparently low on ammunition. The Major shook his head and reminded Kemble of General Maxwell's orders. "You don't have the training," he said. He had no intention of letting us get too close to those murderous British bayonets.

Our last position of the day was a hill with a stone fence on the summit. We could see the Rahway, only a few hundred yards behind us. Around us the hillside was sown with barley growing waist-high. A horseman on a big black horse appeared on the other side of the Rahway, studied us for a moment, and then splashed into the shallow stream. In a moment, Jonathan Gifford was riding through the barley into our little perimeter.

"I shouldn't be here," he said. "If they put a bullet into Thunder, you will have to carry me off. But I couldn't resist the chance to see you fellows fight."

"They have done pretty well," Major Ogden said.

"The King's Own couldn't have done better, Captain," someone said.

A British regiment filed out of the woods and began forming in the pasture below us. "You will have a chance to prove that," Jonathan Gifford said.

The blue facings on the redcoats' cuffs and lapels had instantly identified his old regiment for Jonathan Gifford. "There's Moncrieff," he said.

Sure enough, there was the Major on a white horse, gesturing briskly to his captains with his sword. They began coming up the hill toward us. It was a beautifully executed movement. Four companies swung to the right to get between us and the river. Two worked around our left and one came at us in the center, where most of us were crowded behind the stone wall. Ahead of each company moved a screen of light infantry skirmishers, ducking and dodging through the barley.

Major Ogden raced to direct the fighting on the right flank, where the threat was serious, telling Kemble to take the left and center. Battle fever rose in Jonathan Gifford's blood. "Look at that," he said to Kemble. "Only one company in the center. If you people knew how to use the bayonet, we could chase them halfway to Staten Island."

423

Kemble nodded mournfully. "We had another chance like that earlier today."

Momentary panic flared on the left flank when a half-dozen men were hit in a single volley. Kemble rushed to steady them. Jonathan Gifford was left alone in the center. He could not resist taking command. He rode up to the wall and moved along our line. "Take your time," he said again and again. "Don't shoot until you have a target."

He paused for a moment and studied the fighting. "There's only one company out there. Drive them and they will think twice about pressing so hard on our flanks. Over the wall into the barley. But don't go more than ten yards."

With a shout we leaped into the smoke to take cover in the grain. The ruse worked. The single British company that was skirmishing in the center recoiled. Major Moncrieff, standing at the bottom of the hill, shouted curses and gesticulated at them with his sword. They reformed and moved up the hill again under Moncrieff's personal command. Jonathan Gifford spurred his horse over the wall to join the men in the barley. "They don't have the stomach for it," he said. "Stand up and give them a volley when I say the word."

As the British closed to fifty yards, he shouted: "Fire."

The redcoats broke again and ran down the hill.

We roared with fierce delight, no one louder than Jonathan Gifford. "Give them another round," he shouted, leading us another ten yards down the hill. We obeyed with alacrity.

Suddenly Captain Gifford gave a cry of pain so acute I thought he had been wounded. Major Moncrieff had been hit as he turned to bellow denunciations at his men. He stumbled a few feet and fell, disappearing into the grain. Jonathan Gifford spurred his horse down the hill to where Moncrieff was lying. By the time he got there, the Major had thrashed himself into a sitting position and was clutching a bloody knee.

"Billy—are you all right?" Jonathan Gifford asked.

"I thought it was you, Gifford, you son of a bitch," Moncrieff roared. "I've never seen militia fight like that. Get out of here before I take you prisoner and hang you on the spot."

Jonathan Gifford returned to the top of the hill, and ordered everyone back behind the stone wall. A moment later a messenger from General Maxwell galloped up with good news—Washing-

424

ton's army had arrived from Morristown to block the passes through the Watchung Mountains. We had orders to retreat across the Rahway, where the regulars would support us. We filed off the hill with only a few scattered shots from the British to harass us. In a half-hour we were shoulder to shoulder with other militia regiments and the New Jersey brigade, ranged along the western bank of the Rahway.

We looked like coal miners. Our faces and hands were black with gunpowder. We were so exhausted we could barely cheer. But we managed a parched croak or two. We knew now the British were not going to cross the Rahway. For a while the disgruntled generals concentrated their red- and blue-coated battalions on a hill about a quarter of a mile from the river, trying to decide whether to risk a frontal assault. They counted the casualties they had already taken in the long day's fighting and concluded that the price would probably be too high. We watched the enemy's battle flags disconsolately wheel and begin their retreat toward Staten Island. We sent them on their way with another hoarse derisive cheer.

Kemble suddenly spurred his horse across the Rahway bridge as if he were about to attack their rear guard singlehandedly. I ran after him, wondering if he had gone mad. But he stopped a few yards from the river and swayed there, weeping in one breath and laughing exultantly in the next.

"For Margaret O'Hara," he said. "For Margaret O'Hara."

I looked back and saw Jonathan Gifford watching anxiously from the other side of the river. He yearned to put his arm around his exhausted son and take him home. But he did not know whether the gesture would be welcomed or rebuffed. He sat there, a spectator, while I led Kemble's horse back across the bridge.

There he regained his self-control and rode down the line of our regiment, shaking the hand or slapping the shoulder of every man he knew well. In a mysterious way the pain he was suffering impelled him to affirm his solidarity with these simple farmers, even though none of them would ever know the reason for his tears.

Book
V

CHAPTER ONE

DEAR GIFFORD:

It is nice of you to inquire after my leg, since you did so much to put the bullet into it. It looks like I will keep it, but I will have a limp. It will not be quite as bad as yours, which is some consolation. I have to thank you for it, at all events, because it has gotten me out of this damn army, which has forgotten how to fight a winning war. I am selling my commission while the asking price is still high at home. They don't know we are licked, but I know it and so does every other soldier above the rank of corporal.

I have inquired into the matter of that Irish girl, Margaret O'Hara, for you. They sentenced her to a life term as a convict servant in Jamaica. She received this favor with shocking oaths against King, Queen, lords, commons, and generals. Apparently your son has his father's fondness for the wildest women in sight. Then she lapsed into a Gaelic gloom, refused to eat, and was soon so ill she had to be carried aboard ship. Contrary winds delayed the convoy's departure for three or four days, during which she continued to fail. She died not long after they reached open water and was buried at sea somewhere off your coast.

Moncrieff

Almost every day for a month after Jonathan Gifford gave him this letter, Kemble rode down to Garret Hill, in the highlands not far from Sandy Hook. The view is awesome. The Atlantic's immensity stretches in a great dark blue arc for hundreds of miles. Kemble would stand for hours on the summit brooding upon this image of eternity and the woman who lay beneath it. At Jonathan Gifford's request, I often went along with Kemble on these rides, two loaded pistols in my saddle holsters. There were a lot of Tories in that neighborhood. Sometimes Captain Gifford rode with us. Not once did anyone mention Margaret O'Hara. But his presence—and the fact that Kemble made no objection to it—was evidence of a new wordless sharing that both father and son were loath to name, for fear that it was too fragile to sustain the weight of other feelings, still unresolved.

One day, on the way home, Jonathan Gifford suggested we stop for tea at Kemble Manor. Caroline was out in the fields directing twenty or thirty workmen. She rode in to greet us at Jonathan Gifford's wave. As she dismounted, I noticed a look pass between them that I was too young to understand at the time. It took me a few more years to learn how much lovers can exchange in such glances.

Jonathan Gifford began teasing Caroline about being the hardest-driving foreman in south Jersey. Caroline said she considered that a compliment, and led us into the house. Sukey had tea and corn cakes waiting for us. Caroline quickly got to the point.

"Your father and I think you should run for the assembly, Kemble. He is afraid you will disagree with him, as you do on practically everything. So he has asked me as the family's next most active revolutionist to propose it to you."

"No," Kemble said.

"If we can get an honest man into that legislature, we can force them to investigate Slocum," Jonathan Gifford said. "We can chase him out of the state. Everybody's talking about the way you made a fool out of him in front of the whole regiment."

Kemble shook his head. "We must get someone without blood on his hands. The people are sick of the war. They will only vote for a man who stayed out of it, who disapproved of both sides."

"Like George Kemble?" Caroline said.

Everyone turned to me and asked if I thought my father might run. "I think we can talk him into it," I said.

The next day, Caroline, Kemble, and Jonathan Gifford descended on my father and urged him to run. As usual, he hesitated. He despised Slocum. But he saw no point in abandoning his neutrality in a war that Americans seemed to have lost interest in winning. Jonathan Gifford read him the first part of

Moncrieff's letter to convince him that the British were even more war-weary. But Caroline's arguments were decisive. She forced my father to admit that the legality of independence had little to do with the situation now. The war had become a struggle for dominance between two very different peoples, English and American. Once he conceded this, it was hard for him to deny his American feelings.

My father paced up and down the room looking at our ripped furniture cushions. We had been unable to persuade any Philadelphia upholsterer to venture this close to the British army to mend them. But my father had been impressed by George Washington's uncompromising court-martial of Major Yates.

"Perhaps you're right, Gifford—"

The Captain turned to me. "What do you think he should do, Jemmy?"

"Run," I said.

My father looked at me and for the first time saw I was almost a man. "All right," he said. "By God, I *want* to do it. We will give him a fight."

It was a brawl of an election. General Slocum had antagonized and disgusted a lot of people. The problem was to reach them and assure them that they could vote against Black Daniel without fear of retaliation. Jonathan Gifford persuaded Governor Livingston to write Slocum a letter, forbidding him to station armed men at the polling places. The Captain let my father use Liberty Tavern as his headquarters and distributed gallons of free rum to the crowds that gathered there after church on Sunday and on Thursday market days. They listened—I was going to write "soberly," but that may not be quite the right word—perhaps "intently" would be more accurate—to my father's denunciations of General Slocum as a war profiteer and land jobber.

That summer we proved the old aristocrats could adopt the new democratic style in politics. Up and down the dusty roads in the sultry August heat my father rode, carrying his message to every part of our huge county. It was exhausting work. We worried about his health. My mother repeatedly predicted he was killing himself.

"General Slocum is more likely to do that, my dear," he replied in his dry, indirect way.

"Has he threatened you?" I asked.

431

"I met him on the road to Freehold with a few of his friends yesterday. He told me I would regret every word I ever said against him."

My father was more upset by a letter he received a few days later. I found him in his study brooding over it when he should have been on his way to address a meeting at Liberty Tavern. His expression reminded me of the mixture of anger and regret I saw on his face when Major Yates and his Yankee regiment visited us. "What is it, Father?" I asked.

"A letter from Charles Skinner—with a postscript from his son. They tell me I will be a traitor, from the moment I take a seat in the legislature. Perhaps General Slocum will save me from that embarrassment."

With a sigh he arose and let me drive him to Liberty Tavern. He spoke better that day than I have ever heard him. He was candid about the family's loyalist connections and his own hesitations about joining the Revolution. There were men in the audience with sons in the British army and others with sons in Washington's army. Both sympathized, I think, both shared the pain of what the war had cost and was costing us, no matter which side won. Not that my father implied for a moment that he was now indifferent to an American victory. With a wealth of detail which his lifetime of reading history made it easy for him to cite, he assured his listeners that a British victory meant decades of exploitation. By now the war had cost the British several hundred million pounds. They would get that money back from our sweat if they won. An American victory was our only salvation. But it had to be the victory of honorable men, my father insisted. If we won with men like Slocum in positions of trust, we would turn into a nation of brigands, we would become international outlaws.

Slocum's answer to this assault was characteristic of the man. He ignored all the charges my father was making against him and concentrated on smearing George Kemble and his family and friends as traitors, British secret agents, dupes, thieves. Slocum also talked ad nauseam about his relationship with General Washington, making it sound as if our commander in chief relied exclusively on his judgment. He especially trumpeted his role in our near-victory at Germantown.

We had some answers to these tactics. We pointed out that Congress trusted Dr. Franklin enough to make him Ambassador to France, although his son, the former royal governor of New Jersey, was on the British side. As for the battle of Germantown, Jonathan Gifford procured a letter from Brigadier General Maxwell stating that Slocum and his Jersey militiamen never fired a shot at a single British soldier there. They got lost in the fog on the way to the battlefield (they said) and did nothing more heroic than cover the American retreat.

Throughout the campaign, Kemble rode around the county with my father, lending him the power of his name. He refused to make a speech. But his presence made it clear that the young squire, the man whose name Slocum had used so lavishly in previous elections, was no longer a supporter of our political general. It made a distinct impression on the younger men, for whom Kemble had again become a military hero. Kemble also drew up a list of the men who had slaved for Slocum in the saltworks and visited many of them personally to urge them to vote against the General.

On election day, Slocum had the inevitable barrels of rum at every polling place. He hired brawlers to shout threats at those who voted against his candidates and in neighborhoods where the Slocumites were in the clear majority, to abuse them with their fists as well as their tongues. At Liberty Tavern several ex-salt workers resented the threats and let Slocum's boys know they too could use their fists. The next morning we awoke with a severe collective hangover and a large assortment of black eyes and swollen noses.

That evening chastened drinkers gathered in Liberty Tavern to sip Madeira, small beer, or some other potion likely to rest gently on their stomachs while awaiting the election news from Monmouth Court House. Those in the know drank a special Liberty Tavern restorative, Old Red Rose Water, made by Captain Gifford from an ancient recipe provided by Dr. Davie. Since I was too young to participate in these celebrations as a true son of Bacchus, I cannot vouch for its power, but some swore by it.

Perhaps the reason was hangovers, but no one had much hope. Then at eight o'clock, astonishing news arrived. My father had won by fifty votes. Jonathan Gifford clapped me on the back. "We've got an honest man into the legislature, Jemmy. They will have to listen to him."

But the honest man never reached the legislature. Later that

433

night I awoke to shouts, the shrieks of horses, gunfire, glass breaking. A strange light flickered in the moonless sky. I rushed to the window. Our barns—our new barns that we had spent so much time and money building—were aflame. Men on horseback were riding around the house firing guns through the windows. The glass in front of my face suddenly exploded and a bullet whizzed past my right ear. Downstairs I heard my mother screaming. I ran in that direction and found my father and sister grappling with her by the front door. She was hysterical, howling, "They will burn us. They will burn us." Bullets continued to crash through the windows and thud against the walls. We dragged my mother back to the kitchen and cowered there on the floor.

When they continued to fire into the house, I got mad. "Goddamn them," I said. "I'm getting my gun. I want to get a shot at them."

"No," my father said. "They might use that as an excuse to kill us all."

"Who are they? Loyalists?"

"Slocum, I'm sure," my father said.

"I am getting my gun," I said.

"No, Jemmy!" My father half-rose to his knees as I started to crawl away. I could see him in the flickering light from the burning barns. Suddenly his face twisted, he clutched his throat, and he fell back on the floor. My mother began screaming that he had been shot. But I recognized the symptoms of apoplexy. There was nothing we could do for another fifteen minutes—our incendiary visitors continued to riddle the house. When they finally departed, I rushed out to the barn to see if Johannes Hardenburgh had rescued any of the horses. The old Dutchman looked as though he might go like my father at any moment. He had managed to get three or four horses out of the burning barn but our tormentors had shot the poor beasts. Three were on the ground, dying. One, an old mare named Josie, was bleeding from a shoulder wound that I hoped was superficial. As I saddled her, I asked Johannes if he recognized any of the attackers.

"No. But they not King's men. They shout, 'Goddamn Tory bastard,'" he said.

The old mare lasted until I was about a half mile from Liberty Tavern. Then she slowly descended from a trot to a walk to a shamble and finally sank to her knees and with a great sad sigh expired. I finished the journey on foot, awoke everyone at the tavern, and told them what had happened. Jonathan Gifford turned to Thomas Rawdon. Dr. Davie was no longer well enough to practice medicine. "Will you come?" he asked.

"Of course."

We returned to the house as rapidly as we dared in the dark, Rawdon and Captain Gifford in the chaise and I on horseback. We found that my mother had, with the help of servants, gotten my father upstairs to bed. There was nothing Rawdon could do for him. He vomited black blood, a fatal sign of apoplexy in the third degree. He sank slowly and around dawn died without regaining consciousness.

Jonathan Gifford put his arm around me. "We have lost our honest man, Jemmy. Be proud of him. He died for this country as much as any soldier at Princeton or Brandywine."

I nodded, staring numbly down at the sad, empty face. I remember someone saying that most citizens of New Jersey were "peaceably inclined" when the war began. He was one of those peaceable men. It was not necessary to kill him with a bullet or a bayonet. There are crueler ways to kill peaceable men. I vowed to revenge him.

CHAPTER TWO

MY MOTHER DECIDED she could not live in a country that killed its patriots. All her antagonism to the Revolution flowered into full-blown virulence. She announced she was leaving for England to join the rest of her loyalist Oliver relations. She took my sister Sally but I refused to go with her. I moved into Liberty Tavern and became part of Captain Gifford's family, leaving Johannes Hardenburgh and his hired hands to run the farm.

Slocum blamed my father's death on the loyalists. I blamed it on Slocum and in the early stages of my fury asked Kemble for a rifle from Liberty Tavern's armory. He asked me what I wanted to do with it. I told him I was going to hide in the woods near Slocum's farm and shoot him.

"I've thought of doing something like that," Kemble said. "But as men of honor, Jemmy, we can't descend to Slocum's level. He didn't care whether or not he killed your father, when he fired in your windows. But strictly speaking he did not shoot to kill. Let us wait and see if the General gives us a better reason."

We had drifted far from the soaring ideals of 1776. My father's death cast a sickening pall over our politics. Governor Livingston urged the legislature to investigate the incident. A committee was appointed. But Slocum's henchmen got two of their friends named to it, and they managed to convince the rest of the committee that George Kemble was a secret Tory. The investigation dwindled away after a single hearing. We could not find another candidate willing to risk Slocum's retaliation and one of his yes-men easily won the special election for my father's seat.

The impact on our militia's morale was devastating. Many men swore they would never turn out for Slocum again, no matter how great the emergency. As Samson Tucker put it, "I am through fighting so that murdering son of a bitch can get rich on my blood. I swear I would rather lose the war first."

A few months later, we discovered that losing the war was not our only worry. An outbreak of lawlessness threatened us with anarchy. Early in 1781, Jonathan Gifford and Barney McGovern made one of their periodic trips to Little Egg Harbor to purchase wine and whiskey. On the way back, their wagon loaded with perhaps a thousand (real) dollars' worth of spirits, they were traveling along one of Monmouth's lonely roads through the pines when a half-dozen men leaped out of the woods with leveled guns. There was no hope of resistance. They took the wagon, its contents, the horses, even the money in their victims' pockets and rode off into the forest.

Several of the thieves were wearing remnants of American army uniforms and they carried French muskets, the standard gun for the American foot soldier by this time. They were deserters who had decided the Jersey pines were the perfect place to begin a life of crime. Their numbers grew as sailors from Little Egg heard about the easy pickings. Others were loyalists, exasperated by the persecutions of their Whig neighbors. Once they took to the pines, they became political indifferentists, stealing from Whig or Tory with equal assiduity. Boats were waylaid on the rivers, isolated farms raided, women brutalized, men shot or beaten if they resisted.

Soon it was not safe to travel south of Perth Amboy—which meant that our normal commercial life virtually came to a halt. We had been depending on the blockade-runners and privateers' prizes brought into Little Egg Harbor. We were soon running out of everything from tea and coffee to nails and ammunition. A determined man like Jonathan Gifford coped with the situation by hiring seven of the best militiamen from our local company for an armed escort on his next trip to Little Egg. But most merchants had no stomach for running a gauntlet.

Even more disheartening—and frightening—were the mutinies that shook Washington's army in the winter of 1781. Coming as they did on the heels of Major General Benedict Arnold's defection at the end of 1780, these abortive revolts sent shock waves of alarm through the state. The presence of the army was absolutely essential to preserve the Cause in New Jersey and this made us doubly sensitive to the temper of the troops.

First, the men of the Pennsylvania Line mutinied and were narrowly prevented from marching on Philadelphia to set up a military dictatorship. Next and most shocking to us, our own New Jersey regulars revolted, and had to be suppressed with brutal force, two of the ringleaders being executed before a firing squad.

The soldiers all had the same complaints. They were being paid in worthless paper money when they were paid at all. They were living on loathsome food when they were fed at all. They had signed up for the duration of the war. But no one had told them the war was going to last a lifetime.

Army enlistments dwindled to the vanishing point. In desperation, the state began drafting men from the militia. This provided General Slocum with another source of illicit cash. As militia commander, he had the power to choose who went into the army, who stayed home. For a consideration, he passed over certain names. Most drafted men hired substitutes—indentured servants, even a few slaves. Slocum got into this business too. His constables arrested more than one man who was passing through the county to do some privateering out of Little Egg Harbor. A Slocum judge would pronounce him a vagrant, and sentence him to join the army. Slocum would sell him (without the poor fellow's knowledge) to someone in the market for a substitute.

Watching all this, loyalists like Anthony Skinner went insane. The Revolution in New Jersey seemed ready to collapse—but the British army was expending most of its strength fighting to conquer the South. The loyalists decided to abandon all hope of cooperation with the regulars and fight for New Jersey in their own way. In the spring of 1781, Anthony Skinner landed near Shrewsbury with over a hundred men. He issued a proclamation calling himself a New Jersey patriot. He said he was still loyal to the King —but not to the British army and its greedy generals, who were running the war to line their purses. He hoped that the time would come when an independent New Jersey could return to the Empire—but that would depend on what the King and his ministers offered them. The rebel confederation was about to break up. Now was the time to drive out the New Englanders and Virginians who were plundering the state. Every true patriot who joined him was guaranteed an equal share of the estates which the

438

Congress Party, "by their inveterate hypocrisy, greed, and tyranny, so richly deserved to forfeit."

Madness, you say, from your comfortable decades of hindsight. But it did not sound mad to us. It sounded extremely dangerous and alarming. Skinner was supplied with ammunition and weapons by an organization created by our ex-governor, William Franklin. It was called the Board of Associated Loyalists. Skinner vanished into the pine barrens, where we soon heard rumors that he was recruiting the thieves and robbers in that wilderness into echelons of his little army and building a formidable base camp.

Kemble had helped organize a network of coast watchers along our shoreline to pass intelligence to Washington about the movements of the British fleet. He was one of the first to hear about Skinner's invasion. He told us about it at supper the day after the loyalists landed. Jonathan Gifford's first thought was Kate. He searched her face for a sign that this man's return troubled her.

For almost a year now Kate had been studying medicine with Thomas Rawdon and planning a life totally different from the one Anthony Skinner envisioned for her as the first lady of New Jersey. With Caroline's help, Kate had persuaded two or three of the district's midwives to let her work with them. She and Rawdon were patiently inculcating in them the importance of cleanliness and a thorough knowledge of anatomy to make childbirth safer for the mother and the baby. Rawdon himself was practicing medicine with a small group of patients who trusted Dr. Davie's unqualified recommendation of him.

Jonathan Gifford could find no trace of romantic concern in Kate's manner. "Do you really see him as a threat?" she asked Kemble.

"He has a name and a following. General Slocum has neither, now."

"It is rather shrewd, condemning both sides. I can see that much," Kate said. "He's making war on the war itself."

Kemble nodded glumly. "Most people just want to see it end. They don't care how."

"You can't blame them," Kate said. "Some people are starving. Do you realize that the midwives tell me even babies are going hungry here in New Jersey?"

"Can't Washington send some regulars into the pines and get rid of this fellow?" Lieutenant Rawdon asked.

"Washington's whole army could wander through those pine barrens for weeks without finding an enemy who knows where to hide. It will be up to our militia, I'm afraid," Jonathan Gifford said.

"You don't sound optimistic."

"I'm not."

One by one, in a spreading arc that eventually reached from the outskirts of Little Egg Harbor to Amboy, farmers began receiving messages delivered by night. They were told to contribute hay, oats, wheat, or corn, a horse or a cow or a brace of pigs to a wagon that would be waiting for them at a certain point on a lonely road near their farms at ten or eleven or twelve o'clock. They were promised receipts for these contributions to be redeemed when the people of New Jersey had driven out all "foreign usurpers" and once more governed themselves in "freedom and security." If they failed to cooperate with the "army of the people," they would be considered "enemies of the same" and treated accordingly, in a class with the "usurpers from Virginia and New England and the traitors who were cooperating with them."

Many secret loyalists yielded to Skinner's demands without a murmur. More than one supporter of the Cause wavered when he looked around his isolated farm and asked himself what protection he had if Skinner and his men came out of the night. The answer was soon apparent: none. The first man to defy Skinner was a farmer named Collins who lived near Red Bank. He was dragged from his bed the night after he failed to make his contribution, beaten until he was bloody, then tarred and feathered. His farm was stripped of livestock and his barn burned, leaving him without a seed to plant for the coming year or a morsel of food for his family.

"That is only the beginning," Jonathan Gifford said when we heard the news at Liberty Tavern. "He will soon be demanding other kinds of tribute."

He was right. Gunsmiths were told to deliver guns; blacksmiths horseshoes and nails; storekeepers salt, spices, coffee, tea; tavern keepers casks of rum, pipes of wine. Inevitably, one of these demands arrived at Liberty Tavern. It was couched in particularly insulting terms and the requisition was especially outrageous. A wagon was to be loaded with ten hogsheads of rum and six casks of Madeira, as well as an assortment of brandy, port, and other wines and liquors. That night Jonathan Gifford read it aloud to the drinkers in the taproom and then calmly ripped it into little pieces.

He was one of the few innkeepers with the courage to defy Skinner. Soon Anthony saw himself as the conqueror of New Jersey. He reached for another prize: Kate. Abel Aikin, who had gone back to work as a post rider, was again converted into an unwilling letter carrier. He handed Jonathan Gifford an envelope addressed to Kate in Anthony's bold scrawl. Captain Gifford passed it on to her without comment. She opened it instantly, making no attempt to treat it as a secret communication.

My dearest:
By now you have heard, Kate, that I have come home to relieve my people from a tyranny greater than the Roman, from men like Washington and Slocum and their thieving crew. I also yearn to free you from the tyranny of your father. I could have done so long ago with sword and gun. But I wanted you to come to me freely or not at all. Now is the moment you can repair the hurt your rejection inflicted on me so unjustly. Come to me in the pines, Kate, and tell the world that the best of the Stapletons has remained loyal to the King's soldier in spite of her fanatical brother and scheming father. Search your heart, Kate, in the name of our love and ask yourself how you can refuse my call.

Anthony

Jonathan Gifford could see a faint flush on Kate's cheeks as she handed the letter to her father. "He is so desperate," she said. "I don't know what makes me sadder, the way he lives in the past or the way he tries to use me and love me at the same time."

Despite her reaction, Jonathan Gifford still felt uneasy. He realized that he would feel that way until Anthony Skinner was dead or driven out of New Jersey. His personal concern redoubled the intensity with which he urged an expedition into the pine barrens to rout Skinner and his outlaw auxiliaries from their camps. But no one had the authority to call out the militia except General Slocum, and he was hardly inclined to take Jonathan Gifford's advice. He spent most of his time in Little Egg Harbor, playing financial games with his privateers, and getting richer at it, we heard.

Another reason Slocum did nothing was his unpopularity. He could not turn out more than a hundred men to fight for him anywhere. But the General was not ready to let south Jersey go to Anthony Skinner by default. Slocum let the loyalists ravage us for a month and then announced his answer to them. It was not a march into the pine barrens to fight Skinner to a finish. It was a Slocum invention called the Association for Retaliation.

With a host of pseudo-legal whereases and wherefores supplied by Lemuel Peters, the Association's charter declared it was "a fact notorious to everyone" that loyalists and neutralists were "accessory to the detestable practices" of Anthony Skinner and his fellow loyalists. The Association for Retaliation decreed that they would destroy the house and barn of a "disaffected" person every time the house or barn of a "good subject" was destroyed. They would also rob from the disaffected any article of property, horse, pig, goat, sheep or cloak, silver spoon, or porcelain teacup on a one-for-one basis to match anything stolen by the loyalists. These principles were to be enforced by a nine-man committee elected by the Associates, but actually hand-picked by Daniel Slocum. The General and his colleagues circulated this charter through south Jersey and told people to sign it. Those who refused would be considered among the disaffected, fair game for plunder.

It was nothing less than terror against terror. Anthony Skinner could not have invented a better way to destroy what was left of our revolutionary idealism. He undoubtedly applauded every word of the charter of the Association for Retaliation. It told him that each time he burned a house or barn, stole a horse or cow, he could be assured that another house or barn would be burned, a horse or cow seized from a neutral or a timid Whig or even a staunch Whig whose conscience would not let him join the Association for Retaliation. It was a formula that doubled the damage Skinner was doing and guaranteed perpetual civil war until New Jersey was a desert.

In two weeks Slocum had signed up four hundred and fifty-two members of the Association and was ready to invade Liberty Tavern to recruit still more. He sent dozens of his followers riding through the countryside to round up a large audience and treated them to a ranting roaring speech in favor of the Association. By bad luck, Skinner had raided a recalcitrant Whig farmer in

Middletown the night before and ambushed some militiamen who had turned out to pursue him. People were in a mood to listen to Slocum's diatribe. He pointed out that Skinner had not touched a Talbot farm or a Kemble farm. Of course not. Slocum swore he had proof that loyalists were smuggling Skinner food and ammunition for cash. How much longer were they going to let the Tories and the Quakers get rich on the Revolution while they starved? Slocum urged everyone in the room to come forward and sign the Association's charter.

There was a stir of anticipation, a surge of restlessness, but no one moved. Jonathan Gifford realized that everyone was waiting for him. Without saying a word, he got up and walked out of the room.

"Let me warn you," Slocum shouted after him, "let me warn every one of you who thinks he can play a trimmer's game. There are no neutrals for the Association. Those who are not with us are against us. Anyone who fails to sign is an enemy."

No one followed Jonathan Gifford out the door. No one else had the courage to risk Daniel Slocum's enmity. The mood of the room swayed between revulsion and revenge. There was scarcely a man present who had not lost something to the enemy during the war, a house, a barn, valuable animals, jewelry, silver. Revenge coupled with reimbursement was a tempting proposition.

"Well," Slocum shouted, "are you men or mice? Tories or trimmers?"

Kemble Stapleton stood up. "Gentlemen," he began. "I am a young man. I cannot match General Slocum's years of experience. But I have bled in this Revolution. My friends—" His voice faltered on this word. "—have bled and died. For that reason my opinion deserves a hearing, at least. Let me state it simply. There is only one word that describes General Slocum's plan. Only one word equates retaliation against armed attack by soldiers of the enemy with burning the houses and robbing the possessions of defenseless civilians, driving men, women, and children into the winter cold: cowardice. I cannot believe a man in this district—a real man—will join him."

Slocum was on his feet, roaring invectives. Kemble was a double agent. It was common knowledge that he had sold American secrets to a British whore. His father was on the British Secret Serv-

443

ice payroll. Kemble Manor was a headquarters for a British espionage ring run by Caroline Skinner.

Kemble was wracked by a fit of coughing and called for water. In a way, the sound of that cough was the best possible answer to Slocum. It told all of us the price Kemble was paying for the Cause. But he had no intention of letting Slocum escape the lash of his reply.

He pointed out that this was no court of law and there was no need for him to answer these charges. Instead, he suggested they review the war record of General Slocum. With acid detail, Kemble recalled his visit to Slocum's saltworks. He reminded the audience of Slocum's fraudulent land sales, his lies about his military record. By the time Kemble finished, the General's chances of adding to the Association for Retaliation's membership from Liberty Tavern's neighborhood had vanished.

The following day Caroline Skinner received a demand for tribute from her stepson. Several thousand pounds of oats and hay were to be delivered in installments over the coming weeks. The note was grimly impersonal, in the tone of a military order. Jonathan Gifford was far more disturbed by this note than he was by the insulting and highly personal letter he had received. He said that he would hire a dozen militiamen as guards and pay them hard money for their duty.

Caroline shook her head. "It isn't necessary, Jonathan."

"You mean you will give him what he asks? Then you will go down with him. I assure you that in six months he will be nothing more than an outlaw."

"I did not say I intended to give him anything. If he comes here, I don't think he will abuse me in any way. He may rob me—us—but he will not hurt me. Anthony is my son, Jonathan. If I met him on the road, he would call me Mother."

Jonathan Gifford was staggered by this view of Anthony Skinner. He was discovering a mystery that his masculine mind simply could not comprehend. Women found it difficult to translate the passions of war and politics into personal hatred. Caroline was also speaking out of memories Jonathan Gifford could not share, memories of years when she had been half mother, half older sister to Anthony Skinner, memories of sailing days on Raritan Bay, of long rambling rides through the green

444

countryside, of nights spent reading *Gulliver's Travels* and *Pilgrim's Progress* and *Robinson Crusoe*.

Jonathan Gifford tried—and failed—to understand what Caroline was feeling. He shook his head. "I am afraid I must dispute the idea of letting him rob you. Others may see it as collusion. The Association for Retaliation would love to find an excuse to strip this farm and burn this house over our heads."

"I would rather take my chances with a mob than fight Anthony. The thought of killing him—"

"Caroline," Jonathan Gifford said testily, "isn't Anthony the enemy of everything you believe, of this country's future, of our freedom?"

"Yes. But—"

"Then let me hire the guards. If anyone gets killed it will be on my conscience. A few more dead men won't matter more or less."

She heard the pain in his voice. "No. They will be on mine, too. I—I want them."

Jonathan Gifford understood. By this time their love had become so interwoven in their lives words were no longer necessary to explain how much they wanted to share—and at times wanted to spare—each other's feelings. That was why Jonathan Gifford rode home without telling Caroline that he expected Anthony Skinner to attack him, not her. At Liberty Tavern, Barney, Sam, and a half dozen of our local militia company paid by Jonathan Gifford stood guard constantly. As further insurance, he let it be known that he would pay fifty pounds hard money to anyone who warned him even an hour in advance of Skinner's approach.

Jonathan Gifford also tried to persuade Kate and Kemble to abandon the residence and sleep in the tavern. Kate refused, insisting that this was carrying caution too far. "Anthony will never attack this house as long as I am in it," she said.

This caused Thomas Rawdon to raise an eyebrow. But no one, especially Jonathan Gifford, had any desire to pursue the argument. He let the remark pass and Kate began discussing with Rawdon a trip she was planning to Shrewsbury. There was a midwife down there who had a devoted following among the women of the town. She was an illiterate old crone who scoffed at Kate's educational program.

445

"I'm going to conquer her with kindness," Kate said. "I hear she likes brandy. Can you spare me a bottle, Father?"

"Of course."

Early the next morning Kate rode toward Shrewsbury, the bottle in her saddlebag. Jonathan Gifford watched her go with some misgivings. He told himself he was only remembering another trip to Shrewsbury. This was not the same girl. Still, he wished Lieutenant Rawdon's parole permitted him to travel that far.

It was Thursday, a market day, always a busy time in Liberty Tavern. Jonathan Gifford worked beside Barney until twilight wetting the palates of our farmers, collecting so much paper money that it overflowed the cash drawer into a bushel basket behind the bar. As darkness descended and the crowd dwindled, he left Barney on his own and trudged down to the residence. Instead of a well-lit house, filled with the smell of some favorite dish cooking in the kitchen, Kate sitting at the spinet playing one of the Scottish airs she loved, there was only darkness and silence.

Lieutenant Rawdon's taut voice emerged from the shadows of the porch. "Is Kate at the tavern?"

"No."

"She must have had some trouble on the road. She expected to be back well before dark. Perhaps the old girl was delivering a baby and she stayed to help her."

"Yes," Jonathan Gifford said. "Or her horse might have thrown a shoe. I meant to tell Sam to take a look at him, before she left this morning."

Both men were lying and they both knew it. A few minutes later Kemble arrived and voiced a more realistic worry. "I wish you told me she was going. I would have sent Jemmy with her. The pine robbers held up a man on the Shrewsbury road last night. Shot him and stole his horse. There's not a road south of here that's really safe."

But even Kemble was not voicing his worst suspicion. Perhaps because Jonathan Gifford was troubled by the same fear, he picked up the undercurrent of evasion in Kemble's voice. The hours crept methodically toward midnight without a sign of Kate. Kemble and I were about to saddle horses and ride for Shrewsbury when Barney came to the door with a letter in his hand.

"A fellow handed this in the taproom door and legged it into the night before anyone could get a good look at him," he said.

Jonathan Gifford recognized Anthony Skinner's handwriting. He ripped open the envelope and read the letter aloud.

"Captain Gifford:

I am writing this at Kate's request. Her natural tenderness of heart makes her anxious not to give you even a night's concern about her whereabouts. She has joined me here in the pines, taken her rightful place beside me to let the people of New Jersey know that I have come to their rescue not as a bandit but as a man of peace, who seeks only to right wrongs and mend the broken hearts of our distracted country. She urges you and your friends to waste not a moment in joining the honest men who flock to us daily, in ever growing numbers.

Sincerely,
Anthony Skinner"

Jonathan Gifford saw angry dismay on Kemble's face. On Thomas Rawdon's he could read nothing but pain.

"He is a damn liar," the Captain said. "He's kidnapped her."

Kemble looked gloomy. "I want to believe that. But—"

"I believe it," Rawdon said.

"We will have to go into those pines after her. We will have to fight him," Jonathan Gifford said.

CHAPTER THREE

WITH A GRIM anger that was more formidable than rage, Jonathan Gifford took charge of our little war within the big war. The problem was to find enough militiamen willing to risk a march into the pines to attack Skinner's camp. He rode down to Colt's Neck to ask General Slocum for permission to enlist fifty men and give them the training they needed to succeed. It meant crawling to a man he loathed, but Captain Gifford felt he had no choice. An ex-British officer could not start raising men without official permission. It would be too easy for a Slocum-appointed judge to call it treason.

He found the General on the porch of his house. Slocum had bought up several loyalist estates with his rigged sales and was working them with slave labor. But he had not moved onto any of them. Shrewd politics may have been part of the reason. He knew a display of wealth might cost him more of his already diminished following. But I think it was more attributable to his determination to preside at Kemble Manor. For Slocum the manor was a symbol of ultimate distinction. He never abandoned his passion for it or his hatred of Jonathan Gifford for depriving him of it.

In the privacy of his home, the General was not averse to displaying a little opulence. He met Jonathan Gifford wearing a green silk coat much embroidered with silver lace and a brocade waistcoat of puce, both sprinkled with painted buttons. On his head was a black felt tricorn trimmed in gold lace.

"Gifford," he said with a sneer. "What brings you here?"

"Anthony Skinner. You may have heard that he has kidnapped my daughter."

"I heard she went with him willingly."

"I'm sure that is not true. But let's not argue over it."

Jonathan Gifford explained his plan and asked his permission to enlist fifty men. Slocum rejected the request with a nice mixture of insults and threats. "I would not let a trimmer like you recruit five of my men, Gifford. The next thing you know they would be fighting beside Skinner's robbers. Try to enlist a man, and I will hang you for the traitor you are. I will take back Kemble Manor and string you up on the front lawn."

Wildness, Jonathan Gifford thought, wildness and something else that went deeper than wildness. The spirit of evil was loose in this lovely garden of America. For an hour, riding home, he wondered if he was a fool, risking his reputation, his life, his property, to fight it. Wouldn't it have been better to have retreated to England, to have bought one of those country estates where men cultivated their formal gardens and walled out the world? Corrupt as it was, there was at least order in the Old World, order for a price. Everything was for sale there, even the books from which a man could learn philosophy. Here he was contending with shadows, for love from a son who still seemed to loathe him, from a daughter who may have—in his gloom he added, probably had—succumbed to her dark impulse to self-destruction in the name of mindless desire. By the time he reached Liberty Tavern, Jonathan Gifford was the personification of melancholy.

In the tavern yard, Caroline Skinner was dismounting from her horse. She wore a green riding habit which remarkably suited her black hair and dark complexion. "I rode over," she said, "hoping for some word—"

The sight of her steadied Jonathan Gifford more than a brigade of Washington's army, even though he had no good news to tell her. The love he saw on her face restored his faith in the love he had given Kemble and Kate. He asked her to join Rawdon and Kemble for a council of war in his office.

He told them what Slocum had said. "We will have to spend money," he said. "If we pay enough, I think we can keep it a secret. We will begin recruiting with the work force at Kemble Manor. We will train them there. Everyone else can say he is being hired to dredge a swamp or rebuild a barn, whatever seems most plausible."

He took out a map and let us ponder for a moment the immense breadth of the pine barrens. There were hundreds of square

449

miles of them. "There is no point in marching in there unless we know exactly where Skinner is. Otherwise, we'll wear the men down to nothing or walk into the worst ambush you have ever seen. Either way we will be finished."

"How do we find him?" Rawdon asked.

"We must send someone into the pines who can join him."

He looked straight at Rawdon as he said this.

"Don't they have a quaint habit of shooting people they dislike?" Rawdon asked.

"We must see to it that they like him."

"How do we manage that?"

"That is up to Kemble, our director of espionage."

"I'll work up a disguise that will fool Kate herself," Kemble said.

Jonathan Gifford shook his head. "I don't think you can do it, Kemble, much as I admire your skill. You will be going among men who are on their guard. Some of them, especially Skinner, have known you for years."

"I agree with Captain Gifford," Rawdon said. "I am the only person who can do it with any safety."

"What happens if you find out that Kate has—well, joined Skinner voluntarily?" Kemble asked.

"I have confidence in Kate's affections," Rawdon said.

"So do I," Caroline said.

Jonathan Gifford wanted to join this affirmation. But he remembered too clearly Kate's anguished confession to him after she saw Anthony at the dance in New Brunswick. He could only muster half an affirmation. "I agree with Mrs. Skinner. But even if the worst is true, I cannot conceive that Kate would ever betray you. You would be in no danger from her, Mr. Rawdon."

"I still think I should go. This is not your quarrel, Mr. Rawdon," Kemble said.

"It is now."

"All right," Jonathan Gifford said. "Let's begin."

After a day of discussion, Kemble decided to convert Rawdon into an Irish surgeon from a privateer in Little Egg Harbor. He conferred with Dr. Davie on the kind of medicine he should practice. Dr. Davie advised him to be an activist, in the style of the standard physician of the day. "Bleed them, purge them, lad. Fill them full of calomel, cream of tartar, opium."

"I can't do that," Rawdon said. "They may be outlaws, but my conscience won't permit me to poison them."

"Then take along a half-dozen bottles of pills made from flour and paste but give them the largest possible Greek or Latin names. The average man is so terrified of dying he will swallow anything if you pronounce its name like a professor."

As an added resource, the old doctor gave Rawdon a talisman against enemies. Cast of the purest tin, in the day and hour of Jupiter, it was an engraving of an arm bearing a sword within a mystic triangle. Among its special powers was an ability to give the wearer power to speak with "the most remarkable confidence."

Rawdon had no difficulty mastering a satisfactory brogue. To alter his appearance, Kemble dyed his dark hair red, gave him a red mustache, and added a most convincing scar on his cheek, made from a combination of wax and glue that could only be removed with the aid of a chemical liquid.

While a few intimates at Liberty Tavern watched these interesting preparations, the rest of the state was fascinated by a much larger expedition. Washington suddenly appeared in New Jersey, marching south—with a French army part of his column. People rushed from all points of the compass to see the glittering parade of white-and-gold-uniformed Gauls marching beneath their silken fleur-de-lis. For a year they had been sitting in Newport, doing nothing. Now, went the army rumor machine, their commander, General Rochambeau, had persuaded Washington to march south to battle the British army that had invaded Virginia. No one in the American army had any faith in the expedition. They suspected it was another in the series of pointless exercises into which the French had persuaded us since they entered the war. At Liberty Tavern we were absorbed by our smaller, more poignant drama and paid little attention to history in the making as it marched past us.

A few days after the last Frenchmen crossed the Raritan at New Brunswick, Thomas Rawdon, now known as Dr. Thaddeus Murphy, trudged south into the pine country swinging his satchel. He stopped at a one-room groggery called the Trap Inn, not far from Imlaystown, and asked the proprietor where he could find "the brave Colonel Skinner." He had just come off a privateer which had cruised for six months without taking a single prize, because the captain was a coward. Colonel Skinner, from what he heard of him, was a different sort of man.

The proprietor, an ugly little man with a wen on his forehead, advised him to stay overnight. About 4 A.M., Rawdon was awakened by a lantern shining in his face.

"So you want to join Skinner, eh," growled a voice in the darkness behind the light.

"Why not? The Americans won't have me, and the British are a bunch of lazy dogs."

"We could use a doctor."

Rawdon emerged from the shed in which he had been sleeping to find himself confronting two men in hunting shirts and moccasins. They were both short, with flat monotonous voices and dirty morose faces. They carried new British muskets and had pistols strapped to their waists. They wanted to depart immediately. Rawdon insisted on breakfast. The escorts agreed, if Rawdon paid for it.

The proprietor rushed to serve them. He was obviously terrified of his new guests. "Do you have much money?" he whispered to Rawdon as he paid for breakfast.

"Only a few dollars."

"Don't let them see it. They'll kill a man for a shilling. They killed two men a half mile from here and buried them in the woods last week. My dog found the bodies. Shot through the back of the head."

By eating slowly and talking constantly Rawdon managed to delay his departure until dawn. With daylight he was able to note the landmarks along their route—creeks, swamps, an occasional fisherman's cabin. While he used his eyes, he regaled his morose companions with tales of sea fights and romantic conquests. His guides began to think he was a very entertaining fellow and once or twice actually laughed at his stories. Then they plunged into the seemingly trackless depths of the pine forest. Rawdon was bewildered. "How in God's name do you find your way?"

"We have marked the trees."

The older of his two escorts pointed to a slash three or four feet above ordinary eye level on a nearby pine. A similar mark became visible every hundred yards. From the moment they entered the forest, Rawdon began counting his strides. He was over three thousand and the sun was high in the noon sky when they reached Anthony Skinner's fort. The stockade was about ten feet high and about a hundred and fifty feet long, with a formidable double gate in the center. The other walls were about the same height and length, forming a rough square. On one side was a crude barracks for the garrison. On the other side was a storehouse crammed with food, ammunition, and loot. Behind it in the rear corner was a two-room building, Colonel Skinner's house. There were guards posted on the firing platforms at the four corners of the fort. The front gates were the only entrance. It would not be an easy place to storm.

Anthony Skinner met him at the door of his house. He looked weary and harassed. His green coat was smudged. His shirt, even his hands and face were dirty.

"Ship Surgeon Thaddeus Murphy at your service," said Rawdon with a mock salute. He gave him his privateering history and dilated on his eagerness to serve a man with the courage to defy both sides.

Skinner nodded glumly. "What news do you have of the war?"

"Cornwallis has Virginia beneath his heel by now. With them flattened 'tis the end of the Congress men in the Carolinas."

"What news of Europe?"

"There's talk of peace. The French are out of money and out of patience. The Spaniards tremble for Cuba. If the English take it this time, they won't give it back."

"Good," said Skinner. "You have come to the right place. I admire a man who does not blush to seek his fortune openly. We need a doctor. We have had a fever among us for a month now, laying first one and then another low. I have a sick woman here this very moment."

"Ah," said Rawdon. "I see the Colonel has brought to the wilderness all the pleasures of civilization."

With a growl Skinner grabbed him by the lapel of his coat. "Watch what you say. She's no dockside slut like the rest of the females about this place. They're the scourings of Little Egg's whore houses. She's a lady and if you treat her with anything less than the respect she deserves I will beat you black and blue—as I've already done to one or two of the rabble in this army."

"Sure, you have nothing to worry about. I grew up in Dublin and know a lady when I see one," Surgeon Murphy-Rawdon hastily assured him.

453

"It's the heat and the bad air from the swamp just south of us. It guards our flank but it breeds misery among us."

"A choice of difficulties, like everything else in this damned war."

Skinner nodded. "Let me tell you one more thing, Doctor. Once joined, there is no departing this place. Those two who brought you here know these woods like you know your anatomy. They will hunt you down and shoot you for a traitor."

"Sure, a man like me doesn't come aboard with thoughts of jumping ship. Let me see your young lady."

Skinner led him into the back room of his cabin. Rawdon paused in the doorway, his blood almost ceasing to move in his veins. Now was the moment when he would find out whether Kemble's suspicions of the worst or Caroline Skinner's—and his own—confidence in Kate were justified. Rawdon was too clever to miss the uneasy half doubt in Jonathan Gifford's voice when he talked about Kate and Anthony Skinner. She had loved him once with a totally reckless commitment. It was not easy for anyone to turn her back on such a memory. What if the Captain was even wrong about his certainty that Kate would not betray him? What if she simply recognized him and cried out? That basic male distrust of women almost made Rawdon panic as Skinner introduced him.

Kate was sitting in a straight-backed chair, gazing leadenly out the crude window into the dusty parade ground of the fort. She was still wearing the riding habit she had worn the day she disappeared. It was streaked with dirt and ripped in several places. Her forehead glistened with a feverish sheen. She was sick. But worse than the sickness was the unhappiness that transformed her lovely face into something almost ugly. Her mouth drooped, there were ghastly circles beneath her eyes. Her hair straggled damply across her forehead and down her sallow cheeks.

"Kate," said Skinner. "We're in luck. A doctor has joined our little band. He thinks he has something in his kit to restore your health and spirits."

"There is only one thing that will restore my health and spirits, Anthony. Let me go home."

"Pay no attention to what she says, Doctor. Her mind is a little queer from the fever."

"Thaddeus Murphy at your service, miss," said Rawdon with an elaborate bow as Kate turned to look at him. "Educated in Dublin, with a turn or two in the lecture halls of Edinburgh. If you will be good enough to let me examine the patient, Colonel Skinner."

Skinner retired to the front room. Kate stared at this apparition with its red hair and mustache and disfigured cheek. In her numbed mind she knew who it was, but could not believe it.

"My dear young woman. If you'll be good enough to lie down on the bed."

"Thomas—is it—is it—"

He clapped his hand over her mouth. "Let me take your pulse, my dear. Oh my. Much above normal."

In the next room Skinner called, "I'm going out to inspect our sentries, Doctor. I will be back in a half-hour."

"He will kill you," Kate said, as Skinner clumped out.

"He's never seen me before."

"There are others here who might know you. People who often came to the tavern."

"Kemble says the alteration of a single feature—such as this scar I am wearing—is enough to confuse the average man. People are not observant."

"Ordinarily. I'm not so sure about this place. They know they are hunted men."

"They did—kidnap you?"

For a moment anger made Kate's eyes even brighter than her fever. "Did you ever doubt it?"

"No. Not until I walked into this room. But I think it was panic more than doubt. Are you strong enough to come with me if we try a run from this place?"

Kate shook her head. "I have had this fever for a week. I've eaten nothing but a little bread and milk."

Rawdon gave Kate some of Dr. Davie's worthless pills and urged her to make an elaborate pretense of taking them every hour.

"Let us see signs of health if you can manage them. It will do marvelous things for my reputation."

Kate managed the pretense. The next day she pronounced herself strong enough to take a stroll around the fort on Dr. Murphy-Rawdon's arm. The not quite pseudo-doctor meanwhile briskly plied the garrison's sick with his make-believe pills, giving each a thunderous name. Within a day, a dozen of his patients pronounced themselves much better and abandoned their beds. It was a marvelous example of the mind's power over the body. Of course they all had relapses within a day or two. But a medical charlatan, which was what Rawdon was acting under duress, never lets that worry him. He usually makes arrangements to depart before the relapses occur.

This was precisely what Dr. Murphy-Rawdon was doing, while making a close study of the garrison's routine. He noted that the guards posted at the four corners of the stockade were lazy and unconvinced of the importance of their duty. After midnight, they frequently abandoned their posts or slumped in a corner to snore the night away. Anthony Skinner made impromptu inspections and berated them angrily when he caught them. But he was obviously afraid to impose the kind of punishment that such conduct would have merited in the regular army—the lash or even the firing squad.

The motley garrison was in a surly, semirebellious mood. They had come ashore with Skinner believing his bellicose optimism in an early end to the war and a breakup of the rebel confederation. The summer was dwindling away with the war showing no signs of a swift end. The wary, grudging support they had received from their fellow New Jerseyans did little to nurture the hope that they could organize an army strong enough to defeat the Whigs. More and more of them began to see their best hope in plundering Whigs and loyalists indiscriminately for all they were worth and decamping to the West Indies with their booty.

Dr. Murphy-Rawdon asked for and received a musket, roundly declaring he wanted to earn his share of any loot or glory these fearless fighters might win in the future. The next morning at dawn when the fort's gates were opened, he vanished into the woods, ostensibly heading for the camp privy on the edge of the swamp. As soon as the trees and underbrush concealed him, he shifted direction and hurried to the foot of a tall pine which he had marked with a slash. At its foot beneath the carpet of pine needles he had buried his musket and cartridge box. Loading the gun, he set off at a slow trot through the forest, using the compass Jonathan Gifford had given him for a guide. As he ran, he went over Jonathan Gifford's instructions in his mind. They were drawn from Captain Gifford's Indian-fighting ranger days in Canada.

Every mile, stop, get your breath, and listen. If they are running hard after you, you can hear them a half mile away in the forest. Run hard then until you find a small stream or a hillock on the trail. This is the place for your ambush. Wait until they are close enough. Take dead aim and shoot to kill.

For the first three pauses he heard nothing. He found running at the same steady trot not nearly as tiring as he feared it might become. At the fourth pause he again heard nothing. No. Wait. His civilized ears tried to make sense out of the faint sound of bushes crackling, feet thudding on the pine-carpeted earth. They were coming. He ran hard for the next mile. His breath was a knife in his chest when he found a small swift-running brook beside a stand of cedar trees. The cedars stained the water a dark red-rust color, making it impossible to see the bottom. He crossed it cautiously, sinking to his armpits in the middle. On the other side he crouched behind a cedar and primed his musket. Ten minutes later they became visible through the pines, blurred figures running steadily. They were the same two scouts who had brought him to the fort. As they paused at the stream's edge he studied their empty mercenary faces. One of them pointed to his footprints on the bank and said, "We're catchin' him. Them's fresh."

"It's gonna be an easy five guineas," the other one said.

They stepped into the creek, their guns held above their heads. Rawdon waited until they were halfway across. For a moment he wondered if he could kill a man at such point-blank range. Then he remembered they were hunting him down like an animal for five guineas. He shot the first man in the chest. He gasped and tried to bring his gun to his shoulder. It slipped from his hands and he vanished beneath the coppery water.

The other man blasted a panicky shot at Rawdon. He kept his head down and calmly reloaded his gun. The surviving pursuer, his gun empty, tried to retreat. Rawdon shot him in the back as he was scrambling up the creek's opposite bank. He, too, vanished beneath the cedar-stained water.

At midnight on the same day, Rawdon stumbled into Liberty Tavern almost too exhausted to talk. Within the hour, with the help of some alcoholic restoratives, he had told Jonathan Gifford and Kemble everything he had seen and heard in Anthony Skinner's fort.

"We must not waste a day," Jonathan Gifford said.

Caroline Skinner had already sounded out the work force at Kemble Manor and found twenty were ready to volunteer. Offering five pounds hard money for a bounty, and wages of a dollar a day, Kemble had no difficulty signing up another thirty in the next twenty-four hours. They were all anti-Slocum, pro-Gifford men like Samson Tucker, who was among the first to accept the offer. They gave out the story that they were going to work as hired hands at Kemble Manor and mustered there at dawn, two days after Rawdon's return.

We thought that we would march for the pines within the hour. But Jonathan Gifford had no such intention. "In the first place," he told Rawdon and Kemble, "Skinner will be on his guard, on the chance that Dr. Murphy was a spy. We will give him a week to relax. In the second place, I have no intention of fighting him with untrained men."

He looked at our motley band. We were sprawled around Kemble Manor's lawns. Some of us were straggling into the orchards and the park. "*Form ranks!*" Captain Gifford bellowed in a voice that none of us had heard before. We obeyed with uncommon alacrity. In the same drillmaster's tones, he told us that we would begin training immediately. No one would be permitted to leave the manor for any reason. Training would last five days. We would rest a day, then march.

Within the hour we were hard at work. Captain Gifford gave us his own unique combination of infantry and ranger training. We did no close-order drill or manual of arms. He taught us how to fight in the forest in groups of two and three with one man always reserving his fire. He trained us in responding to signals from a whistle which told us to fight in a square, a circle, parallel lines, an arc.

Above all he concentrated on attacking with the bayonet. Hour after hour in the hot sun we lay on our faces in the manor house park, leaped to our feet and raced forward screaming like madmen to plunge deadly shafts of steel into the straw-filled vitals of a scarecrow. At the end of two hours we ached from head to foot and our throats were raw. Now everyone understood why Jonathan Gifford had paid an incredible five pounds bounty to each volunteer. We were earning it. He knew what he was asking us to do—and he also knew that men who slept in feather beds, got up each morning to have breakfast served to them by loving mothers and sisters would never do it. In five brutal days he was shocking us into becoming the kind of soldiers he needed—men who would attack with ferocity and skill.

We learned to attack with the bayonet in squads. "Always choose the man on your right. That way you know each man will be accounted for." We learned to fight bayonet to bayonet, using blunt wooden sticks on our guns instead of the dangerous steel. When Jonathan Gifford and Barney McGovern demonstrated the rhythm of thrust and counterthrust, how to block and deflect an enemy slash, they used real bayonets. We were hypnotized by the competence with which they handled these weapons. To a casual observer they looked as though they were seriously trying to kill each other. Again and again Barney's bayonet came within an inch of Jonathan Gifford's flesh. Once he drove it straight at his throat. Captain Gifford drew back his head just enough to let the blade pass beneath his chin.

A woman's cry startled us. We turned and saw Caroline Skinner standing at the park gate, her hand to her throat, as if the blade had pierced her there. For a moment we were all members of the same tableau—Caroline at the gate, we hired volunteers with our turned heads and opened mouths, Jonathan Gifford and Barney like a statue of two embattled gladiators. Caroline broke the spell by running headlong to the mansion house. Jonathan Gifford threw aside his musket and told Barney to resume training us with our wooden bayonets.

He found Caroline at the kitchen table. "I'm sorry," she said. "I shouldn't go out there. But I can't help it. I'm—fascinated—horrified—by it all."

Jonathan Gifford heard this as a reproof. Drenched in sweat, dirty and exhausted from the previous four grueling days, his temper was short.

"You don't like the business of war? Does it offend you to discover what dirty work it is to turn men into soldiers? Sometimes I think that's been the trouble with you Americans all along."

"You Americans—?"

"You thought it was all glorious, noble, heroic, defending the rights of man. Well, that's how they're defended, madam, by men who know how to use bayonets—the way I'm teaching them. If you Americans all learned that lesson five years ago this damn war would be over now."

"Jonathan, please don't talk that way. You Americans. It was not just the bayonet coming so close, it was the look on your face. You—you liked it."

They stood there in silence for a long time while all their selves crowded into that hot, still room—the soldier and the woman, the lover and his beloved, another man's wife, another woman's husband.

"I saw the man I never met, the man who—led bayonet charges. Who fought duels. I suddenly wondered if I loved him."

"I have work to do," Jonathan Gifford said and turned to the door. She saw she had hurt him deeply. She flung herself against him from behind, pinning his arms.

"I'm sorry, I'm sorry. I keep thinking of you—and Anthony. The only two people I have ever loved. Really loved. It terrifies me to think you—you may kill him. I used to be so sure I could control my feelings. But you—you have changed that. You have changed me. Please understand, Jonathan."

She was right. He had been enjoying this intense return to soldiering. He had been enjoying the flash of that steel bayonet an inch from his throat. The man he had tried to escape, the killer with his special blend of Irish wildness and English calculation, had been returning to life within him. But it was necessary, he told himself angrily. Necessary to let him live another few days.

"I will try—try to understand," he said.

He left her there in the shadowed kitchen. Caroline felt bereft, as if she had lost him. Outside she heard him roaring, "All right, all right, on your feet now. Time for some work with real bayonets."

CHAPTER FOUR

ON THE SIXTH day, we rested. Jonathan Gifford mustered the staff of Liberty Tavern, Caroline, and Sukey to cook three days' provisions for us. Along with salt pork, and beef, we had a supply of veal glue, an ingenious cake soup that Captain Gifford made from boiling legs of veal into a jelly, which was then laid on fresh flannel to draw out the moisture. A piece the size of a walnut, boiled in a pint of water, made a delicious strong broth.

At twilight we marched south. In his knapsack, along with his provisions, each man carried part of a scaling ladder, made by Black Sam, then broken down to be reassembled at the right time. Jonathan Gifford rode at the head of our little column. Kemble and Thomas Rawdon and Barney McGovern strode in the front rank. By dawn we had reached the Trap Inn below Shrewsbury where Rawdon had met the men who guided him to Anthony Skinner's camp. From there we swung west into the pines, following the slashes on the trees while Rawdon counted his paces. About halfway, Jonathan Gifford called a halt and sent Rawdon and Kemble forward as a scouting party. They got close enough to see the fort through the pines. They marked a path back to our camp by nailing small strips of white cloth to the trees every hundred paces.

Satisfied that we could advance in the dark without losing our way, Jonathan Gifford revealed his plan. We were to attack at dawn. With luck we might be able to blast a hole in the wall. Otherwise we would have to use our scaling ladders. We were to rely on the bayonet. No man was to load his musket. "I guarantee you it will save the lives of some of you. In a fight like this one, you are just as likely to get shot by your friends if everyone is blazing away."

He drew a diagram of the fort on the ground and carefully described its layout. We were to attack their barracks. Skinner's house was to be handled by Kemble and Rawdon.

"No man is to load his musket until he hears three blasts on my whistle," Jonathan Gifford said. "With any luck we will not have to fire a shot. And remember. When we charge. *Yell.* Make them think the whole Continental army is coming after them."

As we formed up for the march, Jonathan Gifford took Lieutenant Rawdon aside and handed him one of his dueling pistols. "You may need this when you go after Skinner in his house."

We marched in a long, carefully planned column. Barney McGovern and three scouts led the way. Twelve men prowled the woods on each side and another carefully picked party of six formed the rear guard. Jonathan Gifford trudged in the middle of the column beside two men who were carrying a keg of gunpowder suspended from a long pole. Nearby were the men with the scaling ladders. It was a five- or six-mile march, agony for a man with a ruined knee. But Captain Gifford never broke his pace.

We arrived within striking distance of the fort at 4 A.M. Rawdon, Kemble, and Jonathan Gifford crept forward to study the situation. As they had hoped, the sentries had vanished from the walls. They could even hear one man snoring.

"Get the gunpowder," Jonathan Gifford whispered.

In five minutes the barrel was deposited beside them. Carefully, silently, they rolled it to the side of the fort, then opened it and ran a fuse back into the woods. The ladder carriers were told to throw aside their burdens. They probably would not need them. The explosion would be the signal to attack.

"Remember," Jonathan Gifford whispered, *"yell."*

The night faded from the sky. A few early birds began to twitter in the trees around us. The shape of the fort became visible.

"Five more minutes," Jonathan Gifford said.

"They beat reveille early," Rawdon said.

"Two more minutes," Jonathan Gifford said.

He counted off the seconds, struck a match and touched the tiny flame to the train of powder. With a whoosh it raced across the twenty yards between our hiding place and the barrel. There was a flash of light and a tremendous explosion that momentarily blinded and stunned us. The fort seemed to vanish in a great gush of smoke. Jonathan Gifford was on his feet running, yes, running on that tortured leg into the smoke. Kemble and Rawdon and Barney ran beside him.

Howling a wordless war cry, we followed them. A ten-foot hole had been blown in the wall. In a moment we were on the parade ground. Skinner's men were pouring from their barracks. Still howling, we opened into a line and charged them. Some of them fired wildly at us. Their bullets whistled harmlessly over our heads.

"My God," one of them screamed, "they're Continentals."

It was a logical conclusion. Never before in the war had militiamen relied on the bayonet with such confident ferocity. They broke and ran before we got close to them.

Rawdon and Kemble raced for Skinner's house. He was as stunned as the rest of the garrison when the explosion flung him from his bed. But he was ready to fight. He grabbed a loaded musket from the wall and shouted to Kate. "Get under the bed."

Kate ignored him. She knew what was happening. She ran to the window. "There are hundreds of them, Anthony. Give up."

He ignored her and crouched in the corner to the right of the door, his musket raised. Thomas Rawdon appeared in the doorway. He had Jonathan Gifford's pistol in one hand and a musket in his other hand.

"Dr. Murphy at your service, Skinner," he said. "I think your best remedy is an immediate surrender."

Rawdon was one step from eternity.

"No, Thomas, he'll kill you," Kate cried and flung herself across the room. She crashed into Skinner as he pulled the trigger.

Rawdon pulled back his head at Kate's cry. The double-shotted musket blasted a hole in the wall an inch from his face, momentarily blinding him with a shower of splinters.

"Bitch," Skinner roared and raised his musket to crush Kate's skull.

Rawdon fired. The pistol's bullet smashed into Skinner's right arm. With a howl of pain and rage he dropped his gun, grabbed Kate by the front of her dress, and hurled her at Rawdon like a projectile. As they tumbled against the wall, he raced past them into the outer room. There he found Kemble, who wasted no time on invitations to surrender. He fired his musket from the hip and another bullet shattered Skinner's right arm. But the recoil of the musket sent Kemble reeling. Skinner got past him and stumbled onto the parade ground.

There he saw at a glance that his dream of conquering New Jersey was over. Most of his men were running or surrendering. A few still fought with an outlaw's desperation, but there was no hope of organizing them to make a stand. They were going down in a series of short, nasty encounters with our bayonets. In the center of the parade ground Jonathan Gifford calmly directed squads to pursue fugitives or attack pockets of resistance.

"GIFFORD," Anthony screamed. He raised his left arm, his fist clenched. "I WILL EVEN THE SCORE, GIFFORD."

"Surrender, Anthony," Jonathan Gifford said, drawing a pistol from his belt and walking toward him.

"Never," Skinner said and ran for the hole in the wall.

Kemble stumbled out of the house. "Shoot the bastard," he roared.

Jonathan Gifford leveled his pistol at Anthony Skinner's back. But he could not pull the trigger. Those words in the manor kitchen, that look of reproach on Caroline's face had forever stilled the wildness, the battle fury that had once made him fearful, even loathsome to himself. He remembered instead Caroline's anguish at the thought of him killing her son. He could never face her with Anthony Skinner's blood on his hands. He lowered his pistol.

"Let him go. I don't think he'll do much more harm."

"He will do harm as long as he lives," Kemble said.

It was impossible to explain to Kemble now. Jonathan Gifford returned his attention to the battle, which was rapidly ending. Most of the garrison had surrendered. A few holdouts in the barracks were soon persuaded to join them by a promise of decent terms. We had killed or badly wounded a dozen of them. Our only casualty was a man wounded in the leg.

Thomas Rawdon reported Kate was weak but basically healthy. Jonathan Gifford decided to send her and the wounded home immediately. He sent Kemble and twenty-five men with them. He gave Kate a note to Caroline, in which he tersely told her of the easy victory, assuring her that he and everyone else in the family were unscathed. He ended with: "A.S. is not among the prisoners. He escaped."

The rest of us stayed to demolish the fort, a job that took two days. We marched home hoping to hear Anthony Skinner had been captured on the run and was safely incarcerated in a local jail. We were greeted by the neighborhood at Liberty Tavern as conquering heroes—but no one had seen a trace of Skinner. Patrols had been sent along the shoreline and a special watch kept on the Shrewsbury, where he was known to have many friends. Tavern keepers were given his description. Daniel Slocum, trying to horn in on our little triumph, offered a reward of $500 for his capture.

Then came news from the South—news of the possibility of a much bigger victory. Instead of retreating from Virginia to the security of their bases in South Carolina, the British had fallen back to the little tobacco port of Yorktown, confident that their fleet could waft them from Washington's grasp, if his attacking army looked too formidable. But a French fleet appeared from the West Indies to blockade the Chesapeake while Washington seized the head of the Yorktown peninsula, cutting off all hope of overland escape. The British were in a sack, and if the French persevered for once, instead of raising our hopes and then sailing away, we had an excellent chance of bagging an entire British army.

Jonathan Gifford was as exultant as the rest of us. He left us studying his maps on the taproom's big corner table, called for his chaise, and rode over to tell the news to Caroline. It was a warm day in late September. Everywhere he looked, Captain Gifford seemed to see a blooming reflection of his happiness. For the first time there was hope, genuine hope that the war might end soon.

In the entrance hall he greeted Caroline with a kiss so hearty it knocked the lace cap off her head.

"What in the world, Jonathan?" she said. She hastily withdrew from his arms, picked up her cap, and fussed with the ribbon. She seemed as diffident and strange as if he had kissed her with her husband in the next room.

"My dearest, I have the most amazing news—" He told her and found himself the amazed one. She barely reacted to it.

"Caroline—what is the matter? Are you still hurt by—"

She shook her head. "That was my fault, not yours."

"What is it then?"

"I will tell you—tomorrow."

465

"I want to know now. Are you thinking that when the war is over—?"

"I will tell you tomorrow, Jonathan."

"You are treating me like a child."

"I am not. Please go and tomorrow—"

"I will have an answer now."

Her eyes filled with tears. "You will hate me."

The words filled him with dread. What was happening? Could someone with so much good sense go mad without warning? All his doubts and fears about women swarmed down his nerves.

"You've heard the news already. Your first thought—if the war ends—was facing Mr. Skinner. There is no need to worry about that, my dearest. I've talked to Governor Livingston. He tells me Congress is resolved no matter what to bar the loyalists forever. It's a sad fate, but they can hope for compensation from the King."

"No, Jonathan, no. That isn't it." She seized his right hand for a moment in her two hands. "I cannot keep it from you. Come upstairs."

He half-knew, as they mounted that graceful, curving staircase, what he would find. She opened her bedroom door. There on the white sheets where they had made love so often in the last years lay Anthony Skinner. He was covered with mud and blood and in a half-conscious stupor, his eyes glazed with fever. He was too weak to raise his head. He tried to sit up and fell back gasping.

"Mother—you promised—" he croaked. "You promised. Why did you? Bastard will sell me—wants to hang me."

"No, no, Anthony," Caroline said. "He won't betray you. You won't, will you, Jonathan?"

Captain Gifford turned his back and walked out of the room. Caroline followed him into the hall, closing the bedroom door behind her.

"He came to the back door last night. He hid first with some loyalists in Shrewsbury but he heard them talking about how much money they could get by betraying him. He came here because there was no one else he could trust. His right arm is black and swollen twice its size."

"You should have sent him away."

"Jonathan, I couldn't. He was sick, dying in front of my eyes."

"You should have sent him away. This is a war. He is an enemy."

"He is still part of my family," Caroline Skinner said. "I can't bear to think of myself as one of those who answers hate for hate. Perhaps that's a woman's weakness."

He waved the self-accusation aside. She had long since dispelled those old ideas from his mind.

"You must leave here this instant. You never saw him," she said.

"Don't be ridiculous. Has Sukey seen him?"

"No. She was visiting friends at the Talbot farm last night. I sent her to Brunswick to buy salt and some other things early this morning. She will be gone all day."

"We must get him out of this house and on his way to New York."

"I have already taken care of that."

"How?"

"I went to the Bellowses'. Anthony told me they would know where to find help. There will be a wagon here at dusk. They will take him to Shoal Harbor where a boat will be waiting."

"Caroline. Don't you see—you've put yourself in their power? You can't trust them. Especially now when it looks like the war may end. Why didn't you send for me, trust me?"

"Because I was afraid of what I saw on your face when you were teaching the men to use the bayonet. Afraid of what you said in the kitchen."

"Some of this is my fault," he said with a sigh. He told her of his inability to shoot Anthony as he fled the fort. "We are in this together," he said. "Let's hope for the best."

At dusk a hay-filled wagon came up the drive. It was driven by George Bellows, the man whom Kemble and his midnight raiders had so cruelly punished in 1777. He held up his arm with its missing hand in a grisly salute.

"Why, Cap'n, what're you doin' here?"

"I'm here to help a family friend, just like you."

"Family friend, hell," Bellows said. "I don't put much stock in friendship any more, Cap'n, or in loyalty to anyone or anything. I told Miz Skinner here it was hard money or nothin'."

"Here's your money," Caroline Skinner said, and handed him a bag of clinking coins.

They lugged Anthony Skinner downstairs, staggering under his dead weight. He was delirious, babbling about England, and his school days there. The slightest jar of his diseased arm made him groan with pain. They covered him with hay and watched the wagon vanish into the twilight.

"It was weakness, I know—but you must love me as I am," Caroline said.

"It was not weakness," Jonathan Gifford said. "It took more courage than any man in this state possesses—the courage to forgive. God knows there is nothing we need more. But I am not sure Anthony or his father will forgive in return. They have lost too much."

"I know," Caroline said sadly. "I sensed it from things he said when he first came to the house."

Jonathan Gifford put his arm around her. "I have no regrets. I've learned a new reason to love you."

In the gathering darkness they embraced, still lovers in spite of disagreement and doubt, those almost inevitable diseases of the heart in a revolution.

CHAPTER FIVE

JONATHAN GIFFORD RODE back to Liberty Tavern later that night, his mind heavy with foreboding. He found a holiday atmosphere. More news had arrived from Virginia. The British fleet had attempted to rescue the army trapped at Yorktown and had been beaten off by the French squadron in a two-day encounter. The British ships had been so badly mauled, they had retreated to New York for emergency repairs. For the next two weeks we—and the rest of America—held our breaths. We knew from the coast watchers along the shore that a revived and reinforced British fleet had sailed south on the thirteenth of October, with Sir Henry Clinton and most of the New York garrison. There seemed a very good chance that the fate of America would be decided down there in Virginia in a titanic land-sea battle.

On October 24, precisely at noon, Abel Aikin, our local Mercury, arrived wearing his usual costume, knitting away in the saddle for a full five minutes after the horse stopped in front of Liberty Tavern. With elaborate care Abel put away his needles and dismounted, hoisted the mail pouches from his nag's back, and stomped into the taproom in his oversized boots.

We crowded around him. "What news? What news from Philadelphia, Abel?"

"From Philadelphia? Why no news at all. The Congress fumbles and grumbles as usual."

"From Virginia, Abel," Jonathan Gifford said. "What news from Virginia?"

"Why nothing at all there either, except Lord Cornwallis and his army are prisoners of war."

With a shout of joy, we hoisted our messenger of victory on our shoulders and paraded him around the taproom, banging his head more than once on the rafters. It was our way of simultaneously forgiving him and getting a little revenge for the perversity with which he had delivered our mail and told us the news for so many years.

We celebrated Yorktown because we were victory-starved—not because we thought it ended the war. Tots who study our history in school these days get the impression that the war ended at Yorktown. We in New Jersey had no such illusions. We sensed a great turning point in the contest had come and gone. But the war continued. The British army and their loyalist allies still controlled New York, Long Island, and Staten Island. The night after we finished celebrating, raiders struck deep into Monmouth County, seizing grain and livestock around Colt's Neck and burning Daniel Slocum's house and barns. Glumly, as the exultation ebbed from our blood, we realized that little had changed.

"It depends on how the King and Parliament react to the news. They still have twenty-five thousand men in America," Jonathan Gifford pointed out that evening at supper with Kemble, Lieutenant Rawdon, and Kate.

"Well, I care not how those dunderheads react," Rawdon said. "I have reacted as follows. I have asked your daughter to marry me as soon as her inclination permits. I've resigned my commission and written a letter to my father, telling him the truth about this stupid war."

"If you find yourself disinherited," Jonathan Gifford said, "I am ready to give Kate her portion of Kemble Manor at a moment's notice and loan you the money to build a house on it."

"I think it would be best if Kate and I lived elsewhere for a few years, Captain. As long as General Slocum is the political ruler of this county, almost anyone could become a victim of his Association for Retaliation. An ex-British officer would be a particularly tempting target. Also, I rather dislike being one of his subjects."

"The devil with Slocum for the time being. Let's drink to your happiness," Kemble said, raising his glass. "If someone told me in 1776 that I would approve the marriage of my sister to a British officer I would have—arrested him."

There was a hearty laugh all around at this confession.

"Where are you going to live, Mr. Rawdon?" Jonathan Gifford asked.

"Dr. Davie has a friend in Somerset County who wishes to sell his practice. He thinks the people up there will be so glad to get a decent doctor, they won't worry about what color coat he's been wearing recently."

"From what I hear, there are more Tories up there than Whigs, anyway," Kemble said.

This produced another laugh. The good cheer died when Kemble broke into a fit of coughing. Rawdon looked solemn. He and Kate had been worried about Kemble for months. But lately his condition had stabilized. Lung disease is an unpredictable malady.

"Perhaps you can spend a winter in the south," Kate said, when Kemble regained his composure. "It would be good for that cough."

"Where?" Kemble said. "The British still hold Georgia and most of South Carolina."

"Bermuda or the Bahamas would be the best place to go, but we must have peace first," Jonathan Gifford said.

Within a month, Kate and Thomas Rawdon were married in the assembly room of Liberty Tavern. Only the family and a few friends were invited. Immediately after the wedding, Jonathan Gifford and Barney hitched up a hired Jersey wagon and drove the newlyweds to their new home in Somerset County, about forty miles northwest of Liberty Tavern, almost in the exact center of New Jersey. The location, far from all possible contact with British or loyalists, had made it easy for Captain Gifford to persuade the state authorities and General Washington to accept the sincerity of Lieutenant Rawdon's resignation from the British army and his readiness to swear allegiance to the United States of America. By evening, Dr. and Mrs. Rawdon were settled in a snug stone cottage on a branch of the Millstone River.

Kate's farewell words to her father as Barney swung the big Jersey wagon into the road were: "Take care of Kemble if you can—and Aunt Caroline."

The next morning Jonathan Gifford decided to heed the second of these directives, telling himself it was much more within his power. But instead of a happy visit at Kemble Manor, he was greeted by tears. What he had dreaded the day Anthony Skinner departed was happening. George Bellows had just left. He was demanding money for his silence. Jonathan Gifford rode to the Bellows' farmhouse and limped into the kitchen, his horsewhip in his hand. George Bellows was cooking something in a pot over the open hearth.

"Bellows," he said, "if you say another word about Anthony Skinner to anyone—above all to Mrs. Skinner—I'll take the skin off your back with this whip."

Bellows retreated into self-pity. He whined that he was a cripple as well as an outcast. The family had lost their farm because they were unable to pay the bonds they had posted for their good behavior, then forfeited by joining Skinner's loyalists in 1777. Daniel Slocum was now their landlord. Their father, Joshua Bellows, had died last year. Another brother was with the British. This left him and one brother to work the farm.

Bellows pointed to his wife Mary sitting in a corner of the kitchen humming a nursery rhyme to herself. She totally ignored two thin, grimy children who sat at the table spooning corn meal mush into their mouths. "I got to take care of her and the kids, as well as carry my share of the farm. You know how she got that way, don't you, Captain?"

He held up the arm with the missing hand. "She's never been the same, since your son, that great patriot Kemble Stapleton, done this to me. All the same, I don't hold a grudge. I helped cut off that other fellow's hand. I suppose I deserved it. But the same way, I think I ought to get what I deserve from you and Mistress Skinner. I did dangerous work for you that night. It was worth a sight more than five pounds."

Jonathan Gifford was more shaken by the wan, sallow faces of the Bellows children than he wanted to admit. He took five Spanish dollars from his pocket and put them on the kitchen table.

"If those children are as hungry as they look, they need this. That's the only reason I'm giving it to you."

He rode back to Kemble Manor and told Caroline what he had done.

"It will never end now, will it? He will whine and threaten us for the rest of our lives."

"No he won't. The moment the war ends and we have decent courts and juries again, and people calm down, I will dare him to tell anyone in the world what we did."

"Not we, I," Caroline said. "I hate myself for forcing you to be a part of it."

"Stop it," Jonathan Gifford said. "You are alone here too much thinking dark thoughts. Why don't you leave this empty old barn for the time being and take Kate's room at our house? We'll get Dr. Davie to cook up a story about an illness that requires daily treatment."

"No," Caroline said. "The less you have to do with me, the better now. And in the future, I fear."

"I will put you over my knee and spank you if you keep talking this way," he said, drawing her to him with a rough sweep of his arm. "We have come this far together. We will go on no matter what."

Caroline freed herself. She had to put some distance between them to disagree with him. "I will stay here. And hope that you can come—more often."

"I will come every day."

It was not good enough, an inner voice warned Jonathan Gifford as he rode back to Liberty Tavern. It was easy to talk about the end of the war. But it showed no sign of ending. If anything, the loyalist reign of midnight terror was growing worse as their frustration and fear of defeat mounted. Worst of all from our point of view at Liberty Tavern was the news that one of the most atrocious raids, in which two Middletown Point farmhouses were burned to the ground, was led by a man with only one arm. Crippled and almost insanely embittered, Anthony Skinner had returned to torment his ex-neighbors.

Kemble organized a troop of light horsemen to defend the district. It meant more sleepless nights and exposure to the weather, at a time when Dr. Davie was insisting that he must rest. The saddest part of it was the near impossibility of catching Skinner. It was like pursuing a will-o'-the-wisp in the darkness. After an exhausting month, Jonathan Gifford cautiously pointed this out to Kemble.

"I know it, Father," Kemble said. "But at least the people feel someone is trying to protect them."

While Kemble was worrying about the people, Daniel Slocum was gleefully expanding his Association for Retaliation. Since he was in charge of dividing the spoils, there can be no doubt that General Slocum found the Association as profitable as it was congenial to his political and military style. Dozens of farms of loyalists and neutralists, Quakers and even Whigs were looted and

473

wrecked. Anyone not in the Association was fair game for the Slocumites. They also showed an ominous appetite for other forms of so-called instant justice. At least seventeen pine robbers, who had returned to simple banditry after Anthony Skinner's defeat, were caught and hanged without benefit of trial by judge or jury.

By this time the Slocumites were utterly indiscriminate about whom they approached. Anyone could join the Association who agreed to abide by its cowardly principles. More than a few loyalist sympathizers, men who had been shunned by the patriots for years, saw a marvelous opportunity to change sides.

Toward the end of December, one of Slocum's relatives strode into Liberty Tavern and posted on the taproom wall a list of names of those who had recently joined the Association. At the top of the list were all the surviving members of the Bellows family. A chill of apprehension ran down Jonathan Gifford's nerves. It was only a matter of time, he thought.

He was right. Early in the new year 1782, a rumor began circulating through the district—a rumor that soon swelled into a detailed story. Exonerating himself, George Bellows told how other unnamed loyalists had come to Kemble Manor at dusk with a wagon and helped Anthony Skinner to escape. The Englishman—the hate name for Jonathan Gifford—was there too, they vowed. He had helped carry Skinner to the wagon. As the story circulated, the loyalists disappeared and Jonathan Gifford played a larger and larger role. He had procured the wagon and driven it to Shoal Harbor. He had hired the boat and sailed it to New York, where he was warmly greeted by his old friends in the British army and well rewarded for rescuing such a valuable partisan leader.

It was vicious stuff but it went from tongue to tongue with frightening rapidity. With that shrewdness which was the most frightening part of his power, Daniel Slocum let the anger fester and swell beneath the surface of our war-weary district for almost a month. Meanwhile he had relatives watching Jonathan Gifford, waiting for him to visit Kemble Manor alone. Slocum soon noted that the Captain had taken to lingering after dinner, often until darkness fell. One cold clear night in late January 1782, Slocum rounded up forty or fifty of the most violent members of the Association for Retaliation, packed them into a half-dozen large sleighs, and rode swiftly down the snowy roads in search of revenge.

Kemble and I were playing chess in Liberty Tavern's taproom when Ambrose Cotter, that ragged remnant of the spirit of 1776, drifted into the tavern and sidled up to us. "I remember a while back your father offered fifty pounds for information that would warn of an attack on him," Cotter said.

"You mean from Skinner?" Kemble said curtly. "Where would he find enough men to attack this place now? There are twenty horsemen sleeping in the barn every night."

"The trouble does not come from Skinner," Cotter said, looking nervously around him. "But the news may be just as serviceable. I hear General Slocum is on his way to Kemble Manor this moment with fifty men. He says he is going to hang your father for treason."

Kemble took three muskets from the armory and told Barney to hitch a two-horse team to a sleigh. We took the back road to the rear of the manor. Jonathan Gifford was having supper with Caroline in the dining room when we burst in with the news of Slocum's intentions.

"How many men did he have with him?"

"Fifty."

"Go home."

"What?" said Kemble. "We can—"

"We can do nothing with guns," Jonathan Gifford said. "The sight of a musket will be the excuse they need to burn us out."

Kemble refused to go home. Barney was even more adamant. "Twenty years I've known and served under you, Captain, and never disobeyed an order. But there's got to be a first time for everything, I suppose."

"Let one of us go back and get the light horse," Kemble said, referring to the twenty men we had on duty at Liberty Tavern.

Jonathan Gifford shook his head. "I don't want anyone killed on my account. This is a private quarrel between me and Slocum. Let's see if we can settle it with words instead of bullets. Put away your guns."

We left the guns in a dark corner of the kitchen. A half-hour later, Slocum arrived with his mob. In the forefront was George Bellows, his round puffy face flushed with anticipation. Other old foes of Jonathan Gifford such as Matthew Leary, the ex-commissioner of confiscated estates were in the crowd. Slocum said he was there "at the request of the good people of this county, to put a stop to the murders and maraudings and thefts by their enemies. We have reason to suspect this house is a headquarters for these fiends. If we find any such proof, summary justice will be executed upon its owner."

Slocum glared at Jonathan Gifford as he said these words. The Captain wondered if he had made a fatal miscalculation. Looking into Slocum's swarthy face, Jonathan Gifford did not have the slightest doubt that the General would hang him if he thought he had even a gambler's chance of getting away with it. There was no ground for hope in the other faces in the crowd. They wore nothing but the worst passions, greed, envy, blind suspicion, a wish, even a need to blame the pain and misery of six years of war on someone.

Slocum turned to his men. "Search the house. Look sharp for guns, ammunition, stolen articles. And bloodstains. From what we hear this place has been a hospital for at least one of their wounded."

The search did not last more than five minutes. Most of the rooms were empty. One man thought he found blood on the dining room floor. Caroline Skinner calmly informed him that it was blood—from a wounded American soldier. Not even the tableware was valuable. It was pewter and it had SR stamped on the back— for Strangers' Resort—a relic of Liberty Tavern's former identity.

They found our guns in the kitchen, and the guns Caroline kept in her bedroom. These were hardly evidence that the house was a loyalist armory. But Slocum was undeterred.

"No doubt their spies warned them of our coming. We'll hear witnesses. Get the serving girl."

Watching, Kemble was filled with loathing and sadness. On the hate-filled faces of the men around Slocum, he saw the death of his dream of American perfection. He had clung to the dream in the face of the war's ruthless and repeated revelation of its impossibility, blaming Slocum, Congress, the Tories. Now he could no longer deny the truth. Expelling old Europe's corruption would not purify these men. The corruption, the weakness, was in their very natures, in their limited minds and unsteady feelings, in their gullibility and pettiness, which let men like Daniel Slocum so easily lead them, in their egotism and greed, which put their own narrow interests ahead of their country. Speechless, our idealist stood there while his dream withered.

Sukey was dragged from the kitchen. She was badly frightened and Slocum did his best to scare her even more by threatening her with the noose if she did not tell the truth. But Sukey did not panic. She despised Slocum too much to give him that satisfaction.

"Did you ever see a Tory refugee in this house? Someone who praised the King, damned Congress?"

"I know what a Tory is. There has never been one in this house since Mr. Anthony went to New York."

"And he has not been back?"

"I have never seen him."

"Did your mistress ever give you sheets or blankets to wash, with blood on them?"

"No."

"You're lying. Do you want to hang along with your mistress and Captain Gifford?"

"You can't hang them. They have done nothing wrong."

"No? Do you know what fornication is?"

"Yes."

"They do that, don't they? Haven't you seen them?"

"You are a disgusting man, General Slocum."

"You will be sorry you said that, you black bitch," Slocum snarled. "Bellows, come forward here."

George Bellows told his story, carefully leaving himself out of it. He was just passing by. He saw the whole thing from the road. He watched Jonathan Gifford and Caroline Skinner carry Anthony Skinner to the wagon. He hid among the bushes at the end of the drive and heard them talking as they drove out. Skinner was telling Jonathan Gifford to head for Shoal Harbor. Bellows even remembered the day and the hour. September 29, at 6 P.M.

"Where were you on that day at that hour, Gifford?" Slocum asked.

"I have no intentions of answering your questions, General. This is not a court of law."

"For you it is," Slocum said. "If you don't contradict this man's story, this will be the last court you ever see."

He turned to the mob crowding around them in the hall. "What do you say, gentlemen of the jury?"

477

"Guilty, guilty," came from every mouth.

"No, he's not."

Caroline Skinner stepped between Jonathan Gifford and his would-be hangmen. She pointed to George Bellows. "This man is implicating Captain Gifford from a low spirit of revenge. But there is this much truth in his story. I did shelter my stepson, Anthony Skinner, when he came here wounded and sick. I arranged for him to escape to New York—with Mr. Bellows' help."

"She's a damn liar," howled Bellows.

"The crime you are confessing is serious enough without attempting to implicate a good citizen," Slocum said, "a man who has had a change of heart and joined the side of his country. Is that why you are attempting to ruin him?"

"I'm telling the truth. I cannot believe that even you, General Slocum, and this mockery of a court would dare to hang a man when a witness has testified to his innocence."

"Caroline—" Jonathan Gifford cried in agony.

"Be quiet, Captain Gifford. I will not permit you to commit suicide on my behalf." She turned to face Slocum and his mob again. "I confess my crime, gentlemen," she said. "If a woman commits a crime when she allows a mother's feeling for her dying son to overcome her patriotism."

"Dying, madam?" roared Slocum. "Is that his ghost that's burned a half-dozen houses and stolen five thousand dollars' worth of horses and cattle in the last few months?"

"He was dying when he came to my door."

"I suggest you go where you sent him, madam. If you think New York is such a fine place for him, why don't you join him there so he can enjoy his mama's love day in and day out? That is the sentence I would pass on you. But I will let the good people of this jury decide for themselves. I think you will hear from them in the next few days."

"There is no need for waiting," shouted a voice at the back of the hall. "Let's escort her to Amboy this night."

"You will do it over my dead body," Jonathan Gifford said.

"I will be ready to go in a half-hour, Captain Gifford," Caroline said. "If this is the price I must pay—I will pay it—gladly."

Seeing the anguish on his father's face, Kemble realized what others had suspected for a long time. Jonathan Gifford and Caroline Skinner were lovers. The man he had accused in his heart of a

478

failure to love—a failure that had darkened their lives—had loved this quiet cool woman so well that she was sacrificing herself for him. Kemble felt the vise of resentment and regret that had made him reluctant to touch this man or be touched by him—he felt this last barrier of knowing, confessing the reality of his father's character—loosen.

He also saw how his dream of a perfect America had stifled his love for this man, because his calm acceptance of human failure had seemed to contradict it. How his very strength, his perseverance in the face of failure, including his son's failures, had been another barrier. These prejudices had been eroding steadily in the years of war, and they vanished totally now in the sympathy and forgiveness that flooded Kemble's heart. Our torchbearer of liberty was free at last to be a son.

Jonathan Gifford knew nothing of this silent drama in Kemble's soul. He only knew that his own heart was shriveling with pain.

"I would like five minutes alone with Mrs. Skinner," he said.

"You will have no such thing," Slocum said. "And you, madam, will have no time to pack anything. You will take nothing but the clothes on your back. Everything else in this house is confiscated and will be sold at auction to repay those who have suffered as a result of your treachery."

Jonathan Gifford, Kemble, Barney, and I could do nothing but stand there, virtual prisoners, while Caroline submitted to this edict. One everyday cloak was all she was permitted to take for an outer garment. As she walked past us to the door, she carefully avoided looking at Jonathan Gifford's anguished face. She spoke only to Sukey.

"You cannot stay here alone. Captain Gifford will give you work at the tavern."

"The hell he will," Slocum said. "She is confiscated with the rest of your property."

"I am not property," Sukey said. "I am as free as you are."

"Her manumission papers are on file at the courthouse," Caroline said.

Slocum growled his disbelief. Weeping, Sukey said she would come with Caroline. "No," she said. "I'm not sure I could protect you. My husband might refuse to recognize your papers and sell you to the West Indies."

Her head bowed, Caroline walked out without looking back at us. In a moment hoofbeats dwindled down the drive. We stood in the silent hall, waiting for Jonathan Gifford to tell us what to do.

The sound of breaking glass came from the south parlor. Another crash in the library. The Association for Retaliation was saying goodbye to Kemble Manor with rocks. Faint shouts of glee reached us, then more breaking glass. But Jonathan Gifford said nothing, did nothing. More than glass was breaking. His resolution, his strength were cracking, crashing to the wintry earth, ripping up the very roots of his manhood.

Through a haze of tears he saw Kemble walking toward him. What was on his face? Anger, accusation? It was logical. He knew his guilty secret now along with everyone else. What else could or would this idealist son do but accuse him of desecrating his mother's memory?

"I'm sorry, Kemble," he said. "She was so—so different—"

There was a hand on his shoulder. An arm that circled his back. "I understand, Father. I—understand," Kemble said.

Through his pain Jonathan Gifford heard—or half-heard—the wider meaning of those words. He reached out blindly for this son who was reaching out to him, returning some of the strength he had tried to give him now that his own strength was failing.

A huge rock smashed out half a window in the north parlor. The house was filled with the sound of destruction. But we saw in that center hall an image that enabled us still to hope: the son lifting up the fallen father, confessing the reality of his tormented love.

CHAPTER SIX

WHAT HAPPENED AT Liberty Tavern in the next month was a hard lesson in the limits of our human ability to comfort and console each other when pain and loss strike hard. In spite of everything Kemble and the rest of our family tried to do for him, Jonathan Gifford withered before our eyes. His vitality, his commanding presence, vanished. He ignored his roses. He lost all interest in his customers and his friends, the news from home or abroad. Not even the report that the British Prime Minister and the Cabinet who had prosecuted the war against America had been ousted, that Parliament had passed a resolution condemning the excessive influence of George III, stirred him. A visit from Kate produced no more than a wan smile, even when she reported that her old nabob of a father-in-law had replied to Thomas Rawdon's letter with grudging affection and no warnings about disinheritance.

Worst of all, Captain Gifford made no attempt to respond to a charge of treason which Daniel Slocum lodged against him in the court of common pleas. If he was convicted, the tavern, the manor, everything he owned, would be condemned and confiscated, to be sold by Slocum's commissioners. With Caroline exiled, he had lost his only favorable witness. With Slocum in control of the judges, it would be a struggle to get an honest jury. Kemble urged his father to hire the best lawyer in the state. Jonathan Gifford wearily agreed, and did nothing.

It was almost unbelievable to see Jonathan Gifford defenseless, unmanned. Kemble's soul was stirred by an emotion much darker than sympathetic grief. He had been brooding about General Slocum for a long time. The man had poisoned the Revolution in our part of New Jersey. I had added to this conviction my own

481

bitter rage for revenge. More than once I told Kemble that Slocum had killed my father as certainly as if he had fired a bullet through his heart. Now he was destroying the man Kemble had come, almost too late, to accept and love as his father.

You will remember back in 1776 Jonathan Gifford had trained me to fire one of the Pennsylvania rifles in Liberty Tavern's armory. One night, about two weeks after Caroline was exiled, Kemble asked me if I had used a rifle lately. I shook my head. "Stay close to home," he said. "We will put one to some use tomorrow."

That night, Kemble took a rifle from the armory and hid it in the barn. The next day we extracted it from the hay and tramped deep into the woods. If ever there was a wicked weapon in its very appearance, it was the rifle of this period. The immense barrel— fifty-two inches long—the gleaming stock with its intricate brass ornamentation gave it a personal, almost living menace. The accuracy with which it could strike a target a quarter of a mile away was awesome. It made the crude muskets with which the average militiamen fought the Revolution seem worse than toys.

Kemble had never fired a rifle. He asked me to teach him everything Jonathan Gifford had taught me. "There is no need for this," I said. "I am ready to shoot him any time you say the word."

Kemble slowly shook his head. "This must be on my conscience —and no one else's."

The darkness and pain on Kemble's face silenced my arguments. All day we fired at paper targets across a clearing in those still woods. I told Kemble everything Jonathan Gifford had taught me about breathing, wind speed, the curvature of a bullet in flight. By the end of the day he was putting ball after ball into a target one foot square, at two hundred and fifty yards.

That night, about 2 A.M., we put on snowshoes and easily covered the thirteen miles from the tavern to Colt's Neck, keeping off the roads. By dawn we were in position about a quarter of a mile from the front door of General Slocum's farmhouse. He had largely repaired the damage done by the loyalist torches, although his barns were still burnt-out hulks. The winter sun rose in a clear blue sky. There was almost no wind. It was perfect shooting weather. The General came out on the porch in his expensive green coat and black felt tricorn. Kemble leveled the rifle and shot

482

him through the heart, killing him instantly. As Slocum slumped to the porch, I saw once more how easy it was to kill a man—and how terrible.

No one ever accused me or Kemble of this deed. It was generally attributed to loyalists or some neutralist victim of the Association for Retaliation. Slocum had legions of enemies. Only Barney McGovern suspected the truth. He happened to meet Kemble returning the rifle to the armory an hour or two after the sensational news of Slocum's death had swept through the tavern.

"Been doing some hunting?" he said.

Kemble nodded.

"Did you hit anything?"

"Only a skunk."

From the vantage point of fifty years, this savagery saddens me. But it did not trouble me in 1782. When you live for six years with guns in your hands, when you see those you love die and suffer, you lose the humanity that is a normal part of your blood. War replaces it with a cold harsh fluid of its own creation.

Without Slocum's vicious energy, the Association for Retaliation began to collapse. The state legislature suddenly discovered the moral courage to condemn it. A hint of another investigation of rigged elections and fraudulent land sales produced resignations of several Slocumite judges and assemblymen. The indictment against Jonathan Gifford was dismissed. There was now no reason why Caroline Skinner could not return to Kemble Manor. Mentally, Jonathan Gifford knew this, but morally he was a paralyzed man. What he dreaded most had happened. Charles Skinner had regained his wife. There was no way that Jonathan Gifford would or could attempt to pirate that wife away from him, even though she represented to him more happiness than he ever hoped to achieve in this world. The depth and the intensity of the joy he had known with Caroline had only redoubled the guilt that pulsed beneath it, like an abscess always ready to erupt. Now the poison was spreading throughout his spirit, and he made no attempt to resist it. He was little more than a walking dead man.

You may think I am exaggerating. You may think that a strong character can resist such feelings. It is true that strong characters can overcome the everyday moods that bedevil many weaker men and women. But when melancholy breaks into a strong spirit, it often takes deeper root, especially when there is an underlying guilt. The sadness is almost welcomed, out of a hidden wish to expiate the guilt.

Every day Captain Gifford rode to Perth Amboy to meet boats from New York. He was hoping for a letter. One finally came. But it was not from Caroline. It was from Charles Skinner.

Dear Sir:

My wife has asked me to write to you and let you know that she is well. She came to me because she had no choice, having neither money nor even a change of clothes, thanks to your good Whig friends and their benign judgment of a mother's mercy. I wish for the sake of our friendship that I could thank you for your kind treatment of her over the last four years. But she has been utterly frank with me, and I find that you have been no more a friend to me than the rankest rebel in New Jersey. In fact, I can now only think of you as my worst enemy. The rebels have taken my property. I can hope that the value of it will be restored to me by the King's generosity. But you have stolen my wife's affections, and she tells me there is no hope of me ever regaining them. This is the worst cruelty I have met in this cruelest of revolutions. How could you do it? Women are children, they are given to us for our consolation and protection. I trusted you with my wife as a father might a daughter. You have betrayed that trust. I despise you, sir. If I had my health, I would call you out to answer for it.

Your friend no longer,
Charles Skinner

Those words about women being children revealed Charles Skinner's appalling ignorance of his wife. They eased Jonathan Gifford's guilt. But the rest of the letter sank him deeper into desolation. There was no hint of forgiveness for Caroline, and the remark about the King's generosity strongly implied that Skinner would shortly join the hundreds of other loyalists who had retreated to England to recoup their losses by pleading for compensation from the Crown. God knows how many years Caroline would spend as a prisoner of this embittered old man. In desperation, Jonathan Gifford wrote a doomed reply to Charles Skinner's letter.

484

My dear old friend,

I knew someday I would have to look you in the face and tell you what had come to pass between your wife and me. It was a deep thing, one of those special friendships that flower into love in spite of everything that both parties do to prevent it. I freely own my responsibility. But this is not the confession of a man who has wantonly seduced a child. It is a responsibility I felt—and still feel—to my love for her, and more particularly to her love for me. You know me. I am not a child. Neither is your wife. I am afraid old soldiers like you and me never knew much about love. Caroline has taught me the difference between old and new ideas, between true feelings and conventional attachments. Let me come see you and tell you this to your face. If I cannot make you understand it, you can blow out my brains.

Your friend,
J.G.

There was no answer to this letter. The madness of war and the various madnesses of love and hate had created a kind of arena in which the Skinners, Caroline, Jonathan Gifford, and Kemble were now trapped. The Skinners spent their days and nights brooding on their ruin. The endless war had exhausted Charles Skinner's funds. He had been forced to sell his fine furniture, his silver, and even most of his splendid clothes. They were living on the loot Anthony brought back from his raids. Soon father and son shared a common delusion. They saw Jonathan Gifford as the worst criminal in New Jersey, the man who had risked nothing, yet had landed on the winning side in possession of their lands. Winning Caroline was the final enormity. Night after night, as Caroline paced like a prisoner in the room above them, father and son got drunk and denounced Jonathan Gifford as Satan incarnate.

Finally Caroline lost all caution and patience. She confronted these two besotted, defeated men, a tiny flaming figure of reproach, and told them what they did not want to hear—it was she who had persuaded Jonathan Gifford to admit his love, she who had offered herself to him from feelings too strong to resist. She told them that Jonathan Gifford would sell Kemble Manor back to the Skinners tomorrow.

"But what good would that do? It would be condemned and

485

confiscated the next day. Admit the truth. You chose the wrong side."

With a roar, Anthony lunged to his feet, his single fist raised to smash her in the face. For him this truth was unbearable. Charles Skinner lurched from his seat and sent him crashing across the room with a swipe of his huge arm.

"She's right," he said. "We chose the wrong side. But Gifford is still a whoremaster. And you—"

He glared at his wife, wavering between rage and regret. Her confession utterly refuted his primitive belief that women were innocent victims of men like Jonathan Gifford. Too drunk to think, Charles Skinner collapsed into sobbing self-pity.

"You see what you have done to him?" Anthony Skinner shouted. "If there is a God in heaven, you and Gifford will pay for it."

He staggered into the night. Charles Skinner stood there in the center of his drab parlor, alcoholic tears streaming down his face. Caroline knew there was no truth in the bitter accusation Anthony had just flung at her. It was British defeat that had unmanned Charles Skinner. It was ridiculous to blame it on the loss of her love when there had been no love to lose. But it was impossible not to pity this suffering man. For a moment she almost regretted the Revolution, facing the pain it had caused her husband. In memory of the first days of their marriage, when there had been at least a hope of love, Caroline went to him and threw her arms around him for a sad solemn moment. She put him to bed tenderly, like a daughter nursing an aged parent.

At Liberty Tavern, Captain Gifford remained a melancholy ghost. Kemble took charge of running the tavern and the manor. He hired workmen to plant the spring crops, rode down once or twice a week to check on the gristmill and the outlying farm at Colt's Neck, replaced the manor house's shattered windows, and presided each evening in the taproom at the tavern. Simultaneously, he refused to abandon his pursuit of Anthony Skinner. At least once, and often twice a week, he was racing across the district on horseback in pursuit of this public and private enemy. Loot was Skinner's primary interest, although he added to his greed a personal taste for sadistic destruction. He rarely left his victims without insulting or abusing them in some way, or burning their houses or barns. He was soon the most hated man in south Jersey, and no one hated him more than Kemble.

Bearing all these burdens, Kemble carefully concealed from his father and everyone else an alarming decline in his health. He had a number of small hemorrhages in his sleep which left him so weak he could barely mount a horse. He went to Dr. Davie and calmly told him what was happening. He wanted to know if there was any medicine he could take that would slow the disease.

"I don't want to distress my father when he's sunk so low. If ever he needed a healthy son, it's now."

Dr. Davie urged him to spend the winter in Bermuda or the Bahamas. Kemble shook his head and ended the conversation with a warning that under no circumstances was Dr. Davie to mention it to Jonathan Gifford. The old doctor retreated to one of his magic cures, this one from the manuscripts of Friar Bacon. He wrote that ancient word, *Abracadabra*, in a pyramidal form on virgin parchment, and each day scraped out one line, saying, "*As I destroy the letters of this chain, so by virtue of this sacred name, may all grief and dolor depart from Kemble.*"

For a few weeks, Kemble improved. No credit should be given to Abracadabra. Bad weather kept Anthony Skinner away from our coasts and Kemble got some rest. But calm seas eventually permitted Skinner's return, which meant, after a few sleepless nights, the revival of Kemble's cough. In desperation, Dr. Davie urged Jonathan Gifford to get a passport from the British army in New York and spend a few months in the West Indies. A sea voyage often cured melancholy. He could take Kemble with him. Jonathan Gifford sighed, nodded, and said he would think about it. It was obvious that he did not believe anything could cure his melancholy.

In despair, Dr. Davie summoned Kate and Thomas Rawdon for a consultation. Rawdon was pessimistic about Kemble. "We don't understand the disease. How can we cure it?" he asked.

Kate somberly agreed. "All we can do is pray," she said. "But I am just as worried about my father. It seems to me we can do more for him."

Rawdon shook his head. "Only time heals the kind of wound your father has received."

"Time? Time is killing him," Kate said. "Has anyone told Aunt Caroline that she can now come home safely?"

"The less said about that, the better, my dear," said Rawdon.

"I agree," said Dr. Davie. "There is already too much talk about it."

Dr. Davie and Rawdon were only echoing the sentiments of most of Jonathan Gifford's friends. They were ready to forgive him for his indiscretion (which is what they considered it) with Mrs. Skinner. But they felt that it should be forgotten as quickly as possible. A tavern was subject to strict regulation by the state. Its owner had to be a man of good moral character.

Kate scoffed at this attitude. "You are joining the ranks of the hypocrites," she told them. "Who cares about talk when a man's happiness—perhaps his life—is at stake?"

Kate abandoned the doctors and strode to the greenhouse, where Jonathan Gifford sat disconsolately staring at his roses. "Father," she said, "why haven't you asked Aunt Caroline to come home?"

"Even if I felt I should, how can I get word to her?" He showed her the letter he had received from Charles Skinner. "I've hurt him enough. He was my best friend."

Kate saw it was futile to argue with him. She mounted her horse and rode to George Washington's headquarters at Rocky Hill. Introducing herself as Jonathan Gifford's daughter, she had no difficulty gaining access to the commander in chief. She had heard that General Washington had an intense interest in the affairs of the heart. She told him the whole story of her father and Caroline Skinner. The General listened with fascination and wrote out a pass, permitting her to go to New York, "on a matter of private business."

Two days later, Kate stood before the Skinner home on Dock Street. She dreaded the thought of seeing Anthony but was ready to risk even that confrontation. She knocked. The door was opened by Jesse, the black butler, wearing a worn, faded relic of his old livery. His lean face brightened at the sight of Kate.

"Why, Miss Stapleton. What a nice surprise."

"Is Mrs. Skinner at home, Jesse? I would like to see her—alone."

"She is alone at this moment. Mr. Anthony and the Squire have gone to buy passage on the next packet. We will all be in England before long."

"Tell Mrs. Skinner I am here."

Caroline threw her arms around Kate like a mother welcoming a beloved daughter. Kate thought she looked as wan and forlorn as Jonathan Gifford. She did not hesitate to say so.

"It would be ridiculous for me to pretend I am happy," Caroline said.

"Daniel Slocum is dead, shot by one of his many enemies. There is no reason why you can't come home."

"Kate—you know there are reasons. Too many reasons."

"None that really matter, when there is a man over there in New Jersey dying by degrees for the want of the sight of you."

For a moment hope created a glow on Caroline's dark face. Then she shook her head sadly. "I can't believe that, Kate. No, I can. But I'm sure he feels, as I do, that it would be best if we never saw each other again."

"Why?"

"You have heard what happened at the manor. We publicly confessed—our attachment. I have embarrassed him enough. He depends on the public for his living."

"Let us talk as married women. Above all, as women. He is sitting over there in his greenhouse, dying, literally dying, like a prisoner bound and gagged and starving in a dungeon by his own arrangement. I love him as much as you do, but he is a *man*. His head is crammed with ridiculous rules about honor and friendship—"

"They are not ridiculous, Kate. They have their place."

"Not here. Not when they are destroying a love that brought happiness to everyone connected with it—to me, Kemble, above all, to you and him. There has been a Revolution in the name of liberty. Are you going to let it make you a prisoner for the rest of your life? And leave him in the same situation?"

"But how could we ever marry?"

"Your case is surely not unique. I cannot believe an American court would refuse you a divorce if your loyalist husband has gone to London and left you in New Jersey."

Caroline wrestled with the memory of those tears on Charles Skinner's ruined face. She had her own guilt, compounded now by pity, to confront. "I don't know, Kate. I must think about this. You're sure Jonathan—Captain Gifford—would welcome me?"

"If he doesn't, I will give up all pretense of being a woman of judgment. I will go back to reading silly novels and consider myself a feminine idiot for the rest of my life. Come with me now. I have money for the stage boat."

Caroline shook her head. "I must be honest with Mr. Skinner."

"He will never let you go. That is asking too much of human nature—especially his nature."

"He has treated me decently, Kate. Coldly but decently."

She was as unreachable as Jonathan Gifford, as lost in her own guilty melancholy. Kate was discovering that strong feelings cannot be changed by argument. Only the shock of events—usually violent events—can break their grasp on the spirit.

"You had better go," Caroline said. "They may come home drunk. If Anthony saw you, I'm afraid he would get very ugly."

Kate retreated to New Jersey so discouraged she did not even bother to send us a message at Liberty Tavern. Within an hour of her departure, Caroline faced the two Skinners like a criminal under investigation. Jesse had told them of Kate's visit. They demanded to know her purpose.

"It is something I wish to discuss with you in private," Caroline told her husband.

"There is nothing I care to hide from my son," Charles Skinner said.

"Very well," Caroline said. "She told me Captain Gifford would welcome me if I chose to go back to him."

"If you chose to go!" Charles Skinner roared. "By God you shall not go as long as there is a lawyer in England and a King on the throne. You are my wife. You may deny me your bed but you shall not deny me your *presence*, madam. As long as there is a breath in this body Anthony will see to that, even if illness enfeebles me. You have *sinned*, madam, and you must pay for it."

"How many times do I have to tell you, Father. There is only one way to settle this business," Anthony said.

Charles Skinner looked at his son with gloomy hesitation. Caroline could not tell what was passing through his mind.

"I guarantee it can't fail. I have the sloop reserved, the men waiting," Anthony said.

A malevolent violence swept Charles Skinner's florid face. "All right," he said. "Do it."

"As for her," Anthony said, glaring at Caroline, "I suggest locking her in her room until we are ready to sail."

"I shall not be treated this way—" Caroline cried.

"You shall be treated as I wish to treat you, madam," Charles Skinner said. "You are my wife. The greatest mistake I ever made was letting you assume airs of independence. Now go to your room or I shall drive you there with a whip. Jesse!"

Genuinely frightened, Caroline retreated to her room and let Jesse lock the door after her. An hour later Anthony Skinner sailed for New Jersey aboard the loyalist sloop *Revenge*. Landing at Woodbridge with three confederates, he rode boldly to Bound Brook on stolen horses, seized a loaded sloop from the wharves there, burned two other ships, and retreated with the tide. Kemble and I and the light horsemen picketed at Liberty Tavern traded bullets with him along the shore. But it was blind shooting and Skinner escaped unscathed as usual.

By the time we returned to Liberty Tavern it was a half-hour after sunrise. Kemble let himself in the side door with his key and checked the downstairs rooms to make sure they were ready for serving breakfast. As he unbolted the big front door, he saw someone had slipped a letter underneath it, addressed to Jonathan Gifford. The handwriting was familiar. He had seen it on many letters to Kate. Why was Anthony Skinner writing to his father? The letter was unsealed. A public insult was scrawled on the envelope: "*To Jonathan Gifford, Trimmer, for all to read.*" Kemble read it.

Gifford:

My father has decided to retire to England on the next packet. I am going with him. But I cannot leave this country without demanding satisfaction from you for the wound you have inflicted on our family's honor. You are a thief and a whoremaster of the lowest, most cunning sort. I still have one good hand to hold a pistol. I hereby challenge you to meet me on the beach below Garret Hill tomorrow morning at dawn. If you kill me, you will be the hero of New Jersey. I give you this opportunity, knowing you may betray me to your fellow thieves and usurpers. I will take the risk to give my father a chance to face his friends again.

A. Skinner

Kemble looked around him. The taproom was empty. The first risers were stirring upstairs. He put the letter in his pocket and told no one about it. Except me.

"You will be my second, Jemmy."

"But why not tell your father?" I asked, inclined to rely on Jonathan Gifford's prowess as a duelist.

"Because it would be sending him to commit suicide. That letter is written with diabolical skill. It is designed to make him hold his fire."

This was Kemble at his most admirable. Then darkness consumed his face. "Besides, I want to kill that bastard. For my father it will be just one more torment—if he did kill him. For me it will be the greatest satisfaction."

The war was still in Kemble's blood. It was in mine, too. We did not sleep much that night. Kemble wanted to talk. At first he poured out to me all the sadness, the regret that burdened his mind and soul. Even though we were on the verge of victory, for Kemble the Revolution was a failure. It had not achieved that purified, virtuous America that he had envisioned in 1776. The paradigm of that failure was his decision to kill Slocum. Its necessity tormented him. He had only one consolation. The act, the crime (let us call it by its right name) was committed more in the name of love than of revolutionary justice. I listened while Kemble struggled with the contradictions between the heart and the mind, between abstract ideals and personal love.

"I always told myself I could never love anything or anyone I did not completely admire. I think that was my original sin—a sin of pride. Now I realize that we can love our country, our friends, our relations with their flaws, their weaknesses, their failures."

I see him now, pacing the floor of that darkened room, the angular face still young, but also old, creased, worn, stained by six years of war. "Perhaps that is why we learn more from defeat, losses, than from what we win. But I don't understand exactly how. It is not purely intellectual. I understand even less how the suffering is passed on to those we love. Perhaps it helps us see them—really see them—for the first time."

Then he began talking about the future, and I saw that Kemble had only begun to resolve his contradictions. He said that there would always be Slocums for Stapletons and Kembles to fight. The time might come—it might be nearer than we thought—

when we would have to use the same solution to eliminate them. I glumly disagreed. "We can't depend on guns, Kemble. Nothing grows from the point of a gun but death and more death." He stopped pacing and stared at me. For a moment I saw the profound weariness, the mortal sadness in his soul. "You may be right, Jemmy. You may be right."

With a visible effort he hardened himself. "But for the time being, guns are necessary."

About 3 A.M. Kemble told me to lie down and get some sleep. He wanted to write a letter to his father. I copy the faded words in Kemble's small, precise script, from the old yellowed paper before me.

Dearest Sir:

The enclosed letter from Anthony Skinner will explain where I have gone. I know you told me never to indulge in such folly. It seems I am fated to go on disobeying you, ignoring your advice. I suppose sons have done thus to fathers since time began. But let me assure you that I do it here not out of disrespect, but from a loving concern for your state of mind, which renders you incapable of meeting this challenge. Since it is part of a quarrel that I was eager to start, and you reluctant, it seems only fair that I should answer it. If the event proves unfortunate, I would like you to know all this— and one thing more. I have come to love you as few sons love their fathers. (Or perhaps like most do but few can admit.) Please understand that I do not in the least see myself as offering a sacrifice in your place. I am Jonathan Gifford's son, and I know how to use a gun. I fully expect to put a bullet between that bastard's eyes.

Kemble

In New York, six or seven hours before Kemble wrote this letter, Caroline Skinner stood between her husband and son, watching Jesse and two husky sailors hauling the last of their trunks out the door. The royal mail packet H.M.S. *Sandwich* was sailing with the morning tide. When the wagon lumbered off with their baggage, Anthony Skinner hired a coach and gave the driver directions to a Hudson River wharf. It was not unusual to go aboard a ship the night before she sailed. Captains were not inclined to lose a favorable wind or an early turning tide for a tardy passenger. Caroline was too miserable to pay much attention to what was happening around her, anyway. The rest of her life stretched before her eyes, a gray pilgrimage to oblivion. She tried to imagine what Jonathan Gifford was doing in New Jersey. One moment she felt consoled by the thought that he was also miserable. The next moment this became the most unbearable part of her despair.

In the darkness she barely noticed the ship they were boarding. Not until she was sitting on a hard chair in the corner of a tiny cabin did she begin to wonder about its size. Mail packets were ocean-going vessels. This was no more than a fishing smack. "Is this the packet?" she asked.

No one answered her. On deck she could hear the captain giving orders to cast off the bow and stern lines.

"Mr. Skinner," she said, "where are we going?"

She walked to the cabin door. Charles Skinner rose from the table in the center of the cabin and blocked her passage. "We are meeting the packet off Sandy Hook tomorrow morning," he said. "We have a debt we must settle in New Jersey."

"A debt? Couldn't you leave the money in New York?"

"This is not a debt that can be settled with money," Anthony said. "Only with these."

He took the lamp from its socket on the table and turned to the bulkhead of the cabin. Caroline saw a rack of gleaming muskets.

The cabin door opened and three men joined the Skinners at the small table. Two were young, squat and thick-bodied, with plain hard faces. They wore greasy sailors' clothing. The third was a big black with a shaved skull and the brand of a runaway slave on his cheek.

"Here is your money, lads," Anthony Skinner said, and counted fifteen guineas into their grimy, outstretched hands. "There's five more for each of you if you do the job well."

"What are you going to do, Anthony?" Caroline asked.

"We are going to settle our debt with your friend, Captain Gifford," Anthony said.

"Anthony—he saved your life."

"Which proves he is a fool—as well as a whoremaster."

"Mr. Skinner. You won't let him do this."

494

For a moment shame flickered in Charles Skinner's eyes. Then his face became as cold and empty as the faces of the three men with the guineas in their hands. He took a flask from the inside pocket of his coat and handed it to the big black. "Drink up," he said. "It will steady your aim."

The ship pitched and rolled wildly as it raced before a strong northeast wind. Caroline sat there listening to Anthony Skinner describe his plan with the help of a map of the Jersey coast. They did not bother to explain it to her. But it was not difficult to grasp. They had found a way to lure Jonathan Gifford to the shore. They were going to wait for him in the marsh grass below Garret Hill and kill him.

Kemble and I left Liberty Tavern about 4 A.M. Jonathan Gifford, staring sleeplessly into the darkness, heard our hoofbeats. He thought nothing of it. Travelers often left the tavern before dawn to catch stage boats from Amboy. But the sound of our horses' hoofs made him decide to do something he had been mulling for two days. He had sent Barney to Amboy to find out when the next packet sailed to England. Today, May 6, was the day. It would be painful to stand on Garret Hill and watch the ship cross the bar at Sandy Hook. But he hoped with the aid of the coast watcher's telescope that he might catch a last glimpse of Caroline standing on the stern looking at the coast of home.

Kemble and I arrived at Garret Hill in time to see the sun rise from behind a bank of gray northeast storm clouds far out on the Atlantic. The waters of the bay were flecked with whitecaps as far as the eye could see. Atlantic-sized waves were crashing on the beach. As the sun rose higher, we saw a ship riding offshore on a straining anchor cable. The coast watcher on duty came out of his hut with his rifle in his hand. He told us the ship was the Tory sloop *Revenge*. She was flying a flag of truce. "But I loaded up just the same," he said, hefting his rifle.

At Kemble's suggestion, each coast-watching station had been equipped with two rifles to give them an advantage over potential attackers.

"Are you here to exchange prisoners?" the coast watcher asked.

Kemble shook his head. "This is a private matter. I give you my word of honor there is nothing illegal about it. You can report the entire thing to General Washington."

The coast watcher was a member of our light horse troop. He

looked baffled by this cryptic guarantee, but he did not argue with us. If it had been anyone but Kemble, he would have demanded to see some authorization to meet loyalists for any reason, public or private.

"There's no one on the beach," I said, sweeping the white sand with the coast watcher's telescope. "I don't see anyone on deck, either."

This was not surprising; wind-whipped spray was flying above the sloop's taffrails.

"They're probably waiting below to make sure there are only two of us," Kemble said.

As we descended the winding path to the beach, the sun rose above the cloud banks on the horizon, sending a blaze of red through the scattered clouds above our heads. Soon the whole world seemed drenched in that ambiguous color, symbol of blood, war, victory, national pride. At the bottom of the hill the wind off the marsh had a damp cutting edge. Kemble broke into a fit of coughing. I saw blood stain his handkerchief.

"Don't worry, Jemmy," he said. "I don't expect to die for a good while yet."

On board the *Revenge*, Charles Skinner dragged Caroline from the cabin and down the spray-soaked deck to the sloop's pitching stern. "I want you to see it, madam," he shouted above the wind. "I want you to see what your faithlessness has done." He pointed to the two tiny figures descending the footpath down Garret Hill. "Coming down that hill is a man I loved more than anyone I ever met in this world. Now I stand here his murderer, thanks to you."

From the foot of Garret Hill, without the coast watcher's telescope, Kemble and I could only make out small formless, faceless figures on the deck of the *Revenge*. I nervously wondered why they were not lowering a boat.

"They want to make us do the waiting," Kemble said.

We walked toward the water on a narrow path through the marsh. Sea birds circled above us uttering wild cries. The thick brown salt hay swayed in the wind. Kemble was a few steps ahead of me.

Four men rose out of the hay, like creatures from the ocean depths, two on the left, two on the right. The nearest one on the right was Anthony Skinner. He balanced his musket on the stump of his right arm. Four guns crashed with a simultaneous blast of

496

smoke and flame. Kemble lunged forward as if he were running through the smoke, miraculously escaping the bullets. But it was like the last leap of an exhausted athlete who would never reach his goal.

"Murderers," I screamed.

They came floundering out of the marsh after me, knives in their hands. I was carrying Jonathan Gifford's pistols in their ivory case. I leveled them at the two shorter men, who were the first out of the muck, being more lightly built than Skinner and the big black. The guns were empty but the cowardly bastards did not know it. They gave a yell of fright and dove back into the salt hay. I ran for the path up Garret Hill. I made it twenty yards ahead of Anthony Skinner and the black. On the crest of the hill, the coast watcher's rifle boomed. His aim was poor. The bullet almost took my head off. But the shot discouraged my pursuers. They gave up the chase and returned to the marsh, where the other two killers were going through Kemble's pockets for money. Anthony Skinner waved them off and the four trotted toward the beach.

"Murderers," I screamed.

The wind flung the word back in my face. Weeping, I ran the rest of the way up the hill. I reached the summit, half choking with grief and exhaustion, to find Jonathan Gifford dismounting from his horse.

On the stern of the *Revenge*, a half mile away, Caroline saw the explosion of smoke and flame in the shoulder-high marsh grass, and Anthony's pursuit of me. "It is done," Charles Skinner said, in a voice that trembled between exultation and grief. "He is a dead man."

There was no reason for Caroline to doubt him. She clung to the rail, tears streaming down her cheeks.

"Captain," shouted Charles Skinner. "Lower away. We must get those fellows off without wasting a minute."

On the summit of Garret Hill, Jonathan Gifford groaned like a man in his death agony as I gasped out what had happened. The red sun glared down like a blind bleeding eye on a toy Kemble. Captain Gifford seized the coast watcher's telescope and focused it on the beach. A boat had rounded the stern of the *Revenge* and was pulling hard for shore. Anthony Skinner and his confederates were at the water's edge, waving exultantly to it.

497

Jonathan Gifford swung the telescope to the *Revenge* and trembled with shock and disbelief. There, close enough so it seemed to speak to her, through the magic of the magnifying lenses, was Caroline Skinner on the ship's stern beside her husband. She was weeping. Her face was contorted with grief.

Captain Gifford sprang into the saddle and spurred his horse down the footpath, which was no more than a yard wide. I grabbed the coast watcher's rifle, mounted my horse and followed him. I was sure we would both end in a tangle of horseflesh and leather in the swamp below us, but we made it to the bottom without a mishap. I thought Captain Gifford would ride hard for the beach to fight it out with Anthony Skinner before the *Revenge*'s boat reached shore. The Captain had two pistols in his saddle holsters, I had the rifle and the dueling pistols. But he stopped, dismounted, and knelt beside Kemble. Three bullets had struck him in the chest. He had died instantly.

With a grief that was terrible to watch, Jonathan Gifford caressed Kemble's upturned cheek. "Son, son," he murmured. "Oh, son."

From my saddle I could see the longboat, about twenty yards from shore. It was having trouble making headway in the surf. Skinner and his cohorts were wading into the water to get to it.

"We can still get a shot at them, Captain," I said.

Jonathan Gifford shook his head. "Enough blood has been spilled, Jemmy," he said.

He remounted and rode slowly toward the beach. By the time we reached the sand, Skinner and his three murderous friends were halfway back to the *Revenge*. Jonathan Gifford paid no attention to them. He rode down the shore until he was directly opposite the sloop. The wind tore at his cloak, lashed his face with blowing spray. He felt nothing, knew nothing but an enormous sadness. The huge sweep of the bay beyond the woman on the stern of that ship was an image of his world, empty of love, and with Kemble's body back there in the marsh, even of consolation now.

Aboard the *Revenge*, Caroline had watched with dazed, uncaring eyes the progress of the boat to the beach, the struggle in the surf as Anthony and his confederates clambered into it. It did not matter to her who died or lived, now. Beside her, Charles Skinner gave cries of alarm, shouts of advice.

A horseman emerged from the swamp. Only one man sat a horse with that instinctive command, only one man had those solid shoulders and that large noble head. Jonathan Gifford. At first Caroline thought he was a hallucination. Then she saw me, behind him. There was no reason why in her torment she should wish Jemmy Kemble into imaginary being. We were real.

She could not see Jonathan Gifford's face. He was too far away. But there was something in the angle of his head, in the unbroken, unmoving intensity of his stare, that spoke grief, longing, agony.

Beside her, Charles Skinner had decided Anthony was safely on his way back to the ship, and turned his eyes to the beach.

"My God, is that Gifford?" he asked.

He never got an answer to that question. With a cry that was as involuntary as the act itself, Caroline flung aside her cloak and leaped into the wild waters of the bay. At first she sank like a stone beneath the weight of her dress and petticoats. But the hours she had spent swimming with Jonathan Gifford had vanquished all her fear of the water. Beneath the surface, she ripped open her dress, untied her petticoats, and struggled free of them. Wearing only her shift, she emerged among the waves and began swimming for shore. Charles Skinner bellowed to the men in the longboat and pointed toward her. Anthony, crouched soddenly in the stern, took command and ordered the oarsmen to come about and pursue her.

The boat gained on Caroline with every stroke of its six oars. It was exhausting work, swimming in such a surf. She stopped to catch her breath, looked back and saw the boat. She struck out again, swimming with all her strength. But it was no contest.

Jonathan Gifford turned to me. "Is that rifle loaded, Jemmy?"

I nodded.

He pointed to the boat. "Pick off that lead oarsman and I will give you half of Kemble Manor."

"I will do it free of charge," I said, springing to the sand.

Caroline was about fifty yards offshore. The boat was about fifty yards behind her now. I knelt on the sand and aimed upwind just enough, I prayed, to hit the man at the bow oar. With maximum care I squeezed the trigger. The rifle bucked against my shoulder. The oarsman pitched forward against the man sitting just ahead of him. They both lost their oars and the boat slewed into the trough of the waves, almost swamping. Jonathan Gifford gave a yell of triumph, kicked off his boots, threw off his cloak and coat, and plunged into the water.

We could hear Anthony Skinner roaring curses at the sailors. They had stopped rowing and were shouting back at him. They had no desire to get any closer to me and the rifle, which I was swiftly reloading.

Captain Gifford reached Caroline with no interference and a minute or two later, was walking back through the shallow water with her in his arms. He wrapped her in his cloak, sat her on my horse, and we turned our backs on the Skinners, leaving them to rendezvous with the packet off Sandy Hook and sail away to their bitter exile in England.

Midway along the path through the marsh to Garret Hill, we found the coast watcher kneeling beside Kemble's body. Even though Jonathan Gifford had prepared her for it, Caroline wept at the sight of him. He lay on his side, his head oddly cradled on his outflung arm, his sightless eyes staring toward the ocean. I like to believe his last thought was of that wild Irish girl who crooned to him in the face of the darkness they were both entering:

> Between us and the hosts of the wind
> Between us and the drowning water
> Between us and the shame of the world.

We buried Kemble the next day in the manor graveyard, beside his mother. It was a private ceremony. Kate and Thomas Rawdon, Caroline and Jonathan Gifford, I and the rest of the Liberty Tavern family were the only mourners. When we returned to the tavern we were surprised to find one of General Washington's aides waiting for us. The coast watcher had written a report of the ambush and the events on the beach, and forwarded it to headquarters. The aide handed Jonathan Gifford this letter:

Dear Sir:

I have heard of your loss, which is also our country's loss. I know how deep such wounds cut, how slowly they heal. I wish to extend my heartfelt sympathy. If your son had a fault, it was an excess of love for his country, and an excess of courage which led at times to recklessness. If these are faults, they are easily forgiven by understanding men. Perhaps they sprang from the want of patriotism and courage in those around him from which alas we have too often suffered in the course of this long war.

You may be consoled to know, sir, that as I sat down to write this letter, word arrived from British headquarters in New York that a new general has taken command there with orders to remain on a strict defensive until peace negotiations are completed in Paris. I think we may fairly rejoice, and I trust you will do so, in spite of your sorrow, that the liberty and safety of our country have been established on a permanent footing.

I also gather from the coast watcher's report that a lady whose feelings on this score as well as on other matters important to your happiness has been restored to you by the fortunes of war. That your future years together may be as contented as a free and prosperous America can make them is the sincere wish of

Your friend,
George Washington

The news of the cessation of hostilities went swiftly through our neighborhood. That night we gathered at Liberty Tavern for a celebration which none of us living have ever forgotten. We drank and laughed and sang and toasted George Washington, the honorable Congress, the United States of America, and the patriots of New Jersey, into the dawn. It was then, I suppose, that we began the process of selective forgetting that transformed our memory of the Revolution into Fourth of July oratory. We let the needless deaths, the random cruelty and crude greed, the halfhearted and the fainthearted slip into history's shadows. I think this was a mistake. It would do us no harm—and perhaps a great deal of good—to remember the dark side of our national character. At the very least, it would give us a new appreciation of those who paid a price in anguish, sorrow, and blood to resist this evil undertow.

But that night we drank to our victory, which grew more glorious with every toast. No matter that some who raised their brimming glasses did not deserve it.

The last toast was the best. Jonathan Gifford gave it in the center of the taproom, his arm around Caroline.

> "Here's to all them that we love
> Here's to all them that love us."

Sorrow and joy mingled in that word *love*. We echoed his deepened timbre as we sang out the response.

> "And here's to all them that love those that love them
> Love those that love them that love us."

The endless war, the hatred, the grief ebbed from our weary hearts. We were at peace at last.